THE BAREFOOT QUEEN

www.**transworldbooks**.co.uk

Also by Ildefonso Falcones

Cathedral of the Sea
The Hand of Fatima

For more information on Ildefonso Falcones and his books,
see his website at www.ildefonsofalcones.com

ILDEFONSO FALCONES

THE BAREFOOT QUEEN

Doubleday

LONDON · TORONTO · SYDNEY · AUCKLAND · JOHANNESBURG

TRANSWORLD PUBLISHERS
61–63 Uxbridge Road, London W5 5SA
A Random House Group Company
www.transworldbooks.co.uk

La Reina Descalza, first published by
Random House Mondadori, S.A. in 2013

First published in Great Britain
in 2014 by Doubleday
an imprint of Transworld Publishers

A CIP catalogue record for this book
is available from the British Library.

ISBN 9780857522269

Addresses for Random House Group Ltd companies outside the UK
can be found at: www.randomhouse.co.uk
The Random House Group Ltd Reg. No. 954009

The Random House Group Limited supports the Forest Stewardship Council® (FSC®), the
leading international forest-certification organisation. Our books carrying the FSC label are
printed on FSC®-certified paper. FSC is the only forest-certification scheme supported by
the leading environmental organisations, including Greenpeace. Our paper procurement
policy can be found at www.randomhouse.co.uk/environment

Typeset in 11.5/15pt Aldus by Falcon Oast Graphic Art Ltd.
Printed and bound in Great Britain by
Clays Ltd, Bungay Suffolk

2 4 6 8 10 9 7 5 3 1

To the memory of my parents

Being flamenco is:
. . . it's another way of seeing the world . . .

Tomás Borrás, 'Elegy for the Cantaor'

MAGNIFICENT GODDESS

1

JUST AS SHE was about to set foot on the dock at Cádiz, Caridad hesitated. She was right at the end of the gangway jutting out of the tender that had taken them ashore from the naval ship named *The Queen*. It had travelled from the Indies laden with riches as escort to six registered merchant ships transporting valuable goods. Caridad looked up at the winter sun that illuminated the bustling, teeming port: one of the merchant ships that had sailed with them from Havana was being unloaded. The sun slipped through the gaps in her worn straw hat, dazzling her. She was startled by the commotion and shrank back, frightened, as if the shouts were being directed at her.

'Don't stop there, darkie!' spat the sailor next in line, overtaking her without a second thought.

Caridad stumbled and almost fell into the water. Another man tried to pass her on the gangway, but she jumped clumsily to the dock, then moved aside and stopped again, while part of the crew continued arriving in port amid laughter, jokes and brazen bets as to which woman would be the one to make them forget the long ocean voyage.

'Enjoy your freedom, Negress!' shouted another man as he passed by her, taking the liberty of a quiet slap on her buttocks.

Some of his mates laughed. Caridad didn't even move, her gaze fixed on the long dirty ponytail that danced on the sailor's back, brushing his tattered shirt to the rhythm of his wobbly stride as he headed towards the Sea Gate.

Free? she managed to ask herself. What freedom? She looked past the dock, the walls, where the Sea Gate opened on to the city: a large part of the more than five hundred men who made up *The Queen*'s crew were crowding together in front of the entrance, where an army of officials – commanders, corporals, inspectors – searched them for contraband and questioned them about the ships' course, to find out if any boat had separated from the convoy and its route in order to smuggle in contraband and evade the royal tax office. The men waited impatiently for them to finish the routine procedures; those furthest from the officials, sheltered by the throng, shouted, demanding to be let through, but the inspectors didn't yield. *The Queen*, majestically docked in the Trocadero channel, had transported in its holds more than two million pesos and almost that many wrought-silver marks, plus more treasures from the Indies, along with Caridad and Don José, her master.

Damn his soul! Caridad had cared for Don José on the voyage. 'The scourge of the sea,' they'd said he had. 'He's going to die,' they also assured her. And his time did come, after a slow agony that ate away at his body, day after day, amid dreadful swelling, fevers and bleeding. For a month master and slave remained locked up in the stern, in a small foul cabin with a single hammock. Don José had paid good money to the captain to have it built with thick planks, taking space from the officers' wardroom. 'Eleggua, force his soul to wander lost, never finding rest,' had been Caridad's plea. She could sense, in that cramped space, the powerful presence of the Supreme Being, the God who rules over men's fates. And it was as if her master had heard her, for he begged for compassion with his bilious eyes and extended his hand in search of the warmth of life he knew was slipping away from him. Alone with him in the cabin, Caridad had refused him that comfort. Hadn't she also outstretched her hand when they separated her from her little Marcelo? And what had the master done then? Order the overseer of the tobacco plantation to hold her down and shout to the Negro slave to take away her little boy.

'And shut him up!' he added on the esplanade in front of the big house, where the slaves had gathered to find out who would be their new master and what fate had in store for them from that point on. 'I can't stand . . .'

Don José suddenly grew silent. The slaves' shock was clear on their faces. Blindly, Caridad had managed to hit the overseer and get free; she seemed to be about to run towards her son, but quickly realized how foolish she was being and stopped herself. For a few moments all that was heard were Marcelo's shrill, desperate shrieks.

'Do you want me to whip her, Don José?' asked the overseer as he grabbed Caridad again by one arm.

'No,' he decided after thinking it over. 'I don't want to bring her with me to Spain ruined.'

He let her go and shot a severe look towards that big Negro – Cecilio was his name – who then dragged the boy towards the shack. Caridad fell to her knees, her cries joining the boy's. That was the last time she saw her son. They didn't let her say goodbye to him, they didn't allow her to even . . .

'Caridad! What are you doing just standing there, woman?'

Hearing her name brought her back to reality and amid the din she recognized the voice of Don Damián, the old chaplain of *The Queen*, who had also just disembarked. She immediately dropped her bundle, uncovered her head and lowered her gaze, fixing it on the worn straw hat she started to crush in her hands.

'You can't stay here on the dock,' continued the priest as he approached and took her by the arm. The contact lasted only an instant; the flustered priest quickly removed his hand. 'Let's go,' he urged somewhat nervously. 'Come with me.'

They walked over to the Sea Gate: Don Damián laden with a small trunk, Caridad with her little bundle and her hat in her hands, not taking her eyes off the chaplain's sandals.

'Make way for a man of God,' demanded the priest to the sailors crammed in front of the gate.

Gradually the crowd moved aside to grant him passage. Caridad followed behind him, dragging her bare feet, black as ebony, her eyes still downcast. The long, greyish shirt of thick coarse burlap that she wore as a dress couldn't hide the fact that she was a strong, shapely woman. She was as tall as some of the sailors, who looked up to take in her thick black curls, while others gazed at her large, firm breasts and voluptuous hips. The chaplain kept walking and merely lifted a hand when he heard whistles, impertinent comments and even the occasional bold invitation.

'I am Father Damián García.' The priest introduced himself, holding out his papers to one of the commanders once he'd got through the seamen. 'Chaplain of the warship *Queen*, of Your Majesty's Armada.'

The commander looked through the documents. 'Father, will you allow me to inspect your trunk?'

'Personal effects . . .' answered the priest as he opened it. 'The goods are duly registered in my paperwork.'

The commander nodded as he rummaged around in the trunk. 'Any mishaps on the journey?' asked the officer without looking at him, weighing up a small roll of tobacco in his hand. 'Any encounters with enemy ships or ships outside the fleet?'

'None. Everything went as planned.'

The commander nodded. 'This your slave?' he enquired, pointing to Caridad after finishing the inspection. 'She's not listed in the documents.'

'Her? No. She's a free woman.'

'She doesn't look like one,' declared the commander, planting himself in front of Caridad, who clung even tighter to her little bundle and her straw hat. 'Look at me, Negress!' muttered the officer. 'What are you hiding?'

Some of the other officers, who were inspecting the seamen, stopped their work and turned towards the commander and the woman who remained before him with her eyes downcast. The sailors who had let them through came over.

'Nothing. She's not hiding anything,' answered Don Damián.

'Silence, Father. People who avoid a commander's eyes are always hiding something.'

'What could this poor wretch be hiding?' insisted the priest. 'Caridad, show him your papers.'

The woman rifled through her bundle in search of the

documents the ship's notary had given her, while Don Damián continued talking.

'She embarked in Havana with her master, Don José Hidalgo, who planned to return to his native land before he died but passed away on the voyage, God rest his soul.'

Caridad handed her wrinkled documents to the commander.

'Before he died,' continued Don Damián, 'as is customary on His Majesty's vessels, Don José made a will and ordered that his slave Caridad be freed. There you have the manumission document.'

Caridad Hidalgo – the notary had written, taking the dead master's last name – *also known as Cachita; Negro slave the colour of ebony, in good health and of strong constitution, with curly black hair and some twenty-five years of age.*

'What have you got in that bag?' asked the commander after reading the documents confirming Caridad's freedom.

She opened up the bundle and showed it to him. An old blanket and a felt jacket . . . everything she owned. Master had given her the jacket last winter and the blanket two winters back. Hidden among them were several cigars she'd been rationing on the journey after stealing them from Don José. *What if they find them?* she thought, terrified. The commander made a motion to inspect the bundle, but when he saw the old fabric his expression soured.

'Look at me, Negress,' he demanded.

Everyone witnessing the scene saw the trembling that ran through Caridad's body. She had never looked directly at a white man when addressed.

'She's afraid,' intervened Don Damián.

'I said look at me.'

'Do it,' pleaded the chaplain.

Caridad lifted her round face with its thick fleshy lips, flattened nose and small brown eyes that tried to look past the commander, towards the city.

The man furrowed his brow and searched, in vain, for her elusive gaze.

'Next!' he said, suddenly giving in, breaking the tension and triggering an avalanche of sailors.

Don Damián, with Caridad close on his heels, entered the city through the Sea Gate flanked by two battlemented towers. *The Queen*, the third-rate ship of the line with more than seventy guns they'd sailed in on from Havana, stayed behind in the Trocadero alongside the six merchant ships it had escorted, their holds stuffed with products from the Indies: sugar, tobacco, cacao, ginger, sarsaparilla, indigo, cochineal, silk, pearls, tortoiseshell . . . silver. The journey was a success and Cádiz had received them with ringing bells. Spain was at war with England; the treasure fleets, which up until a few years earlier crossed the ocean guarded by ships from the Royal Armada, had ceased operating, so the trade was done with register-ships, private merchant vessels that acquired a royal permit for the voyage. That was why the arrival of the merchandise and the treasure, so needed by the Spanish tax office, had sparked a festive atmosphere in every corner of the city.

When they reached Juego de Pelota Street, having passed the church of Our Lady of Pópulo and the Sea Gate, Don Damián stepped out of the floods of sailors, soldiers and merchants, and stopped, turning towards Caridad after he'd put his trunk down on the ground. 'May God be with you and keep you safe, Caridad,' he blessed her.

She didn't respond. She had pulled her straw hat down to her ears and the chaplain couldn't see her eyes, but he imagined them focused on the trunk, or on his sandals, or . . .

'I have things to do, you understand?' he said in an attempt to excuse himself. 'Go and look for some work. This is a very rich city.'

As he spoke, Don Damián extended his right hand, brushing Caridad's forearm; then it was he who lowered his gaze for a second. When he looked up he found Caridad's small brown eyes fixed on him, just as on the nights during the crossing, when after her master's death he had taken responsibility for the slave and hidden her from the crew by order of the captain. His stomach churned. 'I didn't touch her,' he repeated to himself for the millionth time. He had never laid a finger on her, but Caridad had looked at him with expressionless eyes and he . . . He hadn't been able to stop himself masturbating beneath his clothes at the sight of such a splendid female.

Shortly after Don José's passing, the funeral rite was carried out:

they said three prayers for the dead and his corpse was thrown over-board in a sack with two earthenware jugs filled with water tied to the feet. Then the captain ordered that the makeshift cabin be taken down and that the notary inventory the deceased man's assets. Don José was the only passenger on the flagship, Caridad the only woman aboard.

'Reverend,' said the captain to the priest after giving the notary his instructions, 'I am placing you in charge of keeping the Negro woman away from the crew.'

'But I . . .' Don Damián tried to object.

'It's not hers, but you can feed her with the food Mr Hidalgo brought on board,' declared the officer, ignoring his protest.

Don Damián kept Caridad locked up in his tiny cabin, where there was only room for the hammock he hung from one side to the other, which he took down and rolled up during the day. The woman slept on the floor, at his feet, beneath the hammock. The first few nights, the chaplain took refuge in reading the holy books, but gradually his gaze began to follow the oil lamp's beams that, as if of their own volition, seemed to stray from the pages of his heavy tomes to illuminate the woman who lay curled up so close to him.

He fought against the fantasies that waylaid him when he caught a glimpse of Caridad's legs that had slipped out from under the blanket that covered her, or of her breasts, rising and falling to the rhythm of her breathing, or of her buttocks. And yet, almost in-voluntarily, he started to touch himself. Perhaps it was the creaking from the timbers the hammock hung on, perhaps it was the tension gathered in such a small space, but Caridad opened her eyes and all the light from the oil lamp settled inside them. Don Damián felt himself growing red and he remained still for a moment, but his desire multiplied with Caridad's gaze upon him, the same expression-less gaze with which she now listened to him.

'Heed my words, Caridad,' he insisted. 'Look for work.'

Don Damián grabbed the trunk, turned his back and resumed his path.

Why do I feel guilty? he wondered as he stopped to switch the trunk to his other hand. He could have forced her, he'd said to himself whenever he was tormented by guilt. She was only a slave. Maybe . . .

maybe he wouldn't have even had to resort to violence. Weren't all Negro slaves dissolute women? Don José, her master, had admitted in confession that he'd slept with all of his.

'Caridad bore my child,' he revealed, 'maybe two – but no, I don't think so; the second one, that clumsy stupid boy, was as dark as her.'

'Do you regret it?' the priest asked him.

'Having children with the Negro women?' the tobacco farmer replied angrily. 'Father, I sold the little half-breeds at a nearby sugar mill owned by priests. They never worried about my sinning soul when they bought them from me.'

Don Damián headed towards the Santa Cruz Cathedral, on the other side of the narrow spit of land on which the walled city was perched, closing off the bay. Before turning on to a side street, he looked back and caught a glimpse of Caridad as the crowd passed: she had moved to one side until her back was up against a wall where she stood immobile, disconnected from the world.

She'll find a way, he thought, forcing himself to continue and turn the corner. Cádiz was a rich city where traders and merchants from all over Europe met and money flowed in abundance. She was a free woman and now she had to learn to live in liberty and work. He walked a long way and when he reached a point where he could clearly make out the construction for the new cathedral near the old one, he stopped. What kind of a job could that poor wretch find? She didn't know how to do anything, except labour on a tobacco plantation; that was where she'd lived since she was ten years old, after English slave traders had bought her for five paltry yards of fabric from the kingdom of the Yoruba in the Gulf of Guinea, in order to resell her in the bustling Cuban market. That was how Don José Hidalgo himself had explained it to the chaplain when Don Damián asked why he'd chosen her to accompany him on the voyage.

'She is strong and desirable,' added the tobacco farmer, winking at him. 'And it seems she's no longer fertile, which is always an advantage once you're off the plantation. After giving birth to that idiot boy . . .'

Don José had also told him that he was a widower and had an educated son who'd taken his degree in Madrid, where Don José was headed to live out his last days. In Cuba he'd owned a profitable tobacco plantation in the lowlands near Havana that he worked himself, along with some twenty-odd slaves. Loneliness, old age and the pressure from the sugar growers who wanted to acquire land for their flourishing industry had led him to sell his property and return to his homeland, but the scourge attacked him twenty days into the journey and fed viciously on his weak, elderly state. He had fever, dropsy, mottled skin and bleeding gums, and the doctor declared him a lost cause.

Then, as was mandatory on royal ships, *The Queen*'s captain ordered the notary to go to Don José's cabin to bear witness to his last wishes.

'I grant my slave Caridad freedom,' whispered the sick man after ordering a few bequests for the Church and arranging for the entirety of his assets to be given to the son he would now never see again.

The woman didn't even curve her thick lips in a glint of satisfaction at learning she was free, recalled the priest, who had now stopped in the street.

She didn't say a word! Don Damián remembered his efforts to hear Caridad amid the hundreds of voices praying at the Sunday masses on deck, or her timid whispers at night, before sleeping, when he forced her to pray. What could that woman work as? The chaplain knew that almost every freed slave ended up working for their former owners for a miserable wage that barely allowed them to cover their necessities, which as slaves they'd been guaranteed. Or they ended up forced to beg for alms in the streets, competing with thousands of mendicants. And those had been born in Spain: they knew the land and its people; some were clever and quick. How could Caridad find her way in a big city like Cádiz?

He sighed and ran his hand several times over his chin and the little hair he had left. Then he turned around, snorted as he lifted the trunk again and prepared to retrace his steps. *What now?* he wondered. He could . . . he could arrange a job for her in the tobacco factory, she did know about that. 'She's very good with the leaves; she treats them right – affectionately and sweetly – and she knows how to choose the best ones and roll good cigars,' Don José had told him, but that would mean asking for favours and making it known that he . . . He couldn't risk Caridad talking about what had happened on the boat. Close to two hundred cigar makers worked in those factory rows, constantly whispering and finding fault with others as they rolled the small Cádiz cigars.

He found Caridad still up against the wall, unmoving, defenceless. A group of unruly youngsters were making fun of her and the people coming and going did nothing to stop them. Don Damián approached just as one of the boys was about to throw a rock at her. 'Halt!' he shouted.

Another boy stopped his arm; the young woman removed her hat and lowered her eyes.

Caridad distanced herself from the group of seven passengers who had embarked on the ship about to head upstream along the Guadalquivir River to Seville. Weary, she tried to settle in among a pile of luggage on board. The boat was a sleek single-masted tartan that had arrived in Cádiz with a shipload of valuable oil from the fertile Sevillian lowlands.

From the Bay of Cádiz they coasted to Sanlúcar de Barrameda, to the mouth of the Guadalquivir. They waited off the coast of Chipiona, along with other tartans and the local *charangueros* that plied between ports, for the high tide and favourable winds they needed to cross the dangerous Sanlúcar sandbar, those fearsome shoals that had turned the area into a boat graveyard. The captains would only brave crossing that treacherous bar when every one of several specific conditions came together. Then they would sail upriver, taking advantage of the tide's momentum, which could be felt up to the outskirts of Seville.

'Ships have sometimes had to wait up to a hundred days to cross the bar,' said a sailor to one elegantly dressed passenger, who immediately shifted his worried gaze towards Sanlúcar and its spectacular marshlands, obviously desperate not to suffer the same fate.

Caridad, seated among some bags against the gunwale, let herself sway with the tartan's rocking. The sea, though calm, seemed somehow tense, just as the ship's passengers did, and that same atmosphere prevailed in the other delayed boats. It wasn't only the wait; it was also the fear of an attack from the British or from pirates. The sun began to set, tinting the water an ominous metallic tone, and the uneasy conversations of the crew and passengers dropped to whispers. The winter revealed its harshness as the sun hid and the dampness seeped into Caridad's bones, making her feel even colder. She was hungry and tired. She wore her jacket, as grey and faded as her dress and both of rough cloth, in sharp contrast to the other passengers who wore what seemed to her lavish clothes, in bright colours. She realized her teeth were chattering and she had goose-flesh, so she searched in her bundle for the blanket. Her fingers brushed a cigar and she touched it delicately, recalling its aroma, its effects. She needed it, anxious to dull her senses, forget her tiredness, her hunger . . . and even her freedom.

She wrapped herself up in the blanket. Free? Don Damián had put her on that boat, the first he'd found about to depart the Cádiz port.

'Go to Seville,' he said after negotiating a price with the captain and paying him out of his own pocket. 'To Triana. Once you're there, look for the Minims' convent and tell them I sent you.'

Caridad wished she'd had the courage to ask him what Triana was or how she would find that convent, but he practically pushed her aboard. He was nervous, looking from side to side, as if afraid someone would see them together.

She smelled the cigar and its fragrance transported her to Cuba. All she knew was where her shack was, and the plantation, and the sugar mill she went to every Sunday with the other slaves to hear mass and then sing and dance until they wore themselves out. From the shack to the plantation and from the plantation to the shack, day in day out, month in month out, year in year out. How was she going to find the convent? She curled up against the gunwale and pressed her back up to the wood, searching for contact with a reality that had vanished. Who were those strangers? And Marcelo? What had happened to him? And what about her friend María, the mulatta she sang choruses with? And the others? What was she doing in a strange boat at night, in a far-off land, on her way to a city she wasn't even sure existed? Triana? She had never dared to ask the whites anything. She always knew what she had to do! She didn't need to ask.

Her eyes grew damp as she remembered Marcelo. She felt around in her bundle for the flint, steel and tinder to start a flame. Would they let her smoke? On the tobacco farm she could; it was common there. She had cried over Marcelo during the voyage. She had even . . . She had even been tempted to throw herself into the sea, to put an end to her constant suffering. 'Get away from there, darkie! Do you want to fall into the water?' warned one of the sailors. And she obeyed, moving away from the gunwale.

Would she have had the courage to throw herself in if that sailor hadn't shown up? She didn't want to replay the scene in her head again; instead she watched the men on the tartan: they seemed nervous. The tide was high but the winds weren't favourable. Some of them smoked. She skilfully struck the steel against the flint and the tinder soon lit up. Where would she find the trees whose bark and fungus she used to make the tinder? As she lit the cigar and inhaled deeply she realized she didn't know where to get tobacco either. The first draw calmed her mind. The next two relaxed her muscles and made her slightly dizzy.

'Negress, share your smoke with me?'

A cabin boy had crouched down in front of her; his face was dirty but lively and pleasant. For a few seconds, as he waited for an answer, Caridad took in his smile. All she could see were his white teeth, just like Marcelo's when she wrapped her arms around him. She'd had another son, a mulatto born of the master, but Don José sold him as soon as the boy could do without the care of the two old women who looked after the slaves' little ones while they worked. They all went down that same path: the master didn't want to support Negro children. Marcelo, her second son, conceived with a black man from the sugar mill, had been different: a difficult birth; a child with problems. 'No one will buy him,' declared the master when he began to show signs of clumsiness and defects. He agreed to let him stay on at the plantation, as if he were a simple dog, or a hen or one of the pigs they raised behind the shack. 'He won't live long,' everyone predicted.

But Caridad didn't let that happen, and many were the beatings and whippings she got when they discovered she'd been feeding him. 'We provide you with food so you can work, not so you can raise an imbecile,' the overseer said time and again.

'Negress, would you share your smoke with me?' insisted the cabin boy.

Why not? thought Caridad. He had the same smile as Marcelo. She offered him the cigar.

'Wow! Where did you get this? It's amazing!' exclaimed the boy after trying it and coughing. 'Is it from Cuba?'

'Yes,' said Caridad as she took the cigar back and brought it to her lips.

'What's your name?'

'Caridad,' she answered amid a puff of smoke.

'I like your hat.' The boy moved edgily on his legs. He was waiting for another puff, which finally came.

'It's blowing!' The captain's shout broke the stillness. From the other ships similar cries were heard. The southern wind was blowing, perfect for crossing the sandbar. The cabin boy returned the cigar and ran to join the other sailors.

'Thank you, *morena*,' he said hastily. Many in this new country called her that, since her dark skin was the first thing they noticed about her.

Unlike the other passengers, Caridad didn't witness the difficult nautical manoeuvre that required three changes of course in the narrow canal. All along the mouth of the Guadalquivir, both on land and on the barges moored on its banks, fires were lit to guide the boats. She didn't share the others' nerve-racking worry about the crossing: if the wind died down and they were left halfway through, it was likely they would run aground. She remained sitting against the gunwale, smoking, enjoying a pleasant tickle in her muscles and letting the tobacco cloud her senses. As the tartan entered the formidable Canal de los Ingleses, with the tower of San Jacinto illuminating their course on the port side, Caridad began to sing softly under her breath to the rhythm of her memories of the Sunday parties, when after celebrating mass in the neighbouring sugar factory, which had a priest, the slaves from the various estates gathered in the barracks of the plantation they'd come to with their masters. There the white men let them sing and dance, as if they were children who needed to let off steam and forget their rough working conditions. But in every song and every dance step, when they heard the *batá* drums speak – the large *iyá* drum, mother of them all, the slightly smaller *itótele* and the littlest *olónkolo* – the Negroes worshipped their gods, disguised in the Christian virgins and saints, and they remembered their African roots with longing.

She continued singing softly, isolated from the captain's urgent orders and the crew's busy dashing about, and she sang just as she had sung to put Marcelo to sleep. She believed she was touching his hair again, hearing him breathe, smelling his scent . . . She blew a kiss. The boy had survived. He still got yelled at and slapped by the master and the overseer but he had won the affection of the other slaves on the plantation. He was always smiling! And he was sweet and affectionate with everyone. Marcelo didn't know slaves from masters. He lived free, and occasionally looked into the slaves' eyes as if he understood their pain and encouraged them to free themselves from their chains. Some smiled back at Marcelo sadly, others cried in the face of his innocence.

Caridad pulled hard on the cigar. He would be well taken care of, she had no doubt about that. María, who always sang in chorus with her, would look after him. And Cecilio too, even though he had been forced to separate the boy from her . . . All those slaves that had been sold along with the land would take care of him. And her son would be happy, she could feel it. But her master . . . May your soul wander for all eternity without rest, Don José, yearned Caridad.

2

SEVILLE'S TRIANA DISTRICT was on the other side of the Guadalquivir River, outside the city walls. It was connected to the city by an old Muslim bridge built over ten barges anchored to the riverbed and joined by two thick iron chains and various mooring lines stretched from one shore to the other. That outlying district, which had been dubbed the 'garrison of Seville' for the defensive function it had always performed, reached its pinnacle when Seville monopolized trade with the Indies; the difficulties navigating the river led to the House of Trade being moved to Cádiz, which meant a considerable decline in population and the abandoning of numerous buildings. Its ten thousand inhabitants were concentrated on a limited stretch of land on the river's right shore, and bounded on the other side by La Cava, the old trench that, in times of war, comprised the city's first line of defence and flooded with waters from the Guadalquivir to turn the outlying district into an island. Beyond La Cava one could make out sporadic monasteries, chapels, homes and the extensive fertile lowlands of Triana.

One of those convents, on Cava Nueva, was that of Our Lady of Health, with Minim nuns, a humble congregation devoted to contemplation, silent prayer and frugal living. Behind the Minims, towards San Jacinto Street, on a small dead-end alley named after San Miguel, were thirteen tightly packed clusters of apartments around a central courtyard into which nearly twenty-five families were crammed. Twenty-one of those were gypsy families, made up of grandparents, children, aunts, cousins, nieces, grandchildren and the odd great-grandchild; those twenty-one were devoted to ironwork. There were other forges in the Triana district, most run by gypsies, the same hands that in India and in the mountains of Armenia, centuries before emigrating to Europe, had turned that trade into an art. However, San Miguel was the nerve centre of smiths and tinkers in Triana. On to the alley opened the old apartments clustered around a courtyard that were built during Triana's period of splendour in the sixteenth century: some were no more than simple blind alleys of rows of squalid little houses; others were buildings, sometimes elaborate, of two or three storeys arranged around a central court-yard, whose upper levels opened on to it through high corridors and wooden or wrought-iron railings. All of them, almost without exception, offered humble dwellings of one or at most two rooms, in one of which there was a small niche to cook with coal, when it wasn't in the courtyard or passageway itself as a service available to all the neighbours. The washbasins and the latrines, if there were any, were located in the courtyard, for everyone.

Most of these clusters of apartments in Seville were occupied during the day only by women and the children who played in the courtyards, but the smiths in Triana spent their workdays there since their forges were installed on the ground floor. The constant ringing of the hammers on the anvils coming from each of the forges merged in the street into a strange metallic clatter; the coal smoke from the forges, which often emerged from the courtyards or the very door-ways of those modest workshops without chimneys, was visible from every part of Triana. Along the length of the alley, surrounded by the smoke and noise, men, women and children came and went, played, laughed, chatted, shouted and argued. In spite of the tumult, many of them were silent and stopped in the doors of those workshops with their emotions running high. Sometimes you could make out a father holding his son back by the shoulders, an old man with his eyes squinting or several women repressing a dance step as they heard the sounds of the *martinete*: a sad song accompanied only by the monotonous pounding of the hammer whose rhythm it matched; a rhythm and song all their own, which had followed them throughout time and everywhere. Then, with the *quejíos* of the blacksmiths, the hammering became a marvellous symphony that made your hair stand on end.

That 2 February 1748, the feast of the Purification of Our Lady, the gypsies weren't working at their forges. Few of them would attend the church of San Jacinto or the church of the Virgin of Candelaria to ask for blessings on the candles they used to light their homes, but despite that they didn't want any problems with their pious Triana neighbours and even less so with the priests, monks and inquisitors; that was a compulsory day of rest.

'Keep the girl away from the randy *payos*,' warned a gravelly voice.

The words – spoken in Caló, the language of the Spanish and Portuguese gypsies – echoed through the courtyard that opened on to the alley. Mother and daughter stopped in their tracks. Neither of them showed surprise, even though they didn't know where the voice came from. Their eyes ran over the courtyard until Milagros made out in one dark corner the silvery glints coming off the buttons on her grandfather's short, sky-blue jacket. He was standing upright and still, with his brow furrowed and his eyes lost in the distance, as he often did; he had spoken while still chewing on a small, unlit cigar. The girl, splendid at fourteen, smiled at him and spun around gracefully; her long blue skirt with petticoats and her green scarves fluttered in the air amid the tinkling of several necklaces that hung from her neck.

'Everyone in Triana knows that I'm your granddaughter.' She laughed. Her white teeth stood out against her dark skin, the same shade as her mother's, the same shade as her grandfather's. 'Who would dare?'

'Lust is blind and daring, girl. There are many who would risk their lives to have you. I would only be able to avenge you and there isn't enough blood in the world to mend that pain. Always remind her of that,' he added, addressing her mother.

'Yes, Father,' she replied.

Both women waited for a word of farewell, a gesture, a sign, but the gypsy, hieratic in his corner, was silent and still. Finally Ana took her daughter by the arm and left the house. It was a cold morning.

The sky was overcast and threatened rain, which didn't seem to be an obstacle for the people of Triana who were heading to San Jacinto to celebrate the blessing of their candles. There were also many Sevillians who wanted to join the ceremony and, carrying their altar candles, they went over the bridge or crossed the Guadalquivir aboard one of the more than twenty boats that took people from one shore to the other. The crowd promised a profitable day, thought Ana before recalling her father's fears. She turned her head towards Milagros and saw her walking with her head held high, arrogant, attentive to everything and everyone. As a pure-bred gypsy should, she then acknowledged, unable to suppress her pleased expression. They couldn't help but notice her girl! Her thick chestnut hair fell down her back and blended into the long fringes of the scarf she wore over her shoulders. Here and there, her hair was adorned with a colourful ribbon or a pearl; large silver hoops hung from her ears, and necklaces of beads and silver lay over her young breasts, captive in the boldly plunging neckline of her white shirt. A blue skirt clung to her delicate waist and almost reached the floor, where her bare feet could sometimes be seen. A man looked at her out of the corner of his eye. Milagros realized instantly, with feline instinct, and turned her face towards him; the girl's chiselled features softened and her bushy eyebrows seemed to arch in a smile. The day begins, her mother said to herself.

'Shall I tell you your fortune, strapping lad?'

The strong man attempted to continue along his way, but Milagros smiled openly and approached him, getting so close that her breasts almost brushed against him.

'I see a woman who desires you,' added the gypsy girl, staring into his eyes.

Ana reached her daughter in time to hear her last words. A woman . . . What more could a man like him desire, big and healthy but obviously alone, who carried a small candle? The man hesitated for a few seconds before noticing the other gypsy woman who had come over to him: older, but just as attractive and proud as the girl.

'Don't you want to know more?' Milagros regained the man's attention as she looked deeper into his eyes, where she had already seen his interest. She tried to take his hand. 'You also desire that woman, don't you?'

The gypsy girl could tell that her prey was starting to give in. Mother and daughter, in silence, coincided in their conclusion: easy prey. A timid, spineless character – the man had tried to hide his eyes – in a large, bulky body. Surely there was some woman, there always was. They only had to encourage him, insist that he overcome the embarrassment that was holding him back.

Milagros was brilliant and convincing: she ran her finger over the lines on the man's palm as if she were really reading that gullible man's future. Her mother watched her, proud and amused. They got a couple of copper coins for her advice. Then Ana tried to sell him a contraband cigar.

'Half the price they sell them for in the Seville tobacco shops,' she offered. 'If you don't want cigars, I have snuff, too, of the highest quality, clean, no dirt in it.' She tried to convince him, opening the mantilla she wore to show him the merchandise she had hidden, but the man just sketched a simple-minded smile, as if in his mind he were already courting the woman he had yet to dare speak a word to.

All day long, mother and daughter moved through the crowd that travelled from Altozano, near the Inquisition Castle and the church of San Jacinto, which was still under construction on top of the old chapel of the Candelaria, reading fortunes and selling tobacco, always on the lookout for constables and the gypsy women, many of them from their own family, who stole from the unsuspecting. She and her daughter didn't need to run such risks, and they didn't want to find themselves mixed up in one of the many altercations that came about when those pickpockets were caught: the tobacco gave them enough of a profit.

Which was why they tried to move away from the throng when Fray Joaquín, of the Order of Preachers, began his open-air sermon in front of what in time would be the imposing entrance of the church. At that moment, the pious Sevillians crowded on the stretch of ground weren't interested in their fortunes or tobacco; many of them had come to Triana to listen to another of the controversial sermons given by that young Dominican, born of an era in which clear thinking was struggling to forge a path through the darkness of ignorance. From his improvised pulpit outside of the temple, he went beyond the ideas of Fray Benito Jerónimo Feijoo; Fray Joaquín spoke loudly in Spanish and without throwing in Latin phrases, sharply criticizing the atavistic prejudices of the Spaniards and inciting people with his defence of the virtue of work, even as a mechanic or an artisan, against the misunderstood concept of honour that drove Spaniards to laziness and idleness; he aroused women's pride by opposing conventual education and supporting their new role in society and in the family; he affirmed their right to an education and their legitimate aspiration to intellectual development for the good of a civilized kingdom. Women were no longer servants to men, nor could they be considered imperfect males. They weren't evil by nature! Marriage must be founded on equality and respect. In our century, maintained Fray Joaquín, quoting great thinkers, the soul no longer had a sex: it wasn't male or female. People crowded together to hear him and it was then, Ana and Milagros knew, when the gypsy women took advantage of people's fascination to steal their bags.

They got as close as they could to the place from which Fray Joaquín addressed the multitude. He was accompanied by the twenty-odd Dominican friars who lived in the San Jacinto monastery. Many of them looked up every once in a while towards the leaden sky that, luckily, resisted unleashing its water; the rain would have ruined the celebration.

'I am the light of the world!' shouted Fray Joaquín so he could be heard. 'That was what Our Lord Jesus Christ announced. He is our light! A light present in all these candles you have brought and that should illuminate . . .'

Milagros wasn't listening to the sermon. She stared at the friar, who soon noticed the mother and daughter near him. The gypsy women's brightly coloured dresses stood out in the crowd. Fray Joaquín hesitated; for a moment his words lost their fluency and his gestures no longer held the faithful's attention. Milagros noticed how he struggled, in vain, not to look at her; in fact at times he couldn't help letting his eyes linger on her just a bit too long. On one of those occasions, the girl winked at him and Fray Joaquín stammered; on another, Milagros stuck out her tongue at him.

'Child!' her mother scolded, after elbowing her hard. Ana gave the friar priest an apologetic glance.

The sermon, as the crowd had been hoping, went on for a long time. Fray Joaquín, once Milagros had stopped hounding him, managed to make an impression once again. When he finished, the faithful lit their candles in the bonfire that the friars had built. The people dispersed and the two women went back to their schemes.

'What were you trying to do?' her mother asked.

'I like him . . .' answered Milagros, gesturing flirtatiously. 'I like that he stammers, makes mistakes, blushes.'

'Why? He's a priest.'

The girl seemed to be thinking. 'I don't know,' she responded with a shrug, and then smiled.

'Fray Joaquín respects your grandfather and because of that he will respect you, but don't play around with men . . . even if they are religious,' her mother warned.

As was to be expected, the day was fruitful and Ana sold all the contraband tobacco she carried hidden in her clothes. The Sevillians began to cross the bridge or take the boats back to the city. They could still have read a few more palms, but as the crowd thinned it was clear how many gypsies – some drawn and ancient crones, others young women, many boys and girls half-dressed in rags – were doing the same thing. Ana and Milagros recognized the women from the San Miguel alley, relatives of the blacksmiths, but also many of those who lived in the squalid shanties beside the Carthusians' gardens in Triana's fertile lowland and who stubbornly harassed people for alms, blocking their path and grabbing at their clothes while crying out loudly to a God they didn't believe in and invoking a string of martyrs and saints whose names they had memorized.

'I think that's enough for today, Milagros,' announced her mother after moving out of the way of a couple fleeing a group of beggars.

A snotty kid with a dirty face and black eyes who was following the Sevillians crashed into her while still invoking the virtues of Saint Rufina.

'Here,' Ana said to him as she gave him a copper cuarto.

They set off on their return trip as the mother of the little gypsy boy demanded he hand over the coin. The alley was feverish. It had been a good day for everyone; religious holidays softened people up. Groups of men chatted at the doors to their homes drinking wine, smoking and playing cards. A woman approached her husband to show him her earnings and an argument started when he tried to take them from her. Milagros said goodbye to her mother and joined a group of girls. Ana had to settle up the tobacco earnings with her father. She searched for him amid the men. She didn't find him.

'Father?' she shouted once inside the courtyard of the house where they lived.

'He's not here.'

Ana turned and saw José, her husband, in the doorframe.

'Where is he?'

José shrugged and opened one of his hands; in the other he carried a jug of wine. His eyes sparkled. 'He disappeared just after you two did. He must have gone over to the settlement of La Cartuja to see his relatives, like always.'

Ana shook her head. Was he really with them? Sometimes she had gone there to look for him and not found him. Would he return that night or not for a few days, as he'd done so many other times? And in what state?

She sighed.

'He always comes back,' muttered José sarcastically.

His wife straightened up, hardened her expression and frowned. 'Don't start in on him,' she muttered threateningly. 'I keep warning you.'

The man just made a face and turned his back on her.

He usually came back, it was true; José was right; but what was he doing when he disappeared thus on the occasions when he wasn't at the La Cartuja settlement? He never said, and when she insisted, he took refuge in that impenetrable world of his. He was so different now from the father she had known as a child! Ana remembered him proud, fiery, indestructible, a figure she could always depend on. Later, when she was about ten years old, he was stopped by the 'tobacco patrol', the authorities that policed contraband. He was only carrying a few pounds of tobacco leaf and it was the first time he was caught; it should have been treated as a minor offence, but Melchor Vega was a gypsy and they had arrested him outside of the areas designated for those of his race; he dressed like a gypsy, in clothes as expensive as they were flashy, all laden with silver or metal beads; he carried a cane, his knife, wore earrings and, to top it all off, some witnesses swore they had heard him speaking Caló, the gypsy dialect. All of that was illegal, even more than cheating the royal tax office. Ten years in the galleys. That was the sentence they gave the gypsy.

Ana felt her stomach shrink inside as she recalled the agony she went through with her mother during the trial and, above all, during the almost four years between when the first sentence was handed down until they actually carried her father off to the Port of Santa María to board him on to one of the royal galley ships. Her mother had kept up her efforts on his behalf every single day, every single hour, every single minute. That had cost her her life. Ana's eyes grew damp, as they always did when she relived those moments. She saw her mother again, asking for mercy, humiliated, begging judges, officials and prison inspectors for a pardon. They begged for the intervention of dozens of priests and friars, who had refused to even give them the time of day. They pawned everything they had ... they stole, swindled and cheated to pay notaries and lawyers. They stopped eating so they could bring a crust of bread to the jail where her father was waiting, like so many others, for his trial to end and his fate to be decided. There were those who, during that terrible wait, cut off a hand, or even an arm, to avoid going to the galleys and facing the fate of most of the galley slaves permanently fettered to the ships' benches: a painful, miserably slow death.

But Melchor Vega endured the torture. Ana dried her eyes with her shirt sleeve. Yes, he had survived. And one day, when nobody was expecting him any longer, he reappeared in Triana, wasted away, dressed in rags, broken, destroyed, dragging his feet but with his pride intact. He never again was that father who used to tousle her hair when she came to him after some childish altercation. That was what he always used to do: tousle her hair and then look at her tenderly, reminding her in silence who she was: a Vega, a gypsy! It was the only thing that seemed to matter to him in the world. Melchor had tried to foster that same pride in his race with his granddaughter Milagros. Shortly after his return, when the girl was still very young, Melchor anxiously waited for Ana to conceive a boy. 'When's the boy coming?' he would ask again and again. José, her husband, also asked her insistently: 'Are you with child yet?' It seemed that the entire San Miguel alley wanted a boy. José's mother, her aunts, her female cousins . . . even the Vega women at the settlement of La Cartuja! They all pestered her about it, but it wasn't to be.

Ana turned her head towards where José had disappeared after their brief exchange about Melchor. Unlike her father, her husband hadn't been able to recover from what for him had been a failure, a humiliation, and the scant affection and respect there had been in that marriage arranged by the Carmona and Vega families gradually disappeared until it was replaced by a latent rancour that revealed itself in the harsh way they treated each other. Melchor invested all his affection in Milagros, as did José, once he had resigned himself to not having a son. Ana became a witness to the rivalry between the two men, always taking her father's side, whom she loved and respected more than her husband.

Night had fallen; what was Melchor doing?

The strumming of a guitar brought her back to reality. Behind her, in the alley, she heard people bustling about, dragging chairs and benches.

'Party!' shouted a boy's voice.

Another guitar joined in, trying out a few first notes. Soon the hollow tapping of a pair of castanets was heard, and another pair, and another, and even some old metal ones, getting ready, without order or harmony, just trying to wake up those fingers that would later accompany the dancing and singing. More guitars. A woman cleared her throat; hers was the cracked voice of an old woman. A tambourine.

Ana thought about her father and how much he enjoyed the dancing. *He always comes back*, she tried to convince herself. Wasn't that true? He was a Vega, after all!

When she went out into the alley, the gypsies were arranged in a circle around a fire.

'Come on, let's go!' encouraged an old man sitting on a chair in front of the bonfire.

All the instruments were silent. A single guitar, in the hands of a young man with an almost black face and a dark ponytail, started in on the first beats of a fandango.

She was accompanied by the cabin boy with whom she'd shared her tobacco. They docked on a quay in Triana, past the shrimp boats' port, to unload some goods destined for that part of town.

'You get off here, darkie,' ordered the captain of the tartan.

The boy smiled at Caridad. They had smoked together a couple more times over the voyage. Under the tobacco's influence, Caridad had even answered the boy's questions, mostly in timid mono-syllables. He had heard many of the rumours swirling around the port about that distant land. Cuba. Was it really as wealthy as he'd been told? Were there a lot of sugar factories? And slaves, were there as many as they said?

'Some day I will travel on one of those big ships,' he claimed, letting his imagination run rampant. 'And I'll be the captain! I will cross the ocean and see Cuba for myself.'

Once the tartan was docked, Caridad, just as in Cádiz, stopped and hesitated before the very narrow strip of land between the river-bank and the first line of buildings in Triana, some of them so close that their foundations were exposed by the movement of the Guadalquivir's waters. One of the porters shouted at her to move out of the way so he could unload a large sack. The shout attracted the captain's attention, who shook his head from the gunwale. His gaze briefly met the cabin boy's, who was also watching Caridad; they both knew where she was headed.

'You have five minutes,' he conceded to the boy.

The boy thanked him with a smile, jumped on to land and tugged at Caridad. 'Run. Follow me,' he pressed. He knew that the captain would leave him on land if he didn't hurry.

They passed the first line of buildings and reached the church of Santa Ana; they continued two blocks further from the river, the cabin boy nervous, pulling Caridad along, dodging the people who looked at them curiously, until they were in front of La Cava.

'These are the Minims,' indicated the boy, pointing to a building across from La Cava.

Caridad followed the boy's finger: a low, whitewashed building with a modest church; then she directed her gaze to the old defensive moat that stood in her way, sunken, filled with refuse at many points, precariously level in others.

'There are some places where you can cross,' added the boy, imagining what was going through Caridad's head. 'There's one in San Jacinto but it's a bit far away. People cross wherever they can, see?' He pointed to some people who were going up or down the sides of the trench. 'I have to get back to the boat,' he warned Caridad when she didn't react. 'Good luck, Negress.'

Caridad didn't say anything.

'Good luck,' he repeated before heading off as fast as his legs could carry him.

Once she was alone, Caridad looked at the convent, the place Don Damián had told her to go to. She crossed the trench along a small open path among the rubbish. There were no dumps on the plantation, but there were some in Havana; she'd had the chance to see them when her master had taken her to the city to deliver the tobacco leaves to the warehouse in the port. How could white people throw away so many things? She reached the convent and pushed on one of the doors. Locked. She knocked and waited. Nothing happened. She knocked again, timidly, as if she didn't want to be a bother.

'Not like that,' said a woman passing by, who, almost without stopping, pulled on a chain that made a small bell ring.

Soon a latticed peephole opened in one of the doors.

'May the peace of Our Lord be with you,' she heard the caretaker say; from the voice, she was an elderly woman. 'What brings you to our house?'

Caridad removed her straw hat. Although she couldn't see the nun, she lowered her gaze. 'Don Damián told me to come here,' she whispered.

'I don't understand you.'

Caridad had spoken rapidly and incoherently, the way newly arrived blacks in Cuba do when addressing white men. 'Don Damián . . .' she struggled, 'he told me to come here.'

'Who is Don Damián?' enquired the nun after a few moments of silence.

'Don Damián . . . the priest on the boat, on *The Queen*.'

'The queen? What did you say about the queen?' exclaimed the nun.

'*The Queen*, the boat from Cuba.'

'Ah! A boat, not Her Majesty. Well . . . I don't know. Don Damián, you said? Wait a moment.'

When the peephole opened again, the voice that emerged was authoritative and firm. 'Good woman, what did that priest say you should do here?'

'He only told me to come.'

The nun didn't speak for a few seconds. Her voice was then sweet. 'We are a poor community. We devote ourselves to prayer, abstinence, contemplation and penitence, not charity. What could you do here?'

Caridad didn't answer.

'Where do you come from?'

'Cuba.'

'Are you a slave? Where are your masters?'

'I am . . . I'm free. I also know how to pray.' Don Damián had urged her to say that.

Caridad couldn't see the nun's resigned smile. 'Listen,' she said. 'You have to go to the Brotherhood of Nuestra Señora de los Ángeles, do you understand?'

Caridad remained in silence. Why did Don Damián have me come here, she wondered.

'The Brotherhood of the Negritos,' explained the nun, 'yours. They will help you . . . or give you advice. Take note: walk to the church of Nuestra Señora de los Ángeles, near Cruz del Campo. Continue northward along La Cava, towards San Jacinto. There you can cross La Cava, turn to the right and follow Santo Domingo Street until you reach the pontoon bridge, cross it and then . . .'

Caridad left the Minims trying to retain the itinerary in her head. 'Los Ángeles.' They had told her she had to go there. 'Los Ángeles.' They would help her. 'In Cruz del Campo,' she recited in a soft voice.

Absorbed in her thoughts, she went on her way unaware of how people stared: a voluptuous woman with black skin, dressed in greyish rags and carrying a small bundle, who murmured to herself incessantly. In Altozano, awed by the monumental castle of San Jorge by the bridge, she bumped into a woman. She tried to apologize but the words didn't come out; the woman insulted her and Caridad fixed her gaze on Seville, on the other bank. Dozens of carts and pack animals crossed the bridge in one direction or the other; the wood creaked on the pontoons.

'Where do you think you're going, darkie?'

She was startled by the man who blocked her way.

'To the Los Ángeles church,' she answered.

'Congratulations,' he said sarcastically. 'That's where the Negroes are. But to get to your kind, you'll have to pay me first.'

Caridad surprised herself by looking straight into the toll keeper's eyes. Alarmed, she corrected her attitude, removed her hat and lowered her gaze.

'I . . . I don't have money,' she stammered.

'Then you don't get any Negritos. Get out of here. I've got a lot of work.' He made a gesture of heading over to a muleteer who was waiting behind Caridad, but seeing that she was still standing there, he turned towards her again. 'Get out or I'll call the constables!'

After getting off the bridge she was aware that eyes were on her. She didn't have the money to cross over to Seville. What could she do? The man on the bridge hadn't told her how she could get money. In her twenty-five years, Caridad had never earned a single coin. The most she'd ever had, besides the food, clothing and sleeping quarters, was the 'smoke', the tobacco that her master had given her for personal consumption. How could she earn money? She didn't know anything besides tending tobacco . . .

She moved away from the other people, retreating towards the river and sitting on its bank. She was free, sure, but that freedom was of little use to her if she couldn't even cross a bridge. She had always been told what to do, from sunrise to sunset, day after day, year after year. What was she going to do now?

There were many folk from Triana who observed the black woman sitting on the bank, stock-still, with her gaze on the horizon . . . looking at the river, at Seville, or perhaps lost in her memories or meditating on the uncertain future opening out before her. Some of them passed again an hour later, others after two or even three and four, and the black woman was still there.

As night fell, Caridad realized she was hungry and thirsty. The last time she had had anything to eat or drink was with the cabin boy, who shared a hard, mouldy cake and some water with her. She decided to smoke to cover up her craving, as all the slaves on the tobacco plantation did when waylaid by weariness or hunger. Perhaps that was why the master was generous with the 'smoke': the more they smoked, the less food he had to give them. The tobacco replaced many assets and was even bartered for new slaves. The smell of the cigar attracted two men who were walking along the bank. They asked for a smoke. Caridad obeyed and handed them her cigar. They smoked. The men chatted between themselves, passing the cigar, both standing. Caridad, still seated, asked for it back by extending her arm.

'You want something in your mouth, darkie?' said one of the men, laughing.

The other let out a chuckle and pulled on Caridad's hair to lift her head as the first man lowered his pants.

Caridad offered no resistance and fellated the man.

'Looks like she likes it,' the one who had her by the hair said nervously. 'You like it, Negress?' he asked as her pushed her head against his friend's penis.

Then they both mounted her, one after the other, and left her lying there.

Caridad readjusted her dress. Where was the rest of her cigar?

She had seen one of them toss it before grabbing her hair. Maybe it hadn't landed in the water. She brushed through the grasses and rushes, feeling along the ground carefully in case the tip was still burning . . . And it was! She grabbed it and, with her belly flat against the ground, right at the water's edge, she inhaled with all her strength. She sat down again and let her feet go into the water. It was cold, but in that moment she didn't notice; she didn't feel anything. Was she supposed to like it? That was what one of them had asked her. How many times had she been asked that same question? The master had asked when she was just fresh off the boat, recently plucked from her homeland. Then she hadn't even understood what she was being asked by that man who groped her and slobbered before tearing her open. Later, after many more times, after her pregnancy, he replaced her with a new girl, and then it was the overseer and the other slaves who asked her that between their puffing and panting. One day she gave birth again . . . to Marcelo. The pain she felt that time, when her womb tore after hours of labour, told her that she would never have another child. 'Do you like it?' they would ask her on Sundays, at the dance, when some slave took her by the arm out of the hut, there where other couples were fornicating as well. Later they would go back to singing and dancing frenetically, in the hopes that one of their gods would mount them. Sometimes they would leave the quarters again for a repeat. No, she didn't like it, but she didn't feel anything anyway; they had gradually robbed her of her feelings, bit by bit, from the first night her master had taken her by force.

Less than an hour had passed before one of the men returned and interrupted her thoughts.

'Do you want a job in my workshop?' he asked her, illuminating her with an oil lamp. 'I'm a potter.'

What is a potter? wondered Caridad, trying to make him out in the darkness. She only wanted . . . 'Will you give me money to cross the bridge?' she enquired.

The man saw the hesitation on her face. 'Come with me,' he ordered.

That she understood: an order, as when some Negro grabbed her by the arm and took her out behind the hut. She followed him towards Cava Vieja. At the height of the Inquisition Castle, without turning around, the potter questioned her.

'Are you a runaway?'

'I'm free.'

In the castle lights, Caridad could see the man nodding his head.

His was a small workshop, with a living space on the upper floor, on the street of the potters. They went in and the man pointed to a straw mattress in one corner of the workshop, beside the woodpile and the kiln. Caridad sat down on it.

'You'll start tomorrow. Sleep.'

The warmth of the kiln's embers eased Caridad, frozen stiff from the Guadalquivir's dampness, into slumber, and she slept.

Since the Muslim period, Triana had been known for its fired-clay production, especially for its glazed low-relief tiles; the masters sank a greased cord into the fresh clay and achieved magnificent drawings. However, some time ago that artisanal ceramic work had degenerated into repetitive, charmless pieces, which now had to compete with English flint stoneware and people's changing tastes, which leaned towards Oriental porcelain. So the trade was in decline in Triana.

The next day, at dawn, Caridad began to work alongside the man from the night before, a young man who must have been his son and an apprentice who couldn't take his eyes off her. She loaded wood, moved clay, swept a thousand times and took care of the ashes in the kiln. The days passed that way. The potter – Caridad never saw a woman emerge from the upstairs floor – visited her at nights.

'I have to cross the bridge to get to the church of Los Ángeles, where the Negroes are,' she wanted to say to him one night, when the man, after taking her, was preparing to leave. Instead she just stammered, 'And my money?'

'Money! You want money? You eat more than you work and you have a place to sleep,' answered the potter. 'What more could a Negress like you want? Or would you rather be on the street begging for alms like most free Negroes?'

In those days, slavery had almost completely disappeared from Seville; the economic and demographic crisis, the 1640 war with

Portugal (which was the major supplier of slaves to the Sevillian market), the bubonic plague that the city had suffered a few years later (which showed no mercy to the black slaves), along with the constant manumissions ordered in the wills of pious Sevillians: all contributed to a significant decline in slavery. Seville was losing its slaves at the same rate it was losing its economic strength.

You eat more than you work, echoed in Caridad's ears. She then recalled what Master José's overseer on the plantation always used to say: 'You don't work as much as you eat,' was his accusation before letting the whip fall on to their backs. Not much had changed in her life; what good had being freed done her?

One night, the potter didn't come down the stairs. The next night he didn't show up either. On the third night, when he did come down, he headed towards the door instead of towards her. He opened it and let in another man, then pointed him over to Caridad. The potter waited by the door while that man satisfied his desires, charged him and then bade him farewell.

From that night on, Caridad stopped working in the shop. The man locked her up in a miserable little room on the lower floor, with no ventilation, and he placed a straw mattress and a chamber pot beside some debris.

'If you make trouble, if you scream or try to escape, I'll kill you,' the potter threatened the first time he brought her food. 'Nobody will miss you.'

That's true, lamented Caridad as she listened to the man turn the key in the door again: who was going to miss her? She sat on the straw mattress with the bowl of thin vegetable stew in her hands. She had never before had her life threatened: masters didn't kill slaves; they were worth a lot of money. A slave was useful for its whole life. Once trained, as Caridad was as a girl, Negroes reached old age on the tobacco plantations, in the sugar mills or cane factories. The law prohibited selling a slave for more than it had been bought for, so no master, after having taught them a trade, would get rid of them; they'd lose money. One could mistreat them or force them to work to the point of exhaustion, but a good overseer knew his limits and usually stopped short of death. There were those slaves who took their own lives; sometimes at dawn, the light would gradually, unexpectedly, reveal the silhouette of an inert black body hanging from a tree . . . or perhaps several who had together decided to escape their lives once and for all. Then the master would get very angry, as he did when a mother killed a newborn to free it from a life of slavery or when a Negro injured himself to avoid work. The following Sunday, at mass, the priest from the sugar mill would shout that it was a sin, that they would go to hell, as if a hell worse than that existed. Die? *Maybe*, thought Caridad, *maybe the time has come to escape this world where no one will miss me.*

That same night it was two men who enjoyed her body. Then the potter closed the door again and Caridad was left in the most absolute darkness. She didn't think about it. She sang softly through what was left of the night, and when the first rays of light made their way through the cracks in the planks of the miserable little room, she searched among the junk until she found an old rope. This could work, she concluded after pulling on it to test its strength. She tied it to her neck and climbed on to a rickety box. She threw the rope over a wooden beam above her head, pulled it taut and knotted the other end. There had been times when she'd envied those black figures hanging from the trees, interrupting the landscape of the Cuban tobacco plantation, freed from their suffering.

'God is the greatest of all kings,' she called out. 'I only hope not to become a lost soul.'

She leapt off the box. The rope held her weight, but not the wooden beam, which cracked and fell on top of her. The noise was such that the potter soon appeared at Caridad's cell. He put her in irons and, from that day on, Caridad stopped eating and drinking, begging for death even as the potter and his son force-fed her.

The visits from men off the street continued, usually one, sometimes more, until one night an old man who was clumsily trying to mount her got up and off her with shocking agility.

'This Negress is burning up!' he shouted. 'She has a fever. Are you trying to give me some strange illness?'

The potter came over to Caridad and put his hand on her sweaty forehead. 'Get out of here!' he ordered, pressuring her with a foot in the ribs as he struggled to force open and recover the chains that held her captive. 'Right now, this minute!' he yelled once he had managed to free her. Without waiting for her to get up, he grabbed Caridad's bundle and threw it out on to the street.

Was it possible that he had heard a song? It was just a murmur mixed in with the sounds of the night. Melchor pricked up his ears. There it was again!

'*Yemayá asesú . . .*'

The gypsy remained still in the darkness, in the middle of the fertile lowlands of Triana, surrounded by garden plots and fruit trees. The murmur of the Guadalquivir's waters reached his ears clearly, as did the whistle of the wind among the vegetation, but . . .

'*Asesú yemayá.*'

It seemed like a dialogue: a whisper sung by the soloist who then responded like a chorus. He turned towards the voice; some of the beads that hung from his jacket jangled. It was almost completely dark, except for the torches from the Carthusian monastery, a bit further on.

'*Yemayá oloddo.*'

Melchor left the path and entered an orange grove. He stepped on rocks and fallen leaves, he stumbled several times and even loudly cursed all the saints, and yet, despite his shouts echoing like thunder in the night, the sad soft singing continued. He stopped in a patch of trees. It was there, right there.

'*Oloddo yemayá. Oloddo . . .*'

Melchor squinted his eyes. One of the persistent clouds that had covered Seville during the day allowed a faint glimmer of the moon to come through. Then he could make out a greyish form on the ground, before him, just a few paces away. He approached and knelt until he could make out a woman as black as the night dressed in grey clothes. She was sitting with her back against an orange tree, as if seeking refuge in it. Her gaze was vague, unaware of his presence, and she continued singing softly, in a monotone, repeating the same refrain over and over again. Melchor noticed that, despite the cold, her forehead was beaded with sweat. She was shivering.

He sat down beside her. He didn't understand what she was saying, but that weary voice, that timbre, the monotony, the resignation that impregnated her voice revealed immense pain. Melchor closed his eyes, hugged his knees and let himself be transported by the song.

'Water.'

Caridad's request broke the silence of the night. Her singing could no longer be heard; it had died out like an ember. Melchor opened his eyes. The song's sadness and melancholy had managed to take him back to the galley benches. Water. How many times had he asked for the same thing? He thought he could feel the muscles of his legs, arms and back tensing, just as when the galley master increased the pace of the rowing to chase some Saracen ship. His torturous whistle goaded their senses as his whip tore off the skin on their bare backs to get them to row harder and harder. The punishment could last hours. Finally, with all the muscles in their body about to burst and their mouths bone-dry, from the rows of benches there arose a single plea: Water!

'I know what it is to be thirsty,' he murmured to himself.

'Water,' begged Caridad again.

'Come with me.' Melchor got up with difficulty, numb from an hour sitting beneath the orange tree.

The gypsy stretched and tried to orient himself to find the road to La Cartuja – the Carthusian monastery. He had been heading towards its gardens, where many of the Triana gypsies lived, when the soft singing had attracted his attention.

'Are you coming or not?' he asked Caridad.

She tried to get up, grabbing on to the orange tree's trunk. She had a fever. She was hungry and cold. But, more than anything, she was thirsty, very thirsty. Would he give her water if she went with him, or would he trick her like so many others had over the course of her days in Triana? She walked behind him. Her head was spinning. Almost everyone she'd met had taken advantage of her.

A series of lights coming from a cluster of shacks on the road lit up the gypsy's sky-blue silk jacket. Caridad struggled to keep up with him. Melchor didn't pay her special attention. He walked slowly but erect and proud, leaning just for show on the two-pointed staff that marked him as the patriarch of a family; sometimes he could be heard speaking into the night. As they approached the settlement, the beads on Melchor's clothes and the silver edging on his socks shone. Caridad took the shimmering gleam as a good omen: that man hadn't laid a hand on her. He would give her water.

3

THAT NIGHT, the partying in the San Miguel alley went on for a long time. Each of the smithing families insisted on demonstrating their talents at dancing, singing and playing the guitar, castanets and tambourines, as if it were a competition. The García family was there, along with the Camacho family, the Flores family, the Carmonas, the Vargases and many more of the twenty-one surnames that inhabited that alleyway. All the traditional gypsy songs were heard – *romances*, *zarabandas*, *chaconas*, *jácaras*, fandangos, *seguidillas* and *zarambeques* – and they danced in the glow of a bonfire fed by the women as the hours passed. Around the fire, sitting in the first row, were the gypsies that made up the council of elders, headed by Rafael García, a man of some sixty years, gaunt, serious and curt, whom they called El Conde.

The wine and tobacco flowed. The women contributed food from their homes: bread, cheese, sardines and shrimp, chicken and hare, hazelnuts, acorns, quince jam and fruit. These parties were for sharing; when they sang and danced they forgot about the bickering and the atavistic enmity, and the elders were there to guarantee that. The smithing gypsies of Triana were not rich. They were still those same people who had been persecuted in Spain since the time of the Catholic Kings: they weren't allowed to wear their brightly coloured clothes or speak in their dialect, walk the roads, tell fortunes or deal in horses and mules. They were banned from singing and dancing, they weren't even permitted to live in Triana or work as metalsmiths. On several occasions the non-gypsy guilds of smiths had tried to keep them from working in their simple forges, and the royal proclamations and orders had insisted on it, but it was all in vain: the gypsy smiths guaranteed the supply of the thousands of horseshoes essential for the animals that worked the fields of the kingdom of Seville, so they continued smithing and selling their products to the same non-gypsy smiths who wanted to stop them but were unable to meet the enormous demand.

While the half-naked kids tried to emulate their parents at the end of the alley, Ana and Milagros started up a lively *zarabanda* along with two relatives from José's family, the Carmonas. Mother and daughter, one beside the other, smiling when their eyes met, twisted their hips and played with the sensuousness of their bodies to the sounds of the guitar and voice. José, like so many others, watched, clapped and shouted words of encouragement. With each dance movement, as if casting out a net, the women incited the men, following them with their eyes, suggesting an impossible romance. They moved closer and backed away again, they spun around them to the shameless rhythm of their hips, flaunting their breasts, the mother's, lush and the daughter's, pert. They both danced erect, lifting their arms above their heads or twirling them around their sides; the scarves that Milagros wore tied around her wrists took on a life of their own in the air. Some women, in a ring, accompanied the guitars with their castanets and tambourines; many men clapped and crowed at the two women's voluptuousness; more than one failed to contain a lustful glance when Ana grabbed the edge of her skirt with her right hand and continued dancing while revealing her bare calves and feet.

'Look up at the heavens, gypsies, God wants to come down and dance with my daughter!' shouted José Carmona.

The shouts of encouragement kept coming.

'Olé!'

'That's the way!'

'Olé, olé and olé!'

Milagros, spurred on by her father's compliment, imitated Ana, lifting her skirt, and they both circled their dance partners again and again, wrapping them in a halo of passions as the music reached its peak. The gypsies burst into cheers and applause as the *zarabanda* ended. Mother and daughter immediately dropped their skirts and smoothed them with their hands. They smiled. A guitar began to play, tuning up, preparing for a new dance, a new song. Ana stroked her daughter's face and, when she drew near to kiss her cheek, the strumming stopped. Rafael García, El Conde, kept his hand slightly lifted over the guitar. A murmur travelled through the gypsies and even the children approached. Reyes 'La Trianera', El Conde's wife, a fat woman close to sixty years old, with a coppery face scored with a thousand wrinkles, had got one of the other elders out of his chair with a simple, emphatic chin gesture and she had sat down in it.

In the firelight, only Ana was able to make out the look that La Trianera gave her. It lasted a second, perhaps less. The gaze of a gypsy woman: cold and hard, able to penetrate your soul. Ana straightened up, about to face the challenge, but her eyes met El Conde's: *Listen and learn!* his face told her.

La Trianera sang a capella, without music, without anyone shouting, clapping or goading her on. She sang a *debla*: a song to the gypsy gods. Her hoarse old voice, weak, out of tune, nevertheless touched those who heard it deep inside. She sang with her hands trembling and partially open in front of her breasts, as if she were gathering strength through them, and she sang of the many sorrows of the gypsies: the injustices, jail, heartbreak . . . in verses without metre that only found their meaning in the rhythm that La Trianera's voice wanted to give them, always ending with praise in the gypsy tongue. *Deblica barea*, magnificent goddess.

The *debla* seemed endless. La Trianera could have made it go on as long as her imagination or memory allowed, but she finally let her hands drop on her knees and lifted her head, which she had kept tilted to one side as she sang. The gypsies, Ana among them, her throat hoarse, broke out in applause again; many with their eyes flooded with tears. Milagros applauded too, looking at her mother out of the corner of her eye.

In that moment, when she offered her applause and saw her daughter do the same, Ana was glad Melchor wasn't there. Her hands hit each other slackly for one last time and she took advantage of the clamour to slip through the crowd. She rushed as she felt El Conde's and La Trianera's eyes on her back; she imagined them smiling smugly, them and theirs. She pushed aside the gypsies who were still celebrating the singing and, once outside of the circle, she headed to the entryway of her house, and leaned against one of the doorposts.

The Garcías! Rafael García! Her father spat when he heard that name. Her mother . . . her mother had passed away two years after Melchor was fettered to the bench of a galley, and she did so swearing vengeance from the world beyond.

'It was him!' muttered her mother again and again as they begged for alms on the streets of Málaga, in front of the jail where Melchor was waiting to be led to the Port of Santa María to board the galleys. 'Rafael denounced him to the sergeant of the tobacco patrol. Wretch. He violated gypsy law. Son of a bitch! Swine! Mangy dog . . .!'

And when little Ana saw that people were moving away from them, she would elbow her so she wouldn't scare off the parishioners with her yelling.

'Why did he denounce him?' the girl asked one day.

Her mother squinted her eyes and twisted her mouth scornfully before answering.

'The fighting between the Vegas and the Garcías goes way back. Nobody knows exactly why. There are those who say it was over a donkey, others say it was over a woman. Some money? Perhaps. No one knows any longer, but the two families have always hated each other.'

'Just over—?'

'Don't interrupt me, girl.' Her mother smacked her on the back of the neck, hard. 'Listen well to what I am going to say to you, because you are a Vega and you will have to live as one. We gypsies have always been free. Every king and prince of every place in the world has tried to make us submit and they have never been able to do it. They never will; our race is better than all of them, smarter. We don't need much. We take what we need: what the Creator put in this world isn't anyone's property, the fruits of the earth belong to all men and, if we don't like some place, we just move to another. Nothing and no one ties us down. We don't care about the risks; what do laws and decrees mean to us? That is what we Vegas, and everyone who considers themselves gypsy by blood, have always defended. And that is how we have always lived.' Her mother had paused before continuing. 'Shortly before they arrested your father, the head of the council of elders died. The Garcías pressured the others to choose one from their family and your father opposed it. He accused them of not living like gypsies, of working in the forge like *payos*, in accord with them, doing business with them, marrying in the church and baptizing their children. Of renouncing freedom.

'One day Rafael showed up at the settlement; he was looking for your father.' Ana thought she remembered that day. Her mother and aunts had ordered her to move aside, like the other little ones, and she had obeyed . . . but she sneaked back to the place where Rafael had planted himself, threatening, surrounded by members of the Vega family. 'He came armed with a knife and looking for a fight, but your father wasn't there. Someone told him that he'd gone to Portugal for tobacco. The smile that crossed that bastard's face then was proof enough.'

In the San Miguel alley, as the elders got up from their chairs, the men and women began to leave, some to their homes, others scattered through the inner courtyards of the clusters of apartments, in groups, chatting and drinking. The guitars, castanets and tambourines were still heard, but now in younger hands; girls and boys took over and made the party their own.

Ana's eyes swept over the alley: Milagros was dancing happily with other girls her age. She was so pretty! Her grandfather had said the same thing the first time they showed her to him. Less than a day passed between Melchor Vega's return from the galleys – barely a few hours, during which Melchor learned of his wife's death and met his four-year-old granddaughter whom he didn't dare touch, fearing his filthy and cracked hands could hurt her – and his taking up of a large knife and heading, still weak and dishevelled, in search of the man who had informed on him. His daughter had wanted to hold him back, but she didn't dare.

Rafael came out to meet him, armed as well and accompanied by his family. They didn't exchange a single word; they knew what was at stake and why. The men goaded each other, their arms and knives extended, the weapons mere extensions of their bodies. Rafael did it with strength and agility, keeping his hand firm. Melchor's trembled slightly. They spun around each other as their family members remained silent. Few focused their attention on Melchor's trembling knife; most watched his face, his bearing, the anxiousness and decisiveness his entire body displayed. He wanted to kill! He was going to kill! His weakened state didn't matter, or his wounds, his shabby clothes, his filth or his shaking. Melchor would kill Rafael: that much was clear.

That certainty was what led Antonio García, Rafael's uncle and then head of the council, to come between the contenders before either of them launched the first stab. Ana, with Milagros in her arms, held tight against her chest, sighed in relief. After Antonio García's gesture, the elders intervened; the men of the Vega family were warned to deal with the matter before it came to blood. The council, despite opposition from the Vegas and the representatives of two other families who lived in the settlement on the Carthusians' grounds, ruled that there was no proof that Rafael had informed on Melchor, so if he killed Rafael, they would come out in defence of the Garcías and start a war against the Vegas. In addition, they decided that if Melchor killed Rafael, any gypsy could take vengeance and kill another member of the Vega family; in that case gypsy law wouldn't punish him, the council would stay out of it.

As night fell, Uncle Basilio Vega headed over to Melchor and his family. Milagros was sleeping in her mother's arms.

'Melchor,' he said after telling him of the council's decisions. 'You know that we will all support you whatever you decide. No one can make us back down!'

And he handed him the girl, who woke up when placed into her grandfather's arms. Milagros remained still, as if aware of the significance of that moment. *Smile at him!* begged Ana in silence, her hands crossed, stiff, but the girl didn't do it. A few seconds passed before Basilio and Ana saw Melchor purse his lips and stroke the girl's hair with a firm hand. They knew then what his decision was: to submit to the council for the good of the family.

That girl who had thwarted a bloodbath was now dancing and singing in the San Miguel alley. From the door to her house, Ana enjoyed watching her daughter; she found her lovely, proud, decisive, ardent as she danced flirtatiously with a young man . . . Suddenly the woman shook her head violently and moved out of the doorway, confused. The young man was watching her daughter's dance steps unenthusiastically, indifferent to her effort, cold, almost mocking. Didn't Milagros realize? That young man . . . Ana squinted her eyes to focus her vision. He was older than her daughter, dark, attractive, strong, tough. And Milagros danced unaware of her partner's disdain; she was smiling, her eyes twinkled, radiating sensuality. Then, positioned behind the chairs that surrounded the embers of a bonfire, she saw La Trianera, who was clapping with a mocking expression of victory at the girl – a Vega, Melchor's granddaughter – displaying her obvious desire, in public, for one of her grandsons: Pedro García.

'Milagros!' screamed Ana, running towards her.

She grabbed her daughter by the shoulder and shook her until she stopped dancing. La Trianera's mocking expression became a smile. When Milagros seemed about to respond, her mother silenced any complaint with a couple more shakes. The guitarists had almost stopped strumming when La Trianera urged them to continue. Some men approached. Young Pedro García, emboldened by his grand-mother's attitude, wanted to humiliate the Vega women even further and he continued dancing around Milagros as if her mother's inter-vention was nothing more than a trivial setback. Ana saw him coming, let go of her daughter and, just as the gypsy approached, extended her arm and smacked him with the back of her hand. Pedro García stumbled. Milagros opened her mouth but no words came out. The guitars were silent. La Trianera got up. Other gypsy women from various families came over quickly.

Before they got into a fight, the men got between them.

'Bitch!'

'Hussy!'

'Wretch!'

'Slut!'

They insulted each other as they struggled to get away from the men, pushing them away to get to the other women, Ana more than anyone. More men came over, José Carmona among them, and they managed to contain the situation. José shook his wife the way she had their daughter; then, with the help of two relatives, he managed to drag her to the other side of the alley.

'Strumpet!' Ana kept shouting as they pulled her off, wrenching her head round to direct her words at La Trianera.

The gypsy settlement by the grounds of the Carthusian monastery was just a bunch of squalid huts built with clay and pieces of timber – some no more than simple lean-tos made of reeds and fabric – that had gradually extended from the first ones built up against the wall surrounding the monks' land, between the monastery and Triana. Melchor was well received. Many greeted him in the street as he passed; others peeked from the doors of those windowless shacks. The meagre glow of candles illuminating the inside of the houses and a few fires that were lit along the street fought against the shadows.

'Melchor, I have a donkey the tobacco patrol could never catch you on. Interested?' exclaimed an old gypsy seated on a chair at the door to a hut, while he pointed to one of the many pack animals tied or staked along the street.

Melchor didn't even look at the animal. 'For that I'd have to carry him on my shoulders,' he answered, dismissively swatting the air.

They both laughed.

Caridad was walking behind Melchor, her bare feet sinking into the mire. For a moment she thought she wouldn't have the strength to continue through the mud; she was tormented by fever, her throat smarted and her chest burned. Had that man asked anyone for her water yet? She had heard him talk but she couldn't understand a word of the exchange about the donkey. The gypsies were speaking in their tongue.

'Melchor!' shouted a woman who was nursing a baby, both breasts bared. 'There's a black, black Negress following you. Christ, is she black! I hope my milk doesn't sour.'

'She's thirsty,' was all the gypsy answered.

A couple of huts further on, warned of his arrival, a group of men were waiting for him.

'Brother,' Melchor greeted a younger man as they grabbed each other by the forearm.

An almost naked little boy had run over to grab his two-pointed staff, which he was already flaunting to the other kids.

'Melchor!' the gypsy returned his greeting, squeezing his forearms.

Caridad, feeling herself about to faint, watched how the man she had followed greeted the gypsy men and women and tousled the hair of the children that came over to him. What about her water? A woman noticed her.

'And that Negress?' she enquired.

'She wants to drink.'

At that moment Caridad's knees gave in and she collapsed. The gypsies turned and looked at her, kneeling in the mud.

Old María, the woman who had asked about Caridad, snorted.

'It looks like she needs something more than a drink, Nephew.'

'Well, she only asked me for water.'

Caridad tried to keep her vision focused on the group of gypsies; her sight had clouded over; she couldn't understand what they were saying.

'I can't lift her,' said Old María. 'Girls!' she shouted towards the youngest ones. 'Give me a hand picking up this Negress and getting her inside!'

As soon as the women surrounded Caridad, the men washed their hands of the problem.

'A bit of wine, Uncle?' a young man offered Melchor.

Melchor put an arm over the gypsy's shoulders and hugged him. 'The last time I drank your wine . . .' he commented as they headed to the next hut. 'The salt and vinegar they used to treat our wounds in the galleys went down easier than that brew!'

'Well, the donkeys like it just fine.'

They entered the hut amid peals of laughter. They had to bend down to get through the doorway. It was a single room that was used for everything: the bedroom for the young man's family, kitchen and dining room; there were no windows and just a simple hole in the roof for a chimney. Melchor sat down at a chipped table. The older men sat in other seats or benches and the rest stood; more than a dozen gypsies filled the space.

'Are you calling me a donkey?' Melchor picked up the thread of the conversation when his nephew passed a few cups around the table. The invitation was only for the older men.

'You, Uncle, are a winged steed at the very least. The other day, in the Alcalá market,' continued the gypsy as he poured the wine, 'I managed to sell that grey donkey you saw last time you visited, remember? The one that was in such terrible shape.' Melchor nodded with a smile. 'Well, I gave it a bottle of wine and you should have seen how the poor beast ran – looked like a purebred colt!'

'You're the one who must have been running out of that market as fast as you could,' interjected Uncle Juan, seated at the table.

'Like a bat out of hell, Uncle,' admitted the nephew, 'but with some good money, which I won't be giving back, not even to the devil, no matter how fast he makes me run.'

Melchor lifted his glass of wine and, after the others had joined him in his toast, drank it down in one gulp.

'Watch out!' said a voice from the door. 'We wouldn't want Uncle Melchor to run off like a colt.'

'We could sell him for some good money!' replied another.

Melchor laughed and gestured to his nephew to serve him up some more wine.

After a couple of rounds, more jokes and comments, only the older men remained: Melchor, his brother Tomás, Uncle Juan, Uncle Basilio and Uncle Mateo, all bearing the last name Vega, all dark-skinned, each with a face run through with deep wrinkles, thick brows that came together over the bridge of his nose and a penetrating gaze. The others were chatting outside. Melchor unbuttoned his short blue jacket, revealing a white shirt and a sash of shiny red silk. He searched in one of his inner pockets and pulled out a bundle of a dozen medium-sized cigars that he placed on the table, beside the jug of wine that his nephew had given them.

'Pure Havana tobacco,' he announced, and gestured for each man to take one.

'Thank you,' some of them replied.

'Here's to your health,' murmured another.

In a matter of minutes, the hut filled with an aromatic, bluish smoke that overpowered all the other smells in the small dwelling.

'I have a good shipment of powdered tobacco,' commented Uncle Basilio after expelling a mouthful of smoke into the air. 'From the factory in Seville, Spanish, very finely ground. Interested?'

'Basilio . . .' Melchor reproached him with a weary voice, dragging the syllables.

'It's excellent quality!' said the other in his own defence. 'You can get a better price for it than I can. The priests will be snatching it from your hands. They really squeeze us on the prices. What do you care where it comes from?'

Melchor laughed. 'I don't care where it comes from, just how it got here. You know that. I don't want to sell tobacco that someone has been carrying hidden in their arse. Just thinking about it gives me chills . . .'

'It's well wrapped in pig intestine,' insisted his brother Tomás in defence of his business.

The others nodded. They knew he would give in; he always did, he never refused a request from the family, but first he had to complain, drag the discussion out, make them beg.

'Even still. They carried it in their arses! One day they're going to get caught—'

'It's the only way to get around the guards at the factory,' Basilio interrupted. 'At the end of every work day, they strip several workers, at random.'

'And they don't look up their arses?' laughed Melchor.

'Can you imagine one of those soldiers sticking his finger up a gypsy's arse to see if he's carrying tobacco? They can't even imagine doing such a thing!'

Melchor shook his head, but the obliging way he did so showed them that the deal was coming to a close.

'One day one of them is going to burst and then . . .'

'The *payos* will discover another way to use snuff,' declared Uncle Juan. 'Sniffing it up their arse!'

'I'm sure plenty of them would like that better than up their nose,' ventured Basilio.

The gypsies looked at each other over the table for a few seconds and burst into laughter.

The conversation went on long into the night. The nephew, his wife and three little kids came in when the murmurs from the street began to ebb. The children lay down on two straw mattresses in one corner of the hut. Their father noticed that the jug of wine was empty and went to fill it.

'Your Negress has drunk—' the woman started to say to him from the mattresses.

'She isn't mine,' interrupted Melchor.

'Well, whatever, you're the one who brought her here,' she continued. 'Aunt María gave her a potion of barley boiled with egg whites and her fever is going down.'

Then the couple lay down alongside their children. The men continued chatting, with their wine and their cigars. Melchor wanted to know about the family, and the others filled him in: Julián, married to a Vega, a travelling blacksmith, had been arrested near Antequera as he was repairing the tilling tools of some farmers. 'He wasn't carrying any identification!' muttered Uncle Juan. The gypsies couldn't work as blacksmiths, nor leave their homes. Julián was jailed in Antequera and they had already begun the steps to free him. 'Do you need anything?' offered Melchor. No. They didn't need his help. Sooner or later they'd release him; he was eating for free and there was nothing that irked the royal officials more. Besides, they had sought out the help of a nobleman from Antequera and he had committed to intercede on his behalf. Tomás smiled, as did Melchor: there was always some nobleman who gave them a hand. They liked to protect them. Why did they do it? They had discussed it on numerous occasions: it was as if their favours made those men of noble birth feel somewhat gypsy, as if they wanted to show that they weren't like most people and they shared the darker race's lust for freedom; as if they were taking part in a way of life and a spirit denied them in their routine and rigid customs. Someday they would ask for the favour to be repaid, asking them to sing and dance for them at a party in some sumptuous palace, and they would invite their friends and peers to boast of their illicit connections.

'We've had news that about a month ago,' interjected Uncle Mateo, 'near Ronda, the brotherhood confiscated El Arrugado's animals . . .'

'Who's El Arrugado?' asked Melchor.

'The one who's always hunched over, Josefa's son, the cousin of—'

'Yeah, yeah,' interrupted Melchor.

'They took a horse and two donkeys from him.'

'Has he got them back?'

'Not the little donkeys. The soldiers kept them and then sold them. They sold the horse too, but El Arrugado followed the buyer and got it back the next night. They say it was pretty easy: the *payo* who bought it let it loose in a pen, all he had to do was go in and get it. El Arrugado liked that horse.'

'Is it that good a horse?' asked Melchor after a new sip of wine.

'No way!' answered his brother. 'It's a miserable nag that walks stiff as a board, but since they're two of a kind, all hunched over . . . well, he's comfortable with it.'

Other family members, they explained later to Melchor, had taken sanctuary in a chapel on the road to Osuna more than seven days earlier. They were being chased by the Chief Magistrate of Málaga because some *payos* from Málaga had informed on them.

'Now, as usual, they're all fighting and arguing,' reported Uncle Basilio. 'The magistrate wants them for himself; the Holy Brotherhood has shown up at the chapel claiming the gypsies are theirs; the priest says he doesn't want to get involved; and the vicar, whom the priest called, alleges that the law cannot take them from the sanctuary and that they should take the matter to the bishop.'

'It's always the same,' commented Melchor, remembering the times he himself had taken refuge in churches or monasteries. 'Are they going to take them out?'

'Doesn't matter,' answered Uncle Basilio. 'For the moment

they're letting them argue among themselves. They all have cold immunity, so they'll plead that when they come out and they'll have to set them free again. They'll lose their weapons and their animals, but not much more.'

It was already dawn. Melchor yawned. The nephew and his family were sleeping on the straw mattresses and the gypsy settlement was silent.

'Should we continue in the morning?' he suggested.

The others nodded and got up. Melchor just placed one foot on the table and pushed backward until the chair, on just two of its legs, rested against a wall of the hut. Then he closed his eyes as he listened to his relatives leaving. Cold immunity, he smiled to himself before sleep overtook him. The *payos* always fell into the same traps, which was the only way his people, so persecuted and vilified throughout the country, were able to survive. When a gypsy who had taken sanctuary knew that, if he were removed, the sentence would be little or nothing, he would sometimes get the magistrate to remove him by force, thus violating church asylum. From that point on, if the magistrate or the constables didn't return him to the same place he had been removed from, he now enjoyed what was known as cold immunity. And they didn't ever do it. So the next time they arrested him, perhaps for a more serious crime, like simply walking free along the roads, he could claim that the previous time they hadn't restored him to his asylum, and get out of the sentence that way. 'Cold immunity,' repeated Melchor as he drifted off to sleep.

Melchor spent the next morning in the settlement. He sat smoking on a stool in the street, beside women who were weaving baskets with reeds they'd collected on the riverbanks, absorbed in those expert hands braiding baskets they'd later try to sell in the streets and markets. He heard their conversations without joining in; they all knew who Melchor was. Every once in a while, one would disappear and return shortly with a bit of wine for him. He ate at his brother Tomás's house, chicken stew that was a bit past its prime, and he leaned the chair back again for a nap. When he awoke, he got ready to return to the San Miguel alley.

'Thanks for lunch, Brother.'

'No thanks necessary,' answered Tomás. 'Don't forget this,' he added, handing him the pig intestine filled with powdered tobacco they'd talked about the night before. 'Uncle Basilio trusts you'll make a good profit.'

Melchor grabbed it with a disgusted expression, put it in one of the inner pockets of his short jacket and left the hut. Then he started down the street that bordered the wall surrounding the lands belonging to the Carthusian monastery. He would have liked to continue living there, among his own, but his beloved daughter and granddaughter lived with the Carmonas, in the alley, and he couldn't distance himself from the blood of his blood.

'Nephew!' A woman's shout interrupted his thoughts. Melchor turned towards Old María, in the door of her shack. 'You're forgetting your Negress,' she added.

'She's not mine,' he answered wearily; he had already told her that several times.

'She's not mine either,' complained the woman. 'She's taking up my mattress, and her legs stick out the bottom. What do you want me to do with her? Take her with you! You brought her, you take her.'

Take her with me? thought Melchor. What was he going to do with a Negress?

'No—' he started to say.

'What do you mean, no?' Old María interrupted him, her hands on her hips. 'I said she's going with you and she's going with you, understood?'

Several gypsies whirled around them when they heard the ruckus. Melchor looked at the little old woman, gaunt and wrinkled, planted in the door of the hut in her colourful apron, challenging him. He . . . he was respected by everyone in the settlement, but this was Old María before him now. And when a gypsy woman like Old María puts her hands on her hips and skewers you with her gaze . . .

'What do you want me to do with her?'

'Whatever you like,' answered the old woman, knowing she had won.

Several women smiled; a man sighed loudly, another made a face as he tilted his head to one side and a couple of others grumbled under their breath.

'She couldn't move . . .' argued Melchor, pointing to the mud of the street. 'She fell here . . .'

'She can now. She's a strong woman.'

Old María told him that the black woman was named Caridad and she handed Melchor a wineskin with the rest of the barley and egg mixture that she was to take until the fevers went away completely.

'Bring it back next time you come round,' she warned. 'And take care of her!' exhorted the old woman as they set off.

Melchor turned towards her in surprise and questioned her with his eyes. What did she care? Why . . . ?

'Her tears are as sad as ours,' said María, anticipating his question.

And that was how, with Caridad noticeably better behind him and the wineskin hanging from his staff, which was slung over his shoulder like a pole, Melchor arrived at the San Miguel alley, which was flooded with smoke and the ringing of hammers on anvils.

'Who's that woman?' his son-in-law José asked harshly when he saw her enter the courtyard. He still had a hammer in his hand and wore a leather apron over his bare, sweaty chest.

Melchor stood up tall with the wineskin still hanging over his back off his staff, Caridad motionless behind him, unable to understand the gypsy tongue. Since when did he owe any explanations to surly José Carmona? The challenge lasted a few seconds.

'She sings well,' was all he finally said.

4

THE CARMONA FAMILY'S blacksmith shop was located on the lower level of a cluster of apartments in the San Miguel alley. It was a three-storey rectangular building built around a tiny courtyard with a well in the centre. The workshop and the families who lived on the upper floors all made use of its water. However, getting to the well often proved a difficult task, since both the courtyard and the corridors that surrounded it were used to store the coal for the forge and the iron scraps the gypsies gathered to work with: a ton of twisted and rusty pieces piled up because, unlike the Sevillian *payos* who had to buy their raw material in Vizcaya, the gypsies weren't subject to any ordinances or the inspectors who controlled product quality. Behind the courtyard with the well, through a narrow corridor covered by the roof of the first floor, was a small courtyard with a latrine and, beside that, a small room originally used as a laundry; that was the room Melchor Vega had taken as his own when he returned from the galleys.

'You can stay there.' The gypsy pointed Caridad to the floor of the little courtyard, between the latrine and the entrance to his room. 'You have to keep drinking this remedy until you are cured. Then you can go,' he added, handing her the wineskin. 'The last thing I need is for Old María to think I didn't take care of you!'

Melchor went into his room and closed the door behind him. Caridad sat on the ground, with her back resting against the wall, and organized her scant belongings carefully: the bundle to her right, the wineskin to her left, the straw hat in her hands.

She was no longer trembling and her fever had subsided. She vaguely remembered the first moments of her stay in the hut in the gypsy settlement: first they gave her water, but they didn't allow her to sate her burning thirst. They put cold compresses on her forehead until Old María knelt beside the mattress and forced her to drink the thick concoction of boiled barley. Behind her, two women prayed aloud, speaking over each other, entrusting themselves to countless virgins and saints as they drew crosses in the air.

'Leave the saint worship for the *payos*!' ordered Old María.

Then Caridad fell into a restless, confused stupor that transported her to the work on the plantation, the whip, the feasts on the holidays, and all the old gods she used to sing and plead to appeared before her. The Yoruba drums echoed frenetically in her head, just as they had in the sleeping quarters on the plantation in Cuba. She danced in a dream coven that terrified her, and saw the Negroes beating on the skins of kettledrums, their laughter and obscene gesturing, the other slaves who accompanied them with claves and maracas, their faces shouting frantically inches from hers, all waiting for the saint to come down and mount Caridad. And Oshún, her Orisha, finally did mount her, but in her dream it wasn't to accompany her in a joyful, sensual dance as the goddess usually did, but rather she forced Caridad with her movements and gestures towards a hell where all the gods in the universe battled.

She awoke suddenly, startled, soaked in sweat, and found herself amid the silence of the settlement in the dead of night.

'Girl,' said Old María before long. 'I don't know what you were dreaming about, but it scares me just to imagine it.'

Then Caridad noticed that the gypsy woman seated beside her was gripping her hand tightly. The touch of that rough, wrinkled hand calmed her. It had been so long since anyone had held her hand to comfort her . . . Marcelo . . . she was the one who had cradled the little boy. No. It wasn't that. Perhaps . . . perhaps since she had been stolen away from her mother, in Africa. She could barely remember her. What was she like? The old woman must have sensed her uneasiness and she squeezed her hand. Caridad let herself be rocked by the gypsy's warmth, by the feeling she wanted to transmit to her, but she kept trying to conjure up her mother's face. What had become of her mother and her brothers and sisters? What was the land and freedom of her childhood like? She remembered struggling to sketch her mother's features in her mind . . .

She couldn't do it.

In the dusky light that entered the small courtyard, Caridad looked around at the accumulated filth; it smelled of rubbish. She sensed someone's presence and she grew nervous: two women who stood inside the corridor, filling its entire width, observed her with curiosity.

'Just because she sings well?' whispered a surprised Milagros to her mother, without taking her eyes off Caridad.

'That's what your father told me,' answered Ana, her kind expression turning serious when she remembered José's shouting and wild flailing. 'She sings well, he says! The last thing we need is a Negress!' he had howled after dragging his wife inside the smithy. 'You get in a fight with La Trianera, you slap her grandson, and your father brings a Negress home. He set her up in the little courtyard! What is he thinking? Another mouth to feed? I want that Negress out of this house . . .'

But Ana interrupted his rant just as she did every time her husband raged against his father-in-law: 'If my father says she sings well, that means she sings well, you understand? By the way, he pays for his own food, and if he wants to pay for the food of a Negress who sings well, he'll do it.'

'And what does Grandfather want her for?' asked Milagros in a soft voice.

'I have no idea.'

They stopped whispering, and they both, as if they had agreed on it, focused on Caridad, who had lowered her gaze and remained seated on the ground. Mother and daughter contemplated the old dress of faded grey burlap she wore, the straw hat in her hands, and the bundle and wineskin to either side of her.

'Who are you?' asked Ana.

'Caridad,' she responded with her head bowed.

The gypsies had never not looked someone straight in the eye, no matter how eminent or distinguished they were. Gypsies held the gaze of the noblemen when even their closest advisers didn't dare. They always listened to judges serve sentences with their heads held high, proud. They addressed them all with self-confidence. Wasn't a gypsy, just for having been born gypsy, nobler than the best of the *payos*? The two women waited a few seconds for Caridad to lift her gaze. 'What should we do?' Milagros's eyes asked her mother, seeing the Negro woman's stubborn bashfulness.

Ana shrugged.

Finally it was the girl who decided. Caridad seemed like a frightened, defenceless animal and, after all, *If grandfather brought her here . . .* she thought. She approached her, moved aside the wine-skin, sat beside her, leaning to try to see her face. The seconds passed slowly until Caridad dared to turn towards her.

'Caridad,' the girl then whispered in a sweet voice, 'my grand-father says that you sing very well.'

Ana smiled, opened her hands and left them sitting there.

At first Caridad glanced furtively as she tersely answered the girl's naive questions: What are you doing in Triana? What brought you here? Where are you from? As the evening wore on, Milagros felt Caridad fixing her small eyes on her. She searched for some gleam in her gaze, some brilliance, even the reflection of some damp tears, but she found nothing. And yet . . . Suddenly it was as if Caridad had finally found someone to trust, and as she told Milagros about her life, the girl felt her pain.

'Lovely?' replied Caridad sadly when Milagros asked her if Cuba was as lovely as they said it was. 'There's nothing lovely for a slave.'

'But . . .' the gypsy girl wanted to insist, but she grew quiet at Caridad's gaze. 'Did you have family?' she asked trying to change the subject.

'Marcelo.'

'Marcelo? Who is Marcelo? Didn't you have anyone else?'

'No, nobody else. Just Marcelo.'

'Who is he?'

'My son.'

'So . . . you have children . . . And your man?'

Caridad shook her head almost imperceptibly, as if the girl's naivety was too much for her; didn't she know what slavery was?

'I have no man, no husband,' she explained wearily. 'Slaves have nothing, Milagros. They separated me from my mother when I was very young, and then they separated me from my children; one of them was sold by the master.'

'And Marcelo?' Milagros dared to ask after a short silence. 'Where is he? Did they separate you from him?'

'He stayed in Cuba.' He did find it lovely, she thought. Caridad sketched a smile and became lost in her memories.

'Did they separate you from him?' repeated Milagros after a time.

'No. The white men had no use for Marcelo.'

The gypsy girl hesitated. She didn't dare to insist.

'Do you miss him?' she asked instead.

A tear ran down Caridad's cheek before she managed to nod. Milagros embraced her and felt her crying. Hers was a strange sobbing: muffled, silent, hidden.

The next morning, Melchor bumped into Caridad as he left his room.

'Oh hell!' he cursed. The Negress! He'd forgotten about her.

Caridad lowered her head before the man with the sky-blue silk jacket trimmed in silver. Dawn was breaking and the hammering had yet to start, although you could hear people coming and going in the courtyard where the well was located, beyond the covered corridor. Caridad hadn't slept so well in a long time, despite all the people who had stepped over her on their way to the latrine. She remembered the gypsy girl's promise to help her cross the bridge.

'Pay?' Milagros had laughed loudly.

Caridad felt considerably better than the day before and she dared to look at Melchor; his extremely brown skin made that easier for her, as if she were addressing another slave at the plantation. He must be about fifty years old, she calculated, comparing him with the Negroes that age she had met in Cuba, and he was thin and sinewy. She observed his gaunt face and sensed the traces of his years of suffering and mistreatment, just as she had seen in the faces of Negro slaves.

'Did you drink Old María's potion?' asked the gypsy, interrupting her thoughts. He was surprised to see the colourful blanket that covered her and the straw mattress she rested on, but it wasn't his problem where she'd got them.

'Yes,' she answered.

'Keep taking it,' added Melchor before turning his back, heading into the narrow corridor and disappearing towards the door that led out of the cluster of apartments.

That's it? wondered Caridad then. Weren't they going to make her work or mount her? That man, 'the grandfather' as Milagros had called him on several occasions, had said she sang well. How many times had she been complimented in her entire life? *I sing well,* Caridad told herself with satisfaction. 'Nobody will bother you if Grandfather protects you,' the girl had also assured her. The warmth of the sun's rays that filtered into the small courtyard comforted her. She had a small mattress, a beautiful colourful blanket that Milagros had given her and she could cross the bridge! She closed her eyes and allowed herself to fall into a pleasant stupor.

At that time of the day the San Miguel alley was still calm. Melchor walked through it and, when he reached the height of the Minims, as if entering hostile territory, he touched the packet he carried in his inside jacket pocket. It was actually good snuff that Uncle Basilio had given him. The day before, as soon as he'd gone into his room, after leaving Caridad in the small courtyard, Melchor had pulled the powder out of the pig intestine it was wrapped in with a disgusted expression. He'd placed a pinch on the back of his right hand and inhaled deeply: finely ground. He preferred twisted tobacco, but he knew how to recognize quality in powdered tobacco. Probably 'monte de India', he thought, a rough powder brought from the Indies that was washed and treated in the Seville tobacco factory. He had a good amount. Uncle Basilio would make some good money . . . although he could make even more if . . . he searched through his belongings. He was sure he had it. The last time he sold powder he had used it . . . There it was! A bottle of red ochre, fine reddish earth. It was already night. He began to mix the tobacco powder with the red dirt, by candlelight, very carefully, making sure not to go too far.

With San Jacinto in sight, Melchor again patted the packet with satisfaction: he had added weight and it didn't seem the quality had been too affected.

'Good day, Father,' Melchor said to the first friar he met in the area around the church under construction. 'I am looking for Fray Joaquín.'

'He is teaching grammar to the boys,' answered the Dominican, barely turning, focused on the work being done by one of the carpenters. 'What do you want him for?'

To sell him powdered tobacco a gypsy stole from the factory by sticking it up his arse, which you'll surely enjoy sticking up your nose, thought Melchor. He smiled behind the friar's back. 'I'll wait,' he lied.

The friar made a distracted gesture of assent with his hand, still concentrating on the timber being brought to the construction site.

Melchor turned towards the former hospital of the Candelaria, attached to the chapel on which the new church was being raised, and which the preachers were now using as a monastery.

'The friar out there,' he warned the doorman of the monastery, pointing towards the construction, 'says you should hurry. It seems your new church is about to collapse.'

As soon as the doorman ran out without thinking twice, Melchor sneaked into the small monastery. The refrain of the Latin readings led him towards a room where he found Fray Joaquín with five boys who were repeating the lessons in monotone.

The friar showed no surprise at Melchor's sudden appearance; the boys did. Staring at the gypsy from their chairs, one stopped reciting, another stuttered and the others began to jumble their lessons.

'Continue, continue. Louder!' the young friar priest ordered as he walked towards Melchor. 'I have to wonder how you got in here,' he whispered once he was beside him, amid the din made by the boys.

'You'll soon find out.'

'I was afraid of that.' The friar shook his head.

'I have a good bit of powder. Quality. For a good price.'

'OK. We are low on tobacco, and the brothers get very nervous when they don't have enough. Let's meet in the same place as always, at noon.' The gypsy nodded. 'Melchor, why didn't you wait? Why did you interrupt . . . ?'

He wasn't given time to finish his question. The doorman, the friar who was overseeing the construction and two more brothers burst into the room.

'What are you doing here?' shouted the doorman.

Melchor extended his arms with his palms open, as if he wanted to halt the horde that was coming towards him. Fray Joaquín watched him curiously. How was he going to get out of this one?

'Allow me to explain,' requested the gypsy calmly. The priests stopped a step away from him. 'I had to tell Fray Joaquín a sin, a very grave sin,' he said in explanation. Fray Joaquín half closed his eyes and held back a sigh. 'One of those sins that send you straight to hell,' continued the gypsy, 'the kind not even a thousand prayers for lost souls help with.'

'And you couldn't have waited?' interrupted one of the friars.

The five boys looked at each other in astonishment.

'With such a serious sin? A sin like that can't wait,' Melchor defended himself.

'You could have said that at the entrance . . .'

'Would you have listened to me?'

The friars looked at each other.

'Well,' interjected the oldest one. 'So have you confessed yet?'

'Me?' Melchor feigned surprise. 'Not me, your eminence! I am a good Christian. The sin was committed by a friend of mine. It's just that he's shearing some sheep, you understand, and since he was very worried, he asked me to see if I could come by and confess in his name.'

One of the boys laughed. Fray Joaquín made a gesture of impotence towards his brothers before the friar questioning the gypsy exploded, his face flushed.

'Out of here!' shouted the oldest friar, pointing to the door. 'What were you thinking . . . ?'

'Gypsies!'

'Despicable!'

'They should arrest you all!' he heard behind his back.

'This snuff is adulterated, Melchor!' complained Fray Joaquín as soon as he saw the reddish colour of the ochre the gypsy had mixed in with the tobacco. They were on the bank of the Guadalquivir, near the shrimping boat port. 'You told me . . .'

'Of the finest quality, Fray Joaquín,' replied Melchor. 'Fresh from the factory . . .'

'But I can see the red!'

'They must have dried it badly.'

Melchor tried to see the tobacco the friar was holding up. Had he really gone too far? Perhaps the young friar was learning.

'Melchor . . .'

'I swear on my granddaughter!' The gypsy crossed his thumb and index finger to make a cross that he then lifted to his lips and kissed. 'Top quality.'

'Don't swear in vain. And we need to talk about Milagros, too,' noted Fray Joaquín. 'The other day, at the blessing of the candles, she was mocking me as I preached . . .'

'Do you want me to scold her?'

'You know I don't.'

The friar lost himself in the memory: the girl had put him in a difficult spot, that was true. He knew that his voice had turned shaky and he'd lost his train of thought, but he also remembered her chiselled, proud face, as lovely as they come, and that virgin body . . .

'Fray Joaquín.' The gypsy pulled him from his musings. He drew out his words, his brow furrowed.

The friar cleared his throat. 'This snuff is adulterated,' he repeated to change the subject.

'Don't forget that she is my granddaughter,' insisted the gypsy.

'I know.'

'I wouldn't like you to get on my bad side.'

'What do you mean? Are you threaten—?'

'I would kill for her,' Melchor broke in. 'You are a *payo* . . . and a friar as well. You could renounce your vows, but not your race.'

Their eyes met. The clergyman knew that, at just a single sign from Milagros, he would be willing to leave behind his habit and swear loyalty to the gypsy race.

'Fray Joaquín . . .' Melchor interrupted his thoughts, knowing what was going through the friar's head.

Fray Joaquín lifted a hand and forced Melchor to be silent. The gypsy was the real problem: he would never accept that relationship, he concluded. He banished his desires.

'None of that gives you the right to try to sell me this tobacco as good,' he scolded.

'I swear to you . . . !'

'Don't swear in vain. Why don't you tell me the truth?'

Melchor took his time answering. He slipped an arm over Fray Joaquín's shoulder and pushed him a few steps along the riverbank. 'Do you know something?'

Fray Joaquín nodded with an unintelligible mumble.

'I will only tell you this because it's a secret: if a gypsy tells the truth . . . he loses it! He can never get it back.'

'Melchor!' exclaimed the friar, shrugging off his embrace.

'But this snuff is top quality.'

Fray Joaquín clicked his tongue, giving up. 'OK. I don't think the other friars will notice anyway.'

'Because it's not red, Fray Joaquín. See? You are wrong.'

'Don't go on about it. How much do you want?'

Adulterated or not, Melchor made a good profit on the tobacco. Uncle Basilio would be pleased.

'Do you know of any new contraband tobacco arriving in port?' asked Fray Joaquín when they were about to part.

'I haven't been told of any. There must be, as always, but my friends aren't involved. I trust that now, from March on, with the good weather, work will start up again.'

'Keep me informed.'

Melchor smiled. 'Of course, Father.'

After closing the profitable deal, Melchor decided to go and have some wine at Joaquina's tavern before heading over to the gypsy settlement to deliver the money to Uncle Basilio. *What a curious friar!* he thought as he walked. Beneath his preacher's habits, behind the talent and eloquence that people praised so, hid a young man eager for life and new experiences. He had proven that the year before, when Fray Joaquín insisted in accompanying Melchor to Portugal to receive a tobacco shipment. At first the gypsy hesitated, but he found himself forced to allow it: the priests were the ones who financed the contraband operations and, besides, many of them acted as smugglers and could be found loaded down with tobacco on the borders and roads. All the clergy were involved in tobacco contraband, either directly or as consumers. Priests were so fond of tobacco, their consumption was so high, that the Pope had had to prohibit their taking snuff while they officiated at services. However, they were unwilling to pay the high prices that the King established through the tobacco shops. Only the royal tax office could deal in tobacco, so the Church had become the biggest swindler in the kingdom: it participated in the contraband, buying, financing and hiding the smuggled goods in temples and even growing it in secret behind the impenetrable walls of the convents and monasteries.

As he mused Melchor polished off his first glass in one gulp.

'Good wine!' he said aloud to anyone who wanted to listen.

He ordered another, and then a third. He was on his fourth when a woman came up to him from behind and put an affectionate hand on his shoulder. The gypsy lifted his head to find a face that tried to conceal its true features behind rancid, smudged make-up. Nevertheless, the woman had generous breasts emerging from her plunging neckline. Melchor ordered a glass of wine for her as well while he gripped one of her buttocks with his right hand. She complained with a false and exaggeratedly modest pout, but then she sat down with him and the rounds began to flow.

It was two days before Melchor showed up at the San Miguel alley.

'Can you take care of the Negress?' Ana begged her daughter when she noticed that her father hadn't returned that afternoon. 'It seems Grandfather has decided to take off again. Let's see how long it's for this time.'

'And what do I do with her? Should I tell her she can leave?'

Ana sighed. 'I don't know. I don't know what he was planning . . . what your grandfather is planning,' she corrected herself.

'She is determined to cross the pontoon bridge.'

Milagros had again spent most of the morning in the small court-yard. She rushed there as soon as her mother allowed her to, with a thousand questions on the tip of her tongue about all Caridad had told her, everything she'd been wondering about throughout the night. She felt drawn to that black woman, to her melodious way of speaking, to the deep resignation that emanated from her entire being, which was so different from the proud, haughty character of the gypsies.

'Why?' asked her mother, interrupting her thoughts.

Milagros turned, confused. They were in one of the two small rooms that made up the apartment they lived in, on the first floor of apartments off the courtyard. Ana was preparing lunch on a coal stove lodged in an open niche on the wall.

'What?'

'Why does she want to cross the bridge?'

'Ah! She wants to go to the Brotherhood of the Negritos.'

'Is she over her fevers?' asked Ana.

'I think so.'

'Well, after lunch, take her.'

The girl nodded. Ana was tempted to tell her to leave her in Seville, with the Negritos, but didn't.

'And then bring her back. I don't want grandfather to come back and find his Negress gone. That's the last thing I need!'

Ana was irritated: she had argued with José. Her husband had scolded her harshly over the fight she'd had with La Trianera, but he especially condemned her slapping the old woman's grandson.

'A woman hitting a man. Who does that? And he's the grandson of the head of the council of elders!' he shouted at her. 'You know how vindictive Reyes can be.'

'As for the first, I will hit anyone who insults my daughter, whether they're grandsons of La Trianera or the King of Spain himself. Otherwise, you take care of her and keep a close eye out. As for the rest, I don't know what you can tell me about the Garcías' character . . .'

'I've had enough of the Vegas and the Garcías! I don't want to hear anything more about it. You married a Carmona and we're not interested in your disputes. The Garcías rule in the settlement and they are influential with the *payos*. We can't let them take a disliking to us . . . especially not over the old feuds of some crazy old man like your father. I'm fed up with my family throwing it in my face!'

On that occasion, Ana bit her lip to keep from answering back.

The never-ending argument! The same old song and dance! Ever since her father had come back from the galleys ten years earlier, her relationship with her husband had gradually deteriorated. José Carmona, the young gypsy taken by her charms, had been willing to forgo the religious wedding to have her. 'I will never submit to those dogs who didn't move a finger for my father,' she had said. The humiliating disdain with which the priests had treated her and her mother was burned into her memory. Yet, José hadn't been able to stand Melchor's presence, accusing him of stealing Milagros's affection. Milagros saw her grandfather as indestructible: a man who had survived the galleys, a smuggler who outsmarted soldiers and authorities, a free, rambling gypsy. José felt he couldn't compete: he was a simple blacksmith forced to work day in and day out under the orders of the head of the Carmona family and he didn't even have a son to boast about.

José envied the affection between grandfather and grand-daughter. Milagros's immense gratitude when Melchor gave her a bracelet, a trinket or the simplest colourful ribbon for her hair, her spellbound look as she listened to his stories . . . With the passing of the years José ended up taking out the bitterness and jealousy that was eating away at him on his own wife, whom he blamed. 'Why don't you say that to him?' Ana had replied one day. 'Is it that you don't dare?' She didn't have time to regret her impertinence. José had slapped her across the face.

And at that moment, as she was talking to her daughter about the black woman her father had brought home, Ana was cooking food for four on that small, uncomfortable stove: the three people in her family plus young Alejandro Vargas. After keeping her mouth shut when her husband once again threw the disputes between the Vegas and the Garcías in her face, she was surprised at how easy it was to convince José that Milagros's problem lay in that she was no longer a girl. Ana thought that if they engaged her to be wed, the girl would put aside her feelings towards Pedro García, since she was sure that the Garcías would never court a Vega. José told himself the bond between Milagros and her grandfather would fade once she was married, and he supported the idea: the Vargas family had been showing an interest in Milagros for some time, so José lost no time and the next day Alejandro was invited over to eat. 'For the time being there is no commitment, I just want to get to know the young man a little more,' his wife had announced. 'His parents have agreed to it.'

'Go to Uncle Inocencio's house and borrow a chair,' Ana ordered her daughter, interrupting her thoughts of the pontoon bridge Caridad wanted to cross and the Brotherhood of the Negritos that she wanted to reach.

'A chair? For whom? Who . . . ?'

'Go get it,' insisted her mother. She didn't want to tell her daughter about Alejandro's visit beforehand, knowing it would surely lead to an argument.

At lunchtime, Milagros realized why Alejandro was there and received the guest sullenly. She didn't hide her dislike for him – he was timid and danced clumsily – although only Ana seemed to notice her rudeness. José addressed him as if neither of the women existed. The third time the girl used a curt tone, Ana's expression twisted, but Milagros endured the censure and looked at her with her brow furrowed. *You already know which boy I like!* her look said. José Carmona laughed and banged the table as if it were an anvil. Alejandro tried to keep up, but his laughter came out shy and nervous. 'It's impossible,' was Ana's almost inaudible refusal. Milagros tightened her lips. Pedro García. Pedro was the only boy she was interested in . . . And what did she have to do with her grandfather's and her mother's old quarrels?

'Never, my daughter. Never,' her mother warned her through her teeth.

'What did you say?' her husband asked.

'Nothing. Just—'

'She says I won't marry this . . .' Milagros moved her hand towards Alejandro; the boy's mouth was agape, as if shooing away an insect. 'Him,' she finished her sentence to avoid the insult that was already on the tip of her tongue.

'Milagros!' shouted Ana.

'You will do what you are told,' declared José gravely.

'Grandfather—' the girl began to say before her mother interrupted her.

'You think your grandfather is going to let you get anywhere near a García?' she spat out.

Milagros got up abruptly and threw the chair to the floor. She remained standing, flushed, with her right fist tightly closed, threatening her mother. She stammered out some unintelligible words, but just as she was about to start yelling, her gaze fell on the two men staring at her. She growled, turned around and left the room.

'As you can see, she's a filly who badly needs to be tamed,' she heard her father laughing.

What Milagros didn't hear, slamming the door with Alejandro's stupid giggle behind her, was Ana's reply.

'Boy, I'll rip out your eyes if you ever lay a hand on my daughter.' The two men's faces shifted. 'On my honour as a Vega,' she added, bringing her fingers in the shape of a cross to her lips and kissing them, just as her father did when he wanted to convince someone.

Caridad walked stiffly, her gaze fixed on the bridge keeper who was collecting the tolls at the entrance to the pontoon bridge: the same man who had kept her from crossing the last time.

'Come on,' Milagros had called to her shrilly from the corridor, at the entrance to the small courtyard.

Caridad obeyed instantly. She jammed her straw hat on her head and grabbed her bundle.

'Leave them!' The girl hurried her along when she saw her efforts to organize Old María's wineskin, now empty, the colourful blanket and the mattress. 'We'll be back later.'

And now she was again approaching the busy bridge, walking behind a girl as silent as she was determined.

'She's with me,' Milagros proffered, pointing behind her, when she saw the bridge keeper about to address Caridad.

'She's not gypsy,' stated the man.

'Anyone can see that.'

The man was about to turn on her for her impertinence, but he thought better of it. He knew who she was: the granddaughter of Melchor 'El Galeote' – the Galley Slave. The gypsies had always refused to pay the toll – why would a gypsy pay to cross a river? Many years earlier the owner of the rights to the pontoon bridge had been paid a visit from several of them, grim-faced, armed with knives and willing to work out the problem their own way. There was no room for discussion, because really it didn't matter much if a few mavericks crossed from Triana to Seville and vice versa among the three thousand on horse- or muleback each day.

'What do you say?' insisted Milagros.

All gypsies were dangerous, but Melchor Vega more than most. And the girl was a Vega.

'Go ahead,' he conceded.

Caridad released the air she had unconsciously been holding in her lungs and followed the girl.

A few paces on, amid the bustle of sheep and mules, muleteers, porters and merchants, Milagros turned and smiled at her in triumph. She forgot about the argument with her parents and her attitude shifted.

'Why do you want to go to the Negritos?'

Caridad lengthened her stride and in a few paces she was beside her. 'The nuns said they would help me.'

'Nuns and priests, they're all liars,' declared the gypsy girl.

Caridad looked at her in surprise. 'They aren't going to help me?'

'I doubt it. How can they? They can't even help themselves. Grandfather says that before there were a lot of dark-skinned folk, but now there are only a few left and all the money they get they waste on Church nonsense and the saints. Before there was even a

Negro brotherhood in Triana, but it didn't have enough members and it folded.'

Caridad again fell behind as she turned the girl's disappointing words over in her head, while Milagros continued past the bridge and resolutely southward along the wall on the way to the district of San Roque.

At the height of the Torre del Oro, the girl stopped and turned suddenly. 'What do you want them to help you with?'

Caridad opened her hands in front of her body, confused.

'What is it that you think they'll do for you?' insisted the gypsy girl.

'I don't know . . . The nuns told me . . . They are Negroes, right?'

'Yes. They are,' answered the girl resignedly before taking up the path again.

If they are Negroes, Caridad thought, again following in the footsteps of the gypsy girl, keeping her eyes on the pretty coloured ribbons in her hair and the bright scarves that twirled in the air around her wrists, then that place had to be something like the old living quarters where they'd gathered on holidays. There everyone was friends, companions in misfortune even though they didn't know each other, even when they didn't even understand each other: Lucumís, Mandingas, Congos, Ararás, Carabalís . . . What did it matter the language they spoke? There they danced, sang and enjoyed themselves, but they also tried to help each other. What else was there to do in a gathering of Negroes?

Milagros didn't want to go inside the church with her. 'They'd kick me out,' she declared.

A white priest and an old Negro, who introduced himself proudly as the elder brother and the caretaker of the small chapel of Los Ángeles, looked her up and down without hiding their disgust at her dirty slave clothing, so out of place in the pageantry they strove for in their temple. 'What did you want?' the elder brother asked her peevishly. In the flickering light of the chapel's candles, Caridad wrung the straw hat in her hands and faced the Negro like an equal, but both her spirit and her voice were stifled by the cruel way they were staring at her. The nuns? continued the elder brother, almost raising his voice. What did the Triana nuns have to do with it? What did she know how to do? Nothing? No. Tobacco, no. In Seville only men worked in the tobacco factory. Yes, women worked in the Cádiz factory, but they were in Seville. Did she know how to do anything else? No? In that case ... The brotherhood? Did she have money to join the brotherhood? She didn't know she had to pay? Yes. Of course. You have to pay to join the brotherhood. Did she have any money? No. Of course. Was she free or a slave? Because if she was a slave she had to have her master's authorization ...

'Free,' Caridad managed to state as she stared into the Negro's eyes. 'I am free,' she repeated, dragging the words, trying in vain to find in his eyes the understanding of a blood brother.

'Well then, my daughter ...' Caridad lowered her gaze when the priest, who had remained silent up until that moment, finally spoke. 'What is it you expect from us?'

What did she expect?

A tear ran down her cheek.

She went running out of the church.

Milagros saw her cross Ancha de San Roque Street and enter the field that opened up behind the parish church, heading towards the Tagarete stream. Caridad ran, confused, blinded by tears. The gypsy girl shook her head as she felt a stab in the stomach. 'Sons of bitches!' she muttered. She hurried after her. A few steps further on she had to stop to pick up Caridad's straw hat. She found it on the banks of the Tagarete, where she had fallen to her knees, ignoring the fetidness of the stream that absorbed the entire area's sewage. She was crying in silence, just like the previous evening, as if she had no right to do so. This time she was covering her face with her hands and she rocked back and forth as she falteringly hummed a sad, monotone melody. Milagros scared off some raggedy little kids who approached curiously. Then she extended a hand towards Caridad's black curly hair, but she didn't dare to touch it. A tremendous shiver ran through her body. That melody ... Her arm was still outstretched and she watched how the depth of that voice made its little hairs stand on end. She felt tears welling up in her eyes. She knelt down beside her, hugged her awkwardly and sobbed with her.

'Grandfather.'

She had been waiting attentively for more than a day before she saw Melchor returning to the alley. She had run all the way to the settlement by La Cartuja to see if she could find him there, but they had given her no news of him. She came back and leaned against the door to the courtyard; she wanted to talk to him before anyone else did. Melchor smiled and shook his head as soon as he heard his grand-daughter's tone of voice.

'What is it you want this time, my girl?' he asked her as he grabbed her shoulder and moved her away from the building, further from the Carmonas who were bustling about.

'What are you going to do with Caridad . . . with the black woman?' she clarified when she saw his confused expression.

'Me? I'm tired of saying she's not mine. I don't know . . . She can do whatever she wants.'

'Can she stay with us?'

'With your father?'

'No. With you.'

Melchor squeezed Milagros against him. They walked a few steps in silence.

'You want her to stay?' the gypsy asked after a short while.

'Yes.'

'And does she want to stay?'

'Caridad doesn't know what she wants. She has nowhere to go, she doesn't know anybody, she has no money . . . The Negritos . . .'

'They asked her for money,' he said before she had a chance to.

'Yes,' confirmed Milagros. 'I promised her I would talk to you.'

'Why do you want her to stay?'

The girl took a few moments to respond. 'She is suffering.'

'A lot of people are suffering these days.'

'Yes, but she's different. She's . . . she's older than me and yet she seems like a child who doesn't know or understand anything. When she speaks . . . when she cries or sings, she does it with such feeling . . . You yourself say she sings well. She was a slave, you know?'

Melchor nodded. 'I guessed.'

'Everybody has treated her so badly, Grandfather. They separated her from her mother and her children. They even sold one of them! Then—'

'And what will she live off?' interrupted Melchor.

Milagros remained silent. They walked a few steps, the gypsy squeezing his granddaughter's shoulder.

'She'll have to learn how to do something,' he conceded after a little while.

'I'll teach her!' The girl was bursting with joy, turning towards her grandfather to hug him. 'Give me time.'

5

FIVE MONTHS PASSED before Caridad returned to the church of Nuestra Señora de los Ángeles and saw the elder of the Negritos brotherhood again. It was on the eve of the patron saint's day, 1 August 1748. At dusk on that day, among a large group of boisterous gypsy women, including Milagros and her mother, jubilant kids and even some men with guitars, Caridad crossed the pontoon bridge to head towards the San Roque district.

She still had her old straw hat with which she tried to protect herself from the blazing Andalusian sun, despite its many holes and rips. But she hadn't worn her faded grey burlap dress in some time. Grandfather had given her a red shirt and an even redder wide skirt, the colour of fiery blood, both of percale, which she took very good care of and wore proudly. The gypsy women didn't know how to sew; they bought their lovely clothes, although none of them ruled out the possibility that these ones had been left behind by one of Grandfather's lovers.

Ana and Milagros couldn't hide their admiration over the changes Caridad had made. Standing before them all, timid and embarrassed but with her little brown eyes shining in the red reflection of her new clothes, the smile on that round face and those fleshy lips was pure gratitude. Still, it wasn't Caridad's smile that evoked the gypsy women's admiration; it was the sensuality that emanated from her; her shapely curves; her large breasts that pulled the shirt tight exposing a thin line of ebony flesh above the skirt . . .

'Father!' recriminated Ana when she realized that Melchor was spellbound by that line of flesh.

He turned. 'What . . . ?'

'Wonderful!' was Milagros's contribution to the discussion, applauding enthusiastically.

'All of Seville will be gathered today on the Los Ángeles esplanade,' Milagros had explained to Caridad. 'There will be many opportunities to sell tobacco and tell fortunes; people have a lot of fun at that festival, and when they are entertained . . . we make good money.'

'Why?' asked Caridad.

'Oh, Cachita,' answered the girl, using the nickname Caridad had told her they'd called her in Cuba, 'today they'll run the geese!' Caridad looked at her with a puzzled expression, but her only response was, 'You'll see.'

As she headed towards the church, towering over the gypsy women surrounding her, because of her height, which was accentuated by the old hat she refused to get rid of, Caridad watched Milagros at the forefront with the young women. 'This goose tourney must be a really good party,' she then thought, since the girl was laughing and joking with her friends. Milagros had been over-whelmed by sadness for the last month, ever since José Carmona had announced her engagement to Alejandro Vargas for a wedding in a year's time. Melchor, who wanted his granddaughter to marry someone from the Vega family, had disappeared for more than ten days, returning in such a deplorable state that Ana was very worried and sent word to Old María to come and tend to him. Even so, not even Ana herself supported Melchor in that matter: it should be the girl's father who made the decision.

As they surrounded the city's walls and entered the various gates, floods of boisterous Sevillians joined the group of gypsies. When they were getting close to the field between the Tagarete stream and the Negritos' church, their pace slowed, chatting and laughing in groups as they waited for the party to begin. Here and there, men and women were singing and dancing in circles surrounded by spectators. One of the gypsies, still walking, began strumming his guitar. Several women took some joyful dance steps amid whistles and the applause of those around them, and the gypsies continued playing as they walked. Caridad looked from one side to the other: water sellers and wine merchants; vendors selling ice cream, doughnuts, fritters and all types of sweets; sellers of the strangest merchandise, some shouting out to advertise their products, others more surreptitious, keeping a close eye on the officers and soldiers that passed; tightrope walkers; acrobats; dog tamers entertaining the crowds; friars and priests, hundreds of them . . .

'Seville is the kingdom with the most clergy,' Caridad had heard said on more than one occasion, and some of them took part in the festivities by drinking, dancing and singing without the least decorum; while others preached sermons to people who paid them no mind. Almost all of them went about sniffing their tobacco powder as if it were the road to eternal salvation. Caridad also observed some fops wandering through the crowd; mannered young men who dressed in the French court style, delicately covering their mouth and nostrils with embroidered handkerchiefs as they sniffed tobacco.

A couple of those dandies noticed Caridad's interest in them, but they only commented on it among themselves as if it were nothing more than a mild irritation. Caridad looked away quickly, embarrassed. When she looked again she realized that the gypsies had scattered among the crowd. She looked from one side to the other, searching for them.

'Here I am,' she heard Milagros saying from behind her. Caridad turned towards her. 'Enjoy your festival day, Cachita.'

'What—?'

'The men from the brotherhood,' the girl interrupted her, 'the ones who treated you with such arrogance. You'll have the last laugh today.'

'But . . .'

'Come, follow me,' she indicated, trying to make her way through the most tightly packed part of the crowd that had settled in front of the church. 'Sirs!' shouted Milagros. 'Excellencies! Here is a Negress who's come for the festivities.'

People turned their heads and made way for the two women.

When they reached the front rows, Caridad was surprised at the number of Negroes gathered there.

'I have to go,' said Milagros in farewell. 'Listen, Cachita,' she added, lowering her voice. 'You aren't like them. You are with me, with Grandfather, with the gypsies.'

Before she had a chance to respond, the girl disappeared into the crowd and Caridad found herself alone at the front row of a throng that was piled against the back façade of the parish church of San Roque. Between her and the platforms they had set up behind the church there was a wide stretch of open ground. What were these festivities? Why had Milagros whispered that she wasn't like the others? The people began to grow impatient and there were some shouts to hurry it along. Caridad directed her attention towards the platforms: noblemen and the illustrious of Seville, lavishly dressed, members of the cathedral council, adorned in their finery, stood chatting and laughing, unaware of the common people's discontent.

A good while passed and the complaints of the Sevillians intensified until a drum roll was heard behind the parish church of San Roque, where the Negritos' church was located. Those who had been distracted with dancing and fun piled up behind those who were already waiting, as the soldiers and officers struggled to keep the multitudes from breaking through the unstable wood fences.

When a pair of riders, to the sound of fifes and drums and applause from the crowd, came around the corner of San Roque, Caridad felt people pushing to try to get to the front row. Five more pairs of riders followed the first, each one composed of a black rider on the right, the preferential spot, uncomfortably dressed in luxurious clothes, with white sleeves and magnificent feather plumes in their hats. The horses the Negroes rode were also tacked up with pageantry: a fine saddle, bells and coloured ribbons in their manes and tails. On the other hand, the riders accompanying the Negroes paraded in common apparel: floppy Vandyke collars and ordinary hats. Their horses trotted along without the slightest decoration.

After greeting the authorities, the pairs of riders began to gallop in a circle around the open field. Caridad recognized the elder of the brotherhood in the third couple; he was struggling to stay in the saddle, like the others of his race. The people laughed and pointed at them. Men and women shouted taunts at them while the Negroes swayed dangerously while trying to maintain their dignity and composure.

The music continued to play. At one point, the rider accompanying the elder brother, a man with a carefully trimmed white beard who rode with bearing and skill, gave the Negro a hand to keep him from falling.

'Let him fall!' shouted a woman.

'Darkie, you are going to leave your teeth on the ground!' added another man.

'And your black arse!' howled a third spectator, setting off laughter throughout the crowd.

What does this buffoonery mean? wondered Caridad.

'They are knights from the Equestrian Society.' The answer came from behind her back.

Caridad turned and found a smiling Fray Joaquín. He had come over to her when he recognized her red outfit in the crowd. She hid her gaze.

'Caridad,' scolded the young friar. 'I've told you on many occasions that we are all children of God, you don't have to lower your eyes, you don't have to humble yourself before anyone . . .'

In that moment Caridad lifted her head and gestured towards the Negroes who continued galloping amid the taunts and jibes of the spectators. Fray Joaquín understood.

'Perhaps they,' he answered, raising his eyebrows, 'claim to be something they aren't. The Royal Order of Knights of the Equestrian Society of Seville sponsors the Brotherhood of the Negritos; they do it every year. On days like this, Negroes and noblemen, the highest and the humblest classes in the city, exchange positions. But the brotherhood makes some money with the geese that the order gives them.'

'What geese?' asked Caridad.

'Those ones.' The friar pointed.

The six pairs of riders had stopped their display and gathered in front of the authorities. A bit further on, at one end of the open field, where Fray Joaquín had pointed, some men struggled to hang a rope between two large stakes placed on the edges of the field. In the middle of the rope, head down and tied by its feet, a fat goose shook violently. When the men finished hanging the goose, Seville's chief justice officer, nestled in an armchair on the platform, ordered the first Negro to gallop towards the animal.

Caridad and Fray Joaquín, amid the deafening shouts of the crowd, watched the clumsy galloping of the Negro who, as he passed beneath the goose, tried to grab the animal's wriggling neck with his right hand, and failed. He was followed by the equestrian knight who was paired with him. The nobleman spurred on his horse, which took off at a full gallop with its rider howling and standing in the stirrups. When he passed beneath the goose, the knight succeeded in grabbing it by the neck and ripped its head clean off. The Sevillians applauded enthusiastically and cheered while the goose's body shook on the rope. Few noticed, but the chief justice and some of the other noblemen seated on the platform made a chastening gesture to the rest of the knights: they only had six geese and they had to entertain the people.

With those instructions, the goose tourney lasted into the evening to the crowd's delight. None of the Negroes managed to decapitate the animal. One of them was able to grab it by the neck, but not with enough speed, and the goose defended himself by pecking him on the head, which gave rise to the most ignominious taunts from the audience. The six Negroes all fell at some point, as they galloped on the backs of increasingly agitated horses, or when releasing one of their hands and leaning over in the stirrups to grab the goose. As for the geese, they perished each time the chief justice made a signal to the equestrian knights.

'Later the Negritos will sell them and the brotherhood will keep the money,' Fray Joaquín explained to her.

Caridad was absorbed in the spectacle, yet full of contradictory feelings as she watched those clumsy Negroes trying to decapitate geese amid the spectators' shouts. She had found no camaraderie of race in the eyes of the brotherhood's elder, none of the solidarity, compassion and understanding that all Negroes in Cuba shared with their blood brothers.

With the final parade, after the last of the geese died, the people began to scatter and the nobles and religious men who presided over the festivities got up from their seats. *You aren't like them,* Milagros had told her. *You are with the gypsies,* she'd added with that pride that always showed on their lips when they spoke of their race. She was with the gypsies? She was with Milagros. The friendship and trust that the girl showed her had been sealed when she had told her she could stay with Melchor and strengthened when Milagros's father announced her engagement to Alejandro. From that point on, Milagros tried to share the pain she was feeling with Caridad, as if she, who had been a slave, could understand it better than anyone. But what did Caridad know of thwarted love? José Carmona, Milagros's father, looked at her from a distance, as if she were a bothersome object, and Ana, her mother, put up with her as if she were some fleeting whim of her daughter's. As for Melchor . . . who could tell what he was thinking or feeling? He could just as easily give her a red skirt and shirt as pass by her without even glancing, or not speak to her for days. Initially, at the urging of his granddaughter, Melchor allowed Caridad to remain in the corner of the small courtyard, and over time she became the only person who had free access to the grandfather's sanctuary.

One afternoon in May, when spring had flowered all over Triana, the gypsy had found himself near the well, in the entrance courtyard, hidden among old twisted pieces of iron, smoking a cigar and passing the time, lost in those inscrutable worlds where he took refuge. Caridad passed by him on her way out of the main doorway. The scent of tobacco stopped her in her tracks. How long had it been since her last smoke? She inhaled the smoke surrounding the gypsy deeply in a vain attempt to make it reach her lungs and brain. How she yearned to feel the soothing sensation she got from tobacco! She closed her eyes, lifted her head slightly as if trying to follow the smoke's rising path, and inhaled once more. Just then Melchor awoke from his lethargy.

'Here you go.' He surprised her by offering his cigar.

Caridad didn't hesitate; she grabbed the cigar, brought it to her lips and sucked on it with delight. After a few seconds she felt a slight tickle in her arms and legs and a relaxing dizziness; her little brown eyes sparkled. She went to return the cigar to the gypsy, but he gestured for her to continue smoking with a flick of his hand.

'From your land,' he commented as he watched her smoke. 'Good tobacco!'

Caridad was flying by that point; her mind was totally relaxed, lost.

'It's not a Havana,' he heard her say to herself.

Melchor furrowed his brow. What did she mean, it wasn't Cuban? He had paid for a pure Havana! That was the first day Caridad entered the gypsy's room.

People refused to abandon the San Roque district and the field where the festivities were held. Here and there guitars were heard, along with castanets, tambourines and songs; men and women, no matter their gender or age, danced joyfully in groups around the bonfires.

'Where is Milagros?' the friar asked Caridad as they both wandered through the crowd.

'I don't know.'

'She didn't tell you where . . .'

Fray Joaquín stopped himself. Caridad was no longer beside him. He turned and saw her a few paces behind, stock-still in front of a sweets stand. He approached her, full of confusion: this black woman, dressed in red with her shirt hugging her body, was the object of lustful glances and comments from those around her, and yet to the friar's eyes she was like a large girl whose mouth watered at the scent and sight of the sweets: doughnuts, sugar-dusted fritters, sweet biscuits, cinnamon custards . . .

'Give me some *polvorones*,' ordered the friar, pointing to the crumbly shortbread biscuits after glancing at the selection. 'You'll see, Caridad, they're delicious.'

Fray Joaquín paid and they continued strolling, in silence. The friar watched, out of the corner of his eye, as Caridad savoured the oval biscuits of almond, lard, sugar and cinnamon, afraid to interrupt her obvious pleasure. *Had she ever tried them before?* he wondered. Probably not, he concluded as he watched her reaction. It made him recall when Melchor had appeared at the monastery with Caridad in tow, that time with the brother doorman's permission, who had let them through out of sheer fright at the rage oozing from the gypsy's eyes. 'You cheated us!' he shouted as soon as he saw Fray Joaquín. 'This tobacco isn't pure Cuban!' The friar tried to calm the gypsy and took Caridad to the basement that they used as a larder and storehouse. Behind some logs, he hid a couple of leather bags of tobacco leaf – one of them belonging to Melchor as payment for his work – from the incursion they had just made to the place in Barrancos, over the Portuguese border.

Melchor violently cut the ropes that tied one of the bales and, still swearing, indicated to Caridad that she should go over and examine the tobacco. Fray Joaquín remembered that moment: instinctively, Caridad let her eyelids droop and licked her lips, as if she were about to savour a delectable feast. Inside the leather bag, the tobacco was tied up in bunches, but at first glance Caridad saw that the leaves weren't bound with *yaguas*, the flexible royal palm leaves used in Cuba. She had the gypsy cut the cord around the bundle and delicately picked up one of the leaves; both men were surprised by the skill of her long fingers. Caridad examined the tobacco leaf carefully; she held it up to the light of the candle carried by Fray Joaquín to observe its pigments: dark, light or red, matured, light or dry. She stroked it and delicately felt for its texture and moisture; she chewed on the leaf and smelled it, trying to figure out, through its flavour, aroma and the taste of the nicotine, how many years earlier it had been harvested. Melchor hurried Caridad with increasingly agitated gestures, but the friar was spellbound watching the ritual the woman carried out, and the sensations reflected in her face and the pauses she took after smelling and touching the leaf, sure that the passing moments would offer her the solution.

That same ritual was the one that now, walking close to the Tagarete, he slyly observed in Caridad as she ate the *polvorones*: she stopped chewing, half closed her eyes and let some time pass, bringing her lips together, salivating before nibbling on another.

It wasn't pure Havana tobacco, not pure and not mixed, he remembered Caridad declaring that day. Where was it from? She wouldn't know, answered the gypsy with an unusual tranquillity, as if the contact with the tobacco leaves had made him confident; she only knows the Cuban. It's a young tobacco, she declared, slightly fermented, perhaps . . . maybe six months, at most a year. And too blond, with little sun.

Fray Joaquín watched how Caridad brought a new crumbly sweet to her mouth, delicately, as if it were a tobacco leaf . . .

'Cachita!'

Milagros's voice surprised them both. They hadn't even worked out where the voice was coming from when she started to pressure them, 'You are Cuban! You know about tobacco . . .'

'Milagros,' mused the friar, trying to make her out among the people, in the dark.

'Tell them that these cigars are pure Havanas!' the young gypsy urged. 'Come!'

It was Fray Joaquín who first noticed the colourful ribbons in the gypsy girl's hair and the scarves on her wrists twisting in the air as she gestured wildly amid a group of men.

'How dare you say that they aren't Havanas?' complained Milagros, loudly. 'Come, Cachita! Come over here!' Fray Joaquín and Caridad both did. 'They are trying to take advantage of a girl! They want to cheat me! Tell them that they're Havanas!' she demanded as she handed her one of the cigars that Caridad herself had crafted with that blond tobacco that the friar was hiding in the monastery. 'Tell them! She knows about tobacco! Tell them it's Cuban!'

Caridad hesitated. Milagros knew that it wasn't Havana! How could she . . . ?

'Of course it's Havana, gentlemen,' Fray Joaquín came out to rescue her. No one noticed, in the darkness only broken by the faint glow of a nearby bonfire, the complicit smile exchanged between him and the gypsy. 'I myself bought a couple this morning . . .'

'Fray Joaquín,' whispered one of the men gathered when he recognized the famous preacher of San Jacinto.

The five men that surrounded Milagros then turned towards the friar.

'If Fray Joaquín says they are Havanas—' another began.

'Of course they are Havanas!' interrupted Milagros.

At that moment, the flickering light of the fire flashed on the features of the man who had last spoken. And Caridad shivered. And the cigar in question slipped from her hands and fell to the floor.

'Cachita!' scolded Milagros as she was about to kneel to pick it up. But she stopped when she saw Caridad shaking, her eyes lowered and her breathing erratic. 'What . . . ?' Milagros began to ask, turning her head towards the man.

Even in the weak light, Milagros could see the man frown and tense up, but then he shifted his gaze towards the friar and contained himself.

'Let's go!' he ordered his companions.

'But . . .' one of them complained.

'Let's go!'

'Cachita.' Milagros put her arms around her friend as the group of men turned and disappeared into the multitude. 'What's happening to you?'

Caridad pointed to the man's back. It was the potter from Triana.

'What's wrong with that man?' asked Fray Joaquín.

Caridad gently freed herself from the girl's embrace and, with tears streaming down her face, knelt to pick up the cigar that was still on the ground. Why did she always have to cry there, near the Tagarete, in San Roque?

The gypsy and the friar looked at each in puzzlement while Caridad wiped off the dirt that had stuck to the cigar. When they realized that the sobbing woman was now cleaning off sand that only existed in her imagination, the friar urged Milagros with a gesture.

'What happened with that man?' enquired the girl tenderly.

Caridad continued stroking the cigar with her long, expert fingers. How could she tell her? What would Milagros think of her? The gypsy girl had spoken to her about men on many occasions. At fourteen, she had never been with a man and she wouldn't until she was married. 'We gypsies are chaste and then faithful,' she had affirmed. 'There isn't a single gypsy prostitute in the entire kingdom!' she had later said proudly.

'Tell me, Caridad,' insisted Milagros.

And what if she left her? Her friendship was the only thing she had in this life and . . .

'Tell me!' the girl ordered, making Fray Joaquín jump.

But this time Caridad did not obey; she kept her gaze on the cigar she still held in her hands.

'Did that man hurt you?' asked Fray Joaquín tenderly.

Had he hurt her? She finally nodded.

And that was how, question by question, Fray Joaquín and Milagros learned the story of Caridad's arrival in Triana.

6

MILAGROS MISSED CARIDAD. A few days after the goose tourney, Grandfather had received a visit from a galley slave who had rowed with him for several years. The man, like all the convicts who managed to endure the appalling torture of the galleys, appeared as frail as Melchor and, again like all those who survived, knew the ports and peoples of the sea who were like them: traffickers, smugglers and all types of criminals. Bernardo, for that was his name, told Grandfather about the arrival of a substantial tobacco shipment from Virginia into the port of Gibraltar, a rock on the Spanish coast that was under English rule. There, boats with English, Venetian, Genoese, Ragusan or Portuguese flags unloaded tobacco, fabrics, spices and other merchandise on various points of the coast that extended from the Rock to Málaga, by night, when the wind blew hard, to avoid being discovered by the Spanish patrol boats. Bernardo had already made a deal for a good shipment of Virginia tobacco, he just needed funds to pay for it and runners to carry it off the beaches.

'In a few days we will go out in search of a tobacco shipment,' Melchor had announced to Caridad after closing the agreement with Bernardo at Joaquina's tavern, over a jug of good wine.

Caridad, who was in the gypsy's room, sitting in front of a wobbly board on which she continued making cigars with the blond tobacco stored by the friar, just nodded, still rolling her hand over the one she was absorbed in creating.

It was Milagros who seemed surprised as she watched her friend work with the tobacco leaves.

'Are you taking Cachita?' she asked her grandfather.

'That's what I said. I want to get the best tobacco, and she knows how to recognize it,' he answered in the gypsy dialect.

'Won't . . . won't it be dangerous?'

'Yes, girl. It always is,' declared the gypsy, already in the doorway, preparing to leave the room; three people didn't comfortably fit inside.

They looked at each other. *Didn't you know that?* Melchor seemed to be asking his granddaughter, who hid her eyes in shame, aware that the next thing her grandfather's penetrating eyes would ask her was: *When have you ever asked me that?*

Melchor had no problems getting runners and carriers: the Vegas and his relatives in the settlement at La Cartuja were always willing to accompany him; they were tough, bold gypsies and, above all, loyal. He had no problems getting the money either: Fray Joaquín got it for him immediately. What most delayed his shipment, as was often the case, were the pack animals: he needed docile, quiet geldings that didn't whinny in the night at the scent of a mare. But the Vega family set their mind to it and in a few days, with a couple of raids into the meadows around Seville, they made off with enough horses.

'Be careful, Cachita,' said Milagros when it was time to leave. The two women were in the settlement beside the Carthusian monastery, standing slightly apart from the men and the horses.

Caridad shifted uncomfortably beneath the long, dark man's cape that Melchor had dressed her in to hide her red clothes. She had bartered her straw hat for a black slouch hat with a round crown and wide, floppy brim. From her neck hung a lodestone tied with a string. Milagros extended her arm and weighed the stone. The gypsies believed in its powers: smugglers, traffickers and horse thieves swore that if soldiers' patrols showed up, those lodestones would conjure strong dust and sand storms to hide them. What the gypsy girl didn't know was that the Cuban slaves also believed in the powers of lodestone: 'Christ came down to Earth with the lodestone,' they claimed. Caridad would have to baptize it and give it a name, as was the custom in her homeland.

Milagros smiled; Caridad replied with a grimace on her face, all sweaty from the implacable summer heat of Seville. It got hot in Cuba too, but there she never wore so much clothing.

'Stay close to Grandfather,' advised the gypsy girl before approaching to give her a kiss on the cheek.

Caridad seemed startled at the girl's sudden display of affection, yet her thick, fleshy lips widened, turning the initial forced smile into one of sincere gratitude.

'I like to see you smile,' declared Milagros, and she kissed her on the other cheek. 'It's not something you do often.'

Caridad rewarded her by widening her lips again. It was true, she admitted to herself: she had been slow to open up to her friend, but little by little she was putting down roots with the gypsies, and as her anxiety and worries faded, she trusted in her more and more. In the end, the real cause of the change was none other than Melchor. He was the one who had put her in charge of working with the tobacco. 'You don't have to go with the girl and her mother to sell it on the streets any more,' he said in the face of Milagros's insistence on teaching her to do something to contribute to her upkeep. 'I'd prefer you to roll what they sell.' And Caridad felt useful and grateful.

'You be careful, too,' she advised her friend. 'Don't fight with your mother.'

Milagros was about to reply, but her grandfather's shout stopped her.

'Come on, Negress, we're leaving!'

Then she was the one who kissed Milagros.

After Caridad's departure, the girl felt lonely. Since her engagement had been announced, Caridad had become the person who patiently listened to her complaints. She wasn't able to follow the advice she had given her on her departure.

'I won't marry Alejandro,' she assured her mother, practically every other day.

'You will,' Ana would answer without even looking at her.

'Why Alejandro?' she would insist other times. 'Why not—?'

'Because that's what your father decided,' her mother would repeat in a weary tone.

'I'll run away first!' she threatened one morning.

That day, Ana turned on her daughter. Milagros sensed her features would be pinched, serious and icy. She was right.

'Your father gave his word,' muttered her mother. 'Be careful that he doesn't hear you say that; he's liable to chain you up until your wedding day.'

Time passed slowly with mother and daughter angry with each other and constantly arguing.

Milagros couldn't even find comfort in her friends on San Miguel alley, many of whom were also engaged to be married. How could she admit to Rosario, María, Dolores or any of the others that she didn't like the man who had been found for her? They didn't do it either, despite the fact that most of them, before learning of their fate, had freely criticized the boys they would later be promised to. Milagros wasn't exempt from such guilt. How many times had she mocked Alejandro? Now they all lied to each other, kept each other at a distance; it was as if their innocence had suddenly ended. It wasn't that they were growing up or coming of age, it was simply that with their fathers' decision – a word, a simple agreement made behind their backs – what had been true the night before meant nothing at sunrise. Milagros missed the spontaneity of those conversations with her girlfriends, the whispering, the laughter, the knowing looks, the dreams . . . Even the arguments. The last one had happened the night she danced with Pedro García. Most of her friends were horrified when she declared her intention to do it. She was a Vega, Melchor El Galeote's granddaughter, she would never be able to get that boy, they all knew it, so . . . why get involved? But Milagros paid them no heed and threw herself into her dance, until her mother intervened and slapped the boy. Who among the gypsy girls in the alley didn't long for Pedro García, El Conde's grandson? They all did! And yet now, after her engagement, it would be a serious affront to the Vargas family if Milagros encouraged Pedro García to pursue her. Alejandro would have to defend her and his father and uncles behind him; the

Garcías would respond and the men would pull out their knives . . . But Milagros couldn't stop sneaking glances at the boy whenever she saw him walking down San Miguel alley, rambling slowly, as pure-bred gypsies did, haughty, proud, arrogant. Then she missed Caridad, with whom she could have spoken freely about her longing and misfortunes. They said the young man had inherited the age-old gypsy wisdom for working iron, that he knew instinctively when to begin each of the processes, when the iron was ready for forging, cooling, soldering . . . So much so that the elders sometimes consulted him. And yet she was tied to Alejandro. Even Fray Joaquín had wished her the best in her engagement! The friar had given a start when Ana mentioned it to him near San Jacinto. He let out an 'already?'. And Milagros had listened, crestfallen, to how the clear, sharp voice with which he intoned his sermons had cracked when it came time to congratulate her.

'Caridad, I need you,' the girl whispered to herself.

She wasn't paying attention! Beyond the group of girls busy with the countess, Ana glared at her. What was she doing? Why was she hesitating? *She's distracted*, thought her mother when Milagros dropped the delicate white hand the countess's daughter had extended to her and faked a coughing fit. Milagros couldn't remember what it was that she had predicted for her the last time she read her fortune. The little countess and her two girlfriends who encircled the gypsy moved aside with a disgusted expression at the hacking the girl was using to buy time.

'Are you feeling poorly, my daughter?' asked her mother, coming to her aid. Only Milagros noticed the harshness in her tone. 'Excuse me, your excellency,' she apologized to the countess, addressing the group of girls. 'Lately, my girl has had a cough. Let's see, my lovely,' she added after replacing her daughter and grabbing the young woman's hand without ceremony.

The noise of the countess's silk hoop skirt rustling was clear in the large hall when she decided to approach curiously, the little countess's two girlfriends closed the circle and Milagros moved a few steps away. From there, forcing herself to cough every once in a while, she heard her mother skilfully hoodwink the little countess and her two friends.

Men? They would marry princes! Riches, of course. Children and happiness. A few problems, a few illnesses – why not? – but nothing they wouldn't overcome with the devotion to and help of Jesus Christ and Our Lady. With her hand on her mouth and her mother's familiar routine in her ears, Milagros shifted her attention towards the countess's chambermaid, standing beside the doors to the hall, making sure that neither of the gypsies pocketed anything; later, in the kitchens, they would also have to read her palm. Then she looked back at the group of women: her mother, barefoot, dark-skinned, almost black, wearing colourful clothes and with silver beads around her waist; large hoops hanging from her ears and necklaces and bracelets tinkling as she gesticulated and passionately declared the future of those women white as milk, wearing dresses with silk hoop skirts, all decorated with endless embroidery, bows, flounces, ribbons . . . What luxury there was in those clothes, in the furnishings and vases, in the mirrors and clocks, in the chairs with golden arms, in the paintings, in the shiny silver objects placed all around!

The Countess of Fuentevieja was a good client of Ana Vega's. On occasions she would have her called in: she liked to listen to her telling fortunes, she would buy tobacco from her and even some of the baskets that the gypsy women from the settlement made.

Milagros heard one of the little countess's friends giggle nervously, instantly joined by restrained, affected exclamations of joy from the other two and some delicate applause from the countess. The lines of her hand seemed to predict a promising future, and Ana talked at length about it: a good husband, rich, attractive, healthy and faithful. And why didn't she say the same to her, her daughter? Why was she doomed to marry a clod, just because he was a Vargas? The chambermaid, beside the immense doors, jumped when Milagros tightened her fists, furrowed her brow and stomped on the floor.

'Are you feeling better?' her mother asked her with a hint of sarcasm.

The girl answered her with a new, loud attack of coughing.

The evening was becoming unbearable for Milagros. Ana Vega,

not worrying about the time, displayed all of her gypsy wiles for the three girls. Then, when they left, satisfied, whispering among themselves, she directed her efforts at the countess.

'No,' she objected when the aristocrat suggested that Milagros wait in the kitchen, where they would look after her. 'She's better here, isolated, we don't want her to infect your ladyship's servants.'

The new sarcasm infuriated Milagros, but she contained herself. She put up with the long hour that her mother spent talking to the countess; she put up with the farewells and the payment, and she put up with the attentions she then had to pay to the chambermaid and some members of the staff, who bartered tobacco and fortune telling for some food pilfered from the count's larder.

'Are you feeling better?' mocked her mother when they were out on the street, on their way back to Triana, with the summer sun still highlighting the colours of their dresses. Milagros snorted. 'I trust you are,' added Ana, ignoring the insolence. 'Because tomorrow night we are going to sing and dance for the count and countess. They have some guests from abroad, they're . . . English, I don't know . . . French or German, who knows! But they want them to have a good time.'

Milagros snorted again, this time louder and with a touch of peevishness. Her mother continued to ignore her and they walked the rest of the way in silence.

She smiled at her, inviting her to respond in kind. She didn't do it for the Count and Countess of Fuentevieja or for the dozens of guests they had brought with them, who were waiting expectantly in the garden that sloped down to the river, in one of the largest homes in Triana where the count had decided to hold the party. Ana smiled at her daughter after arching her arms over her head and swaying her hips as the first note on the guitar sounded, before the dance had begun, preparing to launch into it once the men were ready. Milagros, facing her, held the invitation without blinking, still, with her arms at her sides.

'Beautiful lady!' one gypsy complimented the mother.

Let's get started! her mother seemed to be saying with an affectionate pout on her lips. Milagros frowned, making her beg.

Another guitar was being tuned. A gypsy woman rattled her castanets. *Come on!* Ana urged her daughter, raising her arms again.

'Lovelies!' they heard the people say.

'My pretty girl!' the mother shouted to her daughter.

The guitars began to play in unison. Several pairs of castanets rang out and Ana straightened her posture more stiffly before Milagros, clapping her hands.

'Come on, girl!' she goaded.

The two women started in sync, turning and flipping their skirts in the air, and when they faced each other again, Milagros's eyes were sparkling and her teeth gleamed in a wide smile.

'Dance, Mother!' shrieked the girl. 'That body! Those hips! I don't see them shaking!'

The Carmonas, who had come to the party, joined the girl in her goading. The count and countess's guests, either French or English, it didn't really matter, were left with their mouths hanging open when Ana accepted her daughter's challenge and twisted her waist voluptuously. Milagros laughed and followed suit. In the night, with the Guadalquivir's water shimmering silver, in the light of the torches arranged throughout the garden, among honeysuckle and four o'clock flowers, orange and lemon trees, the guitars tried to adapt their rhythm to the frenzied pace set by the women; the handclapping echoed powerfully and the male dancers were overwhelmed by the sensuousness and daring with which the mother and daughter danced the *zarabanda*.

Finally, both sweating freely, Ana and Milagros came together in an embrace. They did so in silence, knowing that it was merely a truce, that the dance and the music opened up another world, that universe where the gypsies took refuge from their problems.

One of the count's footmen broke up their embrace. 'Their excellencies want to congratulate you.'

Mother and daughter headed towards the chairs where the count and countess and their guests had watched the dance, as the guitars were strumming in preparation for the next one. Honouring them as his equals, Don Alfonso, the count, stood up and received them with a few courteous claps of his hands, seconded by the other guests.

'Extraordinary!' exclaimed Don Alfonso when the women reached him.

As if out of nowhere, José Carmona, Alejandro Vargas and other members of both families had taken their places behind the women. Before beginning the introductions, the count handed Ana some coins, which she weighed with satisfaction. Ana's and Milagros's hair was dishevelled, they were panting and the sweat soaking their bodies gleamed in the flickering light of the torches.

'Don Michael Block, traveller and scholar from England.' The count introduced a tall, stiff man whose face was tremendously pink where it wasn't covered by a neatly trimmed white beard.

The Englishman, unable to tear his gaze off Ana's damp, splendid breasts, which rose and fell to the rhythm of her still jagged breathing, stammered out a few words and offered his hand to her. The greeting went on longer than strictly necessary. Ana sensed that the Carmonas, behind her back, were stirring restlessly; the count did as well.

'Michael,' said Don Alfonso in an attempt to break the moment, 'this is Milagros, Ana Vega's daughter.'

The traveller wavered but didn't release Ana's hand. She narrowed her eyes and shook her head imperceptibly when she realized that José, her husband, was taking a step forward.

'Don Michael,' she then said, managing to capture the Englishman's attention, 'that which your lordship is set on already has an owner.'

'What?' the traveller managed to ask.

'Exactly what I said.' The gypsy woman, with her left thumb extended, pointed behind her, sure that José would have already pulled out his huge knife.

The pink hue in the Englishman's cheeks shifted to pale white and he let go of her hand.

'Milagros Carmona!' the count hastened to announce.

The girl smiled languidly at the traveller. Behind her, José Carmona arched his brows and kept his knife in view.

'The daughter of the man behind me,' interjected Ana then, again pointing towards José. The Englishman followed her gesture. 'His daughter, do you understand, Don Michael? Daugh-ter,' she repeated slowly, stressing the syllables.

The Englishman must have understood, because he ended the greeting with a dramatic bow towards Milagros. The count and countess and their guests smiled. They had warned him, 'Michael, the gypsy women dance like obscene she-devils, but make no mistake, the moment the music stops they are as chaste as the most pious virgin.' Nevertheless, despite the warnings – the count knew it, the guests knew it, the gypsies knew it as well – that music and those dances, which were sometimes joyful and sometimes sad but always sensual, made those watching them lose all trace of common sense; there were many run-ins with *payos* inflamed by the voluptuous dancing, who had tried to go too far with the gypsy women, and had seen those knives much closer than the Englishman had.

On this occasion, Don Michael, prudently separated from Milagros and with his cheeks recovering their natural pinkness, rummaged in his bag and handed the girl a couple of pieces of eight.

'Go with God!' said José Carmona, bidding farewell on behalf of his daughter.

As soon as the count and countess and their guests took their seats once more, guitars, tambourines and castanets sounded again in the night.

'Would you like a cigar?'

Milagros turned. Alejandro Vargas was holding one out to her. She scrutinized him, from top to bottom, shamelessly: he must be sixteen years old and had the dark skin and haughty demeanour of the Vargas family, but there was something odd . . . His eyes? That must be it. He wasn't able to hold her gaze the way a gypsy should. And he was a bad dancer, maybe because he was too big. Behind him, at a slight remove, she saw that her mother was spying on her.

'It's a pure Havana,' insisted Alejandro to escape her scrutiny.

'Where did you get it from?' asked the girl, focusing on the cigar Alejandro held out.

'My father bought several.'

Milagros let out a laugh. It was one of Caridad's! She recognized it by the green thread her friend had finished off the sucking end with.

'What's so funny?' asked the boy.

Milagros completely ignored him. She frowned at her mother, who was now watching her openly, curious about her laughter. *Was it her?* Milagros wondered. No. It couldn't have been. Her mother wouldn't have dared to trick the Vargases and sell them fake Havanas. It could only have been . . .

'You're wonderful, Grandfather!' she exclaimed with a smile on her lips.

'What did you say?'

'Nothing.'

Alejandro was still holding out the cigar. Caridad had made it with her own hands! She might have been there watching as she did it.

'Hand over that cigar!' Milagros held it up to her eyes and showed it to her mother in the distance. 'Pure Havana,' she affirmed before pursing her features in a funny expression.

'Yes,' she heard Alejandro say.

Ana shook her head and swatted the air.

'It must be good,' ventured Milagros.

'Excellent,' replied Alejandro.

Sure, she thought, *Cachita made it*.

'Light?' he interrupted her thoughts.

Milagros couldn't hold back a resigned sigh. 'Light? Of course I want a light. How else can I smoke?'

Alejandro clumsily pulled the flint and steel from a bag.

'And the tinder?' rushed Milagros.

Alejandro muttered as he rummaged uselessly in the bag.

'Stop! You would have found it by now in that little bag. Can't you see you don't have any? Here. Go light it off one of the torches.'

So you are the one who's going to break in this filly? thought Milagros as she watched him obediently walk over to one of the torches. He walked like a gypsy, slowly, his full height erect, but he wasn't capable of taming even a little donkey. She . . . Her eyes searched for her mother: she was clapping behind one of the guitarists, distracted, animating the dance. She, Milagros, wanted a man!

Milagros didn't manage to shake Alejandro off for the whole rest of the night. They shared the cigar. 'Don't you have another one for yourself?' she complained. But his father had only given him one. And they drank. Good wine, from the abundant supply the count had brought to liven up the party. Milagros danced some more, an upbeat *seguidilla* sung by the women in a lively voice. She danced with other young folk, among them a brave Alejandro.

'I've never heard you sing,' he said to her once the dance was over.

Milagros felt her head spinning: the wine, the tobacco, the party . . .

'You can't have been paying close enough attention,' she lied in a thick voice. 'Aren't you interested in me?'

The truth was that she had never sung in spite of her father's encouraging her to; she sang in groups, hiding her despair over her lack of ability among the voices of other women. 'Don't worry,' her mother had reassured her, 'dance, enchant us with your body; you'll sing some day.'

Alejandro registered the new affront. 'I . . .' he stuttered.

Milagros saw him lower his gaze to the floor. A gypsy never hides his eyes. The image of Caridad came to her mind. To her dizziness was added the embarrassment over the man destined to be her husband. 'That chin!' she shouted. 'Up!'

Yet Alejandro addressed her again timidly. 'I am interested in you. Of course I am.' He spoke just like Caridad when she'd first arrived at the alley, looking down at the ground. 'I would do anything for you, anything at all . . .'

Milagros looked at him, pensive: anything?

'There's a potter in Triana . . .' she said without thinking.

Milagros had talked about it with her mother. She was furious, her temper running high, after she and Fray Joaquín had managed to wheedle out of Caridad, with a thousand questions she answered between sobs, what had happened with the potter.

'That's not gypsy business,' interrupted Ana.

'But, Mother—!'

'Milagros, we already have many problems. The authorities are after us. Don't get us in more trouble! You know we aren't even allowed to dress the way we do; they can arrest us just for our clothes.'

The girl opened her hands and gestured to her blue skirt in confusion.

'No,' clarified Ana. 'Here in Triana, in Seville, we enjoy the protection of some noblemen and we buy the silence of magistrates and justices, but outside of Seville they arrest us. And they send us to the galleys just for being gypsies, for walking on the roads, for forging cauldrons, repairing tools and shoeing horses and mules. Our race has been persecuted for many years; they consider us crooks just because we're different. If Caridad was a gypsy . . . then don't you doubt it! But we shouldn't go looking for problems. Your father would never allow—'

'Father hates Caridad.'

'Possibly, but that doesn't change the fact that she's not a gypsy. She isn't one of us. I'm sorry for her . . . I really am,' insisted Ana in the face of her daughter's desperation. 'Milagros, I am a woman and I can imagine better than you the torment that she went through, but there is nothing we can do, really.'

Fray Joaquín wasn't any more helpful despite Milagros reminding him how furious he had been as he listened to Caridad's story, on that night of the goose tourney.

'And what do you want me to do, Milagros?' he had said in his defence. 'Denounce him? Denounce an honourable artisan who has been working in Triana for years based on the word of a recently freed Negress, who has no roots in this place? Who would testify on her behalf? I know,' he added quickly before she could reply. 'You would and I would believe you, but you are a gypsy and they, the justices and the judges, wouldn't even allow your testimony. All the artisans would take his side. It would be the ruin of Caridad, Milagros. She wouldn't be able to bear it; they would be all over her like wild dogs. Comfort her, be her friend, help her in her new life . . . and forget about this matter.'

However, the next Sunday, invited to preach in the parish of Santa Ana, Fray Joaquín spoke clearly and loudly from the pulpit, knowing that many of those who were listening to him had taken advantage of Caridad. He searched out the potter flesh-peddler with his eyes. He pointed threateningly this way and that. He shouted and shrieked. He lifted his hands to the heavens with his fingers clenched and shouted against ruffians and those who committed the sin of the flesh, particularly against defenceless women! With the support of the parishioners of Santa Ana who had invited him to give the sermon and before a shirking, fearful congregation, he foretold eternal hell-fire for all of them. Then he watched them leave the church amid whispers.

And what did it matter? he grumbled when the church was left empty and plunged into a silence broken only by the sound of his own footsteps. It's all just a hypocritical game! In Seville there were dozens of pardons for plenary indulgences. Any of those men, just by visiting a certain church on a particular day – the church of San Antonio de los Portugueses, any Tuesday, for example – would earn a plenary indulgence and be free of all sin, as innocent and clean as a newborn. Fray Joaquín couldn't hold back a sardonic laugh that echoed throughout Santa Ana. What did they care about repentance or mending their ways? They would run to get their indulgence to clean their souls and they would return convinced they'd escaped the devil, ready to commit some other evil deed.

Milagros and Alejandro were near the soap factory, beside the Inquisition Castle; the penetrating odour of the oils and the potashes used to make the white Triana soaps were beginning to overcome them when, in the light of the torches on San Jorge Castle, the young woman saw her fiancé was walking with a hand gripping the handle of the dagger he wore on his belt. She tried to steady her gait, to walk like an invincible queen beside the three gypsies accompanying her: Alejandro, his younger brother and one of his Vargas cousins, who were also playing with the hilts of their knives.

They had continued drinking, at a distance from the music played for the noblemen and their guests, while Milagros explained to the boy who was willing to do anything for her what had happened to Caridad on her arrival in Triana. Her telling of it was frenzied, even more repugnant – if that were possible – than the version she had told her mother. Alejandro knew Caridad; it was impossible not to notice the black woman who lived in the cluster of apartments with Melchor El Galeote. 'Son of a bitch,' he muttered time and again as Milagros told him in full detail.

'Mangy dog!' he exclaimed when she told him how the man had tied her up. Milagros was silent and tried to focus her gaze on him. Alejandro, also affected by the drink, thought he could make out a trace of affection in those glassy eyes. 'Pig!' he then added.

'Degenerate!' spat Milagros through her teeth before continuing her explanation.

In Alejandro she found the understanding she hadn't got from her mother or Fray Joaquín. She spoke with burning passion. And as for him, he felt her drawing closer and closer to him, seeking out his support, giving herself over to him. The wine did the rest.

'He deserves to die,' declared Alejandro when Milagros ended her story.

From that point on, everything happened very quickly.

'Let's go,' he urged.

'Where?'

'To take revenge for your friend.'

Alejandro grabbed the girl. The simple contact with Milagros's arm emboldened him. In the hall on the way out of the house where the party was being held, he met up with his younger brother and cousin.

'I have a score to settle,' he told them, brushing his fingers along the hilt of his dagger. 'Will you come with me?'

And they had both nodded, either to fulfil gypsy law, or out of the excitement brought on by the party and the wine. Later, as they walked, Alejandro told them about Caridad and the potter. Milagros didn't even think about her mother's warnings.

The neighbourhood was deserted. It was the dead of night. She pointed out one of the houses on the street with an almost imperceptible lifting of her chin. Caridad had shown her which one it was from afar, terrified.

'That's it,' announced Alejandro. 'You guys keep an eye out.'

Then, without thinking twice, he beat his fists against the doors of the workshop. The blows thundered in the silent night.

'Potter!' shouted the gypsy. 'Open up, potter!'

The other two young men paced up and down the street with a calmness that thrilled Milagros. They were gypsies! Alejandro banged on the doors again. The shutter of a facing house opened and the pale light of a candle peeked out. Alejandro's younger brother tilted his head towards the light, as if he were surprised by the neighbour's curiosity. *He can't be more than fifteen years old*, thought Milagros. The shutter closed with a thud.

'Potter, open up!'

Milagros turned her attention to Alejandro and was disconcerted to find that her fine hairs stood on end at his boldness; a shiver that ran up her spine began to temper her drunkenness.

'Who is it? What do you want at this hour?' The voice came from one of the windows on the upper floor.

'Open up!'

Milagros remained spellbound.

'Leave me alone or I'll call the watch!'

'Before they arrive, I'll have set your house on fire,' threatened the boy. 'Open up!'

'Here! Help! Constables! Help!' shouted the potter.

Alejandro thumped on the door again, immune to the screams for help he was drowning out with his banging in the night. Suddenly, Milagros reacted: what had she got herself into? She looked up and down the street. From a nearby workshop came a man in a nightshirt wielding an old blunderbuss. A couple of doors opened. The potter kept shouting and Alejandro kept banging on the doors.

'Alejandro . . .' Milagros managed to say in a halting voice.

He didn't hear her.

'It's some gypsy kids!' shouted the man in the nightshirt then.

'Alejandro,' repeated Milagros.

'Four beggars!'

The brother and the cousin started to back up as men came out of the neighbouring houses, all armed: blunderbusses, sticks, axes, knives . . . One of them let out a laugh at the fear in the boys' faces.

'Alejandro!' shrieked Milagros just as the door to the workshop opened.

Everything unfolded quickly. Milagros only half saw it; enough, however, to recognize the man she had tried to sell cigars to in San Roque on the day of the geese. He was inside the workshop, dressed in worn drawers and with his chest bare; behind him was his son with an old sword in his hand. The man held a blunderbuss whose threatening round mouth seemed immense to Milagros. Then Alejandro pulled his dagger out of his belt and, when he moved to pounce on the potter, a shot was heard. Countless lead pellets destroyed the boy's head and neck, sending him flying.

The men on the street froze. The gypsies, mouths agape, stammering, looked back and forth from the disfigured body on the ground to the potters who had come to help their fellow guild member. Milagros, bewildered, looked at her hands and clothes, splattered with Alejandro's blood and remains.

'You killed a Vargas,' the oldest of the gypsies managed to articulate.

The men looked at each other, as if weighing that threat. Inside the workshop, the potter tried to reload his blunderbuss with trembling hands.

'Let's finish them off!' suggested one of the artisans.

'Yes. That way nobody will find out!' added another.

The Vargas boys kept their knives extended, surrounding Milagros, beside Alejandro's corpse, facing the men who were standing in a semicircle around them. A couple of them shook their heads.

'They are just boys. How are we going to . . . ?'

'Run!'

The oldest gypsy boy took advantage of their indecision: he grabbed Milagros and forced her to run right towards the man who had expressed his doubts, and Alejandro's brother joined them. They bumped into the tentative potter, who fell to the ground, and they leapt over him even before he had finished his sentence. A man pointed his blunderbuss at the boys' backs, but the man beside him pushed his barrel up into the air.

'Are you trying to wound one of our own?' he asked, pointing out the proximity of the curious onlookers who had begun to appear.

When they looked again, the gypsies were already lost in the darkness of the night. In silence, they turned towards the corpse lying in a puddle of blood in front of the door to the workshop. *We killed a Vargas*, they seemed to be saying to each other.

7

TOMÁS VEGA HAD signed up for the party of gypsies led by his brother Melchor that was on its way to the coast near Málaga to receive the tobacco from Gibraltar. The two of them led the march, chatting, apparently carefree yet with all their senses alert to the slightest sign of patrols of soldiers or members of the Holy Brotherhood. Behind them were four young men from the Vega family leading some horses by their halters, which were fitted out with pack harnesses for the load: packsaddles, surcingles and breast-straps; the King had prohibited using horses for transport – it could only be done with donkeys, mules or billy-goats with bells – but he had exempted Seville from that prohibition. The young men joked and laughed, as if their uncles' presence guaranteed their safety. Caridad brought up the rear, walked drenched in sweat beneath her dark cape and hat, constantly worried about revealing a single stitch of her red dress, just as Melchor had warned her before they set out. *It must be the red colour*, thought the woman, because the gypsies wore their colourful garb with no problems. She walked uncomfortably in the old sandals with thin leather soles that Melchor had got for her from the settlement beside the Carthusians; she had never worn anything on her feet before. They had been walking for four days and had already entered the Ronda mountains. On the first day, during a break, Caridad had untied the leather straps that held the soles to her ankles, to keep them from rubbing. Melchor, seated on a large rock beside the road, watched her and shrugged when their eyes met, as if giving her permission to do without them. Then he drank a long sip from the wineskin they were carrying.

The gypsy's attitude didn't shift when the next day, after spending the night out in the open, Caridad changed her mind and tied on the sandals before beginning the day's walk. She knew how to walk barefoot. In Cuba, especially after the sugar harvest, she was careful not to step on any of the sharp edges of the canes that remained hidden, but those Sevillian paths were nothing like the Cuban plantations and fields: they were rocky, dry, dusty and during the dog days of an Andalusian summer they were burning hot, so much so that it seemed few people had much interest in travelling along them, and the trip went off without a hitch.

Despite Melchor taking the rough goat paths, the ascent into the mountains gave them a rest from the heat, although more importantly it allowed the two Vega brothers to relax from the tension of the countryside. An encounter with the authorities along the way would have meant the confiscation of their weapons and horses and surely their imprisonment, but the mountains were theirs; they were the territory of smugglers, bandits, criminals and all types of fugitives from justice. There the gypsies moved freely.

'Negress!' shouted Melchor as they ascended in single file through the thickets, without even turning towards her. 'You can show your colours now, maybe it will scare off the bugs.'

The others laughed. Caridad took the opportunity to take off the cape and hat and breathed deeply.

'I wouldn't let the Negress go around showing off that marvellous dark flesh,' Tomás commented to his brother, 'or we're going to have problems with the other men.'

'In Gaucín we'll cover her up again.'

Tomás shook his head. 'You can start already, right now even a blind man could see her.'

'That would be a nice first sight,' joked his brother.

'The men will be all over her. She knows about tobacco, but was it so important to bring her?'

Melchor was silent for a few seconds. 'She sings well,' was all he said when he finally spoke.

Tomás didn't answer and they continued their ascent, yet Melchor heard him grumble under his breath.

'Sing, Negress!' he then yelled.

Sing, Negro! Caridad remembered. That was the overseers' shout in the sugar mills before cracking the whip against their backs. *If a Negro is singing, he's not thinking,* she had heard the whites say on numerous occasions, and the slaves were always singing: they sang in the cane fields and in the sugar factories at the request of the overseers, but also when they wanted to communicate with each other or complain about the master; they sang to express their sadness and their rare joys; they sang even when they didn't have to work.

Caridad intoned a monotone, deep, hoarse, repetitive song that blended with the beating of the horses' hoofs against the stones and struck a chord in the spirits of the gypsies.

Tomás nodded as he felt his legs trying to match the rhythm of that African song. One of the young men turned towards her with a surprised expression.

Meanwhile, *Sing, Negress,* thought Caridad. It wasn't the same order that the overseers used in Cuba. The gypsy seemed to enjoy her voice. Those nights when he went to the apartment to sleep and found Caridad working the tobacco on the plank, he would drop down on his mattress after taking off his clothes and ask her: *Sing, Negress,* in a whisper. And without pausing in her work under the candlelight, cutting the tobacco leaves and rolling them one over the other, Caridad would sing with Melchor lying behind her. She never dared turn her head, not even when the man's snores and slow breathing indicated that he was sleeping. What was that gypsy thinking about when he listened to her? Melchor didn't interrupt her, he didn't sing along; he just remained attentive, still, soothed by Caridad's sad lullaby. He had never touched her either, although on a few occasions she had perceived something similar to the lust so many others showed in their eyes when they ran them over her body. Would she have liked it if he did, if he touched her, ended up mounting her? *No,* she answered to herself. He would have become just one more. Now he was the first man she had ever known, that she'd had dealings with, who had never laid a hand on her. Throughout her entire life, since they'd ripped her from her homeland and her family, Caridad had worked with tobacco, and yet on those nights when she did so with Melchor lying behind her, the aroma of the plant took on subtleties that she had never noticed before. Then, listening to herself and watching her long fingers handle the delicate leaves, Caridad discovered feelings that had never surfaced in her before, and she breathed deeply. Sometimes she had even stopped her labours until her hands ceased trembling, seized by anxiety in the face of sensations she was unable to recognize and understand.

'Freedom,' declared Milagros one day, reflecting briefly after Caridad explained it to her. 'That's called freedom, Cachita,' she reiterated with a seriousness that was unusual in her.

'Look, Negress, that is the land where you were born: Africa.'

Caridad looked down on the horizon, towards where Melchor was pointing, and made out a blurry line beyond the sea. She covered herself with the cape and the slouch hat pulled down to her ears while the gypsy beside her shimmered in the sun in his sky-blue silk jacket and his silver-edged trousers. In his right hand he held a flintlock musket he had taken out of the saddlebags of one of the horses as soon as they arrived in Gaucín after three days of walking along paths and treacherous cattle tracks.

'And that rock there, by the sea' – Melchor pointed with the barrel of the shotgun, addressing them all – 'is Gibraltar.'

The stately burg of Gaucín, nestled on the King's Highway from Gibraltar to Ronda, was an important enclave in the mountain range. It had close to a thousand inhabitants, and above it, on a hard-to-reach cliff, rose Águila Castle. Caridad and the gypsies enjoyed the view for a few minutes, until Melchor gave the order to head towards the Gaucín inn, a league away from the town, beside the road: a single-storey construction erected on an open field and provided with stables and haylofts.

It was midday, and the smell of roasted young goat reminded them how long it had been since they'd eaten; a long column of smoke rose from the chimney of a large oven bulging out of one of the building's walls. A couple of brats ran from the stables to take care of the horses. The nephews grabbed their belongings, handed over the horses to the boys and hastened to join Melchor, Tomás and Caridad, who were already crossing the inn's threshold.

'I was starting to worry that they'd stopped you on the road!' The shout came from one of the rough tables.

Light streamed into the inn. Melchor recognized Bernardo, his galley mate, seated in front of a nice plate of meat, bread and a jug of wine.

'Haven't see you around here for a while, Melchor,' greeted the innkeeper, extending a hand that the gypsy squeezed tightly. 'They told me you preferred to work on the Portuguese border.'

Before answering, the gypsy glanced around the inside of the inn: only two other tables were occupied, both by several men who were eating with their weapons on the tabletops, always close at hand: smugglers. Some greeted Melchor with a nod, others scrutinized Caridad.

'May God be with you, gentlemen!' said the gypsy. Then he turned to the innkeeper, who was also examining the woman. 'You work where you can, José.' He raised his voice to get his attention. 'Yesterday it was with the Portuguese, today it's with the English. Your family well?'

'Growing.' The innkeeper pointed to a woman and two girls who toiled in front of the large wood stove.

The gypsies, Caridad and the innkeeper walked towards the long table where Bernardo was waiting for them.

'Are they arriving already?' asked Melchor, seeing the women's bustling around the stove and the scarce guests for all that was roasting there.

'They were spotted passing Algatocín a little while ago,' answered José. 'A league away. They'll be here before long. Eat and drink now, before everything's turned upside down.'

'How many are they?'

'More than a hundred.'

The gypsy frowned. That was a significant group. Still standing beside the table, he questioned Bernardo with a look.

'I told you that several boats had arrived at the Rock,' he

explained, turning over the goat leg he was holding, as if the news was of no importance. 'There's a lot of merchandise. Don't worry, our share is guaranteed.'

Before taking a seat, looking towards the entrance, Melchor placed his long musket across the table, banging it perhaps harder than he should have, as if he wanted to make clear that the only thing that could guarantee his business was weapons.

'Sit down next to me, Negress,' he indicated to Caridad as he hit the bench that surrounded the table.

The innkeeper, curious, lifted his chin towards the woman.

'She's mine,' declared the gypsy. 'Make sure everyone knows that and bring us some food. You,' he added to Caridad. 'You heard it: here you are mine, you belong to me.' Caridad nodded, remembering Milagros's words: *Don't leave Grandfather's side.* She noticed the tension in the gypsies. 'Stay well covered, but you can take off your hat. And as for the rest of you . . .' At that moment the gypsy smiled at Bernardo and served himself a brimming glass of wine that he downed almost entirely in a single gulp. 'The rest of you be careful with the wine!' he warned, wiping his lips with the back of his hand. 'I want you alert when the men from Encinas Reales arrive.'

Encinas Reales, Cuevas Altas and Cuevas Bajas were three small towns close to each other and deep in the old borderlands, beside the Genil River, some thirty leagues from Gaucín. The three towns had become a refuge for smugglers, who acted with total impunity. Most of their inhabitants were in that business – primarily with tobacco – and those who weren't were either harbouring them or profiting from it. In those towns, the women and clergymen collaborated in the business, and the authorities, for all their efforts, couldn't impose order in those enclaves of rough, violent, hardened men among whom the laws of silence and mutual protection ruled. The people of the three towns organized constant smuggling parties, sometimes to Portugal, along the route of Palma del Río and Jabugo, in order to cross the border towards Barrancos or Serpa, and on other occasions to Gibraltar, through Ronda and its mountain range. They sought safety in these large groups, bringing together runners and other criminals from Rute, Lucena, Cabra, Priego, and assembled small, fearsome armies that were larger in number and strength than any patrol of royal soldiers, who were mostly corrupt, and often poorly paid, old or crippled.

The only person in the Gaucín inn who didn't notice the uproar of the smugglers before their shouts and laughter flooded the surroundings of the inn was Caridad; the others could hear the murmur from the distance becoming a clamorous riot as the men and horses drew nearer. The four young Vega men stiffened, nervous, looking at each other, searching in Tomás for the calmness their inexperience denied them. Melchor and Bernardo, on the other hand, received the men from Encinas Reales with their hunger sated, with good cigars between their fingers, enjoying the strong young mountain wine, as if with each silent sip, looking at each other in perfect harmony, they sought to reclaim part of those horrific years they had spent fettered to the oars of the royal galley ships.

While all the other diners at the inn moved restlessly on their benches, Caridad nibbled enthusiastically on the bones of the young goat roasted over the wood fire and seasoned with aromatic herbs. She couldn't remember ever having eaten anything so exquisite! Not even the bluish mouthfuls of smoke the gypsy exhaled beside her were distracting, much less the racket made by an approaching party of smugglers. The gypsies didn't usually eat well: their meats were often almost rotten and the vegetables were overripe, but at least there was more variety than the gruel with salt cod that the master fed the slaves day in and day out at his plantation. A little glass of spirits, that was what he gave them in the mornings so they'd be awake and willing to work. No, Caridad certainly wouldn't stay on with the gypsies for the food, although that plus a place to sleep . . . 'Cachita, you can leave whenever you want, you are free, you understand? Free,' Milagros told her time and again. And what would she do without Milagros? A few days before leaving with her grandfather's smuggling party, during a lazy twilight that seemed to resist leaving Seville in darkness, the girl had once again raised the subject of her grief over having to marry Alejandro Vargas. She wanted Pedro García; *I love him*, she had sobbed, the two women sitting on the bank of the Guadalquivir, looking out over the river instead of at each other. Later, Milagros had rested her head on Caridad's shoulder, just as Marcelo used to do, and she had stroked her hair in an attempt to console her. Where would she go without Milagros? The mere memory of what had happened with the potter fogged her thinking; Caridad mentally transported herself to the day she had sat beneath that orange tree waiting for death to overtake her. That night she'd seen Eleggua, the god who governs men's fates, he who decides their lives according to his whims, approaching. How long had it been – she thought at that moment – since she had spoken to the Orishas, since she had made them any offerings, since she had been mounted by them? Then she made an effort and sang to him, and capricious Eleggua spun around her, smoking a big cigar, until he was satisfied with that humble offering and sent the gypsy to help her keep on living. Melchor respected her. He had also been the one who had taken her to San Jacinto and introduced her to Fray Joaquín. There, in that church under construction, was the Virgin of Candlemas: Oyá to the Cuban slaves. Oyá wasn't her Orisha, that was Oshún, the Virgin of Charity, but it was always said that there was no Oyá without Oshún or Oshún without Oyá, and since then Caridad went to pray to the Virgin of Candlemas. She knelt in front of her and, when no one was watching, switched her Hail Marys for the murmuring of the sacred songs to the Orisha the Virgin represented, rocking forward and back. Before leaving, she dropped a stolen tobacco leaf, the only thing she had to offer her. Over the time she'd been in Seville she had seen the free black people of the city: most of them were miserable wretches begging for alms on the streets, lost amid the hundreds of beggars that swarmed the capital, fighting for a coin. She was fine with the gypsies, concluded Caridad, she loved Milagros, and Melchor took care of her.

'Negress, there's no more bone to gnaw on.'

The gypsy's words brought her back to reality and with it came the ruckus going on outside. Caridad found herself with a picked-clean shoulder blade in her hands. She left it on the plate just as the doors of the inn opened and a flood of loud-mouthed, dirty, armed men came in. Caridad made out several mulattoes and even a couple of friars. The innkeeper struggled to accommodate them, but it was impossible to fit them all in. The smugglers shouted and laughed; some callously forced others out of their seats, imposing an authority that was confirmed by the passive acceptance of those ousted. There were some women also, prostitutes who followed them, brazenly selling their charms to those who seemed to be the captains of the various groups that made up the party. The innkeeper and his family started to bring over jugs of wine, liquor and trays brimming with goat to the tables; he worried about serving those who shouted the most and his wife and two young daughters trying to avoid slaps on the arse and unwanted embraces.

Four men went to take the free seats on the long benches adjacent to the gypsies' table, but they failed to do so before three others showed up and stopped them.

'Out of here,' a short, fat man ordered them in a reedy voice. He had a round face with hairless cheeks, and was dressed in a little jacket that looked about to burst, just like the red sash that held back his enormous belly and from which peeked the handles of a knife and a pistol.

Caridad, just like the young gypsies, felt a shiver when she saw how those four rough smugglers had come over to them, full of their own importance, and they stood up with an obedience bordering on servility. The fat man dropped heavily on to the bench beside Bernardo, in front of Melchor; the other two took the spots that were empty. A couple of prostitutes quickly came over. The fat man pulled out of his sash a double-edged cutlass and a miquelet lock pistol with lovely golden arabesque carvings on the barrel. Caridad observed how the man's small, thick fingers meticulously lined up the two weapons on the table, beside Melchor's shotgun. When he seemed satisfied, he spoke again, this time addressing the gypsy.

'I didn't know you were in this business too, Galeote.'

The innkeeper, with no need for shouts or waving, had come over promptly to the gypsies' table to serve the new guests. Melchor waited for him to finish before answering.

'I heard that you were one of the captains and I rushed over. If El Gordo's going, I said to myself, there must be good tobacco.'

One of the men accompanying the captain shifted restlessly on the bench: for some time, ever since he'd started to lead his own band, no one had dared to use that nickname when they spoke to him; there were many who had paid dearly for such slip-ups. They called him 'El Fajado' now, referring to his sash instead of the belly behind it.

El Gordo smacked his tongue. 'Why do you insult me, Melchor?' he then said. 'Is it something I've done?'

The gypsy narrowed his eyes in his direction. 'I'll trade you all the pounds of fat on your belly for my years at the oars.'

El Gordo straightened his thick neck almost imperceptibly, thought for a few seconds and smiled with blackish teeth. 'No deal, Galeote, I prefer my fat. I'll let it go this time, but be careful about calling me that in front of my men.'

Then it was the Vega gypsies who tensed their backs on the benches, wondering how Melchor would react to that threat.

'It'd be best that our paths don't cross again, then,' he suggested.

'It'd be best,' the other agreed, after nodding. 'You are using a Negress as a runner now?' he asked, gesturing towards Caridad, who was witnessing the argument with her mouth and eyes wide.

'What Negress?' asked the gypsy, stock-still, regal.

El Gordo was about to point to her but he stopped himself. Then he shook his head and grabbed a shoulder of goat. That was the signal for the others to pounce on their food and for the prostitutes to approach and start flattering the newcomers.

The inn at Gaucín was the place chosen to await news of the contraband merchandise from Gibraltar landing on the coast of Manilva, a small town some five leagues from the inn that belonged to the municipality of Casares, devoted to fishing and grape and sugar-cane growing. Through their various agents – Melchor had done it with the help of Bernardo – all the parties of smugglers had already acquired the goods they wanted in the British enclave, for a low price, thus evading the Spanish monopoly. Once the deals were struck, the products remained stored and conveniently secured in the warehouses of Gibraltar ship owners, waiting for the right climatic conditions to move them from the Rock to the Spanish coasts.

Two warnings had been sent to Gibraltar: the parties were

gathered in Gaucín. They were just waiting for the ship owners operating on the Rock beneath different flags to confirm the night when the disembarking would take place. Meanwhile, the music of guitars, flutes and tambourines sounding in the inn and the wide field that opened out around it grew in momentum along with the jugs and wineskins that were passed from hand to hand. The men, gathered in groups, bet their future earnings on cards or dice. Quarrels started here and there, but the captains made sure they didn't go any further: they needed their porters. Merchants and traders from the surrounding areas, as well as some prostitutes and criminals, came around in the hopes of easy money.

Melchor, Bernardo and their companions strolled amid that throng noting the cool of the night that drew near. The gypsies weren't going to sleep on the floor in front of the stove, like the captains and their lieutenants would, nor even in the stables or haylofts: they refused to sleep near *payos*; it was their law. They would head off to take shelter among the trees and sleep out in the open; but until that moment came, Melchor, leading the procession, stopped to listen to music in a corner, to watch the betting in another and to chat here and there with acquaintances among the smugglers.

'Want to bet your Negress in a game of dice with me, Galeote?' proposed the captain of a small party from Cuevas Bajas, crammed with other men around a wooden plank.

Caridad's head turned in fear towards the smuggler. *Would he accept the bet?* crossed her mind.

'Why do you want to lose, Tordo?' That was what they called the captain. 'You'd lose your money if I won, and your health if I lost. What would you do with a woman like this?'

El Tordo hesitated for a moment before replying, but he ended up adding a forced smile to the guffaws of the men playing with him.

Melchor left the improvised dice table behind and the nasty comments still audible around it and continued strolling.

'Melchor, have you gone crazy? We are going to end up with problems,' Tomás whispered, making a gesture towards Caridad.

Despite the cape that covered her, the woman was unable to hide her large breasts and the voluptuous curves of her hips, which excited the imagination of all who watched her move.

'I know, Brother,' answered Melchor, raising his voice so the other gypsies could hear him. 'That's exactly why. The sooner we have those problems, the sooner we can rest. Besides, this way I'll be the one who chooses who to have them with.'

'Are you that interested in the Negress?' asked Tomás, surprised.

Caridad pricked up her ears.

'Didn't you hear her sing?' answered the gypsy.

And Melchor chose: a runner old enough to be obliged to defend his manliness, the value that earned them a place in the tacit hierarchy of criminals; he was grim-faced, with a shabby beard and bloodshot eyes that showed how much wine and liquor he had consumed. The man was chatting in a group, but he had turned his attention towards Caridad.

'Stay alert, Nephews,' murmured Melchor under his breath while he handed his musket to Bernardo. 'What are you looking at, you pig?' he then shouted at the runner.

The reaction was immediate. The man put a hand to his dagger and his companions tried to do the same, but before they could, the four Vega nephews had pounced on them and were already threatening them with their weapons. Melchor remained immobile before the runner, with his hands empty, challenging him only with his gaze.

Silence fell around the group. Tomás, a step behind his brother, grabbed the handle of his knife, still in his sash. Caridad was trembling, to one side, with her eyes fixed on the gypsy. Bernardo was smiling. Some distance away, out in the field, someone called El Gordo's attention, who turned his gaze towards where they pointed. *He's got some guts!* he admitted.

'She's my Negress,' muttered Melchor. The runner moved his extended dagger threateningly towards the gypsy. 'How dare you look at her, you scum?'

The new insult made the man charge at Melchor, but the gypsy had the situation under control: he had seen him move clumsily, inebriated, and it was so crowded that the man could only move in a straight line, towards him. Melchor stepped aside nimbly and the runner passed to one side, stumbling, with his arm awkwardly extended. It was Tomás who put an end to the quarrel: with rare speed he pulled his dagger from his sash and launched a stab at the attacker's wrist, making him fall to the floor, disarmed.

Melchor approached the wounded man and stepped on his already bleeding wrist. 'She's mine!' he announced in a loud voice. 'Anyone else planning on imagining her in his arms?'

The gypsy ran narrowed eyes over the scene. Nobody answered. Then he released the pressure of his foot, while Tomás kicked the runner's knife out of his reach. After a sign from Melchor, the nephews stopped menacing the other smugglers and they all disappeared as one into the crowd. Caridad felt her knees grow weak; she was still terrified but above all confused: Melchor had fought for her!

A few paces past where the altercation had taken place, Bernardo returned the musket to his companion. 'So many years in the galleys,' he commented then, 'so many years struggling to stay alive, watching so many fall by our side, on our very benches, after unbearable agony, and you risk your life for a Negress. And don't tell me she sings well!' he said, anticipating his response. 'I haven't heard her yet.'

Melchor smiled at his friend.

'Can she outdo you?' asked Bernardo then. 'Does she sing better than you?'

They both were lost in their memories, of when Melchor, as they rowed out at sea in the silence of a calm wind, started an interminable gloomy wailing lament as if pulled from the spirits of all those unfortunates who had died in the galleys. Even the slave driver stopped whipping the rowers then. And Melchor sang without words, modulating his cry and intoning the lament of men destined to die and add their souls to the many left chained to the oars and the timbers of the galley for ever.

'Better than me?' wondered the gypsy aloud after a pause. 'I don't know, Bernardo. What I can tell you is she sings with the same pain.'

*

The tower built on Chullera Point for coastal observation and defence was used, as on so many other occasions, as an improvised lighthouse to guide the smugglers' ships through the night from Gibraltar. The lookout on the watchtower, more concerned with tending the garden that surrounded it, was pleased to get the money the smugglers paid him, as were the local magistrates, corporals and justices of the nearby towns and garrisons.

And while a man waved a lantern from the top of the tower, at his feet, on the beach, the hundred smugglers who had come from Gaucín with their horses waited in the darkness of the night for the boats to arrive. They had spent two days at the inn, playing, singing, drinking and fighting as they waited for news from Gibraltar but on the beach most of them were scanning the black horizon, because while they could act with impunity on land, it wasn't the same at sea, with the Spanish coastguard ships controlling the shoreline. The most delicate moment of the operation had arrived and they all knew it.

Caridad, among whispers and the occasional whinny from the horses, heard the murmur of the waves breaking on the shore and repeated the gypsy's instructions to herself over and over: 'Some *faluchos* will show up,' he had told her, 'perhaps, for this amount of people, even a xebec . . .'

'*Faluchos?*' she'd asked.

'Ships,' Melchor had clarified brusquely, nervous. She didn't dare ask anything more and kept listening. 'They will unload leather bags filled with tobacco on to the beach. Eight are ours, two per horse. The problem is that each vessel will unload many more, so we have to divide them up on the beach. That's where you come in, *morena*. I want you to choose the highest quality ones. Did you understand me?'

'Yes,' she answered, although she wasn't very sure. How long would she have to smell and feel the leaves? 'How much time will I have . . .' she started to ask. One of the gypsies' horses launched a kick at another who was nibbling on his rump.

'Boy!' muttered Melchor. 'Deal with the animals!'

Caridad stopped paying attention to the horses when his nephews separated them.

'Were you saying something, *morena*?'

She didn't hear him. And how was she going to check the colour and the different tones on the leaves? It was pitch black; you couldn't see a thing. Besides, there were all those men waiting impatiently beside them. Caridad sensed the pent-up tension on the beach. Would they give her enough time to choose the tobacco? She knew she was able to recognize the best plants. Don José always called her over to do it, and then even the master remained silent during the time it took, while she, now the lady of the plantation, savoured the aromas, textures and colours.

'Melchor . . .' she tried to clear up her doubts.

'Let's go!' he interrupted.

The order caught her off guard.

'Get going, *morena*!' urged the gypsy.

Caridad followed them.

One of the nephews stayed behind, guarding the animals, just as one in each of the other groups did. Only the men went down to the shore, since it was so chaotic that the horses would get frightened, kicking each other and squandering the goods.

Suddenly, many lanterns were lit along the beach. No one was being cautious any longer; the lights could betray them to any coast-guard boat in the area. They just had to hurry. In the footsteps of the gypsies, surrounded by smugglers, Caridad made out several boats around which crowded the most diligent. She stopped a few steps from the shore, beside Melchor, amid shouts and splashing. Bernardo moved quickly in search of his merchandise. He called them, waving a lantern, and they all headed over to where they were piling up the leather bags unloaded from one of the several boats that had come close to the beach.

'Get started, *morena*!' urged Melchor as he pushed aside several smugglers and cut the cords that bound one of the sacks with his knife. 'What are you waiting for?' he shouted after he had cut the cords off the next one and Caridad still hadn't moved.

Protected by Tomás and the three remaining nephews, who tried to keep the others from making off with the tobacco before Caridad could check the merchandise, she tried to get close to the first bag. She couldn't see. The shouting distracted her and the pushing was annoying. She still managed to introduce a hand into the first leather sack. She was hoping to get to feel the leaves, pick up one of them and . . . It was Brazil tobacco! She had first encountered it in Triana, although she had heard about it before that. Rope tobacco: black Brazilian tobacco leaves wrapped in big rolls. Caridad smelled the cloying sweet treacle syrup used to treat the leaves so they could be rolled. The Spaniards liked it: they ground up the rolls and wrapped another leaf around it. It could also be chewed, but it didn't compare to good tobacco . . .

'Negress!' This time it was Tomás who called her attention, his back up against hers, to withstand the pushing of the other men. 'Hurry it up or one of these men is going to mistake you for a leather bag and load you on to one of the horses.'

Then Caridad cast aside that first sack and a couple of smugglers pounced on it. In the lantern light and confusion, the Vega nephews looked at their Uncle Tomás in surprise. He shrugged. Brazil tobacco, the most sought-after smoking tobacco on the market!

After looking through a couple more sacks, Caridad found leaves. They weren't Cuban, it was Virginia tobacco. It pained her to rip the leaves roughly, but Tomás and Melchor were constantly rushing her while Bernardo tried to calm the agent who had unloaded them. She rejected the ones that seemed too dry or too damp; she quickly sniffed them, trying to calculate how long ago they'd been harvested, she held them up to the faint light to check their colour, and she began to chose: one, two, three . . . And the nephews took them aside.

'No!' she corrected. 'Not this one, that one.'

'For crying out loud!' one of them shouted at her. 'Make up your mind!'

Caridad felt tears come to her eyes. She hesitated. Which was the last one she had chosen?

'*Morena!*' Melchor shook her, but she couldn't remember.

'That one!' she pointed without being sure, her eyes flooded with tears.

Some distance away, on a dune, while his men had taken care of the contraband that belonged to them, El Gordo and his two lieutenants watched the huge commotion the gypsies had started with interest. Caridad continued with her selection, crushing the tobacco leaves, barely knowing which bag they had come out of. The nephews set aside the ones she pointed to and the other smugglers made off with the rejected sacks. Melchor and Tomás hurried Caridad, and Bernardo argued with the agent who was wildly pointing to the other ships already leaving the beach, all eyes on the horizon, looking out for the lights of a coastguard vessel.

Finally, the gypsies managed to gather their eight leather bags. The agent and Bernardo shook hands and the agent ran towards a boat that was already starting to row towards the *faluchos*. The ruckus continued over the tobacco Caridad had discarded. That was when El Gordo squinted his eyes. Each bag could weigh more than a hundred pounds and there were only six men: five gypsies and Bernardo. He looked towards where the other gypsy was waiting for them with the horses. They had to cover a good stretch of beach, each of them with a bag; they couldn't carry any more. Then he turned to his lieutenants, who understood him without the need for a single word.

'Wait here, *morena*,' ordered Melchor while he threw one of the bags on to his back with difficulty and joined the line headed by Tomás, each with his own bundle.

Caridad was sobbing, terrified. Her body was drenched in sweat and the red of her dress showed through her open cape. Her legs trembled and she still clenched pieces of tobacco leaf in her hands. El Gordo watched as the line of gypsies set off, then he shifted his gaze to his lieutenants: one of them, with the help of two other smugglers, drove an unloaded horse on through the water, behind Caridad's back; the other walked over to her.

'Distract her,' El Gordo had ordered him. 'You don't have to hurt her,' he added at the man's surprised expression.

However, seeing how his henchman drew closer to Caridad, the lanterns gradually going out as the parties left the beach with their goods, he understood that if the woman realized the trick and put up a fight, his caution would have been in vain. When the smuggler was only a few steps away from Caridad, El Gordo again calculated the timing: the gypsies hadn't yet reached their horses. He smiled. He was about to let out a laugh: they advanced slowly, as erect as they could walk beneath the bags, haughty and proud as if they were strolling down the main street of a town. The men who were driving the horse through the water had already disappeared into the darkness, so they must be very close to the bundles. They had little time, but he was already rubbing his thick hands together: he sensed it was going to be easy.

'Negress!'

Caridad jumped. The smuggler who had shouted did as well: her breasts, large and firm, struggled to burst through her red shirt with each laboured exhalation of breath. The man forgot the speech he'd prepared, absorbed in the sight of her and his sudden desire for those voluptuous curves. Caridad lowered her gaze and her submissive attitude inflamed the man's passions. Beneath the increasingly dim light, the woman shone from the sweat that ran down her body.

'Come with me!' the smuggler proposed naively. 'I'll give you . . . I'll give you whatever you want.'

Caridad didn't answer and, all of a sudden, the smuggler saw how his companion, who had already arrived, was waving wildly with open hands, incredulous at what he had just overheard. El Gordo shifted restlessly on the dune and turned towards the gypsies: they were already loading up the horses, but it was unlikely they could see Caridad from where they were. The one behind the woman waved his hand, wanting nothing to do with it, and picked up one of the leather bags. Caridad noticed and was about to turn around, but then the lieutenant reacted and pounced on her, immobilizing her with a hand on the nape of her neck and bringing the other to her inner thigh. For a moment he was surprised that she didn't scream or defend herself. She only wanted to turn towards the tobacco. He didn't let her and bit her lips. They both fell on to the sand.

El Gordo made sure the other lieutenant and the men he had with him were quickly loading the leather bags on to the horse and disappearing into the darkness. The first shouts were heard from the gypsies. Only one of his men remained . . . *Good-for-nothing!* he thought. If the gypsies caught him, they would know that he was behind the theft, and he didn't want that. He was relieved to see that the lieutenant reappeared in the night and grabbed the man by his hair, almost lifting him off the ground, and separated him from the woman. They escaped shortly before Melchor and his men got to Caridad. It was unlikely that they had recognized them.

'You're old, Galeote,' murmured El Gordo before turning his back to the sea and disappearing into the night as well, trying mockingly to imitate the gypsies' gait.

8

'*S*ING, *MORENA*!'

It wasn't Melchor asking her this time, but Bernardo, after three days of walking in the most stubborn of silences, with one horse's pack saddle empty, reminding them at each stride what had happened on the beach at Manilva.

Melchor hadn't allowed the bags to be distributed evenly among the horses and he walked beside the horse without bags, downcast, as if that were part of his penance. Caridad obeyed, but her voice came out strangely: her lower lip was destroyed by the smuggler's biting, her body bruised and her precious red clothes torn to shreds. Even so, she wanted to please the gypsy and her mournful singing further accentuated the dryness of the summer fields they had decided to cross to avoid the main roads. It also intensified the pain of her scabbed, parched lips, although they didn't pain her as much as the torn shirt she protected with the dark cape. What were the bites of a smuggler compared to the lashings of an infuriated overseer? She had experienced that sharp, intense pain many times, it lingered long before finally abating, but her red clothes . . . Never in her twenty-five years had she had clothes like those! And they were hers, all hers . . . She remembered Milagros's applause when she'd showed them to her and her mother; she also remembered the way the people of Triana looked at her, so differently than they had when she wore those greyish slave clothes, as if they revealed what she was. Dressed in red she had managed to feel a twinge of that freedom she was struggling so hard to recognize. Which was why, more than her injured lips, it hurt her to feel how one of her breasts fell free over the fabric and the torn shreds of the skirt brushed against her legs. Would she be able to fix it? She didn't know how to sew, and neither did the gypsy women.

She observed the row of gypsies with horses in front of her. Despite the sun, their brightly coloured clothes didn't shine either, as if exuding the anger and disappointment of those who wore them. She had to sing. Perhaps that was her punishment. She had expected it on the beach, when the smuggler released her body and she saw that the bags had vanished. She had let them down! She curled up on the sand, not daring to look the gypsies in the eye when they came back; that was when the lashing should have come . . . or the kicks and insults, like on the plantation, like always. But it wasn't like that. She heard them shout and curse; she heard Melchor's instructions, and the others running around the beach with the gypsy's indignant panting over her.

'The hoof prints come out of the sea and disappear into it again,' lamented one of the nephews.

'We have no way of knowing which way they went,' panted another.

'It was El Gordo!' accused Tomás. 'I thought I saw him lagging behind . . . I told you the Negress would bring us—!'

Caridad couldn't see the authoritative gesture with which Melchor stopped his brother's accusation, but: 'Get up, *morena*,' she heard him order.

Caridad got up with her eyes lowered; the light of the lanterns the gypsies carried focused on her.

'Who was the man who threw himself on to you?'

Caridad shook her head.

'What did he look like?' Melchor enquired then.

'White.'

'White!' That was Bernardo. 'What do you mean white? That's all? Did he have a beard? What colour was his hair? And his eyes? And—?'

'Bernardo,' interrupted Melchor in a somewhat weary voice, 'all you *payos* are the same.'

And there it all ended, without punishment, without even any recrimination. The gypsies went back to where the horses were waiting for them and they set off, far behind the other parties; they wouldn't meet up with them again as they each went their own way. No one said anything to Caridad: not 'Follow us', not 'Come on', not 'Let's go'. She joined them like a small dog that follows whoever feeds it. They spoke little along the way back to Triana. Melchor didn't utter a single word after his last on the beach. Caridad walked with Melchor's back as her focal point. That man had treated her well, respected her, given her the red clothes and defended her on several occasions, but why hadn't he whipped her? She would have preferred that. Everything ended after a lashing: back to work until there was a new mistake, until a new fit of anger from the overseer or the master, but this way . . . She looked at the gypsy's sky-blue silk jacket and the lyrics of her song stuck in her throat.

They waited until night fell to approach Seville. The return had gone off without a hitch but, even at night, they couldn't cross the pontoon bridge to Triana with three horses loaded down with contraband tobacco. When the sky filled with stars and they continued, Melchor spoke for the first time.

'Let's go to Santo Domingo de Portaceli.'

The convent, of the same order as San Jacinto, was outside the city walls, in the district of San Bernardo, beside the Huerta del Rey and the Monte Rey; it was the least populated of the six in Seville since only sixteen Dominicans lived there. The place seemed tranquil.

'The monastery, the Huerta del Rey, the Monte del Rey,' complained one of the young gypsies as he pulled on his horse, 'everything belongs to priests or to the King.'

'Not in this case,' Melchor corrected him. 'The monastery belongs to the priests. The garden used to belong to the Moorish King of Niebla, although I guess that now it belongs to the King of Spain again. You can't enter with weapons. There is a tile forbidding it on the door. As for the Monte del Rey, it's not called that, it's Monte Rey: not property of the King.'

They walked a few paces more, all waiting for an explanation.

'Why?' asked another of the nephews before long.

'You explain it to him, Tomás,' urged Melchor.

'We used to come here as kids,' Tomás began. 'It's called Monte Rey because it is the tallest of all the hills in Seville. Do you know what all those hills in Seville are made of?' No one answered. 'Corpses! Thousands of corpses piled up and covered with dirt from the plague last century. The years passed, people lost their fear of contagion and their respect for the unburied dead, and they started rummaging around the hill looking for treasures. And there was plenty. During the epidemic people perished by the thousands, and not many dared to pick around on a stinking recently dead body, so some of the corpses were piled up with their jewellery and their money. We found some coins, remember, Melchor?' He nodded. 'You can still see the hill now,' added Tomás, pointing towards something in the night. 'But it's quite a bit smaller.'

Finally they arrived at the monastery. Melchor rang the bell at the large entrance gates; the tolling broke the stillness. He didn't seem to care. He rang again, insistently, three times in a row. After a long wait, the gleam of a lantern behind the gates indicated that someone was headed towards them. The spyhole opened.

'What brings you here at this time of the night?' asked the friar after examining the gypsies.

'We are carrying Fray Joaquín's goods,' answered Melchor.

'Wait. I'll go and look for the prior.'

The friar was about to close the spyhole, but Melchor intervened.

'Fray Genaro, don't leave us here,' he requested, drawling his words. 'You know me. This isn't the first time. The bell could have alerted someone, and if we have to wait here while you consult the prior . . . Remember that the money is yours.'

At the mere mention of the money, the locks moved.

'Come in,' invited the friar. 'Stay right here,' he warned while he lit up a narrow path beside the garden. He turned his back on them and ran to the monastery in search of the prior.

'I don't want to hear a word, understood?' muttered Melchor when the cleric was far enough away. 'No nonsense about hills or gardens, and nobody contradict me.'

Caridad didn't even move; she remained standing behind the last horse, the one without a load. Except for asking her to sing, none of the gypsies had paid any attention to her during the way back; they seemed to be letting her stay with the group just for Melchor's sake. She had her eyes on the horse's hindquarters when Fray Genaro returned accompanied by half the members of the religious community. A tall man with thick white hair greeted Melchor with a simple nod; the others stayed a little behind.

'Good evening, Fray Dámaso,' the gypsy replied, 'I have Fray Joaquín's order.'

The prior ignored him and just moved among the horses considering the bags. He reached the last one. He looked at the horse. He walked around it to see its other side and looked brazenly at Caridad. Then he feigned surprise and, as if addressing a class of children, began to count the bags out loud, pointing to them each with a finger: one, two . . .

'Fray Joaquín told me that there were eight on this trip, Galeote,' he protested when he finished his ludicrous count.

'There were, yes,' answered Melchor from where he stood, at the head of the row of horses.

'So?'

That stupid Negro woman let them steal two of them, Caridad was afraid he would respond.

However: 'The Chief Magistrate of Cabezas kept the other ones,' she heard Melchor answer in a firm voice.

The prior brought his hands together with his fingers extended, as if praying. He covered his mouth and rested his fingertips on the bridge of his nose. He remained that way for a few seconds, scrutinizing the gypsy in the light of the friar's lanterns. Melchor wasn't intimidated; he withstood the gambit.

'Why didn't he keep them all?' asked Friar Dámaso after a pause.

'Because making off with all eight would have cost him the lives of some of his men,' replied the gypsy.

'And he was satisfied with two?'

'That was the value I placed on the lives of mine.'

The prior let the seconds slip away; none of those present made the slightest movement.

'Why should I believe you?'

'Why wouldn't you, your reverence?'

'Perhaps because you're a gypsy?'

Melchor frowned and clicked his tongue, as if he had never considered that possibility. 'If you wish, your eminence, we can ask God. He knows everything.'

The friar remained unruffled. 'God has more important matters than confirming the lies of a gypsy.'

'If God doesn't want to intervene, the gypsy's word stands . . .' This time it was Melchor who let the seconds slip away before continuing. 'Which your reverence could confirm by going to the authorities to denounce the Chief Magistrate of Cabezas for stealing some of your tobacco. The King's authorities don't listen to gypsies.'

Fray Dámaso snorted and ended up acquiescing. 'Unload the merchandise,' the prior ordered the other friars.

'One bag is mine,' warned the gypsy.

'You lost two and you still think . . . ?'

'The risk of the business is yours,' interrupted Melchor in a hard voice. 'I am just the bearer,' he added in a softer tone.

The cleric weighed the situation: a group of friars against six armed gypsies (he mistakenly included Bernardo). There was little he could do against them. He didn't believe a word of what El Galeote had told him, not a single word! He had warned Fray Joaquín on numerous occasions, but that young, stubborn preacher . . . The gypsy had taken those two missing sacks and now he planned on stealing another! Fray Dámaso turned red with rage. He shook his head repeatedly and counted the gypsies again: six . . . and a Negro woman covered in a dark cape with a floppy hat pulled down to her ears. On an August night in Seville! Why was that woman looking at him? She was staring insistently!

'What is that Negro woman doing here?' he bellowed suddenly.

Melchor wasn't expecting that question. He stammered.

'She sings well,' responded Tomás for his brother.

'Yes,' confirmed Melchor.

'Really well,' put in Bernardo.

'We can lend her to you for the choir,' offered El Galeote.

The four Vega nephews exchanged a smile above their horses' withers; the rest of the friars watched the scene with a mix of fear and fascination.

'Enough!' shouted the prior. 'Do you realize that this will be your last trip subsidized by the Dominicans?' Melchor just showed the palms of his hands. 'Unload!'

The friars unloaded the five bags in a flash.

'Get out!' shouted Fray Dámaso then, as he pointed to the gates.

'You really don't want us to leave you the Negress?' joked one of the Vega nephews as he passed with his horse beside the prior. 'We don't need her. She's not ours.'

'Boy!' Tomás scolded him, trying to repress a laugh.

Once outside, Melchor avoided heading for Triana, instead turning towards the outskirts of Seville. The others followed him with the horses.

'How do you plan on getting this tobacco through?' worried Tomás.

When the contraband originated in Portugal, there was no problem getting to Triana since coming from the west didn't involve crossing the Guadalquivir over the pontoon bridge. When it came from Gibraltar, they usually stored the goods in the Portaceli monastery and later Fray Joaquín would give them to Melchor in Triana but, given the circumstances, Tomás understood why his brother hadn't wanted to leave his share in the monastery.

'Go to the house of Justo, the boatman, and wake him up. Pay him well. You and one of the boys will go in the boat. The others can cross the bridge . . .'

'Go? Pay him? What do you mean by that?'

'I'm leaving, brother. I have a score to settle with El Gordo in Encinas Reales.'

'Melchor, no . . . I'll go with you.'

The gypsy shook his head and patted his brother's arm and then Bernardo's, grabbed his musket from the horse, lifted it as a farewell gesture to his nephews and left them right there. However, he had only gone a couple of paces before turning and pointing to Caridad.

'I'm forgetting! *Morena . . .*' Caridad felt her throat tightening. 'Here,' he added after searching in his jacket and pulling out a colourful handkerchief that he had managed to buy at the inn in Gaucín after haggling extensively with one of the pedlars who followed the smugglers.

Caridad approached him and took the handkerchief.

'Give it to my granddaughter and tell her that I love her more than ever.'

Caridad kept her gaze lowered, her injured lip burning as she bit it. She thought that . . . she thought that . . . She felt Melchor grab her by the chin and force her to lift her head.

'Don't worry,' he tried to reassure her. 'It wasn't your fault. But you can already get started with twisting the tobacco. When I return I expect to find you've multiplied our profit.'

Caridad remained still as his sky-blue jacket disappeared into the night. *When I return*, he had said. He would come back . . .

'*Morena*, are you coming or not?' urged Tomás.

The group was already far ahead.

When dawn had broken, Caridad crossed the pontoon bridge with Bernardo and three of the Vega nephews pulling the geldings; the tobacco had crossed the river a couple of hours earlier, by boat, with Tomás and the most strapping of the boys. The bridge's toll collector, like many of the Sevillians and Trianeros who came and went, was surprised to see her covered with the cape in such weather, but what could she do? The man's brazen expression brought her back to reality. How would she dress from then on? she thought, again feeling the torn fabric brush against her beneath the cape that hid it. Milagros would help her, surely. She smiled, overcome with the desire to see her friend. She quickened her step, thinking of the imminent reencounter and remembering their conversations. She could tell her so many things now. Once she got past the toll collector she found Triana just starting to bustle. The imposing Inquisition Castle was to her right.

'*Morena!*'

Caridad stopped short and turned her head, confused. She had passed Altozano Plaza and, absorbed in her thoughts, she'd continued straight along the street that led to San Jacinto on her way to the San Miguel alley. However, Bernardo and the gypsies, with the horses, had turned on the street that bordered the castle, heading to the settlement by the Carthusians. They were separated by several paces, and people were crossing between them.

'Go home if you want,' shouted one of the nephews to her, 'but remember what Uncle Melchor told you.' The boy mimed rubbing his hands together, with a slight space between them, as if he were twisting tobacco. 'Come by the settlement at La Cartuja to work.'

Caridad nodded and watched spellbound as the gypsies raised their hands in farewell and went on their way. People passed by her, some giving her strange looks because of her attire, just like on the bridge.

'You're going to roast under that cape, *morena*,' said a little boy who passed her.

'Out of the way!' shouted a cart driver behind her.

Caridad jumped to one side and sought refuge beside the wall of a building. *Go home*, the gypsy had said to her. Did she have a home? She didn't have a home . . . or did she? Hadn't her feet led her towards the San Miguel alley? Milagros was waiting for her there; Melchor lived there. She had spent months in that alley, twisting cigars by night. They fed her and she went to San Jacinto to pray to the Virgin of Candlemas, to visit Oyá, to offer her pieces of tobacco leaf, and they had given her clothes, and she went out with the gypsies, and . . . and Milagros lived there. She felt a strange, pleasurable sensation travel up her body, a lovely tickle. She had a home, the gypsy had said so, although it was only that wretched space in front of the latrine. She peeled her back off the wall and mingled among the people.

José Carmona stormed out of the forge as soon as he found out that Caridad was back.

'What are you doing here, Negress?' he shouted at her in the courtyard. 'How dare you? You have ruined us! And Melchor? Where is that crazy old man?'

Caridad wasn't able to answer any of those questions, nor the ones he kept spitting at her, endlessly. Even if she had wanted, she wouldn't have been able to: the gypsy was beside himself, the veins on his neck about to burst, sputtering out each word as he shook her.

'Why are you wearing a black cape in the middle of August? What are you hiding, Negress? Take it off!'

Caridad obeyed. Her torn clothes were revealed when she removed the cape.

'Good Lord! How can you go around like that, you dirty Negro? Get dressed! Take off those clothes before they arrest us all and put on the ones you came with.'

José kept silent as she stripped off her clothes until she was completely naked, revealing her firm breasts, her voluptuous hips, her flat stomach above a pubis that the gypsy focused his attention on shamelessly. Only her back lined with scars broke the charm of Caridad's sensual body, which she finally sheathed in her old long shirt, there in the small courtyard with the latrine. The man's panting, which she thought she had heard as she stood nude before him, turned back into shouts as soon as she was covered with her slave shirt.

'And now get out of here!' José shouted at her. 'I don't want to ever see you again as long as I live!'

She knelt to stuff the torn clothes into her bundle. And Milagros? Where was Milagros? Why hadn't she come to her aid? On her knees on the floor, she turned her head towards José. *And Milagros?* she wanted to ask him, but the words refused to emerge from her mouth.

'Get lost!'

She left the building with tears in her eyes. What had happened? Milagros's father had always looked at her like an overseer on the plantation: with scorn. Perhaps if Melchor had been there . . . She grimaced: she was still a slave; the only thing she had in the world was a piece of paper that said she was free. How could she have got her hopes up over having some place that was like a home? With those thoughts she left behind the smoke and the sound of hammers beating on anvils that filled the alley.

Come by the settlement of La Cartuja to work, she remembered one of the gypsies had said to her. Why not? Besides, the Vegas would give her news of Milagros.

After Alejandro's death, Milagros was dragged to the house where the party was being held. She didn't want to go, but the Vargas boys pulled her there, blindly, bewildered, running through the streets of Triana as if trying to escape a monster on their trail. She managed to get free of their hands and their pushing; she wanted to think, she needed to focus, but all attempts were stifled by the haste and the shouts that broke the night. They killed him! He's dead! They killed Alejandro!

And with each shout she quickened her pace and she ran as fast as the Vargas boys did, without wanting to, stumbling, getting up with their hurried assistance, stuttering, complaining, always with the image of Alejandro's bloody corpse treading on her heels.

The party hadn't ended, but it was winding down. When the boys burst into the home, the count and countess and their guests had left their chairs and were strolling through the garden chatting with the gypsies; the guitars were strumming faintly, as if saying goodbye; no one danced or sang.

'They killed him!'

'They shot him!'

Milagros, behind the Vargas boys, panting, her heart about to burst, closed her eyes when she heard those heartrending words and kept them squeezed tightly shut, hidden behind the hand she used to cover her face, when all the gypsy men, women and children thronged around her.

Questions and answers, all rash, all urgent, swirled around her.

Who? Alejandro! Alejandro? How? Who did it? One of the potters. Dead? A hair-raising howl rose above the other voices. *His mother?* wondered Milagros. The count and countess and their guests, after hearing the first words, hastily left the house. The boys struggled to respond to the thousand questions that rained down on them. The women's shrieks could be heard all over Triana. Milagros didn't need to see them: they pulled at their hair until it came out in handfuls, they scratched at themselves and tore their shirts, they shouted at the heavens with their faces contorted in anguish, but meanwhile the men continued their interrogation and she knew that at some point . . .

'Why? Why did you go to the potters' quarter?' asked one of them.

'I told you not to do it.'

Her mother's recrimination, whispered in her ear with icy breath, kept her from hearing the answer, but she caught the questions that followed.

'Milagros? El Galeote's granddaughter?'

'Why?'

Milagros tried not to heave.

'Open your eyes!' muttered her mother as she elbowed her in the ribs. 'Face up to what you've done!'

The girl uncovered her face to find that she had become the focus of all eyes, her father's serious, barbed gaze among them.

'Why did Milagros take you to the potters' quarter?'

'To settle a score with someone who had forced himself on a woman,' answered the eldest Vargas.

Even some of the hysterically screaming women were suddenly quiet. A gypsy woman had been raped? That was the worst offence a *payo* could commit against them. The boy who had answered sensed the misunderstanding that his words had provoked.

'No . . . it wasn't a gypsy woman,' he clarified.

The questions came tumbling out again. 'Why? What did you care if she wasn't a gypsy? What were you hoping to achieve – you're just *boys*?' Several of them, however, were asking the same question. 'What woman?'

'The Vega grandfather's Negro woman.'

Milagros felt herself fainting. The silence during which the gypsies took in the revelation stretched out for several seconds, and she saw her father heading towards her.

'You – wilful idiot!' he insulted her, and gave her a look, his eyes shot through with blood. 'You can't even imagine the consequences of what you've done.'

From that point on, the gypsies argued heatedly among

themselves, but not for long: after a few minutes, several of the Vargas men left crying out for revenge with their knives already in their hands and accompanied by the oldest of the boys.

They didn't find the potter or his son; they had fled, leaving the workshop open. In front of the open doors lay a large puddle of blood and Alejandro's destroyed corpse. A couple of gypsies searched the building, others grabbed the boy's body and headed towards the San Miguel alley, and the rest remained standing in the street, facing the terrified gazes that came from the rest of the houses.

Someone handed a lit torch to Alejandro's father, who entered the workshop and threw it on to the dry firewood prepared for the ovens that would never be used again. The fire was soon blazing.

'Tell that son of a bitch child-killer,' he then shouted from the middle of the street, diabolically illuminated by the tongues of fire that began to rise from the building, 'that there is no place in Spain where he can hide from the vengeance of the Vargas family!'

When the gypsies left, the potters poured out on to the street with all kinds of buckets and containers filled with water to tame the fire that threatened to spread to the surrounding houses; no local magistrate, no constables, no patrols showed up in the neighbourhood that night.

Rafael García, El Conde, seated in the tallest chair with the other members in a circle around him, presided over the council of elders charged with dealing with Alejandro's death. Among the parade of witnesses and accusers that came before the gypsy tribunal, El Conde ran his gaze over the courtyard packed with gypsies despite the twisted pieces of iron stored there; then he looked up at the upper floors, on whose railings, with clothes hung out to dry and pots of wilted flowers, many more jostled to follow the trial from the adjacent halls that opened on to the courtyard. That was the gypsy courtroom, the only one that should judge the members of their race according to gypsy law. Rafael García, as representative of the community, had been forced to argue with governors and justices about Alejandro's death. The potter and his son had fled. The gypsies had passed a sentence of death on him, and the order to execute it if anyone found him had been spread by the various families. However, rumours of what had happened also spread throughout Triana, and El Conde had to fight with the authorities to get them to forget about the matter; no *payo* had reported the altercation.

The Vargas family attacked Milagros mercilessly before the elders' council. She shouldn't have put a gypsy boy's life in danger over a simple Negro, they accused her; she had tried to take advantage of the gypsy people to benefit a *paya*, they shouted; she hadn't asked her elders for permission to take revenge. And what if Alejandro had killed the potter? All the gypsies would have suffered for it!

The Carmonas found no arguments to defend her. Without Melchor or Tomás (who were out on a smuggling run), the Vegas designated Uncle Basilio to convince the elders, although his speech faded into stammering when he realized how little influence the gypsies from the settlement of La Cartuja had in a council dominated by blacksmiths. The members of the other families supported the Vargas family. The father of the girl, standing behind the elders like many other men, calmly witnessed a trial that extended throughout an endless evening; her mother, unable to submit herself to such an ordeal, waited along with other members of her family in the San Miguel alley, at the door to the cluster of apartments where El Conde lived and in whose courtyard the council meeting was being held. Ana withstood the passing hours with her face clenched and tense, trying to hide her true feelings. Milagros was confined to the house.

Rafael García listened to the opinion of what seemed to be the last witness sprawled out in his chair, occasionally sketching a half-smile with his lips. Melchor's granddaughter, the thing the old man loved most in the world. El Galeote wouldn't be able to blame him. All the families agreed; it wouldn't even be he who'd have to suggest the punishment; she would be expelled, undoubtedly, and with her . . .

A commotion at the entrance to the courtyard where they were gathered interrupted his thoughts. The man who was speaking fell silent. Attention centred on the two boys who stood watch and tried to keep the curious out.

'What's happening?' shouted El Conde.

'Old María Vega, the healer,' explained one of the gypsies who was closest to the door. 'She wants to come in.'

El Conde questioned the other elders with his gaze. A couple of them answered with shrugs, another looked afraid.

'Tell her that women cannot intervene—' Rafael García began to order.

But the scrawny, bony old woman in a colourful apron had managed to move the boys aside and was already inside the courtyard. Behind her, Milagros's mother peeked her head in through the doorway.

'Rafael García,' cried out the gypsy woman, interrupting El Conde, 'what gypsy law says that women cannot intervene on the council?'

'It has always been that way,' he replied.

'You lie.' The old woman spoke slowly. 'You are looking more and more like the *payos* you live among, you trade with and whose money you accept without thinking twice. Remember this!' she shouted, moving through the courtyard with one of her fingers half extended, stiff, in the shape of a hook. 'Gypsy women are not submissive and obedient like the wives of the *payos*, and you wouldn't want us that way either, isn't that true?' Among the men there were some signs of agreement. 'Since we came out of Egypt, gypsy women have had a voice in council matters, my mother told me that, and she had been told by her mother, but you . . . you, Rafael García,' she added, pointing to El Conde with her finger, 'who acts from spite, I accuse you of forgetting our tradition and law. How many of you have come to me so I could cure you, you or your wives or children? I cure, I have that power! If there is anyone here who would deny me the right to speak before the council, let him say so now.'

A murmur ran through the crowd. Old María Vega was respected among the gypsies. Yes, she could cure and she did; they all knew it, they had all sought her help. She knew the earth, plants, trees and animals, stones, water and fire, and there she was: challenging the patriarchs. The gypsies didn't believe in the Christian God, nor in the saints, virgins or martyrs, but in their own god: Devel. But Devel wasn't the Creator. The mother of all the gypsies, who existed even before the divine itself, was the Earth. Mother Earth: a woman! The gypsies believed in nature and in her power, and in healers and witches – always women, like the earth – as intermediaries between the world of men and that other marvellous, higher being.

'Speak, crone,' someone in the crowd said.

'We are listening.'

'Yes. Say what you have to say.'

María frowned at Rafael García.

'Speak,' he conceded.

'What that girl has done,' she began to say, 'is all your fault.'

The gypsies complained, but she continued, ignoring them.

'Yours, José Carmona,' she added, pointing at him, 'and yours, Ana Vega.' She turned, knowing that the mother was behind her back. 'All of you. You have settled down and you work like the *payos*, you even marry in the Catholic Church and baptize your children to get their approval. Some of you even go to mass! Few of you blacksmiths of Triana walk the roads and live with nature as our ancestors always did, as is emblematic of our race, eating what the earth produces, drinking from wells and streams and sleeping beneath the sky with a freedom that has been our only law. And with that you are raising weak, irresponsible children, just like the *payos* have, children who disregard gypsy law, not because they don't know it, but because they don't feel it or live it.'

Old María paused. The silence in the courtyard was absolute. One of the elders on the council tried to defend himself.

'And what can we do, María? The law forbids walking the paths, wearing our clothes and living the way those ancestors you speak of did. You know full well that they consider us bad people simply for being born gypsy. Just three years ago we had to leave Triana by proclamation of Seville's chief justice, who declared us bandits. Three years! Who of us here doesn't remember that? We had to flee to the fields or take sanctuary. Do you remember?' A murmur of agreement arose from the men. 'They threatened to kill anyone who had weapons and punish the rest with six years of galleys and two hundred lashes—'

'Didn't we all come back?' interrupted Old María. 'What do we care about the laws of the *payos*? Since when have they affected us? We have always got around them. There are thousands who still live like gypsies! And you all know it, and you know them. If you in Triana want to submit to the King's laws, go ahead, but there are many others who don't and never will. That is exactly what I am telling you: you live like *payos*. Don't blame the children for the consequences of your . . .' They all knew the next word the old woman would use, and they all feared hearing it. '. . . cowardice.'

'Watch your tongue!' warned El Conde.

'Who is going to forbid me to speak? You?'

Their eyes locked in a challenge.

'What is it that you propose for the girl?' asked another of the council elders, keen to break up yet another of the atavistic quarrels between the Vegas and the Garcías. 'What are you getting at? Did you ask to speak just because you wanted to insult us?'

'I will take the girl to the settlement of La Cartuja to make her into a gypsy who knows the secrets of nature. I am old and I need . . . you all need someone to take over for me when I'm gone.'

'Choose another woman,' intervened El Conde.

'I will choose whom I wish, Rafael García. My grandmother, a Vega, taught my mother, another Vega, and I, Vega and childless, want to transmit my knowledge to someone who has Vega blood. The girl will leave the San Miguel alley until the day you require her presence . . . and you will, I assure you. The council and the Vargas family will have to be satisfied with that. Otherwise, don't any of you ever come looking for my help again.'

'I forbid you!' Ana yelled. Milagros, after seeing her Vega cousins arrive at the settlement with the horses, had asked them about her grandfather and Caridad and then decided to go and look for her friend, fearing for her safety. Having heard the story of the theft by El Gordo, as well as Melchor's departure, Milagros was worried about Caridad.

'Father will kill her if Grandfather isn't there,' complained Milagros.

'That doesn't concern you,' answered her mother.

The girl tightened her fist and blood rushed into her face. Mother and daughter challenged each other with their eyes.

'It does concern me,' she muttered.

'Haven't we suffered enough because of that Negress?'

'It wasn't Cachita's fault,' argued Milagros. 'She didn't do anything, she didn't—'

'It's up to your father to decide that,' declared her mother.

'No.'

'Milagros.'

'No.' The gleam in her gypsy eyes indicated that she wouldn't let her arm be easily twisted.

'Don't argue with me.'

'I'll go to the alley . . .'

That was when her mother forbade it with a shout that echoed through the settlement at La Cartuja, yet the girl kept insisting stubbornly.

'I'm going, Mother.'

'You will not,' ordered Ana.

'I will . . .'

She didn't get to finish her sentence: her mother smacked her hard across the face. Milagros tried to hold back her sobs, but was unable to repress the trembling of her chin. Before she burst into tears, she ran towards Triana. Ana did nothing more to stop her. She was drained after the outburst; she had been under such stress since Alejandro's death. With her arms hanging by her sides, her whole body feeling the pain of the slap she had inflicted on her daughter, she let her go.

Caridad recognized Milagros from a distance, on the road that led to the settlement at La Cartuja, near where Melchor had found her that night the potter had kicked her out of his workshop. She was walking barefoot and dressed like a slave again, with her greyish burlap shirt and her straw hat. In her bundle she carried the rest of her few belongings, including her shredded red clothes.

Milagros didn't have any trouble recognizing her friend even with her eyes flooded with tears. She hesitated, expecting her to be dressed in her showy red clothes, but her doubt dissipated almost instantly: there was no woman in Triana, nor in the whole of Seville, as black as the one who advanced slowly towards her.

The girl wiped away her tears with her forearm and then touched her cheek. It still burned from her mother's slap.

Milagros threw herself into Caridad's arms. Caridad was waiting ... hoping ... she needed an explosion of joy and affection yet, amid the girl's sobs and babbling, she sensed that Milagros was seeking help and understanding from her.

On the road that led from Triana to the gypsy settlement at La Cartuja, Caridad let Milagros embrace her. The girl buried her head between Caridad's breasts and broke out in inconsolable sobs, as if she had been holding back her feelings until then, without anyone she could pour out her pain and misfortune to.

Caridad had managed to calm the girl down a bit and they were sitting by the side of the road, among the orange trees, glued to each other. She listened to Milagros's faltering account of what had happened, beginning at the count and countess's party.

'Holy Mother of God,' murmured Caridad when the girl told her how she had asked Alejandro to avenge her.

'He deserved to be punished!' exclaimed Milagros.

'But . . .' she tried to counter.

The gypsy girl didn't let her continue. 'Yes, Cachita, yes,' she insisted between moans. 'He raped you, he prostituted you and nobody was willing to do anything about it.'

'They killed him over me?' The splintered question came out of Caridad's throat when Milagros told her about the boy's death.

'It's not your fault, Cachita.'

It wasn't your fault: those had been the very words Melchor had said to her that same night as he bid her farewell. On the plantation, they put an end to mistakes with the whip, and then it was back to work. But now she was overcome by unfamiliar feelings: because of her, Melchor had gone out to seek vengeance; because of her, Milagros had also demanded vengeance. Vengeance! How vital it was to the gypsies!

'But it was all because of me,' she said, interrupting Milagros's account of what had happened in the council of elders.

'And because of me, Cachita. Me, too. You are my friend. I had to do it! I couldn't . . . I kept thinking about what that man had done to you. I felt your pain as if it were mine.'

Her pain? The only pain she was suffering in that moment was the pain of Melchor having left, of him no longer being with her. The nights in the small courtyard's cramped room, twisting tobacco and singing softly while he remained in silence behind her flashed into her mind's eye. Milagros was still talking about Rafael García, about the elders and some healer. Should she interrupt her and tell her about it? Should she confess that her stomach was in knots at the mere thought of Melchor getting hurt in the confrontation with that smuggler? She lost the thread of the conversation, remembering El Gordo and his lieutenants sitting at the table in the Gaucín inn, all of them violent brutes, while Melchor . . . He had gone alone! How could he . . . ?

'Are you OK?' asked Milagros, noticing how Caridad's body trembled.

'Yes . . . no. Alejandro is dead.'

'He was a true gypsy in the end: brave and reckless. You should have seen him beating on the potter's door . . . And he did it for us!' Milagros let a few seconds pass. 'Do you think he loved me?' she suddenly suggested.

Caridad found herself surprised by the question. 'Yes . . .' she stammered.

'Sometimes I sense his presence.'

'The dead are always with us,' Caridad then murmured as if reciting something she had learned by heart. 'You must treat him well,' she continued, repeating what they said about the spirits in Cuba. 'They are unpredictable and if angered they can be dangerous. If you want to distance him, you can light a bonfire in front of your house at night. Fire frightens them, but you shouldn't burn him, just beg him to leave.'

'At night?' asked the girl, surprised. Then she looked up at the sky, in search of the sun. 'The night isn't the problem, it's noontime.'

Caridad looked at her, puzzled. 'Noontime?'

'Yes. The dead appear right at noon, didn't you know that?'

'No.'

'Noon,' explained Milagros. 'When the shadows disappear and the sun leaps from the east to the west, time doesn't exist and everything belongs to the dead: the roads, the trees . . .'

Caridad felt a shiver and looked up at the sun.

'Don't worry!' Milagros tried to reassure her. 'I think he loved me. He won't do me any harm.'

The girl stopped speaking when she saw how her friend kept looking up at the sun, calculating how long it would be before the shadows disappeared; her breathing had accelerated and her hand was at the lodestone she still wore around her neck.

'Let's go to the settlement,' she then decided.

Caridad bounced up as if on a spring, terrified because in Spain ghosts also came out at noon.

Not even a minute had passed when Milagros turned her head towards her friend, who had quickened her step. She didn't know what she had been up to all that time; she hadn't given her a chance to speak, to explain her adventure with Grandfather.

'And why were you coming to the settlement?' she asked.

'Your father kicked me out of the alley.'

Milagros imagined the scene, lowered her eyelids and shook her head. And there was still the problem of her mother. What would she say when she showed up at the settlement? Ana went there frequently, much more than one would expect of a married woman; she even slept with Milagros and María some nights in the healer's hut. After Alejandro's death and the sentence that left the girl in the healer's care, Ana's relationship with her husband seemed to have taken a path with no return: for him, Melchor's taking in that Negress on a whim had ruined his life for ever. No. Her mother wouldn't like seeing Caridad. She wouldn't allow it. Milagros feared how she would react.

'And your new clothes?' she enquired, trying to push away the anxiety that had suddenly overtaken her.

Despite her wariness over the sun reaching the highest point in the sky, despite their haste, Caridad stopped in the road, rummaged around in her bundle and pulled out the torn shirt, which she held out towards the girl with her arms high.

Surrounded by fertile gardens and orange trees, Milagros couldn't see Caridad's head or torso, hidden behind the shirt she dangled in front of her. What she could see were the rips in the blouse. An uncontrollable, tender shiver swept over her as she realized how the gesture revealed Cachita's innocence.

'What . . . what happened?' Milagros asked after clearing her throat a couple of times.

But before she could answer, Milagros went on, 'We'll fix them, Cachita. I'm sure we can.' She had already heard about how El Gordo had managed to steal those two bags of tobacco from the Vegas and that Melchor had set out in search of vengeance.

As they were about to resume their walk, Caridad carefully stuffed the blouse back into her bundle and came across the handkerchief that Melchor had given her to deliver to his granddaughter.

'Wait. This is for you, from your grandfather.'

Milagros looked at the large, colourful handkerchief with affection and squeezed it between her fingers. 'Grandfather,' she whispered. 'He's the only one who loves me. And you, too, of course, I mean – I guess,' she added, flustered.

But Caridad wasn't listening. Did the gypsy love her as well?

9

AT THE SETTLEMENT, Caridad spent her time twisting tobacco and making cigars. Tomás put her up in the shack of an old married couple, both dour and surly, who lived alone and had a bit of extra space. He also got her all the tools needed for her work but, above all, he was the one who defended her against Ana's aggression when she saw her arriving with Milagros.

'Niece!' shouted Tomás, getting between the women and gripping Ana by the wrists to get her to stop hitting Caridad, who was curled up, trying to shield her head from the gypsy woman's shouts and blows. 'When Melchor comes back, he will decide what should be done with the *morena*. Meanwhile ... meanwhile,' he repeated, shaking her to get her to listen to him, 'she will be working with the tobacco; those were your father's orders.'

Ana, flushed with rage, managed to spit in Caridad's face. 'I refuse to sell a single cigar made by that Negress!' she declared, escaping Tomás's hold. 'So they'll all rot, and you along with them!'

'Mother!' exclaimed Milagros as she saw her flee towards Triana. The girl rushed after her.

'Mother.' She tried to stop her. 'Caridad did nothing,' insisted the girl, tugging on her clothes. 'It's not her fault.'

Ana pushed her away and continued down the road.

Milagros watched her go and then returned to where a fair number of gypsies had gathered. Tears streamed down her cheeks.

'Always marry a woman from a good family!' declared Uncle Tomás. 'She's just like her father: a Vega. She'll get over it.' Milagros looked up at him. 'Give it some time, girl. This issue with the Negress isn't a question of gypsy honour: it will pass.'

And while Caridad was shut away in the hut, choosing leaves and removing their stems and veins, moistening them and drying them just right, cutting them, twisting them and finishing off the cigar's mouth with thread, Milagros learned the basics of the potions and remedies from the healer by following her around everywhere: to gather herbs in the fields or visit the ill. Old María didn't allow the girl the slightest lapse in concentration or attitude, and she controlled her: her mere presence was enough to make Milagros submit to her will. Later, at night, she allowed her some time to relax, and Milagros would run in search of Caridad. Together they would leave the settlement and lose themselves in conversation or just smoke and look up at the starry sky.

'Do you steal them from Grandfather?' the girl asked one night after taking a long puff, the two of them sitting side by side on the bank of the Guadalquivir, near a rundown fishing pier, listening to the murmur of the water.

Caridad's hand stopped in mid-air as she was about to take the cigar the girl was passing her. Steal?

'Yes!' exclaimed Milagros at her friend's hesitation. 'You steal them! It's OK, don't worry, I won't tell anyone.'

'I don't . . . I don't steal them!'

'Well, how do you explain it, then? If the tobacco isn't yours . . .'

'It's my smoke. They belong to me.'

'Go on, take it,' insisted the gypsy girl, pushing the cigar closer to her. Caridad obeyed. 'What do you mean by your smoke?'

'If I make them . . . I can smoke, right? Besides, these aren't made of twisted tobacco, I just use the veins from the leaves and the remains, all chopped up and wrapped in a leaf. On the plantation that's how it was. The master gave us our smoke.'

'Cachita, this isn't the plantation and you have no masters.'

Caridad exhaled some long scrolls of bluish smoke before speaking. 'So, I can't smoke?'

'Do whatever you want, but if you stop bringing your smoke, I won't see you any more.' Caridad was silent. 'It's a joke, *morena*!' The gypsy girl let out a laugh, hugged her friend and shook her. 'How could I stop seeing you? I couldn't!'

'I co-co-could . . .' Caridad stammered.

'What?' prompted the girl. 'What? Spit it out, Cachita!'

'I couldn't either.' She managed to get the words out in a rush.

'For all the gods, saints, virgins and martyrs in all the heavens, it's about time!'

Milagros, with her arm still around Caridad's back, pulled her closer. Caridad awkwardly allowed it.

'It's about time!' repeated the gypsy girl, giving her a loud kiss on the cheek. Then Milagros took Caridad's arm and forced it over her shoulders while grabbing her around the waist. Caridad even forgot about the cigar she held between her fingers. Not wanting to break the spell, Milagros let the time pass, feeling how her friend returned the embrace, both of them with their gazes on the river. Nor did she want Caridad to notice the sobbing she was struggling to hold back.

But Caridad surprised her with a question nonetheless, her voice projecting out on to the water. 'Your mama?'

'Yes,' answered Milagros.

Ana hadn't set foot in the gypsy settlement again; Milagros couldn't go to the alley.

'I'm sorry.' Caridad blamed herself, and squeezed her friend tighter when Milagros could no longer hold back her sobs.

Caridad remembered shedding similar tears the day they separated her from her mother and her people as they forced her and hundreds of unfortunates like her to wait for a boat at the trading post; but when had she stopped crying – was it during the voyage . . . ?

She blocked the memories when she noticed that the cigar was burning her; she sucked on it again. In Cuba she had searched for her mother's spirit in the parties, when she was mounted by one of the saints, but here, in Spain, she only tried to remember her face.

Milagros and Caridad's affection for each other grew as they sat together by the river, but those evenings didn't last long.

'Girl.' The healer stopped her one night when she was about to leave the hut. Milagros turned back. 'Listen to me: don't distance yourself from your kind, from the gypsies.'

Caridad received a similar message that day from Tomás.

'*Morena*,' he warned her, entering the hut as she was carefully wrapping a cigar in leaf, 'you shouldn't take Milagros away from her blood brothers. Do you understand what I'm referring to?'

Caridad's long fingers stilled and she nodded without lifting her head.

From that day on the two women strolled along the street of the settlement without going farther, Caridad behind the girl, converted into her shadow, mingling with those at the doors of their huts who chatted, played, drank, smoked and, above all, sang. Some voices were accompanied by guitars, others by the unembellished sound of palms hitting some object, most by the warmth of simple clapping of hands. Caridad had witnessed some of the celebrations in the San Miguel alley, but it was different in the settlement: the songs didn't turn into a party or a competition. They were simply a way of life, something that was done as naturally as eating or sleeping; they sang or danced and then went back to their conversation only to start singing again or they'd all get up from their seats and go over to encourage and applaud the two scantily clad little girls who were dancing off to one side, already showing some flair.

Caridad feared that they would ask her to sing. Nobody suggested it, not even Tomás. They accepted her – with some misgivings, certainly, but they did: she was the Negress of Grandfather Melchor; he would decide what to do with her on his return. For her part, Milagros was growing used to being burdened by grief; she missed her parents, her grandfather and her girlfriends from the alley. Yet what tormented her most was her internal struggle. She had ended up putting Alejandro on a pedestal in order to compensate for a death that she knew was a result of her whims; nevertheless, she kept thinking about Pedro García night and day . . . What was he doing? Where could he be? And most importantly: which of her girlfriends was seeking his favours? Alejandro was watching her closely and knew her desires. Ghosts knew everything, Caridad had told her, but the thought of Pedro García being flattered by other girls ate away at her so much that she pushed away those feelings and took advantage of any errand Old María sent her on to approach the San Miguel alley furtively.

She saw a lot of gypsies, including her girlfriends. One day she had to hide quickly in a doorway with her heart pounding when she saw her mother. She must have been going out to sell tobacco. *I should be going with her*, she thought as she watched her slow, determined gait. She dried a tear. On one occasion she saw Pedro, but she didn't dare go out to meet him. She saw him again another day: he was walking with one of his uncles towards the pontoon bridge, as handsome and dapper as ever. Milagros had regretted not going over to him on that first day. The council of elders' sentence, she reminded herself, was to stay with the healer and not set foot in the alleyway. But Old María felt free to send her on errands to Triana . . . She ran along a street parallel to the one Pedro was on, circled a block of houses and before turning the corner took a deep breath, straightened her skirt and smoothed her hair. Did she look pretty? She almost ran right into them.

'Aren't you supposed to be at the settlement, with the healer?' spat out Pedro's uncle as soon as he saw her.

Milagros hesitated.

'Get out of here!'

'I . . .'

She wanted to look at Pedro, but his uncle's eyes had ensnared hers!

'Didn't you hear me? Leave!'

She lowered her head and left them behind. She heard them speaking as she started walking again. She wished Pedro had bothered to look at her.

'You have to do it!'

Old María's shout echoed inside the dwelling. José Carmona and Ana Vega avoided looking at each other over the table where the three of them sat. The healer had showed up at their house unannounced that morning.

Neither of the parents had dared to interrupt Old María's words.

'The girl is sick,' she warned them. 'She doesn't eat. She doesn't want to eat,' she added, seeing in her mind the gypsy girl's protruding cheekbones and her increasingly pointed nose since her frustrated encounter with Pedro. 'She's just a girl who made a mistake. Have you two never made one? She couldn't foresee the consequences. She feels alone, abandoned. She no longer even finds comfort in the *morena*. She is your daughter! She is wasting away in plain sight and I don't have a cure for grieving souls.'

Ana played with her hands and José repeatedly rubbed his mouth and chin when the healer referred to them.

'Your problems shouldn't affect the girl; what happens between you isn't her fault.'

José seemed about to say something.

'I'm not interested,' María said before he could speak. 'I'm not here to solve your disagreements, or even to give you advice. It's not my intention to find out what brought you to this situation; I only want to know: don't you love your daughter?'

And after that meeting, on a cool dusk in late September, Ana and José Carmona showed up at the settlement. Caridad saw them before Milagros did.

'Your parents,' she whispered to the gypsy girl despite the fact that they were still quite a distance away.

Milagros froze; some of the boys she was chatting with fell silent and followed her gaze, locked on Ana and José, who approached along the street, between huts and shacks, greeting those still sitting at their doors whiling away the time. When José stopped to talk to an acquaintance, her mother stepped ahead of him and, when she was a few paces away from her daughter, opened her arms. Milagros needed no further invitation and launched herself into them. Caridad felt a knot in her throat, the boys released the breath they'd been holding and there was even someone, from the shacks, who applauded.

José approached them. Milagros hesitated when she saw him, but the shove that Ana gave her encouraged her to walk towards him.

'Forgive me, Father,' she mumbled.

He looked her up and down, as if he didn't recognize her. He brought a hand to his chin, with feigned seriousness, and scrutinized his daughter again.

'Father, I . . .'

'What's that over there?' he shouted.

Terrified, Milagros turned to where he was pointing. There was nothing out of the ordinary. 'I don't . . . what? What are you talking about?'

Some gypsies were curious. One of them got up and started to approach the spot José was pointing to.

'I'm talking about that! That, don't you see?'

'No! What?' screamed the girl, looking for help from her mother.

'That, girl,' he said, pointing to an empty chair at the door to one of the shacks.

'That chair?'

'No,' answered her mother. 'Not the chair.'

An old guitar was leaning against the chair. Milagros turned towards her father with a smile on her face.

'I won't forgive you,' he said, 'until you get every gypsy in this settlement to kneel before your charms.'

'Let's get started!' accepted Milagros as she straightened her back proudly.

'Gentlemen!' José Carmona then howled. 'My daughter is going to dance! Prepare yourselves for the sight of the most lovely of all gypsy women!'

'Is there any wine?' said someone from one of the huts.

Old María, who had witnessed the scene and was already dragging a rickety stool over to where the guitar was, let out a laugh.

'Wine?' exclaimed Ana. 'When you see my daughter dance, you'll steal all the grapes on the Triana plantation to offer them up to her.'

That night – with Caridad in attendance, watching from behind the gypsies, trying to keep her legs from moving to the sound of the music with the joy she saw brimming in Milagros – José Carmona had no choice but to be true to his word and forgive his daughter.

After the party, life continued in the gypsy settlement on the grounds of Triana's Carthusian monastery. Ana agreed to sell the cigars rolled by Caridad, in a sort of truce following the outburst of rage she had received her with; that forced her to go and see her daughter frequently. And Caridad saw her workload increase when Fray

Joaquín showed up with a couple of bags of tobacco unloaded on the beaches of Manilva.

'You owe me,' was all he said to Tomás. The gypsy was about to reply, but Fray Joaquín didn't let him. 'Let's leave things the way they are, Tomás. I have always trusted you; Melchor has never failed me, and I want to think that you had some problem that I know you will never reveal to me. I have to make back the community's money, you understand? And the cigars that Caridad makes increase the tobacco's value.'

Then he went to see her.

'The Virgin of Candlemas has been waiting a long time for your visits,' he said as soon as he entered the hut.

Caridad got up from the chair where she was working, brought her hands together in front of her and lowered her gaze to the floor. The Dominican watched the two old people who shared the hut with her out of the corner of his eye. He was surprised to see Caridad in her old slave clothes. He remembered her dressed in red, kneeling before the Virgin, moving rhythmically, forward and back, when she thought no one was looking. He knew, from the brothers who had lived in Cuba, about the mix of African religions with the Catholic one, and the Church's tolerance of it. *At least they believe and come to the religious celebrations!* he had heard on numerous occasions, and it was true: Caridad went to church, while most of the gypsies didn't set foot in there. What had happened to her red clothes? He didn't want to ask.

'I brought more tobacco for you to work with,' he announced instead. 'For each bundle of fifty cigars you make, one will be for you.' Caridad was surprised to find herself looking at the friar, who smiled at her. 'One of the good ones, one of the twisted ones that you make with leaf, not from the scraps.'

'And what is there for us, who put her up in our home?' interjected the old gypsy.

'OK,' accepted the clergyman after letting a few seconds pass, 'but you both have to come to mass every Sunday, and on the holy days of obligation, and pray the rosary for the souls in purgatory, and—'

'We're too old to be running this way and that,' snapped his wife. 'Wouldn't your reverence be satisfied with a little prayer at night?'

'I would be, but the man upstairs, no,' smiled Fray Joaquín, ending the discussion there. 'Are you OK, Caridad?' She nodded again. 'Will I be seeing you again at San Jacinto?'

'Yes,' she confirmed with a smile.

'I trust I will.'

He hadn't yet seen Milagros. He bid them farewell and before he was out of the door he heard the gypsies demanding that Caridad give them a share of those promised twisted cigars. He clicked his tongue; he had no doubt that she would give in to them. He asked for the hut of the healer and it was pointed out to him. He knew what had happened in the potters' quarter because it had caused quite a stir in Triana. Rafael García made sure that no one spoke to the authorities about either the murder of the gypsy boy or the fire: the gypsies were all sworn to silence through the various patriarchs of each family; the *payos* who had witnessed or been involved in the fight were sent a few intimidating messages which were enough to keep them quiet: none of them wanted to end up fleeing in the night, ruined, like the potter who had shot the gypsy boy. Despite all that, the rumours had spread as quickly as the fire in the ceramics workshop and Fray Joaquín's stomach had knotted when he found out about Milagros's part in it. He prayed for her. Finally he managed to discover the decision made by the council of elders based on the intervention of Old María and he again fell to his knees to thank the Virgin of Candlemas, Santa Ana and San Jacinto for the painless punishment she was given. The nights he'd spent worrying about her being banished from Triana dragged on endlessly; he was racked with the fear he'd never see her again!

Why couldn't I fall asleep on those nights? he asked himself yet again as he pulled aside the curtain and distractedly went over the threshold of the shack that had been pointed out to him. Milagros and Old María were leaning over a table sorting herbs; they both turned their heads towards him. Suddenly his insomnia didn't matter any more; all his worries vanished at the sight of her wonderful smile.

'May God be with you,' greeted the friar without approaching, as if he didn't want to interrupt the women's work.

'Father,' answered Old María after looking carefully at him for a few seconds. 'I have been waiting for more than fifty years for that God you speak of to deign to come to this shack and grace me with some relief from poverty. I have dreamed of the thousand ways it could happen: surrounded by angels or through one of the saints.' The old woman lifted her hands and fluttered them through the air. 'Encircled in blinding light . . . And,' she added, shrugging her shoulders, 'the truth is I never thought that he would send a friar to stand in the doorway like a dumbfounded fool.'

Fray Joaquín was slow to react. Milagros's stifled laugh made him blush. Dumbfounded fool! He straightened up and adopted a serious expression.

'Woman,' he declared with a much stronger tone than he had intended, 'I want to speak with the girl.'

'If she doesn't mind . . .'

Milagros got up without thinking twice, smoothed her skirt and hair and walked towards the preacher with a mocking expression on her face. Fray Joaquín let her pass.

'Father,' called out Old María, 'what about my riches?'

'Believing that God will one day visit you is the greatest wealth that anyone can aspire to in this world. Seek no other riches.'

The gypsy waved a hand in the air dismissively.

Milagros waited for the friar outside.

'What do you want to talk to me for?' she asked, flattering him slightly while maintaining her mocking expression.

What did he want to talk to her for? He had gone to the settlement about the tobacco and . . .

'What are you laughing at?' he asked instead of answering her question.

Milagros arched her brows. 'If you could have seen yourself in there . . .'

'Don't be impertinent!' The friar squirmed. Must he always look foolish in front of that girl? 'Make no mistake,' he tried to defend himself, 'my expression was just . . . seeing you there making potions with herbs. Milagros—'

'Fray Joaquín,' she interrupted, speaking in a slow drawl.

But the priest had already found an excuse for his untimely visit. He straightened up seriously and walked down the street with the girl beside him. 'I don't like what you are doing,' he scolded her. 'That's why I wanted to speak with you. You know that the Inquisition keeps a close eye on witches . . .'

'Ha!' laughed the girl.

'It's no laughing matter.'

'I'm no witch and I'm not planning on becoming one. Old María isn't either, and she is against those spells used to trick *payos*. You know, the hidden treasures, the love potions, they're just scams to part fools from their money. She only cures with herbal remedies . . .'

'It's similar. What about the evil eye?'

Milagros's expression soured.

'Did you know that the Inquisition just arrested a gypsy for giving the evil eye to livestock, here, in Triana?'

'Anselma? Yes, I know her. But they also say she makes spells to dry up the milk of *paya* mothers and that they have seen her naked, riding a stick and flying out of windows.' Milagros was silent for a few seconds to gauge the priest's reaction. 'Naked and flying on a stick! Do you believe the part about the stick? It's all lies. She isn't a witch. Did you know what would have to happen for a gypsy to become a witch?'

The friar, with his gaze on the dirt road they walked along, shook his head.

'Witches transform in their youth,' explained Milagros. 'And everybody knows that Anselma Jiménez wasn't one of the chosen. There are some water and earth demons who will choose a young gypsy girl and, as she sleeps, fornicate with her. That is the only way to become a true witch: after fornicating, the gypsy acquires the powers of the demon who has lain with her.'

'That means you do have witches,' replied the priest, suddenly stopping in his tracks.

Milagros frowned. 'But I'm not one. No demon has fornicated with me. And the witch doesn't have to work with herbs.' She gesticulated broadly to keep the friar from putting in his twopenn'orth. 'That doesn't have anything to do with it: anyone can be chosen.'

'I still don't like it, Milagros. You . . . you are a good girl . . .'

'I have no choice. I suppose you know about the ruling by the council of elders?'

'Yes, I know.' He nodded. 'But we could find another solution . . . If you wanted . . .'

'As a nun, perhaps? Would you marry me off? Would you get me a good dowry from one of your pious parishioners? You know I could never marry a *payo*. Fray Joaquín, I'm a gypsy.'

And there was no getting away from that fact, the priest had to acknowledge despite himself, ruffled by the insolence and arrogance with which Milagros addressed him. The seconds passed, both of them standing almost at the point where the settlement road entered the garden plots, her trying to figure out what was going through the friar's mind, he with her last words still ringing in his head: *I could never marry a* payo. Some women who were making baskets at the doors to their huts, who until then had only been watching them out of the corner of their eyes, stilled their skilful hands and observed the situation.

'Fray Joaquín,' warned Milagros in a whisper, 'the women are watching us.'

'Yes, yes, of course,' was the priest's reaction.

And they started to walk back.

'Fray Joaquín . . .'

'Yes?' he asked in the silence that followed.

'Do you think that any of your parishioners would be willing to give me a dowry so I can marry?'

'I didn't say . . .' He hesitated.

What was Milagros trying to do? The last thought in his head was the idea of finding a husband for her; he'd heard about the death of Alejandro, her fiancé, and he still felt remorse over his . . . happiness? *How can I be happy over the death of a boy?* He tortured himself over and over again in the silence of his nights.

'We could find someone,' he declared nonetheless, to please her. 'We could . . .'

But the girl left him with the words on the tip of his tongue and ran off towards Old María's hut. Before the friar understood what was going on, Milagros had returned, running again, and she stopped before him, panting, offering him Caridad's red clothes, carefully folded.

'If you could get me a dowry . . . could you get one of your parishioners to mend Cachita's clothes?'

Fray Joaquín grabbed the clothing and laughed; he laughed to keep himself from caressing the girl's tanned face or her hair adorned with ribbons, so he didn't take her by the shoulders and pull her towards him, and kiss her on the lips, and . . .

'I'm sure I can, Milagros,' he confirmed, banishing his desire.

Caridad worked tirelessly. The old couple she lived with treated her with indifference, as if she were nothing more than an object, not even a bothersome object. They both slept in a rickety bed with legs, which the old woman was inordinately proud of; it was her most prized possession, since in that shack there was little more than a table, stools and a rudimentary hearth for cooking. They pointed to a spot on the dirt floor where she could lay out the mattress that Tomás had given her, and they didn't feed her unless he gave them the necessary foodstuffs beforehand. Even the candles whose light allowed Caridad to work at night had to be provided by Tomás. 'If there is a single tobacco leaf missing,' he warned the old couple incessantly every time he showed up at their hut, 'I'll slit your throats.' Yet, every once in a while, Caridad would address their constant, insistent complaints and give them one of the cigars from her smoke, and see how they shared it eagerly, despite their laments over having to smoke cigars made with the veins and leaf scraps. But Caridad didn't even manage to win them over that way, and the old couple thought that all the cigars that Caridad set aside for her smoke were for them; actually, she hid the ones for her own consumption just as she had on the plantation so the other slaves wouldn't steal them.

As time passed, Caridad began to miss the nights in the San Miguel alley, when Melchor would ask her to sing and then fall asleep behind her, peaceful, trusting, and she could work and smoke at the same time, feeling how the smoke invaded her senses and transported her to a state of placidity in which time didn't exist. It was then when the work of her long fingers, as she cut, handled and twisted the leaves, mingled and mixed with the hum of her songs, with the aromas and her memories, with the gypsy's breathing and with that freedom Milagros had spoken of and which now seemed to be fading away in a strange hut.

Where is Melchor? she thought in the silence of the nights.

An excited, sweaty Milagros, in a break during the party her father had thrown to forgive her, had spoken about him.

'I have news about Grandfather,' she commented. 'A gypsy from Antequera, a travelling blacksmith, showed up. He needed to have a new document forged for him or something like that, I don't know . . . Well, it turns out that he ran into Grandfather while working in the Osuna region and they spent a couple of days together; he says he's fine.'

Caridad asked the same question that Milagros did when her mother told her about the travelling blacksmith: 'No message?' The girl used the same sarcastic reply on Caridad that her mother had used on her: 'From Grandfather?'

Since then Caridad had had no news of him. She did know his objective, she had talked about it with Milagros: to kill El Gordo. 'You'll see! You don't know Grandfather; there isn't a man alive who can rob him and get away with it!' she'd added proudly. That prediction haunted Caridad. She had seen El Gordo's men, his lieutenants, his army of smugglers: how could Melchor take them all on? She didn't tell the girl, but every night she remembered his sky-blue silk jacket; it shone before her as if she could touch it just by extending her hand. That same blue that had guided her to the gypsy settlement when Eleggua decided to allow her to live, the jacket that the gypsy hung on a rusty nail before going to bed at night and she glanced at every so often. Caridad sadly savoured the memory of his insolence and his slow, arrogant gait. They were a different race, as they never tired of repeating; hadn't Melchor proved that in the Gaucín inn when he confronted the runner? And he had done it for her! Yet how could Grandfather beat El Gordo's army? If she had . . . She didn't know they were planning to steal the tobacco! And besides, what could she have done against a white man?

She appealed to Saint Jacinto; she knelt before the Virgin of Candlemas and prayed to Oyá for Melchor Vega. 'My goddess,' she murmured, her fingers scattering part of a tobacco leaf on the floor as an offering, 'may nothing bad befall him. Bring him back to me, please.'

That day she returned to the settlement with three good cigars that Fray Joaquín had given her in payment for her work.

'Sell them, Cachita,' suggested Milagros. 'You'd get good money for them.'

'No,' murmured Caridad. 'You and I are going to smoke these.'

'But they'd pay you a lot . . .' replied the gypsy as she began to prepare the flint and tinder.

Caridad stilled her expert hands and fixed her gaze on Milagros. 'I don't know a thing about money,' she argued.

'But what's the point—?' Milagros cut her question short. Caridad's little eyes, the need for affection her whole self revealed, answered her in silence. Milagros smiled tenderly. 'All right, then,' she declared.

10

THE RAIN HAD been relentless for several days in Triana and many of the inhabitants went to the river to check its water level and gauge the risk of it overflowing, as had happened so many times – with dramatic results. In the gypsy settlement by the Carthusian monastery, a persistent drizzle mixed with the columns of smoke that rose from the huts. On that inclement morning in early December of the year 1748, only some old squalid horses were out. And the half-naked kids, immune to the cold and the water soaking them to the skin, played in the mire the street had become, sinking up to their ankles in the mud. The older folk took shelter from the rain and waited it out idly.

Mid-morning, however, the children's shrieks broke the idleness imposed by the bad weather.

'A bear!'

The shrill screams of the children echoed among the splashing of their races through the mud. Men and women stuck their heads through the doors of their huts.

'Melchor Vega is bringing a bear!' exclaimed one of the gypsy kids, pointing towards the road that led to the settlement.

'Grandfather Vega!' shrieked another.

Milagros, who had already risen from the table, leapt outside. Caridad dropped the knife she was using to cut a large tobacco leaf. Melchor Vega? The two women found each other outside on the street.

'Where?' the girl asked one of the boys, whom she managed to catch as he ran.

'There! He's almost here! He's bringing a bear!' he answered as she clutched him, until he managed to escape her and vanish into the hubbub; some looked on in surprise, others ran to greet Melchor and yet others rushed to move their animals, which were braying and whinnying and pulling at their halters, frightened by the presence of the large beast.

'Let's go!' Milagros urged Caridad on.

'What is a bear?'

The girl stopped and pointed. 'That.'

At the top of the street – he'd already reached the first of the shacks – Grandfather was walking and smiling, the blue of his silk jacket darkened by the rain. Behind Melchor's two-pointed staff, an immense black bear followed him on all fours, patiently, with its ears pointed, looking curiously at all those who surrounded him at a prudent distance.

'Holy Virgin of Charity!' muttered Caridad, backing up a few paces.

'Don't be afraid, Cachita.'

But Caridad kept backing up as Melchor, surprise showing in his face upon discovering her at the settlement, approached them.

'Milagros! What are you doing here? And your mother?'

The girl didn't even hear him; she just stood there frozen. Melchor reached his granddaughter but the bear, who was now ahead of him, got there first and brushed his snout against the gypsy's calf.

Milagros backed away just as her friend had done, keeping her gaze on the animal.

'And you, *morena*, you're here too?'

'It's a long story, Brother,' answered Tomás from amid the group of gypsies who had followed him along the length of the street.

'Is my daughter OK?' the grandfather asked immediately.

'Yes.'

'And José Carmona?'

'He's fine.'

'That's a shame,' he complained, stroking the bear's head. Someone laughed. 'But if my daughter and my granddaughter are fine, let's leave the long stories for priests and women. Look, Milagros! Look how he dances!'

Then the gypsy moved away from the bear and lifted both the animal's arms.

The bear rose up on its back legs, extended its front ones and followed the rhythm marked by Melchor, who seemed small beside the beast twice his height. Milagros backed away even further, to where Caridad stood.

'Look!' shouted Melchor nonetheless. 'Come here with me! Come closer!'

But Milagros didn't.

During the rest of the morning and in spite of the drizzle that never stopped, Melchor played with the bear: he forced it to dance again and again, to walk on its back legs, to sit down, to cover its eyes, to roll in the mud, and many other skills that amused and impressed the crowd.

'And what are you planning to do with that animal?' some of the gypsies asked him.

'Yes, where will you keep him? Where will he sleep?'

'With the *morena*!' answered Melchor very seriously.

Caridad brought her hands to her chest.

'It's a joke, Cachita,' laughed Milagros, elbowing her affectionately. Then she thought it over again. 'It is a joke, isn't it, Grandfather?'

Melchor didn't respond.

'How will you feed it?' shouted one of the women. 'It's been raining for so long that the men don't go out and we haven't even got half a chicken around here for all of us.'

'Well, then we'll feed him children!' Melchor pretended he was going to let the animal go so he could grab one of the bolder little kids, who had come close and now ran away shrieking. 'A boy in the morning and a girl at night,' he repeated, furrowing his brow towards all the other runny-nosed kids.

As the morning wore on, the mystery was cleared up: a family of gypsies from the south of France showed up at the settlement with a caravan to pick up the bear. Melchor had borrowed it to amuse his people.

'How'd you come up with that idea? It could have carved you up with a single paw swipe. You don't know anything about bears,' Tomás began to scold him when the caravan was leaving the settlement.

'Not a chance! I've been living with them for a month. I've even slept with that bear. He's harmless, at least more so than most *payos*.'

'And even some gypsies,' noted his brother.

'Well, what about that long story you had to tell me?'

Tomás nodded.

'Get started!'

'That *morena* is mixed up in all our misfortunes,' commented Melchor when his brother finished explaining the events that had led Milagros to the settlement.

They were gathered around a jug of wine with the other Vega elders: Uncle Juan, Uncle Basilio and Uncle Mateo.

'That Negress is jinxed!' exclaimed Mateo.

'But she handles tobacco well,' alleged Tomás in her favour. Melchor arched his eyebrows in his brother's direction and Tomás understood. 'No, she hasn't been singing. She works in silence. A lot, even at night. More than any *payo*. She makes money for us, but I haven't heard her singing.'

'What are you planning on doing about your granddaughter?' asked Mateo after a few moments of silence.

Melchor sighed. 'I don't know. The council is right. The girl is a scatterbrain, but the Vargas boys who went with her are clueless. How did they expect to give that potter a lesson in the middle of his neighbourhood, protected by all his own kind? They should have waited to catch him alone and slit his neck, or entered his house in silence . . . Kids today are losing their talent for these things! I don't know,' he repeated. 'Perhaps I'll talk to the Vargas family; only with their forgiveness—'

'José told me that he already tried that . . .'

'He's not capable of lighting a cigar without my daughter's help. Well,' he added as he served himself another glass of wine, 'the only thing that worries me is that she's separated from her mother. If it wasn't for that, it's not a bad thing that my granddaughter is here, with her kind. María will teach her what her father never could: to be a good gypsy, to love freedom and how to not make more mistakes. I'll leave things the way they are.'

Basilio and Mateo nodded.

'Good decision,' agreed Tomás. Then he paused. 'And you?' he asked after a few seconds. 'How'd it go? It doesn't look like you got back the tobacco El Gordo stole from us.'

'How were you expecting me to bring two bags full?' he asked as he searched inside his jacket and pulled out a bag, which he dropped on to the table.

The muffled clinking of the coins silenced any further interventions. Melchor made a gesture urging his brother to open it: several gold escudos rolled out on the tabletop.

'El Gordo won't be pleased,' commented Tomás.

'No,' agreed Uncle Basilio.

'Well, this is only half of it,' revealed Melchor. 'The rest the bear took.'

The Vegas asked him to explain.

'I spent quite a few days around Cuevas Bajas, where El Gordo lives with his family; I even walked through the town at night, but I couldn't find a way to give that son of a bitch a lesson: he's always accompanied by one of his men, as if he needs them even to just take a piss.

'I waited. Something had to come up. One day, some Catalan gypsies who were passing through told me about the French guy with the bear who wandered through nearby towns making the animal dance. I found him, made a deal with him and we went back to wait for El Gordo to organize another smuggling party. When El Gordo and his men were gone and the town was in the hands of old men and women, the French gypsy came in with the bear and did his performance, and while they were all enjoying themselves with his dancing and juggling games, I slipped into El Gordo's house with no problem.'

'Empty?' interrupted Uncle Basilio.

'No. There was a trusted guard who, without leaving his post, was trying to watch the bear from a distance.'

Basilio and Juan gave Melchor a questioning look; the others mockingly feigned mournful expressions: if Melchor had El Gordo's money, that guard had not met a good end. For a few seconds, the gypsy thought about that. It had been difficult to get the man to talk. First he caught him off guard: he primed and loaded his musket, approached him from behind and threatened him, pointing the barrel at the nape of his neck. He brought him inside the house and disarmed him. The man was lame, which was why he hadn't gone with the smuggling party, but that didn't mean he was weak. They knew each other from before he got the limp and the nickname El Cojo along with it.

'This will be the end of you, Galeote,' predicted the guard while Melchor, with the barrel of his weapon beneath the man's throat, used his free hand to pull a pistol and a large dagger out of the man's sash and dropped them to the floor.

'If I were you I'd be worried about my own end, Cojo, because you either collaborate or you'll be going out before me. Where does that thief hide his treasures?'

'You are crazier than I thought if you think I'm going to tell you that.'

'You will, Cojo, you will.'

He forced him to lie down on the floor with his arms extended. Cheers and applause for the bear's tricks came in through the window.

'If you scream,' warned Melchor aiming at his head, 'I'll kill you. You can be sure of that.'

Then he stomped on the little finger of his right hand. El Cojo gritted his teeth while Melchor felt his bones snapping. He did the same to the four other fingers, in silence, twisting his heel into them. Sweat dripped from the man's temples. He didn't speak.

'You're going to be one-handed, not just lame,' Melchor told him, moving on to his left hand. 'Do you think El Gordo will appreciate it, will he feed you when you can no longer do it for yourself? He'll toss you aside like a dog, you know it.'

'Better an abandoned dog than a dead man,' muttered the man. 'If I tell you, he'll kill me.'

'That's true,' affirmed the gypsy, putting his heel on the left little finger and keeping his musket always aimed at his head. 'It's a tough choice: either he'll kill you or I'll maim you,' he added without putting any pressure on. 'Because after this we'll continue with your nose and the few teeth you have left, and end with your testicles. I'll leave your eyes so you can see how people look at you with scorn. If you withstand it, I give you my word as a gypsy that I will leave this house with my hands empty.' Melchor gave the man a few seconds to think. 'But you have another possibility: if you tell me where the money is, I'll be generous with you and you can escape with something in your bag . . . and the rest of your body intact.'

And the gypsy was true to his word: he gave El Cojo several gold coins and let him go; with that money in his bag El Cojo wouldn't turn him in and he'd have enough time to escape.

'Then,' said Tomás when his brother ended the story, 'El Gordo has no way of knowing whether it was you who robbed him or if he was betrayed by his own trusted man.'

Melchor tilted his head and instinctively brought a hand to one of his earlobes, smiled, drank wine and spoke: 'What satisfaction could we get from revenge if the victim doesn't know we were the ones who took it out on him?'

After El Cojo left the house, Melchor had taken off one of the large silver hoops that hung from his ears and placed it right in the centre of the small chest he had emptied of his possessions.

'He knows,' Melchor answered his brother. 'As sure as the devil, he knows that it was me! And at this moment, right now, he'll be cursing my name and raging, just as he'll do at night, and when he wakes up, if he's ever able to get any sleep, and—'

'And he will hunt you down and kill you,' declared Uncle Basilio.

'Undoubtedly. But now he has more pressing problems: he can't pay for his contraband, or pay his men. He has lost a large part of his power. Let's see how his enemies, who are legion, respond.'

Basilio and Tomás nodded.

Melchor didn't want to go back to the San Miguel alley; nothing tied him to the blacksmiths' place and, if he had to choose between his daughter and José Carmona on one hand and Milagros on the other, he'd choose his granddaughter. After talking to the Vegas, he headed towards the shack where the girl lived. Night was already falling.

'Thank you for what you did for the girl, María,' he said as soon as he entered. They were cooking something in a pot that looked like a piece of meat.

The old woman turned towards him and shrugged. Melchor stopped one step in front of the coarse curtain that served as a door and watched his granddaughter for a good long while; she turned her head occasionally, looked at him out of the corner of her eye and smiled.

'What do you want, Nephew?' asked the old woman with a weary voice, behind him.

'I want . . . a palace where I can live with my granddaughter, surrounded by a vast tobacco plantation . . .' Milagros was about to turn, but the old woman elbowed her in the side and forced her to keep her attention on the fire. Melchor squinted his eyes. 'I want horses and colourful silk suits; gold jewellery – tons of it; music and dance and the *payos* serving me my food every day. I want women, also by the dozens . . .' The old woman elbowed Milagros again before she could turn around. That time Melchor smiled. 'And a good husband for my granddaughter, the best gypsy man in the land . . .' Her back still to her grandfather, Milagros tilted her head from left to right gracefully, as if she liked what she was hearing, and was urging him to continue. 'The strongest and the bravest, rich and healthy, completely free, and who'll give my granddaughter many children . . .'

The girl continued nodding until Old María spoke.

'Well, you aren't going to find any of that here. You're in the wrong place.'

'Are you sure?'

The old woman turned and Milagros turned with her. In one of Grandfather's hands, his arm extended, hung a lovely necklace of small white pearls.

'You have to start somewhere,' Melchor then said, and he approached his granddaughter to place the necklace around her neck.

'It's so sad to get old and know that your body no longer excites men!' complained the healer as Milagros stroked the pearls that gleamed on her tanned neck.

Melchor turned towards the old woman. 'Let's see if with this . . .' he started to say as he searched in one of the inner pockets of his blue jacket, 'you can manage to attract some gypsy into your bed, to warm up that body that no longer—'

The old woman didn't let him finish his sentence: as soon as Melchor pulled out a gold medallion inlaid with mother of pearl, she grabbed it from his hands and, almost without looking at it, as if she were afraid he would change his mind, put it in the pocket of her apron.

'Not many men would come to me because of that trifle,' she let fly later.

'Well, here is one who needs supper and a corner to sleep in.'

'I'll give you food, but forget about sleeping in this house.'

'The medallion's not enough?'

'What medallion, you lying gypsy?' she responded with mock seriousness before turning back to the pot.

Milagros could do nothing more than shrug her shoulders.

'Sing, *morena.*'

Caridad, absorbed in her work by candlelight, sketched a wonderful smile that lit up her face. Standing in the doorway, Melchor examined the shack: the old couple was already resting in their bed, from where they looked at him expectantly.

'Antonio,' he said to the old man as he threw a coin the other caught on the fly, 'you and your wife can sleep on Caridad's straw mattress. She and I will take yours, it's bigger.'

'But . . .' the old man started to complain.

'Give me back the money.'

The old man caressed the coin, grumbled and elbowed his wife. Caridad couldn't help smiling again as the two old grim-faced gypsies reluctantly relinquished their prize possession.

'What are you laughing at?' the old woman snapped, her gaze going right through Caridad, whose face fell. And while the old couple covered themselves awkwardly with a blanket on Caridad's mattress, Melchor went to the table and handled some of the cigars that were already prepared. He winked at Caridad and brought one to his lips.

Then he took off his blue jacket and his boots and he lay down in the bed, with his head against the headboard, where he lit the cigar and filled the shack with smoke.

'Sing, *morena*.'

Caridad had wanted him to ask her for that again. How many nights had she yearned to work with that man at her back! She cut the tobacco leaf for the wrapper with extraordinary skill and began to sing softly. But, without planning it or even thinking about it, she abandoned the monotone African songs from her homeland and, just as when she'd worked on a tobacco or sugar plantation, she used her music to narrate her worries and her hopes like the Negro slaves did in Cuba, only able to talk about their lives in song. And meanwhile she continued working, focused on the movement of her hands, attentive to the tobacco, her feelings flowing freely into the lyrics of her songs. *And those two old gypsies steal my slave smoke*, she protested in one, *and then while they suck on the veins, they complain about the tobacco . . .*

She also asked for forgiveness for having allowed them to steal the tobacco: *And even though the gypsy says it's not my fault, it was, but what could the Negress do against the white man?* She cried over her torn red clothes and she celebrated Milagros's getting them mended. She confessed her uneasiness about Melchor's leaving to take revenge. She thanked him for the tranquil nights in the San Miguel alley. She sang of her friendship with Milagros and the hostility of the girl's parents, and of their reconciliation, and of Old María who took care of the girl, and of the parties and the bear and—

'*Morena*,' interrupted Melchor. Caridad turned her head. 'Come here and smoke with me.'

Melchor patted the mattress and Caridad obeyed. The wooden bed frame creaked, threatening to give when she got on it and lay beside the gypsy, who passed her the cigar. Caridad took a hard puff and felt the smoke filling her lungs completely; she held it there until she started to feel a pleasant tickle. Melchor, with the cigar again between his fingers, exhaled the smoke towards the reed and straw roof that covered them and gave it back to Caridad. *What should I do?* she wondered as she took another drag. *Should I keep singing?*

Melchor kept silent, his gaze lost on that roof through which the rain dripped. She hesitated between singing or offering her body to him. Every time she had ever got into a bed, it had been for some man to enjoy her body: the master, the overseer; even the young son of another white master took her on a whim one Sunday. She smoked. She had never been the one to offer herself; it had always been the white men who called her and took her to bed. Melchor smoked too; the cigar was already burning when he passed it to her again. He had invited her into the bed . . . but he wasn't touching her. She waited a few seconds for the cigar to cool down. She felt the contact of the gypsy's body, on his side next to her, both crowded in, but she didn't notice that accelerated breathing, that panting with which men usually pounced on her; Melchor breathed calmly, as always. And yet wasn't her heart beating harder? What did it mean? She smoked. One drag right after the other, with gusto.

'Morena,' he then said, 'finish the cigar. And make sure not to move too much during the night or I'll have to pay those two for a new bed. Now sing . . . the way you used to in the alley.'

Melchor kept his eyes fixed on the reed roof: all he had to do was turn over and he would be on top of her, he thought. He felt the desire: hers was a young, firm, voluptuous body. Caridad would accept him, he was sure of that. She began to sing and the sad slave melodies filled Melchor's ears. How he had missed her singing! If he leapt on her, she would stop. And from that point on, nothing would be the same, as always was the case with women. The affliction and pain that oozed from that music provoked other feelings in the gypsy, feelings that clouded his desire. That woman had suffered as much as he had, maybe more. Why break the spell? He could wait . . . for what? Melchor was surprised at the situation: he, Melchor Vega, El Galeote, wondering what to do. That *morena* really was special! Then he placed a hand on her thigh and slid up its length, and Caridad was silent and remained still, waiting, tense. Melchor could feel it in her leg muscles as they hardened, and in her breathing which stopped for a few moments.

'Keep singing, *morena*,' he requested, lifting his hand.

*

He didn't seek out her body again, in spite of the ardour he felt when he awoke in the night and found they were entangled, both embracing each other against the cold, and the woman's breasts and buttocks were tight up against him. Hadn't she noticed his erection? Caridad's tranquil, unhurried breathing was answer enough. And Melchor hesitated. He pushed her away from him but she kept sleeping, only muttered something in a language unfamiliar to the gypsy. Lucumí, she had told him one morning. She trusted him, slept placidly and sang to him at night. He couldn't let her down, he again concluded, surprised on each of those occasions, before pushing her away from him.

Melchor felt comfortable in the settlement, with his granddaughter and other relatives, and where his daughter Ana regularly visited. She was the one who came running over to him one day to warn him that a couple of men had appeared at the alley pretending to be interested in some cooking pots; but not even the least sharp of the gypsies believed that they'd come there to buy anything. Amid their dealings they'd said that they knew Melchor and they asked about him, but no one, that Ana knew of, had given them any information.

Tomás increased the vigilance over the settlement. He had taken that measure when he found out about his brother's revenge on El Gordo's assets, but now he urged the young Vega men to be increasingly zealous. The gypsies of La Cartuja were used to being on a constant state of alert: the settlement was frequented by all sorts of delinquents and fugitives from justice seeking refuge, trying to blend in with the members of a community who proudly lived outside the laws of the *payos*.

Yet Melchor told his brother, 'Don't worry.'

'How can I not? They must be El Gordo's men.'

'Just two? You and I can take them. You don't need to bother the young men, they have things to do.'

'We have plenty of money now . . . for a while. Two of them accompany Old María and your granddaughter when they go out to collect herbs.'

'All right, pay those ones well,' Melchor corrected himself.

Tomás smiled.

'You are very calm,' he said later.

'Shouldn't I be?'

'No, you shouldn't, but it seems that sleeping with the *morena* does you good,' he affirmed with a crafty expression.

'Tomás,' said Melchor, running an arm over his brother's shoulder and pulling his head close to his own, 'she's got a body that would satisfy the frenzied passion of the best lover.'

Tomás let out a laugh.

'But I haven't laid a hand on her.'

Tomás freed himself from the embrace. 'What . . . ?'

'I can't. I see her as innocent, insecure, sad, shattered. When she sings . . . well, you've heard me say this before. I like to listen to her. Her voice fills me up and transports me back to when we were boys and we used to listen to the Negro slaves singing, do you remember?' Tomás nodded. 'The Negroes today have lost those roots and just try to turn white and become *payos*, but not my *morena*. Do you remember how Mother and Father were crazy for their music and their dancing? Then we would try to imitate them in the settlement, remember?' Tomás nodded again. 'I think . . . I think if I lay with her the spell would be broken. And I prefer her voice . . . and her company.'

'Well, you should do something. The settlement is a rumour mill. Think of your granddaughter . . .'

'The girl knows we haven't done anything. I'm sure of that. I would be able to tell.'

And that was true. Milagros, like all the gypsies in the settlement, knew about the deal her grandfather had struck with the old couple, who complained to anyone who'd listen about how little Melchor had paid them to have their bed to share with the *morena*. Who had ever heard of a Negress sleeping in a bed with legs? Milagros couldn't stand the idea of her grandfather and Cachita . . . Three days passed before she made up her mind and went in search of Caridad, and found her alone in the hut, working the tobacco.

'You are fornicating with my grandfather!' she rebuked her right from the doorway.

The smile Caridad had greeted her friend with faded on her lips. 'No . . .' she managed to say in her defence.

But the gypsy girl didn't let her speak. 'I haven't been able to sleep thinking that you two were there: fucking like dogs. You, my friend . . . ! I trusted you.'

'He has not mounted me.'

But Milagros wasn't listening to her. 'Don't you realize? He's my grandfather!'

'He has not mounted me,' repeated Caridad.

The girl furrowed her brow, still enraged. 'You haven't . . . ?'

'No.'

Would she have liked him to? That was the question that crossed Caridad's mind. She enjoyed Melchor's touch; she felt safe and . . . did she want him to mount her? Beyond the physical contact, she felt nothing when men did that. Would it be the same with Melchor? As soon as he'd taken his hand off her leg that first night and asked her to sing, Caridad again felt the spell established between them to the rhythm of the Negro songs, their souls united. Would she like him to touch her, to mount her? Perhaps yes . . . or no. In any case, what would happen afterwards?

Milagros misinterpreted her friend's silence.

'Forgive me for having doubted you, Cachita,' she apologized.

She didn't ask again.

Which was why Melchor could maintain to Tomás that his granddaughter knew he wasn't having sexual relations with Caridad. No explanations had been necessary on any of the many occasions that the gypsy came to see her.

'I'm stealing her from you,' he would announce to Old María when he entered the hut where they were working with herbs; then he would take the girl by the arm, paying no mind to the healer's complaints, and they would stroll by the riverbank or the Triana lowlands, mostly in silence, Milagros afraid her words would break the spell surrounding her grandfather.

Melchor would also ask her to dance when he heard some hand-clapping, he would treat her to wine, he would surprise her when she and Caridad hid to smoke at dusk and he would join them – 'I don't have the friar's cigars,' he would joke – or he would go with her and the old gypsy healer to gather herbs.

'These weeds won't cure anybody,' grumbled the old woman on those occasions. 'Get out of here!' she would shout at Melchor, shooing him off with her hands. 'This is woman's work.'

And he would wink at his granddaughter and move a few paces away until he was beside the gypsies Tomás had ordered to watch over the women. They were already familiar with the healer's crankiness and bad temper. But before long Melchor would be close to Milagros again.

They were returning from one of those strolls when they heard the news of young Dionisio Vega's death.

There was a place in Triana that Melchor hated; there gathered, all mixed and crowded together, pain, suffering, impotence, rancour, the smell of death, hatred for all of humanity! Even when he was walking around Seville, near the Gold Tower, with the wide Guadalquivir in between, the gypsy turned his face towards the city walls to avoid seeing it. However, that spring dusk, after the dramatic wake for young Dionisio Vega, an irrepressible impulse led him there.

Dionisio hadn't even been sixteen. Surrounded by the relentless cries of grief from the women of the settlement and the San Miguel alley, all gathered to bid their final farewell to the boy, Melchor remembered the liveliness and intelligence in his dark penetrating eyes and his always smiling face. He was the grandson of Uncle Basilio, who endured the gathering with composure, trying to keep his gaze from meeting Melchor's. When, at the end of the ceremony, Melchor headed over to his relative, Basilio accepted his condolences and for the first time in that day faced him. Basilio said nothing but the accusation floated through the settlement: *It's your fault, Melchor.*

And it was. Those two men El Gordo had sent, the ones Ana had told him about, had disappeared. Maybe because they saw that Melchor was never alone, maybe when they saw the security measures. But over time, the vigilance Tomás had ordered ceased. How could they think that El Gordo would forget the offence? Spring came and one day, young Dionisio, with two friends, left the settlement and went on to the fertile plain of Triana in search of a hen to steal or some iron scraps to sell to the blacksmiths. Two men cut them off. The boys were obviously gypsies from their dark faces, their colourful clothes and the trinkets that hung from their ears and around their necks. Not a word was exchanged before one of the men stuck a dress sword through Dionisio's heart. Then the same man addressed the other boys.

'Tell that coward, El Galeote, that El Fajado does not forgive. Tell him to stop hiding among his people like a frightened woman.'

Stop hiding among his people like a frightened woman. The boys' words, repeated thousands of times since they appeared at the settlement with Dionisio's corpse, stuck like red-hot needles in Melchor's brain while many of the gypsies avoided his eyes when they passed him. *They think the same thing!* Melchor tortured himself with the thought. And they were right: he had hidden like a coward, like a woman. Was he getting old? Was he like Antonio, who for a mere coin had given up his prized bed so Melchor could sleep with the *morena*? The wake lasted three days, the women howling incessantly, tearing their dresses and scratching at their arms and faces. Melchor kept apart even from Milagros and Ana, who couldn't keep the recrimination out of their eyes; he even came to believe he saw scorn on his own daughter's face. Nor did he have the courage to join the parties of gypsies who, fruitlessly, went out in search of El Gordo's men. Meanwhile he tormented himself over and over with the same question: had he turned into someone like old Antonio, a coward who could cause the death of boys like Dionisio? Even his own daughter tried to avoid him!

He witnessed the burial, in a nearby open field, crouched among the other gypsies. He saw how the boy's father, accompanied by Uncle Basilio, put an old guitar in Dionisio's limp arms. Later, in a heartbroken voice, addressing his son's lifeless body, he cried out, 'Play, son, and if I have done wrong, let your music deafen me; but if I have acted correctly, be still and I will be absolved.'

In the earsplitting silence, Basilio and his son waited a few moments. Later, when they turned their backs on the corpse, the other men buried him along with his guitar. When the earth completely covered the simple pine coffin, Dionisio's mother went over to the head of it and carefully piled up the dead boy's few personal possessions: an old shirt, a blanket, a knife, a small silver horn that he had worn around his neck as a child to ward off the evil eye and an old two-cornered hat that the boy had loved and which his mother kissed tenderly. Then she set fire to the pile.

As the flames began to die out and the gypsies leave, Melchor went over to the bonfire. Many stopped and turned their heads to watch El Galeote take off his sky-blue silk jacket, pull the money out of its pockets and put the coins in his sash, and throw the jacket on to the fire. Then he offered his hand to Uncle Basilio with the heavens as his witness.

Pain, anguish and guilt led his feet to the Triana bank of the Guadalquivir. He needed to be there!

'Where's he going?' Milagros asked her mother in a whisper.

The two women, and Caridad with them, hastened to follow Melchor as soon as he bowed his head to Basilio with a resigned expression and headed off towards Triana. They did so at a distance, making sure he didn't see them, not imagining that Melchor wouldn't have noticed their presence even if they were walking right beside him.

'I think I know,' answered Ana.

She said no more until the Grandfather passed the pontoon bridge and the bank and stopped in front of the church of the old Seafarers' University, where they taught boys about the sea and took care of sick seamen.

'It was there,' whispered the mother, keeping a close eye on the silhouette of her father set against the last lights of the day.

'What was there?' enquired Milagros, with Caridad behind her.

Ana was slow to respond.

'That is the church of Our Lady of Bonaria, the patron saint of seafarers. Look . . .' she began to address her daughter, then corrected herself to include Caridad as well. 'Look at the main entrance. Do you see the uninterrupted balcony looking on to the river above it?' Milagros nodded; Caridad said nothing. 'From that balcony, on holy days of obligation, they said mass to the boats in the river; that way the seamen didn't even have to disembark . . .'

'And neither did the galley slaves.' Milagros finished the sentence for her.

Ana sighed. 'That's right.'

Melchor continued to stand tall before the door to the church, his head lifted towards the balcony and the river almost licking the heels of his boots.

'Your grandfather never wanted to tell me anything about his years in the galleys, but I know, I overheard some conversations he had with the few others who survived that torture. Bernardo, for example. During the years that Grandfather was at the oars, there was nothing that hurt him more, of all the hardships and disasters he had to endure, than being chained to the galleys listening to mass docked at Triana.'

Because Triana was freedom incarnate and there was nothing more precious to a gypsy. Melchor endured the lashings of the slave driver, suffered thirst and hunger covered in his own excrement and urine, with ulcers all over his body, rowing through exhaustion. *So what?* he wondered in the end. *Wasn't that the gypsies' fate, be it on land or on sea? To suffer injustice.*

But when he was there before his Triana . . . when he could smell, practically touch, that air of freedom that naturally drove the gypsies to fight against all the ties that bind, then Melchor ached from all his wounds. How many blasphemies had he repeated in silence against those priests and those sacred images from the other side of freedom? How many times right there, on the river, in front of the retablo of Our Lady of Bonaria flanked by paintings of Saint Peter and Saint Paul, had he cursed his fate? How many times had he sworn that he would never again lift his eyes towards that balcony?

Suddenly, Melchor fell to his knees. Milagros wanted to run towards him, but Ana held her back.

'No. Leave him be.'

'But . . .' the girl complained. 'What is he going to do?'

'Sing,' Caridad whispered behind them, to their surprise.

Ana had never heard her father sing his 'galley lament'. He had never sung it once he was free. Which was why, when the first long, doleful wailing flooded the dusk, Ana fell to her knees just like him. Milagros felt all the little hairs on her body stand on end. She had never heard anything similar; not even the heartfelt *deblas* of La Trianera, El Conde's wife, could compare to that lament. The girl shivered, searched out her mother and rested her hands on her shoulders; Ana grasped them. Melchor sang without words, weaving moans and whimpers that sounded deep, cracked, broken, all tinged with the taste of death and misfortune.

The two gypsies remained cowering inwardly, aware how that profound and indescribable song, marvellous in its melancholy, cut them to the quick. Yet Caridad was smiling. She knew it: she was sure that everything the grandfather was incapable of putting into words he could express through music; like her, like the slaves.

The galley lament lasted several minutes, until Melchor ended it with a final mournful cry that he let die on his lips. The women saw him get up and spit at the chapel before starting to walk downriver, away from the settlement. Mother and daughter stayed still for a few more moments, drained.

'Where is he going?' asked Milagros when Melchor vanished into the distance.

'He's leaving,' Ana managed to choke out, her eyes flooded with tears.

Caridad, with the laments still echoing in her ears, tried to keep the gypsy's back in sight. Milagros felt her mother's shoulders convulse with sobs.

'He'll come back, Mother,' she tried to console her. 'He's not . . . he's not carrying anything; he has no jacket, no musket, not even his cane.'

Ana didn't speak. The murmur of the river's water in the night surrounded the three women.

'He'll come back, won't he, Mother?' added the girl, her voice now cracked.

Caridad perked up her ears. She wanted to hear yes. She needed to know that he would come back!

But Ana didn't answer.

SONG OF BLOOD

11

DEVASTATED BY THE unbearable summer heat, city life passed languidly. Those who could had already moved their furnishings, clothes and essentials from the upper floors of their homes to the lower ones, where they tried to fight against the heat and the wind from the east. The rest, who were most of the population, moved closer to either of the Guadalquivir's banks, the Seville side or the Triana side, where at least they could find a glimmer of life in the people bathing in the river, looking to cool off a little, beneath the watchful gaze of the guards sent there by the city council to avoid the frequent deaths by drowning. The people were whiling away the day when a rumour began to spread through them: the army was taking the city. It wasn't constables or the chief justice of Seville, but the army! Suddenly, armed soldiers stationed themselves at the thirteen gates and in the two side doors of the capital's walls and warned those people who were outside the city walls to get inside. Swimmers, merchants, seamen and dock workers, traders, women and children . . . The crowd hastened to obey the orders of the military men.

'We're going to close the gates of the city!' shouted corporals and sergeants heading armed detachments.

But beyond the warnings, none of the officers gave any other explanations; the soldiers used their rifles to push away the Sevillians crowded around the gates, asking what was going on. The agitation reached crisis point when someone shouted that the army had the entire city surrounded. Many looked towards Triana and saw that it was true: there on the other side of the river, they saw people running among the white soldiers' uniforms, and the pontoon bridge was a throng of horses rushing back and forth, incited by the soldiers.

'What's going on?'

'Is it war?'

'Are they attacking us?'

But instead of replies the people got shoves and blows – because the soldiers didn't know why either; they had merely received the order to force the inhabitants inside and close the gates to the city. Only two were to be left open: Arenal and Carne.

'Go home!' shouted the officers. 'Go to your homes!'

Various patrol units had been giving the same order on the streets inside Seville and Triana, an order which on that 30 July of 1749 was proclaimed through the entire length and breadth of Spain in a meticulous secret military operation devised by the Bishop of Oviedo and Don Gaspar Vázquez Tablada, President of the Council of Castile, and the Marquis of Ensenada, who a few years earlier had toughened the sentences for gypsies arrested outside of their home town: death. By virtue of that new proclamation of 1749, that same day, the royal troops took every city in the kingdom where they knew gypsies lived.

After a few hours, the gates of Seville had been shut except for the Arenal and Carne gates, which were heavily guarded. Triana had been besieged by the army; the good citizens ran to take refuge in their homes and the pickets stationed themselves strategically on certain streets. That was when the soldiers finally received direct instructions from their superiors: arrest all gypsies as dangerous and despicable persons, regardless of their gender or age, and confiscate all their assets.

Previously they had dispatched the pertinent secret official letters to the Chief Magistrates of all the towns in the kingdom where the census data registered gypsies, so Seville's chief justice, as the city's highest-ranking magistrate, had already pointed out to the military authorities the homes and places where they should proceed with the arrests.

As was happening all over Spain, the gypsies were in shock as they witnessed the vile measure being implemented: in Seville they were arrested without opposition, as were the blacksmiths of San Miguel alley and those that lived on La Cava and the surrounding area in Triana. Those in the settlement of La Cartuja had better luck, however; many of them managed to escape, leaving behind their meagre belongings. Two were shot and killed by soldiers as they fled, another was wounded in one leg and a fourth drowned in the river while his wife looked on impotently, his small children wailed and the contemptuous troops did nothing.

Close to 130 gypsy families were arrested in Seville in the massive raid of July 1749.

Inside the shack, Caridad heard the shouts of army officers rising above the tumult.

'Arrest them all!'

'Don't let them get away!'

She stopped working Fray Joaquín's tobacco. Frightened by the commotion of gypsies and soldiers running, the shrieks of children and women and the occasional shot, she got up from the table and rushed towards the door just as Antonio and his wife ran limping in the other direction, helping each other.

'What . . . ?' she tried to ask them.

'Out of the way!' The old man pushed her.

She stood there, frozen, transfixed, watching as the soldiers pounced on women and threatened men with rifles. Many managed to escape and ran fearlessly through the line of soldiers surrounding the settlement. She looked all around for Milagros without success, and saw how Uncle Tomás was distracting a group of soldiers so that one of his sons could flee, taking his family with him. There was no trace of Milagros. Some gypsies escaped by jumping over the roofs of shacks in order to fall behind the monastery's garden wall and start a frenetic race towards freedom. Antonio and his wife pushed her again as they left the hut. Caridad followed them with her gaze: the old woman was dropping tobacco and cigars that she had stolen. She watched them run with difficulty towards . . . the soldiers! One of them laughed as he saw them approach, old and bumbling, but his face changed when Antonio brandished the large knife in his hand. A blow with the rifle butt in the old man's stomach was enough to get him to drop the knife and fall to the floor. The soldier and his two companions laughed as if they considered the fight over just as the old woman dropped her bag and surprised them, leaping with an astonishing strength and agility born of hatred and rage, her claw-like hands as her only weapon, on the soldier who had hit her husband. The men were slow to react. Caridad saw some furrows of blood on the soldier's face. They struggled to subdue the old woman.

'What are you doing here?'

Absorbed in what was happening to Antonio and his wife, Caridad hadn't realized that the operation was almost finished and that the rest of the soldiers were already entering the shacks. The arrested gypsies were in groups on the street and surrounded. She lowered her gaze before the soldier who had addressed her.

'What are you doing here, Negress?' he repeated when Caridad didn't reply. 'Are you a gypsy?' Then he looked her up and down. 'No. How could you be a gypsy? Hey!' he shouted to a corporal who was passing by on the street. 'What do we do with this one?'

The corporal approached and asked her the same questions. Caridad still didn't answer or even look at them.

'Why are you in the gypsy settlement? Are you the slave of one of them?' He himself rejected the idea, shaking his head repeatedly. 'You ran away from your masters, right? Yes, that's what it must—'

'I'm free,' Caridad managed to say in a reedy voice.

'Are you sure? Prove it.'

Caridad entered the hut and returned with her bundle, which she rummaged through until she found the documents that the notary on *The Queen* had given to her.

'It's true.' After examining and handling them, as if he could recognize by touch that which he was unable to read, he accepted them as valid. 'What have you got there?'

Caridad handed him the bundle, but just as had happened in the seaport of Cádiz, the soldier stopped looking as soon as his hand came across the rough, worn blanket she used to protect herself from the cold in winter and just weighed up and shook the bundle to see if something inside jingled, but the contents – the blanket, her red clothes, some cigars that Fray Joaquín had given her in payment for her work and the straw hat that was tied to it all – didn't weigh much or jingle.

'Get out of here!' he shouted at her then. 'We've got enough problems with this scum.'

Caridad obeyed and started walking towards Triana. She lingered on the street when she passed the arrested gypsies. Was Milagros among them? The soldiers took their weapons and their jewels and beads while a new army, this time of notaries, tried to write down their names and their belongings.

'Whose is this mule?' shouted a soldier with the tether of a scrawny mule in his hand.

'Mine,' screamed one of the gypsies.

'Shut up, liar!' spat out a woman. 'That belongs to a labourer from Camas!'

Some gypsies laughed.

How can they laugh? thought Caridad, astonished, as she continued searching for Milagros among them. She saw Uncle Tomás, and Basilio and Mateo . . . most of the older Vegas. She also saw Antonio and his wife, hugging each other. But she didn't see Milagros.

'OK,' said the soldier with the mule, holding his ground, 'who does it belong to?'

'To him,' answered someone, pointing to the first gypsy.

'To the guy from Camas,' said another.

'Mine,' was heard from somewhere in the group.

'No, it's mine,' laughed another voice.

'No, the other one is yours.'

'No, that's the one that belongs to the guy from Camas.'

'The guy from Camas had two mules?'

'It's the King's!' added a young man. 'The King's,' he repeated to the soldier's exasperation. 'It's the one we save for him to ride when he comes to Triana!'

The gypsies burst into laughter again. Caridad widened her lips in a smile, but she was still worried about Milagros.

'They didn't arrest her,' shouted Uncle Tomás, imagining what was worrying her. 'She's not here, *morena*.'

'Who's not here?' rudely interrupted the same corporal who had interrogated Caridad; he'd now come over to the chaos.

Caridad stammered and lowered her eyes.

'The King's mule, captain,' Tomás then answered with mock seriousness. 'Don't let them trick your excellency: really the mule the guy from Camas has is the King's.'

'Laugh!' shouted the corporal, addressing all those arrested. 'Laugh now, because you won't be laughing where you're headed to. I promise you that!' Then he turned to Caridad. 'And you, didn't I tell you to—'

'General,' he was interrupted by a voice from the group, 'where we're headed, can we bring the King's mule?'

The corporal turned red and, amid the laughter and mocking, Tomás silently urged Caridad to escape.

Triana was also seized by the royal army. A large part of the troops were in the San Miguel alley and on Cava Nueva, places with primarily gypsy populations, but there were still patrols going through the streets in case anyone had escaped or hidden in some *payo*'s house. The King had foretold grave consequences for those who helped them, and anonymous denunciations, both founded and unfounded, began as a result of old quarrels between neighbours.

Caridad could only think of one place to go and she headed there: the monastery of preachers at San Jacinto. But the churches and monasteries were also under surveillance by the soldiers. So she tried entering Triana along Castilla Street and passing in front of the church of Our Lady of O. Caridad always carefully watched that sober church: she didn't know of any Orisha personified by the Virgin of O, but Fray Joaquín had imbued her with the affection that he himself felt for that temple: 'It was built exclusively with alms collected by the brotherhood,' he commented to her one day. 'That is why she is so beloved in Triana.'

Caridad evaded the patrol of soldiers stationed in front of the main façade of the church, and she heard an officer heatedly arguing with a priest. The same thing was happening in the parish of Santa Ana, and in Sancti Espiritus, and in Remedios, and in Victoria, at the Minims, the Martyrs and San Jacinto. The King had managed to get a papal bull that allowed the soldiers to remove the gypsies who were taking sanctuary, so all those who had fled and sought their salvation in ecclesiastical asylum were being removed, not without vehement arguments with the priests who were defending the privileges of that atavistic institution the gypsies resorted to so often.

The situation at San Jacinto was worse than at the church of Our Lady of O. Given its proximity to the San Miguel alley and to Cava Nueva, there were several gypsies who had taken asylum in that church before the troops entered. Almost all of the twenty-eight friar preachers who made up the community were huddled together with their prior, determined to impede access into the temple under construction to a lieutenant who kept showing his order from the King. Fray Joaquín soon noticed Caridad's presence, since her old straw hat stood out amid the crowd waiting to see how the dispute was resolved. The young clergyman left his brothers and ran towards her.

'What happened in the gypsy settlement?' he asked even before reaching her. His features were pinched with worry.

'The soldiers came . . . They were shooting. They arrested the gypsies . . .'

'And Milagros?'

His shout attracted people's attention. Fray Joaquín grabbed Caridad by the arm and pulled her a few paces aside.

'And Milagros?' he repeated.

'I don't know where she is.'

'What do you mean? They're arresting all the gypsies. Was she arrested?'

'No. Arrested, no. Tomás told me . . .'

The clergyman's sigh of relief interrupted her words. 'Glory be!' he exclaimed, lifting his eyes to the heavens.

'What can I do, Fray Joaquín? Why are they arresting the gypsies? And where could Milagros be?'

'Cachita, wherever she is, she's better off than here. Of that you can be sure. And as for why they're arresting them—'

Applause and cheers interrupted the conversation and forced them to turn towards San Jacinto. The prior had given in and three gypsy men, several children and a woman with a baby in her arms left the church escorted by the soldiers.

'They're arresting them for being different,' declared the friar when the group of military men and gypsies had vanished in the direction of La Cava. 'I can assure you that they are no worse than many of those they call *payos*.'

Fray Joaquín didn't have much problem getting a devout family of shrimpers on Larga Street to take Caridad in for a few days; some coins from the preacher's own pocket helped them to make their decision. Caridad set herself up in the shed in a tiny garden behind the fisherman's house. Sitting among some old tools and fishing supplies piled up there, she had little to do besides smoke and worry about Milagros. The hospitality of those 'good Christians', as Fray Joaquín called them, disappeared as soon as the preacher did.

The day after the arrests, all of Triana came out to witness the gypsies' departure over the pontoon bridge. Mixed into the crowd, Caridad saw Rafael García – El Conde – dragging his feet with his gaze lowered, at the head of a long row of men and boys over seven years old who walked behind him, all tied together with a thick rope. Their destination: Seville's royal jail. Many of the townspeople insulted them and spat on them. 'Heretics! Thieves!' they shouted as the gypsies passed, while they threw rubbish and litter that had piled up on the streets. Caridad couldn't make out in the gypsies any of the sarcasm she had been surprised to see the day before at the settlement. Now they all knew the royal orders: from the jail they would be transferred to La Carraca, the military arsenal of Cádiz, where they would be committed to forced labour for the rest of their lives.

In addition to keeping them from taking sanctuary and confiscating their goods to sell at public auction and pay the expenses of the raid, the soldiers had also repossessed the documents that identified them as 'old Castilians' and the residency papers from those who had them. Those official documents were the only way the gypsies could prove they weren't vagrants or delinquents; re-possessing them – even though many were forged – meant that from that point on they couldn't even confirm their identity and status. From one day to the next, most of the gypsy blacksmiths from the San Miguel alley and many others who had spent years working and living with the *payos* had become criminals.

Walking halfway along the rope, Caridad recognized Pedro García, Milagros's impossible love. What would the girl say if she saw him there? Milagros's eyes sparkled in the night when she remem-bered him, especially once Alejandro's ghost had stopped tormenting her. Caridad also saw José Carmona, downtrodden, hiding his face amid the insults.

After the men came the women along with the girls and the boys under seven, all tied with ropes and watched over by the soldiers almost more closely than the men were. Caridad recognized Ana, Milagros's mother, and so many others that she knew from the alley, some with their little ones on their backs. She felt a shiver as the gypsy women passed: they had not lost their pride. They weren't silent, they hurled abuse and spat back despite also knowing what awaited them: imprisonment for an unspecified length of time in a women's jail.

Caridad heard someone shout out, 'Witches!'

Instantly, the rope curved and several gypsies pounced on the women in the crowd who had insulted them. Seized by panic, the women tried to back up into the people packed behind them; the soldiers had to stop them.

In the ruckus, Ana saw Caridad. They had heard rumours of shots fired, deaths and struggles in the settlement.

'And my girl?' she screamed.

Caridad was focused on avoiding the soldiers' blows.

'*Morena!*' This time Caridad did hear her. 'How's Milagros?'

Caridad was about to answer when all of a sudden she realized that many of the people who surrounded her were staring, as if condemning her for speaking to the gypsy women. She hesitated. She couldn't take on the crowd . . . but Milagros . . . and Ana was her mother! When she lifted her head, the rope had already started moving and she could only manage to see Ana's back.

Behind the people crowded together on both sides of the street, Caridad followed the rope the women were tied to. She got ahead of Ana and stationed herself in the Plaza del Altozano, in the front row, in front of the Inquisition Castle, where it was impossible for the gypsy woman not to notice her. But when she saw her approaching and the shouts and insults of the crowd intensified around her, she was once again overtaken by fear.

Ana saw her. And she saw her lower her head as the rope passed.

'Help me,' she urged the women on the rope with her. 'I have to get over to where that Negro woman is, over to my father's *morena*, there, to the left, do you see her?'

'The one who works the tobacco?' someone asked her from further up on the rope.

'Yes, that's the one. I need to know about my daughter.'

'You'll be so close you could smoke a cigar with her,' someone assured her from behind.

And she was. When Ana passed in front of Caridad, the gypsy women threw themselves to the left and caught the soldiers off guard. The rope curved again and some fell to the ground taking a few soldiers with them. Ana imitated them and rolled on the ground.

'Caridad!' she shouted in a firm voice, lying at her feet.

The Negress reacted to her urgent tone.

'Come closer!'

She did and then knelt beside her.

'What about Milagros? What's become of my girl?'

The soldiers began to regain order, some lifting the fallen gypsy women, others inserting themselves between the ones who remained standing, but the gypsies, keeping an eye on Ana, resisted and insulted the crowd, leaping on to them again and again.

'What news do you have of her?' insisted Ana. 'Was she arrested?'

'No,' affirmed Caridad.

'She's free?'

'Yes.'

Ana closed her eyes for a second. 'Find her! Take care of her!' she then begged Caridad. 'She is just a girl. Find Melchor with her and seek out the protection of the gypsies . . . if there are any left. Tell her that I love her and I will always love her.'

Suddenly, Caridad went flying backwards from a soldier's boot to her shoulder. Ana allowed herself to be lifted up and made an almost imperceptible gesture to the other women. The fighting stopped, except for a little girl who kept kicking a soldier.

Before going back to her position on the rope, Ana turned; Caridad had fallen to the ground and was trying to recover her hat amid the people's feet. Had Ana just asked her to take care of her daughter? she wondered as she noticed that her entire body was soaked in cold sweat.

12

OLD MARÍA HELD Milagros back when she tried to return to
Triana.

'Be still, girl,' she ordered in a whisper when she saw the infantry
soldiers approaching them. 'Get on your knees.'

They were off the path, collecting licorice. It wasn't the best
season for it, the healer had complained, but she needed those roots to
treat coughs and indigestion. There were those who said they were
also aphrodisiacs, but María avoided mentioning that property to
Milagros, telling herself that there would be time later for learning
such things. In the silence of the wide Triana lowlands, among
grapevines, olive and orange trees, the two women had pricked up
their ears to catch the murmur that became louder and louder. Soon
they saw a long column of armed infantry soldiers advancing stiffly,
dressed in white dress coats whose front coattails were folded back
and fastened with clasps, tight waistcoats beneath, breeches, gaiters
buttoned above the knees and black three-cornered hats over complicated white wigs with three horizontal curls on each side that went
down to their necks and covered their ears.

Milagros watched the soldiers with their serious faces, sweating
under the summer sun that beat down on them, and wondered what
reason there could be behind such a deployment.

'I don't know,' answered Old María as she got up with difficulty
after the army had marched past. 'But I'm sure we are better off
behind their rifles than in front of them.'

It wasn't long before they found out. They followed them at a prudent distance, both attentive and quick to hide. They watched how the soldiers divided into two columns when they were out of Triana and they exchanged a horrified look when they noticed that one of the columns was taking up position around the gypsy settlement of La Cartuja.

'We have to warn them,' said Milagros.

The old woman didn't answer. Milagros turned towards her and found a wrinkled, trembling face; the healer kept her eyes half-closed as she thought hard.

'María,' insisted the girl. 'They are going after our people! We must warn them—'

'No,' interrupted the elderly woman with her eyes on the settlement.

Her tone, and the refusal exhaled from her very innards, was that of a resigned old gypsy tired of fighting.

'But . . .'

'No.' María was emphatic. 'It will just be one more time, another detention, but we will move on, as always. What do you want to do? Stand up and scream? Risk one of these bastards shooting you? Run to the settlement? They'll arrest you . . . And what good would it do? Our people are already surrounded, but they know how to defend themselves. I'm sure that your mother and your grandfather would support my decision.' Then, doubting her obedience, she gripped the girl's forearm tightly.

Crouched behind some brush, they waited for the assault to happen; it was as if they were being forced to witness the downfall of their people, to experience their pain. They couldn't see anything. For a long while all they could hear was the coming and going of people in the settlement mixed with Milagros's muffled sobs, which became uncontrollable crying when the captain ordered the assault. María pulled on Milagros when she tried to peek out and struggled to keep the girl quiet, but what did it matter now? The shooting and the screaming thundered through the plains. The old woman grabbed Milagros's head, hugged her tightly and rocked her. The gypsies that managed to get past the siege ran towards where they were; no one chased them, except for random bullets.

'Mother . . . Father . . .' the healer could hear Milagros say as the commotion died down. 'Mother . . . Cachita . . .'

With each moan, a mouthful of warm breath caressed the old woman's chest.

'The *morena* isn't a gypsy,' she thought to say. 'Nothing will happen to her.'

'And my parents?' The girl turned after escaping the old woman's embrace. 'The same thing must have happened in Triana. You saw how the soldiers split up . . .'

With her palms open, the old woman grabbed the girl's flushed face with bloodshot eyes and tears streaming from them.

'They are, girl. They are gypsies. And that means they are strong. They will prevail.'

Milagros shook her head. 'And me? What will become of me?' she sobbed.

María hesitated. What could she tell her: *I'll protect you*? An old woman and a fifteen-year-old girl . . . What would they do? Where would they go? How would they make enough to live on?

'At least you are free,' she said, choosing to scold her instead, and dropped the hands that held her face. 'Do you want to go with them? You can. All you have to do is walk a few paces . . .' She ended the sentence by pointing towards the settlement with her hooked finger.

Milagros took the blow. Scrutinized by the old woman's penetrating gaze, she sniffled, wiped her nose on her forearm and straightened her neck.

Then: 'I don't want to,' she said.

The healer nodded, satisfied. 'Cry for your parents' misfortune,' she said. 'You should. But defend your freedom, girl. That is what they would want. Freedom is the only thing we gypsies have.'

They waited for sunset hidden among the thicket.

'You can't run,' Milagros said to the old woman. 'It's better that we wait for night to fall.'

They chewed on licorice roots to calm their tension. At noon, when the sun moved from east to west and the land belonged to no one, with the sound of the soldiers' shots and the gypsies' screams still floating in the air, Milagros remembered Alejandro and the blunderbuss shot that destroyed his neck and head. It had been a year since his death. Crouched on the ground, the girl delicately smoothed her blue skirt, where faint bloodstains could still be seen, however much she washed it. If it hadn't been for that event, they would have arrested her, as they had surely done to the gypsies in San Miguel alley. She thought she could feel his presence in the shiver that ran up her spine; it was his moment, that of the souls of the dead. However, a surprising feeling of tranquillity overcame her after the shiver, as if Alejandro had come to defend her with the same bravery he had shown beating on the potter's door.

Good gypsy! she told herself just as laughter from the settlement, prompted by the discussion over the King's supposed mule, brought her back to reality. Before giving María a quizzical look, she checked that the sun had already passed its peak.

The old woman shrugged at the sound of laughter, paradoxical under such circumstances.

'You hear them? They're laughing. They can't keep us down,' she declared.

The village of Camas was barely half a league from where they were hiding; however, in the night, walking slowly in the moonlight, being startled by and hiding from even their own noises, it took them more than an hour to reach the outskirts.

'Where are we going?' whispered Milagros.

María tried to get her bearings in the night.

'There is a small farmhouse nearby . . . That way.' She pointed with her atrophied finger.

'Who are they?'

'An unhappily married couple, with more kids in their house than fruit trees on the land they've leased.' The healer now walked with firm, decisive steps. 'I made the mistake of taking pity on them and refusing a couple of eggs they wanted to give me the first time I cured one of their runny-nosed kids. I think that every time they've called me since then, they've offered me the very same eggs.'

Milagros answered with a forced laugh. 'That's what you get for doing favours,' she said.

Should I tell her that it was her grandfather Melchor who begged me to go and cure that boy? wondered the old woman. *And that his skin was of a darker shade than his siblings'?* In any case, she laughed to herself, there weren't many resemblances to be found among any of that peasant woman's other children either, and she was known for her exuberant flesh and loose ways.

'A common mistake,' Old María replied. 'I don't know if you know but something similar recently happened to me, with a young gypsy girl who had got herself into a bind. The council of elders was about to banish her.'

María didn't want to see the expression the girl's face twisted into. 'There it is,' she said instead, pointing to a couple of small buildings that could barely be seen in the darkness.

They were greeted by some barking dogs. Instantly, a faint light appeared in one of the windows. A piece of canvas that was the only thing separating it from the night was pushed to one side. The figure of a man was silhouetted inside of what was nothing more than two shacks together, as miserable if not more so than the ones in the gypsy settlement.

'Who's there?' shouted the man.

'It's me, María, the gypsy.'

The two women continued advancing, the now calm dogs trotting between their feet, while the farmer seemed to be consulting with someone inside the shack.

'What do you want?' he asked after a little while, in a tone that didn't please María.

'From your attitude,' answered the healer, 'I think you already know.'

'The law has threatened to jail anyone who helps you. They have arrested all the gypsies in Spain at once.'

Milagros and María stopped a few steps from the window. All the gypsies in Spain! As if wanting to accompany the bad news with his presence, the man came out into the light. He was gaunt with thin hair, a long messy beard and bare torso that clearly showed his ribcage, proof of his hunger.

'Maybe you'd be better off in jail, Gabriel,' spat out the healer.

'What would become of my children, crone?' he complained.

Let their fathers take care of them! she was tempted to reply.

'You know them, you've cured them; they don't deserve that.'

She knew them, of course she knew them! One squalid little abandoned girl, her large eyes sunken in their sockets, had begged her for help over the two long days it took for her to die in her arms; she could do nothing for her. 'All the thankless sons of bitches like you should be in jail!' she answered, remembering the girl's eyes.

The man thought for a few seconds. Behind him appeared two boys who had been awoken by the conversation.

'I won't turn you in,' assured the peasant farmer. 'I swear! I will give you something to help you continue on your way, but don't ruin my life, crone.'

'Now he's going to offer you those two eggs again,' whispered Milagros. 'Let's go, María. We can't trust this man, he'll sell us out.'

'Your life is already in ruins, you wretch,' shouted the old woman, ignoring the girl.

They couldn't continue walking. It was pitch black. They had no money: the little they'd had was left behind in the settlement – for the soldiers, lamented the healer, including the lovely medallion and pearl necklace that Melchor had given them. *All the gypsies in Spain*, the farmer had said. She was tired; her body could take no more . . . She needed to think, to organize her thoughts, find out what had happened and where those who had escaped were.

'Are you going to refuse help to the granddaughter of Melchor Vega?' she said all of a sudden.

Milagros and the farmer were both surprised. Why had María mentioned Grandfather? What did he have to do with it? But the healer knew what she was doing: she knew that those who knew Melchor – and in that house he was well known – grew to appreciate him as much as they feared him.

'Do you know what would happen to you if Melchor finds out?' insisted María. 'You'll wish for the worst of jails.'

The man hesitated.

'Let them in!' It was a woman's voice.

'The gypsy must have been arrested,' he tried to oppose his wife.

'El Galeote arrested?' The woman laughed. 'You'll always be an idiot! I said let them in!'

And what if they arrested him in some other gypsy settlement? wondered Milagros then. It had been four months since anyone had heard from him; no news had reached them although both she and her mother, and even Caridad, had asked every gypsy that showed up in Triana. No. Melchor Vega couldn't have been arrested.

'But tomorrow at daybreak, without fail, they will leave.' The farmer gave in, interrupting Milagros's thoughts, before disappearing from the window.

The two women waited for the man to remove the planks he used to close the shack. Amid the sounds of wood moving and muttered insults, Milagros felt she was being watched: the two boys that had appeared behind their father were now by the windowsill, and they undressed her with their eyes. Instinctively, the girl, feeling the weight of their gaze, moved closer to María.

'What are you looking at?' The old woman scolded them as soon as she noticed what Milagros was doing. Then she took her by the arm and led her inside; kneeling to enter through a space that the farmer had managed to open.

María knew the shack but Milagros grimaced at the penetrating odour that hit her as soon as she entered and at what she could make out in the light of a guttering candle: three or four sweaty children slept on the floor, on straw, between the legs of an emaciated donkey who rested with its neck and ears drooped; it was probably the only possession those people had. *There's no need for you to hide the burro,* thought Milagros. *Not even a starving gypsy would go near it.* Then she turned her head towards a broken stool and what used to be a table where a candle rested atop a twisted mountain of wax, both near the straw mattress where a woman lay. After squinting her eyes to try to make out some trace of Melchor in the girl's features, she indicated with a halfhearted sweep of her hand for them to settle in wherever they could.

Milagros hesitated. María pulled her towards the donkey, getting it out of the way with a slap to the rump, and they sat against the wall with the children. The peasant, now that he'd put the door planks back up, didn't lie down with his wife. Despite the summer heat he curled up next to a little blonde girl who grumbled in her sleep at his touch. María sucked her teeth in disgust.

'Get out of here,' she said later, when the boys from the window, dirty and in rags, tried to lie down near Milagros.

Before they decided where to lie, the farmer's wife extended her arm and snuffed out the candle by pinching the wick with her fingertips; the sudden darkness made Milagros better able to hear the murmur of the two older boys' complaints and stumbling.

Shortly after, the only sounds heard in the shack were the slow and deliberate breathing of the children and the donkey, occasional coughing, the peasant's snores and his wife's sighs as she tried to get comfortable, time and again, on the straw mattress amid the shadows visible in the moonlight that entered through the worn canvas on the window. All those sounds and images were unfamiliar to Milagros. What were they doing there, beneath the miserable roof of some *payos* who had only reluctantly taken them in? Their law forbade it; Grandfather would say: you shouldn't sleep with *payos*. Would María sleep? she wondered. As if she knew what was passing through the girl's head, the old woman searched out her hand. Milagros responded, grabbing it and squeezing it tightly. Then she sensed something more in those thin atrophied bones: María, plunged into the unknown just as she was, was also looking for solace. Fear? Old María couldn't be frightened! She had always, always been a bold, resolute woman. Everyone respected her! Nevertheless, the gaunt hand that jabbed her palm clearly showed the opposite.

Far now from the shots, the commotion of the settlement and the need to flee, surrounded by unfriendly strangers in a disgusting shack, in the darkness and gripping a hand that suddenly had turned old on her, the girl understood her true situation. Nobody would help them! The *payos* had always repudiated them, so now, when they were threatened with jail, it would be even worse. Nor would they find gypsies they could take shelter with; from what that man said, they'd all been arrested, and the few that had managed to escape would be in the same situation as they were. A tear, long and languid, ran down her cheek. Milagros felt it brushing against her; its slow sliding seemed to want to drown her further into vulnerability. She thought of her parents and of Cachita. She yearned for her mother's embrace, to be close to her, wherever she was, even in a jail. Her mother had always known what to do and she would have consoled her . . . Old María was already sleeping. Her hand was limp now, and her laboured breathing and snores told Milagros that she was alone in her desperation. Milagros gave in to sobs. She didn't want to think any more. She didn't want . . .

A blow to her thigh stopped even the tears in their tracks. Milagros remained stock-still while the possibility that it had been a rat ran through her head. She reacted when she felt fingers clawing at her inner thigh, over her clothes. *One of the sons!* she said to herself, violently releasing Old María's hand and searching in the darkness for the scoundrel's head. She found him on his knees by her side. The boy pressed and pinched her pubis hard, and when Milagros tried to scream he silenced her by covering her mouth with his other hand. His panting stopped abruptly when she pulled out some locks of his hair. His pain gave Milagros the chance to get free of the hand covering her mouth; she pounced on him, drove her teeth into the skin beneath one of his ears and scratched his face. She heard a repressed howl. She tasted blood just as he lifted her skirt and petticoats. She twisted, without letting go of her prey, at the stab of pain she felt when he reached her vulva. She had never been touched there by anyone . . . Then she bit him viciously until he left her privates alone because he had to use both hands to defend himself from her bites, which was when Milagros took the opportunity to push him away with her foot.

The sound that the peasant farmer's son made when he fell didn't seem to disturb anyone in the shack. Milagros was sweating and panting, but above all trembling with an uncontrollable shivering. She heard the boy moving and knew for certain that he would attack her again: he was like an animal in heat, blind.

'I have a knife!' she shouted as she tried to find the one the old woman used to cut plants in María's apron pockets. 'I'll kill you if you come near me!'

María woke up, startled by the shouts and agitation. Confused, she stammered out some unintelligible sounds. Milagros finally found the knife and bared it, with a trembling hand, to the rat who was once again at her side; the blade shone in the moonlight that entered the shack.

'I'll kill you!' she muttered in rage.

'What . . . what is going on?' Old María managed to ask.

'Fernando.' The voice came from the mother's bed. 'She will do it, she will kill you, she's a gypsy, a Vega, and if she doesn't, her grandfather surely will. But before he does, Melchor will castrate you and rip out your eyes. Leave the girl alone!'

With the knife trembling before his face, Milagros saw him back up like the animal he was: on all fours. Then her hand fell like a dead weight.

'What happened, girl?' insisted the old woman even though she was pretty sure of the answer.

She had never been touched there, and she never imagined that the first time would be a disgusting, pathetic *payo*. The dawn found the two women awake, just as they had been the rest of the night. The light gradually revealed the poverty and filth inside the shack, but Milagros paid no attention to that; the girl felt dirtier than her surroundings. Had that bastard stolen her virginity? If so, she could never marry a gypsy. That possibility had obsessed her through the long hours of the night. She went over and over in her mind a thousand times the confused scenes and a thousand times she scolded herself for not having done more to keep it from happening. But she had kicked, she remembered that; maybe it was in that moment . . . surely that had been when the boy was able to reach her virtue. At first she hesitated, but later she confided in María.

'How far did he get?' the old woman questioned her in the darkness, not hiding her concern.

María was one of the four women who always took part, for the Vega family, in checking brides' virginity. Milagros shrugged, her palms up, which the old woman couldn't see. What did she know? How far did he have to get? She only remembered the pain and terrible sensation of humiliation and helplessness. She felt unable to define it; it was as if in that very instant, just a mere second, everything and everyone had disappeared and she was facing her own disgraced body insulting her.

'I don't know,' she answered.

'Did he dig inside of you? For how long? How many fingers did he stick in?'

'I don't know!' she shouted. Milagros shrank back at the light that was starting to enter the shack.

'When it's light,' the healer whispered to her, 'check to see whether your petticoats are stained with blood, even if it's only a few drops.'

And what if they are? The girl trembled.

Gabriel, his wife and children began to get up. Milagros kept her head bowed and made sure to avoid eye contact with the two older boys. She did look at a small dark-skinned boy with blond hair who didn't dare to come over to her but who smiled at her with strangely white teeth. María's expression soured again when the little blonde girl the farmer had been embracing in his sleep showed tiny budding bare breasts when she stretched in front of her father. She had treated Josefa, that was the girl's name, a few months earlier for some tapeworms. The girl, flustered, hid from the healer when she realized she was there.

The peasant farmer, scratching his head, went over to the planks he used to close the door, followed by the tetherless donkey. María gestured towards the door with her chin.

'Go,' she said to Milagros, who got up and waited beside the animal.

'Where do you think you're going?' growled the farmer.

'I have to go out,' answered the girl.

'With those colourful clothes? You'd be recognized a mile away. Forget about it.'

Milagros sought the old woman's help.

'She has to go out,' María affirmed, already by the girl's side.

'Not a chance.'

'Cover yourself with this.'

Gabriel and the gypsies turned towards his wife. The woman, standing, her hair messy, dressed in a simple shirt beneath which you could see large hips and immense fallen breasts, tossed a blanket at Milagros that the girl caught on the fly and threw over her shoulders.

The peasant farmer swore under his breath and let them through the door when he had finished with the last plank. The first to go out was the donkey. Then Milagros, and as María was about to follow her, the two older boys tried to get ahead of her.

'Where do you think you're going?' enquired María.

'We need to go out, too,' answered one of them.

The old woman saw the wound beneath his ear and stationed herself in the doorway, small as she was, with her legs open and her penetrating gypsy gaze in her eyes.

'Nobody leaves here, is that understood?' Then she turned towards Milagros and indicated that she should head off towards the fields.

It took the young gypsy girl some time to check whether she had lost her virtue. She took so long that Old María, aware of the lust oozing from the boy who had attacked her during the night, understood how serious a predicament they were in: they had made it through the night but they would only get through this moment if the young man, who was shifting restlessly from foot to foot, didn't push her over and run out to force himself on Milagros again. Nobody would be able to stop him.

Suddenly she knew she was vulnerable, tremendously vulnerable; it wasn't like among her people, she wasn't respected here. A father who slept with his young daughter? He wouldn't do anything to stop it – he might even join in happily. She watched the wife: she was distractedly tearing off bits from a crust of bread, detached from it all. If they killed them, Melchor would never find out . . . If they survived this morning, what would happen the next day, and the next? How could she protect Milagros? The girl was beautiful; she emanated sensuality with every movement. They wouldn't even be able to walk a couple of leagues before men started pouncing on her, and she would only be able to respond with shouts and insults. That was the crude reality.

A noise from behind her back made her turn her head. Milagros's smile confirmed that she was still a virgin, or at least she thought so. Old María didn't let her come any closer.

'Let's go,' she ordered. 'The blanket is instead of the eggs you owe me,' she added to the peasant woman, who just shrugged and continued picking at the crust.

'Wait,' requested Milagros when the old woman was heading towards her. 'Did you see that blond boy with the brown skin?' María nodded as she closed her eyes. 'He seems smart. Call him over. I thought he could do something for us.'

Fray Joaquín observed the warm embrace that united Caridad and Milagros.

'Thank God you are all right!' exclaimed the priest when he reached the peripheries of the solitary chapel of the Virgen del Patrocinio, nestled in the fertile valley, on the outskirts of Triana, before Milagros and Caridad ran to each other.

'Leave God out of it!' exclaimed María then, which made the friar's face fall as he turned to her. 'The last time your reverence spoke of God you told me that he was going to come to my house and instead the King's soldiers showed up. What God is this who allows women, old people and innocent children to be arrested?'

Fray Joaquín stammered before opening his arms helplessly. From then on the friar and old woman remained silent, ignoring each other as Milagros showered questions on Caridad, who was barely able to respond.

The dark peasant boy from Camas ran his alert gaze over both couples, nervous at the healer's startling reaction and his anticipation of the silver bracelet that Milagros had promised him if he brought Fray Joaquín, from San Jacinto – the girl had repeated it several times – to the chapel of the Virgen del Patrocinio. Old María didn't like the clergy, she distrusted them all, the secular ones and the regular ones, the priests and the friars, but she gave in to Milagros's wishes.

'What about my mother? And my father?'

'Arrested,' answered Caridad. 'They took everybody, tied with a rope, escorted by soldiers. The men went one way, the women and children the other. Your mother asked me about you . . .'

Milagros stifled a sigh, imagining proud Ana Vega being treated like a criminal.

'Where are they?' she asked. 'What are they going to do with them?'

Caridad's round face turned towards the friar in search of help.

'Tell them what your God has in store for them,' muttered the healer.

'God has nothing to do with this, woman,' said Fray Joaquín, this time defending himself. He spoke in a low voice, however, without confronting the old gypsy. He knew that what he'd said wasn't true; there was a rumour that the confessor of King Ferdinand VI had approved the raid on the gypsies to calm the monarch's conscience: 'The King will be making a great gift to Our Lord God,' answered the Jesuit to the question posed, 'if he manages to wipe out those people.'

But the words caught in the friar's throat, with Milagros and Caridad listening, one afraid of knowing, the other afraid she knew.

'What is going to happen to our people?' pressed Old María, convinced that he would give her an answer.

And he did, the words tumbling out of him.

'The men and boys over seven years old will be sent to forced labour in the arsenals, the Sevillians to La Carraca, in Cádiz; the women and others will be locked up. They are planning to send them to Málaga.'

'For how long?' asked Milagros.

'For life,' stammered the friar, sure that his revelation would bring on a new outburst of tears. He hated to see Milagros cry, yet he also felt close to tears himself.

But, to his surprise, the girl gritted her teeth, moved away from Caridad and planted herself right in front of him. 'Where are they now? Have they taken them already?'

'The men are in the royal jail; the women and children in a shepherd's shed, in Triana.' They were both silent. The girl's sweet eyes were now irate, steady, penetrating, as if blaming the friar for her misfortune. 'What are you thinking, Milagros?' he enquired, besieged by guilt. 'It's impossible for them to escape. They are guarded over by the army. There isn't a chance.'

'And Grandfather? Does anyone know anything about my grandfather?'

Grandfather will know what to do, she thought. *He always . . .*

'No. I have no news of Melchor. None of the tobacco men have seen him.'

Milagros lowered her head. The boy from Camas approached her, anxious over the turn the situation was taking and about the bracelet he'd been promised. Fray Joaquín was about to push him aside, but the girl stopped him.

'Here,' she whispered after removing the bracelet.

The boy had come through. What did a bracelet matter now? she concluded when the boy ran off with his treasure without even saying goodbye.

The three women and the friar watched him go, each immersed in the whirlwind of worries, hatred, fears and even desires that hung over them.

'What are we going to do now?' asked Milagros when the boy disappeared among the fruit trees.

Caridad didn't answer, nor did Old María; they both kept their eyes on the distant horizon, where the boy must still be running. Fray Joaquín . . . Fray Joaquín had to jab the fingernails of one hand into the back of the other and swallow hard before speaking.

'Come with me,' he suggested.

He had thought it out. He had decided it as soon as the boy from Camas had come to him with the message from the girl. He had weighed it during the walk to the chapel and his steps had lightened and he'd smiled at the world as he convinced himself of that possibility, but when the moment arrived his arguments and desires sank under the weight of the surprise jolt he saw in Milagros's shoulders, who didn't even turn, and the shouts of the old woman, who pounced on him like a woman possessed.

'Wicked dog!' she barked into his face, on her tiptoes, still gesticulating wildly with her arms.

The young friar wasn't listening to her, he didn't see her; his attention remained fixed on Milagros's back, until she finally turned with confusion on her face.

'Yes,' insisted the friar, taking a step forward and away from the healer, who stopped shouting. 'Come with me. We will escape together . . . To the Indies if need be! I will take care of you now that—'

'Now that what?' interjected María from behind him. 'Now that her parents have been arrested? Now that there are no gypsies left?'

The old woman continued to curse him while Milagros's gaze met the friar's and she shook her head, upset. She knew that he liked her, she had always been aware that he was attracted to her, but he was a friar. And a *payo*. She went to stand by Caridad, who was watching the scene with her mouth agape, for support.

Then: 'My grandfather would kill you,' Milagros managed to say.

'He wouldn't find us,' the friar let slip.

He instantly understood his mistake. Milagros stood tall, her chin lifted and firm. Old María stopped growling. Even Caridad, waiting for her friend, turned her face towards him.

'It is impossible,' the girl declared.

Fray Joaquín sighed deeply. 'Flee, then,' he said, trying to feign a serenity and a composure he didn't feel. 'You can't stay here. The soldiers and constables of every kingdom are looking for gypsies that escaped arrest. They have declared pain of death on the spot, without trial, for those who don't turn themselves in.'

Two gypsies, Old María thought then, one a lovely, desirable young one, the other an old woman unable to remember when was the last time she had run like that little boy from Camas, if she had ever been able to. And with them, walking the roads, a Negro woman, so pitch-black she would attract attention from leagues away. Flee? She sketched a sad smile.

'First you want to run away with the girl and now you're trying to get us killed,' she spat out cynically.

Fray Joaquín looked at his hands and pursed his lips at the four small, long cuts that showed on the back of his right one. 'Would you rather turn the girl over to the soldiers?' he suggested, switching his gaze from the old woman to Milagros, who remained defiant, as if her mind had frozen at the possibility of never seeing her grandfather again.

A silence followed.

'Where should we flee to?' asked the old woman after a while.

'Portugal,' he responded without hesitation.

'They don't want gypsies there either.'

'But they're not arresting them,' alleged the friar.

'They just banish them to Brazil. Does that sound welcoming to you?' Old María regretted her words as she realized they didn't have many alternatives left. 'What do you say, Milagros?'

The girl shrugged her shoulders.

'We could go to Barrancos,' proposed the healer. 'If there is any place we can find Melchor or get news of him, it's there.'

Milagros started: she had heard that name from her grandfather's lips a thousand times. It was a nest of smugglers on the other side of the Portuguese border. Caridad turned towards the old healer with her eyes bright: finding Melchor!

'Barrancos,' Milagros confirmed.

'And you, *morena*?' asked María. 'You're not a gypsy, no one is after you, would you come with us?'

Caridad didn't hesitate for even a second. 'Yes,' she said emphatically. How could she not go in search of Melchor? And with Milagros, besides.

'Then we'll go to Barrancos,' decided the old woman.

As if trying to cheer each other up, María smiled and Milagros nodded her head. Caridad seemed euphoric. She looked at Milagros beside her, and draped an arm over her friend's shoulders.

'I will pray for you,' intervened Fray Joaquín.

'Do so if you desire,' replied Milagros before Old María had a chance to blow up at him. 'But if you truly wish to help me, keep an eye on what happens to my parents: where they are taken and what becomes of them. And if you see or hear of my grandfather, tell him that we will be waiting for him in Barrancos. We will also try to send that message through the smugglers; everyone knows Melchor Vega.'

'Yes,' the friar whispered then, focusing his attention on the wounds on the back of his hand. 'Everyone knows Melchor,' he added with a voice that trembled between regret and irritation.

Milagros slipped out from under Caridad's arm and went over to the friar; she was sorry to have hurt his feelings. 'Fray Joaquín . . . I . . .'

'Don't say anything,' he begged her. 'It's not important.'

'I'm sorry. It just could never be,' she declared anyway.

13

THEY HAD BEEN on the road for four days, rationing the water and salted pork that Fray Joaquín had given them before they left. Even Old María doubted whether the preacher could have been right about his gods and devils when, after they decided to flee to Portugal, they drew up their itinerary along with a downcast Fray Joaquín who, nonetheless, insisted on helping them as if it were a way to purge the mistake he had made.

'There are two main routes you should avoid,' he advised, 'the Ayamonte road, towards the south, and the Mérida one to the north. These have the most traffic. There is a third one that forks off the Ayamonte road near Trigueros to head to Lisbon through Paymogo, near the border. Search for that, the one that crosses the Andévalo, always heading west; go around the mountain range towards Valverde del Camino and then further west. There you'll have fewer possibilities of running into the constables or soldiers.'

'Why?' asked Milagros.

'You'll see. They say that when God created the earth, he was tired after the effort of making the Andalusian coasts and decided to rest, but so as not to interrupt creation he let the devil continue his work. And that was how the lands of the Andévalo were born.'

And indeed they did see.

'Why couldn't your friar's God have had just a little more energy, girl!' Old María complained yet again, dragging her feet – bare just like those of the other two – along the dry, barren paths beneath the August sun.

They avoided the roads and towns and walked without a single tree beneath which to take shelter, for the flocks of sheep and goats and the herds of pigs gathered where the holm-oak woods and cork oaks grew, and they were watched over by shepherds, and the women didn't want to run into anyone.

'Of all the luck! We had to get a lazy God!' muttered the old woman.

But except for those pastures, most of the fields that weren't near towns were fallow: large stretches of uncultivated land. Beyond Seville there were only a few occasions when they had spotted a labourer from a distance, who would always lean on his hoe, using his hand as a visor, wondering about those who walked by – but never came near.

They travelled in the early morning and at dusk, when the suffocating heat seemed to lessen. Four or five hours each stretch, which wasn't nearly enough time to cover the four or five leagues they'd set out to, but they had no way of knowing that. Walking through those barren fields, alone and without points of reference, they began to be somewhat discouraged: they didn't know where they were or how long it would be until they arrived; they only knew – this Fray Joaquín had told them – that they had to cross the Andévalo heading west until they reached the Guadiana River, whose course marked most of the border with Portugal.

They walked in single file; Milagros headed the march. At one point, when Caridad was trying to match her pace, she had ordered her: 'Take care of María,' pointing back with one of her thumbs.

Milagros didn't have a chance to regret the tone she used or notice the disappointment her friend was unable to hide. Her thoughts were too full of her parents, separated from each other, separated from her . . . she was afraid to even imagine where they were and what they were doing. And she cried. She picked out the paths with her eyes flooded in tears and she didn't want anyone to bother her in her pain. Forced labour for the men, Fray Joaquín had said. She didn't know what they did in the arsenal of La Carraca in Cádiz. What were they forcing her father to do? She remembered the last time he had forgiven her, like so many other times throughout her life! 'Until you get every gypsy in this settlement to kneel before your charms,' he had demanded. And she had danced in search of his approval, moving her body to the rhythm of the pride sparkling in her father's eyes. And her mother? Her throat tightened and her legs seemed to baulk at the mere thought of her, as if she was betraying her by fleeing. A thousand times she thought of going back, turning herself in, searching for her and throwing herself into her arms . . . but she didn't dare.

When the sun beat hard or when night fell, they searched for somewhere to take shelter. They ate salted pork, they drank a few sips of hot water and they smoked the cigars that Caridad still had in her bundle. Then, exhausted by the heat, the girl would sob in silence; the others respected her grief.

'Fray Joaquín must have been right: this land could only have been the work of the devil,' she commented with disgust at the end of that day as she pointed to a lone fig tree silhouetted against the sunset.

From behind, the old woman groaned. 'Girl, the devil has tricked us: he was reincarnated into the friar who set us off on his paths. May that damn priest rot in his own hell!'

The girl didn't respond; she had quickened her step. Caridad, behind her, hesitated and turned towards the healer: she was limping and hunched over, cursing under her breath at every step. She waited for her.

Old María, exhausted from the effort, slowly reached Caridad, stopping with an exaggerated groan and tilting her head to one side. She looked up at the worn straw hat Caridad wore.

'Morena, with that mat of hair you've got on your head, I don't know what you want with a hat.'

Caridad took it off and held the hat in front of her greyish dress of coarse burlap, along with her bundle.

'You are so dark!' exclaimed the healer. 'Were you sent by the devil, too?'

'No!' she quickly replied, with fear in her face.

A sad expression crossed the old woman's face at Caridad's denial: the morena was obviously innocent. 'Of course not,' she tried to reassure her. 'Help me.'

María went to offer her her forearm, but Caridad put her hat back on and, before the old woman could protest, she lifted her up in the air, held her in her arms like a little girl and started marching behind Milagros, who was substantially ahead of them by that point.

'Do you think the devil would carry you in his arms?' asked Caridad with a smile.

Old María nodded.

'It's not a litter in the style of the great Sevillian ladies,' commented the old woman once she'd recovered from Caridad's sudden lift. She had run an arm around the black woman's neck and even got comfortable. 'But it'll do. Thank you, *morena*, and as that deceitful friar would say, may God reward you.'

María kept talking and complaining about the state of her feet, her old age, the friar and the devil, the *payos* and that rough, fallow land until Caridad stopped suddenly several paces from the fig tree. María felt the tension in Caridad's arms.

'What . . . ?'

She was silent as she looked towards the tree: against the reddish light that was already falling on the fields, Milagros's figure was silhouetted in front of another, taller one, a man's, surely, who was grabbing her and shaking her.

'Put me down on the ground, *morena*, slowly,' she whispered as she searched in her apron pocket for the knife she used to cut plants. 'Have you ever fought?' she added, now standing with the knife in her hand.

'No,' answered Caridad. Had she fought? She thought of the times she had been forced to defend her smoke or her daily ration of cod gruel from the other slaves: simple quarrels among the hungry. 'No,' she reiterated, 'I haven't.'

'Well, now's the time for you to learn,' said the old woman, handing her the knife. 'I no longer have the strength or the youth for such things. Stab him in the eye if you have to, but don't let him touch the girl.'

Suddenly Caridad found herself with the weapon in her hand.

'Hurry up, demon Negress!' screamed the old woman,

gesticulating wildly at the man, who was already pulling the girl towards him.

Caridad stammered. Stab him in the eye? She had never . . . but Milagros needed her! She was about to take a step when María's scream alerted the girl to their presence. Then she freed herself from the man, lifted an arm and greeted them with a wave.

'Wait!' called the healer, seeing how calm the girl was. 'Maybe today is not the day you'll have to . . . prove your valour.' She dragged the last few words out.

He was a gypsy named Domingo Peña, an itinerant blacksmith from the Puerto de Santa María, one of the towns where many gypsies had been arrested, and he had spent a couple of weeks shoeing horses and fixing farm tools in the Andévalo region.

'Except for the big towns, of which there aren't many,' explained the gypsy, as they all sat beneath the fig tree's large leaves, 'the blacksmiths have disappeared, even though they are essential to the work in the fields,' he added as he pointed to his tools: a tiny anvil, an old bellows made of ram's skin, some tongs, a couple of hammers and some old horseshoes.

The healer still was watching him with some suspicion.

'What was that man doing to you?' she had accused Milagros in whispers as soon as she was close enough.

'He was hugging me!' the girl said in her defence. 'He has been in the Andévalo for some time and knew nothing about our raid. He was crying over the fate of his wife and children.'

'Even so, don't let men hug you. It's not necessary. Let them cry on your shoulder.'

Milagros accepted the reprimand and nodded, her head bowed.

Beneath the fig tree, Domingo questioned them about the gypsies' arrest. They were speaking in Caló, the gypsy tongue that Caridad had started to understand in the settlement. Yet what caught her attention was the desperate gesturing and the anguished expression on the face of the man; he was as gaunt as he was sinewy, with a smith's strong arms with long veins that swelled in the tension of the moment. Domingo had left behind three boys over seven, the age at which, according to what the women had just told him, they would be separated from their mother and destined to forced labour. 'Juan,' he enunciated in a thin voice. María and Milagros, cringing, let him speak. 'The youngest, a lively lad. He liked to the hit the iron scraps against the anvil and sometimes he would even softly sing something like a *martinete* to the rhythm marked by the hammer. Francisco, ten years old, introverted but intelligent, cautious, always aware of everything around him; and the oldest, Ambrosio, just a year older than his brother.' His voice cracked. The boy had fallen from a crag and his legs were deformed from the accident. Had Ambrosio also been separated from his mother and sent to forced labour in the arsenals? Neither the old woman nor the girl dared to respond, but Domingo insisted, obliviously repeating the question: Were they capable of that? And when he was answered by silence again he brought his hands to his face and broke out in sobs. He cried in front of the women without trying to hide his weakness. And he howled up at the already starry sky with screams of pain that split the warm air around them.

'I will turn myself in,' Domingo said at dawn. He didn't see himself capable of travelling through the towns to continue smithing in exchange for a meagre coin knowing that his children were suffering. He would search for them and he would turn himself in.

Caridad sensed in the gypsy's tone of voice and expression what he meant.

'I don't know if I should do it, too,' admitted Milagros.

Old María wasn't surprised by her confession: she'd had a feeling it was coming. Four days crying incessantly over her parents' arrest was too much for the girl. She had heard her at night, when Milagros thought they were sleeping; she had noticed the stifled sobs in the long hours of the day when they took shelter from the heat and she had observed, as she walked behind the girl, how her shoulders trembled and her body shook. And it wasn't the desperation and the implacable pain that comes from the death of a loved one, the old woman said to herself; suffering over this separation could be remedied: by turning oneself in.

'I can't stop thinking—' Milagros started to add before the blacksmith interrupted her.

'Don't do it, girl,' the gypsy urged her. 'I wouldn't want my children to turn themselves in. I'm sure your parents don't want it either. Keep your freedom and live; that's the best thing you can do for them.'

'Live?' Milagros opened her hand to take in the arid fields that were already threatening to burn their feet over the course of another day.

'Leave the Andévalo region and go down to the coast, towards the flat lands . . .'

'They'll arrest us!' objected the girl.

'What could we do there?' interjected the old woman with interest.

'You'll find gypsies there. Maybe the King arrested everyone who lived in towns and cities, but there are many more, those who walk the roads; they haven't found them. There are also many settled in towns where gypsies weren't allowed to reside, they must have all left those places. They'll be in the flat lands, I know it. It's a richer land than the Andévalo.'

'We are headed to Barrancos.'

The gypsy arched his eyebrows towards Milagros. 'Why?'

'We trust we'll be able to find my grandfather there.'

María was half listening. There were gypsies in the flat lands and Domingo knew where. It was what she had been wanting all those days on the road: to meet up with her people. Despite the decision they'd made in Triana, the old woman was wary of going to Barrancos. She had had four long days to think on it: Melchor might not show up or not for a long time, which would leave them just as alone to face the dangers that threatened them as they were now.

'You only trust? You're not sure?' the man asked, surprised. Then he looked Milagros up and down, shook his head and turned to the old woman. 'Barrancos is a town of smugglers. It's between ravines . . . totally isolated. Do you realize what you are getting your-selves into?' He accompanied his question with an expressive look towards Milagros and Caridad, who was hovering on the margins of the conversation. 'A young, desirable, beautiful gypsy girl . . . virgin, and a voluptuous Negress. You won't last two days. What am I saying? Not even two hours.'

For a few moments the four listened to what seemed to be the crackle of the dry land around them.

'He's right,' affirmed the old woman after a short while.

'What do you mean?' the girl snapped, seeing María's intentions. 'Grandfather—'

'Your grandfather is a gypsy,' the old woman interrupted. 'Melchor will seek out his own kind. If we spread the word among our people, at some point we will find him or he'll find us, but we shouldn't go to that town, girl.'

Stop hiding like a frightened woman. For months before the big raid, the jibe tormented Melchor's every step after he had sung his galley lament before the open chapel of the Virgin of Bonaire in Triana. With the silent condemnation from Uncle Basilio for the death of his grandson Dionisio and, above all, the look of scorn from his daughter Ana burned into his conscience, the gypsy headed to the Portuguese border; there he would run into El Gordo when the smuggler least expected it and then . . . Melchor spat. Then they would see who was a frightened woman! He would kill him like the dog he was and he'd cut off his head . . . his testicles and maybe a hand, anything he could offer publicly to Uncle Basilio in amends.

Along the way, he avoided inns and towns, except for one where he stopped only long enough to buy some food and tobacco, cursing his luck at having to pay for it, in a small shop where the King forced them to sell it for a tenth its price, as was the case in all those towns where it wasn't worthwhile setting up a tobacconist's shop. He slept under the stars for three nights before arriving at the capital of Aracena, nested among the foothills of the Sierra Morena. Melchor knew the town: he had been there on many occasions. About four leagues away lay Jabugo, the spot for loading contraband tobacco, and seven, the Portuguese border, with the towns of Barrancos and Serpa, centres of the illegal trade. Aracena, subject to the Count of Altamira, had some six thousand inhabitants spread out over the twenty-odd streets scattered beneath the remains of an imposing castle that dominated the city; four squares; the parish church of the Assumption, unfinished despite the people's efforts; some chapels, two convents and two monasteries.

The gypsy felt the cold of the mountains; the spring temperatures there weren't the same as in Triana and he was walking without his blue jacket, which had joined young Dionisio's belongings in the bonfire at his ill-fated funeral. Every Saturday they held a market, mostly for grain. Sellers travelled from Extremadura to sell them in that region where hardly any cereals grew. He would find some kind of a jacket, although he was unlikely to find anything like the one he had sacrificed for the boy ... or was it for himself? 'It's Thursday,' answered a townsperson. He would wait until Saturday. He had no intention of staying in the town; it was somewhat off the tobacco route. He headed towards a small tavern he knew and whose owner he felt was discreet. He didn't want his presence known and to reach the ears of El Gordo or his men.

'Melchor,' the owner greeted him without stopping his work.

'What Melchor?' he asked. The man just squinted his eyes for an instant. 'I haven't seen anyone named Melchor, have you?'

'No, not me either.'

'That's good. Is your back room free?'

'Yes.'

'Well, bring me some food and drink.'

The gypsy handed him a coin, enough to cover the expenses and his silence, and locked himself in the tiny room that the tavern keeper offered to his few guests. He smoked, he ate and he drank. He smoked again and drank until his memories and his guilt became blurry, incoherent stains. He tried to sleep but couldn't. He drank more.

The dawn slipping in through the room's only little window found him humiliated and frozen stiff, sitting on the floor, his back against the wall, at the foot of the rickety old bed. He grabbed the jug of wine beside him: empty. He tried to shout for more wine, but all that came out was a muffled rasping that scratched at his throat. He tried to swallow; his mouth was dry, so he got up as best he could and went out to the tavern, still closed to the public, where he got another jug of wine and returned to the little room. Standing, he endured a succession of heaves that overcame him after the first long, eager gulp. And while his stomach punished him, he let his back slide down the wall until he was back where he had woken up. After spending the days smoking and drinking, escaping his reality, without even trying the food the tavern keeper brought him, Saturday found him with one thought obsessing his intoxicated, revenge-fuelled mind: buying the best short jacket he could find in the Aracena market.

The Plaza Alta was filled with traders from Extremadura, on the other side of the mountains, who offered the wheat, barley and rye that wasn't grown in that region. Alongside them, people from neighbouring villages announced their wares. Melchor was stunned by the racket. Dirty and with bloodshot eyes, he walked past the town hall and realized he had no documentation that would allow him to be there, or in any other town; he hadn't thought to grab any of his identification papers. Then he forced his eyes, dry as they were, to look over to the other side of the square, in front of the town hall, towards the parish church of the Assumption, which was the same as ever, unfinished, with the beginnings of the pillars and the walls of the third and fourth gallery open to the air and at different heights, like jagged teeth surrounding the two and a half finished naves that were used for worship. It had been that way for more than a hundred years. How were they going to arrest him in a town where they weren't even able to finish their main church? With his hand over his eyes to protect himself from the sun, he looked around at the different stalls and stands and the people that moved among them. The breeze was chilly. He found the stall of a second-hand-clothes dealer and headed over to it: used items, dark and patched and many times mended by the shepherds who'd worn them. He rummaged through them without much conviction; anything blue, red or yellow, or with gold or silver filigree would have stood out in the pile.

'What are you looking for?' the trader asked him. He had already noticed that Melchor was a gypsy, as evidenced by the rings in his ears and his breeches trimmed in gold.

Melchor lifted his dark, lined face towards the second-hand-clothing dealer. 'A good short jacket in red or blue. Doesn't look like you have any.'

'In that case, move along,' urged the dealer with a contemptuous flick of his hand.

Melchor sighed. The disdain roused him from the hangover of two long days drinking harsh, strong wine. 'You should have what I want.' He said it in a low, deep voice, his gypsy eyes challenging the man, who gave in first and lowered his; he could shout or call the constable, but who could be sure there weren't more gypsies who would come for him later? They always travelled in groups!

'I . . . don't . . .' he stuttered.

'What is it you want so badly that you're threatening this good man?'

The question came from behind Melchor's back. A woman's voice. The gypsy remained still, trying to find some sign in the used-clothes dealer's face that would reveal who was behind him. There were many people slipping through the narrow aisles between the stalls. A single woman? Several people? The constable? The second-hand-clothing dealer didn't seem too relieved; it was probably a woman alone, but a bold one, thought Melchor before turning and answering.

'Respect. That is what I want.'

She was short and strong, with a sun-beaten face and white hair that stuck out of a headscarf. Melchor figured she was about fifty years old, the same age as her shabby clothes. From her right arm hung a basket filled with grain she had bought at the market.

'Don't overreact!' exclaimed the woman. 'Gyps— Men,' she corrected herself quickly, 'are so touchy lately. I'm sure Casimiro didn't want to offend you. These are difficult times. Isn't that right, Casimiro?'

'That's right,' answered the used-clothes dealer.

But Melchor ignored him. He liked the woman's insolence. And she had generous breasts, he thought, looking at them openly.

'And who are you to talk about respect?' she rebuked him for his brazenness. However, the smile on her lips didn't match her words.

'What is more respectful than admiring what God offers us?'

'God?' replied the woman looking towards her breasts. 'I'm the only one offering this, God has nothing to do with it. They're mine and I do what I want with them.'

Melchor let out a laugh. The second-hand-clothing dealer saw people pass without approaching his stall where the pair stood. He opened his hands to hurry the woman up, but she remained focused on the gypsy, who rubbed his chin and then replied, 'That's too bad. The priests say that God is extremely generous.'

Now she was the one who laughed. 'What are you getting at? We're just two ... loners, right?' Melchor nodded; the woman thought for a second and screwed up her face before looking the gypsy up and down. 'You and me together? Even God would be frightened.'

'Nicolasa, I'm begging you,' whined the dealer, urging her to leave his stall.

Melchor lifted an arm, ordering him to be quiet. 'Nicolasa,' he repeated as if he intended to remember that name. 'Well, if God is so easily frightened, let the devil accompany us.'

'Hush!' she protested, looking to either side to see if anyone had heard his proposal. Casimiro begged her to leave, again. 'How dare you place yourself in the devil's hands?' she whispered after giving in to the dealer's pleas and pulling the gypsy away from the stall, while the trader offered his wares in a shout, as if trying to make up for lost time.

'Woman, to be with you I'd go down to hell and drink a glass of wine with Lucifer himself.'

Nicolasa stopped short, amid the people, with a confused look. 'I've been courted many times—'

'I have no doubt about that,' Melchor interrupted.

'As a young girl, they promised me the moon . . .' she continued, 'then they only gave me a couple of suckling pigs, several children who abandoned me and a husband who died on me,' she complained. 'But nobody has ever promised to go down to hell for me.'

'We gypsies know it well.'

Nicolasa looked at him lewdly. 'Skinny as a stick,' she teased. 'Have you got anything besides arms and legs?'

Melchor tilted his head to one side. She imitated him. 'Keep in mind that the devil kicked me out of hell. That was after he saw what isn't arms and legs.' She pushed him with a giggle. 'It's true! Have you heard talk about Lucifer's knob? Well, it's nothing compared to . . .'

'Joker! We'll see about that!' exclaimed the woman, hanging from his arm.

14

ONCE THE GYPSIES had been rounded up, their troubles really began. They still trusted they would overcome them, as they had so many other times. On the morning of 16 August 1749, almost three hundred Sevillian gypsy men were led by the soldiers from the royal jail to the city's port. There, as people harassed and insulted them, they were boarded on to barges to be transported down the Guadalquivir to the arsenal of La Carraca, in Cádiz. Later that same day, more than five hundred women and young children set off in wagons, carts and caravans, guarded by the army, to Málaga's citadel, where the Marquis of Ensenada planned to have them imprisoned.

The same thing was happening all over Spain. Nearly twelve thousand gypsies, vile criminals according to the authorities, had been arrested in the terrible round-up of late July with a single objective: the men and boys older than seven were taken to La Carraca, if they were Sevillian. Those in the east were sent to Cartagena, and those in the kingdom of Galicia to El Ferrol; others were destined to the mines in Almadén and forced to extract the mercury used to treat the silver coming over from the Indies. The women and young children were taken to Málaga or Valencia, to the castles of Oliva and Gandía. They were considered even more dangerous than the men: *Be particularly careful* – said the June 1749 order – *to secure and apprehend the women, said diligence being highly advisable for achieving this ruling that is so very important for the peace of the kingdom.*

Those people were just part of the Spanish gypsy community, and furthermore they were the ones who were most assimilated with the *payos* and adopted their culture. Originally from India, the gypsies had arrived in Europe in the fourteenth century, some through the Caucasus and Russia, others through Greece, crossing the Balkans or even travelling along the African coast on the Mediterranean. They arrived in Spain in the late fourteenth century as groups of exotic nomads led by those they called counts or dukes of 'little Egypt' and proffered letters of presentation from the Pope and several kings and nobles stating that they were pilgrims. At first they were well received and the lords whose lands they travelled through treated them kindly and guaranteed their safety, but that situation didn't last long. It was the Catholic Kings who pronounced the first proclamation against those they called 'Egyptians': they were forced to leave the kingdom within sixty days unless they had a recognized trade or were in the service of the feudal lords. Floggings, cutting-off of ears, banishment and slavery were the punishments for those who disobeyed the royal decree. Throughout the sixteenth century they had to repeat the decrees; the clever gypsies didn't follow the royal orders, their desire for freedom and independence trumped any obstacle. Their determination to maintain their atavistic way of life led successive monarchs to pass numerous new laws trying to control them: they prohibited their language and their way of dressing, their nomadism and even simple travelling, their trade in animals, blacksmithing and business . . . All these laws and their consequent regulations, many of them contradictory, benefited the gypsies: the justices of the towns and places where they travelled or resided didn't know which to apply or whether they had to apply any. They also tried to tell them where they could live: the gypsies could only reside and be included in the census in certain towns within the kingdom, and that was the error that King Ferdinand VI and the Marquis of Ensenada made: the big round-up of July 1749 focused on the gypsies who followed the decrees, who resided in the places designated by the authorities and were conveniently registered in the census. The nomadic or migrating ones, those not in the census or who lived in unauthorized places, were exempt from the army's persecution.

On that 16 August 1749, Ana Vega grabbed tightly the hand of a young child who had got lost in the confusion. As dusk fell, after the men had headed on barges to La Carraca, the soldiers appeared with almost thirty wagons at the doors of the stockade where the women and children under seven had been locked up for two weeks. Complying with the decrees that forced towns and cities around the kingdom to provide the army with wagons and pack mules for the transport of the troops and their supplies, porters and mule drivers from Seville had put at the army's disposition several wagons. Eight of them were large four-wheeled caravans, some covered with tarpaulins and pulled by six mules; the rest were carts and two-wheeled wagons pulled by two or four mules. A crowd of curious onlookers gathered in the area. The military men tried to get the gypsies and their children to leave the stockade in an orderly fashion, but things got complicated quickly.

'One of them confronted the soldiers. 'Where are you taking us?'

'What are you going to do with us?' asked others.

'And our men?'

'My children are hungry!'

The soldiers didn't answer. People were gathered outside the stockade, a simple roof on pillars and open on the sides, and they insulted the women. Ana found herself getting squashed: the women were bunched up against each other.

'You won't get us out of here!'

'Justice! We've committed no crime!'

'And our men? What have you done with them?'

'And our children?'

Outside the shouting worsened. The soldiers consulted each other in glances, the corporals to the sergeants and the sergeants to the captain.

'To the wagons!' shouted the captain. 'Get them in the wagons!'

The six-year-old boy gripped Ana's thigh when the soldiers set upon the women with blows and the butts of their rifles. It was total chaos. Ana helped an old woman, who was on her knees on the ground, stand up.

'Whose boy is this?' she shouted repeatedly.

She watched as a group of soldiers pushed Rosario, María,

Dolores and some others of Milagros's friends out of the stockade; they tried to cover their young bodies as the shreds of clothes they still possessed after half a month locked up left them exposed: heaped up, without water, they had slept on top of a thousand layers of dried cattle excrement. A soldier grabbed Rosario by the shirt and violently pulled her out. Her shirt tore and was left in the soldier's hand, who looked at it incredulously and then burst out in laughter while the crowd whistled and applauded the fleeting glimpse of the girl's ample breasts.

Ana, blind with rage, went to pounce on the soldier; she had forgotten about the runny-nosed kid gripping her thigh and only managed to drag him along the ground. The soldier noticed her and made an authoritative gesture for her to come out of the stockade. There were few women left inside. She obeyed. The wagons, set up in a long line and guarded by the army to keep people from rushing at them, were already full to bursting. The colourful clothes the gypsy women wore looked dull even under the bright August sun; all of them had been stripped of their jewellery and beads; even the belts on their dresses had disappeared. Cries, sobs, screams, complaints and pleas came from the women and their little children. Ana's knees grew weak; what miserable future was in store for them?

'Whose is this . . . ?' she started to scream. But then she broke off and squeezed the little boy's hand; it was a wasted effort.

'Get into the wagon!' they shouted at her as they pushed her with a shotgun crossed against her back.

Get into the wagon? She turned slowly and found a fresh-faced young man with a cockeyed white wig. She looked him carefully up and down.

'Tobacco!' she shouted at him. 'I sell tobacco at a good price!' she added, miming searching inside her skirt. 'The best!'

The boy stammered something and shook his head naively.

'Tobacco!' Ana then howled towards the crowd, pretending to smoke a cigar.

Behind her, the gypsy women in the wagon stopped sobbing.

Then she smiled, as if the blood had started running through her veins again, when one of the women in the wagon joined her farce.

'Fortunes! I read palms! Would you like me to read yours, lad?'

From wagon to wagon, the gypsy women started to react.

'Alms for the poor!'

'Baskets! Would you like a basket, my lady?' one asked a huge matron who was watching the scene dumbstruck, as was the puny man who accompanied her. 'You can carry your husband in it!'

The crowd laughed.

Little by little, the women and children transformed their crying into laughter. Ana winked at a young soldier.

'We'll have a smoke together some other day,' she said to him before turning and helping the little boy into the last of the wagons. Then, when the captain ordered the start of the march, she got on as well.

Beside Ana, in the wagon, Basilia Monge offered the crowd imaginary sweet fritters. 'Bring me the pan and the dough,' she shouted at the soldiers on horseback who brought up the rear. 'I'll get the fat to fry them in off your sergeant's belly.'

Ana Vega ignored the soldiers' laughter and the sergeant's indignation and she knelt down to the height of the boy she'd been dragging along with her. 'What's your name, little one?' she asked him as she tried to clean, with saliva-dampened fingers, the dirty streaks that ran down his face from the tears that she hadn't even had the chance to acknowledge before then.

The caravan of gypsy children and women took almost a week to reach Málaga. The battered coach road that went south allowed them to be insulted and spat on by the authorities and the inhabitants of El Arahal, Puebla de Cazalla, Osuna, Álora and Cártama before reaching the famous city on the banks of the Mediterranean. The King had ordered that the expenses of the gypsies' food and transport be covered by the sale of their belongings, but there wasn't time to auction them. The local Chief Magistrates and their deputies refused to provide, on the account of a King who wasn't likely to pay them back, more than was strictly essential for keeping those women from dying in their jurisdictions and creating problems for them; so hunger started to take its toll on the gypsies, who had to look on helplessly as the soldiers stole their rations. They put aside the little that was left to feed their children.

On the first night, Ana searched the line of wagons for Francisco's mother – that was the boy's name – whom she ran into making the same search but in the opposite direction and asking at each wagon for her little one. For a moment she forgot how desperate her situation was as she received her son with outstretched arms. Still hugging him, she looked at Ana. 'Thank you . . .'

'Ana,' she introduced herself. 'Ana Vega.'

'Manuela Sánchez,' said the other.

'He's a good boy,' commented Ana, mussing Francisco's dirty hair. 'And he sings very well.'

Ana had kept him entertained with songs throughout the endless and uncomfortable wagon journey.

'Yes, just like his father.'

Manuela's smile disappeared. Ana knew she was thinking about her man. And José? She again felt the uneasiness that had hounded her during the days of imprisonment in the shepherd's stockade, surrounded by the constant complaints and laments of the gypsy women at being separated from their husbands. She . . . Well, tears didn't spring to her eyes when she thought of José. What had become of her life? Where was the love she once believed she felt for her husband? Only Milagros united them. She pursed her lips. At least the girl was free. That was her only comfort; the rest didn't matter much if the girl was still free. She straightened up. They had to fight! The King had taken her father from her when she was a child, and now another King was stealing her . . . her own freedom. She was unwilling to submit, to beg and plead and grovel before the *payos* and the priests and the friars as she had done with her mother when she was a girl. No! She wouldn't do it. Time . . . or death would resolve the situation.

'Show us how you sing, Francisco,' Ana asked the boy then, to Manuela's surprise. She began to clap her hands softly, her fingers extended and tense.

'Sing, boy,' his mother added sweetly.

The boy felt self-conscious and kept his eyes glued to the ground as his bare toes played with the sand, yet he began to hum the same songs they had used to fight off the tedium of the journey. Ana clapped harder.

'Come on, Francisco!' his mother encouraged him with a catch in her voice and tears in her eyes.

The gypsy women began to come over, but no one dared to interrupt the little boy, not even to cheer him on. There were no guitars or castanets, they didn't have even a measly tambourine; all that was heard was Ana's clapping and the boy's humming through his teeth. He hesitated as he looked up and met his mother's face, flooded with tears.

'Like your father, Son, sing like him,' she managed to request.

And Francisco broke out in song, a capella, with his high child-like timbre, lengthening the vowels until he had to stop to take a breath, just as his father used to do, just as when he used to sing with him. But there no one smiled, no one cheered, no one danced; the little boy found himself surrounded by downcast, weeping women who, in the faint light of the sunset, grabbed their children as if they were afraid they'd be taken from them. When one of those women fell to her knees with her hands covering her face, Francisco's voice gradually faded until it broke completely and he launched himself into his mother's arms.

'Very good,' she rewarded him, squeezing him to her.

Ana continued her handclapping.

'Bravo,' cheered someone in a weary whisper from among the group of gypsy women.

Almost no one moved. The little bit that Francisco had sung had transported them back to their homes, with their husbands, grand-parents, parents, uncles, cousins and children; many had thought they could hear the laughter of their older sons who'd been taken with the men.

Ana clapped harder.

'Sing!' she urged. 'Sing and dance for the soldiers of the King of Spain!'

'Gypsy, are you trying to mock us?'

The question surprised Ana, who turned and, in the light of

the bonfires, saw the face of a soldier peeking above the wagon.

'No . . .' she had started to respond when the soldier was hit hard, right in the forehead, by a rock.

Ana turned her head again, and in the half-light, a bit further back, she was able to make out La Trianera, who mocked her with her cynical smile before throwing a second rock. She didn't have time to react.

'They're attacking us!' one of the soldiers yelled.

Ana herself had to get down on her knees to avoid the rain of rocks that came flying, amid insults and shouts.

The soldiers sounded the alarm.

Manuela, kneeling beside Ana, screamed like a woman possessed, and even little Francisco was throwing rocks . . . Ana sought out the protection of the wagon when the soldiers on horseback came through and pushed the women, scattering some, sending others to the ground and trampling them. Shots into the air intimidated most of the women. Barely a few minutes had passed; the cloud of smoke from the shotgun fire was still floating in the air when the riot was already controlled.

Ana listened, with her heart clenched, to the moans of pain and the sobs, and she made out the shadows of children and women trying to get up from the ground and hobbling around looking for their family members. Just an isolated insult, which the soldiers were now laughing about, had brought on that punishment. She turned her head in search of La Trianera and saw her slip away with unusual agility. She was fleeing. Why . . . ?

The answer came from behind her back as a pair of strong arms gripped her.

'This is the one who started it, my captain,' she heard a soldier say as he shook her before presenting her to the officer who had approached on the back of a horse that still snorted loudly, nervous from the charge. 'I heard her mocking us and inciting the others to dance for the King. Then they threw rocks at us.'

'No . . .'

'Shut up, gypsy!' The captain's order merged with a blow to the head from the soldier grabbing her, as he tried to nip her excuses in the bud. 'Chain her up and take her to the first wagon.'

'Bastard!' she muttered as she spat at the horse's feet.

The soldier hit her again. Ana turned and launched on him with her teeth bared. Others came to his aid, as he did what he could to get her off him. Between them they managed to immobilize her: they grabbed her by the arms and legs as she howled and insulted them between flying gobs of spit. It took four men to drag her to the first wagon and her clothes were ruined in the struggle, leaving her legs and breasts exposed.

She made the rest of the trip to Málaga inside it, with bread and water, almost naked, with shackles on her wrists and ankles and a third chain joining them.

15

NICOLASA LIVED ON the outskirts of the town of Jabugo, just over eight leagues from Barrancos. After walking almost three hours during which they spoke little and exchanged many a lustful glance, Melchor nodded with satisfaction when she pointed to a lone hut on the top of a hill with a view of the surrounding hummocks: jumbled forests of oak and chestnut trees that came together with the scrubland of holm oaks. When Melchor saw the place, he thought it could offer him the privacy he sought while allowing him to keep an eye out for any sizeable party of smugglers heading towards the Portuguese border.

Along with two large dogs who rushed to greet Nicolasa, they climbed the hill to the hut. It was a small, circular stone construction, windowless, with a single low, narrow door, and a conical roof made of brushwood over a framework of logs. Inside you couldn't take more than four steps in a straight line.

'My husband was a pig herder . . .' Nicolasa started to say as she put down the grain she'd bought in Aracena on top of a stone bench beside the hearth.

Melchor didn't let her continue; he squeezed her hard from behind, wrapping his arms around her and reaching for her breasts. Nicolasa remained still and trembled at his touch; it had been a long time since she had had relations with a man – her husband's blunderbuss, always at the ready, convinced those who might think to try anything – and she had long ago stopped touching herself on the lonely nights: her crotch was dry, her imagination destitute, her spirit frustrated. Had she made a mistake by inviting him? She didn't have time to answer as the gypsy's hands were already running all over her. How many years had it been since she had taken care of her body? she berated herself. Then she heard passionate whispers, erratic from Melchor's accelerated breathing, and she was surprised to realize that the pace of her own breath matched that almost silent panting. Could it be true? He desired her! The gypsy wasn't faking it. He had stopped at her thighs, curved over her, squeezing and caressing them, sliding his hands to her pubis and then down her legs again. And as her doubts began to dissolve, Nicolasa gave in to forgotten sensations. The 'devil's knob', she smiled to herself as she rubbed her large buttocks against him. Finally, she turned and pushed him violently to the straw mattress on which she had squandered her nights in recent years.

'Call the devil, gypsy!' she almost shouted out when Melchor fell on to the mattress.

'What?'

'You're going to need his help.'

Nicolasa was humming as she worked in the pigsty, a small enclosure to the rear of the hut. She had four good breeding pigs and some piglets that she fed farm-bought acorns, plus herbs, wild bulbs and fruits. Like many people in Jabugo and the surrounding areas, she lived off those animals, off their ham and cured pork, which she made in a ramshackle salting room, opening or closing its windows to the mountain air as dictated by her years of experience.

As she worked, Melchor let the days slip by, sitting in a chair at the door to the hut, smoking and trying unsuccessfully to frighten off the two large woolly dogs that insisted on staying beside him, as if they wanted to thank him for the shift in mood he had brought on in their owner. The gypsy glanced at them with a frown. *It doesn't work on these animals*, he said to himself over and over, remembering the effects his furious looks had on people. He also growled at them, but the dogs wagged their tails. And when he was sure that Nicolasa couldn't see him, he gave them a kick, softly so they wouldn't yelp, but they just took it as a game. 'Damn beasts,' he muttered then, remembering how Nicolasa had punched him the first time he really tried to kick them hard.

'You won't see a single wolf anywhere around,' the woman explained afterwards. 'Those dogs protect me, me and my pigs. Be very careful about mistreating them.'

Melchor hardened his features. He had never been hit by a woman. He made as if to return the blow, but Nicolasa spoke first.

'I need them,' she added, sweetening her tone of voice, 'as much as I need you and your knob.' The woman brought her hand to the gypsy's crotch.

'Don't ever do that again,' he warned her.

'What?' enquired the woman in a syrupy voice, searching in his drawers.

'Hit me.'

'Gypsy,' she said just as sweetly, noting how Melchor's member began to respond to her caresses, 'if you mistreat my animals again, I'll kill you.' She gripped his testicles harder. 'It's simple: if you can't live with them, continue on your way.'

Sitting at the door to the hut, Melchor kicked at the air again, and one of the dogs responded by getting up on his hind legs and prancing about. He had no doubt that Nicolasa would make good on her threat. He liked that woman. She wasn't a gypsy, but she had the character of someone hardened by the solitude of the mountains . . . And, at night, she pleased him with a wild passion he never could have imagined when he saw her there in front of the used-clothing stall. He just missed one thing: Caridad's singing in the dark silence of the night. *That* morena, *she's a good woman.* Some nights he imagined her offering him her body the way Nicolasa did, demanding more and more, as he had wanted when he woke up holding her in the gypsy settlement. Except for those songs for which he had renounced enjoying Caridad's body, he couldn't ask for anything more. He had even come to an agreement with Nicolasa when she demanded he work.

'As long as the knob you've got between your legs keeps up its end of the bargain,' she said, standing in front of him with her hands on her hips, 'my body is free . . . but you have to earn the food.'

Melchor looked her up and down, displeased: short, with wide hips and shoulders, exuberant flesh and a dirty face that made her look friendly when she smiled. Nicolasa tolerated the inspection.

'I don't work, woman,' he spat out.

'Well, go hunt wolves. In Aracena they'll pay you two ducats for every one you kill.'

'If it's money you want . . .' Melchor searched beneath his sash until he found the bag that held what he'd stolen from El Gordo. 'Here,' he said, throwing a gold coin at her. She caught it in mid-air. 'Is that enough for you to stop pestering me?'

Nicolasa was slow to answer. She'd never had a gold coin before. She handled it and bit it to make sure it was real. 'It's enough,' she finally admitted.

Since then Melchor had been free to do what he pleased. Some days he spent sitting at the door to the hut, drinking the wine and smoking the tobacco she brought him from Jabugo. Nicolasa would often sit with him, after she finished with the pigs and her other chores. She sat on the ground – they only had one chair – and respected his silence, letting her gaze wander around a setting she had never imagined she would enjoy again.

Other days, when Nicolasa hadn't been to Jabugo in some time, Melchor went out and checked the mountains to see for himself if El Gordo was approaching. That was the only information he had given Nicolasa.

'Every time you go into town,' he told her, 'find out if anyone knows about any large group of smugglers. I'm not interested in the little runners who cross the border and load up in Jabugo.'

'Why?' she asked.

The gypsy didn't answer her.

And that was how they spent the rest of the spring and part of the summer. Melchor felt the days growing long. After the initial weeks of passion, there had since been times when Nicolasa had rejected him with a vehemence equal to that of her lust. The woman's ardour was replaced by affection, as if the relationship the gypsy considered temporary was for her permanent. So that was why, when the news of the gypsy round-up reached the town, Nicolasa decided to keep it to herself. Not only to protect him, but also because she was afraid, and rightly so, that the gypsy would leave in search of his family as soon as he found out.

Every time he went out on to the road, Nicolasa watched him worriedly, with a distress she didn't try to hide, and ordered one of her dogs to follow him, but Melchor didn't go near the town. The gypsy had come to accept the canine company, which warned him with low growls when there was a person or animal on the deserted mountain paths.

Nicolasa had given him an old army dress coat with epaulettes and gilding that still had some of their original yellow. Melchor smiled gratefully, touched by her childish nervousness when she handed it to him. 'Casimiro told me what you were looking for at his stall in the Aracena market,' she confessed, trying to hide her anxiety behind a forced smile. The two dogs witnessed the scene, tilting their heads from one side to the other. Melchor put on the jacket, which was huge on him and hung from his shoulders like a sack, and adopted an expression of approval, pulling on the lapels and looking at himself. She asked him to turn around so she could see him. That night it was Nicolasa who sought out his body.

But time continued to pass and Nicolasa shook her head every time she came back from Jabugo. Melchor, who knew the contraband routes, only came across a few miserable runners transporting merchandise from Portugal to Spain by foot, under cover of night. 'Where are you, Gordo?' he muttered whenever he went out. The dog, glued to his calf, let out a long howl that broke the silence and made its way through the trees; he had heard that new master mention the name El Gordo many times, with a hatred so bitter it could cut through stone. 'Where are you, you son of a bitch? You'll come. As sure as the devil exists, you'll come! And on that day . . .'

'I brought you cigars,' announced Nicolasa on her return from Jabugo, almost a week later, as she extended a small bundle of *papantes* tied with their characteristic red string: the medium-sized cigars made in the factory in Seville, considered among smokers to be the best.

She kept her eyes hidden, looking at the floor. Melchor furrowed his brow and grabbed the bundle, still seated at the door to the hut. Nicolasa was about to go inside when the gypsy asked her, 'You have nothing more to tell me?'

She stopped. 'No,' she answered.

That time she was unable to avoid his gaze. Melchor saw that her eyes were watery.

'Where are they?' he asked.

A shiny tear slid down Nicolasa's cheek. 'Near Encinasola.' She didn't dare to lie about that. Melchor had asked her to inform him if she found out anything, so she added with a shaky voice, 'Some of the men from Jabugo have gone to join them.'

'When are they expected in Encinasola?'

'One, two days at the most.'

Standing in front of him, her legs together, her hands intertwined over her belly, with her throat seized and tears now running freely down her face, Nicolasa saw the transformation of the man who had changed her life: the wrinkles that lined his face grew tense and the sparkle in his gypsy eyes, beneath their furrowed brows, seemed to sharpen as if it were a weapon. All the fantasies of a future that the woman had naively entertained faded as fast as Melchor got up from the chair and pulled on the tails of his yellow jacket, his gaze lost in the distance, all of him lost.

'Keep the dogs with you,' he said in a whisper that to Nicolasa sounded deafening. Then he searched in his sash and pulled out another gold coin. 'I never thought that the first one I gave you was enough,' he declared. He grabbed one of her hands, opened it, placed the coin in her palm and closed it again. 'Never trust a gypsy, woman,' he added before turning his back on her and beginning his descent down the hill.

Nicolasa refused to admit the end of her dreams. Instead, she focused her blurry gaze on the bundle of *papantes* with their red strings that Melchor had forgotten on the chair in front of the hut.

It depended where they decided to spend the night. There were barely two leagues between Encinasola and Barrancos, and Melchor knew that El Gordo – if it was his party – would do everything possible to get to Barrancos. Unlike Spain, in Portugal there was no government tobacco store. There the trade was leased out to the highest bidders, who, in turn, opened two types of establishment: those that sold to the Portuguese and those devoted to selling to Spanish smugglers. Melchor remembered the large building in Barrancos with warehouses for the smoking tobacco from Brazil, rooms, places for the smugglers to rest and many, well-appointed stables. Méndez, the owner, didn't charge for all those comforts he lavished on his customers, especially if they were large parties like those from Cuevas Bajas and the surrounding area, although he didn't charge the modest runners either, and sometimes he even financed their shady dealings, or gave them tobacco on credit.

Yes, El Gordo is going to try to reach Barrancos to fill up his belly with good food, get drunk and lie with women, well sheltered from those inept but always annoying royal patrols, concluded Melchor as he sat on a tree stump halfway between Encinasola and Barrancos. The two towns seemed to be having a distant face-off, both located on bluffs, with their castles, the one in Encinasola in the town itself and the one in Barrancos at a slight distance, rising high to overlook the valley that separated them: a valley that had little in common with the wild nature of Jabugo and its surrounding area.

It was past midday and the sun was beating down. Melchor had got far enough ahead of the smugglers and he'd been sitting on that uncomfortable stump since dawn, by the shore of the Múrtiga River, where he'd found a grove of trees that protected him from the sun. Sometimes he looked towards the town, even though he knew there was no need: their uproar would precede them. It wouldn't even take much noise, since the silence was so absolute that Melchor could hear his own breathing. A few country folk paraded past him on their way to their fields and labours. Melchor barely moved his head in reply to their frightened greetings in the local dialect. They already knew how close the smugglers were, and that gypsy with large hoops hanging from his ears and wearing a faded yellow jacket could only be one of them. Meanwhile, between fleeting glances towards Encinasola and evasive nods to the peasants, Melchor remembered Uncle Basilio, young Dionisio and Ana. His daughter had never blamed him for anything before, no matter what he had done! What would he do when El Gordo's party arrived? He tried not to worry; he'd decide that later. His blood was boiling. Nobody was ever going to say that Melchor Vega, of the Vega family, hid from anybody! They would kill him. Perhaps El Gordo wouldn't even let him challenge him: he would order one of his lieutenants to shoot him right there and then continue along his way with a smile on his lips, maybe a laugh. He would probably spit down on his corpse from way up on his horse, but Melchor didn't care.

A small group of women loaded down with baskets of bread and onions for El Gordo's men passed by him in silence, their heads downcast. He had lived too long, he thought, gazing at their backs. The gypsy gods – or maybe the priests' God – had given him a few years. He was living on borrowed time. He should have died in the galleys, like so many others, but he hadn't perished rowing in the King's service . . . He pursed his lips and looked at his hands, covered in dark spots that stood out even on his dark gypsy skin. He tried to get comfortable on the stump but all his muscles hurt, stiff from the hours of waiting; perhaps he was nothing more than an old man, like the one who had given up his bed in the settlement for a lousy coin. He felt an eerie itching in the scars left by the galley slave driver's whip on his back. He sighed and turned his head towards Encinasola.

'If I didn't die in service to the son-of-a-bitch King,' he said aloud to himself, addressing some place far beyond the town in front of him, 'what better way to do it now that I'm nothing more than a shell? This way I'll silence all those who would compare me to a woman.'

As he'd suspected, he heard them long before they were visible, on the road leaving Encinasola in the late afternoon. A long and chaotic column of men: some on horseback; most leading horses, mules and donkeys by their halters. Among them were many simple runners. Shouts, insults and laughter accompanied them, but the rejoicing in Melchor's eyes ceased as soon as he recognized El Gordo, flanked by his lieutenants, leading them. *Morena*, he then thought with a half-smile on his lips, *what a mess you've got me into*. The murmur of Caridad's mournful, monotone singing filled Melchor's mind, driving out all other sounds. The gypsy, with his eyes locked on the approaching column, widened his smile.

'The only thing I'm regretting is that I'm going to die without having tasted your body, *morena*,' he said out loud. 'I'm sure we would have made a good couple: an old galley slave and the blackest woman in the Spanish empire.'

El Gordo and his men soon reached him but were slower to recognize him because the sun was in their eyes. The column of men crowded together behind their captain when he and his lieutenants halted suddenly in their saddles.

Melchor and El Gordo challenged each other with their eyes. The lieutenants, after their initial surprise, looked at their surroundings – trees and thickets, stones and uneven ground – to see if it was an ambush. Melchor saw how uneasy they were. He hadn't thought about that possibility: they thought he wasn't alone.

'El Galeote . . .' The murmur ran through the rows of smugglers. 'El Galeote's here,' they whispered to each other.

'So you've come out of your hidey-hole?' asked El Gordo.

'I've come to kill you.'

A low sound rose through the smugglers until El Gordo let out a laugh that silenced them.

'You alone?'

Melchor didn't answer. He didn't even move.

'I could finish you off without even dismounting,' El Gordo threatened him.

The gypsy let a few seconds slip away. He hadn't done it. He hadn't shot him. El Gordo was hesitating; the others were, too.

'Just you and I, Gordo,' said Melchor after a pause. 'We have nothing against the others,' he added, pointing to the other two.

The use of the plural forced the lieutenants to look around the area again; the scamper of some animal running off, the whisper of the wind amid the foliage: the slightest noise attracted their attention, just as El Gordo's eye was drawn to the simple flutter of a little bird. There could be gypsies hiding, aiming their guns at him. He knew about the massive round-up but he also knew that many from the settlement had managed to escape, and that most of them were from the Vega family, who were loyal to the death when it came to their blood. All it would take was one of them aiming at his head right then! El Galeote couldn't have come alone to challenge an entire party of men, he wasn't that crazy. Where could they be? Among the branches of the trees? Lying behind some rock?

Melchor took advantage of that moment of indecision and got up from the stump. His muscles responded as if the risk, the proximity of the fight and its uncertain outcome had injected them with a strange vitality.

'You can run away, Gordo,' he shouted so that everyone would hear him. 'You can spur your horse on and maybe . . . maybe you'll get lucky. Do you want to try it, you disgusting sack of blubber?' he yelled again.

Only the brushing of the men's restless feet on the dirt road and the snort of a horse broke the silence that followed his insult.

'I came here to kill you, son of a bitch. You and I alone.' The gypsy pulled his knife out of his sash and opened it slowly, until the shining blade emerged from its bone handle. 'Nobody else has to get hurt. I came here to die!' howled Melchor with the open knife in his hand. 'But there will be consequences for many of you if I die any way other than hand-to-hand with your captain. Isn't that the best way to solve problems?'

Among the few murmurs of agreement behind him, El Gordo noticed that his two lieutenants weren't reining in their horses enough; they were now a significant distance away from him.

Melchor, standing firmly a few paces from his horse, the faded yellow of his jacket revived by the sun that shone behind his back, noticed it as well. 'Are you thinking about running away like a scared woman?' he challenged him.

If he tried that, he would lose the respect of his men and with it all possibility of leading a party ever again, and El Gordo knew it. He exhaled a long, weary snort, spat at the gypsy's feet and dismounted with difficulty.

He hadn't even touched the ground when the men broke out into cheers and started placing bets. The lieutenants moved to one side of the road. The others tried to place themselves in a circle around the contenders, but Melchor didn't allow it; he had to maintain the pretence of an ambush. If the men surrounded El Gordo . . . Melchor stepped back a few paces with his hand extended, indicating to the approaching crowd that they should stop.

'Gordo!' he shouted when the first few obeyed him. 'Before your men can surround us, someone will blow your head off! Do you understand? Everyone behind you, on the road . . . Now!'

The smuggler made an authoritative gesture to his lieutenants, who made sure the others stayed on the road. Many of them mounted the animals they had been leading by the halter, for a better view. Those in the last few rows shouted for those in front to sit down, and then, in a sort of crescent moon which extended beyond the road as their amphitheatre, they applauded and cheered on their captain when he opened up a large knife and pointed it at the gypsy. Some peasants and their women, on their way back from town, watched in amazement from a distance.

The two contenders sized each other up, moving in a circle, arms and knives extended, trying to keep the sun out of their eyes. El Gordo moved with surprising agility, observed Melchor. He shouldn't underestimate him. He wouldn't be the captain of a party of smugglers from Cuevas Bajas if he didn't know how to fight and defend his position day after day. These thoughts were running through his mind when El Gordo pounced on him and launched a stab at his liver, which Melchor avoided but not easily. He stumbled as he moved away from the attack.

'You're old, Galeote,' El Gordo said as Melchor tried to regain his balance and the shouts and applause from the crowd died down. 'Didn't you just compare me to a woman who wanted to run away? Have you fought with them so much that you've forgotten how real men do it?'

The smugglers' laughter at their captain's words infuriated the gypsy, but he knew he shouldn't get carried away with his rage. He frowned and continued moving around the other, testing him with his weapon.

'The last woman I fought with,' he lied as he prepared himself for the next attack, which was surely coming, 'was the whore I paid with your wife's medallion. Do you remember it, you sack of fat? I fucked her on your account, thinking about your wife and daughters!'

His answer, as Melchor expected, was quick in coming. El Gordo paid more attention to the tense silence of his men than to prudence and he launched his knife, cutting through the air. Melchor swerved, went around him and wounded him with a gash at chest height that turned his white shirt the colour of the red sash around his enormous belly.

I've got him! the gypsy said to himself when he saw how El Gordo turned, with his face flushed and blood flowing from his chest, stabbing at the air. Melchor dodged his blind attacks once, two, three times. He wounded him again, on his left thigh, and then he let out a guffaw that broke the silence the smugglers maintained.

'And your wife's pearls . . .' The gypsy jumped from one side to the other, confusing his enemy even further. He felt young and strangely agile. He dodged a new attack and jammed his knife into El Gordo's right armpit, forcing him to take the knife with his left hand. 'My granddaughter is flaunting them, you filthy dog!' shouted Melchor after moving several paces away from him.

'I'll kill her when I'm done with you,' answered the other, refusing to give up, 'but first I'll give her to my men to enjoy. Did you bring her with you?' he added, pointing with his knife past the road, towards the trees.

Melchor decided to finish him off, grabbed his weapon tightly and approached his opponent ready to deal the final blow.

'When we're done with her she'll wish she'd been arrested last month in Triana along with all the other gypsy riffraff . . .'

El Gordo didn't finish his sentence. The decisiveness with which Melchor approached him faded at his words. The smuggler sensed the confusion in the gypsy's face; his arms and legs were paralysed. He didn't know about it! He hadn't heard about the round-up! El Gordo took advantage of his opponent's hesitation, moved quickly and sunk the entire length of his knife into his belly.

Melchor, with surprise in his face, leaned forward, brought his free hand to his wound and stepped back a few paces.

'There are no gypsies!' screamed El Gordo excitedly amid

the cheers and applause of his people after his stab. 'He's alone!'

'He's all yours!' encouraged one of his lieutenants. 'Finish him off!'

The shouting was deafening.

Bloodied, with his right hand hanging by his side, the smuggler pounced on Melchor, who in his attempt to avoid the attack, tripped and fell to the ground, on to his back. The men, no longer afraid of an ambush, got up and started to run towards where El Gordo was standing above Melchor. The smuggler's cynical grin was back. Many of his men could see how the gypsy was curled up and grabbing his stomach with both hands, submissive; others, however, could only manage to make out the fleeting trace of two large dogs that appeared out of nowhere and sprang on the captain. One leapt on his thigh, where he was bleeding from the wound Melchor had given him; the other went straight for his neck when El Gordo fell from the first dog's attack.

Most of the men were frozen in place; some tried to approach the dogs, but stopped when the animals growled without releasing their prey. El Gordo was still close to Melchor. He was as motionless as the two huge dogs, bred to fight mountain wolves; both had their powerful jaws clenched just enough, as if they were waiting for the definitive order to sink their fangs into the smuggler's flesh.

'Shoot them!' suggested someone.

Without daring to speak, El Gordo managed to frantically gesture in the negative with one hand, from beneath the animal that was clamped on to his thigh.

'You could wound El Fajado!' one of his lieutenants objected at the same time. 'Nobody shoot, or even go near.'

'Bite,' Melchor struggled to mutter. The dogs didn't obey but they greeted his voice with a wagging of their tails that the gypsy couldn't see. 'Bite, goddamnit!' he managed to howl in a cry of pain.

'They won't do it.'

The smugglers turned towards Nicolasa, who had appeared on the edge of the road with her late husband's gun in her hands.

'They won't do it . . . unless I order them to.'

Her voice trembled as she spoke. The pain she had felt in her own stomach when she saw the smuggler sink his knife into Melchor's had now transformed into a tremendous knot. She had set the dogs on El Gordo as soon as she saw Melchor fall to the ground and she understood that his die was cast. Then she went out to the road, blind, determined to fight for the gypsy, but suddenly she found herself surrounded by rough, grim-faced men, all enormous compared to her.

'If it's the woman who has to give the order . . . let's kill her!' proposed one of the smugglers, making a move to leap on Nicolasa.

The shot thundered and the man went flying backwards, his face destroyed by the blunderbuss's pellets.

Nicolasa didn't dare to look at the others. She had shot the way she did when wolves came close to the shack: without thinking. She had never shot a man before, as much as she threatened it when anyone came close to her territory. The dogs' growling brought her back to reality. El Gordo was again frenetically beating his free hand against the road. She reloaded her weapon, trying to control the trembling in her hands, keeping one eye on the men who surrounded her.

'Nobody do a thing,' one of the lieutenants again ordered.

Nicolasa breathed hard as she tamped the barrel of the blunderbuss for the second and last time with the ramrod. Then she began to place the fine gunpowder in the weapon's flash pan. They were all watching her closely . . . her and the dogs. She cleared her throat.

'If anyone tries to hurt me . . .' She cleared her throat again; she was having trouble speaking. 'The dogs will come to my aid, but first they will finish off that wretch just as they do with wolves. They never leave an enemy alive.' She checked the gun, nodded and took it up again. Some of the men moved away and she felt strong. 'A single squeeze of that jaw and your captain will die,' she added, addressing the place where Melchor lay. Then she lifted her gaze towards one of the lieutenants, still on his horse, and found a face that seemed to encourage her. What was that she saw reflected in his eyes? Ambition! 'Or perhaps you'd like him to die?' she speculated in a lower voice, directly to the lieutenant. 'What are you going to do with a cowardly, obese captain who only has the use of one hand? I saw the fight. That wound in his armpit isn't going to heal.'

The lieutenant brought a hand to his chin, thought for a few seconds, grabbed his weapon tightly and nodded.

Nicolasa sketched a half-smile as she realized she was going to make it out of that sticky situation alive.

'What . . . ?' the second lieutenant tried to object when a sudden shot from the other silenced his complaints and took him off his horse with a bullet to the chest.

A murmur ran through the men, but none of them raised their voices: it was between the leaders, as they had seen many times before.

'You and you' – the woman addressed two nearby smugglers and then pointed to Melchor – 'load him up . . .' She gasped for breath when she saw the gypsy's hands, soaked in blood and tense against his stomach. 'Load him on a horse!' she managed to finish.

'Do it,' confirmed their new captain, pointing to El Gordo's horse.

Melchor couldn't keep himself in the saddle. They put him across it like a bundle, his head hanging down.

'You are going to die, Gordo,' the gypsy spat out before his face contorted in pain.

And while El Gordo beat on the ground again with his hand, Nicolasa grabbed the reins of the horse that carried Melchor and headed off into the trees with him.

No one dared to move for a long time. The two dogs remained on top of their prey, who now accompanied his weakened banging with moans. After a while a high-pitched whistle was heard from among the trees. Then one of the dogs pulled on his leg, as if trying to rip it off his torso, and the other sunk his teeth into El Gordo's neck. All the animal had to do was jerk its head violently a couple of times to know that its prey had perished. Unlike the wolves, who fight for their lives, the man had let himself be killed like a pig. Then the two dogs ran off in pursuit of their owner.

Before the animals reached Nicolasa, in the thicket, Melchor spoke. 'Did you know about the gypsies?'

She didn't answer.

'Let me die,' he whispered.

'Shut up,' said the woman. 'Don't strain yourself.'

'Let me die, woman, because if you manage to heal me, I will leave you.'

The dogs' arrival, with bloodied snouts, allowed Nicolasa to relax her throat, which had seized up when Melchor's life was threatened.

'Good boys,' she whispered to the animals as they ran through the horse's legs. 'You're lying, gypsy,' she then said.

16

MÁLAGA WAS A town of little more than thirty thousand in-habitants that formed part of the kingdom of Granada and had been established on the shores of the Mediterranean by the Phoenicians in the eighth century BC. After the passage of the Carthaginians, Romans, Visigoths and Muslims, the town of Málaga of the eighteenth century, busy demolishing its mag-nificent Nazarite walls, took the shape of a cross, with the Plaza Mayor in the centre and numerous large religious buildings along the arms.

Nevertheless, the former Phoenician city wasn't prepared to take in the arrested gypsy women. The round-up had taken place in late July, but the secrecy with which it had been carried out meant that the order that had designated that city as the repository for the gypsy women and their children didn't reach the authorities until 7 August, with no time to make any preparations. And to the despair of the city council, caravans of wagons loaded with women were arriving at the capital from Ronda, Antequera, Écija, El Puerto de Santa María, Granada, Seville . . .

La Alcazaba, the castle chosen by the Marquis of Ensenada as a prison, turned out to be dangerous because the army's gunpowder was stored there, something that the nobleman hadn't taken into account. So, the first women were locked up in the royal jail, but the constant influx meant that it was soon full. Then the city council requisitioned some houses on Ancha de la Merced Street, and they weren't enough either. And while their space calculations had been way off, their estimates for maintaining that huge number of people were even worse. The council presented a formal request to the marquis to stop sending women while he asked for the funds necessary to deal with those who had already arrived. The nobleman decreed that the new parties of gypsy women be diverted to Seville: 'Directly and safely,' he ordered.

In the end, on the outskirts of the city, outside the walls, the authorities requisitioned the houses on Arrebolado Street and closed off the exits, thereby creating a large jail into which they crammed more than a thousand ragged, hungry and sick gypsy women with their children under seven. Ana Vega, however, was locked up in the royal jail awaiting trial as the instigator of the riot on the way to the city.

And while the situation in Málaga was desperate, the same could be said of the arsenal in La Carraca. José Carmona, along with six hundred gypsies – five hundred men and a hundred boys – from various places, arrived in Cádiz in late August. But unlike Málaga, where the city council could requisition houses to lodge the unforeseen arrivals, the arsenal in La Carraca was nothing more than an enclosed military shipyard that was constantly guarded to keep the convicts from running away and to make sure the slaves carried out their forced labour. As in Cartagena, the gypsies didn't fit in La Carraca; however, while in the arsenal in Murcia they could put them into useless, disgusting old beached galleys, in the one in Cádiz they grouped them into courtyards and all kinds of outbuildings. The briefs the governor of the arsenal presented to the council, stressing the inadequacy of the facilities and the risk of mutiny, did him little good.

In that age of reason and civility, the response from the authorities was absolute: where before they had fitted so many convicts, they could now fit the gypsies. The governor was ordered to fire the hired labourers and replace them with that dangerous, lazy human mass; in that way they would obtain the results sought by the Bourbon monarchy, who wished to transform Spanish society. Until that point, the poor had endured their plight with pious resignation, their only relief being through alms. The Bourbons believed that work was honourable. These days, when Spaniards were starting to leave behind the age-old concept of honour that had kept them from devoting themselves to manual – and therefore base – labour, no one was allowed to be idle, least of all gypsies, who should be useful to the nation like the vagrants who were arrested throughout the kingdom and destined to forced labour.

Much against his will, the governor of La Carraca obeyed: he increased the security troops, installed stocks and gallows in the arsenal as deterrents for the gypsies; he fired the hired labourers and proceeded to replace them with the new arrivals. However, terrified of the possibility of rebellions, he refused to take off their shackles and chains.

The measures produced no results. The arsenal in La Carraca, the oldest of the Spanish shipyards, stood in the narrow channels and navigable tributaries that headed inland from the bay of Cádiz; it was a swampy area because of the sedimentation around an old carrack sunk in the region. The Marquis of Ensenada himself had decided to expand those shipyards by incorporating the island of León, which was also on a bed of mud.

José Carmona, like the other gypsies, was forced to work up to his hips in mud preparing the pilings of the docks and helping the pile-driving machines force the long, sturdy oak trunks into that unstable bottom. The gypsies struggled to move in the quagmire, and their chains made something that seemed impossible from the outset even harder. They were trying to extract as much mud as possible from the previous marked-off piling site, in order to drive in the pilings that would support a framework of logs to create the base of the construction. As the overseer shouted and whipped, José, like many others, struggled valiantly with sludge up to his stomach to move with a basket filled with mud. They could have faked that effort and loafed in the mire, but they all wanted to get away from the pile driver's dangerous drop hammer, which was hoisted again and again and then dropped heavily on the head of the pile. They had already witnessed one accident: the unsteady ground had made the pile twist from the impact of the large iron hammer and the two operators next to it had been seriously injured.

On other occasions, José worked in the cranes used to load and unload the heavy artillery from the ships. Four men had to turn the wheel with levers that pulled the rope that ran along the crane's wooden arm. The twenty-four calibre cannons could weigh up to two and a half tons! The guards whipped them at the slightest hesitation while the cannon were moved through the air from the boat to the dock.

And when he wasn't working in the mud or with the cranes, he had to work the bailing pumps or in the boats' rigging, always in chains – the governor kept the gypsies in shackles even when they were sent to the infirmary – and then spent his nights lying out in the open, trying to take shelter among the rotted timber that was piled up in front of one of the arsenal's warehouses. There José collapsed with exhaustion, but he had trouble falling asleep, like most of those who lay there amid the timber. On the esplanade that opened out in front of the warehouse, various stocks held those gypsies who had revolted. And how could they rest with their gypsy brothers forced to watch them with their heads locked in a stock?

'They're almost all from the settlement,' José heard one of the blacksmiths from the San Miguel alley say in an accusing tone one night. 'They and their rebellion are the reason we're all here.'

No one spoke out in agreement with him.

'I'd like to have their guts,' lamented another after a few seconds of silence when many of them exchanged glances with the punished men.

Guts? José held back a reply. Of course it had been them! And those others who wandered the roads and had escaped arrest. The Vegas. It had been people like the Vegas – Melchor, and even Ana – who were responsible for the fact that their ankles were bleeding right now beneath the fetters. José Carmona tried to adjust the irons so they did not chafe his wounded legs. *Damn them all!* He spat out at a stabbing pain.

The governor didn't yield about the chains, but, to his desperation, the gypsies didn't submit, neither the men nor the boys, because when they had sent the little ones to learn boat-repairing trades, the carpenters and caulkers outright refused to allow the gypsy boys into their guild.

Meanwhile, the uprisings and revolts kept happening at the arsenal. They were all repressed cruelly. None of the escape attempts were successful and the gypsies continued to be forced to work, even more than the Moorish slaves they shared their imprisonment with – because the Moors communicated with Algiers about the work conditions the Spaniards imposed on them and the Berber authorities reciprocated: the captive Spaniards in Barbary were treated equally as badly as the Moors in the Spanish arsenals. And Bourbon diplomacy endeavoured to find a middle ground that would satisfy the interests of both sides.

Unlike the Moorish slaves, the gypsies had no one they could turn to. Their only defence was their solidarity. In rags, almost naked, hungry and in chains, wounded, many of them sick, they prevailed over the initial shock of their arrest until their proud, haughty character reasserted itself: they didn't work for the King or for the *payos*, and there wasn't a whip in the world that could force them to.

17

IT WAS LATE October of 1749 and Old María felt the threat of winter travelling in the clouds as she rubbed her hands together. Her knotted fingers got tangled up in each other; they were starting to hurt. She and the others had stopped, when night had almost completely fallen, in a place that seemed remote and far enough from the road between Trigueros and Niebla, among the scarce bushes and pines characteristic of that region. Santiago Fernández had led them there. Santiago was the head of a family of almost two dozen members, and he knew the area intimately, as every patriarch of a group of nomads must.

María squeezed her fingers together to loosen them up. It was all perfectly planned, just like each time they stopped somewhere for the night: the men unharnessed and hobbled the horses, the kids ran here and there in search of dry branches to make a fire, and the women, towards whom the old lady headed, skilfully set up the tents that would be their shelter for the night, with fabric tied to stakes sunk into the ground, or simply to bushes and trees. That night, however, they all seemed to be in more of a rush than usual and they worked amid jokes and laughter.

'No, no! You stick to your herbs,' said Milagros when María tried to help her with some ropes. 'Cachita!' she then shouted, completely ignoring the old woman. 'Come over when you can, and pound this stake in deeper. We'd hate to have the devil sneeze tonight and blow our tent away.'

'Cachita, I need you first!' came from another woman.

María searched for her friend in the small clearing they had stopped in for the night. Cachita here, Cachita there. And she came and went. Once they'd got over their initial misgivings, the gypsy women had found the strong and always willing Caridad to be of invaluable help in all sorts of tasks.

The old woman remained beside Milagros.

'Move aside,' the girl scolded her again as she tried to move to the other side of what was already taking shape as a tent as irregular as the fabric they were using. It was flat and very low, just barely enough to provide shelter to the three women. 'Cachita!' Milagros shouted again. 'I asked first!'

María saw that Caridad had come to a halt among the unfinished tents and the kids piling up firewood and scraps.

'*Morena*,' said the other woman who had called her, 'if you don't help me I'll steal your precious red dress.'

Caridad swatted at the air and headed towards the woman who had threatened her. Milagros let out a laugh. *Everything's changed so much*, thought María when she heard the joyful sound of the girl's laughter. Domingo, the travelling blacksmith, had offered to accompany them down to the lowlands until they found Santiago and his people. The man didn't have to go too far out of his way to Puerto de Santa María, and he wasn't in any rush to turn himself in to the *payos*, he confessed in terrible anguish.

They had joined Santiago and his family two months ago, and they weren't the first. A Vega cousin, his wife and two-year-old child who had managed to escape the settlement had come before them, although they'd left behind a four-year-old girl who had slipped from her mother's arms in the frantic escape: María had heard, a thousand times, their sobbing and the excuses the young married couple gave each other as they tried to rid themselves of the guilt. Two boys from Jerez and a woman from Paterna completed the list of refugees in the Fernández tribe.

Throughout those weeks the old woman had witnessed a trans-formation in Milagros, although she still held back sobs on the nights when she didn't fall asleep as soon as her head hit the pillow. *Cry*, she would encourage her in silence, *never forget your loved ones*. All in all, the migration seemed to have changed the girl's character; her personality had bloomed, as if her life in the settlement had held her back. 'Blessed freedom,' muttered the old woman as she watched Milagros run, or sing and dance at nights around the fire in a camp like the one they were setting up. During the day, busy with typical gypsy bustling about, Milagros's face only clouded over when she failed to get news of the fate of the detained gypsies from the walkers she passed or the people in the towns, as if they didn't give those gypsy bastards a second thought. As for Melchor, Santiago had promised Milagros he'd do everything in his power to obtain news of him.

Life was rough for the gypsies. Selling the baskets and utensils that hung from the mules and horses; getting the day's food – buying it when they had some money or stealing it when they didn't; a fandango or a *zarabanda* in an inn or on a street corner for some coins; reading palms; trading with whatever they found along the roads, always on the lookout for Chief Magistrates and their deputies, justices and soldiers; buying favours; always ready to pick up their camp and flee at the drop of a hat . . . Where were they headed and for how long?

'You see that, girl? That is our route,' Santiago had told Milagros while he pointed to the horizon line at nothing in particular. 'For how long? What does it matter? The only important thing is the present moment.'

Only when she was alone beneath the tent, at night, surrounded by the sounds of the countryside, did Milagros recall her home. And looking at the uncertain future, she was unable to hold back her tears, even though during the day she tried to live the way Santiago had taught her to – which was also how, she realized, her grandfather lived.

That night they were at least a league from the town of Niebla, setting up their new camp amid laughter, joking and shouting. Milagros struggled to make the tent fabric as taut as possible so that the wind, the devil's sneeze, didn't lift it during the night. Old María looked over the scene, and Cachita ran from one side to the other helping everyone until a commotion among the men attracted her attention: two of them had grabbed a ram they'd stolen from the town of Trigueros, and Diego, one of Santiago's sons, headed towards it with an iron bar in his hand. The animal didn't even have time to bleat: an accurate and definitive blow to the head made him drop down dead.

'Women!' shouted Santiago as they all moved away from the ram's body as if they had done their part. 'We're hungry!'

Gazpacho with mutton roasted over the fire. Wine and stale bread. Fried blood. A piece of cheese that someone had kept hidden and decided to share. That was how the first part of the evening was spent, the gypsies eating their fill around the bonfire, their features fragmented by the flickering flames, until the strum of a guitar announced the start of the music.

Milagros shivered when she heard the first chords.

Several of the gypsies, old Santiago among them, looked at the girl, encouraging her; a couple of girls rushed to switch spots and sat on the floor next to her.

The guitar insisted. Milagros cleared her throat and then took several deep breaths. One of the girls who had run to her side began to clap boldly in time with the instrument.

And Milagros started with a long, deep wail, her face flushed, her voice cracked and her hands open in front of her, tensed, as if she were incapable of transmitting everything she wanted to with merely her voice.

That clearing surrounded by low thickets and pines was overtaken by their frenzy; the shadows of the men and women dancing in confused movements silhouetted against the fire, the guitars wailing, the clapping echoing against the trees and the songs scraping together feelings: all these made Caridad's heart clench.

'You did it, *morena*,' Old María, who was sitting beside her and guessed what was going through her head, whispered into her ear.

Caridad nodded in silence, her eyes fixed on Milagros, who contorted voluptuously in a frenetic dance; in some of those lustful movements she recognized what she'd been teaching her over those past months.

'Teach her to sing,' the healer had suggested as soon as they had joined Santiago's party, pointing with her chin at Milagros, who was walking with the group sadly, dragging her feet.

Caridad was surprised by the suggestion.

'Melchor liked how you sang and, what with the way she is, it would be good for her to learn.'

Caridad was absorbed for a few seconds in remembering Melchor, and those lovely nights they'd spent together . . . Where could he be now?

'What do you say?' insisted the old woman.

'About what?'

'Will you teach her?'

'I don't know how to teach,' objected Caridad. 'How . . . ?'

'Well, give it a try,' the healer said authoritatively, knowing by that point that Caridad only heeded orders.

As for Milagros, she just shrugged her shoulders at the idea of María's project, and from that day on, at every opportunity, the old healer dragged the two far from the group, in search of some isolated spot to sing and dance. The first few days the little girls in the group spied on them, but they soon started to join in.

'*Guineos, cumbés, zarambeques, zarabandas* and *chaconas*,' the gypsies explained to Caridad the first day, after Milagros danced one of them reluctantly, accompanied only by the awkward hand-clapping of a healer with atrophied fingers. They were the Negro dances and songs brought to Spain by slaves. The words of the songs were nothing like what they sang in Cuba, but Caridad was able to find in them the African dances she knew so well.

Caridad didn't hide her confusion from the gypsies, her arms at her sides.

'Come on!' María spurred her on. 'You move now!'

She hadn't danced in a long time; she missed the drums and the other slaves. Yet she ran her gaze around: they were in nature, under an open sky, surrounded by trees. It wasn't the lush Cuban country-side, with its banyan trees, kapoks and royal palms, where the gods and spirits lived, but . . . all nature was sacred. All thickets and grasses, even the smallest stalk, held some spirit. And if that was the case in

Cuba and the other islands, in all of Africa, in Brazil and in many other places, why would it be any different in Spain? A shiver ran up Caridad's spine when she understood that her gods were here, too. She turned around and she could feel them in the life and nature that surrounded her.

'Morena . . . !' Old María started to scold her impatiently, but Milagros hushed her by putting a hand softly on her forearm: she sensed the transformation that was happening to her friend.

Which one of these trees holds Oshún? wondered Caridad. She wanted to feel her inside again, could she mount her here? Dancing. She would do it. *But the countryside is sacred*, she said to herself, *you must go into the countryside with respect, like into a church.* She needed an offering. She turned towards the gypsies and stuck a hand into her bundle, at María's feet. As the other two women watched her attentively, she searched around inside. She had . . . There it was! The remainder of a cigar that one of the gypsies had given her. She headed off and, among some pine trees, she lifted her hand with the cigar in it.

'What is she going to do?' whispered María.

'I don't know.'

'Fool,' the healer whispered when she saw Caridad breaking up the cigar between her fingers and letting the tobacco fly away. 'That was the only cigar we had,' she complained.

'Shush.'

Then they saw her search among the trees, until she returned to them with four sticks in her hands. She handed two to Milagros. 'Listen,' she asked them.

And she hit the sticks against each other in the simplest rhythm she could remember: the one marked by the clave; three spaced-out taps and two close together, again and again. A couple of times, Milagros joined in. Caridad was already moving her feet when she offered the sticks to María, who took them and started hitting them against each other.

Then the former slave closed her eyes. It was her music, different from the gypsy music and the Spanish music, which had melody. The Negroes didn't look for melody: they sang and danced on just percussion. Caridad, little by little, was able to imagine that those simple clave beats were the boom of the batá drums. Then she searched for Oshún and danced for the Orisha of love among her gods, feeling them near, in the presence of two astonished gypsy women, their eyes wide at the frenetic and lewd movements of that black woman who seemed to be flying.

A couple of days later, with two little gypsy girls banging the claves together, Milagros began to imitate Caridad in her Negro dances.

It was harder to get the girl to sing.

'I don't know how,' lamented Milagros.

The three women were seated in a circle on the floor, beneath a pine tree, as the dusk tinged the fields and forests with melancholy.

'Show her,' the old woman ordered Caridad.

Caridad hesitated.

'How do you want me to do it?' Milagros said in her defence. 'All I have to do to learn her dances is pay attention and repeat what she does, but when I say I can't sing it's because I pay attention to those who do know how and, the more I pay attention, the more I know I don't know how.'

Silence overtook the three women. Finally, María opened her hands, as if giving in; she had already managed to distract the girl with the dancing. That was her goal.

'I don't know how to sing either,' Caridad added.

'Grandfather says you sing very well,' contradicted Milagros.

The other woman shrugged. 'All Negroes sing the same way. I don't know . . . it's our way of talking, of complaining about life. There, on the plantations, while we worked, they forced us to sing so we wouldn't have time to think.'

'Sing, *morena*,' the old woman asked again after a new silence.

Caridad remembered Melchor with nostalgia, closed her eyes and sang in Lucumí, with a deep, weary, monotone voice.

The gypsies listened in silence, shrinking increasingly inward, into themselves.

'Now you do it,' Old María begged Milagros when Caridad

ended her whispering. 'Do it, girl,' she insisted when the girl tried to object.

The old woman didn't want to talk to her about pain. She had to find it herself. What were the *deblas, martinetes* or galley laments but songs of anguish? Who would dare to deny that the gypsy people were as persecuted as the Negroes? Hadn't that girl suffered enough?

'Come with me,' Caridad encouraged her, standing in front of her and offering up her hands, inside which Milagros's hands took refuge.

Caridad began again and soon Milagros was humming the song hesitantly. She searched for help in her friend's small brown eyes but, despite the fact that she was staring right into them, they seemed lost somewhere far away, as if they were able to bypass anything that got in her way. She felt the touch of her hands: they weren't holding tight, yet she felt that hers were trapped. It was . . . it was as if Caridad had disappeared, converted into her own music, merged with those African gods who had stolen her. And she understood the grief she distilled through her voice.

That day ended with Milagros confused but with Caridad and Old María convinced that the girl would be able to pour her feelings out into the songs.

And so she did. The first time that Milagros tore at their emotions with a song, the group of gypsy kids who tagged along at their lessons broke out into applause.

Milagros was caught off guard and stopped singing.

'Go on, keep going until your mouth tastes of blood!' Old María spurred her on, scolding the kids with a harsh look, who scampered off behind the trees.

From that point on it was all easy. What up until then had been nothing more than upbeat ditties, sung with a misunderstood passion, became pure pain and heartbreak: for the imprisonment of her parents and her love for Pedro García; for her grandfather's disappearance; for Caridad's rape and Alejandro's death; for the constant fleeing amid the *payos'* gobs of spit; for the hunger and the cold; for the injustice of the rulers; for the past of her persecuted people and their uncertain future.

That night, camped on the outskirts of the town of Niebla,

Caridad and Old María, sitting beside each other around the fire, experienced conflicting feelings as they witnessed Milagros's new way of dancing, lascivious yet filled with joy, and the depth of emotion in her songs of gypsy hardship.

18

NIEBLA, THE TOWN that gave its name to the county then belonging to the House of Medina-Sidonia, had been an important Arab and medieval military enclave. It was surrounded by strong, high walls and defensive towers and it had an imposing castle with its tower keep. By the mid-eighteenth century, however, it had lost its original importance and its population had dropped to little more than a thousand inhabitants. Yet, it still maintained its tradition of three festivals a year: San Miguel's, the Feast of the Immaculate Conception, and All Saints' Day, all three devoted to the buying and selling of livestock, sackcloth and leather.

The festivals had followed the same path as the town and no one hesitated in describing them as 'fallen on hard times'. They were used mostly for supplying old animals for the nearby city of Seville. Santiago headed there with his group of gypsies. On the first of November, All Saints' Day, Diego and Milagros, along with a boy about eight years old – skinny and dirty but with mischievous black eyes – named Manolillo, and other members of the Fernández family, loaded down with baskets and pots as if they intended to sell them, reached the walls of the town, outside of which, on an esplanade, the fair was held. Hundreds of heads of livestock – cows and oxen, pigs, sheep and horses – were offered for sale amid the crowd's hustle and bustle. The old patriarch, Caridad, María, the smaller kids and the old women remained hidden on the roads.

Manolillo latched on to Milagros when they were stopped by the deputy magistrate accompanied by a constable: gypsies were not allowed to go to fairs, especially livestock fairs. As Diego complained and gestured, begging and pleading in the name of the Lord Our God, the Virgin Mary and all the saints, Milagros and the boy separated discreetly from the group so that neither the deputy nor the constable would notice the sacks they were carrying, which held four sleeping weasels that they had managed to hunt en route. Finally, Diego dropped a couple of coins into the warden's hand.

'I don't want any altercations,' the deputy warned them all after he had hidden the money.

As soon as they'd got past the Niebla authorities, Diego Fernández gestured the other gypsies to scatter throughout the fairgrounds; then he winked at Milagros and Manolillo: 'Let's go for it, kids,' he encouraged.

More than three hundred horses were crowded in precarious enclosures made of timber and thatch. Milagros and Manolillo headed towards them, feigning a calm they weren't feeling, among the merchants, buyers and the curious. Reaching the end of the pens, which met the town's outer walls, they looked around and slipped in amid the horses. Protected among them, Milagros handed her sack to the boy, pulled a flask filled with vinegar out from under her skirt and emptied it out in the sacks. Then she shook them vigorously and the weasels, who hadn't been fed since their capture, started to shriek and squirm. The boy and girl sought shelter near the walls and let them loose. The weasels jumped crazily, shrieking and biting their feet. The horses, in turn, neighed and reared up against each other. Confined, they kicked and bit each other. The stampede was fast in coming. The three hundred animals easily broke through their fragile enclosures and galloped frantically through the fair.

In the chaos the horses caused, Diego and his men managed to make off with four of them and drove them quickly to where the patriarch was waiting, on the outskirts of town. Milagros and Manolillo, who couldn't help laughing once the tension was broken, were already there.

'Get moving!' shouted Santiago, knowing that the deputy magistrate wouldn't hesitate even a second before blaming them.

They set off, loaded down with their cauldrons, baskets and

utensils, along with some clothes and blankets that the gypsies had managed to steal in the confusion. One of them proudly showed off some shoes with leather soles and silver buckles.

The patriarch ordered them to head towards Ayamonte.

'Yesterday I found out,' he explained, 'that a rich nobleman passed away, setting out in his will close to five thousand reals for his funeral: burial and masses for his soul – he was so sanctimonious, he paid for more than a thousand masses to be read! Plus mourning textiles and alms. They are calling all of the priests and chaplains from town as well as the friars and nuns from a couple of monasteries and convents – the halfwits are going to take his good money. There will be a lot of people . . .'

'And a lot of alms!' one of the women said.

They walked parallel to the coach road that led to Ayamonte, although before reaching San Juan del Puerto they had to take it to cross the Tinto River in a rowing boat; the boatman didn't even dare to argue over the price Santiago offered him to take them to the other shore. That same afternoon they managed to sell off two of the horses cheaply to one of the customers and the owner of an inn on the way; neither asked where they had come from. They also scrounged a few coins from the scarce patrons who had gathered at the inn after Milagros performed: she sang and danced suggestively, as Caridad had taught her, to incite the crowd's desire. It wasn't the deep, broken song the gypsies used to rekindle their passions and pain at night around the campfire, but even the old patriarch was surprised to find himself clapping and smiling when the girl started her cheery fandangos and *zarabandas*.

Despite the cold, Milagros's face, arms and upper breasts were beaded with sweat. Diego observed her as she walked among the tables where the patrons were drinking, and when she took a seat, with a long weary sigh, at the table where Caridad and María had been watching her performance, the innkeeper invited her to a glass of wine.

'Bravo, girl!' María congratulated her.

'Bravo,' added the innkeeper as he served her the wine. 'After the round-up,' he continued, his eyes distracted by the girl's cleavage, 'we were afraid we wouldn't be able to enjoy your dancing any more, but since the liberation . . .'

The chair went flying, the wine went flying and even the table went flying. 'What liberation?' shouted the girl, now standing in front of the innkeeper.

The man opened his hands before the circle of gypsies he suddenly found himself in the middle of. 'You don't know?' he enquired. 'Just that . . . they are freeing them.'

'Not even the King of Spain can take us on and win!' the gypsies yelled.

'Are you sure?' asked Santiago.

The innkeeper hesitated. Milagros waved her arms frantically in front of him.

'Are you sure?' she repeated.

'Am I sure . . . ? That's what they are saying,' he added, shrugging his shoulders.

'It's true.'

The gypsies turned towards the table where the confirmation had come from.

'They are letting them free.'

'How do you know?'

'I came from Seville. I saw them. I passed them on the pontoon bridge on their way to Triana.'

'How do you know they were gypsies?'

The man from Seville laughed sarcastically at the question. 'They were coming from Cádiz, from La Carraca; they looked a wreck. They were accompanied by a notary who carried their discharge papers and several justices who were escorting the group—'

'And the women in Málaga?' Milagros interrupted.

'I don't know anything about the women, but if they are freeing the men . . .'

Milagros turned towards Caridad. 'Let's go home, Cachita,' she whispered in a voice choked with emotion. 'Let's go home.'

The gypsies weren't profitable in the arsenals. They didn't work, complained the governors. Both in Cartagena and in Cádiz, they claimed, they had let go the expert staff to replace them with that ignorant workforce unwilling to make an effort, who weren't working enough to pay for the food they were eating. The gypsies, they insisted, were problematic and dangerous: they fought, argued and plotted escape. They didn't have enough troops to control them and they feared the desperation of men imprisoned for life, taken away from their women and children, would lead to a mutiny they would be unable to snuff out. The gypsy women were just as problematic as the men if not more so; they didn't even work, and their maintenance costs were a huge burden on the scarce resources of the municipalities they were being held in.

The briefs from those in charge at the arsenals and jails didn't take long to reach the hands of the Marquis of Ensenada.

But it wasn't only those officials who were complaining to the powerful minister of Ferdinand VI. The gypsies themselves were as well and from their places of imprisonment they presented complaints and petitions to the council. In addition there were some noblemen who protected them, clergy members and even whole town councils who saw how their communities had been left without workers to perform necessary tasks: blacksmiths, bakers and simple farmers. Even the city of Málaga, which wasn't one of the places legally authorized to take in gypsies, decided to support the petitions of gypsy smiths residing there and refuse to detain them.

The pleas and petitions piled up in the offices of the royal council. In little less than two months the inefficiency, danger and extremely high cost of the big round-up were exposed. Besides, they had arrested assimilated gypsies, who lived according to the laws of the kingdom, while many others, the undesirables, still camped freely around Spain. So, in late September of 1749, the Marquis of Ensenada backtracked and blamed the subordinates who had carried out the round-up: the King had never wanted to harm those gypsies who lived in accordance with the laws.

In October, the council passed the orders necessary to liberate those unjustly arrested: the Chief Magistrates in each place had to process secret files on the life and habits of each one of the detained gypsies indicating whether they conformed to the laws and proclamations of the kingdom; the files had to be accompanied by a report from the corresponding parish priest, also secret, in which most importantly it must be stated whether the gypsy was married by the Church.

Those who complied with all those requirements would be freed, returned to their places of origin and their seized assets restored, although they were expressly prohibited from leaving their towns without written authorization, and from ever attending fairs or visiting markets.

Those who didn't get past the secret reports would stay in prison or be sent to labour on public works or projects of interest to the King; those who fled would be immediately hanged.

They also gave specific orders for the gypsies who hadn't been rounded up: they gave them a span of thirty days to come forward, otherwise they would be deemed 'rebels, bandits, enemies of the public peace and notorious thieves'. They would all receive the death penalty.

The gypsy settlement had been destroyed. At night, Milagros, Old María and Caridad stopped at the start of the street that ran along the wall of the Carthusians' gardens against which the shacks leaned. None of them spoke. The hope and illusions that had grown over two days of walking, with each of them spurring the others on, promising a return to normality, vanished at the mere sight of the settlement. After the round-up and the seizure of assets, the looters had been quick to take what they wanted from even the most miserable shacks. They were missing roofs, even those made of brushwood, and some walls had collapsed owing to the pillaging of the items the soldiers hadn't taken: built-in iron bars, the few wooden frames, cupboards, hearths ... Even so, they could see that some shacks were still inhabited.

'There are no children,' noticed the old woman. Milagros and Caridad remained silent. 'They aren't gypsies, they are criminals and whores.'

As if they wanted to prove her right, a couple emerged from one of the nearby shacks: he was an old mulatto; she, who had come out to say goodbye to him, was a raggedy, dishevelled woman with her breasts bared.

Both groups exchanged glances.

'Let's go,' the other two women urged the healer. 'This is dangerous.'

Chased by a string of obscenities from the mulatto and the whore's peals of laughter, they rushed towards Triana.

Once they had left the Carthusian monastery far behind, the three women crossed the outskirts slowly. On their way to the church of Our Lady of O, their distress over seeing their humble homes turned into a refuge for outlaws began to transform into consternation: the Vegas would never have allowed it. Once they were freed they would have kicked all those undesirables out of there. Old María became ever more pessimistic; Milagros, who didn't dare to say aloud what they both were fearing, clung to the possibility that her family was waiting for her in the alley; her father was a Carmona and didn't live in the settlement, but if they hadn't freed the Vegas . . .

That cold November night – colder, it seemed to the three women, than any of the preceding nights – was upon them. The San Miguel alley greeted them with an inhospitable silence; only the faint gleam of some candles behind the windows, here and there, spoke of a human presence. Old María shook her head. Milagros escaped the group and ran towards her house. The well in the courtyard, always hidden behind twisted, rusty iron pieces, greeted her now like a lonely, proud beacon. The girl stared at it for a long time before going upstairs.

Shortly after, Caridad and María found her prostrate on the ground: she hadn't dared to take even a single step inside the house, as if the completely empty space had hit her and knocked her down right there. She trembled in rhythm to her sobs and covered her face tightly with her hands, terrified of facing the reality.

Caridad knelt by her side and whispered in her ear. 'Don't worry, it will all work itself out. You'll see how they'll come home soon.'

The hammering on the anvils woke them up; the sun had already risen. After María managed to calm Milagros down and stop her going to other homes that might be occupied by delinquents, they had all three slept together, with Milagros crying every so often, covered with a blanket and the tent fabric that Santiago had given them for their journey. The sunlight insulted them by revealing the place without a stick of furniture; only some broken plates on the dust-covered floor testified to the fact that a family had once lived there. Still lying down, the three women stopped to listen to the tapping of the hammers: it was nothing like the frenzy of the smiths they were used to; these were scarce and slow, one might even say weary.

Despite her knotted fingers, Old María surprised them with a hard, loud clap. 'We've got things to do!' she exclaimed, taking the initiative and getting up.

Caridad followed suit, but Milagros pulled up the tent fabric and covered her head.

'Didn't you hear, girl?' said the old woman. 'If they are working with iron, they must be gypsies. No *payo* would dare to do that here, in the alley. Get up.'

María indicated to Caridad with a look that she should uncover the girl. She took a few seconds to obey, but finally pulled off the fabric and the blanket to reveal Milagros in a foetal position.

'Your parents could be in another house,' continued the healer without much conviction. 'They could have their pick, and here' – she turned and waved her hand over the place – 'they don't even have a damn chair.'

Milagros sat up with her eyes bloodshot and her face flushed.

'And if they aren't,' continued María, 'we have to find out what is going on and how we can help them.'

The hammering came from the Carmona smithy, which they reached from the same courtyard all the apartments shared. Inside, the effect of the seizure of assets during the round-up was clear: the tools, the anvils and the forges, the cauldrons, the basins for tempering . . . all had disappeared. Two young men were on their knees, working on the forge; they hadn't spotted the women. Milagros noticed that they used a portable forge like the one carried by Domingo, the gypsy from Puerto de Santa María they had come across in the Andévalo: one of them was banging a horseshoe on a tiny anvil and the other used a ram-skin bellows to fan the incandescent coal that glimmered in a simple hole cut into the ground.

The girl recognized them, as did the old woman. They looked familiar to Caridad. They were Carmonas. Milagros's cousins. Their names were Doroteo and Ángel but they had changed. They worked the iron with bare torsos that showed their ribs and their cheekbones jutted out of their wasted faces. The women didn't need to announce their presence. Doroteo, the one who was hammering on the anvil, missed the mark, cursed, leapt up and dropped the hammer.

'It's impossible to work with this . . . !'

He stopped mid-sentence when he saw them. Ángel turned his head towards where his cousin was looking. María was about to say something, but Milagros beat her to it.

'What do you know about my parents?'

Ángel put down the bellows and stood up as well. 'Uncle didn't get out,' he answered. 'He's still being held at La Carraca.'

'How is he? Did you see him?'

The young man didn't want to answer.

'And my mother?' asked Milagros in a thin voice.

'We haven't seen her. She isn't around here.'

'But if they haven't freed Uncle, they won't have freed her either,' added the other.

Milagros felt herself fainting. She turned pale and her legs shook.

'Help her,' María ordered Caridad. 'And your parents,' she added after making sure that Caridad was holding up Milagros before she collapsed, 'are they free? Where are they?' she asked when they nodded.

'The elders,' responded Doroteo, 'are negotiating with Seville's chief justice officer to get back what they took from us. We've only been able to get this' – the young man looked indignantly at the small anvil – 'useless portable anvil. The King has ordered that they return our goods to us, but those who bought them don't want to do it without getting back the money they paid for them. We don't have any money, and neither the King nor the chief justice officer wants to contribute.'

'And the women?'

'All those who aren't at the town hall went to Seville at dawn, to beg for alms, work or to get food. We have nothing. We are the only Carmonas here. This thing' – he pointed at the anvil again half-heartedly, 'only lets two people work. In other workshops they have also managed to get some old forges like the ones the travelling smiths use, but we need more iron and coal . . . and to work out how to use them.'

At that moment, as if the other had reminded him, Ángel knelt down again and blew on the coal, which launched a cloud of smoke into his face. Then he picked up the horseshoe that Doroteo had been working on, now cold, and stuck it among the embers again.

'Why didn't they free them?' The question emerged from Milagros's still pale lips as she escaped Caridad's arms and walked haltingly towards her cousin. Doroteo didn't beat around the bush.

'Cousin, your parents aren't married according to the Catholic rites, you know. That is an essential requirement for release. It seems your mother never allowed it . . .' he said, clearly angry. 'I don't know of any Vega from the settlement who has been freed. Besides the church wedding, they ask for witnesses to declare that they didn't live like gypsies . . .'

'Don't repudiate our race, boy,' the healer warned him then.

Doroteo didn't dare answer; instead he extended his hands as silence overtook them.

'Doroteo,' interjected Ángel, breaking that silence. 'We're out of coal.'

The gypsy shook one hand in a gesture that demonstrated both his desire to work and his sense of helplessness at the situation; he turned his back on them, searched for the hammer and made as if to kneel beside the anvil.

'Do you know anything about Grandfather Vega, about Melchor?' asked the old woman.

'No,' he answered. 'I'm sorry,' he added to the women standing before him anxious for some good news.

They went out into the alley through the door to the workshop. Just as Doroteo had told them, intermittent, faint hammer blows echoed in other smithies; otherwise, the place was deserted.

'Let's go and see Fray Joaquín,' suggested Milagros.

'Girl!'

'Why not?' she insisted, walking towards the exit. 'He'll have forgotten all about that crazy idea.' She stopped; the old woman refused to follow her. 'María, he is a good man. He will help us. He did before . . .'

She looked to Caridad for help, but the Negress was absorbed in her own thoughts.

'We have nothing to lose by trying,' added Milagros.

It reassured her that people weren't surprised by her presence; they knew that the gypsies had returned. In San Jacinto, however, Milagros and Caridad's hopes were thwarted again. Fray Joaquín, the doorman informed them, was no longer in Triana. He didn't seem willing to give them much more information, but Milagros, who even went so far as to tug on his habit, got the brother to reluctantly tell them something more, mostly to get rid of them.

'He left Triana,' he told them. 'He suddenly went crazy,' he confessed with a wave of his hand. He thought for a few seconds and decided to explain further. 'I could see it coming,' he burst out, with obvious presumption. 'I told the prior on several occasions: that young man is going to bring us problems. The tobacco, his friendships, his comings and goings, his insolence and those sermons of his . . . so irreverent! So modern! He wanted to hang up his habit. The prior convinced him not to. I don't know why the prior liked that boy that much.' Then he lowered his voice. 'They say he knew Fray Joaquín's mother quite well; some say too well. Fray Joaquín claimed that there was nothing to keep him here any longer, in Triana! What about his community? And his vocation? And God? Nothing to keep him here . . .' he repeated with a snort. The brother interrupted his harangue, closed his eyes and shook his head, bewildered, angry at himself when he realized that he was explaining something to two gypsies and a Negro woman, who listened in astonishment.

'Where did he go?' enquired Milagros.

He didn't want to tell her. He refused to continue talking to them.

They returned downcast to the alley, Caridad bringing up the rear, her eyes on the ground.

'Oh, so he forgot about that crazy idea, huh?' said María sarcastically on the way.

'Maybe it wasn't about—' Milagros started to retort.

'Don't be naive, girl.'

They continued walking in silence. Except for the two coins that Santiago had given them, they had no money. They had no food either. They had no relatives! There wasn't a single Vega in Triana, according to Doroteo. The old healer couldn't hold back a sigh.

'Let's buy something to eat and go and collect some herbs,' she then announced.

'And where will we prepare them?' asked Milagros sarcastically. 'In your—?'

'Shut up!' interrupted the old woman. 'You have no right to question me. We're all having a hard time. When someone gets sick, they'll be running to find a place to prepare them.'

Milagros shrank back at the reprimand. They were walking towards La Cava, where the rubbish was piling up. María looked at the girl out of the corner of her eye and, when she heard her first sob, made a gesture to Caridad to console her, but Milagros quickened her step and left them behind, as if fleeing.

Caridad didn't catch Old María's look. Her thoughts were still on Melchor. *I'll find him in Triana,* she had repeated to herself over and over again during the journey back. She imagined meeting him again, singing for him again, his presence . . . his touch. If he had been arrested, as they had assumed so many times over the course of their flight, they would have freed him like the others, and if he hadn't been arrested, why wouldn't he come to Triana as soon as he found out that his people had been freed? But he wasn't there, and the young Carmona men assured them that no Vega had left the arsenal. A thousand times that very morning her stomach had turned at the image of those gaunt faces and scrawny torsos on Milagros's cousins. If that was the toll on young men, what would Melchor be like? She felt her eyes grow damp.

'Go with her,' asked the healer, pointing to Milagros.

Caridad tried to hide her face.

'You too?' asked María with desperation.

Caridad sniffled and tried to hold back her tears.

'Why are you crying, *morena*?'

Caridad didn't answer.

'If it were about Milagros you would already be with her. I doubt that José Carmona treated you kindly even once, and as for Ana Vega . . .' María stopped suddenly, tensed her old neck and looked at her in astonishment. 'Melchor?'

Caridad couldn't hold it back any longer and she burst into tears.

'Melchor!' exclaimed Old María incredulously as she shook her head. '*Morena!*' she finally called out. Caridad made an effort to look at her. 'Melchor is an old gypsy. A Vega. You'll see him again.' A smile flickered over Caridad's face. 'But now she is the one who needs you,' insisted the healer, turning to point at Milagros as she headed off.

'I'll see him again? Are you sure?' Caridad managed to babble.

'With other gypsies I wouldn't dare to predict, but with Melchor, yes: you will see him again.'

Caridad closed her eyes; satisfaction was already invading her features.

'Go on, run after her!' urged the old woman.

Caridad gave a start, rushed ahead, reached her friend and draped an arm over her shoulders.

No one consoled Fray Joaquín on the unpleasant morning when he left Triana, shortly before Milagros and her companions returned to the settlement. He carried in his bag the official letter issued by the Archbishop of Seville; Fray Pedro de Salce, the famous preacher, walked by his side singing litanies to the Virgin, as he always did when he went out on missions. He was accompanied in his prayers by two lay brothers who each led mules loaded down with chasubles, crosses, books, torches and other objects needed for their evangelizing.

Some of the walkers they passed fell to their knees and crossed themselves as Fray Pedro blessed them without stopping, others matched their rhythm to that of the religious men and prayed with them.

'Are you troubled?' asked the preacher between songs, aware of the other man's pain.

'I'm immensely happy for the opportunity to serve God that your eminence has given me,' lied Fray Joaquín.

The friar, satisfied, lifted his voice to sing the next prayer while Fray Joaquín's mind filled only with Milagros, again, as it had ever since the day following the round-up. He should have gone with her! Milagros was going to have to contend with the Andévalo until she reached Barrancos. Where was she now? He trembled as he thought of the fate the girl could have suffered at the hands of the soldiers or the bandits who populated those lawless lands. Bile rose in his throat at the mere image of Milagros at the mercy of a band of fiends.

A thousand biting and anxious questions like those had been haunting him since the very moment when he'd lost sight of Milagros's back. He wanted to run after her. He hesitated. He couldn't decide. He lost his chance. And on the way back to San Jacinto he sank into melancholy; he was distracted, uneasy, inconsolable. Milagros never left his mind and, finally, he decided to go to the prior and renounce his vows.

'Of course it makes sense for you to stay in the order!' the prior contradicted him after Fray Joaquín confessed his sins and doubts. 'It will pass. You aren't the first. Great men of the Church have made bigger mistakes than yours. You haven't had carnal contact with her. Time and Saint Dominic will help you, Joaquín.'

And in the end, the prior of San Jacinto found a solution for that lost soul. He'd watched him wander around the monastery and teach grammar lessons to the boys without the slightest conviction; Fray Joaquín needed something to galvanize him, thought the prior. The solution appeared when he heard about the death of Don Pedro de Salce's companion. Don Pedro was the most celebrated of all the missionaries who walked the lands of the kingdom of Seville preaching the gospel and Christian doctrine. The prior persuaded the archbishop to name Fray Joaquín, also renowned for his sermons, as his new companion. It wasn't difficult; nor did he have any trouble convincing the friar to accept his nomination.

Fray Pedro de Salce and Fray Joaquín were headed to Osuna. Before choosing a town, the expert priest studied those places that hadn't been evangelized in recent years; Osuna and its surrounding area met the requirement. It took them three days to reach it, and they were approaching when night had already fallen. The silence was absolute; the houses were sketched in silhouette against the moonlight. Fray Joaquín was tired, and Don Pedro stopped. The young man was about to ask him where they would sleep when he saw that the brothers who led the mules had begun to rummage around in the saddlebags.

'What—?' asked Fray Joaquín, surprised.

'You follow me,' interrupted the missionary while he put on a chasuble and urged him to do the same.

They put together a large cross that they carried in pieces and Fray Pedro ordered Fray Joaquín to carry it. The lay brothers lit two torches made of straw and tar that burned with a smoke blacker than the night and, then, the priest carrying a bell in his right hand, they walked towards the town.

'Arise, sinners!'

Fray Pedro's shout broke the calm as they reached the first door. Fray Joaquín was shocked by the harshness of a voice that during the three days of walking, almost without pause, had been whispering psalms, hymns, prayers and rosaries.

It didn't look as though they were going to rest. Fray Joaquín resigned himself as the preacher urged him to raise the cross.

'Lift it up, show it to everyone,' he added, ringing the bell. 'Neither the adulterer nor the young man with ugly sins will enter the kingdom of heaven!' he then shouted. 'Arise! Follow me to the church! Come to hear the word of the Lord!'

And in response to his loud invocations and calls, his threats of eternal hellfire and all manner of ills for those who didn't follow them, and the tolling bell in Don Pedro's hands, people came out of their homes or peeked from their balconies, dazed, surprised. The church bell, which the parish priest rushed to ring as soon as he heard the missionaries' call, accompanied those who had already joined the procession, barefoot, sketchily dressed or covered in blankets, while the friars, holding the cross high between the torches of the lay brothers, went through the streets of Osuna, which was plunged into absolute chaos.

'Neighbours of Osuna: I have called you, says the crucified one,' shouted Fray Pedro, pointing to the cross, 'and you haven't listened; you have scorned my advice and threats, but I too will laugh at you when death comes knocking!'

And the people knelt to cross themselves repeatedly and beg loudly for forgiveness. Fray Pedro gathered them all in the church, and there, after a fervent sermon and the reciting of several Hail Marys, he announced the start of a mission that would last sixteen days. Neither the parish priest nor the town council could oppose him, since he carried a letter from the archbishop. The priest ordered that before the mission began the church bells be rung for half an hour and that the authorities convene the inhabitants of neighbouring towns to leave their lands, trades and labours and, guided by their parish priests, heed the call of the Lord.

The idea was, as Fray Pedro explained to Fray Joaquín that very night, to surprise the folks in the middle of the night and frighten them so they would come to the missions. The rumours, which he himself and others like him had started from the pulpit over the years, spread among the humble, illiterate people: a shoemaker who had died for not following the missionaries; a woman who'd lost her son; a man whose harvest had failed while another who had complied and left his crops in God's hands saw how they prospered on his return.

'They are sinners! We must strike fear into them,' the priest lectured him after listening to Fray Joaquín's civilized sermons. 'Fear of sin and hell has to take hold of their souls.'

And Fray Pedro certainly achieved that! Those poor souls abandoned their tasks for more than two weeks to come to mass every day and listen to him preach. And those from the nearby towns travelled leagues to enter the chosen town in organized processions, singing the rosary behind their respective parish priests.

During those weeks mass was celebrated daily; there were

sermons in the churches, streets and plazas, and general processions, with hymns and prayers, attended by thousands of people that culminated in the perfectly ordered penitence procession: first the children from all the towns with their teachers, carrying a baby Jesus on a litter and followed by the men who didn't have a special outfit for the procession. Behind them came the penitents in white, purple or black robes, or a simple sheet covering those without robes, carrying crosses, crowns of thorns on their heads and ropes around their necks; they were followed by those who wrapped their bodies in brambles, walked on their knees or even dragged themselves along the ground; then those with their arms outstretched and tied to poles; those who practised 'dry flagellation', among which there were ten-year-old boys who whipped their backs with five-tailed ropes, and between those and before the clergy, the authorities, the women and the choir that brought up the rear of the procession, were the blood flagellants, who flayed their skin with lashes of their whips.

Prior to that exalted public manifestation of contrition, the missionaries had been preparing the faithful. Halfway through the mission, and with the people's guilt exacerbated by the preachings, the church bell called to flagellation at nights and the men came to the temple. Once they were all inside, the doors were closed and Fray Pedro went up to the pulpit.

'It's not enough that your hearts repent!' he warned loudly during the sermon. 'Your senses must also suffer, because if you leave the body without punishment, the temptations, the passions and the bad habits will bring you to sin again.'

When the priest finished his sermon, he rang a little bell to indicate that the candles and torches lighting the church would be put out, which was when Fray Joaquín, like the hundreds of men clustered in the temple, took off their clothes. 'We clergy must set an example,' Fray Pedro exhorted him. In the darkness, the bell rang out three times and the sound of the straps and whips on flesh mixed with the Miserere intoned by the choir in doleful ceremony.

In the dark, tremendously distressed by the sound of the whiplashes and the laments of the congregants, by the Miserere inciting them to repent, by the powerful voice of Fray Pedro above all those sounds calling them to atone for their sins, Fray Joaquín clenched his teeth; and when Milagros's luminous and phantasmagorical face appeared before him he punished his flesh harshly at the sight. But the more he flagellated himself, the more the girl smiled at him, and she would wink an eye and mock him by sticking out her tongue mischievously.

After leaving San Jacinto without getting any more information about Fray Joaquín's whereabouts, María was only able to keep Milagros collecting herbs for a couple of hours. November wasn't a good time of the year, although they found rosemary and dried elderberry; in any case, thought the healer, Mother Earth would offer them nothing good with one of them oozing hate, cursing and crying, since the girl had moved from grief and sobs to insulting the Church, Jesus Christ, the Virgin and all the saints, the King, the *payos* and the entire world. The old woman knew that that wasn't the way to approach nature. Illness originated with the demons or the gods, so one mustn't displease the earth spirits that gave them the remedies against the wishes of those superior beings.

She couldn't get Milagros to stop. The first couple of times that she remonstrated with her, the girl didn't even answer.

'What do I care about the spirits and their damn herbs!' Milagros spat the third time the old woman scolded her. 'Ask them to set my parents free!'

Caridad crossed herself three times at that affront to nature; María decided that they would return to Triana.

Once they were there, however, she wondered if it wouldn't have been better to stay in the fields, even at the risk of offending the spirits.

'Do I know anything about your mother?' repeated Anunciación, a Carmona whom they ran into in the courtyard they shared with their neighbours, near the well.

Before answering, the gypsy questioned María with her gaze. The old woman nodded: whatever that look meant, the girl would find it out sooner or later.

'They arrested her and jailed her for sedition when they reached Málaga. They shut the rest of us up in a neighbourhood on the outskirts that was closed off and guarded.' Anunciación grew quiet for a few seconds, lowered her eyes to the ground, sighed as if gathering strength and looked up again to face Milagros. 'I saw her a month before they freed me: they had whipped her . . . not too badly!' she added quickly when she saw Milagros's terrified expression. 'Twenty or twenty-five lashes from what I understand. And . . . they had shaved her head. They brought her to us and they put her in the stocks for four days.'

Milagros closed her eyes tightly, trying to banish the image of her mother in the stocks. María, however, saw it vividly: her back bleeding, kneeling on the ground, with her wrists and throat trapped between two large blocks of wood with holes, her head shaved and her hands hanging on either side.

An agonizing lament thundered through the building. Milagros brought both hands to her hair and, as she screamed, she pulled out two thick clumps. When she was about to do it again, as if wanting to share in her mother's shame, Anunciación came over and stopped her.

'Your mother is strong,' she said. 'No one made fun of her in the stocks. No one spat on her or hit her. We all . . .' Her voice choked. 'We all respected her.' Milagros opened her eyes. Anunciación let go of the girl's hands and brought a finger to her face to wipe away a tear that ran down her cheek. 'Ana didn't cry despite the fact that many did when they saw her. She always stayed strong, with her teeth clenched, when she was in the stocks. Not a single lament left her mouth!'

Milagros sniffled.

Anunciación kept quiet the fact that she had often been gagged.

'How many times did they punish her?' asked María, surprised.

'Quite a few,' admitted Anunciación. Then she pursed her lips in a half-smile and swiped at the air. 'I wouldn't be surprised if she was back in the stocks right now.' Even Caridad straightened when she heard those words. 'Yes, she confronts the soldiers if they go too far with any woman. She demands more and better food, and that the surgeon treat the sick women, and clothes that we needed and . . .

everything! She's not afraid of anyone; nothing intimidates her. That's why it's not surprising they punish her in the stocks.'

'Didn't she give you any message for the girl?' enquired María after a brief silence.

'I know she spoke with Rosario before they freed us.'

María nodded, remembering Rosario: the wife of Inocencio, the Carmona patriarch.

'Where is Rosario?'

'In Seville. She'll be back soon.'

Never forget that you are a Vega. That was the terse message that Rosario Carmona gave her at the entrance that led to El Conde's courtyard. Almost all the freed gypsies had already returned to the San Miguel alley and El Conde – Rafael García – had called together the council of elders.

'That's all?' asked Milagros, surprised.

'Yes,' answered the old Carmona woman. 'Think about it, girl,' she added before turning her back on her.

As the people went into the courtyard and passed her by, some even pushing her, Milagros remained still. She tried to understand her mother's words. What should she think? She already knew she was a Vega! *I love you*, is what she would have said to her, that's the first thing she would have conveyed. She would have liked . . .

'That includes it all,' she heard María say as the healer grabbed her by the forearm and pulled her away from the entrance.

'What?'

'Those words include everything your mother wanted to tell you: that you are a Vega. That you are a gypsy, from a family proud to be gypsies, and that you must be strong and brave like her. That you must live like a gypsy, and with the gypsies. That you must fight for your freedom. That you must respect the elders and follow their law. That—'

'Doesn't she love me?' interrupted Milagros. 'She didn't say that she loves me or misses me . . . not even that she wanted to be with me.'

'Does she need to tell you that, girl? Do you doubt it?'

Milagros turned her head towards Old María. Caridad was listening to the conversation in front of the other two, who were now up against the wall of El Conde's house as the parade of men and women continued.

'Why not? I know that I'm a Vega, what need was there for her to remind me of that?'

'Yes, girl, but that, that you are a Vega, you could forget some day. But you will take your mother's love to the grave with you, whether you want to or not.' The girl furrowed her brow pensively. María let a few seconds pass and then said, 'Let's go inside or we won't get a spot.'

They joined the gypsies who were already gathered in front of the door and were entering gradually, packed tightly together.

'You, no,' the old woman warned Caridad. 'Wait for us in the house.'

The courtyard was full; the stairs to the upper floors were filled; the corridors that led to the patio were full. Only the central circle, where the elders sat presided over by El Conde, had any breathing room. Three chairs stood empty as evidence of those who remained in the arsenals. When not a single person more could fit in, and some were even climbing up on bars and windows, Rafael García started the council.

'We calculate . . .' He lifted a hand and waited for silence. 'We calculate,' he then repeated, 'that close to half of the arrested gypsies have been freed.'

A murmur of disapproval greeted his words. El Conde waited again, running his gaze over those present, and came across Old María and Milagros, who had managed to slip into the front rows. He pointed to the girl; the finger that once flaunted an impressive gold ring was now bare, since the seizure of goods.

'What are you doing here?' His voice silenced the comments that could still be heard.

Many turned towards the women; others, from behind, asked what was going on, and some leaned over the corridor railings to be able to see better.

'You cannot be in the alley,' he added.

Milagros felt herself shrink and she moved even closer to the old healer.

'Rafael,' intervened María, 'you have to put aside your grudge. Consider the situation. The girl's parents are still imprisoned and—'

'And they'll stay that way!' interrupted El Conde. 'It's their fault we've been arrested and find ourselves in this situation, without goods, without tools, without food or money, without . . . without clothes even.' El Conde indicated his raggedy shirt, pulling on it with both hands. The murmurs rose again. 'And all because of the Vegas, and others like them, insisting on staying away from the *payos* and not following their laws.'

'The only law that we have to follow is gypsy law, our law!' screamed the healer, silencing everyone.

The gypsies debated among themselves: they felt that it should be that way, that it had always been that way. That was what they all wanted! But . . .

'Leave her be.' It was Rosario who spoke, addressing her husband, the Carmona patriarch seated to the left of El Conde. 'That law of which María Vega speaks is what led the girl's mother to defend us in Málaga. And she will continue to do so, I know it.' Then Rosario searched among those present for Josefa Vargas, Alejandro's mother, the young man who had lost his life because of Milagros's whim. 'What do you say?' she asked her after finding her in the crowd.

The woman spoke slowly, as if she was reliving the scene. 'Ana Vega fought with a soldier who dared to touch my daughter.' Milagros felt her little hairs stand on end and her throat seize up. 'It cost her a beating. I don't know whether the Garcías or the Vegas are right about what law we should follow, but leave her daughter alone.'

'So be it,' added the Vargas patriarch, Alejandro's great-grandfather.

Those words meant Milagros was pardoned; Rafael García could do nothing. Near him, La Trianera, his wife, shot him a critical look. *I warned you*, it seemed to be saying. El Conde stammered for a few seconds, but he took up the thread of the meeting again.

'I do know what laws we should follow. The gypsy law, of course, our law. Nobody will put the García blood in doubt!' he exclaimed, challenging María. 'But we also must follow the *payo* laws. There is no contradiction in that. Above all, we must go to their church, even if it is a trick. We thought about it,' he added, pointing to the other patriarchs, 'and we decided that we should create a brotherhood . . .'

'A brotherhood?' cried out an indignant voice.

'It was the priests who arrested us!' shouted another. 'They are the ones who free us or keep us imprisoned.'

María shook her head.

'Yes,' stated El Conde as if he were answering her directly. 'A brotherhood of penitents. The Gypsy Brotherhood. Just like the *payos* have, like the Brotherhood of All-Powerful Christ, of the Five Stigmata of Christ or of the Holy Christ of the Three Falls; like any of the many brotherhoods that participate in the Holy Week processions. It won't be easy, but we have to do it. And all this' – he pointed to María, who continued shaking her head – 'while still complying with our laws and without renouncing our own beliefs, do you understand, crone?'

'And how are we going to pay for all that?' asked a gypsy.

'The brotherhoods are very expensive,' warned another. 'You have to get a church to accept us, buy the statues, take care of them, provide the candles and lanterns, pay the priests . . . A procession can cost up to two thousand reals!'

'That's a different question,' answered El Conde. 'We are just talking about establishing it. It will take us time, years probably; besides which, the way things are now, they won't allow us to. And it's true, we don't have money. They aren't going to return the goods they seized from us.'

El Conde used his speech to deliver that bit of news. That was the real reason they were holding this council meeting: the gypsies wanted to be updated on the negotiations with Seville's chief justice officer. Now the audience started shouting.

Rafael García and the other patriarchs waited for everyone to calm down. 'Let's get everything back ourselves!' he said finally.

'No.' It was Inocencio, the head of the Carmonas, who objected. 'One of us stabbed a baker from Santo Domingo because he didn't give back two mules. He was imprisoned.'

'We aren't going to get anything,' lamented the Vargas patriarch.

Rafael García took the floor again. 'They threatened to lock us up in La Carraca again if we reclaim our goods.'

'But the King said . . . !'

'It's true. The King said they should give them back to us. And? Are you planning on going to get them?'

The gypsies started arguing among themselves again.

'This is the law you want us to comply with, Rafael García?' It was María's voice, again, that rose above the arguments.

El Conde waited, his eyes fixed on the old healer. 'Yes, crone,' he spat angrily after a moment. Milagros shrank with fear. 'That's the one. The same law they've been applying to us all our lives. Does it really surprise you that much? The *payos* have always done what they want. Whoever wants to can go to the Royal Court to reclaim their goods. I won't do it. You already heard what's happening in Málaga with the women. In La Carraca they treated us worse than the Moorish slaves. No, I won't claim them; I would rather work for the Sevillian blacksmiths. They need us. They will give us what we need. My grandchildren won't rot in that arsenal working their entire lives, like dogs, for the King and his damn Armada.'

Milagros followed Rafael García's hand, which he had pointed towards his family as he was speaking. Pedro! Pedro García! She hadn't noticed his presence among so many people. Just like his Carmona cousins, he was gaunt and frail, and yet . . . his entire being radiated strength and pride.

The girl didn't hear the rest of the council meeting. Selling out to the Sevillian blacksmiths? They'd bleed them dry. But what other choice did they have? Milagros couldn't take her eyes off Pedro García. His grandfather, Rafael, surprised everyone by announcing that he was negotiating with the *payos* so his family could start working as soon as possible. Finally, the young man realized he was being observed. How could he fail to notice that gaze, which seemed to want to reach out and touch him? He turned towards Milagros. 'What will happen to those who are still in custody?' someone asked. The elders couldn't hide their pessimism; they shook their lowered heads or pursed their lips as if unable to answer. 'We will insist that they are freed,' promised El Conde without conviction. Pedro García remained impassive on the other side of the courtyard, in front of Milagros, who was feeling slightly weak-kneed with anxiety. 'How are we going to insist on their freedom if we can't even claim what belongs to us?' cried out a fat gypsy woman. When the gypsies again started arguing, the girl thought she saw Pedro squint his eyes briefly before looking away from her. Did that mean something? Had he noticed her?

19

THEY HAD NO food. The two coins that Santiago had given them only lasted a few days. Nor could they go to the other gypsies: everybody was in the same boat; few had any money and they all had many mouths to feed in their own families. The negotiations with the Sevillian blacksmiths were dragging on and the smiths on the alley continued working with portable ram-skin bellows. The authorities, however, had decided to give the gypsies coal and they worked the iron, hammering it over simple rocks that eventually broke. They were also intimidated: the threat of being arrested and returned to Málaga or La Carraca dissuaded men and women from stealing – even though there were those who still risked it – and from the rest of their tricks. Women and children just joined the army of beggars that populated the streets of Seville to await the meagre coin the Church gave out. But to get any – except on one narrow street where the Carthusian monks managed to get them to line up for their alms and exit on the other end once they had received it – they had to fight not only with the truly lost causes, but also with the innumerable artisans, bricklayers and labourers who preferred living off the charity of the generous city to working up a sweat. Seville was swarming with the voluntarily unemployed. Even what had previously been the surest thing – stealing tobacco powder – had failed.

In the old tobacco factory in San Pedro, in front of the church of the same name, more than a thousand people worked in shifts night and day. It was the largest manufacturing industry in Seville and one of the most important in the entire kingdom: it had stables for two hundred horses who worked the mills, its own jail, chapel and all the spaces needed for working the tobacco: receiving and storing the bundles of leaf tobacco, opening up the bundles, stretching the tobacco out on the roofs, storing it again once it was dry, grinding it in the mills, sifting it in the sieves, washing, drying again and then giving it a very fine last grinding with stone mills. However, since the seventeenth century, the factory had been growing haphazardly with the increasing demand for tobacco, which in fifty years had multiplied six times for powder consumption and fifteen times for cigars. The factory had become a neighbourhood inside the city, composed of a confusing network of passageways and narrow streets and not very useful rooms, so they had begun to build a new factory outside the city walls, beside the port of Jerez, which would be able to deal with the surge in cigar demand, but the construction, begun twenty years ago, still hadn't got past the base. Meanwhile, the San Pedro factory had to continue operating and, above all, controlling the stealing and fraud. Their security procedures were routine but effective: when they left work, in a line, one by one, all the workers were thoroughly searched by the door guards looking for tobacco. In addition, the superintendent named one or more workers to choose some of those who had already been searched for a second control. If they found tobacco on a worker, the guard who hadn't found it in the first control would be fired and substituted by the one who had; and the well-paid guard jobs were highly sought after.

The recently freed gypsies were the ones most often subject to second searches. And one of them, thinking only of the need to feed his family, didn't take the necessary precautions when creating the sleeve of pig intestine that, jammed with tobacco powder, he had introduced into his anus. 'Take off your clothes. Come here. Sit down. Now stand. Your shoes, take them off too. Bend over so we can see your hair. Bend down more. Get on your knees.' And the compressed block of tobacco powder, with all that moving around, ended up tearing. The gypsy howled in pain, doubled over with his hands gripping his stomach. The guard was surprised to see powdered tobacco diarrhoea sliding down the thief's bare thighs. Some time later, the gypsy was condemned to death, which was the punishment from then on for all who stole tobacco using that method.

The news of the gypsy and the torn tobacco casing reached Milagros the same day she had decided to go to request the support of the Countess of Fuentevieja. On the way to the palace she remembered her grandfather, who had already foreseen that sooner or later that would happen. Where could he be? Was he even alive? She was surprised to find herself smiling at the memory of his warnings about the tobacco that came out of gypsy bums. She hadn't smiled since arriving in Triana – they'd had nothing but bad news and problems – but, since they had exchanged glances during the council of elders, she'd had hopes about Pedro García. She spied on the alley from the window of her house to see him and she had even managed to come up with a way to cross paths with him, but the young man didn't seem to notice her. Yet she didn't smile when she imagined herself strolling and chatting with him; she only . . . she only felt a worrying, empty feeling in her stomach that disappeared as soon as María's complaining woke her from her daydreaming.

As for her friends, many of them had come back from the prison in Málaga, all of them dirty and without their adornments. Their clothes were in rags and sadness had taken hold in their souls. None of them laughed any more. There was no place for parties in the alley or for gatherings or adventures with girlfriends; the only thing that interested them, just like their mothers, sisters, aunts and cousins, was the thought of getting their hands on some money.

The countess wouldn't see her. Old María waited out on the street. They had decided that Caridad would not go with them, and Milagros had trouble getting into the palace through the tradesman's entrance.

'The daughter of Ana Vega? Who is Ana Vega?' a servant girl asked her after looking her up and down peevishly.

After much insisting, someone finally recognized the gypsy who read their palms and they allowed her into a hall that led to the kitchens. The countess was getting dressed, they told her. Wait? It would take hours; the hairdresser hadn't even arrived!

They left her there, and Milagros was forced to dodge the constant flow of servants and suppliers coming in and out. Her stomach growled over the baskets filled with meats and vegetables, fruits and cakes that passed by her: they could eat for an entire year with all that food! Finally, someone must have complained about the barefoot, dirty little gypsy who was getting in the way, and then someone else must have remembered her and talked to a third, who in turn spoke to a butler so that, in the end, the count's secretary appeared, grim-faced, as if she were a minor irritation that had to be dealt with rapidly. It was a cutting, quick conversation, right there in the hall, although no one dared to pass by while it was going on. 'Their excellencies have already interceded on behalf of the gypsies,' affirmed the secretary after listening to Milagros nervously struggle to keep her tone of voice even. For whom? He didn't know, he would have to review the correspondence and he was unwilling to do so, but there had been several letters, he had prepared them himself, he commented indifferently. 'Two more? Your parents? Why? Friends of the countess?' he repeated incredulously.

'Friends . . . no,' rectified Milagros at the scornful sneer with which the man dressed head to toe in black received the idea. 'But they have been in her private drawing rooms, telling fortunes to her and the little counte . . . her excellency's daughter and her excellency's friends, and they danced for the count and countess and their guests in Triana, and they rewarded them with money—'

'And if they've enjoyed such privileges from their excellencies,' said the secretary, interrupting the girl's hurried speech, 'why weren't your parents freed along with the rest of the gypsies?'

Milagros hesitated and the man sensed her indecision. She remained silent and the man in black insisted again. *What does it matter?* thought the girl.

'They weren't married by the Church,' she said.

The secretary shook his head, failing to hide his smug expression at being able to get the lords out of the petitions of another detestable beggar.

'Girl, it's one thing interceding on behalf of gypsies who comply with the kingdom's laws, that . . . that is nothing more than a hobby for their excellencies.' He humiliated her by fluttering a hand affectedly. 'But they will never help those who violate the precepts of our Holy Church.'

When Old María saw her leaving the palace, enraged, squirming with the desire to cry or burst out in insults against the count and countess, she shook her head. 'What did you expect, girl?' she muttered under her breath before Milagros reached her.

They'd thought that the countess was their last chance. Some days earlier, Inocencio, the Carmona patriarch, had snorted when María and Milagros went to him in search of help.

'I think highly of your father,' he conceded. 'He's a good man, but there are still many imprisoned, including several members of our family. We are fighting to get them freed, but it is becoming more and more complicated. The authorities keep putting up obstacles. It seems . . . it seems as if they don't want to release anyone else. Despite the recommendations we made at the elders' council meeting, there are many gypsies all over Spain who are demanding the return of their goods, and that worries the King, who is unwilling to pay. It's as if he salved his conscience enough with the first releases. Please understand,' he then said, his voice growing cold, 'we have very little money to buy favours, and as head of the family I have to put all my efforts into those who have a real chance of getting out. Your father has very little.' He accompanied those final words with an even colder look at María, obviously implying that José's situation was a result of marrying a Vega who had refused to be wed by the Church.

Milagros, after protesting to the patriarch without success, swore that she would appeal to the chief justice officer of Seville, the archbishop and the King himself if it came to that. But Inocencio Carmona convinced them that her begging for José's freedom wasn't a good idea.

'Don't do it, girl,' he advised her, obviously sincere in his concern. 'You don't have documents. You aren't listed as one of those arrested in the July round-up, nor as imprisoned in Málaga and freed. For them you are a gypsy on the run. The new royal decree obliges you to present yourself before the authorities within thirty days. And, given your parents' circumstances . . . it wouldn't be surprising if they put you in jail. Are you baptized?'

Milagros didn't answer. She wasn't. She reflected for a few seconds. 'At least I would be with my mother,' she whispered then.

Neither María nor Inocencio doubted that the girl was seriously considering making the sacrifice.

'No.' Inocencio's words disappointed her. 'They haven't sent any women to Málaga for some time now. After the first expeditions, the others were jailed right here, in Seville. They would jail you far from her, Milagros: in Triana, among the other gypsies, you go unnoticed, you're just one more, and they'll think you are one of the freed, but if you make a mistake, if they catch you on the roads, they'll arrest you and you won't even be able to get them to take you to where your mother is.'

The Carmonas, her family, wouldn't defend them. The count and countess wouldn't either. Fray Joaquín had disappeared and their hands and feet were tied. If Grandfather were here ... what would Grandfather do? He would surely free his daughter, even if he had to burn down all of Málaga to do it.

Meanwhile they were hungry.

Milagros and Old María were returning from the Count of Fuentevieja's palace. They turned on to Cava Nueva at San Jacinto and went along it silently as they headed to the San Miguel alley. María was the first to see her: black as jet in the late autumn sun, with her straw hat pulled down to her eyebrows and the tails of her greyish shirt tucked up, rummaging through the garbage accumulated in the trench that had once been a defensive ditch for the area. The old woman stopped and Milagros followed her gaze just as a vagrant grabbed something out of Caridad's hands that she had just found. She didn't even threaten to fight over the treasure; she hung her head, submissive.

Then Milagros allowed the tears she hadn't cried as she left the palace come rushing to her eyes.

'*Morena!*' Old María tried to call Caridad but her voice was choked. Milagros turned towards her in surprise, her eyes flooded. The old woman tried to wave it off, cleared her throat a few times and shouted again, this time in a strong voice, '*Morena, get out of there before they mistake you for a black mule and eat you!*'

Hearing María's voice, Caridad, in the ditch, lifted her head and looked at them from beneath the brim of her hat. Sunk in the garbage up to her calves, she smiled sadly.

They sold the little they had – coloured ribbons, bracelets, necklaces and pendants – for a pittance, but that wasn't the solution, and Milagros knew it. If they had at least had the pearl necklace and gold medallion that Melchor had given them . . . But those jewels had been left in the settlement, for the soldiers to steal. Surely they hadn't been inventoried but just ended up in one of their bags. The days passed in that house without furnishings or even basic essentials, just the bedspread, Caridad's threadbare blanket and the tent cloth spread out for sleeping. Caridad would glance mournfully at the bundle that rested in one corner. Inside it were her red clothes and the lodestone that Melchor had given her, the only thing she had ever owned in her life and she was loath to sell it.

Hunger continued to drive them on. Their earnings from their last sale of a beaded necklace and a little silver bracelet had been used not for food but for a dark, mended skirt for Milagros. Only Caridad's old long shirt from when she was a slave seemed to withstand the passage of time; the gypsies' clothes frayed and tore. María decided that the girl couldn't go around showing her thighs through her ruined skirt and petticoats, and her breasts seemed about to burst out of a shirt that just a few months earlier had seemed loose. Her torso could be covered with the old woman's large tasselled scarf, but her legs, the focus of so much gypsy desire, no. She needed a skirt, even at the risk of going hungry.

At least, the old woman tried to console herself, they weren't being charged rent. No one had ever tried to collect rent for those homes in the San Miguel alley. And that wasn't because of their race: it was just that no one knew whom they really belonged to. This was a situation that was repeated throughout Seville, where neglect by the proprietors, most of them institutions – from charities to schools – had led to their true ownership being forgotten over time.

Nevertheless, as the days passed they ran out of bread. Milagros didn't know how to beg, and María wouldn't have allowed her to.

Caridad didn't know either, but if she had she would have done so, rather than keep going to La Cava to sift through the rubbish. The healer, who was only called in to ply her trade for extremely serious cases, found herself unable to demand payment when it was clear the gypsies were penniless.

Finally, the old woman was forced to accept the suggestion Milagros had made some time back, remembering the coins that she'd occasionally earned with the Fernández family.

'You will sing,' she announced to her one morning, after waking up and finding they had nothing for breakfast.

Milagros nodded with a couple of joyful claps in the air, as if she was already getting ready. It had been some time since she'd sung. Guitars were no longer heard in the alley for the simple reason that nobody had one. Caridad sighed in relief: she thought of her bundle, still in a corner. It was the last thing left to sell, and her efforts to obtain scraps of food on La Cava were turning out to be entirely useless.

However, neither of the two women imagined how difficult it had been for María to make that decision: the Sevillian nights were extremely dangerous, even more so for a girl like Milagros and an exuberant Negress like Caridad, who were looking to inflame men's desires so they would loosen their purse strings and give them some coins. When the girl had sung on the roads with the Fernández family, far from constables and justices, they were protected by gypsies willing to stab anyone who went too far, but in Seville . . . Besides, the gypsies were forbidden to dance.

'Wait for me here,' she told the other two. 'And you,' she added, pointing to Caridad with her atrophied finger, 'stop going through the rubbish or they are really going to eat you.'

Instinctively, Caridad brought a hand to her forearm and hid the bite marks she'd received from a vagrant when she tried to defend a small bone with something resembling meat stuck to it. All she'd done in return, however, was to naively turn her back on him. The beggar bit her, Caridad dropped her find and he got what he wanted.

The inn stood in a small neighbourhood outside the city walls in front of the Arenal Gate, between the Resolana, the Guadalquivir

River and the Baratillo, where they were building Seville's bull-fighting arena. The Arenal Gate was the only one of the thirteen in the city's walls that remained open at night. On the other side of it was the old brothel, where, despite the ban, they continued plying their trade. It was a humble community, with people who worked in the port, farmers passing through and all kinds of ruffians. Its mouldy buildings showed the damage caused by the frequent flooding from the river, against which they had no defence. She didn't like to, but María had to ask for favours; she was owed quite a few.

Bienvenido, the innkeeper, was as old, skinny and shrunken as she was. His expression soured when he heard the old woman's request and his wife, a big woman who was his third or fourth – María had lost track – slid silently towards the kitchen.

'What's your secret?' asked the old woman, pointing to his wife in a vain attempt to please Bienvenido, who ignored the compliment.

'Do you know what you are asking me?' he replied instead.

María breathed in the foul air of the inn. It was still morning, and unemployed sailors and port labourers drank among tired prostitutes who were trying to extend their shift from the night before, which perhaps hadn't been as lucrative as they would have liked.

'Bienvenido,' answered the gypsy after a pause, 'I know what I can ask you for.'

The innkeeper avoided María's eyes; he owed her his life.

'A young gypsy girl,' he then murmured. 'And a Negress! There will be fights. You know it. And I guess that, as always, they will come accompanied by gypsy men. I . . .'

'Of course we'll come with men,' interrupted María, thinking about which ones she should bring, 'and we'll need a guitar at least and . . .'

'María, for God's sake!'

'And all the saints!' she said to silence him. 'The same ones you put yourself into the hands of when you had fevers. Did they come to your aid?'

'I paid you.'

'That's true, but I told you then: it wasn't enough. You had spent everything you had on doctors, surgeons, masses, prayers and who knows what other dumb stuff, do you remember? And you agreed. And you told me that I could count on you.'

'I can't pay you now . . .'

'I'm not interested in your money. Make good on your word.'

The innkeeper shook his head before sweeping his gaze over his customers in order to avoid looking at María. *What was his word worth? Had any of them ever made good on theirs?* he seemed to be wondering at the same time.

'We're old, Bienvenido,' argued María. 'Maybe tomorrow we'll bump into each other in hell.' The old woman let a few seconds pass as she sought out the innkeeper's bilious eyes. 'We'd better settle our debts up here, don't you think?'

And there, at Bienvenido's inn, the two women and the girl met up a couple of nights after María had reminded him of hell's eternal flames: the old woman feeling in the pocket of her apron for the knife she used to cut plants – she'd kept her hand on it since they'd crossed the pontoon bridge and entered the Sevillian night; Milagros with her green gypsy skirt (María had managed to get someone to lend her a petticoat); and Caridad dressed up in the red outfit, which was tight around her large breasts and revealed an exciting strip of black at her belly, where the shirt didn't reach the skirt. They were accompanied by two gypsy men – Fermín and Roque, one a Carmona and the other from the Camacho family – whom the old woman had convinced with arguments similar to those she'd used on Bienvenido. Both of them knew how to play the guitar; both were strong and intimidating, and both were armed with knives that María had also got from the innkeeper. Even so, the old woman was still nervous.

Her distrust grew when she entered the inn and saw sailors, artisans, cardsharps, friars and dandies squeezed around the small tables of rough wood. They were playing cards and shooting dice, chatting, laughing loudly as if competing between tables for who had the most raucous guffaw. Some argued in bold voices or simply sat there staring vacantly at some unspecified point in the distance. They ate, smoked, or did both at the same time; they negotiated with the prostitutes who came and went displaying their charms, or they grabbed the buttocks of Bienvenido's daughters who were waiting on the tables. But all of them, without exception, were drinking.

A shiver ran up the healer's spine as she noticed, amid the dense blanket of smoke that floated in the air, how Milagros was trembling. The frightened girl backed up a step towards the threshold she had just crossed. She bumped into a stunned Caridad. 'This is crazy!' declared María then and there. The old woman was about to tell Milagros that if she didn't want to she didn't have to . . . but an outburst of shouting and laughter from the nearby tables prevented her.

'Come here, lovely girl!'

'How much for the night?'

'The Negress! I want to fuck the Negress!'

'Suck me off, girl!'

Fermín and Roque moved up until they were flanking Milagros and they managed to silence some of the shouting. The two men threateningly stroked the hilts of the knives stuffed into their sashes and they fixed a piercing gaze on anyone who addressed the girl. Arrogant in the face of the danger, the two gypsies ignored the possibility of being attacked, and challenged the crowd as if they didn't believe them capable of it. María took her attention off the girl and looked around the inn until she found Bienvenido near the kitchen, beyond the entrance door, listening to the unfamiliar shouting. The innkeeper, up against the wall, shook his head. *I warned you*, the old woman thought she could read on his lips. María didn't move; she kept her lips pressed firmly together. Then Bienvenido extended his hand and invited them to join him.

'Let's go,' said the healer without turning around.

'Come on, girl,' one of the gypsies said. 'Don't worry, nobody is going to touch a hair on your head.'

The firmness of those words calmed the old woman down. In a line, avoiding chairs, barrels, drunks and prostitutes, the group of five headed to where Bienvenido had cleared a table to make some room for them: María at the head, Milagros between the two gypsy men and, bringing up the rear, as if she were completely unimportant, Caridad. They tried to get comfortable in the small nook that

Bienvenido had arranged for them; leaning against one of the walls behind them, were two old guitars.

'That's the best I could do,' said the innkeeper before the old woman had a chance to complain.

Then he left them alone, as if what might happen from that point on had nothing to do with him. Fermín picked up one of the guitars. Roque made a move to do the same, but the other shook his head.

'One is enough,' he told him. 'You keep an eye out, but first bring me a chair.'

Roque turned and, without a word, lifted up a young dandy by the scruff of his neck as he was conversing with two others just like him. The Frenchified fop was about to complain but he shut his mouth when he saw the gypsy's grimacing face and the knife in his hand. Someone let out a giggle.

'Now you'll have your arse in the air, pansy!' spat one of the men at the next table.

Roque handed the chair to Fermín, who rested one foot on it and tried out the guitar on his thigh, attempting to tune it and get used to it. No one in the inn seemed to be the least bit interested in listening to music, because the uproar continued at full volume; only the brazen lustful looks at Milagros and Caridad and the occasional sharp remark proved that the customers knew the gypsies were there. When Fermín gestured to her, the guitar at the ready, María gathered her strength to face Milagros. She had avoided doing so up until that point.

'Ready?'

The girl nodded, but her whole being contradicted her: her hands trembled, she was breathing heavily and even her dark complexion looked pale.

'Are you sure?'

Milagros clenched her hands tightly.

'Breathe deeply,' the old woman advised her.

'Let's start, precious,' encouraged Fermín as he started playing. 'With *seguidillas*.'

The guitar made no sound! It couldn't be heard over the commotion. María started to clap her stiff hands and made a movement of her chin indicating that Caridad to do the same.

Milagros didn't know how to start. Bienvenido's place was nothing like the inns where, protected by the Fernández men, she had sung in front of a few patrons. She cleared her throat several times. She hesitated. She had to go forward into the tiny circle that opened out in front of her and sing, but she remained rooted beside María. Fermín repeated the guitar's entrance, and then again. The girl's hesitation captured the attention of the closest spectators. Milagros sensed their eyes on her and she felt ridiculous facing their smiles.

'Come on, girl,' encouraged Fermín again. 'Or the guitar's going to get tired.'

'Never forget that you are a Vega,' María said, spurring her on with the message from her mother.

Milagros moved into the circle and began to sing. The old woman closed her eyes tightly in desperation: the girl's voice was trembling. It wasn't enough. No one could hear her. She lacked rhythm . . . and joy!

Those that had been smiling were now swatting the air with their hands. Someone whistled. Others booed.

'Is that how you pant when you're getting fucked, little gypsy?'

A chorus of laughter accompanied the remark. Tears welled up in Milagros's eyes. Fermín questioned María with a look and the old woman nodded with her teeth clenched. She had to get going! She knew she could do it! But when rotten vegetables started flying towards the girl, Fermín made a gesture to stop strumming the guitar. María observed the crowd, which was drunk and over-excited.

'Dance, *morena*!' she then ordered.

Caridad seemed hypnotized by the atmosphere and continued clapping like an automaton.

'Dance, goddamnit!' screamed the old woman.

Caridad's appearance in the circle, her large breasts showing up dark beneath her red shirt, brought on a chorus of applause; cheers and all types of rude shrieks echoed in her ears. She turned towards Milagros: tears were running down her cheeks.

'Dance, Cachita,' she begged her before stepping out and leaving her the space.

Caridad closed her eyes and the commotion in the room began to make its way into her the way the howls from the slaves at the Sunday parties had done, when the high point was reached and someone was mounted by an Orisha. The sound of the guitar intensified behind her, but she found her rhythm in those incoherent shouts, in the people banging on the tabletops, in the lust that floated, almost tangible among the smoke. And she began to dance as if calling Oshún, the goddess of love, her goddess, to come to her: displaying herself shamelessly, thrusting her pubis and hips into the air, twisting her torso and head. Roque had to work hard. He pushed away some men who came forward to grope her, kiss her or embrace her, until he had no choice but to take up his knife, brandishing it to keep the men from leaping on her. Yet the more frantic the crowd became, the more Caridad danced.

The spectators gave her a standing ovation after the first dance: clapping, whistling and demanding more wine and liquor. Caridad was forced to repeat her dance. She was shiny with sweat and her red clothes were soaked, clinging to her breasts and outlining her nipples.

After the third dance, Bienvenido came out into the circle with both arms raised, waving them to announce the end of the performance. They knew what the old innkeeper and his three sons who kept things in line were like, and mumbling and joking they started to take their seats around the tables.

Caridad was panting. Milagros remained downcast.

'Go pass the hat,' María told Caridad. 'Quickly, before they forget.'

The old woman had been muttering insults while she watched the dances and the naive look that was Caridad's response made her even more furious.

'Go with her!' she ordered Roque and Fermín brusquely.

Bienvenido stayed with María and Milagros while the others went from table to table.

Caridad walked timidly with one of the men's hats while the gypsies tried to offset her ingenuousness by frowning and silently threatening those who weren't forthcoming. She got coins, but also propositions, rude remarks and the occasional fleeting grope, which

Caridad tried to evade and which the gypsies, in return for more generosity, overlooked. After all, Caridad wasn't a gypsy woman.

'Didn't you say she sang like the angels?' Bienvenido asked María, as they both counted the money dropping into the hat from a distance.

'She'll sing. As sure as we're not yet rotting in hell, she will. I promise you that,' answered the old woman, raising her voice without turning towards Milagros, to whom her statement was really directed.

Fermín and Roque were satisfied with the cut that María gave them, so much so that the next day several men and women passed by Milagros's house trying to join the group. The old woman refused them all. She was about to do the same with a woman from the Bermúdez family who showed up with a babe in arms and two almost naked kids clinging to her skirt, which was faded and ragged like all the ones worn by the gypsies who had returned from Málaga, but first she peeked her head inside the apartment: Milagros was lying hidden beneath a blanket. She had spent the entire day like that, sobbing every once in a while. Caridad, seated in a corner with her bundle, was smoking a *papante*. María had rewarded her with four of them when she was finally able to go and buy provisions: food and a candle. They said the *papantes* were made with Cuban leaf, and it must have been true, given the satisfaction with which Caridad, removed from all that was going on around her, exhaled large mouthfuls of smoke. María pressed her lips together, thought for a few seconds, nodded imperceptibly to herself and turned back to the Bermúdez woman, who was trying to keep her little ones quiet; she had seen her around, she knew her a little.

'Rosa . . . ? Sagrario?' the old healer tried to remember.

'Sagrario,' she answered.

'Come back at nightfall.'

The woman's gratitude was clear from her wide smile.

'But . . .' María pointed to the children. 'Come alone.'

'Don't worry. The family will take care of them.'

The rest of the day passed with the same apathy as the blacksmiths, still without the proper tools, showed towards their hammering. Caridad and the old woman ate sitting on the floor.

'Leave her be,' María told Caridad, who kept looking at the shape covered in a blanket lying a few paces from them.

What would she say to the girl if she got up and ate with them? Their return the night before had been taciturn; only Fermín and Roque exchanged a few funny anecdotes. Tired, the three women had gone to bed without even mentioning what had happened at Bienvenido's inn. Would she be able to sing tonight? She had to; they couldn't depend on Caridad: she wasn't a gypsy, anyone could tempt her away and she would leave them in the lurch. The old woman observed her as she ate: she smoked between bites. Her thoughts . . . where were they? On Melchor? Was she thinking about Melchor? She had cried over him. Is it possible that there was something between them? The old healer was only sure of one thing: at the rate she was smoking, Caridad would polish off the four *papantes* soon. She asked her for a drag.

'Are you still thinking about the gypsy?' she then asked.

Caridad nodded. There was something about that old woman that pushed her to tell the truth, to confide in her. 'I don't know if he would have liked seeing me dance at the inn,' was all she said.

The healer stared at her. That young woman was in love, there was no doubt about it. 'You know something, *morena*? Melchor would know that you did it for his granddaughter.'

The *morena* loved Milagros, thought María after exhaling a mouthful of smoke, but she wasn't gypsy, and that was reason enough to be wary of her. The two strong drags on the cigar clouded her mind. Yes, the girl would sing and dance that night, she said to herself as she handed the cigar to Caridad, and she would surprise all those drunks with her voice and the way she moved her body. She had to! And she would, that was why María had let Sagrario join them: the Bermúdez woman sang and danced like the best of them. María had heard and seen her in some of the many parties that had been so frequent before the arrest.

After eating, Caridad and the old gypsy lazed around waiting for night to fall. Every once in a while Caridad's gaze drifted towards Milagros, but María kept her from going over to console her, even with her mere presence. They no longer heard her sobbing. Milagros was still beneath the blanket and tent cloth until, eventually and suddenly, she moved jerkily as if trying to call attention to herself. Just like a capricious, sulky child, thought María, who smiled as she imagined her wanting to know what was going on in the persistent silence that surrounded her sanctuary. She must be hungry and thirsty, but she was stubborn like her mother . . . and her grandfather. A Vega who never surrenders! *Tonight you'll demonstrate that*, she promised as she watched her shivering under the blanket again.

Sagrario and the two men arrived together. María made them wait on the threshold.

'Let's go, Milagros!'

The girl responded with a violent kick beneath the blanket. María had had a lot of time to think about how Milagros would react and how to deal with her: only hurt pride and the fear of great shame would get her to obey. She approached, planning to uncover her, but Milagros clung to the blanket. Even so, the old woman was partially successful.

'Look at her!' she said to those at the door, still pulling on the blanket the girl was grabbing. 'Girl, do you want all the gypsies to know what a coward you are? The rumours will spread so far they'll reach your mother's ears!'

'Leave my mother out of this!' shouted Milagros.

'Girl,' insisted María in a firm voice; the blanket covering Milagros was now taut in one of her hands. 'There isn't a single Vega in Triana. At this point I am the elder of the family and you are nothing more than a gypsy girl without a man to depend on; you must obey me. If you don't get up, I'll tell Fermín and Roque to carry you, do you hear me? You know I'll do it and you know they'll obey me. And they'll take you through the alley like a spoiled child.'

'They won't do it. I'm a Carmo—!'

Milagros didn't get to finish the sentence. When she'd heard it, María had opened her hand and released the blanket with a scorn the girl couldn't see but could sense in all its intensity. Had she been about to repudiate being a Vega? Before the old woman had turned around, Milagros was already on her feet.

And she sang. She sang beside Sagrario, whose voice – aided by the effects of a glass of red wine that Old María forced the girl to drink as soon as they entered the inn – was powerful and joyous enough to cover up her fear and shame. Caridad also danced again, and again she ignited the crowd, which was somewhat larger than the night before. Word had spread. But not as much as it had by the third night, when Sagrario, after dancing with Milagros, moved out of the circle and introduced the girl with an exaggerated bow as she had planned with the old woman. Milagros found herself alone, amid the applause that still hadn't waned. She was panting, gleaming . . . and smiling! noticed María with her heart on tenterhooks. Then the girl lifted a hand, adorned with some coloured ribbons, like her hair, and asked for silence. The healer felt a shiver run through her stiff limbs. How long had it been since she'd felt that pleasure? Fermín, with his foot on the chair and the guitar over his left thigh, exchanged a victorious look with the old woman. The audience was reluctant to quiet down; someone tapped on a glass with a knife and shushing followed.

Milagros endured having all eyes on her.

'Come on, pretty girl!' they urged from one of the tables.

'Sing, gypsy!'

'Sing, Milagros,' encouraged Caridad. 'Sing like only you know how.'

And she began, a capella, before Fermín joined in with the guitar.

'I know how to sing the story of a gypsy . . .' Her lively voice, with its extraordinary timbre, filled the entire inn; Fermín and the others immediately recognized the gypsy *seguidilla* but they let her finish the verse unaccompanied, savouring her singing. '. . . who fell in love with a lad of the pale race.'

When Milagros was about to launch into the second verse, the crowd received the guitar's entrance with applause and compliments for the girl. The women in the group joined in with the handclapping. María was crying as she clapped, Caridad biting down hard on one of her *papantes*. Milagros continued singing, confident, firm, young, beautiful, like a goddess who enjoyed knowing she was adored.

Seville was a singing school, a music university, a workshop where all styles came together before heading out into the world. Caridad could arouse the men with her provocative dances, as the gypsy women did with their *zarabandas* – deemed sacrilegious by the priests and the sanctimonious – but no one, none of those men or women, prostitutes and criminals, washerwomen and artisans, friars and maids, could remain unmoved by the marvellous spell of a song that captured their emotions.

And the crowd went wild: cheers, acclaim and applause. And as the girl's performance reached its climax she was showered with countless promises of eternal love.

20

'SHE'S A VEGA,' El Conde whispered to keep from waking the other family members sleeping with them.

Rafael García and his wife remained with their eyes open in the darkness, stretched out fully dressed on a pile of straw and dried branches that served as a mattress. Reyes covered herself with a worn blanket. She was old and felt chilled. The forges had always kept the upper floors warm, but Rafael hadn't yet reached a definitive agreement with the *payo* blacksmiths and they were still working with portable anvils and holes in the floor.

'We could be making a lot of money,' insisted La Trianera.

'She's El Galeote's granddaughter!' objected Rafael again, this time raising his voice.

This shout prompted the sounds of bodies stirring and the odd unintelligible word spoken in dreams. Reyes waited until the murmur of their breathing quieted down.

'It's been months since anyone's heard anything from Melchor. El Galeote must be dead, someone must have killed him—'

'Son of a bitch,' her husband interrupted, again in a whisper. 'I should have done it myself long ago. Even so, the girl is still his granddaughter, a Vega.'

'The girl is a gold mine, Rafael.' Reyes let a few seconds pass and snorted towards the flaking ceiling; her next words were very hard for her. 'She is the best singer I've ever heard,' she managed to admit.

Milagros's success had spread by word of mouth and, like many other gypsies, Reyes was curious and had gone to listen to her at the inn. She stood in the door, huddled behind the audience that was larger every night. And while she couldn't see her, she did hear her. Lord, did she ever!

'OK, she sings well, so what?' asked El Conde as if he wanted to put an end to the conversation. 'She is still a Vega and she hates us as much as her grandfather and her mother do. May she turn mute!'

'Let's marry her to Pedro,' she insisted, reiterating the suggestion that had started the argument.

'You are insane,' repeated Rafael in turn.

'No. That girl is in love with our Pedro. She always has been. I've seen her spying on him and following him. She melts when he's around. Trust me. I know what I'm talking about. What I'm not sure is if Pedro would be willing to—'

'Pedro will do what I tell him to!'

After that show of authority, El Conde remained silent. Reyes smiled again at the chipped ceiling. How simple it was to steer a man, no matter how powerful he was . . . All it took was some goading to his pride.

'If she marries Pedro, she will have to obey you as well,' said Reyes then.

Rafael knew it, but he liked hearing it: him ordering around a Vega!

Reyes had picked up on a change in his attitude; he was no longer raging at the mere mention of the Vegas. Rafael was already fondling the money. 'And how do we arrange it?' he might now ask. Or perhaps, 'María, the healer, will object.' 'I will go to the council of elders if need be.' Any of those sentences could be his next.

The old woman. He chose the old woman.

'That grumpy old hag?' was all Reyes said. 'Actually, the girl is a Carmona. Without her parents around, it will be Inocencio, as the patriarch of the Carmonas, who decides. He wouldn't dare if El Galeote or the mother were around, but without them . . .'

'And the Negress?' El Conde surprised her by saying. 'She's always with her.'

Reyes held back a laugh. 'She's just a stupid slave. Give her a cigar and she'll do whatever you want.'

'Even so, I have a bad feeling about that Negress,' grumbled her husband.

One afternoon, in the alley, Pedro García came out of his family's smithy as Milagros was passing and smiled at her. Since she had begun singing at the inn there were many who now smiled at her or stopped to talk to her, but not Pedro. Even her girlfriends had tried to coax their way into the musical group by flattering her. 'Did any of them do anything for you when the council forbade you from living in the alley?' said Old María, ending the matter.

That afternoon the old woman frowned over the encounter with Pedro, much as she had when listening to Milagros's idea about dancing with some of her girlfriends at the inn. She suspected the meeting was no accident and tugged at the girl's arm, but Milagros didn't budge; she had stopped, spellbound, a few steps from the young García. Old María saw her stammer and turn red like . . . like some ridiculous, shy little girl.

'How are you?' the boy feigned an interest before María snorted in his direction.

'Fine, until now!' the old woman answered curtly. 'Can you move it along? Don't you have things to do?'

The young man ignored the old gypsy's presence and words. He widened his smile, revealing perfect white teeth that stood out against his dark skin. Then, as if he had to leave against his will, he half closed his eyes and brought his lips together in what could be seen as a hint of a kiss.

'See you soon,' he said in parting.

'Don't you go near her,' warned María after the young man had turned his back to them. *She's not for you*, she was about to add, but the tremendous beating of Milagros's heart, which she could feel in the forearm she was holding on to, bewildered her, so she stopped.

Then: 'Let's go,' insisted the old woman, pulling on her arm. 'Come on, *morena*!' she shouted to Caridad.

The effort María had to employ to get the girl to keep walking was in sharp contrast to La Trianera's smug expression. She was hiding behind a small window on the upper floor of the smithy, and she nodded in satisfaction as she watched them cross the alley and head to the building where the Carmonas lived: the healer cursing ostentatiously, Milagros as if floating, and the *morena* . . . the *morena* behind them, like a shadow.

They were going to see Inocencio. If it was money that was needed to free Milagros's parents, they now had it. And they trusted they'd have more, despite the bribes they were forced to pay to the constables so they'd allow them to continue singing at the inn and not investigate whether they'd been arrested in the round-up and freed in Málaga. María patted her pocket with the coins; they had only had to give in on one point.

'The Negress has to stop dancing,' Bienvenido had warned her one night. He too was pleased with the profits.

The old woman had grumbled.

'They'll close down my inn,' Bienvenido had insisted. 'We can bribe the officials to let a girl sing, and even dance, but several friars and priests have already denounced Caridad's dancing; they're appalled and there's nothing we can do about them, María. I promised the constable that she wouldn't dance again. He won't give me another chance.'

And they wouldn't have given it to him, the old woman had admitted to herself. Since Seville had lost the monopoly on trade with the Indies in favour of Cádiz, there was less wealth. The shopkeepers were poor and the difference between those who lived in absolute misery – the vast majority – and a minority of corrupt officials, haughty noblemen who owned vast lands and thousands of clergymen, both regular and secular, had heightened. The clergymen saw it as a favourable moment to stress the Christian doctrine of resignation to the people with sermons, masses, rosaries and pro-cessions. There had never been so many public sermons threatening the faithful with all kinds of fire and brimstone as retribution for their licentious lives. And unlike the court in Madrid, with its two comedy theatres and their permanent companies of actors – the Cruz and the Príncipe – the Archbishop of Seville had managed to ban theatre, opera and comedies in his archdiocese.

'As long as no comedies are shown in Seville, its people will be free of the plague,' a fervent Jesuit father had already prophesied at the end of the last century. And the city that had been a cradle of the dramatic arts, that had erected the first covered theatre in Spain, was now forced to hide and arrive cloaked to enjoy the singing of a young gypsy virtuosa. But Caridad's dancing, with her breasts swaying and her lower belly and hips thrusting, was a carnal provocation worthy of eternal hellfire.

'You won't be dancing any more,' María had told Caridad, although the crowd was already demanding her presence.

María had scrutinized the Negro woman's face for some reaction. She hadn't been able to discern any; perhaps the news made her happy? Amid the shouting, catcalls and the obvious satisfaction of a constable hidden in the crowd, Caridad had seemed to receive her words with absolute indifference.

As for Milagros now . . . she was still dumbstruck, with a stupid smile on her lips. María found herself forced to admit that Pedro García could probably dazzle any woman. He was a proud, haughty gypsy with tanned skin, long black hair and intense ebony eyes; he was handsome and strong despite the effects of hunger on his seventeen-year-old body.

'You are a Vega!' María stopped in front of the door to Inocencio's house; the reproach came out of her mouth at the mere thought of the girl and that . . . that rogue kissing her and touching her and . . . 'And he is a García!' she then shrieked. 'Forget about that boy!'

Young Pedro García stood inside the smithy, his legs spread and his hands on his hips, in front of his grandfather and his father, Elías, at a distance from the other members of the García family, who were wrangling with their portable anvils.

'I won't have any problems with that girl,' the young man boasted, smiling.

'Pedro, we aren't talking about another fling,' warned El Conde, worried by the memories of his grandson's love affairs, luckily all with *paya* women, when he'd had to come to his aid. Sometimes it was enough to threaten the fathers or cuckolded husbands, other times he'd had to fork out some money that later, in front of the other family members, he had pretended to recoup by giving the boy extra work. He liked Pedro; the boy was his favourite. 'You will marry the girl,' he declared. 'You must comply with gypsy law: you cannot touch her until the wedding has been celebrated.'

The young gypsy responded with mocking theatricality. His grandfather and father hardened their features at the same time, which was more than enough for the boy to understand the importance of what was being planned.

'You could . . . you should talk to her, even give her a gift, but nothing more. You are not allowed to leave the alley together unless accompanied by adult members of the families; I don't want complaints from the old woman or the Carmonas. I promise you won't have to endure a long engagement. Do you understand?'

'Yes,' he confirmed seriously.

'Good gypsy,' his grandfather congratulated him with a pat to the cheek.

El Conde was about to turn when he noticed the expression on his grandson's face: the boy's eyebrows were raised, asking a question.

'What?' he asked in turn.

'And meanwhile?' enquired Pedro, wagging his head from one side to the other. 'Tonight I have a date with the wife of a Sevillian carpenter . . .'

Both father and grandfather let out loud guffaws.

'Enjoy yourself while you can!' encouraged El Conde, laughing. 'Mount her for me too. Your grandmother doesn't—'

'Father!' reproached Elías.

'Do you want to come with me, Grandfather?' suggested the grandson. 'I can assure you she's woman enough for both of us.'

'Don't talk such nonsense!' the young man's father intervened again.

'You haven't seen her!' insisted Pedro while El Conde smiled. 'She's got this arse and this pair of tits—'

'I meant—'

The grandfather swatted the air with his hand. 'We know what you meant,' he interrupted his son. 'In any case, Pedro, be careful not to make the Vega girl mad; if she's even the slightest bit like her grandfather, she'll be proud,' he added, his expression souring at the memory of El Galeote. 'The girl must not know about your escapades.' Rafael García took the moment of seriousness to warn his grandson, 'Pedro, your grandmother and I, your father, our family has a lot invested in that marriage working out. Don't let us down.'

'Hag!'

They were many who called her 'hag' but María could tell when it was being used affectionately and when it was meant to offend. On that occasion there was no doubt that it was the latter. She ignored the shout that had come from the smithy and continued crossing the shared courtyard, alone. Milagros had refused to go shopping with her and, to her dismay, she had stayed upstairs whispering with Caridad . . . about Pedro García, no doubt.

For several days now the young man had arranged to bump into Milagros on the San Miguel alley, not trying to hide it from María or from anyone else. Milagros seemed not to realize that it was planned and time and again she would melt in his presence, until María scared him off. Then came the arguments, which the old healer would settle by parroting the words of Milagros's mother: *Never forget that you are a Vega.* She was referring to the hatred between the two families. But she couldn't stop Milagros from whispering with Caridad, who always listened attentively, impassive with her cigar in her mouth, and that irritated María so much that she had been thinking about not buying her any more tobacco.

'Hag!' she heard again, this time from the courtyard itself.

She turned and recognized Inocencio in the doorway of the blacksmith workshop whose back opened on to the courtyard, where pieces of old rusty iron were already starting to pile up again, even though the gypsies were unable to work with the tools they had.

'Mind your tongue, Inocencio!' She turned back.

'I haven't said anything that could bother you,' replied the Carmona patriarch as he approached.

'But you are going to, am I right?'

'That depends on how you take it.'

Inocencio had reached her. He was also old, like all the patriarchs. Perhaps not as old as El Conde and much less so than María, but he was definitely an old gypsy, used to giving orders and having them obeyed.

'Tell me what you have to say,' she pressed.

'Stop getting in the way of Milagros and the García boy.'

The old woman hesitated. She had never expected such a warning. 'I'll – I'll do what I think is best,' she stammered. 'She is a Vega. She is under my—'

'She's a Carmona.'

'The same Carmonas who defended her to the council of elders?' She laughed sarcastically. 'You banished her from the alley and you gave her to me. Even her father agreed. The girl is under my protection.'

'So why is she living in the alley, then?' replied Inocencio. 'The punishment has been lifted, you know that. The Vargas family has forgiven her. She is a Carmona and she answers to me, like all of them.'

Perhaps he's right, reflected María; she couldn't avoid a shiver at the thought.

'Why haven't you asserted your authority before? It's almost a month that we've been . . .'

'The girl feels she is a Vega,' admitted Inocencio. 'I'm not interested in her money and certainly not interested in getting into a conflict with the Vegas, although now . . .'

'Melchor will return,' said María, trying to intimidate him.

'I wish that crazy old guy no harm.'

He seemed sincere.

'Then, why now? Why do you want to encourage her relationship with Pedro García? Can't you find another man for Milagros? Someone who's not a García, someone who's not that libertine – everyone knows about his adventures. You will find many suitors for the girl that all the families could agree on.'

'I can't.'

María asked for an explanation by extending one of her knotty hands out in front of her.

'You asked me to free Ana and José, and for that I need Rafael García's help.'

The old woman's hand, at the height of her dry breasts, began to tense up. Inocencio noticed.

'Yes,' he affirmed then. 'El Conde has made the marriage of his grandson to the girl a condition.'

María clenched her hand and shook it furiously. Her hooked fingers didn't allow her to make the fist she wanted to beat Inocencio with. She felt as if her arguments were escaping through those gnarled fingers.

'Why is Rafael's intervention necessary?' she enquired, despite knowing the answer.

'He is the only one who can get the parish priests of Santa Ana to provide a marriage certificate for the girl's parents. Without that piece of paper there is no freedom. He has always been the one who dealt with them, in the name of the council of elders; they won't even see me. And that is his only condition: Milagros and Pedro must marry.'

'Ana Vega would never consent to regaining her freedom in exchange for that union.'

'Ana Vega will submit to her husband's orders,' said Inocencio resolutely, 'and the Carmonas have nothing against the Garcías.'

'Until her mother gets back, I will not allow this relationship,' retorted the healer.

In the morning light that entered the courtyard and slipped through the twisted iron scraps, they stared each other down. Inocencio shook his head.

'Listen, hag: you have no authority. You will do what I tell you; otherwise we will exile you from Triana and I will take care of the girl even if I have to do it by force. She wants her parents to return ... and I understand that she isn't against a relationship with Rafael's grandson, either. What more can you hope for? José Carmona belongs to my family: he is my cousin's son and I will do everything in my power to free him, like all the others. I am not going to let your stubbornness make El Conde back out. He is obtaining the freedom of a Vega! The daughter of El Galeote, his bitter enemy! Do you want me to talk to Milagros?' María took a step back, as if Inocencio had pushed her with his threat; she scratched her bare feet on one of the pieces of iron. 'Do you want me to tell her that you are jeopardizing her parents' freedom?'

The old woman suddenly felt dizzy. Her mouth filled with saliva and the ochre colour of the iron, drowning out the sun's brilliance, danced in every corner of the courtyard, wavering before her eyes. Inocencio made a gesture to help her, but she refused it with a clumsy swipe. What would happen if he did talk to Milagros? The girl was enthralled by the García boy. She would lose her. She felt herself fainting. The figure of Inocencio blurred before her. Then she pressed her foot hard against the iron she had stepped on, until she felt one of its corners gouging into her and blood running down her calloused sole. The real, physical pain revived her so she could face the Carmona patriarch, who silently watched a small dark puddle form around the old woman's foot and soak into the ground.

They both knew what the harm the old woman was inflicting on herself – as she tried to keep the pain from showing in her face – meant: she was giving in.

'Save your blood . . . María. You are too old to waste it,' recommended the Carmona patriarch before turning his back on her and returning to the smithy.

Hours later, the old woman stepped away from Milagros as soon as Pedro García came out to meet her. She did so in silence and limping, her foot bandaged, yet trying to hold her head up. Milagros was surprised at the sudden freedom offered to her by the person who, up until that point, had fought dauntlessly to keep her from talking to the young man. And . . . she even wasn't muttering curses! The smile and warm look with which Pedro invited her to come over and chat with him made her forget all about the old woman and even gesture imperiously with her hand for Caridad to move aside as well. La Trianera stood at one side of the alley, and Inocencio at the other, both in full view, like witnesses verifying a pact being fulfilled, and they exchanged satisfied looks when María withdrew.

That night, even the old woman was forced to admit that the

voice with which Milagros intoxicated the audience at the inn was tinged with a depth of feeling that it had never had before. Fermín, on the guitar, turned his head and his expression asked what had happened; so did Roque and Sagrario. María didn't answer any of them. She hadn't explained her change in attitude to Milagros. She didn't want to, and the girl hadn't asked, perhaps afraid of breaking the spell if she did.

That same night El Conde spoke with his wife again as they lay on the mattress of straw and branches. He had got the marriage certificate and the priests' promise that they would testify in the secret file in support of José Carmona and the Vega woman; he also had assured the backing of the constable of Triana. Reyes congratulated him.

'You won't regret it,' she added.

'I hope not,' he said. 'It cost a lot of money. More than Inocencio gave me. I had to sign documents forcing me to pay that debt.'

'You'll make that money back in spades.'

'I also had to promise the priests that they'll marry in the church as soon as they are freed, that the girl will be baptized and will sing carols in the Santa Ana parish church this Christmas. They have heard talk about her.'

'She will do it.'

'They want to make sure that we are really getting closer to the Church, that our efforts are public, so that everyone can witness and appreciate them. They forced me to confess! I don't know—'

'Isn't that what was agreed upon in the last council meeting? Did you talk to them about creating a brotherhood?'

'They laughed. But I think deep down it pleased them.' El Conde was quiet for a few moments. 'And if Ana Vega refuses to be married by the Church?'

'Don't be naive, Rafael! They are never going to free Ana Vega. Since she's been in Málaga she's been racking up more convictions than a criminal. If she weren't with the gypsies she would be in jail. They won't free her.'

'Then . . . she won't be able to marry.'

'Better for you. Ana Vega would never do it.'

Reyes turned her back on him, ending the conversation, but Rafael insisted.

'I made a promise. If she doesn't marry . . .'

'And what can you do if they don't free her? You already have your excuse, and by then Pedro will be married to the girl,' she interrupted. 'If the priests want Ana Vega to be married in church so badly, they can talk to the King to get her pardoned.'

In mid-December, when they had confirmation that the secret file had been processed and sent to La Carraca and Málaga, the García and Carmona families gathered the neighbours of the bride in the shared courtyard. It had been cleaned of twisted, rusty iron pieces as befitted the occasion; Inocencio had ordered them moved to the smithy. Days earlier, he had approached María again.

'Do you want to tell her or should I?' he asked her.

'You are the patriarch,' blurted out the old woman without thinking. But then, before Inocencio had a chance to speak, she changed her answer. 'I'll do it.'

The apartment was still as empty as when they came back to Triana; the biggest change had been a pile of coal beneath the niche that held the cooking oven, an old cooking pot and a large spoon, three chipped Triana crockery mugs, all different, and some food placed in a built-in cupboard that the soldiers were unable to take with them.

'Wait for us downstairs,' María ordered Caridad.

As soon as Milagros heard the old woman curtly getting rid of Caridad with those severe words, she headed to the window that opened on to the alley and leaned her elbows on the sill. She didn't want to hear her ranting. She knew that they had been avoiding talking about it for days, but she was living some of the best days of her life: Inocencio had assured her that her parents would be freed, she was singing and she was admired almost as much for her voice as for her relationship with Pedro García. The other gypsy girls, her friends, envied her! She leaned her top half out of the window, as if she wanted to flee the old woman's complaints. What did Old María know of love? What did she know of the spell cast between her and Pedro when they got together? They talked and laughed over every little thing: people's clothes, a simple twisted piece of iron, a little boy who tripped . . . They laughed and laughed. And they looked at each other tenderly. And sometimes they brushed up against each other. And when that happened it was like the burn of a cinder jumping off the anvil: a pinprick. Milagros had never been hit by those anvil sparks, but Pedro described the feeling that way one day when they'd got closer than was advisable. He pulled away feigning discomfort, while Milagros had wanted that moment to last for ever. They had both returned to the alley in case someone had seen them. 'Yes, like a cinder!' she agreed, her legs still trembling. It had to be that. What did the old woman know about cinders that pricked like needles? No! She didn't want to hear María's sermons.

However, the old woman spoke. 'In a few days . . .'

Milagros moved to cover her ears.

'Inocencio will promise you in marriage to El Conde's grandson.'

Milagros's hands hadn't yet reached her ears. Did she just hear what she thought she just heard? She leapt round. María forgot her speech when she saw the girl's overjoyed expression.

'What did you say?' she asked, almost shrieking. Her high-pitched tone annoyed the old healer.

'You heard me.'

'Say it again.'

She didn't want to.

'You are going to marry him,' she said eventually.

Milagros let out another high-pitched little scream and brought her hands to her face; she immediately pulled them down and extended them to the old woman, inviting her to share in her joy. She stopped when she saw the healer's impassive face. She cried and paced back and forth with her fists clenched. She twirled and shouted through her sobs. She stuck her head out of the window and looked up at the heavens. Then she turned towards María, somewhat calmer but with tears running down her cheeks.

'You can object,' the old woman dared to tell her.

'Ha!'

'I would help you, I would support you.'

'You don't understand, María: I love him.'

'You are a—'

'I love him! I love him, I love him, I love him.'

'You are a Vega.'

The girl stood firmly in front of her. 'Those quarrels were many years ago. I don't have anything to do with—'

'It's your family! If your grandfather heard you . . .'

'And where is my grandfather?' The shout was heard all the way to the alley. 'Where is he? He's never here when I need him.'

'Don't—'

'And the Vegas, where are those Vegas you're always talking about?' interrupted Milagros, angry, spitting her words. 'There isn't a single one left, not a single one! They are all in jail, and the ones that aren't, like the ones we found with the Fernández family, prefer living with another clan than returning to Triana. What Vega are you talking about, María?'

The old woman didn't know how to respond.

'That young man isn't good for you, girl,' she chose to say, knowing her warning was useless. But she had to say it, even knowing how the girl would react.

'Why? Because he is a García? He's not to blame for what his grandfather did! Because you decided so? Or perhaps because my grandfather decided it, wherever he is?'

Because he is a hypocritical scoundrel and a womanizer who only loves your money and who'll make you miserable. The answer went through the old woman's head. The girl wouldn't believe it. *And, yes, a García, the grandson of the man who sent your grandfather to the galleys; grandson of the man who brought death to your grand-mother and misfortune to your mother.*

'You don't want to understand,' she lamented instead.

María left the girl with her reply still on her tongue. She turned around and left the apartment.

Now Milagros, in the courtyard emptied of iron scraps, while the Carmonas and the Garcías congratulated each other and drank wine they'd bought with the earnings from her last night at the inn, was missing the old woman. She hadn't seen her since then. Five days she'd spent asking after her. She had even dared to go to the settlement with Caridad, to no avail; then she had searched the streets of Seville, also without luck. Apart from Pedro, who had spent a few minutes with her before devoting himself to drinking, chatting and laughing with the other gypsies, and Caridad, Milagros felt strange among those people. They wore colourful clothes and ribbons and flowers in their hair; the gypsies were hungry, but they weren't going to dress like *payos*. She knew them all, that was true, but . . . what would her life be like with them? What would her days be like once she had crossed the alley, into the building where the Garcías lived? She observed La Trianera, as fat as she was self-satisfied, moving through the people as if she were a true countess, and her stomach shrank. She wanted to seek Pedro's support when the two patriarchs, Rafael and Inocencio, called for silence. And while the people milled around her, Rafael called his son Elías and his grandson Pedro to his side. The Carmona patriarch called for her.

'Inocencio,' announced Elías García loudly and in a formal tone, 'as head of the Carmona family, I want to ask, on behalf of my son Pedro here, for the hand of Milagros Carmona, daughter of José Carmona. My father, Rafael García, head of our family, has promised in his name and in mine to pay for the freedom of Milagros's parents, and with this expenditure we consider gypsy law fulfilled and the girl's price paid.'

Before Inocencio could answer, Milagros gave Pedro a nervous glance. He smiled at her in encouragement. His serenity managed to calm her down.

'Elías, Rafael,' she heard Inocencio respond, 'the Carmonas consider sufficient the price of the payment to obtain the freedom of one of our family members and his wife. I present you with Milagros Carmona. Pedro García,' added Inocencio, addressing the young man, 'I am bestowing upon you the most beautiful girl in Triana, the best singer that our people have ever had. A woman who will give you children, who will be faithful and will follow you wherever you go. The wedding will be celebrated as soon as the new year comes in. May you be happy with her.'

Then Inocencio and Rafael García went forward and publicly

sealed the pact, face to face, in a long, vigorous handshake. At that moment, Milagros felt the strength of that alliance as if each of the two patriarchs were gripping her body. And what if María was right? She was overcome with doubt. *Never forget that you are a Vega.* The words her mother had wanted to convey to her went through her head like a flash of lightning. But she didn't have time to think about it.

'May no one dare break this engagement!' she heard Rafael García exclaim.

'Damn any who try!' added Inocencio. 'May it live on in the heavens as on earth!'

And with that gypsy oath received with applause, Milagros knew that her fate had just been decided.

It was the first party celebrated since the liberation of the gypsies from the arsenals and jails. The gypsies of the San Miguel alley brought the little food and drink they had. A couple of guitars appeared, along with some castanets and tambourines, all broken and worn. In spite of that, the men and women made an effort to get into the spirit, scratching on their instruments until they got music out of them that compared to the music they used to make so long ago. Milagros sang and danced, cheered on by all, tipsy from the wine, stunned by the succession of congratulations and advice she kept getting; she danced with other gypsy women and several times with Pedro, who instead of moving to her rhythm, accompanied her with short, sharp movements that were proud and haughty, as if instead of dancing for the gypsies who clapped their hands he was shouting out to all of them that this woman was going to be his and only his.

As night fell, La Trianera began an unaccompanied *debla* that went on and on until her cracked voice brought tears to the women's faces and the men raised their forearms to their eyes to hide theirs. Milagros was no stranger to those painful feelings that surfaced in them and she trembled like the others. On several occasions she thought that Pedro's grandmother was challenging her. *Up until now your success is nothing more than the fruit of the silly, cheerful tunes you sing in a wretched inn*, she seemed to be spitting at her. *And what about the pain of the gypsy people?* La Trianera challenged her. *What about the heartbreaking, deep songs we gypsies keep to ourselves?*

Milagros accepted the challenge.

The long wail that sprang from her silenced the applause that had broken out as soon as La Trianera's voice stopped, as if its sudden hush were a consolation. Milagros sang without even placing herself in the centre of the circle, with Caridad and gypsy women at her sides. She didn't feel free! In fact, the voice of old Reyes had managed to transport her to that evening on the riverbank, in front of the church of the Virgin of Bonaire, and her grandfather down on his knees. *Where are you, Grandfather?* she thought as her voice broke in her throat and emerged tormented, like a ragged, rough lament. *Keep going until your mouth tastes of blood,* María had told her. And the old woman? And her parents? Milagros thought she could taste that blood just as La Trianera hung her head in defeat. She didn't see her do it but she knew, because the gypsies were silent for a long time when she was finished, waiting for the reverberation of her last sigh to disappear from the alley. Then they cheered her the way the Sevillians at the inn did.

In the clamour, Pedro García told his grandfather in an aside, 'I'm leaving.'

'Where to, Pedro?'

The young man winked an eye.

'Today is not the day to—' he tried to object.

'Say that you sent me on an errand.'

'No, Pedro, not today.'

'For a Vega?' the young man flung into his face. Rafael García gave a start as his grandson sweetened his features and smiled before continuing. 'You were just like me, isn't that right? We are the same.' Pedro draped an arm over his shoulders and pulled his grandfather to him. 'Are you going to keep me from having my fun just to keep up appearances in front of a Vega?'

'Go and have fun,' the patriarch gave in quickly.

'To the church. Say that I went to pray a rosary,' joked the young man, already on his way out of the alley.

When Pedro was near the Plaza del Salvador, after crossing the pontoon bridge and entering Seville, his grandfather had no choice but to go over to Milagros: the girl had obviously been looking around for her fiancé for some time.

'He went to talk to the Santa Ana parish priest about your baptism,' he said to reassure her.

Not even Milagros was going to believe that Pedro had joined one of the more than a hundred processions that went through the streets of Seville singing Hail Marys and saying the rosary! But Milagros knew she would have to be baptized; Inocencio had mentioned it when he told her that she must sing carols in the parish church at Christmas. It was one of the conditions for freeing her parents. And just as Pedro was crossing the Plaza del Salvador and reaching Carpintería Street, she accepted El Conde's excuse and went back to join the party.

Hidden in the corner of the Plaza del Salvador, Pedro studied the street where the carpenters lived, some of whom had become luthiers, before crossing it to reach the house where the exuberant but un-satisfied wife of an artisan was waiting for him. A tiny piece of yellow fabric left behind the bars of one of the workshop windows told him when she was alone. His heart beat wildly and not only with desire: there was a risk that her husband would show up, usually drunk – as had happened once; he'd had to hide until his wife could get him off to sleep – and that increased both of their pleasure. Pedro smiled in the dark, remembering the last time. *He's going to show up now*, the woman had shrieked nervously as Pedro mounted her frenetically, her legs lifted, hugging his hips with her thighs, *he'll open the door and we will hear his footsteps*, she laughed, panting, *he'll catch us and . . .* Her words were drowned in a long moan as she reached orgasm. That night the carpenter didn't show up, remembered the young man with another smile when the shadow he was watching vanished beyond Cuna Street and Carpintería Street was left empty. Then he rushed down it.

He left the house an hour later and walked the streets distracted, with the touch, taste, smell and moans of the woman still clinging to his senses, until he reached a retablo dedicated to the Virgin of the Forsaken painted on that street.

'Disgusting dog!'

The insult surprised him. He hadn't seen the shrunken shadow beside the retablo. Old María continued speaking.

'Not even on your engagement day are you able to suppress your . . . your lust.'

Pedro García looked the old healer up and down. She stood arrogantly, expecting a respect that . . . She was alone on a remote street of Seville, in the middle of the night! What respect could she be expecting, no matter how old she was?

'I swear by the blood of the Vegas that Milagros will not marry you!' threatened María. 'I'll tell her . . .'

The gypsy boy stopped listening. He trembled at the very thought of his grandfather and father, enraged if the girl refused to marry him. He didn't think twice. He grabbed the healer by the neck and her voice muted into an unintelligible gurgle.

'Stupid old hag,' he muttered.

He squeezed with just one hand. María gasped and sank her atrophied fingers into the arms of her aggressor as if they were hooks. Pedro García ignored her hands. How easy it was, he discovered as the seconds passed and the old woman's eyes threatened to pop out of their sockets. He squeezed more, until he felt something crunch inside the old woman's neck. It was simple, fast, and silent, tremendously silent. He let her go and María collapsed into a small, wrinkled pile.

The brotherhood that took care of the retablo's altar would deal with the corpse, he thought before leaving her there, and they would tell the authorities, who would exhibit her, or perhaps not, somewhere in Seville to see if anyone claimed her. Most likely she would be buried in a mass grave, paid for by gifts from pious parishioners.

21

THE SANTA ANA parish, in the heart of Triana, had the largest
congregation in Seville – more than ten thousand – and was
served by three parish priests, twenty-three presbyters, a subdeacon,
five minor clerics and two tonsured monks. But despite the large
number of faithful and priests, Santa Ana made Milagros tremble. The
building was a solid rectangular Gothic construction with three naves,
the central one narrower and taller than the others, interrupted in the
middle by the choir. It had been erected in the eighteenth century by
order of King Alfonso X to show his gratitude to the mother of the
Virgin Mary for having miraculously healed his eye.

To Milagros it was a dark place filled with golden retablos, statues
and paintings of sorrowful, wounded Christs, saints, martyrs and
virgins who scrutinized her and seemed to be interrogating her. The
girl was trying to shake off that oppressive feeling when she noticed
that her bare feet were walking on a rough surface; she looked at the
floor and jumped to one side, holding in a swear word that came out
as a snort: she was on top of one of the many stones beneath which
rested the remains of the church's benefactors. She pulled closer to
Caridad and they both remained still. A priest appeared beneath the
arch of Our Lady of Antigua, in the nave of the Gospel, behind which
was the sacristy. He did so in silence, trying not to disturb the faithful,
who were mostly women praying and commending themselves to
Saint Ann for nine days in a row, either to achieve their desired
fertility or to protect their obvious pregnancies; it had been known
in Triana and throughout Seville since ancient times that the

Holy Mother of Mary interceded for women's conception.

Milagros observed the priest and Reyes whispering a few paces from them; Reyes pointed at her again and again, and the priest looked at her with disapproval. La Trianera had come to replace Old María in her life. *Where is that stubborn old woman?* Milagros asked herself again, as she had done a thousand times in the last few days. She missed her. Surely they would be able to forgive each other – why not? She tried to banish the old woman from her mind when the priest made an authoritative gesture for her to follow him: María wouldn't have liked her being there, entrusting herself to the Church and preparing her baptism; surely not. When she passed Reyes, La Trianera tried to move Caridad aside.

'She comes with me,' said Milagros, pulling on her friend so she wouldn't stay with Reyes.

After Old María's disappearance and until her parents returned, Cachita was the only person she had left, and the girl sought her out more than ever, sometimes even at the expense of meeting Pedro. She was forced to admit that since the two families had agreed on the wedding, her young fiancé's attitude had changed, albeit subtly: he still smiled at her, talked to her and let his eyes drop in that tender gesture that thrilled her, but there was something . . . something different in him that she couldn't quite put her finger on.

The priest was waiting for her beneath the arch of the Virgin of Antigua.

'She comes with me,' repeated Milagros when he too was about to object to Caridad.

The reproachful expression with which the man of God took in her words indicated to the girl that perhaps she had been too harsh in her tone but, still, she went into the sacristy with Caridad. She was starting to be tired of everyone telling her what to do; María didn't do that, all she did was complain and grumble, but Reyes . . . she went everywhere with her! At Bienvenido's inn she even wrote down the songs she should perform. She tried to object, but the guitars obeyed La Trianera and she had no choice but to submit to them. Fermín and Roque were no longer part of the group, nor was Sagrario. They had all been replaced by members of the García family, and only the

Garcías took part. La Trianera had even forbidden Caridad from joining in with the songs and dances. *What does a Negro know about clapping fandangos and* seguidillas? she spat at Milagros. And during the performance, Caridad stood motionless, as if attached to the wall of the inn's kitchen, without even a bad cigar to put in her mouth. Reyes had taken over the management of all the money they made. She handed it over to Rafael, the patriarch, and unlike Old María, El Conde didn't seem willing to reward Caridad with *papantes*.

The only moment when Milagros could escape La Trianera's control was at night, when she was sleeping. Inocencio had refused to let her move into the Garcías' part of the alley until the wedding was concluded, and she and Caridad remained in the old, desolate dwelling she'd grown up in. However, La Trianera had saddled them with an old widowed aunt to keep an eye on Milagros. Her name was Bartola.

'What are the commandments of the Holy Church?'

The question brought Milagros back to reality: they were both standing inside the sacristy in front of a carved wooden table. The priest sat behind it, interrogating her with a stern expression. He didn't have the courtesy to invite them to sit down in the chairs. The girl had no idea about those commandments. She was about to admit her ignorance but then she remembered a piece of advice her grandfather had given her once when she was very young: 'You are a gypsy. Never tell *payos* the truth.' She smiled.

'I know them . . . I know them . . .' she then replied. 'I've got them on the tip of my tongue,' she added, touching it. The priest waited a few seconds, his fingers crossed on the tabletop. 'But they don't want to come out, those d—'

'And the prayers?' the priest interrupted her before the girl said something inappropriate. 'What prayers are you familiar with?'

'All of them,' she answered confidently.

'Tell me the Our Father.'

'Father, you asked me if I'm familiar with them, not if I know them.'

The priest's face didn't change. He knew what gypsies were like. He regretted having accepted the responsibility for helping this insolent gypsy girl, but the principal parish priest seemed very interested in baptizing her and bringing the gypsy community into the church fold, and he was just a simple priest without a curacy or benefice. His lack of reaction emboldened Milagros, who reached a similar conclusion: the priests wanted her to be baptized.

'What three people make up the Holy Trinity?' the man insisted.

'Melchior, Caspar and Balthasar,' exclaimed Milagros, stifling a giggle. She had heard that joke from her grandfather, in the settlement, when he was making fun of Uncle Tomás. They all would laugh.

But this time even Caridad, who remained a step behind Milagros, in her slave shirt with her straw hat in her hands, gave a start. The priest was surprised by her reaction.

'Do you know?' he asked her.

'Yes . . . Father,' answered Caridad.

The priest tried to urge her to list them with his gestures, but Caridad had already lowered her gaze and kept it on the floor.

'Who are they?' he ended up asking.

'The Father, Son and the Holy Ghost,' she recited.

Milagros turned towards her friend and listened to the following questions, all directed at Caridad.

'Are you baptized?'

'Yes, Father.'

'Do you know the Creed, the other prayers and the commandments?'

'Yes, Father.'

'Well, teach them to her!' he exclaimed, pointing to Milagros. 'Didn't you want her to accompany you? As a priest, when an adult . . . or something similar,' he added sarcastically, 'wants to enter into the holy sacrament of baptism, I am obliged to meet that person and testify that their life is governed by the three Christian virtues: faith, hope and charity. Listen: the first is what every good Christian should believe, and that is in the Creed. The second refers to how you must act, for which you must know the commandments of the Lord and of the Holy Church; and lastly, the third: what you can expect of God, and that is found in the Our Father and other prayers. Don't come back here without having learned them all,' he added, abandoning the idea of indoctrinating the gypsy in the catechism of Father

Eusebio. He'd settle for that brazen girl being able to recite the Creed!

Without giving her a chance to reply, the priest got up from the table and repeatedly shook both hands with his fingers extended, as if scaring off a couple of pesky little animals, to indicate that they leave the sacristy.

'How did it go in there?' asked La Trianera, who was waiting for them at one of the church doors, where she had used her time well, discreetly asking for alms, predicting fertility for each of the young female parishioners who went inside.

'I'm already half baptized,' responded Milagros seriously. 'It's true,' she insisted to the suspicious woman. 'All I need is the other half.'

But Reyes was no dull *paya* and she wasn't about to be outdone. 'Well, be careful, girl,' she answered, pointing at her with a finger that slid through the air from side to side, at the height of the girl's waist, 'that they don't cut you up to baptize the other half, and your witty repartee doesn't get lost in the shuffle.'

Milagros had trouble retaining the prayers and commandments that Caridad tried to teach her, reciting them wearily just as she had at Sunday mass at the Cuban sugar mill. Bartola, the old aunt, grew tired of listening to her faltering morning repetitions as she sat in the dilapidated chair she'd brought with her from the other side of the alley and set up beside the window in Milagros's house as if it were her prize possession. One morning she solved the problem with a shout.

'Sing them, girl! You'll remember them if you sing them.'

From that day on, the apathetic stammering turned into ditties and Milagros began to learn prayers and precepts to the rhythm of fandangos, *seguidillas*, *zarabandas* and *chaconas*.

It was precisely that natural facility, that talent she had for absorbing music and songs, that brought her the most problems and heartaches when it came time to learn the Christmas carols she was to sing in Santa Ana.

'Do you know how to read sheet music?' Before Milagros could answer, the choirmaster himself waved his hand through the air when he realized how ridiculous his question was.

'The only thing I know how to read are palms,' replied the young woman. 'And I can already see much misfortune on yours.'

Milagros was tense. Every member of the Santa Ana choir was judging her, and it hadn't been difficult to imagine what everyone in the choir, the tenor, and the organist – except for the boys, they were all professional musicians – were thinking of her. *What was a barefoot, dirty gypsy girl doing singing Christmas carols in their church?* was what the girl read in their faces.

And what she could now read in the bald, paunchy choirmaster's was a triumphant expression that transformed into a deafening shout.

'Reading palms? Get out of here!' The man pointed to the exit. 'The church is no place for gypsy sorcery! And take your Negress with you!' he added, indicating Caridad, positioned at a distance.

Even La Trianera herself, who now begged for alms openly outside the church while she waited for them, as if the fact that Milagros was going to sing Christmas carols gave her some sort of licence, ran to tell her husband about the girl's expulsion.

'If she were already married to Pedro, I would slap that fickle girl,' she added.

'You'll have your chance,' assured her husband tersely, rushing to Santa Ana before the parish priest summoned him to be rebuked.

He returned blind with rage: he had had to ask for forgiveness a thousand times and humiliate himself before an incensed cleric. Back in the alley, on that bright winter day, Rafael saw Milagros listening entranced to Pedro, as if nothing had happened. He decided against approaching her then and sought the help of Inocencio, who returned with him to where the young couple was chatting.

The girl didn't even see them arrive, but Pedro did, and from his grandfather's gait and snorting he could see what was coming; he moved a few steps away.

'They won't free your parents,' El Conde spat at Milagros. He was improvising.

'What . . . ?' she stammered.

'They're not going to free them, Milagros,' lied Inocencio in support of El Conde, who had promised the parish priest that Milagros would come back and behave.

'But . . . why? They said that the files had already been sent to Málaga and La Carraca.'

'All they have to do is say that a new witness has shown up, who challenges all the other secret information,' answered El Conde. 'They not only had to be married by the Church, they also had to prove they weren't living as gypsies, which with the Vegas will be easy to refute.'

Milagros brought her hands to her face. *What have I done?* she asked herself, inconsolable.

'What difference does it make if I sing in the church or not?' she tried to defend herself.

'You don't understand, girl. There is nothing more important to them than recovering for God the sheep that have gone astray. And nowadays those sheep, after having expelled the Jews and the crypto-Muslims, are us: the gypsies. They haven't sung Christmas carols in several years at Santa Ana, and the priests have agreed to restore the tradition, with a gypsy singing them! You singing Christmas carols in a church means publicly showing that they have managed to bring us into the fold. Even the Archbishop of Seville was aware of the project! But now . . .'

The two patriarchs exchanged a look of complicity as soon as they saw the trembling in Milagros's chin; the girl was about to burst into tears. Both of them made as if they were leaving.

'No!' She stopped them. 'I will sing! I swear! What can be done? What can I . . . ?'

'We don't know, girl,' answered Inocencio.

'Maybe if you went to ask for forgiveness . . .' mused Rafael, twisting his mouth to say that even with that there was little chance.

And she asked for forgiveness. Of the priests. Of the choirmaster. Of all the members of the choir, including the boys. Caridad watched her: standing, head bowed, browbeaten before them, not knowing what to do with those hands that were used to fluttering happily around her, scratching out each one of the words that Inocencio had recommended she say.

'I'm sorry. Forgive me. I didn't mean to offend anyone and least of all Jesus Christ and the Virgin in their own home. I beg you to forgive me. I will make an effort to sing.'

La Trianera had stopped chasing the townspeople for alms and had entered the church to enjoy the girl's humiliation. 'You'll have your chance,' her husband had assured her, and by God would she get her chance to give her the smack she deserved.

After several boys in the choir and some of the older musicians accepted her apologies, one of the priests urged her to kneel on the floor in front of the high altar and pray to atone for her mistake. There, in front of the sixteen panels that comprised the retablo that fitted into the octagonal apse of the church, Milagros, during the two long hours that the choir practice lasted, babbled the ditty she had learned. Christmas was approaching and everything had to be ready.

Despite Milagros's apologies, the next few days, in which Rafael arranged for her not to sing at the inn so that she could focus on Santa Ana, were a real trial for the girl, who, with her parents' freedom on her conscience, had to bite her tongue at the choirmaster's shouts. He stopped the rehearsals again and again to blame and insult her, crying out to the heavens at the misfortune of having to work with an ignoramus who knew nothing about reading music, or singing, and was unable to replace handclapping and guitars for the organ.

'A gypsy!' he shouted, pointing to her. 'A dirty beggar who is used to singing vulgar ballads for drunks and prostitutes! They're all thieves!'

Milagros, exposed to ridicule in front of everyone, tolerated it without even hiding the tears that ran down her cheeks and when the music played again she made an effort in body and soul. She felt . . . she was sure that the choirmaster and everyone else didn't want her to sing for Christmas and they would do everything they could to keep it from happening.

Her suspicions were confirmed three days before Christmas. The choirmaster arrived at rehearsal with the three parish priests at Santa Ana; other presbyters were positioned beside the sacristy. He didn't insult her that day, but his complaints and interruptions were constant, all of them followed by desperate glances at the priests trying to transmit to them the impossibility of the concert going off well.

'I'm not even trying,' lamented the choirmaster on one occasion, 'to get her to sing an aria in the Italian style, although that is what this great temple deserves. I chose a Spanish Christmas carol, a classic with *coplas* and *seguidillas*, but she can't even do that!'

Milagros saw the priests talking among themselves and was terrified to see how, with the choirmaster's wild gesticulations, their anxiety was turning into the certainty that they had made a mistake. She wasn't going to sing! She shook all over. She looked at Caridad, who stood stock-still in the same place. She observed with horror how the first priest opened his hands in an unequivocal gesture of surrender.

They were leaving! Milagros thought she would faint. The choir-master hid a smile as he made a small bow when the parish priests passed him. 'Son of a bitch,' muttered the girl under her breath. Her faintness turned into rage: *Son of a bitch!*

'Son of a . . . !' she burst out before another shout interrupted her.

'Master!' Reyes, as fat as she was, was running through the church. She stopped to make a clumsy genuflection and cross herself in front of the high altar, then got up and continued making crosses on her forehead and chest until she reached them. 'Reverend Fathers,' she panted, opening her arms to keep them from walking, 'do you know what my people say?'

The choirmaster sighed; the parish priests remained impassive, as if they were granting her the favour of allowing her to speak.

'The oldest donkey gets the heaviest load and the worst tack,' said La Trianera.

Someone in the choir laughed, perhaps one of the boys.

'Do you know what it means?'

Milagros ran her eyes over them, incredulous.

'Tell us,' allowed the first priest again with a look of acquiescence.

'Yes. I will tell you, Reverend Father: it means that the old folk: those' – she pointed towards the singers, who had their eyes glued on her – 'are the ones who have to bear the heaviest load and the worst tack. Not the girl. You won't get her to do it,' she added, addressing the choirmaster. 'She is just a simple gypsy, as your honour keeps repeating, a sinner who wants to be baptized. We, the gypsies, are the ones who want to come to this church and hear one of our own sing to honour the Baby Jesus on the day he was born. Listen. Listen, all of you. She does know them. She knows the carols. Silence, everyone!' Reyes dared to insist. Astute, she sensed that her speech had pleased the priests, now . . . now Milagros's singing had to please them too. 'Sing, girl, sing as you know how.'

Milagros started off with a carol, in her own way, forgetting about the choirmaster's complicated instructions. Her voice rose and echoed inside the mostly empty church. The parish priests turned towards the girl. Behind them, in the sacristy, one of the other presbyters leaned on the wall and closed his eyes and let himself be carried away by the song; another, older, clapped along. They didn't cheer like at the inn, no one shouted out rude remarks, but as soon as the carol ended, the girl knew that she had them captivated.

'Did you hear that?' Reyes challenged the choirmaster.

The man nodded with a frown, not daring to look at the priests.

'Well, based on that, load up the old donkeys!'

Milagros, unable to move a single muscle to check, wondered if any of them were smiling now.

'Let the old donkeys adapt to the girl's rhythm, to her tone, to her way of reading music or whatever you call it; she's just an ignorant gypsy, the young donkey.'

For a few seconds both Reyes and Milagros thought they could even hear the priests thinking it over.

'Let it be so,' declared the first priest after exchanging a look with the others. 'Maestro, the girl will sing her way, the way she just did, and let the others adapt to her style.'

And Milagros was there on that Christmas morning of 1749, dressed in a black cloak of rough cloth borrowed from the priests, with sleeves, that covered her from her head to her bare toes. The day before she had been baptized after proving she knew how to recite the prayers and commandments. They didn't demand more knowledge from her and, since she was an adult, they sprinkled her with water instead of dipping her in the baptismal font in the presence of her godparents: Inocencio and Reyes. Now the girl was looking out of the corner of her eye nervously at the people who were gradually accumulating inside Santa Ana, all clean and dressed in their finest clothes. The men were all in black, in the Spanish style, since there were few Frenchified men who dressed in military style in that neighbourhood; the women were sober, covered in black or white mantillas, with rosaries of mother of pearl or silver, some gold, and countless fans that fluttered constantly in their gloved hands. Milagros tried to imagine that she was at the inn, where with the help of Old María and Sagrario she had managed to control the trembling of her hands and the tightness in her chest that barely let her breathe, but the atmosphere in the church was nothing like the chaos of wine and liquor flowing from table to table and the men pouncing on prostitutes. All of Triana was meeting at the church, all of Triana was anxious to hear the gypsy sing, restoring a tradition that had been lost some years back.

She focused her attention on the bald, paunchy choirmaster. He wore some glasses that she had never seen at rehearsals and they gave him a serious air that contrasted with his frantic comings and goings as he organized and reorganized the choir. He didn't deign to look at Milagros through those new glasses. Amid the murmur of people waiting for the start of mass and the sound of the hundreds of fans and rosary beads clinking together, the already nervous girl worried that the choirmaster might do something underhand to disrupt her. The final rehearsals, accommodated to her way of singing, had been magnificent, or at least the girl had thought so, but who could be sure that the choirmaster, his pride wounded, wouldn't take his revenge on the day when all of Triana was watching her? The priests would get angry and her parents' freedom would again be imperilled.

What the girl didn't know was that the others had thought the same thing after Reyes told them how she publicly challenged the choirmaster. Rafael and Inocencio only needed to exchange a look, and on Christmas morning, at dawn, three gypsies, two Garcías and a Carmona, were waiting for the maestro at the door to his house. Few words were needed to make the man understand that he had to make that performance the most splendid of his life.

The mass had begun, solemnly concelebrated by the parish priests of Santa Ana, all three dressed in luxurious chasubles embroidered with gold thread; the other deacons followed the ceremony from the same high altar or from the choir, almost at the end of the main nave. Milagros observed the rows of the faithful closest to the apse, where Triana's illustrious families sat. On one end of the first she recognized Rafael and Inocencio with their wives, humble in their dress and demeanour, as if on this occasion they had left their gypsy arrogance at home. The others, Caridad included, must be at the back of the temple, supposing they were able to get in, since Santa Ana wasn't large enough for all its faithful.

The music began with liturgical hymns: music and songs in the Italian style that, since the arrival of the Bourbons to the Spanish throne, sought more to please the parishioners than to inspire them to spiritual passion as composers had done before with their use of counterpoint; reason versus ear, that was the fashionable discussion among the choirmasters of the large cathedrals. Milagros found the serenity she needed in the light melody. Standing still beside the musicians, it was as if they were speaking to her before anyone else; their notes reached her ears clearly, free of whispers, noises or murmurs. She closed her eyes, and let herself be carried away by the marvellous polyphony of voices from the boys' choir until she was wrapped in a musical delirium of which, for the first time in a long while, she wasn't the protagonist.

Then, suddenly, the marvellous choir that filled the church stopped singing and gave way to the words of the officiants. When Milagros heard the voice – supposedly gentle but actually gruff – she opened her eyes, which were damp with tears she hadn't even felt well up. She looked around her. Her vision was blurred but she did nothing about it, as if she wanted to extend the moment she had just experienced. Then she sensed his presence; she sensed it just as a few moments earlier she had vibrated to the sound of the violins. Although her eyes kept showing her a blurry spot between Rafael and Inocencio, she knew it was he. Finally she wiped them with her forearm and there he was: her father's smile lessened the effect of his emaciated appearance, the dried wound that crossed one of his cheeks to his forehead, his swollen black eye and the improvised, absurd clothes it was clear he had been lent to wear to the church. Milagros wanted to run to him, but he stopped her with a gesture. *Sing,* he mouthed. *And Mother?* she mouthed back to him. His expression froze her blood. Suddenly Milagros realized: the choirmaster was looking at her incredulously, as were those in the chapel and even the priests in front of the high altar; the singers . . . The entire church was staring at her! She hadn't come in when she should have. She trembled.

'Sing, my girl,' encouraged her father before the people's whispering broke the silence.

Milagros, spellbound by the immense, enveloping love she felt in those three little words, took a step forward. The choirmaster signalled for the musicians to begin again. The first note came out of the gypsy girl's throat cracked and timid. The second swelled when she heard her father's sobs as he listened to that voice he thought he'd never hear again. She sang to the newborn child. When the choirboys launched into the chorus she had a chance to run her eyes over the faithful and she could tell they were captivated. Later, when the choir stopped, she extended her hands and straightened up as if she wanted her voice to come from the very ribs of the arches of Santa Ana's vaulted ceiling to continue singing the miracle of Jesus's birth.

The parish priest had to clear his throat a couple of times before continuing the mass when Milagros ended the Christmas carol, but she only paid attention to her father, who struggled to hold back his tears and remain dignified.

At the back of the church, crammed between two men in the huge crowd, Caridad, with gooseflesh, wondered what had happened to Old María and Melchor. Even though it was in a church, she was sure they would have enjoyed hearing Milagros sing.

22

HE COULD JUST disappear, as he used to do in Triana. Nobody had ever asked him for any explanations. He could do it right then, while Nicolasa was in Jabugo. She would return, find the shack empty and she would understand that he had finally followed through on his threats. *Didn't you tell me never to trust a gypsy? You're lying. You'll stay with me . . .* Those were the woman's replies, sometimes when she wanted to downplay the importance of Melchor's threats, and other times as if she were searching in his eyes for his true intentions. He had told her to let him die. He had actually said that! He was prepared for it. He'd warned her that he would leave her and she'd decided to ignore him: she'd brought him to the shack, at death's door, as Nicolasa told him when he regained consciousness after quite a few days of fevers and flirting with death. She had found a surgeon for him, she also said, and she'd spent all of the money from El Gordo that Melchor had left on paying him.

'All of it?' shouted Melchor from the mattress he was lying on. The pain over the loss of his stash was worse than the excruciating tear he felt in the sutures of his wound.

'Surgeons don't want to heal gypsies,' she answered. 'In the end, what does it matter? If you had died you wouldn't have it either. I did what I thought was best.'

'But I would have died rich, woman,' he complained.

'So?'

'Who knows what lies beyond death? I'm sure they let us gypsies come back for what's ours so we can pay the devil.'

Two months later, when Nicolasa could carry him from the mattress to the chair beside the door to the shack for some air and the surgeon stopped visiting because he considered him cured, the woman confessed to Melchor that she had also had to give him El Gordo's horse . . . and her two gold coins.

'He threatened to denounce you to the constable.'

Enraged, Melchor made as if to get up from the chair, but he couldn't even move his legs and almost fell to the floor. The dogs barked before Nicolasa scolded him. It would still be another couple of months before he was walking with ease.

'Wait until spring arrives,' she recommended after another attempt to leave. 'You are still very weak, winter is hard and the mountains dangerous. The wolves are hungry. Besides, perhaps they've freed some of your people; take your time.'

Nicolasa had been passing along to him the news she'd gathered in Jabugo about the gypsies' fate; runners and smugglers knew things. First she was forced to confirm El Gordo's words that had almost cost Melchor his life: yes, all the gypsies in the kingdom had been arrested at the same time; Seville, and Triana with it, had been no exception. Melchor didn't ask her why she hadn't told him at the time: he already knew the answer. In November, however, Nicolasa came running to tell him the good news: they were freeing them!

'I'm positive,' she reiterated. 'People are talking about parties of gypsies from Cáceres, Trujillo, Zafra and Villanueva de la Serena who have returned to their people and to the tobacco trade. They have seen them and talked to them.

'Take your time,' she again begged him that day.

Nicolasa was only asking for time. *Why?* she asked herself – to no reply. Melchor's mind was made up; she saw it in his eyes, in the efforts that the lazy gypsy, who used to spend hours sitting by the door of the shack, made to walk again; in the melancholy tangible in him when he looked out on to the horizon. And what about her? She just prayed for one more day . . . she prayed that, when she returned from wherever she'd gone, she would still find him there. Secretly, she had ordered the dogs to stay with Melchor, but the animals, sensitive to her uneasiness, disobeyed her and stayed glued to her legs, as if promising her that they would never let her down. What did she want that time for? she asked herself whenever she had a fateful feeling and came running from the pigpen or the salt house to make sure, hiding in the shadows, that he hadn't yet abandoned her? But she loved him; she had cried over him the tears she had denied her own children during the endless days when she was forced to nurse their fevers and delirium; she had fed him like a baby bird; she had washed his body and dressed his wound and sores, made a thousand promises to Christ and all the saints if they let him live! Time . . . she would have given one of her hands for just another day by his side!

'OK,' yielded Melchor after reconsidering. He felt he should leave even with the risk of cold and his weak state. His instinct told him that this was the moment, but Nicolasa . . . the woman's dirty face convinced him. 'I'll leave when spring comes,' he stated, sure that would be the end of the discussion.

'You aren't tricking me?'

'You don't seem to want to understand, woman. How would you know that I'm not lying if I reassured you about that?'

Before spring arrived, Milagros heard – without daring to look out of the window – the pandemonium grow in the San Miguel alley with the hundreds of gypsies who had come for her wedding. Despite the circumstances, the Garcías and the Carmonas inviting their scattered families brought on a massive influx of gypsies from all corners of Andalusia and even further: some had even come from Catalonia! Milagros looked at her simple dress: white, like the *paya* brides, adorned with some colourful ribbons and flowers; after the mass she would change it for a green and red one that her father had given her.

A few tears ran down the girl's cheeks. Her father came over to her and took her by the shoulders.

'Are you ready?'

José Carmona had supported the commitment made by Inocencio; he was aware that his freedom was a result of that wedding and he wouldn't break the patriarch's word.

'I wish she were here with me,' answered Milagros.

José squeezed his daughter's shoulders, as if he didn't dare come closer and dirty her white dress. Just as La Trianera had predicted, Ana had not been freed and José had received the news with concealed satisfaction. Ana Vega would never have allowed the wedding, and the arguments and problems would have multiplied. With Ana in Málaga and Melchor absent, José enjoyed his daughter as he never remembered having enjoyed her in his life. Overjoyed with her engagement to Pedro García, Milagros had shared her happiness with her father; since he had come back from La Carraca, José lived enraptured by the affection his daughter constantly showed him. Why would he want them to free his wife? Yet, in order to calm Milagros, they both went to make claims to the authorities, though their attempts were in vain. What did it matter that this Ana Vega was married and there were witnesses who swore that she had lived according to the laws? Impossible! They were lying! She had been condemned by the Málaga courts and since then the list of denunciations and punishments she had racked up was endless.

'The day before the Chief Magistrate of Málaga answered our letter,' a functionary told them as he tapped on the papers spread out on his desk, 'your wife pounced on a soldier and bit off half of his ear. How do you expect them to release such an animal? Be careful about what you say, girl!' the man said before Milagros replied. 'Be careful it isn't you who ends up in the city jail and your father back in La Carraca.'

Milagros asked her father if they could go to Málaga to try to see Ana.

'We aren't allowed to travel,' he objected. 'In a little while you are going to be married, what would happen if they arrested you?'

She lowered her eyes. 'But . . .'

'I'm trying to get to her through third parties,' lied José. 'We are all doing everything possible, my girl, don't you doubt it.'

José Carmona was one of the last gypsies freed. Beginning in 1750, reports of pressures from the gypsies to influence the secret files were brought before the Council, and the authorities considered that all those who hadn't passed the test before the month of December should be considered guilty . . . of being gypsies. From that point on, thousands of them, Ana Vega included, were facing lifelong slavery.

'Your mother will always be with us,' said José on the day of her wedding, trying to sound convincing. 'She'll come back one day! I'm sure of it!'

Milagros frowned; she wanted to believe her father. His assertion echoed strangely inside the Carmona house, unlike the rest of their conversation where they'd battled to hear each other over the noise. Father and daughter looked at each other: silence reigned in the alley.

'They're coming,' announced José.

Reyes and Bartola for the Garcías; Rosario and another old woman named Felisa for the Carmonas. The four gypsy women had solemnly crossed the alley towards the house of the father of the bride. The people made way for them and fell silent as they approached the building. The moment their figures vanished beyond the shared courtyard at the entrance, men and women crowded around in silence beneath Milagros's window.

'I love you, my girl,' said José Carmona in farewell when he heard the gypsy women's footsteps already at the open door. He didn't need the women to send him away. 'Let's go, *morena*,' he added to Caridad, already heading down the stairs.

Caridad gave Milagros a forced smile – she knew why the old women were coming, the girl had told her – and she followed in José's footsteps. After finding out about how she'd helped his daughter during the arrest and subsequent flight, José had finally accepted Caridad's living with them.

La Trianera didn't beat about the bush. 'Are you ready, Milagros?' she enquired.

She didn't dare to look the women in the eyes. How different it would have been if Old María were among them! She would be grumbling and complaining, but in the end she would treat her with a tenderness Milagros wasn't expecting from those women. She had begged her father to search for María, to find out what had happened to her. She also kept asking any new gypsies who appeared in Triana about the healer, in case she had decided to go somewhere else. Nobody knew anything; nobody confirmed her suspicions.

'Are you ready?' repeated La Trianera, interrupting her thoughts.

'Yes,' she stammered. Was she ready?

'Lie down on the mattress and lift up your skirt,' she heard them order her.

That young scoundrel in Camas had hurt her with his groping, when he stuck one of his disgusting fingers inside her. She had felt disgraced . . . and guilty! And at that moment she was overtaken by fear again.

'Milagros,' Rosario Carmona spoke sweetly to her, 'there are a lot of people waiting in the alley. Let's not make them impatient, thinking that . . . Lie down, please.'

And what if that boy in Camas had taken her virginity? She couldn't marry Pedro; there would be no wedding.

She lay down on the mattress and, with her eyelids trembling from the effort of keeping them closed, she lifted her skirt and petticoats and revealed her pubis. She felt someone kneel beside her. She didn't dare to look.

A few seconds passed and no one did anything. What . . . ?

'Open your legs,' La Trianera said, interrupting her thoughts again. 'How do you expect . . . ?'

'Reyes!' Rosario reprimanded her for her tone. 'Girl, open your legs, please.'

Milagros half opened them timidly. La Trianera lifted her head and shook it in Rosario Carmona's direction: *What do I do now?* she asked with an impertinent gesture. A few days earlier, Rosario had tried to talk to Milagros. 'I already know what it is,' she answered, avoiding the conversation. Every gypsy girl knew that! Besides, Old María had told her what it involved, but she had never prepared her for it or gone into detail, and now, lying on the straw mattress, naked from the waist down, she was immodestly showing her private parts to four women who at that moment felt like total strangers to her. Not even her mother had seen her like that!

'Girl . . .' Rosario was starting to beg.

But La Trianera interrupted her, grabbing Milagros's legs and opening them as best she could.

'Now pull up your knees,' she ordered, accompanying her words with a firm hand movement.

'Don't bite your lip, girl!' warned another of the women.

Milagros obeyed and stopped doing it just as La Trianera's fingers, wrapped in a handkerchief, began touching her vulva until they found the entrance to her vagina, where she drove them in which such force that she felt like she'd been stabbed: she arched her back, with her fists tightly closed at her sides and tears mixing with the cold sweat that soaked her face. As she felt the fingers scratching at her vagina she held back a howl of pain. She opened her mouth extremely wide when La Trianera dug inside her.

'Don't scream!' demanded Rosario.

'Bear it!' admonished another.

A sharp prick. The fingers come out from inside her.

Milagros let her back drop down on to the straw mattress. The heads of the four gypsy women hovered over the handkerchief while Milagros filled her lungs with the air she had desperately needed from the very beginning. She kept her eyes closed and moaned as she shook her head from side to side on the straw mattress.

'Good, Milagros!' she heard Rosario say.

'Bravo, girl!' the others congratulated her.

And while Rosario pulled down her skirt and petticoats, Reyes García headed to the window and triumphantly showed the blood-stained handkerchief to the gypsies waiting below. The cheers were immediate.

Milagros had kept them hidden and surprised Caridad with them before leaving for the church, after La Trianera and the other three gypsy women allowed her father and her friend back into the apartment: a coral necklace, a little gold bracelet and a mantilla of black satin patterned with colourful flowers that she had borrowed for the wedding. The girl's mouth widened into a smile when she entered the Santa Ana church and saw Caridad, seated in the front row beside her father, trying to remain as erect as the gypsies that surrounded her. She was wearing her red dress, the mantilla over her shoulders and the jewels on her neck and wrist. What the girl didn't notice was how forced the smile Caridad gave her was: the *morena* sensed that after she was married, their friendship would wane.

'Will we still be friends after the wedding?' Caridad had dared to ask her, in a trembling voice, after a long circumlocution plagued with throat clearing and stammering, a few days before the wedding.

'Of course!' declared Milagros. 'Pedro will be my husband, my man, but you will always be my best friend. How could I forget what we've been through together?'

Caridad stifled a sigh.

'You will live with me,' Milagros had then assured her.

The gratitude and affection in her friend's little eyes was so deep that she couldn't admit that she hadn't even broached the subject with Pedro.

'I love you, Cachita,' she whispered instead.

Nevertheless, it was true that they had been growing apart. Milagros hadn't sung in the parish again, or even in the inn, after the Christmas service. Once in a while Rafael García would hire her out for private parties in the homes of nobleman and illustrious Sevillians, which made more of a profit than the paltry coins she got from Bienvenido's customers. Caridad had been excluded from those parties by order of La Trianera. With that money and more that the parents of the bride and groom had borrowed, they could pay for the pageantry of a three-day-long wedding; there wasn't a gypsy family in Spain that didn't spend their last dime when celebrating a marriage.

In the fleeting exchange of glances, Milagros couldn't tell that her friend's smile was faked: her attention was focused on Pedro García; the young gypsy was a magnificent presence, dressed in a short purple jacket, white britches, red socks, square-toed shoes with silver buckles and a *montera* hat in his hand, and filled her with confidence as he reached her side, before the altar. *Was she that lovely and elegant?* she wondered.

Pedro stretched out a hand and her apprehension over her appearance vanished amid a thousand sparks, as if the embers of the largest forge in Triana had burst around her. He squeezed her hand as they turned towards the priest and Milagros blocked out everything that wasn't the touch of his hands, his scent, his thrilling closeness;

she hadn't been able to sense all that in the whirl of the gypsy ceremony they had just celebrated, in which Pedro's grandfather had split bread in two parts so that, once it was salted, they could exchange them and be considered married according to their law. There, in the church, the respectful silence of the place contrasting with the shouts of congratulations that still echoed in her ears, Milagros remained distant from the sermons and prayers, and she listened to the mass with mixed feelings. In front of the altar, about to marry a García, her mother, grandfather and Old María attacked her soul; none of them would have consented to that marriage. *Never forget that you are a Vega* echoed in her memory. At each wave of doubt, Milagros took refuge in Pedro: she squeezed his hand and he responded; a happy future opened out before them, she could feel it, and she looked at him to rid herself of her grandfather's vexed face. He was so handsome! *I told you, Mother, I love him, what can you reproach me for? I warned you. I love him, I love him, I love him.*

The peal of the bells marking the end of the celebration put an end to her internal struggle. She looked at the ring she wore on her finger; Pedro had put it on her, smiling at her, caressing her with his gaze, his presence promising her happiness. Her man! From the church she was carried almost through the air to the alley. She didn't have time to change her clothes as she had planned. As soon as she arrived, the women received her with baskets of cakes that the gypsies ended up throwing at each other. She danced with her new husband in the Garcías' courtyard, on a bed of egg-yolk sweets that they stomped on until their feet were sticky and they were splattered all over. Pedro kissed her passionately and she shivered with pleasure; he kissed her again and Milagros thought she was melting. Later, in the same courtyard, on top of the egg sweets, she danced with the other members of the two families. She had no time to think before she found herself forced out into the alley packed with gypsies drinking, eating, singing and dancing. There, at a frenetic pace, as if the world was ending, she was passed from hand to hand until nightfall; she didn't even see Caridad, she didn't even get a chance to dance with Pedro again and to dissolve in another of his wonderful kisses.

The large influx of guests meant that all the houses on the alley were filled to bursting. But they had reserved a room for the newly-weds in El Conde's apartment. As soon as Pedro grabbed her by the hand and pulled her, publicly interrupting one of her dances with yet another stranger, they were bombarded with obscene comments from the young gypsies following them to the apartment door. But Milagros, who was exhausted, dizzy from the wine, the shouting and all the spinning she had been subjected to throughout the day, could barely make them out.

She tried to sit down somewhere when they were alone; she was afraid of collapsing, but her young husband didn't allow it.

'Take off your clothes,' he urged as he removed his shirt.

Milagros looked at him without seeing him, amid a thick cloud, her head whirling.

Pedro started to take off his trousers. 'Come on!'

Milagros could hear him urging her amid the deafening roar of those young gypsies who were now beneath the window.

Pedro's member, large and erect, made her react and she stepped back.

'Don't be afraid,' he told her.

Milagros didn't hear any tenderness in his voice. She saw him approach her and struggle to get her dress off. His penis brushed against her again and again as he wrestled with her clothes. Then she was naked once more, like that morning with La Trianera, but this time above the waist as well. He squeezed her breasts and brought his mouth to her nipples. He ran his hands over her buttocks and inner thighs. He was panting. He sucked some dried remains of sugared yolk that was stuck to her skin as his fingers played with the lips of her vulva searching for . . . A shiver ran through Milagros's body when he reached her clitoris. What was that? She felt her vulva grow wet and her breathing speed up. The tiredness that kept her at a distance vanished and she dared to throw her arms around her husband's shoulders.

'I'm not afraid,' she whispered.

Without separating their bodies, they staggered and laughed until they were lying on a bed with legs that Rafael and Inocencio had borrowed for the occasion. Milagros opened her knees, as she had done with Reyes that morning, and Pedro penetrated her. The pain she felt was lost in her laboured declarations of love.

'I love you . . . Pedro. How . . . how I've dreamed of this moment!'

He didn't answer the promises that came from Milagros's mouth. Leaning on the bed with his hands, his torso raised over her, he looked at her with his face flushed as he secured maximum contact with her pubis, pushing firmly, trapping her to merge with her. Milagros's pain disappeared along with her words. A pleasure hitherto unknown, impossible to imagine, began to flow from her lower belly to install itself in the most secret corners of her body. Pedro continued pushing and Milagros shivered at a pleasure that seemed terrifying . . . because it was never-ending. She panted and sweated. She felt her nipples stiffen, as if they were trying to burst and couldn't manage it. She pushed against him and clawed her nails into his forearms, trying to free herself of sensations that threatened to drive her crazy. What end could there be to that pleasure that required satisfaction, that demanded she reach an unknown pinnacle? Suddenly Pedro exploded inside her with a howl that extended through his final thrust and Milagros's uncontrollable anxiety ended up vanishing, disappointed amid the shouting that hadn't stopped and which again filled the room to remind her that it was over. Pedro dropped down on her and covered her neck with kisses.

'Did you like it?' he asked, bringing his lips to her ear.

Had she liked it? She wanted more, didn't she? What was she supposed to expect?

'It was wonderful,' she answered in a whisper.

Suddenly, Pedro got up, put on his britches and with his torso still bare he leaned out of the window, and greeted the gypsies waiting below. The second time in the same day that someone had bragged publicly through the window over her, lamented Milagros when she heard the cheers intensify. Then he came over to the bed and stroked her cheek with the back of his hand.

'The most beautiful gypsy in the world,' he flattered her. 'Sleep and rest, my lovely, you still have two more days of festivities ahead of you.'

He finished dressing and went down to the alley.

'Come warm me up, *morena*,' ordered José Carmona.

Caridad stopped twisting the cigar. She had been working for José since practically the very day when, after the wedding party, El Conde had flatly refused to let her remain by Milagros's side and live with the Garcías. Then José Carmona had taken her into his house, moved by his daughter's sobs, although Caridad wasn't sure if her friend's tears were over her or from the smack that La Trianera had given her to shut her up. Later, José got tobacco leaves for her to twist as a way to fatten up his extremely empty pockets. Less than a week passed between that and his calling her over to his bed to keep him warm.

'Didn't you hear me, *morena*?'

Caridad's skilful fingers tightened around the leaf that was the cigar's wrapper. She always chose the best leaves for the wrappers, since that was what the buyer noticed first. She had never done anything like that: ruining a good tobacco leaf, but it was as if her fingers had a life of their own, and she watched in astonishment as her fingernails tore into it.

She got up from the table where she was working and headed to the mattress where José Carmona lay. She knew that the gypsy would grope her for a while, mount her from the front or from behind, then again complain about her indifference. 'It'd be better to fornicate with a mule,' he had told her the last time, and then he would end up snoring, still clutching her.

She removed her slave shirt with her teeth clenched and her eyes damp and lay down beside the gypsy. José stuck his head between her breasts and pecked at her nipples. His little bites hurt her and yet she did nothing to stop them; she deserved that punishment, she repeated night after night. Caridad had changed. What had previously not aroused any feeling in her – being passed from one hand to the next like the animal she had been taught to be on the tobacco plantation – now disgusted and repulsed her. Melchor! She was betraying him. José Carmona ran his hands over her body. Caridad couldn't help shrinking back, tense. The gypsy didn't even notice. What had become of Melchor? Many assumed he was dead, among them Milagros. The rumours of a clash between smugglers that he seemed to have been involved in had reached Triana, but no one was able to confirm anything for certain. They all were talking about what someone else had told them, news that had in turn been obtained from third parties. However, she knew that Melchor wasn't dead. José didn't let her sing, he said that Negro songs annoyed him, although he gave up trying to keep her from softly humming those rhythms that, along with the tobacco's aroma, took her back to her roots. And Caridad sang softly as she worked, imagining that the man lying behind her was Melchor. In the darkest hours of the night, when José was sleeping deeply, she searched for her gods: Oshún, Oyá . . . Eleggua, he who arranges men's lives at his whim, he who had allowed her to live when Melchor found her beneath a tree. Then she would smoke and sing until her senses were intoxicated and she was able to receive the presence of the greatest of the gods. Melchor was alive. Eleggua confirmed it for her.

José Carmona slithered on top of Caridad, trying to enter her. She didn't want to open her legs.

'Move it, damn darkie!' the gypsy demanded tonight, yet again.

And she did, with guilt destroying the last corner of her consciousness. But what else could she do? She would lose Milagros. José would kick her out. Rafael García would banish her from the alley without a second thought. It was there, with his people, with the gypsies, close to his granddaughter, that she should wait for Melchor. She closed her eyes, resigned to the re-encounter with the feeling that was so new and strange to her as a man mounted her: repugnance.

'Morena!'

Caridad half opened her eyes. The burgeoning light of dawn still left most of the house in shadow. She struggled to understand. José was snoring, hugging her. She tried to clear her vision. A yellow spot, blurry, was standing beside her.

'What are you doing there?'

Caridad leapt up when she recognized the voice.

'And my daughter? Where is Ana?'

Melchor! Caridad sat on the mattress before him, her breasts exposed. She pulled on the blanket to cover them; a wave of suffocating heat rushed to her face. José grumbled in his dreams.

The old gypsy wasn't able to keep his gaze from focusing on those black breasts and the large areolas that surrounded their nipples. He had desired them . . . and now . . .

'Why are you sleeping with that . . . that . . . ?' He couldn't get the words out; in their place he pointed to José with a trembling hand.

Caridad remained silent, hiding her eyes.

'Wake that scoundrel up,' he then ordered.

The woman shook José, who was slow to understand.

'Melchor,' he greeted him with slurred voice as he got up, dishevelled, and tried to fix his shirt. 'About time you came back. You've always had a talent for disappearing in the most—'

'And my daughter?' the grandfather interrupted him, his face flushed. 'What is the *morena* doing in your bed? And my granddaughter?'

José brought a hand to his chin and stroked it before answering. 'Milagros is well. Ana is still in prison in Málaga.'

José turned his back to his father-in-law and headed to the cupboard to serve himself a glass of water from a pitcher that Caridad always kept filled.

'They won't let her out,' he added, facing him after drinking a sip. 'It seems that Vega blood always causes problems. The *morena*?' he added with a contemptuous gesture towards Caridad. 'She warms my nights; not much more could be expected of her.'

Caridad surprised herself by daring to scrutinize Melchor: the wrinkles that lined his face seemed to have multiplied, but despite the yellow dress coat that hung from his shoulders like a sack, he hadn't lost his proud gypsy bearing or that gaze that could cut through stone. Melchor felt Caridad's interest and turned his head towards her. She couldn't hold his gaze and lifted the blanket covering her breasts up higher. She had failed him, his eyes reproached her.

'She sings well,' said Melchor then with a tremendous sadness that made Caridad's hair stand on end.

'You call that singing?' laughed José.

'What would you know!' muttered Melchor, dragging out the words, his eyes still on Caridad. He had come to desire her, but he had renounced her body in order to continue hearing those songs that oozed pain, and now she was in José's hands. He shook his head. 'What have you done to free my daughter?' he suddenly spat in a weary voice.

With that question Caridad knew that she was no longer the focus of Melchor's attention and she lifted her gaze to watch the two gypsies in the light of dawn: the gaunt grandfather in his yellow dress coat; the blacksmith, with his strong chest, neck and arms, planted arrogantly in front of the old man.

'For my wife . . .' José corrected him slowly. 'I have done all that can be done. It's your fault, old man: the stigma of your blood has been her undoing, like all Vegas. Only a pardon from the King would get her out of jail.'

'What are you doing here then, enjoying my Negress, instead of at the court getting that pardon?'

José just shook his head and pursed his lips, as if what Melchor suggested were impossible.

'Where is my granddaughter?' Melchor then asked.

Caridad trembled.

'She lives with her husband,' answered José, 'as is her duty.'

Melchor waited for an explanation that didn't come.

'What husband?' he finally asked.

The other man straightened up, threateningly. 'Don't you know?'

'I walked day and night to get here. No, I don't know.'

'Pedro García, El Conde's grandson.'

Melchor tried to speak but his words came out in an unintelligible stammer.

'Forget about Milagros. It's not your problem,' spat out José.

Melchor gasped in search of air. Caridad saw him raise a hand to his side and double over with a grimace of pain.

'You're old, Galeote . . .'

Melchor didn't listen to the rest of his son-in-law's words. *You're old, Galeote*, the same words El Gordo had spat at him on the Barrancos road. Caridad in the arms of José, his daughter imprisoned in Málaga, and Milagros, his girl, whom he loved most in this damn world, living with Rafael García, obeying Rafael García, fornicating with the grandson of Rafael García! The wound he'd thought was healed now struggled to burst his stomach. He had renounced taking revenge on Rafael García for Milagros, the child that Basilio put in his arms when he came back from the galleys. What good had it done? His blood, the Vega blood, that very girl's, would mix with that of those who had betrayed him and stolen ten years of his life. He twisted in pain. He wanted to die. His girl! He stumbled. He searched for some place to rest. Caridad leapt up to help him. José took a step forward. Neither of them reached him. Before they could, the pain shifted to wrath; berserk, blind with rage, he pulled his knife from his sash and as soon as he opened it he pounced on his son-in-law.

'Traitor! Son of a bitch!' he howled as he sank the weapon into José's chest, into his heart.

He only realized the magnitude of what he had done when he saw José Carmona's surprised eyes, knowing his death was near. He had just murdered his granddaughter's father!

Caridad, naked, remained still, out of reach, and watched the convulsions that announced the gypsy's death, lying on the floor with a large pool of blood forming around him. Melchor tried to stand up straight, but he couldn't quite manage it, and he brought the bloody hand that held the knife to the wound that El Gordo had given him.

'Traitor,' he then repeated, more for Caridad than the corpse of José Carmona. 'He was a traitorous dog,' he said to defend himself against the terror in her face. He thought for an instant. He ran his eyes over the room. 'Get dressed and go get my granddaughter,' he urged. 'Tell her that her father wants to see her. Don't tell her about me; nobody should know that I'm here.'

Caridad obeyed. As she crossed the alley and returned with Milagros, worried by the Negro woman's persistent silence in response to her questions, Melchor dragged José's corpse with great difficulty over to the next room to hide it. How would Milagros react? Carmona was her father and she loved him, but he had asked for it . . . Melchor didn't have time to clean up the trail of blood that streaked the floor, or the large stain that shone damply in the middle of the room, or his knife blade, or his yellow dress coat; Milagros only saw him and leapt into his arms.

'Grandfather!' she screamed. Then her words caught in her throat, mixed with sobs of joy.

Melchor hesitated, but in the end he hugged her too, and rocked her. 'Milagros,' he whispered again and again.

Caridad, behind them, couldn't help following the trail of blood with her eyes, before focusing again on granddaughter and grandfather, and then back at the bloodstain in the middle of the room.

'Let's go, girl,' said Melchor suddenly.

'But you just arrived!' responded Milagros, leaning back from him with a wide smile on her lips, her arms still holding him, to get a better look at him.

'No . . .' corrected Melchor. 'I mean let's leave . . . Triana.'

Milagros saw her grandfather's stained coat. Her expression soured and she checked her own clothes, impregnated with blood.

'What . . . ?' The girl looked beyond Melchor.

'Let's go, girl. We'll go to Madrid, to beg for your mother's freedom—'

'What's that blood?' she interrupted him.

She pulled away from her grandfather and kept him from tugging her back. She discovered the trail. Caridad saw her first tremble and then bring her hands to her head. Neither Caridad nor Melchor went into the next room, from which a shriek emerged, blending with the hammering of the blacksmiths who had already begun their working day. Caridad, as if her friend's heart-rending scream was pushing her, backed up until she was against the wall. Melchor brought a hand to his face and closed his eyes.

'What have you done?' The accusation emerged cracked from Milagros's throat; the girl searched for support in the lintel of the doorway between the rooms. 'Why . . . ?'

'He betrayed us!' reacted Melchor, raising his voice.

'Murderer.' Milagros was dripping with rage. 'Murderer,' she repeated, dragging out each syllable.

'He betrayed the Vegas by marrying you—'

'It wasn't him!'

Melchor straightened his neck and squinted his eyes towards his granddaughter.

'No, it wasn't him, Grandfather. It was Inocencio. And he did it to free Mother from prison in Málaga.'

'I . . . I didn't know . . . I'm sorry . . .' Melchor managed to say, awed by his granddaughter's pain. Yet he rallied instantly. 'Your mother would never have accepted that arrangement,' he declared. 'A García! You married a García! She would have chosen prison. Your father should have done the same!'

'Families and their quarrels!' sobbed Milagros, as if detached from her grandfather's words. 'He was my father. He wasn't a Vega or a García or even a Carmona . . . he was my father, do you understand? My father!'

'Come with me. Leave behind those—'

'He was all I had,' she lamented.

'You have me, girl, and we will get your mother's free—'

Milagros spat at her grandfather's feet before he could finish his sentence.

The contempt in that gob of spit, from the person he most loved in the world, made his face quiver and his eyelids tremble. Melchor was silent even when he saw her shout and pounce on Caridad.

'And you?'

Caridad couldn't move; frozen in that spot as she was, she wouldn't have anyway. Milagros screamed in her face.

'What did you do? What did you do?' she demanded again and again.

'The *morena* didn't do anything,' intervened Melchor in her defence.

'That's it!' shrieked Milagros. 'Look at me,' she demanded. And since Caridad didn't lift her eyes, she smacked her. 'Fucking nigger! That's it: you never do anything. You've never done anything! You let him murder him!'

Milagros started to beat her breasts with both fists, up and down. Caridad didn't defend herself. Caridad didn't speak. Caridad couldn't look at Milagros. 'You killed him!'

For the first time in her life Caridad felt pain in all its intensity and she realized that, unlike the wounds inflicted by the overseer and the master, these would never heal.

One girl screamed and hit; the other cried.

'Murderer,' sobbed Milagros, letting her arms fall to her sides, unable to hit her even one more time.

For a few seconds the only sound to be heard was the hammering that came from the forges. Milagros collapsed on the floor at the feet of Caridad, who didn't dare move; nor did Melchor.

'*Morena*,' she heard him say. 'Gather your things. We're leaving.'

Caridad looked at Milagros, hoping, yearning for her to say something . . .

'Go,' was all she spat out. 'I never want to see you again as long as I live.'

'Gather your things,' insisted the gypsy.

Caridad went to find her bundle, red outfit and straw hat. While she grabbed her few belongings, Melchor, without daring to look at his granddaughter, calculated what effect his actions would have: if they caught them in the San Miguel alley or in Triana, they would kill them. And even when they fled, the council of elders would pronounce a death sentence against him and most likely the *morena* as well, and they would let all the families in the kingdom know about it. It was in Milagros's hands whether they would be able to escape Triana alive.

Caridad returned with her things and looked for the last time at the only friend she had ever had. She hesitated as she passed by her, huddled, crying, cursing between moans. She couldn't have stopped Melchor. She remembered running towards him, and the next thing she had seen was José's badly injured body.

Milagros had told her that she didn't want to ever see her again. She tried to tell her that it hadn't been her fault, but at that moment Melchor pushed her out of the apartment.

'I'm sorry for you, girl. I trust that some day your pain will ease,' he said to his granddaughter before leaving.

Then they both left the building, hastily. They needed time to flee. If Milagros sounded the alarm, they wouldn't even make it out of the alley.

THE VOICE OF FREEDOM

23

THEY FLED TRIANA over the pontoon bridge and entered the streets of Seville. Melchor headed to the house of an old notary public who no longer practised.

'We need fake passports to get to Madrid,' Caridad heard him asking the old man, openly.

'The Negress, too?' he enquired, pointing at her from behind a solid wood desk piled with books, folders and papers.

Melchor, who had sat in one of the chairs on the other side of the desk, turned his head towards her. 'Are you coming with me, *morena*?'

Of course she wanted to go with him! But . . . Melchor guessed at the thoughts going through Caridad's mind.

'We'll go to Madrid to get Ana freed. My daughter will fix everything,' he added, convinced.

How is Ana going to fix José's death? wondered Caridad. Yet she clung to that hope. If Melchor trusted in his daughter, she wasn't going to be the one to object, so she nodded.

'Yes,' confirmed Melchor to the notary, 'the Negress too.'

The old man took half the morning to forge the documents that would allow them to travel to Madrid. Using an old provision of the Royal Court of Seville he elevated Melchor to the rank of 'old Castilian' based on the merits of his ancestors in the wars of Granada, in which some gypsies had accompanied the armies of the Catholic Kings as blacksmiths. He added a second document: a passport that authorized him to go to Madrid to procure his daughter's freedom. He turned Caridad, who showed him the manumission documents that they had given her on the boat, into a maid. Even though she wasn't a gypsy, she still needed a passport.

As he put together the documents, the couple waited in the front hallway of the house. Caridad leaned on the wall, exhausted, yet not daring to slide down the tiles until she was seated on the floor, to hide her face and try to make sense of what she had experienced that morning. Melchor seemed to be trying to get away from the blood staining his dress coat as he paced up and down in the small space.

'He's a good man,' he commented to himself, without looking to see if Caridad was listening. 'He owes me a lot of favours. Yes, he's good. The best!' he added with a laugh. 'You know what, *morena*? Notaries public make their living off the fees they charge for trial papers: so much per page, so much per letter. Those damn letters get expensive! And since they charge for the papers, many notaries provoke lawsuits, quarrels and rows between people. That way there are trials and they make a profit. Every time I passed through his district, Eulogio would ask me to start up some trouble: denounce someone; steal from somebody and stash the booty in somebody else's house . . . Once he gave me the address of a ruffian who was exploiting his wife's charms. A magnificent female!' he exclaimed after stopping, lifting his head and shaking his chin. 'If she were mine . . .'

He interrupted himself and turned towards Caridad, who kept her gaze on her trembling hands. The ruffian's wife had never been his, but Caridad . . . When he had surprised her in bed with José he had felt as if she had indeed once been his and that Carmona had stolen her from him.

Caridad didn't take her eyes off her hands. She didn't care about Melchor's shady dealings with the notary public. She could only think of the terrible scene she had witnessed. It had all happened so quickly . . . ! Melchor's appearance, her own shame at being naked, the fight, the stabbing and the blood. Milagros had followed her to her father's house, all the while asking why, as she stammered excuses, and then . . . She clasped her hands tightly together to keep them from shaking.

Melchor resumed his pacing along the hallway, now in silence.

They obtained the documents plus a letter of recommendation that the old notary addressed to a colleague who worked in Madrid.

'I think he's still alive,' he commented. 'And he is entirely trustworthy,' he added, winking at the gypsy.

The partners in crime said goodbye to each other with a heartfelt embrace.

To avoid going through Triana, they left Seville through the Macarena Gate and headed west, towards Portugal, along the same road that Milagros, Caridad and Old María had taken almost a year earlier. *Whatever happened to her?* thought the former slave as soon as her gaze took in the open field. If Old María had been there maybe Milagros, whom she loved so much, wouldn't have sent her away after screaming and beating her. Caridad stroked one of her breasts – but what harm could her friend's fists do to her? She hurt inside, in the deepest, most private part of her being. If at least María had been there . . . But the old woman had disappeared.

'Sing, *morena*!'

They took a lonely path among gardens and fields of crops. The gypsy was walking in front of Caridad with his huge, faded yellow dress coat hanging from his shoulders; he hadn't even turned towards her.

Sing? She had reason to sing, to use her voice, as the Negro slaves did, to cry out her sadness and lament her misfortune, but . . .

'No!' she shouted. It was the first time she refused to sing for him.

After stopping for a second, Melchor took a couple of steps.

'You killed Milagros's father!' Caridad yelled at his back.

'Who you were sleeping with!' screamed the gypsy, turning suddenly and accusing her with one finger.

The woman opened her hands in a gesture of incomprehension. 'What . . . ? And what could I do? I lived with him. He forced me.'

'Refuse!' replied Melchor. 'That's what you could have done.'

Caridad wanted to respond that she would have done that if she'd had any news from him. She wanted to tell him that she had been a slave for too many years, an obedient slave, but her words contorted into a sob.

Then it was the gypsy who opened his hands. Caridad was planted before him, just a few steps away. Her worn burlap shirt rose and fell to the rhythm of her sobbing.

Melchor hesitated. He went over to her. '*Morena*,' he whispered. He made as if to hug her, but she took a step back.

'You killed him!' she accused him again.

'It wasn't like that,' he replied. 'He sought out his own death.' Before Caridad could interject, he continued. 'For a gypsy there is a big difference.'

He turned around and continued along the path.

She watched him head off.

'And Milagros?' she shouted.

Melchor clenched his teeth tightly. He was sure that the girl would get over it. As soon as he freed her mother . . .

'What's going to happen to Milagros?' insisted Caridad.

The gypsy turned his head. '*Morena*, are you coming or not?'

She followed him. With Seville at their backs, she dragged her bare feet behind the gypsy, allowing herself a dry, deep sobbing, just as when they separated her from her mother and from her little Marcelo. Then it had been the white masters who had sealed her sad fate, but now . . . now it was Milagros herself who had rejected her friendship. Her doubts about her guilt hounded her: she had only obeyed, as she always did. In pain she relived the applause with which Milagros had received her the first time she wore her red outfit. The laughter, the affection, the friendship! The suffering after the gypsies were arrested. So many shared moments . . .

She continued such musing until they reached a monastery where Melchor forced her to wait at the door.

He came out with money and a good mule fitted out with saddlebags.

'More friars, like the ones in Santo Domingo de Portaceli,' commented the gypsy once they were on the road again, 'who won't ever trust me again when they see that I don't bring them the tobacco I promised.'

Caridad remembered the episode and the tall, white-haired prior who hadn't had the guts to challenge the gypsies who had brought him fewer bags than they'd agreed on. *All my fault*, she said to herself accusingly.

'But my daughter comes first,' continued the gypsy. 'And we need this money to multiply it and buy favours in the court. Surely their God will understand it that way, and if their God understands it, they'll have to understand it too, right?'

Melchor spoke as they walked, not expecting a reply. However, when they stopped, he fell into the melancholy that Caridad knew so well. Then he talked to himself, even though sometimes he turned to her in search of an approval she didn't concede.

'Do you agree, *morena*?' he asked her again. Caridad didn't answer. Melchor shrugged it off and continued. 'I have to get them to free my daughter. Only Ana will be able to bring that girl into line. Marrying a García! The grandson of El Conde! You'll see, *morena*, everything will be the way it was as soon as Ana appears . . .'

Caridad stopped listening to him. *Everything will be the way it was.* The tears clouded her image of the gypsy pulling the mule in front of her.

'And if the friars don't like it,' said Melchor, 'they can come looking for me. They can join up with the Garcías, who will be after me too. No doubt about it, *morena*. By this time the council of elders will already have gathered to pass our death sentences. Maybe you'll get lucky, but I doubt it. I can imagine the smug smiles on the faces of Rafael and his bitch of a wife. They will hide the corpse so that the King's justice doesn't intervene and they will set gypsy justice in motion. Shortly every gypsy in Spain will find out about our sentence and any of them could carry it out. Although not every gypsy obeys the Garcías and the elders of Triana,' he added after a while.

They went through towns without stopping. They bought tobacco and food with the money from the friars and they slept out in the open, always heading northwest, towards the Portuguese border. At nights, Melchor would light one of the cigars and share it with

Caridad. They both inhaled deeply until their lungs were filled; they both let themselves be carried away by the pleasant feeling of lethargy the tobacco gave them. Melchor didn't ask her to sing again and she didn't.

'Milagros will get over it,' she heard Melchor declaring one of those nights, suddenly, breaking the silence. 'Her father was not a good gypsy.'

Caridad remained quiet. Day after day, in silence, in utmost privacy, she again felt Milagros beating on her breasts and her dreams were disturbed by the young woman's angry face insulting her and screaming out that she never wanted to see her again.

They reached the Aracena mountain range. Melchor avoided the outskirts of Jabugo and took a detour to reach Encinasola and from there to Barrancos, in that no man's land between Spain and Portugal that the blacksmith – the one they had met as they fled through the Andévalo – had told them about.

The gypsy was kindly received by the owner of an establishment that provided tobacco to Spanish smugglers.

'We'd given you up for dead, Galeote,' said Méndez after greeting him affectionately. 'El Gordo's men told us of your wound—'

'It wasn't my time. I still have things to do around here,' interrupted Melchor.

'I never liked El Gordo.'

'He stole two leather bags of my tobacco on the beaches of Manilva, then he ordered the killing of my cousin's grandson.'

Méndez nodded pensively.

That was how Caridad found out about the death of the captain of the smugglers' party who had tricked her on the beach, causing such trouble and problems. She noticed that Melchor was looking at her out of the corner of his eye when Méndez asked him about the woman armed with a blunderbuss who had challenged an entire party of men and shot a smuggler, and the two large dogs that had killed El Gordo in their jaws, and how that woman had fled with what everyone assumed was his corpse.

'She saved your life,' declared Méndez. 'You must be grateful.'

Caridad perked up her ears. Melchor sensed her interest and gave her another sidelong glance before answering.

'You *payos*, your women included, have the wrong idea about gratitude.'

They stayed in the tobacco seller's place and, just as at the inn in Gaucín, Melchor made sure to make it clear to every runner and smuggler who showed up that Caridad was his and therefore untouchable. Melchor spent the first three days in meetings with Méndez.

'Don't go too far, *morena*,' the gypsy told her. 'There are always bad people wandering around here.'

Caridad listened to him and hung around the stables and the surrounding area, looking at the landscape that stretched away from her feet and thinking of Milagros; watching the people who came and went with their sacks and backpacks, and remembering Milagros again; taking refuge from her pain in the tobacco that was plentiful there and thinking of her . . . and of Melchor.

'Who was the woman who saved you from El Gordo?' she asked one night as they lay on adjoining straw mattresses in a large room they shared with other smugglers. She didn't have to lower her voice; at the other end of the room, a runner was enjoying one of the many prostitutes that followed the scent of money. It wasn't the first time that had happened.

For a few moments only the sound of the couple's panting was heard.

'Someone who helped me,' answered Melchor when Caridad had already given up waiting for an answer. 'I don't think she'd do it again,' he added with a twinge of sadness that didn't go unnoticed by Caridad.

The panting turned into muffled howls before reaching ecstasy. Those women enjoyed being with men, thought Caridad, something that seemed out of her reach.

'Sing, *morena*,' said the gypsy, interrupting her thoughts.

Could he have known what she was thinking? She wanted to sing. She needed to sing. She wanted everything to be the way it used to be.

They were awaiting the arrival of a shipment of French snuff, explained Melchor when Caridad asked him how long they would be there and why they weren't going to Madrid to get Ana freed.

'It usually comes in through Catalonia,' continued the gypsy. 'But the tobacco patrol is getting more and more vigilant and it's complicated. It is very difficult and expensive to get, but we'll make a good profit.'

The consumption of snuff, the thick powdered tobacco produced in France, was illegal in Spain; only the very fine Spanish powder was allowed, the colour of gold and perfumed with orange-flower water in the tobacco factory in Seville, better than any snuff according to many. Although there were other types of powders – one made with stems and ribs, one mixed with mud, one doused with a diluted aromatic vinegar, one mixed with red ochre – the gold-coloured one was the best. However, the appeal of all things French, including snuff, won out over even the orders from the Crown, and the first ones to disobey them were the courtiers themselves. The King had ordered severe penalties for snuff consumption: aristocrats and noblemen could be punished with stiff fines and four years of exile for the first offence; twice the fine and four years of prison in Africa for the second, and perpetual exile and loss of all assets for the third. The others, the common people, were sentenced with fines, whippings, galleys and even death.

But the elegance of sniffing snuff instead of Spanish powder, together with the risk and appeal of the forbidden, meant that in the parlours of most courtiers and noblemen, they continued to do so. How could a fop bear to humiliate himself with Spanish powder, despite its quality being recognized throughout Europe? And snuff consumption was so high in the court itself that the authorities naively began to allow secret denunciations: the denouncer had the right to receive the fine imposed on the accused and the judge had to hand it to them personally and keep their identity secret; but Spain was no place for keeping secrets, and snuff continued to be smuggled in and sniffed.

Méndez had promised them a good variety: dark powder as thick as sawdust, made in France using techniques that each factory kept confidential. The thickest, fleshiest tobacco leaves were mixed with some chemical elements (nitrates, potash and salts) and natural elements (wine, liquor, rum, lemon juice, treacle, raisins, almonds, figs . . .). The tobacco and the mixture from each factory was wetted down, cooked, allowed to ferment for six months, pressed into rolls and aged again for another six or eight months. The French aristocrats personally scraped the rolls or *carottes* with small rasps, but that wasn't the style in Spain, so the snuff came already prepared and ready to blacken the nostrils, beards and moustaches of those who consumed it, to the extent that in the court they no longer used white handkerchiefs, but grey ones instead, to hide the mucus brought on by the constant sneezing.

'Are we going to bring it to Madrid?' asked Caridad.

'Yes. We'll sell it there.'

Melchor hesitated, but finally decided to hide from her what could happen to them if they were arrested with a shipment of snuff in their possession. They were both sitting in the sun, on a large rock from which they could see the entire Múrtiga River valley, indolently whiling away the hours.

'How long do we have to wait?'

'I don't know. It has to arrive from France, first in boat and then get here.'

Caridad sucked her tongue in annoyance: the sooner they got to Madrid, the sooner they would free Ana and Milagros's mother could fix things. Melchor misinterpreted the gesture.

'Do you know what, *morena*?' he said then. 'I think we could do something useful while we're waiting.'

As dawn was breaking the next day, in the first light, loading sacks on their backs like simple runners, Caridad and Melchor crossed the border and entered Spanish territory. Méndez informed the gypsy that the priests in Galaroza needed tobacco.

'From now on, *morena*,' warned Melchor as soon as they started the descent from Barrancos along a steep hidden goat path, 'silence, watch your step and . . . don't even think about singing.'

She couldn't hold back a nervous little giggle. The idea of smuggling with Melchor thrilled her.

They were perhaps the most wonderful days of Caridad's life. Magic, intimate days: the two of them walking in silence along lonely paths, among trees and fields of crops, listening to the sound of each other's breathing, brushing against each other, hiding when they heard horses approaching. Then they smiled at each other when they were sure it wasn't the tobacco patrol. Melchor told her about the paths, the tobacco, smuggling and its people, explaining things to her in more detail than he ever had with anyone before. Caridad was captivated; every once in a while she stopped to gather some herbs with the intention of drying them once they returned: rosemary, pennyroyal . . . and many others she was unfamiliar with but whose aroma convinced her to pick them as well. Melchor let her do her thing; he put down the sack and he sat to observe her, drawn by her movements, her body, her voluptuousness. His apprehension over the José matter was gradually fading.

They were in no rush. Their time was theirs. The roads were theirs. The sun was theirs, and the moon that illuminated their first night out in the open, which they shared with the distant howling of wolves and the busy nocturnal animals.

It took almost a month, which to them seemed too short, for the promised snuff to arrive. Melchor and Caridad went back out smuggling through the area several times.

'Sing, *morena*,' the gypsy requested.

They had stopped for the night on their way back from Barrancos, already freed of their load of tobacco and the risk that the patrol might catch them with it. The spring was in full bloom and they could hear the flowing waters of the brook Melchor had decided to set up camp by. After eating some meat with sauce and bread, and taking some sips of the wine they carried in a leather wineskin, the gypsy lay down on the ground, atop an old blanket.

Caridad smoked by the side of the brook, a few paces away. She turned to look at him. She had agreed to sing every time Melchor asked her to since she had first decided to sing shortly after reaching Barrancos. However, as soon as she began the first laments, the gypsy would lose himself in his own world and his presence would fade. Caridad had spent days sharing his lively company. She didn't want him to plunge into that hole that seemed to demand his attention so anxiously; she wanted to feel him alive.

She approached him, sat by his side and offered him a smoke. The gypsy took a drag and gave her back the cigar. The murmur of the brook's waters mingled with the thoughts of each. Gradually, her breathing made her desire known.

'And what if everything changes and you don't sing the same way?'

Caridad couldn't find the words to answer. It would change, undoubtedly, but it was something that she yearned for with her entire body.

'Do you mean that my singing won't be sad any more?' she asked.

'Yes.'

'I would like to be happy. A happy woman.'

Melchor was surprised to find himself approaching her with a tenderness he had never shown any woman: delicately, as if afraid to break her. Caridad surrendered herself to his kisses and caresses. She delighted in them, discovering a thousand hidden corners of her being that seemed to want to respond passionately to the mere brush of a fingertip. She knew she was wanted. Melchor made love to her gently. Melchor spoke sweetly to her. She cried, and the gypsy remained stock-still until he realized that those tears weren't tears of grief, and he whispered in her ear lovely things she'd never been told before. Caridad panted and howled just like the wolves in the mountain's thick vegetation.

Later, in the light of the moon, naked, with the brook's water licking her knees, she insisted until she got Melchor to come over. She kicked water on to him, just as Marcelo did with her on the plantation as soon as they stepped into a puddle. The gypsy complained and Caridad splashed him again. Melchor pretended he was about to lie down again, but then turned suddenly and leapt on her. Caridad let out a shout and ran off down the river. They played naked in the brook, running and splashing like little kids. Exhausted, they drank and smoked, gazing at each other, getting to know each other, and they made love again and stayed in each other's arms until the sun was high in the sky.

'You don't sing the same any more.' He reproached her in the room at Méndez's house. They had brought their straw mattresses together, but, as if they had agreed on it without ever having discussed it, they didn't make love there where the smugglers and runners slept with the prostitutes. They preferred to go out in search of the cover of sky.

'Would you rather I stopped?' she asked, interrupting her song.

Melchor thought about his answer; she gave him an affectionate punch on the shoulder to get him to reply.

'*Morena*, never hit a gypsy.'

'Negro slaves can hit our gypsies,' she declared categorically.

And she continued singing.

There is a coach road that links Madrid with Lisbon via Badajoz. From Barrancos it would have been easy to head to Mérida through Jerez de los Caballeros, follow it to Trujillo, Talavera de la Reina, Móstoles, Alcorcón and enter the capital through the Segovia Gate; they were little more than seventy leagues from Madrid, about two weeks of walking. It took them almost the same amount of time moving quickly along solitary paths that were new to Melchor. They left behind the tranquillity they had enjoyed in Barrancos; they had the snuff and they needed to free Ana. However, a gypsy dressed in yellow, a Negress and a mule loaded with a large sealed earthenware jar that smelled of perfumed tobacco couldn't travel along the main roads.

But while the gypsy had to use all of his instincts, often leaving Caridad and the mule in a safe place while he went to inns or farm-houses to ask for directions, it wouldn't be the same in Madrid: he had been there twice. 'I know Madrid,' he assured her. Besides, it was often the subject of conversation among the smugglers, who exchanged all types of experiences, addresses and contacts. A great deal of money moved through Madrid: that was where the King lived surrounded and served by a large court; almost the entire Spanish nobility; ambassadors and foreign traders; thousands of clerics; a veritable army of high-ranking officials with sufficient resources and a burning desire to feign a high birth they lacked, and above all countless

Frenchified fops whose only objective seemed to be enjoying life's pleasures.

They stopped less than half a league from Madrid. Melchor took a good sample of the snuff and they buried the earthenware jar in a thicket.

'Are you going to remember where . . . ?' Caridad was worried when she realized that the gypsy planned to leave the jar hidden there.

'*Morena,*' he interrupted her seriously. 'I assure you that I'll remember how to get back to this place faster than how to return to Triana.'

'But what if someone—?' insisted Caridad.

'Jinx!' interrupted the gypsy again. 'Don't invite bad luck!'

Further on, at an inn, they sold the mule.

'We'll attract enough attention with you at my side without pulling along that animal,' joked Melchor sweetly. 'Besides, I don't think we can cross by night with the mule.'

With the city in their sights, they hid among the vegetable gardens on the outskirts. Melchor sat against a tree and closed his eyes.

'Wake me up when it gets dark,' he said after an exaggerated yawn.

From the other side of the lowlands of the Manzanares, Caridad ran her gaze over the Madrid that rose before them. Its highest point was a palace in construction at whose feet she could make out a large city with all sorts of jumbled houses. What awaited them there? Her thoughts returned to Milagros . . . and to Ana. Was Melchor right when he maintained that Ana would fix everything?

A couple of hours passed before the sun began to set over Madrid, tinting its buildings and bringing up reddish glints from its belfries and the pointed tips of the towers that projected above them.

In the moonlight they headed towards the Toledo Bridge. Since they were coming from Portugal, they should have crossed the Segovia Bridge, but Melchor ruled it out.

'It's very close to what was the citadel of the kings and many noblemen and important courtiers live there, and there is always more surveillance in those areas.'

They crossed the bridge stealthily, hunched over, up against the parapet, so much so that instead of travelling in a straight line they followed the little semicircular balconies that opened over the Manzanares River. There were no guards, although between the river and the Toledo Gate that led to the city there was a considerable area covered with vegetable gardens and hills both small and large, over which the last buildings of Madrid rose.

Since Madrid didn't have suburbs, its outline was perfectly delineated by those last buildings: it was forbidden to build beyond the wall that surrounded the city, and the growing population accrued inside. Melchor remembered that wall well. It wasn't wide like the one around Seville and many of the kingdom's cities and even humble towns, but just a simple masonry wall. And the truth was that Madrid's walls, which were interrupted by and combined at many points with the very faces of the city's last buildings, was only respected by the citizens in the case of epidemics. In those cases they did close the entrances into the city, but while there was no such danger, the wall offered countless gaps along its length, and as soon as they were repaired, more showed up in another stretch. It was as easy to open up a hole in a wall as it was to count on the complicity of one of the owners of the houses whose façades made up parts of it.

Melchor and Caridad crossed the vegetable gardens and arrived at the Toledo Gate: a couple of simple rectangular openings, closed at night, without any decoration and set into the wall that enclosed the street with the same name. To the right, instead of the wall, there was a slaughterhouse for cattle and rams, with several doors that opened out and allowed the animals to enter directly from the field.

You just have to wait until some runner who knows how to get in shows up, Melchor remembered hearing from a smuggler, in an inn. *Then you join him, you pay and you go in.* Someone asked, *And what if nobody shows up?* The first guy laughed out loud. *In Madrid? There's more traffic at night than during the day.*

They stationed themselves in front of the slaughterhouse and waited hidden beside a corral that was used as a place to store straw and dry skins; Melchor remembered being assured that many people slipped in through the doors of that slaughterhouse.

However, time passed and nothing indicated that anyone planned on going through the Madrid wall that night. *And what if they are quieter than we are?* thought Melchor.

'Morena,' he then said aloud, willing to attract the attention of anyone moving about there but indicating with a finger to his lips that Caridad remain silent. 'If I didn't hear you breathing, I'd think you weren't with me. You are so black and silent! Behind these doors and the slaughterhouse are the neighbourhoods of El Rastro and Lavapiés. They stretch over this whole part of Madrid. Good people live there; *manolos* they call them. What a name! Arrogant and reckless, ready to get into a knife fight over a wrong word or an indiscreet glance at their women. And what women!' He sighed as he opened his knife, making sure to silence the clicking of the mechanism; he had heard suspicious noises. Then he moved closer to Caridad and whispered, 'Be on the lookout and don't approach anyone. And what women!' he repeated almost in a shout. 'I tell ya, they'd only be better if they were gypsies! The last time I was in Madrid, after the King honoured me by allowing me to row his galleys . . .'

The attackers thought they were going to catch the gypsy unawares. Melchor, in a state of tension, with his senses alert and gripping his knife, didn't want to kill either of the two men whom he thought were approaching; he needed them.

'You . . . !' one of the bandits interrupted Melchor's speech.

He didn't have a chance to say anything more. Melchor turned and dealt him a stab to the hand in which he saw the flash of a blade, and almost before the weapon hit the floor he was already behind the man and pressing his knife against his throat.

The gypsy wanted to threaten him but the words wouldn't come out: he was panting. *I'm not so young any more!* he thought resignedly. And, as if wanting to refute his own weakness, he pressed the knife against his captive's neck so it was he, in the end, who screamed instead.

'Stay still, Diego!' he begged his companion, surprised just a step away from them.

This Diego hesitated as he tried to get his eyes accustomed to the darkness.

'Diego . . . for Our Lady of Atocha . . .' repeated the first man.

Once he had caught his breath, Melchor was able to speak. 'Listen to him, Diego,' advised the gypsy. 'We don't want to hurt you. This can all end well. We just want to get into Madrid, like you.'

Melchor had forgotten to mention to Caridad that the people called *manolos* were not only bold, proud and indolent, but they were also loyal. They had become leaders of the atavistic forms of Spanish life, and found themselves in constant struggle against what they considered the superficiality and frivolity of the nobility and the Frenchified influential classes. That sense of honour, which had been shown throughout Spain's history in so many epic chapters, and which was now threatened by the authorities, meant that when they made a commitment they felt obliged to fulfil it, as if their identities depended on it.

'Word of honour!' Melchor heard them both say.

That is what sets a manolo *apart from a gypsy,* Melchor said to himself, smiling, while loosening his grip on the man's throat with total confidence, closing the knife and hiding it again in his sash: a gypsy giving a *payo* his word meant nothing.

Melchor even helped to bandage the wound on Pelayo's hand – that was the name of the first *manolo* – using a strip ripped from the man's shirt. Later, he and Caridad followed them to the slaughterhouse at the Toledo Gate, where, after an exchange of passwords, a man allowed them through. Melchor haggled over the payment the man from the slaughterhouse demanded.

'I'm not trying to buy one of your cows,' he reproached him as he counted out some coins.

Diego and Pelayo didn't pay with money; instead they opened the sack they were carrying, rummaged around inside it and handed the slaughterman a tiny stone that glittered red in the light of the lantern he held. Between the money and the stone, the man was satisfied and he accompanied them to Arganzuela Street through a narrow alley that crossed between the houses that bordered the back of the slaughterhouse.

'Fake stones, that's your trade?' enquired Melchor once they were on the street.

'Yes,' admitted Pelayo. 'It's a good business; even fake they sell for a lot of money.'

Melchor knew that; he was well acquainted with the price of glass beads. Except pearls, which weren't considered precious stones, the King had banned the use or buying and selling of all fake stones: diamonds, rubies, emeralds, topazes.

'The women and men who can't afford the real ones, which is most of Madrid,' continued Pelayo, 'still like flaunting the fakes. It's a very profitable trade.'

The gypsy took note of that, while Caridad inspected their surroundings. The darkness was almost absolute: a few candles and oil lamps struggled to illuminate the interiors of some single-storey houses whose pitched roofs could be seen against the moon. Among the shadows, however, she sensed the presence of people moving from one side to the other and she heard laughter and conversations. On the street, beyond them, a couple lit their way with a lantern. But what most attracted her attention was the stench she was breathing in, and she wondered where it was coming from. Then she understood that what she was stepping in with her bare feet was nothing less than excrement accumulated on the dirt floor.

'We have to go,' announced Pelayo. 'Where are you headed?'

Melchor knew a gypsy related to the Vegas who lived in Madrid: El Cascabelero, a member of the Costes family who had married a Vega cousin more than twenty-five years ago; several of the Vegas on the settlement in the Carthusian monastery grounds, himself included, had gone to the large wedding that had sealed the alliance between the two families. Even so, he had been haunted by doubt since he'd come up with his plan in Barrancos, when Méndez told him about the snuff shipment he was waiting for. What if they'd also arrested the gypsies in Madrid and he couldn't find any? He told himself that the capital was different: it wasn't considered an officially authorized place of residence for gypsies, so they wouldn't have arrested anyone there. Despite the fact that living in Madrid was forbidden for gypsies, the royal proclamations ordering their expulsion from the capital had been repeated many times, owing to the gypsies stubbornly remaining there.

Surely there were gypsy descendants of that cousin in Madrid? But since his last visit, before being sent to the galleys, they could well have married into other families that were enemies of the Vegas. He would have to check. But Melchor was sure that, until he did, the Madrid gypsies shouldn't know about Caridad's presence; the death sentence that had undoubtedly been passed by the Triana council of elders would already be known even there. Milagros had spat at his feet and Ana was jailed in Málaga. He couldn't risk losing his *morena*, too.

'Pelayo,' said the gypsy, 'I'll buy one of those stones off you if you take us somewhere safe to sleep. Somewhere discreet.'

They agreed. They all went along Toledo Street and a bit further on they turned right on to Carnero. Hearing the shrieks of the animals being slaughtered at night, they reached the little hill of the Rastro, a mound of earth that rose between the buildings, beside the old abattoir, which was kept uncultivated to let the area breathe. They splashed in the stream of blood that descended from the slaughterhouse along Curtidores Street and, always staying to the right, crossed Mesón de Paredes and Embajadores Streets. There they bade farewell to Diego, who went into a house with his fake stones. Pelayo continued with Melchor and Caridad to a secret hostel on Peligros Street. According to what he told them, he knew Alfonsa, the widow who ran it, so they wouldn't have any problems. She wouldn't inform the constables of their presence, as innkeepers were required to do with all guests.

They had trouble waking Alfonsa up.

'Were you expecting the Duke of Alba?' spat Melchor as she looked askance at them after talking to Pelayo.

The woman was about to answer back, but she closed her mouth when she saw the money the gypsy held out to her. Pelayo said goodbye. Alfonsa charged them, and Caridad and Melchor followed her up a dark staircase as narrow as it was steep, the three in single file brushing the damp, chipped walls, until they reached the attic: a filthy little room that they had to share with three other sleeping guests. Alfonso pointed them to a rickety old bed.

'That's all I have,' she claimed without a hint of apology before turning her back to go down to her house, on the lower floor.

'Now what?' asked Caridad.

'Now I hope you'll snuggle up on one side of that bed so we can sleep a little. It's been a rough day.'

'I mean—'

'I know what you mean, *morena*,' interrupted Melchor as he tugged at her arm, trying to navigate the belongings scattered on the floor by the other guests. 'Tomorrow we'll see who can give us a hand.'

24

SHE HAD BEEN cooped up there for five days. There was nothing she could do in that disgusting little room she shared with a brick-layer, his sister, who claimed she worked washing clothes in the Manzanares River, and a third guest who was surely involved in shady activities but maintained, as fervently as the washerwoman, that he was a cutter, though he didn't specify whether he worked in a slaughterhouse or in a tannery.

'I'm going to look for the notary. Don't leave the hostel,' Melchor had whispered to her the first morning, when the other guests were still stretching. 'Don't talk to anyone or tell them about me and especially not about the snuff.'

He started to leave but then stopped. He fingered the hilt of his knife and launched a murderous look at the others, including the washerwoman, all three of whom had their eyes glued on the couple. Then he turned and kissed Caridad full on the mouth.

'Did you understand, *morena*? I might take a while, but I will be back, no doubt about it. Wait for me and keep an eye on the bed – don't let Pelayo's friend sell it as "half with clean".'

Caridad didn't know what 'half with clean' meant and Melchor didn't explain before heading down the stairs. It was an expression coined in the underbelly of Madrid, populated with beggars and layabouts, criminals and all sorts of people without resources who drifted through the big city, some waiting for an actual royal favour – revenue, a job in the administration, the results of a lawsuit – others waiting on some risky business that would line their pockets, and the rest looking to pilfer or sell junk, when not just to outright steal. Many of them, come nightfall, would head to one of the houses where for two bits they could rent half of a bed they shared with someone clean: that was someone without lice, scabies or ringworm.

Madrid was unable to absorb the constant immigration. Enclosed by the wall that surrounded it, beyond which it was forbidden to build, two-thirds of the property were split between the Crown and the Church; the remaining third, in addition to what those two institutions decided to lease, had to be fought over by the almost one hundred and fifty thousand inhabitants that packed the capital at mid-century. The houses they fought over were poorly put together, with tiny dark rooms devoid of any comforts, all the result of the construction of 'houses of malice', a scheme that Madrileños had used in previous centuries to get around the lodging privileges that forced them to give the King, free of charge, a part of their dwellings for the use of the members of the court. So, despite the royal proclamations regarding the quality of the buildings that should adorn the kingdom's capital, more than half of the ten thousand houses erected in Madrid the century before were only one storey high, therefore ineligible to welcome ministers or servants of the Crown. Well after the turn of the eighteenth century, when the lodging privileges were replaced by economic contributions, the houses of Madrid were renovated and the single-storey buildings were reconstructed or simply raised to accommodate the immigration that continued to arrive in the capital.

These secret hostels, like the one where Melchor and Caridad were staying, were born out of that need. While the city had enough taverns and bars, there weren't many public hostels, and they were both expensive and constantly watched over and regulated by the royal magistrates and the constables during their rounds. That was why the secret hostels sprang up and, although no one knew for sure how many there were, it was known that they were all dirty and messy like the little attic room where Caridad whiled away the hours. She didn't even have a cigar to smoke and calm her hunger, which was far from sated by the watery, rotten stew that Alfonsa fed her guests.

The chickpeas, turnips, onions and heads of garlic didn't seem to have left any room for pork, mutton, beef or chicken.

Melchor had left the hostel five days ago and Caridad was gripped by anguish. Had something happened to him? Milagros and her mother had faded in her mind as the days passed. Melchor, Melchor and Melchor: the gypsy was all she thought about! He had told her not to leave the hostel, she reminded herself over and over again as she paced up and down the little room, oppressed between those walls, disgusted by the stench that came up from the street. Her only contact with the outside was the hustle and bustle and traffic that she could hear through a little window far above her head. She cursed that useless window. She sat on the bed. He had told her to keep an eye on it . . . She smiled sadly. *Where did you go, damn gypsy?* She could go out, but she didn't know where to go or what she would do. She couldn't go to the constables to report the disappearance of a gypsy smuggler. Besides, Melchor had told her not to talk about him to anyone. Even the gleam of the fake sapphire he had given her, and which she kept clenched in her fist, seemed to have faded.

Over the course of those days, the bricklayer and the woman he said was his sister had given up trying to get more than a mono-syllabic answer out of her, but Juan, the cutter, insisted on wheedling her and interrogating her over and over, persistent despite the silence and lowered gaze with which Caridad received his questions.

'Where is your master? What business brought him to Madrid?'

The cutter surprised Caridad by returning to the hostel the morning of the fifth day after the other two had already left. Juan was a middle-aged man, tall, bald, with a pockmarked face and teeth as black as the long nails that extended from his fingers and which at that moment were in sharp contrast to the large loaf of white bread he was holding. Caridad couldn't keep her eyes from drifting briefly towards the loaf: she was hungry. He noticed her gaze.

'Do you want a piece?'

Caridad hesitated. What was the cutter doing there?

'I bought it at the San Luis junction,' said the man as he broke it in two and offered her one of the halves. 'You and I could get a lot like this one. Take it,' he insisted, 'I'm not going to do anything to you.'

Caridad didn't do so. The cutter approached her.

'You are a desirable woman. There are few real black women in Spain, they've all got whiter over time.'

She backed up a few steps until her back hit the wall. She saw the cutter's eyes light up, boring into her before he could.

'Here, take the bread.'

'I don't want it.'

'Take it!'

Caridad obeyed and grabbed it with the hand that didn't hold the fake sapphire.

'That's it. Why were you going to refuse? It cost me good money. Eat.'

She nibbled the half-loaf. The cutter watched her do so for a few seconds before trying to grab one of her breasts. He didn't manage to; Caridad had foreseen it and batted his hand away. The cutter persisted and she rebuffed him again.

'You want to make it hard for me?' muttered the man, as he threw the bread on to one of the beds, visibly excited, and rubbed his hands together. His black teeth stood out in his lewd smile.

The bread and the sapphire fell to the floor when Caridad put her arms out to repel the cutter's onslaught. After a struggle, she managed to stop him by grabbing his wrists. Her own reaction surprised her and made her hesitate: it was the first time she had challenged a white man! He took advantage of her indecision: he freed himself, shouted something incomprehensible and smacked her. It didn't hurt. She looked him in the eyes. He hit her again and she kept looking at him. The woman's passive reaction to his violence excited the cutter even more. Caridad thought that he was going to hit her again, but instead he held her and started to bite her neck and ears. She tried to get away from him, but couldn't. The man, frenetic, grabbed her curly hair and searched out her mouth, her lips . . .

All of a sudden he let her go and doubled over. She tilted her head to one side, as if she wanted to listen more carefully to the long muffled wail that came from the cutter's throat. She had seen her friend María – the mulatta she sang with – do it one Sunday back at the sugar factory: María had allowed the Negro harassing her to get close, holding her and getting excited, and then she had jammed her knee into his testicles. He had doubled over and howled just like the cutter, with both hands grabbing his crotch. Caridad breathed heavily while she searched for her sapphire. She knelt and extended her arm to grab it; her hands were trembling. She couldn't control them. The rage seemed to want to burst from inside her. She grabbed the stone and the bread and got up, confused at the whole sequence of new feelings inside her.

'I'll kill you!'

She stared at the cutter: he was recovering and almost able to stand up straight. He would do it, he would kill her; his contorted features made that clear; the knife that glittered in one of his hands galvanized her as if he was already about to stab her. The hostel owner was her only hope of salvation! Caridad ran downstairs. The door of the woman's apartment was locked. She beat hard on it, but her blows were drowned out by the screams of the cutter who was coming down behind her.

'Whore! I'm going to cut your throat!'

Caridad leapt down the last flight of stairs. She ran into two women as she burst out on to Peligros Street, a narrow thoroughfare no more than five paces wide. The women's complaints merged with the bedlam that she'd been listening to for five days, which now exploded in all its rawness. She looked both ways, back and forth repeatedly, not knowing what to do. One of the women tried to pick up the countless chickpeas that had scattered on the ground when they crashed into each other; the other screamed insults at her. Onlookers crowded around to watch the scene. So did the cutter, who had stopped in front of the building. They were separated by barely three steps. Their eyes met. Caridad tried to calm down: he wouldn't dare to kill her in public. She saw in the man's resigned face, as he put away the knife and brought a hand to his chin, that he had reached the same conclusion. Caridad let out a snort, as if she had been holding it in since she started to descend the staircase.

'Thief!' then echoed between the buildings. 'My bread! She stole my bread!'

Caridad's gaze ran from the half-loaf of bread, still in her hand, to the cutter, who was smiling.

'Get the thief!'

The shout came from behind her back and stopped her attempting to deny the accusation. Someone tried to grab her arm. She got away. The woman picking up chickpeas looked at her and the one who was insulting her jumped on her, as did the cutter. Caridad dodged the woman and pushed her against the cutter, taking advantage of the momentary confusion to escape and rush down the street.

The others chased after her. She ran, blindly. She bumped into men and women, avoiding others and shoving aside those who tried to stop her. The noise and the shouts of those trying to catch up to her spurred her on in a reckless race. She got to the end of Peligros Street and found herself on a wide avenue. There she was almost run over by a luxurious carriage pulled by two saddled mules. From the driver's seat, the coachman swore at her as he cracked his whip in her direction. Caridad tripped. More carriages were passing: coaches, calashes and curious litters with a mule in front and another behind. Caridad snaked through them until she found another side street and ran down it. She could still hear the shouting; she wasn't aware that she had already left it far behind.

They were no longer chasing her. It wasn't worth the bother for a common darkie who'd stolen a piece of bread. So the cutter found himself in the middle of Alcalá Street surrounded by all kinds of carriages, drivers and footmen. Those accompanying noblemen were dressed in livery; the others, escorting those who had obtained royal permission to use coaches but weren't noble, wore none. The shrieks with which he had been urging on the mob he thought was with him drowned in his throat when he saw the scornful looks he was getting from most of the drivers and footmen who walked alongside the carriages. He, a dirty, common ruffian, had more to lose if he drew attention to himself there, among the grandees.

'Step aside!' shouted out a driver in warning.

One of the footmen made as if to come at him. The cutter acted as though nothing had happened and disappeared whence he had come.

Caridad only stopped her frantic race when she could hardly breathe any more and the pressure in her chest grew unbearable. She stopped, leaned her hands on her knees and started coughing. She held back a heave between coughs. She turned her head and could see only some people who looked curiously before continuing on their way, indifferent. She stood up and tried to catch her breath. In front of her, at the end of a narrow street, rose two towers, one on each side, crowned by spires with crosses. The one on the left also had a belfry: a church. She thought, before glancing behind her again, that she could take refuge there. No one was following her, but she didn't know where she was. She closed her eyes tightly and felt the accelerated beating of her heart in her temples. She felt as though she had crossed all of Madrid. She was a long way from the hostel and didn't know how to get back there. She didn't know where the hostel was. She didn't know where she was. She didn't know where Melchor was. She didn't know . . .

Right before her, a few steps away, she saw an iron gate on to a large courtyard behind the church. It was open. She headed towards it, wondering if they would allow her into that temple. She was just a barefoot, sweaty Negress dressed in slave's rags. What would she tell the priest if he asked questions? That she was fleeing because they accused her of stealing bread? She still carried the half-loaf in her hands.

A rotten smell, worse even than the streets of Madrid over-flowing with excrement thrown from the windows, attacked her senses as she went through the iron gate into the church cemetery. No one was policing the burials at that moment. *Maybe it is safer here than in the church,* she thought as she hid between a small headstone and a wall of niches. She recognized the stench: it was decomposing corpses, like those of the runaway slaves they sometimes found in the reed beds.

As she bit on the bread the smell of death mixed in with her saliva, so dense she could almost chew it, and she started to reflect on what had happened and think what she could do next. She had time before it got dark, when the ghosts would come out . . . and there must have been hundreds there.

Not far from the cemetery of the San Sebastián parish, where five days later Caridad would take refuge, was the parish church of Santa Cruz, whose 144-foot-tall tower dominated the small plaza of the same name. It was there that on Holy Saturday, before they were buried in the church cemetery, the Brotherhood of Charity displayed the skulls of those who had been condemned to death and had their throats slit, after rescuing the bodies from the roads where they were left out to intimidate people. The parish of San Ginés took care of the hanged and that of San Miguel was responsible for those executed by garrotte.

In the same small Santa Cruz Plaza, beneath its arcades, was the largest market for domestic labourers. There unemployed servants would station themselves, especially wet nurses, waiting for someone to hire them. Madrid needed many wet nurses to nourish the increasingly high number of foundlings and abandoned children, but mostly they were hired by women who didn't want to nurse their children so their breasts wouldn't suffer. The 'vanities of the boob' was what advocates of mother's milk called it.

But in that square there was also one of the wholesale tobacconist's shops that brought the highest profits to the royal tax office, along with the ones in Antón Martín, Rastro and the Puerta del Sol, of the twenty-two spread all over Madrid. The sale of tobacco was complemented by two state warehouses that sold powdered or leaf tobacco wholesale, never in measures of less than a quarter-pound, so only consumers able to afford such a quantity shopped there.

The same morning that Caridad left the hostel, Melchor confirmed that the Santa Cruz tobacconist's shop, which only sold powder, seemed more like an apothecary for the supply of medicines and remedies than the others, which sold the popular, unprocessed smoke tobacco used by the humbler classes. In the middle of the counter, in full view – as was required – stood a precision scale to weigh tobacco powder; on the wall shelves were the tin or glazed earthenware vessels that kept it from losing its fragrance, which is what would happen if it were stored in little paper bags, which was strictly forbidden.

Ramón Álvarez, the tobacconist, made a face when he saw the gypsy – his faded yellow dress coat, the hoops in his ears, the thousands of wrinkles that crossed his tanned face and those penetrating eyes – but he reluctantly agreed to talk to him at the insistence of Carlos Pueyo, the old notary public who accompanied him. Pueyo and the tobacconist had already done some deals as shady as they were profitable. Álvarez's wife took over serving in the shop while Carlos and Melchor followed the tobacconist's lethargic ascent to the upper floor of the establishment, where he lived.

Any trace of suspicion disappeared when Ramón Álvarez sniffed a sample of Melchor's snuff. His face lit up at the mere mention of the number of pounds of it the gypsy had.

'You'll never regret doing business with me,' the notary reproached the tobacconist for his initial reluctance.

Melchor fixed his gaze on the old notary. Those were the very words that had marked the end of their meeting when he had gone to the notary's office, on Eulogio's recommendation, to discuss his daughter Ana's situation in the gypsy prison in Málaga. He'd told the notary about the jar of snuff when negotiating the payment of his fees and those of the fixer who would be needed to intercede with the authorities to free Ana. *Fixers are expensive, but they are at home at court and they know who needs to be bought,* declared Carlos Pueyo.

At that moment, in that apartment that masked the stench of Madrid's streets with the aromas of the tobacco that had been stored below for years, Melchor recognized in the tobacconist's face the same greed the notary had shown.

'Where do you have the snuff?'

The notary had asked the same exact question. The gypsy, with the same gravity, repeated his response: 'Don't worry about that. It is safely hidden away, just like the money you are going to buy it with.'

Ramón Álvarez moved quickly: he knew the market, he knew who would be interested in that outlawed merchandise and, above all, he knew who could pay its high price. He was just a tobacconist, in the service of the Crown, who made a few silver reals a day, like all those whose establishments had a healthy turnover. There were others: those who sold less, or those that, in towns where there wasn't enough business to support their salary and expenses, were forced by the Crown to provide tobacco in shops that sold other things as well and who got ten per cent of the total sold.

While the tobacconists enjoyed a privileged position – they were free of burdens and obligations, they didn't have to deal with deliveries and pack mules, and couldn't be called up for military service; they didn't have to pay tolls on roads, bridges or boats and were protected from wrongs and offences – those reals weren't enough to match the ostentatious, luxurious lives of those who enjoyed similar privileges. Madrid was an expensive city, and a shipment of quality snuff like Melchor's was one of the best deals they could do because it didn't affect the sales of Spanish tobacco powder.

While the tobacconist collected the money – *I'll have it tonight and we will close the deal*, he promised so Melchor didn't take his business elsewhere – Melchor got ready to go in search of his relatives.

Comadre de Granada Street. He would always remember that name. Surprising: why would a street in the capital have such a strange name? That was where El Cascabelero lived with his family, as did many other gypsies, so if they weren't living there any more, he could surely get news of them. He asked for directions. 'Downhill. Pretty nearby,' he was told. Comadre de Granada Street belonged to the humble Madrid of the day labourers. Both sides of what was nothing more than a simple, dreary dirt road that ended at the Embajadores gully were lined with wretched low houses, with narrow façades and small patches of garden to the back, when there weren't other buildings added on, which shared rooms and a back door. Melchor realized that he was going to reveal his presence in Madrid, but the truth was he couldn't handle the operation alone. They could rob him; just take the jar and kill him.

'Go further up,' indicated a woman after he had gone up and down the street a couple of times without finding the house. 'And once you pass Esperancilla Street, it's the second or third house . . .'

And even if they didn't rob him, how was he going to transport the jar to Madrid and get around town with it? He could count on Caridad, but he didn't want to involve her; he preferred to run the risk of being betrayed. He needed someone else's help, and it was best if they were relatives, even if very little Vega blood ran through their veins.

Any trace of doubt vanished at the profound look exchanged between Melchor and El Cascabelero. They grabbed each other by the forearms, and their grasp indicated affection and promised loyalty. They were surrounded by a respectful silence, which told Melchor that his relative had become the patriarch; and El Cascabelero's mere touch told him that the man was aware of the death sentence hanging over him.

'And Aunt Rosa?' asked Melchor after communicating everything he could with his eyes.

'She passed away,' answered El Cascabelero.

'She was a good gypsy.'

'Yes, she was.'

Melchor greeted the members of El Cascabelero's extensive family one by one. His sister, a widow. Zoilo, his oldest son, a picador in the bullfights, as his father proudly introduced him before pointing to his daughter-in-law and grandchildren. Two daughters with their respective husbands, one of them with a baby in arms and other little ones hidden behind her legs, and the fourth, Martín, a boy who received his greeting with a look of admiration.

'Are you El Galeote?'

'We've been talking about you a lot lately,' acknowledged El Cascabelero as Melchor nodded to the question and patted the boy's cheek.

Close to twenty people were packed into that small house on Comadre de Granada Street.

As the women prepared the food, Melchor, the patriarch and the other men settled into the small back garden, beneath the eaves, some in rickety chairs, others on simple cushions.

'How old are you?' Melchor asked Martín, who was peeking out through the lace curtain that served as a door to the yard.

'Almost fifteen.'

Melchor looked for El Cascabelero's consent.

'You are already a gypsy man,' he said when he saw his father nod. 'Come with us.'

That same afternoon, in the notary's office, Carlos Pueyo assured him that the tobacconist had the money to buy the snuff.

'He's capable of selling his wife and daughter to get it for tonight,' added the notary when he saw the gypsy's doubt. 'He won't get much for the wife,' he joked. 'But the daughter has a certain charm.'

They agreed to complete the sale after eleven at night, which was the shop's closing time.

'Where?' asked Melchor.

'In the shop, of course. He has to check the quality, weigh the snuff . . . Is there any problem with that?' added the notary, seeing that the gypsy was pensive.

There were seven hours until then.

'Not at all,' he confirmed.

Along with El Cascabelero and all the men in his family, including young Martín, Melchor left Madrid through the Toledo Gate. He smiled, thinking about Caridad, when he reached the thicket where the jar was still hidden. *You see how it's there, my Negress?* he said to himself while Zoilo and his brothers-in-law dug it up. What would they do after closing the deal? Zoilo and his father had been unequivocal.

'Now that you've set foot on Comadre Street, you can be sure that the Garcías know you are in Madrid.'

'Are there Garcías here?'

'Yes. A branch, nephews of El Conde. They came from Triana.'

'It must have been . . .'

'Around the time you went to the galleys. Your Aunt Rosa hated them. We started to hate them and they hated us.'

'I didn't want to make problems for you,' said Melchor.

'Melchor,' the patriarch spoke seriously to him, 'the Costes and those with us will defend you. Do you want the ghost of your aunt to come beat me at night? The Garcías will think twice before starting trouble.'

Would they defend Caridad as well? When they told him about the sentence they had included the woman, but no one had asked about her: she wasn't a gypsy. While in Madrid he would always have to be protected by El Cascabelero's men, and live with them, but he doubted they would be willing to stick their necks out for a Negress.

They whiled away the time until nightfall before returning with the jar. They would leave Madrid, Melchor decided during the wait. He would set the matter of Ana in train and the two of them would go and smuggle tobacco, hand in hand, without joining up with any band. He had never enjoyed running tobacco as much as he had with his Negress in Barrancos! The risk . . . the danger took on another dimension with the mere possibility that she could be arrested, and that breathed life into him. Yes. That's what they would do. Every once in a while, he would return to Madrid, alone, and check on the progress of the proceedings to free his daughter.

They reached the capital through a hole in a house that made up part of the wall. They didn't even pay.

'Another picador,' explained El Cascabelero.

They headed to the Santa Cruz Plaza carrying the jar. If someone on the dark streets of Madrid were tempted to make off with that treasure, they would surely be dissuaded by the entourage he had with him.

After eleven, Melchor and his relatives were upstairs at the tobacco shop, serious and silent, threatening, just like the two escorts the tobacconist had procured. He and his wife checked the quality and weighed the pounds of snuff to their satisfaction. Ramón Álvarez nodded and, in silence, handed Melchor a bag with the money. The gypsy poured the coins out on to a table and counted them. Then he took some gold ones and offered them to the notary.

'I want my daughter Ana free in a month's time,' he demanded.

Carlos Pueyo didn't allow himself to be intimidated, nor did he take the coins.

'Melchor, if you're looking for miracles, cross the plaza and go into the Santa Cruz church.' They locked gazes for a moment. 'I will do what I can,' added the notary. 'That's the most I can promise you. I've told you that several times.'

The gypsy hesitated. He turned towards Zoilo and El Cascabelero, who shrugged. Eulogio had recommended the notary and he seemed like a person who got things done – the quick sale of the snuff was good proof of that – yet, when the moment came to hand over the money, his confidence waned. He thought of Ana locked up in Málaga and his rejection by his beloved granddaughter Milagros, bound to the Garcías in matrimony, and he told himself that the money wasn't important. He could make thousands if that was what his family needed!

'Agreed,' he conceded.

The tension disappeared as soon as the notary stretched out his hand and Melchor dropped the coins into it. Later, right there, he gave others to the Costes men, not forgetting young Martín, who only dared to take them when his father nodded.

'We have to celebrate!' Zoilo shouted.

'Wine and a party,' added one of his brothers-in-law.

The tobacconist brought his hands to his head and his wife went pale.

'The patrol . . . the magistrates,' he warned. 'If they catch us with the snuff . . . Silence, I beg of you.'

But the gypsies didn't quiet down.

'Melchor, there in front,' interjected the notary, pointing to one side, 'is the High Court jail. There are constables there and it is where the patrols gather. Except for the palace of Buen Retiro, with the King and his guards, you are choosing the worst place in the city to raise a ruckus.'

Melchor and El Cascabelero understood and silenced the gypsies with hand gestures. Then, ejected by the tobacconist and his wife, they left the building, unable to hold back a few comments and some laughter under their breath.

'In a few days I will come by your office to find out how things are going with my daughter's case,' Melchor warned the notary, who was sheltering with the tobacconist behind the shop door.

'Take your time,' he answered.

Melchor was about to reply when the door closed and they were left in front of the majestic building – two storeys plus the attic and three large towers crowned by spires – that held the jail of the High Court, where they administered justice. They had skirted it when they were carrying the jar and now they realized that the notary was right: the constables came and went around it, with thick clubs in their hands and wearing suits with ruffs, as they had worn in the past, their necks erect and trapped in strips of lined cardboard, which the King had forbidden for the common people.

'Let's go and have some fun with the young folks,' El Cascabelero suggested to Melchor.

El Galeote hesitated. Caridad would be waiting for him.

'Do you have something better to do?' insisted the other.

'Let's go,' said Melchor, giving in because he was incapable of saying that he had a Negro woman waiting for him, no matter how beautiful she was. After all, they would be leaving Madrid the next day.

They stationed themselves beside one of the walls of the Santa Cruz church where, above Atocha Street, rose an atrium that opened on to the temple's main portico where some homeless people slept. At a signal from Zoilo they slipped away, going around the atrium and heading down Atocha Street. They knew they were taking a risk: in the streets of Madrid, after midnight (which the bells had announced some time ago), anyone found armed, as they were, and without a lantern lighting their way, would be arrested. However, when they'd passed the atrium of the monastery of the Calced Trinitarians and had left the jail and its many officials far behind, they began to chat carelessly, sure that no patrol would dare confront six gypsies. They laughed loudly as they crossed the small Antón Martín Plaza, where one of the district magistrates was often stationed, and they continued down Atocha Street, carefree, ignoring the drunk men and women, tripping over beggars lying on the ground and even challenging those muffled in long capes, their faces hidden in the night beneath wide-brimmed slouch hats, waiting for some dupe to rob.

At the end of the street, they passed by the General Hospital and entered the Atocha meadow. There, the wall around Madrid didn't end with the last buildings in the city but opened out behind the gardens and olive groves to surround the Buen Retiro Palace with its many buildings and adjoining gardens. They soon heard the music and commotion: folks from Lavapiés and the Rastro got together in the open fields to drink, dance and have fun.

They had money on them. Melchor's concern about Caridad disappeared as the party went on, with wine, liquor and even chocolate from Caracas. He heard El Cascabelero demanding the best hot chocolate, with sugar, cinnamon and a few drops of orange-blossom water. They ate the sweets hawked by the street vendors: doughnuts deemed 'stupid' or 'clever' depending on whether they were sweetened in a bath of sugar, egg white and lemon juice; rolled wafers and cream-filled pastries. Seeing that their purses seemed to never grow thin, no matter how many coins came out of them, other gypsy men joined them, along with some women. The men flirted but nothing more, since the patriarch was always vigilant about his daughters' honour.

'You go ahead,' the others encouraged young Martín, 'you've got money and you're single. Enjoy those *paya* women!'

But he excused himself and remained beside Melchor, the galley slave who had survived torture and smuggled tobacco, who was capable of killing his own son-in-law for the honour of the Vega family. Martín listened attentively to him, laughed at his jokes, felt proud to be able to talk to him. Over the course of the night, Melchor and Martín spoke about the Vegas, about honour, about pride, freedom, the gypsy settlement and about how pleased Melchor would have been if his granddaughter had chosen someone like Martín instead of a García. 'She must be confused,' declared Melchor. 'For sure,' agreed the boy. Fandangos and *seguidillas* sounded until dawn, and they were surrounded by all types of people. The gypsies, dressed in their brightly coloured clothes, mixed with *manolos*, in their colourful short jackets and waistcoats, silk sashes, tight britches, white knee socks, shoes with large buckles almost at the tip, striped capes and cloth caps, always armed with a good knife and a perennial cigarette between their lips; and *manolas* wearing bodices, fine dresses and very flouncy skirts over them, hair nets and mantillas and silk shoes.

Melchor missed the gypsy spirit more than his companions did;

the bewitching spell of those cracked voices that spontaneously emerged from the most unexpected corner of the gypsy settlement by La Cartuja. Nevertheless, the joy and hubbub continued echoing in his ears when the music stopped and the light of day found them in a field where only the stragglers remained.

'Are you hungry?' Zoilo asked then.

They sated their appetites at the San Blas inn, also on Atocha Street, amid cartwrights, muleteers and carriers from Murcia and La Mancha who frequented it. Just as they had done during the party the night before, they bragged about their purses and started with toast fried in lard and sprinkled with sugar and cinnamon. This they followed with chicken stewed in a sauce of its chopped livers until the main dish was ready: a lovely lamb's head split in half, seasoned with parsley, crushed garlic cloves, salt, pepper, and salt pork strips beneath the gristle, then tied up again to be roasted in sheets of brown paper. They made short work of the brains, tongue, eyes and attached meats, some tender, others gelatinous, all washed down with undiluted Valdepeñas wine, strong and harsh, as befitted that inn filled with dirty, loud-mouthed men who watched them out of the corners of their eyes with obvious envy in their faces and gestures.

'A round for everyone here!' shouted Melchor, sated and tipsy. Before the men had a chance to thank him for his generosity, a shout boomed through the inn:

'We don't want to drink your wine!'

Melchor and El Cascabelero, seated with their backs to the door, saw the tension in the faces of Zoilo and his two brothers-in-law, who were facing it. Martín, beside Melchor, was the only one in the group who turned his head.

'I didn't think they'd be that fast,' the patriarch commented to Melchor.

Most of the clients, intrigued by the impending quarrel, moved away from the gypsies and made space for the newcomers. Only a very few left the inn. El Cascabelero and Melchor kept their eyes straight ahead.

'The sooner, the better,' Melchor said as he stifled a sigh of regret at not having gone home sooner. If he had, he would be with Caridad, safe. Or would he? Maybe not, who knew? He clicked his tongue. 'What's done is done,' he muttered to himself.

'What did you say?'

'They're waiting for us,' answered El Galeote, standing up, his hand already on his knife.

El Cascabelero did the same, and all the others followed suit. There must have been eight Garcías, perhaps more: he couldn't be sure when he saw them bunched up in the doorway.

'Idiots!' spat Melchor as soon as his gaze met the eyes of the man who seemed to be leading the party. 'Wine paid for by a Vega will only be spilled on the García graves, where you'll soon all be.'

'Manuel,' said El Cascabelero, surrounded by his men, 'you are about to make the biggest mistake of your life.'

'Gypsy law—' the man tried to reply.

'Shut up!' interrupted Melchor. 'Come for me, if you've got the balls.'

One of the onlookers cheered his bravado.

The click of several knives opening at the same time was heard inside the inn; the blades shone in the penumbra.

'Why . . . ?' El Cascabelero started to ask Melchor.

'They don't have enough room here,' he answered. 'We will be more or less even. Outside they would crush us.'

He was right. Although the Garcías pushed aside tables and chairs in their path, their group couldn't fully spread out in front of the Vegas. Six against six, seven at the most. *The rest will come later,* thought Melchor as he launched the first stab, which easily cut open the forearm of the García in front of him. The others continued feinting, not really jumping into the fight. Then he realized something else, even more important: they didn't know how to fight. Those gypsies hadn't ranged through mountains and fields; they lived in Madrid, comfortably, and their fights weren't with smugglers and criminals who fought viciously, with no concern even for their lives. He stabbed again, his arm extended, and the wounded García backed up into the relative behind him.

Right then, a cold sweat drenched Melchor's back. Martín! He was still beside him, as always, and while the others still hadn't joined the fray, he could see how the young man was launching himself, wildly, blindly, on one of the Garcías. He wasn't experienced with a knife . . . He heard a terrified howl from the mouth of El Cascabelero when his adversary's blow hit his youngest son's wrist, disarming him.

'Stop!' shouted Melchor just as the García was about to go for the boy's neck.

The knife stopped in mid-air. The entire world seemed to stop for Melchor. He dropped his weapon and sketched a sad smile towards the frightened face of the young Vega.

'Here you have me, swine.' He then gave himself up, opening his arms.

He didn't look at Martín, he didn't want to humiliate him, but he knew that El Cascabelero had his eyes downcast, looking at the floor or perhaps his own knife. Melchor approached the Garcías, and before they pounced on him, he had the chance to run a hand through Martín's hair.

'The Vega blood has to continue to flow in you, not in old men like me,' he declared before they took him out of the inn amid insults, kicks and shoves.

She didn't dare to clear her throat, for fear of being discovered, although the stench of death had a firm grip on her dry throat. The spring night had fallen and she was thirsty, very thirsty. Yet that urgency disappeared as soon as a soft breeze began to caress her body and lift her fine hairs; then she trembled, convinced she was being surrounded by the ghosts emerging from the many tombs of that cemetery. And while the men behind the tombstone that protected Caridad made their bets and stakes in whispers that seemed to her like howls, she shivered again and again from the contact with the living dead.

They had entered the cemetery just as she was about to leave it to search for a fountain to quench her thirst. Five, six, seven men – she wasn't able to count them – who were allowed in by the sacristan himself. Throughout the course of the night, she heard some of them leave the cemetery, probably having lost all their money, and other new ones joining the game. A simple lantern hung on a memorial cross lit up the gravestone where they had been playing cards for a couple of hours already. The sacristan acted as the lookout for the street patrol. On a couple of occasions he warned them of approaching constables and, in the sudden deepest darkness, Caridad held her breath, just as they all did, until the danger passed and they started up their illegal game again.

It was on those two occasions, when the faint light of the lantern was extinguished in haste and fear, that Caridad felt the presence of the spirits most strongly. She prayed. She prayed to Oshún and to Our Lady of Charity, because the dead not only rested in their graves, but they also mingled with the earth on which she sat, the same earth that she had played with to pass the time, on which she had dropped the rest of the loaf of bread and that she distractedly wiped off before continuing to gnaw on it. She had heard it from the mouth of the furtive card players:

'This smell is unbearable,' one of them whispered.

'That's exactly why we are here,' was the response. 'This is the worst one in Madrid. Few people come anywhere near.'

'But . . .' the first tried to insist.

'You can go to another cemetery if you'd like,' replied a different voice calmly. 'This one at San Sebastián is the best for getting around the gambling laws. They've run out of room to bury the dead and every spring they dig them up; the last time was just a few days ago. They take out the corpses that have been buried for two years and move them to the mass grave; a lot of the remains get mixed up with the dirt and nobody worries about it. That's why it smells like this: like death, for fuck's sake! Are you playing or not?'

And Caridad couldn't do anything to free herself from all the dead that surrounded her, the stench that scratched at her throat, filling her with bad omens. Melchor! What had happened to him? Why had he left her at the hostel? Something serious must have happened to him, or . . . ? Was he capable of . . . ? No. Surely not. The last kiss he gave her before leaving and the happy times in Barrancos flooded her mind and banished thoughts of that possibility. And meanwhile, just as she had done in Triana, silently, with her dark hand on the stone he had given her, she tried to concentrate and summon her gods: *Eleggua, come to me, tell me if Melchor is still alive, if he is well*. But all her efforts were in vain and she felt that the ghosts were fondling her . . . All of a sudden she leapt up. She jumped up off the ground as if a large crossbow had launched her towards the heavens. She feared that the dead were coming for her. She scrubbed her hair, her face, her neck . . . hard. A sticky, warm liquid was soaking her head.

'Holy Mother of God!' echoed through the cemetery. 'What is this?'

The exclamation came from the man who had climbed on the grave whose stone Caridad was hiding behind. He didn't dare to move, shocked, terrified, unable to make out in the darkness what that frenetically shaking black spot was. The stream of urine that had managed to do what the ghosts had been unable to – make Caridad reveal her hiding place – gradually grew thinner until it was a tiny thread.

Caridad was as slow to react as the man was to adapt his vision to the darkness. When they both had, they found themselves face to face: she smelling her arm once she realized what had happened; he with his now shrunken penis still in his hand.

'It's a Negro woman!' said one of the players who had come over to see what the fuss was all about.

'Black as night,' added another.

A smile appeared on Caridad's face, revealing her white teeth in the darkness. Despite her disgust, they were humans, not ghosts.

Standing there in front of the men, the oil lamp one of them held illuminating her, she heard their comments:

'And what was she doing hiding there?'

'Now I understand why my luck was so bad.'

'She's got some great tits on her.'

'That's not bad luck. You don't even know how to hold the cards in your hand.'

'Speaking of hands, are you going to hold your knob all night long?'

'What do we going to do with the darkie?'

'We?'

'She has to go and wash. She's drenched in piss!'

'Negroes don't mind that.'

'Gentlemen, the cards are waiting.'

A murmur of approval rose among the men and, without paying any more attention to Caridad's presence, they turned their backs on her to gather again around the grave over which they were playing.

'A bit further down, along Atocha Street, in the Antón Martín Plaza, you'll find a fountain. You can wash there,' said the man who'd urinated on her, hiding his member in his trousers.

Caridad turned her head at the mention of the fountain: her tremendous thirst was unrelenting and the dryness in her throat reasserted itself, along with the urgent need to wash herself. The card player was about to go with his companions when Caridad interrupted him.

'Where?' she asked.

'In the plaza . . .' he started to repeat before realizing that Caridad didn't know Madrid. 'Listen: you go out of the cemetery and turn the corner towards the left . . .' She nodded. 'Good. It's the narrow street behind here.' He pointed to the wall of niches that enclosed the cemetery. 'Del Viento. Keep walking and go around the church, always towards the left, and you will reach a larger street. That's Atocha. Go down it and you'll find the fountain. You can't miss it. It's very close by.'

The man didn't wait for a reply and turned his back on her as well. But: 'Oh!' he exclaimed, turning his head. 'And I'm sorry. I didn't know you were hiding there.'

Caridad's thirst pushed her on.

'Goodbye, Negress,' she heard the players say as she slipped briskly away from the cemetery, beneath the surprised gaze of the sacristan who was watching over it.

'Clean yourself off well.'

'Don't tell anyone you saw us.'

'Good luck!'

Turn left twice, Caridad repeated to herself as she went around the bell tower and church of San Sebastián. *And now go down the large street.* She passed a new side street and she could make out the small square in the light of the street lamps from two buildings. In its centre she saw the fountain: a tall monument crowned by an angel, statues of children below and water spouting from the mouth of large fish.

Caridad was only thinking about washing herself and quenching her thirst. She didn't notice a couple of cloaked figures hiding from the gleam of the building's torches. But they didn't take their eyes off her when she climbed into the fountain's basin to bring her lips to the pipe that came out of the mouth of one of the dolphins. She drank and drank, while the two men approached her. Then, with her legs and the lower part of her slave shirt already wet, she got on her knees, stuck her head beneath the stream and let the fresh water run over the back of her neck and her hair, down her shoulders and her breasts, feeling herself purified, freed from the filth and all the spirits that had been pestering her in the cemetery. Oshún! The river Orisha, who rules over the waters; she had paid tribute to her many times in Cuba, there on the tobacco plantation. She stood, looked up at the heavens above the angel that topped the fountain.

'Where are you now, my goddess?' she prayed out loud. 'Why don't you come to me? Why don't you mount me?'

'If she doesn't, I'd be happy to mount you.'

Caridad turned in surprise. The two men, standing by the basin, opened their eyes widely, full of lust at the sight of the body beneath the drenched greyish shirt that stuck to her voluptuous breasts, stomach and wide hips.

'I can give you dry clothes,' offered the other.

'But first you'll have to take those off,' laughed the first in a brazen tone.

Caridad closed her eyes, desperate. She was fleeing from a cutter who wanted to force himself on her and now . . .

'Come here,' they encouraged her.

'Come closer.'

She didn't move. 'Leave me alone.'

Her request was somewhere between a plea and a warning. She scrutinized the space beyond the two men: deserted, dark.

The men looked at each other and nodded with a smile, as if planning a crude game.

'Don't be afraid,' one said.

The other waved his hand, calling her to come closer. 'Come with me, little Negress.'

Caridad backed away towards the middle of the fountain until her shoulders hit the statue.

'Don't be silly, you'll have fun with us.'

One of them jumped over the basin.

Caridad looked both ways: she couldn't escape; she was trapped between two of the large dolphins that emerged from the water.

'Where would you go?' asked the other man, realizing what she intended to do, while he also leapt over the basin, on the opposite side, trapping her. 'I'm sure you don't have anywhere to go.'

Caridad shrank back even more against the monument and felt the stone scratching her back just before they both pounced on her. She tried to defend herself with kicks and punches, the costume jewel from Melchor imprisoned in her fist. She couldn't. She screamed. They grabbed her and she felt disgusted listening to them laugh heartily, as if forcing themselves on her wasn't enough and they had to humiliate her even more by mocking her. They groped her and tugged at her shirt, fighting to remove her clothes: one tried to rip the shirt, the other to pull it over her head. She felt them sink their fingernails into her inner thigh and squeeze her breasts as they continued laughing and spewing obscenities . . .

'Halt! Who goes there?'

Suddenly she sensed she was alone although the shirt over her face didn't allow her to see. Violent splashing told her that the men were running off. When she pulled the shirt down from over her eyes, she found herself before two men dressed in black, illuminated by the oil lamp one of them carried. The other held a truncheon. Both wore rigid cardboard collars that had once been white at their necks.

'Cover yourself,' ordered the one with the oil lamp. 'Who are you?' he enquired as she struggled to cover her bare breasts. 'What were you doing with those men?'

Caridad lowered her gaze towards the water. The white man's

authoritarian tone caused her to react as she had on the tobacco plantation. She didn't answer.

'Where do you live? What is your occupation?'

'Come with us,' decided the other, his voice weary with the fruitless questioning, as he tapped his truncheon on the edge of the basin.

They set off walking down Atocha Street.

25

'PROSTITUTION!'
That was the charge that one of the constables alleged to the sentry at the door of La Galera, Madrid's women's prison, after he had let them in. The prison was right there on Atocha Street, a bit beyond the plaza where she had been arrested. Caridad, downcast, didn't see the immediate, exaggerated reaction of the guard after giving her a quick glance.

'No room for any more,' he claimed.

'Of course there is,' objected one of the constables.

'You released two women yesterday,' the other reminded him.

'But—'

'Where is the warden?' the constable with the truncheon said, interrupting the sentry's complaints.

'You know perfectly well where he is: sleeping.'

'Go get him,' he ordered.

'Don't start fucking with me, Pablo!'

'Then keep her.'

'The rooms are full,' insisted the sentry, without much conviction; it was the same song and dance every night. 'We can't even feed them all—'

'You are keeping her,' Pablo cut in with a tone of voice similar to the one the other had used.

The guard let out a long sigh.

'She's a Negro! How many women like this one do you have in there?' joked the second constable.

The three men walked towards a gloomy little room to the left of the entrance, where the thick black smoke given off by a tallow candle clouded the light meant to illuminate a decrepit desk. Caridad walked in the middle of them.

'Negroes like this one...' answered the sentry as he went around the desk to sit down, 'none. At most we have a couple of mulattas. What's her name?' he added after dipping the quill in the inkwell.

'She didn't want to tell us. What's your name?'

'Caridad,' she responded.

'Well, it turns out she does know how to talk.'

'Caridad what?' asked the sentry.

She was just named Caridad. Nothing more. She didn't answer.

'You don't have a last name? Are you a slave?'

'I'm free.'

'In that case you have to have a last name.'

Hidalgo, she then remembered the commander at the Sea Gate in Cádiz reading in her papers; Don José's last name.

'Hidalgo. That is the last name they gave me on the boat, when Master died.'

'Boat? You used to be a slave? If you say you're free now, you must have a deed of manumission.' The sentry looked her up and down: still wet, barefoot, wearing only her grey shirt. He snorted. 'Do you have the deed?'

'It is in my bundle, with my things, in the room...' Her voice tailed off.

'What room?'

Caridad merely gestured with her hands as she recalled Melchor's warning. *Don't say anything to anyone,* he had told her.

'What do you have in your hand?' the sentry surprised her by asking, seeing that she kept it constantly tightly clenched. She lowered her gaze. 'What have you got there?'

Caridad didn't answer, her chin trembling, her teeth gritted. The truncheon hit her back.

'Show it to us,' the constable ordered her.

She felt that that stone was the last thing tying her to Melchor, to the days they had shared in Barrancos and on the road to Madrid. The bundle, her red dress, her documents and the contraband money Melchor had shared with her in Barrancos and which she had guarded zealously: she'd left everything she had at the hostel. The truncheon hit harder against her kidneys. She opened her hand and showed them the fake sapphire.

'Where did you get that?' said the sentry, leaning over the table to grab it.

'What does all that matter now?' interjected the constable. 'It's late and we have to continue our rounds. We aren't going to spend all night here. Just record her name, the date and time she came in, assets you find on her and reason for her arrest. That's all that matters.'

With her gaze fixed on the blue stone that the sentry left on the desk, Caridad heard the scratching of the quill as it slid across the paper.

'And what is the reason for the arrest?' the man finally asked.

'Prostitution!' The reply echoed through the room.

La Galera, the royal prison for scandalous and dishonest women, was located in a two-storey rectangular building with a central courtyard. Beside it, on the same block, was the hospital of La Pasión, also exclusively for women, which in turn, via an arch that crossed over Niño Perdido Street, linked to the General Hospital, the last building in Madrid before the Atocha Gate.

Once the constables signed the record and left to continue their rounds, Caridad followed the sentry to the upper floor. The man had taken a truncheon and the candle from the desk, which he used to try to illuminate a long hall, with a gallery whose windows overlooked the interior courtyard and the street; it was filled with sleeping women, some on cots, most on the floor. Caridad heard the sentry complain to a female guard who should have been watching over the prisoners. She was sleeping. 'Same as ever,' the man seemed to reluctantly accept. As if he didn't want to take another step further, he used the candle to illuminate the corner near the door, on his right side, where two women were curled up together. He used the truncheon to wake them up. They both grumbled. 'Make room!' he ordered.

The one closer to the wall pushed the other as the sentry hit her on the back to get them to obey. He stopped when a small space opened up between the woman and the wall.

'Squeeze yourself in there,' he indicated to Caridad with the truncheon.

Before she had crouched down, the man was gone and, with him, the light of the smoking candle, which was gradually replaced by the gleam of the moon and the thousand shadows it cast.

Caridad lay down on the floor, trapped between the wall and the other woman. She struggled to move her arm and place it beneath her head as a pillow. The accusation of prostitution came to her mind as soon as she managed to settle in. She was no prostitute. She was tired, yet found some comfort in the contact with the woman she was huddled beside. Her worries intensified: fear of what was going to happen to her, fear for Melchor, who would return to the hostel and not find her there. She listened to the sounds of the night. Coughs and snores. Sighs and words revealed in dreams. Like in the shack on the tobacco plantation, when she slept with the other slaves. The same sounds. All she was missing was Marcelo . . . She stroked her hair just as she had her son's and closed her eyes. She was convinced that someone was taking care of him. And, in spite of everything, exhausted, she fell asleep.

They forced her to her feet at five in the morning, when a point of light began to slip in through the windows. Several guards chosen from among the trusted prisoners went through the various galleries of the second floor and woke the rest by shouting. Caridad took a few seconds to realize where she was and why there were thirty or forty women in front of her, standing in a corner beside the door, yawning, stretching or chiding the guards.

'New girl, huh?'

The words came from the woman who had slept by her side: she was about forty years old and gaunt, with features forged by poverty and as dishevelled as the other woman she pointed out Caridad to. There were no more words or introductions; instead, the tone of the chatter intensified, occasionally blending in with shouts or arguments. Caridad observed the women: many of them had joined a queue to pee into a chamber pot. One after the other they lifted their skirts without the slightest modesty and crouched over the pot, the others urging on the one whose turn it was, who was slowing everyone up by defecating. Then they took the chamber pot, clambered on to a box to reach the high window and poured out the urine before putting it back in place for the next woman.

'Gardy loo!' she heard some of the women shout as they threw the piss down to the street.

'Let's see if you can hit the warden's bald head!'

The remark was met with some laughter.

Caridad felt the need to urinate and joined the queue.

'There were no Negro women here yesterday, were there?'

The comment came from a fat woman who had queued up behind her.

'I can't remember any,' came from some other point in the line.

'Well, this one would be hard to forget,' laughed the fat woman behind her.

Caridad felt many eyes on her. She tried to smile, but no one paid her any heed. The prisoner who was using the chamber pot right before her looked at her insolently the entire time.

'All yours,' she said after getting up. She didn't empty the pot.

Caridad hesitated.

'Negress,' intervened the fat woman behind her, 'Frasquita's quite a pisser. Watch that you don't overflow the pot when you go, getting your fanny wet and spilling it everywhere. Then you'll have to clean it up!'

Caridad threw Frasquita's piss out of the window, urinated and repeated the operation. She moved away from the queue. No one had told her what to do next, so she watched how many of the prisoners went downstairs and she rejoined the group. Behind her, the guards' shouting chivvied those who remained upstairs.

Mass. She heard mass in a small chapel, on the lower level, packed with close to 140 standing prisoners, whom the priest constantly scolded for their disrespectful behaviour – talking and even the occasional loud laugh – during the service. Then they prayed a Station to Jesus, a prayer Caridad didn't know. They left the chapel and again made a long queue at the entrance to another room in which there was a hearth for cooking. They were each handed a piece of leathery bread that was days old. They could also drink with a ladle from a bucket of water. As the queue moved forward, Caridad saw that the sentry from the night before was pointing at her while he spoke to a couple of guards, who nodded along with his words as they stared at her. She finished off the bread before even reaching the gallery of the upper floor.

'Do you know how to sew, Negress?' one of the guards there asked her.

'No,' she answered.

And while the other prisoners began sewing the white linens for the hospitals of La Pasión and El General – sheets, pillowcases and shirts – Caridad was put to scrubbing and cleaning. At twelve they called her for lunch: some meat and another piece of old bread. Back to work until six in the evening, when they supped on a few vegetables, prayed the rosary and Salve Regina and went to bed. She returned to the same corner she had slept in the night before.

The next day, before lunch, the guard from her gallery brought her to the sentry. There a constable was waiting for her and, without a word, he led her up Atocha Street. Caridad stopped in the street; the sun, high in the sky, dazzled her. The constable pushed her, but she didn't mind much. For the first time since she had arrived, she began to look at the city that Melchor had told her was so important; the other times she had passed through it at night or like a bat out of hell with the cutter on her heels. She pursed her lips sadly at the memory: she had managed to escape him only to end up imprisoned as a prostitute. That was what the sentry had written on the papers.

'Watch out, Negress!'

The shout came from the constable. Caridad stopped before she collided with a rickety cart with two wheels, loaded with sand and pulled by a mule headed in her direction. She ran her gaze down the street and was overcome with anxiety at the size of the crowd coming and going. The houses, most with businesses on the ground level, extended on both sides of one of Madrid's widest streets. They left behind the two hospitals, the women's prison and the monastery of clerics for the dying poor across from it. Following in the constable's footsteps, she shifted her gaze towards the businesses: a chandler's shop, a shoe shop, a carpenter's shop, bars, taverns and even a bookshop, as well as a lay monastic community and the Orphanage for Waifs and Strays. People came in and out loaded down with baskets or earthenware jars of water; they chatted, laughed or argued in a universe that was beyond Caridad. Soon she could make out in front of her the fountain topped by the angel that she had leapt into thirstily before she was arrested. From that point on, the look of the street changed: between the homes rose impressive buildings. Caridad kept looking from her left to her right: the convalescent hospital shortly before reaching the square; the Our Lady of the Love of God Hospital devoted to venereal diseases, and the Our Lady of Montserrat, which took in natives of the kingdom of Aragón and whose highly decorated façade made her feel tiny; the Loreto School to the right once she had left the square. Then the Antón Martín hospital and the church of San Sebastián, with its cemetery where she had hidden. There she almost stopped short when she saw the church's atrium: congregated on the platform elevated over the street that led inside was a huge group of chatting dandies. She had seen them in Seville, but never so many in one place . . . She was surprised by their colourful attire, their white wigs, the way they moved, laughed and gestured as they chatted with each other.

'Come on, Negress,' the constable pressed, after allowing her to enjoy the sight for a few moments.

After the atrium came the monasteries of the Trinity and of Santo Tomás, on the next block. The church of Santa Cruz . . .

'We've arrived.'

'Where?' she asked without thinking.

'To the Court jail.'

Caridad turned towards the left: the imposing red-brick building rose from the triangular plaza of La Provincia, with a fountain in the middle. They crossed the plaza dodging the people and carriages that filled it.

'Are they moving me to another jail?' Caridad then asked.

'Here's where you will be tried,' explained the constable.

The sudden calm that came over Caridad as she went beneath the classical pediment that covered the building's three doors – after the commotion of the crowded plaza – faded as soon as she found herself at the feet of the stairs that divided the building in two, thronged with mace-bearers, constables, notaries, barristers, attorneys and public prosecutors; detainees and prisoners, their families; vendors and even noblemen. They were all coming and going, rushing, tense, shouting, loaded down with files or dragging prisoners. Caridad shrank; many looked at her, others pushed her out of their way without thinking twice. She followed the constable to an antechamber where they stood waiting for her. The constable spoke with one of the mace-bearers and pointed to Caridad; the man observed her, then checked his papers and nodded.

Every morning, early, the various constables notified Madrid's district magistrates, who were their superiors, of the results of their night rounds: those arrested and any incidents that might have occurred. Each morning, Madrid's district magistrates gathered in the High Court and prepared a report for the Council of Castile in which they recorded all of those incidents: the deaths, including the natural or accidental ones; what had happened in the theatres and in the streets; the results of the magistrate's inspection of the official second weighing, making special mention of the supply and the price of the provisions sold in the Plaza Mayor, at the butcher's shop and other public stalls. Each morning, after hearing mass in the chapel, the magistrates, divided into two halls, judged criminals and heard civil cases.

Caridad was taken to the second hall.

After witnessing, alongside the constable, how the criminals entered the room and exited a few minutes later, some remorseful, others angry, her turn finally came. She sank her gaze into the dark wooden floorboards as soon as she saw the interior: men dressed in black with square hats and wigs, all on an upper level, seated behind imposing desks from which she felt scrutinized. Yet they paid her very little attention. Prostitution, a minor charge among those they judged and sentenced quickly, without more formalities, coming down hard on the accused.

'Don Alejandro,' said one of the men who sat in front of her, 'lawyer for the poor. Don Alejandro will defend you.'

Disconcerted, Caridad looked up and, at what seemed like an insurmountable distance in that large room, seated in a stand above all the others, she saw a man who pointed to her right. She followed the direction of his finger and found another man who didn't even meet her eyes, absorbed as he was in reading some papers. 'Caridad Hidalgo . . .' Before she even had time to look down again, the notary had begun to read the accusation made against her by the arresting constable. Then the public prosecutor interrogated her:

'Caridad Hidalgo, what were you doing in the small hours of the morning, alone, on the streets of Madrid?'

She hesitated.

'Answer!' shouted the magistrate.

'I . . . was thirsty,' she mumbled.

'She was thirsty!' It echoed through the room. 'And you hoped to quench your thirst with two men? Is that what you were thirsty for?'

'No.'

'They arrested you almost naked with two men kissing and groping you! Is that true?'

'Yes,' she stammered.

'Were they forcing themselves on you?'

'Yes. I didn't want to . . .'

'And this? What is this?' howled the public prosecutor.

Caridad looked up from the floor and at the prosecutor. In his hand shone the fake sapphire.

A few seconds passed before she tried to answer.

'That . . . no . . . It's a gift.'

The prosecutor let out a laugh. 'A gift?' he asked cynically. 'You want us to believe that someone would give stones, even fake ones, to a woman like you?' He lifted his hand and showed the sapphire to the members of the court.

Caridad shrank before them, barefoot, dirty, wearing only her slave shirt.

'Isn't it really true,' spat the prosecutor, 'that this stone was the payment for giving your body to those two men?'

'No.'

'So?'

She didn't want to talk about Melchor. Those men who governed Madrid mustn't know anything about him . . . if he was still alive. She was silent and lowered her gaze. She didn't see how the prosecutor shrugged and opened his hands towards the magistrates who presided over the room: not much more to decide, he transmitted with that gesture.

'What is your job?' asked one of the magistrates. 'How do you make a living?' he insisted without giving her time to answer.

Caridad remained silent.

'Are you free?' they enquired.

They said she maintained she was free.

'Where are your documents?'

The questions came one after the other, stinging, shouted. Utterly dejected, she didn't answer any of them. Why had Melchor left her alone? By that point tears had been streaming down her cheeks for some time.

'Only comparable to the most unspeakable of sins!' she heard the prosecutor shout at the end of a short speech he began as soon as they had finished interrogating her.

'Does the honourable defender of the poor have anything to say?' asked one of the magistrates.

For the first time since the trial had begun, the lawyer for the poor looked up from the papers he had been immersed in. 'The woman refuses to speak before this illustrious room,' he pointed out in a monotone. 'What argument could I give in her defence?'

The magistrates exchanged a look. That was all it took.

'Caridad Hidalgo,' the president pronounced her sentence, 'we condemn you to two years of imprisonment in the Royal Women's Prison of this city. May God take pity on you, protect you and lead you along the path of righteousness. Take her away!'

26

MILAGROS DROPPED INTO a chair and squeezed her hand over her belly, as if trying to keep the baby she carried inside from coming out too soon. She calculated that she was five or six months from giving birth, but the succession of brusque, violent contractions she'd had when she found out that her grandfather had been arrested in Madrid made her fear she would lose it. The news had travelled from mouth to mouth in the San Miguel alley until it reached the Garcías' forge and from there to the upper floors, where it was celebrated with cheering and hugs. The gypsy girl breathed deeply. The pain lessened and her heartbeat started to calm.

'Death to El Galeote!' she heard from one of the adjoining rooms.

She recognized that high-pitched, shrill voice: it belonged to a boy, one of Pedro's nephews; he couldn't be more than seven years old. What could that little brat have against her grandfather? She was gripped by conflicting feelings again, now that her fury over her father's death had given way to deep, lonely, tormenting grief. Yes, her grandfather had killed him, but should he die as well for what he had done? *A fit of rage, that's what it was, a fit of rage,* she often said to herself as she fought against her grief. She admitted that he deserved to be punished, but the idea of seeing him dead terrified her.

She pricked up her ears to listen to the conversations in the next room, which was full with the arrival of the men who worked in the forge. A trusted courier who made the route between Madrid and Seville, one of those men who transported packages and ran errands for others, had brought the news: 'The relatives in Madrid have seized Melchor Vega,' announced the courier. *How could you let yourself get caught, Grandfather?* lamented Milagros amid the shouts of joy. *Why did you allow it?* Someone commented that the family members wanted to know what to do with him: they couldn't bring him in a wagon, with other people, and the voyage to Seville with a shackled man would be slow and dangerous. 'Kill him!' 'As soon as possible!' 'Have them castrate him first!' 'And rip out his eyes!' added the little nephew amid the others' shouts.

'The revenge is for the Carmonas. Have them bring him here, however they can, no matter how long it takes. The sentence must be carried out here, in Triana, before all those present.'

Rafael García's order put an end to the discussion.

Why? cried Milagros in silence. *Who were the Garcías to decide the fate of her grandfather?* She felt seething hatred towards her new family: it was almost palpable; everything was impregnated with rancour. She stroked her belly, wanting to feel her child; not even that baby, fruit of the marriage between a Vega and a García, seemed to diminish the atavistic hatred between the two families. Her mother had warned her: *Never forget that you are a Vega.* She had argued with Old María about it. She hadn't heard anything from the healer in so long but she thought of her increasingly often as her pregnancy advanced. Her mother's words drilled into her conscience even at the altar, but she sought refuge in Pedro. How naive she had been. There was the answer: in the shouts of joy over her grandfather's disgrace that continued in the next room! She hadn't heard from her mother until her father had been killed. Reyes, La Trianera, had enjoyed sending to Málaga the news of Milagros's marriage to a García and the death of José Carmona by Melchor's hand. *Tell my daughter she is no longer a Vega.* La Trianera's smug expression as she conveyed her mother's message was burned into Milagros's memory.

She didn't want to believe it. She knew that it was true; she was certain that that had been her mother's response, but she refused to admit that she would disown her. She worked every night, non-stop. She sang and danced where El Conde decided she should: inns, homes and palaces, parties . . . Milagros of Triana was what people called her.

She stole some of the coins, her own money, which was controlled by greedy La Trianera, who never left her side. Milagros secretly convinced a gypsy from the Camacho family to go to Málaga. 'There is enough for you to bribe whomever you need to and then to give my mother a bit of money,' she told him.

'I'm sorry. She doesn't want to have anything to do with you,' he told her on his return. 'She says you are no longer her daughter. She doesn't want it,' he added as he gave her back the money intended for Ana.

'What else did she say?' asked Milagros in a thin voice.

'That you shouldn't waste more money trying to contact her; that you should give the coins to the Garcías so they can pay someone to kill your grandfather.

'She said it was ironic,' added the Camacho, shaking his head almost imperceptibly, 'that a Vega was supporting the Garcías. And that she preferred to be in Málaga, in prison, suffering alongside women and their children who'd been unable to obtain their freedom because they were gypsies, than return to Triana to be with a traitor.'

'Me, a traitor!' interrupted Milagros.

'Girl . . .' The man's face took on a serious expression. 'The enemies of someone in your family, the enemies of your grandfather, your mother, are also your enemies, every member of that family is. That is gypsy law. Yes, I also consider you a traitor. And there are many who feel the same way.'

'I am a Carmona!' she tried to defend herself.

'Your blood is Vega, girl. The blood of your grandfather, El Galeote . . .'

'My grandfather killed my father!' shrieked Milagros.

The Camacho swatted at the air. 'You shouldn't have married the grandson of your enemy; your father shouldn't have allowed it, even if only because of the blood that flows through your veins. He knew what the deal was: his freedom for your engagement to the García boy. He should have refused and sacrificed himself. Your grandfather did what he had to do.'

She no longer had any of her family or close friends: her mother, her grandfather, her father, María . . . Cachita. She perked up her ears:

nobody in the next room was talking about Cachita. She was also condemned to death, but they didn't seem to care much about her. She would have liked to share her incipient motherhood with her friend. Her grandfather had said that she hadn't done anything. It had to be true: Cachita was incapable of hurting anyone. She had been unfair to her. How many times had she regretted allowing herself to get carried away by rage! And now, when she found out that her grandfather had been caught, she couldn't stop thinking about the *morena*: if she hadn't been captured with him . . . Where was Cachita? Alone?

Alone or not, she was probably doing better than Milagros was, she tried to convince herself. That very night she would sing, given that she couldn't dance much in her condition. She would perform in an inn near Camas, La Trianera had told her in passing, without asking her opinion or much less her consent. She would go surrounded by members of the García family, but not Pedro, who never accompanied her: 'I'm afraid I would end up killing one of those cocky men who drool watching you dance,' had been his excuse from the start of their marriage. 'You'll be fine with my cousins.' But he didn't go with her when she wasn't dancing for *payos*, either. Pedro barely worked in the forge any more; he didn't have to, what with his share of his wife's earnings, which Rafael and Reyes made sure to claim for him. He loafed about in the inns and bars of Triana and Seville, and there were many nights when he arrived home at dawn. How many times had she had to block her ears to the whispers of harpies about her husband's running around! She didn't want to believe them! They weren't true! It was just envy. Envy! What was it about Pedro that his mere touch destroyed her resolve? Just a trace of a smile on that beautiful dark face with its hard features, a compliment, a bit of flattery – 'Pretty girl!' 'Lovely!' 'You are the most beautiful woman in Triana!' – some trifling gift, and Milagros forgot her anger and saw her bad mood over her husband's abandonment transformed into pleasure. And making love . . . God! She felt as though she was dying, or going insane. Pedro brought her to ecstasy, once, twice, three times. Of course the other women whispered when her moans filled the Garcías' house, the building, the entire San Miguel alley! But then he would disappear again. Milagros lived in an endless, desperate back and forth between loneliness and unbridled passion, between doubt and blind devotion.

Milagros didn't have anyone to talk to or to confide in. La Trianera controlled her day and night, and as soon as she saw her chatting with someone in the alley, she quickly came over to put in her twopenn'orth. Milagros often passed by San Jacinto and sadly contemplated the church and the friars coming and going. She would have been able to talk to Fray Joaquín, tell him about her life, her worries, and he would have listened, she had no doubt. But he had vanished from her life as well.

Fray Joaquín had been on missions for almost a year, travelling all over Andalusia with Fray Pedro, surprising humble folk in the middle of the night, threatening them with every possible evil, forcing men to punish their bodies in the churches while the women were to do it in the privacy of their homes with stinging nettles hidden in their clothes, wormwood in their mouths, pebbles in their shoes and rough cords, knotted ropes and wires wrapped tightly around and cutting into their bellies, breasts and extremities.

Milagros was never out of his mind.

General confession, the ultimate goal of the missions, ended up breaking the friar's will and spirit. The letter issued by the Archbishop of Seville allowed him to forgive all sins, including those whose extreme seriousness meant they were usually dealt with by higher-ranking officials of the Church. He listened to hundreds, thousands of confessions through which people strove to obtain general absolution of sins they had never told their usual parish priests, since the latter couldn't forgive them. But, poor and humble as they were, they had no access to bishops and prelates to confess such sins as incest and sodomy. 'With a child?' Fray Joaquín shouted on one occasion, piquing the curiosity of those waiting. 'How old?' he added, lowering his voice. Then he regretted having asked. How could he forgive him after hearing the age? But the man remained in silence awaiting absolution. 'Do you repent?' he asked without conviction. Murders, kidnappings, bigamy, a string of evils that were eroding his principles and bringing him closer, step by step, mission by mission, to believing, just as Fray Pedro did, that they were all irredeemable sinners, who only reacted out of fear of the devil and the flames of hell. What remained of the Christian virtues, of joy and hope?

'You have been slow to realize that this is not the path that Our Lord has called you to,' Fray Pedro said when Joaquín told him he intended to abandon the missions. 'You are a good person, Joaquín, and after all this time I have come to appreciate you, but your sermons do not call people to contrition and repentance.'

Fray Joaquín didn't want to return to Triana. His excitement over his last trip back, a few months after first leaving – when he'd heard the news of the return of the assimilated gypsies – had ended when he found out about Milagros's marriage. He locked himself in his cell, fasted and punished his body as much as he had on the missions. Angry, disappointed, his fantasies frustrated, he came to understand the fits the penitents claimed as excuses for their mortal sins when it came time to confess: jealousy, rage, spite, hatred. He didn't go back; he preferred to continue dreaming of the girl who mocked him by sticking out her tongue than face the torment of running into her one day with her husband on the streets of Triana. His next few breaks were spent with Fray Pedro, far from his home, while the preacher speculated about the reasons his assistant refused to reveal.

'I've heard from a nobleman in Toledo, close to the archbishop, who needs a private Latin teacher and tutor for his daughters,' he suggested when Fray Joaquín admitted he didn't know what to do.

Fray Pedro took care of everything: his prestige opened doors. He got in touch with the nobleman, gave Joaquín documentation, both from the lay authorities and from the Church, a mule and enough money for the trip, and on the morning Joaquín was going to depart he showed up to say goodbye with a package beneath his arm.

'Hold on to it so it can guide your life. May it soothe your doubts and calm your spirit,' Pedro wished him as he held it out.

Fray Joaquín knew what it was. Still, he pulled away the canvas that covered the upper part. The crowned head of an Immaculate Virgin appeared in his hands.

'But this—'

'The Virgin wants to accompany you,' the priest interrupted.

Fray Joaquín contemplated the sculpture and its perfect rosy face that looked at him sweetly: a valuable work of considerable size, masterfully carved, with a crown of gold and diamonds. The faithful thanked the missionaries with many gifts and a great deal of money for the absolution of their sins. Fray Pedro, moderate in his habits, refused all those that weren't essential for his survival, but his integrity had wavered when a rich landowner placed this in his hands. 'After all, what better place for Our Lady than working for the missions?' he told himself to justify breaking his rule of austerity. When he handed it over to Fray Joaquín, he felt that he was liberating himself of a burden.

27

IN THE BARQUILLO district of Madrid, to the northeast of the city, in humble single-storey houses, lived the *chisperos*, who were as haughty, proud and arrogant as the *manolos* from the Rastro and Lavapiés, but dedicated to blacksmithing and the trade in iron utensils. That was where the Garcías lived along with many other gypsies, and that was where young Martín Costes had been wandering for the last ten days, with his arm bandaged and trying not to attract attention to himself as he went up and down the deserted, dirty streets.

His father and his brother Zoilo told him that they understood what he was doing, that they were with him, but that that was just the way things were. 'It didn't work out well,' admitted El Cascabelero, ashamed. Later they tried to convince the young man not to continue. 'It'll be a waste of time,' said one. 'Uncle Melchor is already dead or on his way to Triana,' assured another. 'What do I have to lose by trying?' replied the young man.

He asked discreetly and found the house of Manuel García, on Almirante Street. From the first moment he knew that El Galeote was still inside: unlike the other homes, there were always a couple of gypsies going in and out and loitering around without ever getting very far from the door. At midday, they were replaced by others, just as if it were a changing of the guard: they whispered among themselves; they pointed at the house. Often one of the new arrivals would go inside, come back out and the whispering would start up again until the others left with smiles on their faces, patting each other on the back as if they were already savouring the wine they were planning on drinking.

'Have you seen him?' El Cascabelero asked his youngest son.

No. He hadn't seen him, he had to admit. He should make sure. One night, when Almirante Street was shrouded in pitch-blackness, Martín drew close beneath the window that opened on to it.

'They are waiting for instructions from Triana,' he told his father after waking him up at an ungodly hour when he returned home. 'He is inside that house, I'm positive of it.'

They weren't going to unleash a war between families. That was the decision that, much to the young gypsy's desperation, his father explained to him after taking the question to the heads of the other friendly families.

'Son,' El Cascabelero tried to excuse himself, 'I saw death in your eyes. I hadn't been in a situation like that in a long time. I didn't want you to die. I don't want any of my family members to die. No one is willing to let one of his own die for a gypsy from Triana condemned to death for killing his daughter's husband! Uncle Melchor ... El Galeote is made of stronger stuff. He gave himself up for you. What will he think if after all that, after handing himself over to the Garcías, you or other Vegas died for him?'

'But ... they are going to kill him!'

'Tell me: is he alive today?' asked his father in a serious voice.

'Yes.'

'That is what matters.'

'No!' The young gypsy got up from his chair.

'Promise me,' his father begged, trying to hold him back by grabbing his shirt, 'that you won't do anything that could put you in danger.'

'You want me to promise it to the memory of my mother, a Vega?'

El Cascabelero let him go and lowered his eyes to the floor.

Since then, Martín kept patrolling around the house where they were holding Melchor. He couldn't confront the Garcías. If he caught them by surprise maybe he'd be able to take on one, but not both, of the guards. Besides, there were women inside, and maybe more men.

He even thought about starting a fire, but El Galeote would die with the others. He tried to get in through the back. He slipped into a tumbledown forge and studied the interior kitchen gardens. Impossible. There was only a little window and he didn't even know if he would find El Galeote behind it. And what if he took his father's horse, the one he used in the bullfights? He smiled at the image of himself attacking the little house on horseback. He also considered the possibility of reporting it to the constables, but his shoulders trembled at the mere thought, as if they wanted to shake off the idea. The days passed and Martín only managed to come up with harebrained schemes. A fifteen-year-old boy, alone, against an entire family. And when night fell, he would return to Comadre Street, defeated, mute, to find an even more oppressive silence; even the children seemed to have lost the spirit that pushed them to shout, play and fight.

He didn't give in. He kept going to Barquillo to insult the Garcías under his breath. At least he would be there. 'It could take them over a month to get the instructions from Triana that you say they are waiting for,' Zoilo said. 'Are you going to be there that whole time?' He didn't answer his older brother. Of course he would be there! He owed his life to El Galeote! Perhaps then he would have an opportunity, when they took him out of the house to take him to Triana or when . . . Or were they going to kill him in their house?

The night of the tenth day, after losing hope while patrolling the García house, Martín headed back towards Comadre Street. The whisper he thought he had heard became clearer as soon as he turned the corner of Real del Barquillo: a chorus singing the rosary in the street, just as he had heard so many times in the distance. Twice a day, morning and night, processions of Madrileños went from the many churches to roam the streets praying the rosary. There were close to fifteen hundred brotherhoods of all types in Madrid. The procession was heading up Barquillo Street, in the opposite direction. Martín thought about changing his route and taking a detour, as he always did. The street rosaries were known for pressuring those they met along the way to join them, sometimes with slaps if they were unwilling. The last thing he needed was to end that night praying the rosary with a pack of brutes! If two of those processions crossed paths, the groups of faithful would often end up punching and beating each other with sticks – that's when they didn't pull out their knives.

Martín was about to change direction, but he stopped. An idea went through his head; *why not?* he thought. He ran towards them and blended in with the people praying.

'To Almirante Street,' he said through gritted teeth.

Someone in front of him asked why.

'There . . . those people are most in need of the . . .' He hesitated, not remembering what it was called. '. . . the illumination of Our Lady!' he managed finally, provoking a murmur of approval.

'To Almirante Street,' he then heard transmitted from one brother to the next until it reached the head of the procession. Amid the chanting of the mysteries, Martín was surprised to find himself trying to look at the image of the Virgin that made its way between the torches. Did he want her help?

He felt his knees grow weak as they approached the García house, walking slowly, all jammed together in the narrow alley. What if he wasn't successful? He was gripped by doubt. The monotonous, repetitive chants made it hard for him to think clearly. They were almost there! El Galeote. The gypsy had saved him from certain death. He stepped out of the line and in the dark he kicked the door to the house hard, and it opened wide; he jumped in and, without even worrying about the surprised Garcías inside, he shouted as loudly as he could.

'Fucking Virgin! Fuck the Virgin and all the saints!'

The Garcías didn't have time to lay a hand on him. They had barely stood up when a flood of angry, yelling people came into the house. Martín knelt down on the ground and started to cross himself desperately.

'Them! It was them!' he howled, pointing to them with his free hand.

The knives that Manuel García and his people showed were of no use to them. Dozens of indignant, enraged people leapt on the gypsies. Martín got up and looked for Melchor. He saw a closed door and went around the people who were mercilessly attacking the Garcías to reach it. He opened it. Melchor was standing there waiting for him, shocked, with his hands tied behind his back.

'Let's go, Uncle!'

He didn't give him time to react: he pushed him out of the room and pulled him towards the door. The members of the procession were busy with the Garcías; even so, some tried to block their way. 'It's them, them!' shouted Martín, distracting them as he slipped through the crowd. In a few steps they were in front of the door to the street, which was blocked by the throng.

'This man . . .' Martín started to say, pointing to Melchor.

The people at the door looked at him expectantly, waiting for his next words. Melchor understood the young man's intentions and they both pounced on them at the same time, as if they were a wall.

Several of the men fell to the floor. Martín and Melchor did too. The ones behind backed away. Others stumbled. Outside darkness reigned. The Virgin lurched. Most of the brothers shifted their attention to her image. Martín, covered by arms and legs, grabbed Melchor again, who couldn't move with his hands tied behind his back, helped him up, stepped on several brothers and ran.

Many didn't understand what had happened. Among complaints and cursing they heard the sound of laughter disappearing down Almirante Street.

Young Martín was surprised when Melchor, after thanking him for his help with a couple of sincere kisses, refused to go to El Cascabelero's house and instead asked him to take him to Peligros Street.

'OK, Uncle,' agreed the boy, stifling his curiosity. 'But the other Garcías . . . when they get word of your escape . . .'

'Don't worry. You just take me there.'

Eleven full days and nights. Melchor had kept track. *Will she still be at the hostel?* he thought as he hurried the boy. A dishevelled Alfonsa, whom they got out of bed after banging repeatedly on the door to her apartment, dashed the gypsy's hopes. 'She went with the cutter,' she said. 'That's what the washerwoman told me.' Caridad was gone. The guests came and went at the whim of their purses, which was often, by the way, she added when Melchor wanted to see the washerwoman. She knew nothing of the cutter either. Had she asked him for references when he showed up in the middle of the night with Pelayo and some black woman? There were countless possibilities as to Caridad's fate that had occurred to Melchor while he was locked up, each more disquieting than the one before, yet none of them were that she had voluntarily left with another man.

'It can't be!' he spat out.

'Gypsy,' replied the innkeeper with feigned weariness, 'you abandoned her; you left her alone for several days. Why are you surprised she went off with another man?'

Because I heard her sing. Because I was the only company she had. Because I loved her and she . . . Did he love Caridad? He had never admitted it, but he was sure he did, because of all the women he had known throughout his life, he had never felt, until being with Caridad, that union of body and spirit that gave his pleasure a hithertofore unknown dimension. If he didn't satisfy his desire completely, he could quell that frustration by merely brushing the back of his hand on the *morena*'s cheek. It was absurd and alarming: constant desire and satisfaction, endlessly intermingling. Of course she loved him! Because he had heard her scream with pleasure; because she smiled at him and caressed him; because her singing was starting to lose the grief and affliction that seemed to haunt her.

Alfonsa held the gypsy's gaze, now saddened, missing the spark it had held the night he had showed up with Caridad. She had thrown out the cutter after finding out what had happened; she didn't want scandals in her hostel. Then she had gathered Caridad's things and taken the money she had in her bundle. Her documents ended up burning in the stove, and the red clothes and hat were sold off cheaply to a second-hand clothes' shop. If the woman ever came back and denied her version, all she had to do was insist that that was what the washerwoman had told her. And if they asked about the bundle, she would just say that the cutter and the washerwoman had divided it up among themselves . . .

'Uncle . . .' Martín tried to attract Melchor's attention from the dismay he sensed in him. 'Uncle,' he had to insist.

'Let's go,' said the gypsy, finally reacting but not before shooting a look, his eyes sparkling again but now with a terrifying gleam, at the innkeeper. 'Woman, if I find out that you've tricked me, I will come back to kill you.'

The boy headed towards Comadre Street.

'Wait,' urged Melchor when they reached Alcalá Street. It was pitch black and an almost absolute silence reigned. El Galeote took Martín by the shoulders and faced him. 'Are you planning on taking me to your father's house?'

Martín nodded.

'I don't think I should go there,' objected the gypsy.

'But . . .'

'You freed me and I will be grateful all my life, but you were the only one there, no other Costes men, no gypsies allied with the Costes family.' Melchor let a few seconds pass. 'Your father . . . your father decided not to fight for me, right?' The boy's gaze, glued to the ground, was enough of a reply for Melchor. 'Going to his house now would only mean humiliating and shaming him, him and all your family.'

Melchor left out the misgivings that were also filling him: if they hadn't helped him, what guarantees did he have that they wouldn't sell him out to the Garcías? Maybe not El Cascabelero, but those around him, those he had surely consulted before making the decision to abandon him to his fate. It wasn't something he could have settled alone.

'Do you understand?' he added.

Martín lifted his head. He felt ashamed of his family's attitude. 'Yes,' he answered.

'Don't worry about me, I'll land on my feet. I have to . . . I have to find someone.'

'The *morena*?' Martín interrupted.

'Yes.'

'Is it the one they also condemned in Triana?'

'Yes. Don't mention it to anyone.'

'I swear to it on my Vega blood,' declared the boy.

He will be true to his word, Melchor told himself. 'Good. The problem now is you.'

Martín was confused by his words.

'You have to disappear, boy. Here, in Madrid, they will kill you, one day or another. I know what I am going to say will pain you, but don't trust anyone, not even your father. He, probably . . . surely he wishes you no harm, but he could find himself forced to choose between you and the rest of his family. You must leave Madrid. Go, say goodbye to your father and leave, this very night if possible. Don't look for protection in your family even in other cities, even if your father insists, because they will find you. I don't know where there are other Vegas – I'm afraid they've all been arrested. But there is a place on the border with Portugal, Barrancos, where you will find protection. Take the road to Mérida and then head towards Jerez de los Caballeros. From there it is easy to reach. Look for a tobacco dealer named Méndez and tell him I sent you; he will help you and teach you the art of smuggling. Don't trust him either, but as long as you are useful to him you won't have any problems.'

Melchor looked the boy up and down. He was only fifteen, but he had just shown greater fearlessness and valour than his own father. He was a gypsy. A Vega, and those of his line could take care of themselves.

'Did you understand me?'

Martín nodded.

'Well, this is where we part, although I have the feeling we will meet again, if the devil doesn't get me first.'

Melchor still held him tightly by the shoulders. A slight tremble was transferred to the palms of his hands. He drew close to the boy and hugged him hard. The grandson his daughter hadn't given him!

'One more thing,' he warned him after they separated. 'There are worse people out there than the Garcías. Don't wield your knife until you've learned to use it well.' Melchor was shaken by the memory of the sudden attack at the inn, how he'd held the knife out in front of him like a pike. 'Don't let yourself be blinded by your rage in quarrels, that will only lead to mistakes and death, and remember that bravery is worth nothing if it's not matched by intelligence.'

*

The dawn found Melchor leaning against the wall of the salt-cod warehouse at the gap in the wall near Embajadores, with the gully behind the wall opening up at his feet. There the city ended; there he had hidden to spend the rest of the night after bidding farewell to young Martín. Weary, he had fallen into a sleep that was constantly interrupted by Caridad's image. At some moments Melchor tried to convince himself of the impossibility of her running off with the cutter; at other times he was gripped by anguish when he tried to imagine where she could be. Remaining still, he tried to organize his thoughts: they would look for him – the Garcías and their allies would be looking for him; he couldn't go to anyone for help and he didn't have a penny. He didn't even have his knife or his yellow dress coat. He sighed. Bad start. The Garcías had taken everything from him. He had to find Caridad. *It's not possible that she went off with another man*, he told himself once again in the light of day, but then . . . why hadn't she waited at the guesthouse? Ten, eleven, twenty days if need be. The *morena* was capable of that, she was as patient as the best of them and she had enough money to deal with all expenses. As a shiver ran up and down his spine, he rejected the thought that something bad had happened to her, that someone had forced himself on her and killed her. No. The law, perhaps. Had she been arrested? In that case they would have arrested Alfonsa too for hiding her in a secret guesthouse; besides, the *morena* had her documents in order and never got into trouble – at least not voluntarily, smiled the gypsy, remembering the beaches of Manilva and the bags of tobacco they had stolen from her. He could only imagine . . . She was a tremendously desirable woman, voluptuous, black as ebony, showy and fascinating for a lusty city like Madrid. Any ruffian could make quite a profit off her. His stomach shrank and he trembled as he imagined Caridad being passed from man to man, disgracefully sold in any disgusting hole in the wall. He would find her! He got up stiffly, leaning on the wall. Absorbed in his thoughts, he hadn't realized that the people of Madrid were already up and working. Below the gully, in a meadow, they were trading livestock. He extended his neck and the breeze brought him the market's hubbub and the neighing and braying of the animals, but not their scent, which was cancelled out by what came from the salt-cod warehouse. The water the workers for the Provisions Board soaked the salted cod in, so it could later be sold, was tossed into the gully. Madrid consumed more cod than any other fish, including sardines, hake and tuna. The pious Spanish Christians paid enormous sums of money to their bitter enemies, the heretical English, for the supply of enough salted cod for their countless days of abstinence. The horses and the scent of fish made him think of Triana, the Guadalquivir, the pontoon bridge that linked it to Seville, the San Miguel alley and the gypsy settlement. There, among the orange trees, he had found Caridad. And Milagros, what had become of his girl? Had she forgiven him yet? José Carmona had deserved that stabbing. He sighed as he thought that Ana was the only one who could fix it. She was her mother. Milagros would listen to her . . . if he could get her freed.

Madrid lived in its streets, which ended up becoming the gypsy's home as well, blending into the army of beggars that populated them; he wore a splint on his right leg under his britches to fake a limp, and an old cloth cap and a worn blanket, both stolen, to cover part of his face even in the summer heat.

Melchor set out in search of Caridad. He travelled through the neighbourhoods of Madrid's eleven districts. Whether in Lavapiés, in Afligidos, in Maravillas or any other, he spent the days sitting in the streets and plazas, attentive to the patrols of magistrates who could arrest him, as much as to the daily comings and goings of Madrid's women: to mass, to buy food, with jugs for water, to bake bread, to wash clothes, to sell the darning they did at home and on all sorts of errands; few of them remained inside their gloomy dwellings more than strictly necessary, and the gypsy listened to the din of their conversations and witnessed their numerous disputes.

Men. They were the cause of the bitterest fights between women in a society where women who were single, widowed or abandoned outnumbered the married by thousands. He told himself often that it wouldn't be hard to recognize a Negro woman among them. He saw several; some he ruled out from a distance, others he followed limping until he was sure of his disappointment. On feast days and holidays, almost one hundred a year thanks to ecclesiastical zeal, he saw the women of Madrid leave their homes smiling and proud, all spruced up and dressed in the Spanish style: narrow waists and generous necklines, mantillas and combs, and he followed them to the Migascalientes copse, to the Corregidor meadow or the fountain of La Teja, where they flirted with men and snacked, sang and danced until the men got into quarrels and started throwing rocks at each other. He didn't find his *morena* there either.

However, it was at night when Melchor searched most. He was looking for prostitutes.

'You are lovely,' he would flatter them. 'But . . .' he pretended to hesitate, 'I'm looking for something special.'

Before they insulted him or spat at him as some had done, Melchor showed them his money.

'Like what?' they would respond once they'd seen the coins.

'A virgin girl . . .'

'You'll never have enough money for that.'

'Well . . . a black girl. Yes, a black girl. Do you know of any?'

There were some. They took him around, to dark alleys and squalid rooms. On every occasion, he squandered on the matchmakers the few coins he had been able to gather with his hustling.

'No! A real Negro,' he then insisted if he sensed that the woman might be able to help him. 'I want a black, black girl. Young, beautiful. I'll pay whatever it takes. Find her for me and I'll pay you well.'

Money. That was his biggest problem. Without money he couldn't sustain the greed of the various women of the night he had sent in search of Caridad. His sustenance was taken care of by the Church, but it had been some time since he'd smoked a cigar or drunk a good jug of wine. *I must really love you*, morena! he told himself as he passed the many taverns and bars without stopping. When he was hungry he would join the long lines of indigents at the doors of a monastery waiting for the watery slop that was handed out daily at most of them. He also kept an eye out for the bread and egg patrol that left the church of the Alemanes every night to attend to the needy. Three brothers from the Brotherhood of the Refugio – one of them a priest – along with a servant who lit up the street with a lantern, alternated neighbourhoods in their rounds to pick up the dead, take the sick to hospitals, offer spiritual comfort to the dying and feed the rest: a piece of bread and two hard-boiled eggs; big eggs as was to be expected of a prestigious brotherhood, because the little ones, those that fit through a hole that the brothers had made in a wooden board to check their width, were rejected.

He stole, and everything, except for a knife he decided to keep, was used to pay for the search for Caridad. He remembered the way Martín had freed him and he slipped into the rows of rosary singers on the streets, just as the boy had, until he managed to trick two of them into fighting with each other, one from San Andrés, and the other from the monastery of San Francisco, as they crossed each other in the little square at the Moros Gate. In the chaos of the fight he managed to make off with several objects that he later sold. He used a similar trick with a group of blind people. Melchor felt drawn to that army of the sightless that roamed Madrid's streets and plazas; Spain was a country filled with the blind, so many that some foreign doctors laid the blame for it on the practice of bleeding to flaunt pale skin or to rebalance the body's humours. The blind went around in groups offering to recite stories, play music and sing, always with a string of sheets pinned to a cord printed with the lyrics of the songs or the text of the works they recited, which they produced in small secret work-shops, without authorization, without paying the royal taxes or censoring them. They sold the pages at a very low price to those who listened to them, and the humble folk bought them from them; they spoke of themselves, of the *manolos* in the capital, extolling their gallantry, their customs and their valour in keeping alive the Spanish spirit while mocking and disdaining everything that was the least bit Frenchified. The blind were distrusting by nature, and all it took was passing them a fake coin for the canes and then the fists to start flying. The gypsy pulled it off on a few occasions, when he took advantage of the ruckus to steal all he could, but the third time it was as if the blind could smell him and they shouted insults at him before he could even get close.

Some prostitutes also began to recognize him. 'You still stuck on your black girl?' one of them let fly. 'Don't bother me!' shouted a second. 'Go tell your lies to someone else, imbecile!'

How long had he been searching for the *morena*? The summer and part of the autumn had passed; the cold got worse and he had even had to seek shelter at night in one of the many hospitals in Madrid. He missed the temperate climate of Triana. Sometimes they refused to admit him, claiming that it was already full, and he had to head to the large hospital run by the Alemanes, where the bread and egg rounds started, which took up an entire block between the Corredera Baja de San Pablo and Ballesta Streets.

Caridad wasn't there, he had to admit to himself one day that dawned leaden and cold. Every once in a while he would interrupt his search to find out about the procedures for freeing his daughter; he went to Carlos Pueyo's office so often, at the arcade on Mayor Street where second-hand clothes were sold, that the notary refused to see him and sent him to a dour clerk who got rid of him rudely. One day he received him to tell him that the fixer wanted more money, dashing Melchor's hopes. The gypsy protested. The other shrugged. Melchor shouted.

'We can just leave it at that and not continue, if you prefer . . .' interrupted the notary.

Melchor pulled out his knife. The notary's clerk saw him and got behind him and aimed a musket at him.

'That's not the way, Melchor,' Carlos Pueyo cut in calmly. 'Officials are greedy. They demand more money, that's all.'

'You'll have it,' spat the gypsy as he put his knife away and weighed whether he should threaten him or not. He didn't. 'Give me time,' he asked instead.

He had all the time in the world. What was left to him? He hadn't found Caridad despite having travelled all over Madrid and its brothels again and again. He had been yearning more and more strongly to see his daughter free – it had reached the point of obsession, and he was dependent on that notary who was bleeding him dry, sheltered behind a fixer he hadn't even ever met. That day he spent his last few reals on cigars and wine, and drank with his face exposed, without any blanket covering him, with his right leg tickling him constantly, freed from the pressure of the planks that had kept it straight for months. Tobacco, he concluded to himself as he turned an empty jug of wine round and round in his hands; that was the only way to get the money the notary demanded of him. Later, with his senses dulled, far from the bustle of people, he crossed the city towards the Segovia Gate. He didn't have anything to gather for his trip, no one to say goodbye to. He was alone. Before crossing the bridge over the trickling Manzanares River, he looked back at Madrid.

'I didn't pull it off, *morena*,' he whispered in a hoarse voice. The royal palace under construction rose on a hill above him, blurred by the tears that came to his eyes. 'I'm sorry. I really am, Cachita.'

28

CARIDAD WAS JUST finishing the first year of her sentence at La Galera, Madrid's royal jail for women.

That morning, as they both worked seated on the floor of the gallery where they slept, Frasquita shifted her attention from the sheet to focus on Caridad. Frasquita, who was over fifty, felt a twinge of tenderness seeing that woman absorbed in the garment, her agile fingers sewing ceaselessly. She had been among those who'd tried to humiliate her when they sent her back to La Galera after the sentence handed down by the High Court. Each morning, in the line that formed for the chamber pot, she would cut right in front of Caridad so she would have to empty her stools. And Caridad did it, without complaining, until her patience managed to soften Frasquita up. And the day that Frasquita decided to put an end to the humiliation and take a different spot in the queue, Caridad called her over to the place where she had stood day after day. Perhaps with another prisoner she would have responded angrily, but that round face as black as jet smiled at her without the slightest trace of bitterness, mockery or challenge. She went to where Caridad had indicated, urinated and threw the liquid out of the window herself, to the shout of 'Gardy loo!' Many of the other prisoners were pleased by her decision; in the end, they said in silence, they were all equal: women sharing the same misfortune.

And yet . . . Caridad didn't seem unhappy; she had confessed that some time ago, when Frasquita had to explain to her the reasons behind some of the women's complaints.

'When they were sentenced they were given an indefinite jail term. They have spent years locked up without knowing when they will be set free.' Caridad nodded as if that were normal; for someone who had been a slave, it wasn't so strange. 'But even if you have a release date,' continued the other, 'if you don't have a respectable man who takes responsibility and vouches for you, they don't let you out anyway.'

Caridad looked up from her sewing.

'It's true,' interjected Herminia, a slight, blonde woman who had taught Caridad how to sew.

The other two exchanged a glance when they saw that Caridad took up her sewing again as if trying to console herself with it.

'Do you have anybody out there?' asked Herminia.

'No . . . I don't think so,' she responded after a few seconds had passed.

In her life she had only had her mother, some siblings and her first Cuban baby whom they had taken away from her, then Marcelo, Milagros and Melchor . . . It had been a year since she'd heard from him. Sometimes her gods told her that he was alive, that he was fine, but she still had her doubts. Every once in a while her stomach would clench, but the tears that ran down her cheeks brought back happy memories. After all, what could a Negro slave expect? How could she have been so naive as to fantasize about a happy future?

'I'm fine here,' she murmured.

Yes. That was her way of life, what she knew and befitted her, what the white men had taught her with their whips: sleep, wake up, hear mass, breakfast, work, lunch, pray . . . Fulfil a series of daily routine obligations. She had no great worries. Sometimes she could even smoke. Saturdays, the inmates could sew for themselves and earn some money, a pittance, but enough for the sentry or the *demandera*, who ran errands for them outside of La Galera, to get them some tobacco.

Besides, since Frasquita had started throwing her own waste out of the window, most of the other prisoners seemed to have accepted Caridad.

'Don't go near certain people,' Frasquita warned her one day as they walked through the central courtyard; when there was good weather they let them do that before going to bed. Then she pointed to an inmate who was standing alone, with a bad-tempered expression and gaze. 'Isabel, for example. She is not a good woman: she killed her newborn son.'

'In Cuba many mothers kill their children. They aren't bad people; they do it to save them from a life of slavery.'

Frasquita analysed her words. Then she spoke slowly and deliberately, as if she had never thought about it that way before. 'Isabel says something similar: the father didn't want to take responsibility, she couldn't support the child, and in the foundling hospital eight out of every ten orphans dies before the age of three. She says she couldn't bear imagining her son sick and neglected, dying a slow death.'

Despite everything, Caridad avoided Isabel and two other inmates who had done the same thing. But she couldn't avoid a prostitute that Frasquita had also warned her against. One morning the woman happened to be behind her in mass, surrounded by other whores with whom she formed a feared group within the prison. Caridad heard them whispering openly until the priest yelled at them; then they laughed under their breath and, after a few seconds, started up their chattering again. *Who was that Mary Magdalene, who the father called them to imitate in sermon after sermon?* thought Caridad. In Cuba they didn't talk about her.

'Sinners!'

The shriek echoed in the small chapel where the forced faithful were packed in. Startled by the shouts of the priest demanding penitence, repentance, contrition and a thousand other sacrifices, Caridad jumped when she felt someone put a hand on her shoulder. She didn't dare look behind her.

'They say you were condemned as a whore,' she heard.

She feared that the priest would notice and shout at her. She didn't answer. The woman shook her.

'*Morena*, I'm talking to you.'

Frasquita wasn't with her. That morning she'd arrived late and was in one of the rows at the back of the chapel. Caridad lowered her gaze, fearful, sorry she hadn't waited for someone who could protect her.

'Leave her alone,' the inmate next to her spoke up in her defence.

'You stay out of other people's business, bitch.'

Another of the prostitutes pushed the woman who had interfered – hard. The woman went flying into those in front of her, who staggered in turn.

The priest stopped the sermon at the commotion; the sentry made his way through the women to come over to them.

'Exotic black whores like you are the ones who steal our customers,' Caridad heard the one who had grabbed her shoulder accusing her, indifferent to the truncheon that the sentry used to open a path in the crowd. 'Tell me how much they pay you for sleeping with them.'

'Herminia, come with me!' ordered the man when he reached them.

'I don't . . .'

'Silence!' shouted the priest from the altar.

The truncheon pointing at her was enough for Herminia to give in and she prepared to go with him. Caridad shot her a grateful look. That woman had tried to defend her and she felt indebted to her.

'I don't steal,' Caridad spat at the prostitute. 'They never paid me anything!'

Her surprise grew when she turned and saw a docile woman opening her hands towards the sentry in a gesture of innocence.

'Morena, you come with me as well,' she heard him say.

'Stupid darkie.'

The prostitute's insult behind her back blended in with the priest's words, who continued his mass.

That was how Caridad became friends with Herminia: sharing a week of bread-and-water punishment with her.

'Who is Mary Magdalene?' she asked her new friend one day.

'Which one?'

Caridad looked confused.

'Here we have two Magdalenes they insist on lecturing us about,' explained Herminia.

'The one in mass, the one the priest is always talking about.'

'Oh! That one!' Herminia laughed. 'A whore. They say she was Jesus Christ's lover.'

'Jesus!'

'The very same. It seems she ended up repenting and they made her into a saint. That is why they use her as an example day in and day out. They didn't tell you about her in Cuba?'

'No. There they didn't ask us to repent for anything, they just told us that we had to obey and work hard because that was what the Lord wanted.' Caridad let a few seconds pass. 'And the other Magdalene?' she asked finally.

Herminia snorted before answering.

'She's worse than the first! Sister Magdalene of San Jerónimo' – she uttered the words in disgust – 'a nun from Valladolid who created women's prisons more than a hundred years ago. Since then all the kings have followed her instructions with fervour: equal punishment to men and severe discipline until they break us; humiliation, cruelty if necessary; hard work to pay for our maintenance. Did you notice that we can't see the street because the windows are so high?'

Caridad nodded.

'That was this Sister Magdalene's idea: isolate us from the good people. And along with all that, mass and sermons to convert us and make us useful as good maids . . . That is our fate if we ever get out of here: service. God save us from the Magdalenes!'

But except for those who had decided to cut short their children's sad, sure fate, the group of prostitutes and the odd other violent and nasty criminals, most of those 150 women were locked up there as a result of minor mistakes made out of ignorance or necessity.

She found out what Frasquita had been condemned for: immodest living, declared the magistrates.

'They arrested me one night strolling with a shoemaker,' she explained to Caridad. 'A good man . . . We weren't doing anything! I was cold and hungry and just looking to sleep indoors. But they caught me with a man.'

Frasquita pointed out many other women toiling in La Galera for their crimes against morality, a catalogue as extensive as it was vague.

They condemned them for being wanton or being scandalous, layabouts, libertines, dissolute, lecherous, unbridled, harmful to the State . . . Since, unlike men, they couldn't be sent to the army or to public works, they ended up in the women's prison.

The only crime Herminia, the small blonde who came from a nearby town, had committed was trying to sell a couple of strings of garlic on the streets of Madrid. She needed the money, she confessed to Caridad with resignation. There were many pedlars like her among the prisoners: women who were only trying to make a living by selling vegetables, which was against the law.

Caridad met two other women. A simple quarrel without real consequences had brought them to La Galera. Insults and fighting were also prohibited, as were frequenting inns or walking alone at night. They locked them up for not having a known job or address; for being poor and not wanting to work in service; for begging . . .

One Saturday, the day they divided up the week's tasks among the inmates – scrubbing, mopping, lighting or putting out the oil lamps, serving the food – Caridad got the job of handing out the stale bread. They paired her with a young woman who still had the glow and vigour of her youth. Caridad had noticed the girl: she seemed even more timid and defenceless than she herself did. They were both waiting beside the breadbasket for the sentry to authorize them to distribute it to the others.

'My name is Caridad,' she introduced herself over the noise of the women lined up.

'Jacinta,' answered the girl.

Caridad smiled and the other made an effort to return it. With a wave of his truncheon, the sentry allowed them to begin handing the bread out.

'Why are you here?' asked Caridad as they distributed the crusts of bread. She was curious. She was hoping the woman would say that it had been something petty, like so many others. She didn't want to have to think of her as a bad woman.

'What are you waiting for, girl?' One of the prisoners chivvied Jacinta, who had been distracted by Caridad's question.

She hadn't wanted to lie with her employer. That was what

Jacinta explained when they finished serving the bread and collecting the baskets as the others ate. Caridad questioned her with her gaze: it seemed a strange crime when most of them were condemned for just the opposite.

'I gave in on other occasions and I got pregnant. Don Bernabé's wife beat me and insulted me, she called me a whore and a slut and much more; then she forced me to give the child to the foundling hospital.' The explanation came out of the girl's mouth as if she still was unable to understand what had happened to her. 'Then . . . I didn't want to have another child!'

She stifled a sob. Caridad knew that pain. She stroked the girl's forearm and felt her tremble.

Thousands of girls like Jacinta suffered the same fate in the big capital; it was estimated that 20 per cent of the working population of Madrid was made up of servants. Young girls were sent by their families from all over Spain to serve in Madrid's homes or workshops. Most of them were hounded by their employers or their employers' sons and they couldn't refuse. Later, if they got pregnant, some of them dared to go to court to get a dowry if the man who had impregnated them was married or a nobleman, or to marry them if he was single. The wives and mothers accused the maids of tempting the men to gain money and position, and that was what Don Bernabé's wife charged Jacinta with after insulting and beating her. She was just a girl from a small town in Asturias who'd been sold by her parents. She lowered her gaze towards her young, full breasts when the woman pointed to them as the cause of her husband's lust and resulting mistake. And she felt guilty, standing there, under attack, in the parlour of a house that seemed like a palace compared to the miserable shack she came from. What were her parents going to say? What would the Asturian relative who lived in Madrid and had recommended her think? And so she allowed it. She kept quiet. One night she gave birth in the hospital of the Orphanage for Waifs and Strays, on Atocha Street as well. There they took in orphans older than seven, piled up in forty beds the decrepit, terminally ill old ladies who came to die in the only place in the capital for them, and there was also a room where the disgraced like Jacinta could give birth.

Many women died in childbirth; many babies suffered the same fate. Jacinta survived. The Congregation of God's Love hid the fruit of her womb in the foundling hospital, where the boy ended up passing away, and the girl went back to service.

'But if you didn't want to lie with your master . . .' insisted Caridad. 'Why did they lock you up?'

'Don Bernabé decided to do it. He said he didn't want me working in the house, that I was a bad maid and that I was disobedient.'

That was how Caridad found out that, along with the criminals and the desperate, there was another group of inmates whose only crime had been being born a female subordinate to a man. Women who, like Jacinta, had been locked up simply by the will of a husband, father or employer. Like María, almost an old lady, imprisoned for having sold a shirt without the consent of her man; Ana, who was there for having left her conjugal home without permission; and a third whose only crime was having struck up a friendship with a fisherman. Most of these decent women who ended up in jail because of an accusation from their husbands were sent to the San Nicolás and Pinto jails, but some of them ended up in La Galera. The only difference between them and those who had committed some crime was that the High Court consulted the man who'd asked that they be put away regarding the sentence they should receive. That man also had to pay the costs of maintaining the inmate while she was imprisoned. In some cases, after some time, they were pardoned and left the jail.

'Don Bernabé warned me, before I was put in here,' Jacinta confessed, 'that when I was ready for him, he would pardon me.'

Caridad looked the girl's body up and down. How long would it be before she lost the beauty that the gentleman was so attracted to, locked up in a place like this?

The day that Herminia asked if she had anyone outside the jail, Caridad, knowing she was being observed by her fellow inmates, kept sewing the hospital gown in silence. Her fingers, so expert in rubbing tobacco leaves and then twisting them delicately, quickly grew accustomed to sewing. She was fine inside there: she was surrounded by many women she could talk and even laugh with; most of them were good people. They fed her, although not much and badly. Some of the inmates complained and even rebelled, which brought them severe punishment. Caridad tried to understand their attitude: she had heard them talk about the hunger and misery that many blamed on their imprisonment and she couldn't see why they were complaining. She remembered the gruel and never-ending cod that she had eaten, day in and day out for years, in the tobacco plantation.

And freedom . . . thought Caridad. That thwarted freedom, which many of them spoke so much of, had only brought her to inhospitable lands and offered her the company of strange people who had eventually abandoned her. What had become of Milagros? Sometimes she thought of the young gypsy girl, although each time she seemed further away. And Melchor . . . She felt her eyes grow damp and she hid it from the others by feigning a coughing fight. No, freedom wasn't something that she missed.

RESTRAINED PASSION

29

MILAGROS HADN'T RETURNED to the palace of the Count and Countess of Fuentevieja since the day she had done so to request help in freeing her parents. Almost three years had passed and that girl whom the dour secretary to his excellency had not allowed past the gloomy hallway that led to the kitchens was now at ease in its luxurious rooms. Among those rich noblewomen who regularly bled themselves just to make their cheeks paler and who wore dresses plumped out with crinolines, women with corseted waists and torsos and tall, complicated and profusely ornate hairdos, which threatened to win out over the wire framework that held them up and collapse on to their bejewelled and beribboned heads, the gypsy felt observed and desired by the men invited to the count's party. His secretary, when receiving her that late February night along with one of the doormen, had directed a lascivious look at her breasts.

'You.' The gypsy wanted to get revenge on him, as she wondered if he recognized in her the girl he had mocked years earlier. 'What are you drooling over?'

The man reacted by straightening his head, embarrassed.

'These pearls are not for such swine,' Milagros spat at him.

Some of the gypsies who accompanied her showed their surprise. The doorman stifled a laugh. The secretary was about to respond when Milagros fixed her eyes on him and challenged him in silence:

Do you want to offend me and risk my leaving? How would that make your lord and lady look in front of their guests? The secretary gave in, not before directing a disdainful look at the group of gypsies.

Of course he hadn't recognized her! Three years and the birth of a lovely daughter had transformed the splendid body of the eighteen-year-old woman, still young but now full-bodied. Tanned, with pronounced, beautiful features and long chestnut-brown hair falling wildly down her back, everything about her emanated pride. Milagros didn't need corsets or elegant clothes to show off her charms: a simple green shirt and a long flowered skirt that almost covered her bare feet hinted at the voluptuousness of her legs, shoulders, hips, stomach . . . and her firm, turgid breasts. The tinkling of her many beads followed the steps of the doorman and the secretary to the large salon where, after dinner, the count and countess and their illustrious guests were waiting as they chatted, drank liqueurs and snorted snuff. After greeting the hosts and all the curious who came over to meet the famous Milagros of Triana, while the gypsies got settled and tuned their guitars, she wandered around among the people, looking at herself in the huge mirrors or indifferently touching some figurine, displaying herself before men and women in the light of the imposing crystal chandelier that hung from the ceiling, flaunting that sensuality that would soon explode.

The already rhythmic strumming of several guitars demanded her presence in one corner of the parlour expressly cleared for the group of four men and a few other women. La Trianera remained vigilant, her abundant flesh lodged in a wooden armchair carved with gold and upholstered in red silk, as if it were a throne. As soon as she'd seen it her eyes had grown wide and she had forced a couple of servants to bring it over to her from the other side of the room.

Reyes and Milagros exchanged cold, hard looks; however, all disquiet disappeared from the young gypsy's mood as soon as she began her first song. That was her universe, a world in which nothing and no one mattered in the slightest. Music, song and dance bewitched her and transported her to ecstasy. She sang. She danced. She shone brightly. She enchanted the audience: men and women who, as the night went on, shed their rigid bearing and their aristocratic airs to join in with the gypsies' shouts, hoots and clapping.

In the short breaks, the gypsies from the García family put down their guitars and surrounded her as she flirted with the men who approached her. Pedro wasn't there; he never was. And Milagros scrutinized the men, seeking in their faces, and in the desire she could smell, which of them was willing to reward her in exchange for a naughty wink, a daring gesture, a smile or a bit more attention than she gave the others. Some coins, a small jewel or whatever accessory they had on them: a silver button, perhaps a well-carved snuffbox. Those civilized, cultured nobleman satisfied their vanity by wooing her shamelessly in front of their wives, who, off to one side as if it were another performance, whispered and laughed at the enormous efforts their husbands made to rise above the others and claim the spoils.

A pocket watch. That was the trophy she won that night, and it passed quickly into La Trianera's hands, who weighed it and hid it among her clothes. Milagros allowed the winner to take her hand and brush his lips on the back of it. Out of the corner of her eye, she saw a woman with a large gold bow at her neckline that matched a number of other small bows adorning her hair, which was caught up in a bun; she was being congratulated by some of her companions as she gestured in an offhand manner, as if to make light of the fact that her husband had just given away such a jewel. *They enjoy it*, thought Milagros: affluent nobles, courtly and civilized, united by marriages of inclination.

The gypsies continued playing their guitars, clapping castanets and palms, and Milagros sang and danced for the nobles. They would keep it up until Don Alfonso and his illustrious guests grew weary, although seeing the soups, cakes, sweets and chocolate that the servants continued to serve, Milagros knew it would go on for a long time. And it did: the party lasted until dawn, long after she had grown exhausted and had given up her spot to the women who accompanied her, who struggled in vain to emulate her.

La Trianera, who was dozing on her throne, got up for the first time in the whole night when Don Alfonso brought the party to a close. The old gypsy woman woke up instinctively the minute the count directed a barely perceptible look towards his butler. The count had to pay them, although it was he who decided on the price. Many guests had already retired. Among those who remained, some had lost their noble bearing owing to the liquor. Don Alfonso, the bag of money in his hand, didn't seem to be too drunk and neither did the man with whom he approached the group of gypsies.

'An enjoyable evening,' the count congratulated them, extending the bag.

Reyes ripped it from his hand.

'An interesting night,' added his escort.

Without paying attention to La Trianera, Don Alfonso addressed Milagros. 'I believe I have already introduced you to Don Antonio Heredia, Marquis of Rafal, here visiting in Seville.'

The gypsy observed the man: old, powdered white wig, serious face, open black dress coat, narrow and embroidered on the cuffs, waistcoat, lace tie, britches, white stockings and low shoes with silver buckles. Milagros hadn't noticed him; he hadn't been one of those who had besieged her.

'Don Antonio is the Chief Magistrate of Madrid,' the count added after giving the gypsy a few seconds.

Milagros acknowledged his words with a slight bow of her head.

'As Chief Magistrate,' Don Antonio then explained, 'I am also the exclusive Judge Protector of Madrid's comic theatres.'

Before the Chief Magistrate's expectant expression, Milagros wondered if she should act impressed by his revelation. She arched her eyebrows to signal her lack of comprehension.

'I was impressed by your voice and' – the Chief Magistrate turned a couple of fingers in the air – 'your way of dancing. I want you to come to Madrid to sing and dance in the Coliseo del Príncipe theatre. You will form part of the company—'

'I . . .' the gypsy interrupted him.

Then it was the count who arched his eyebrows. The Chief Magistrate lifted his head. Milagros was silent, not knowing what to say. Go to Madrid? She turned towards the gypsies, behind them, as if waiting for some help from them.

'Woman . . .' the count's voice sounded harsh in her ears. 'Don

Antonio has just made you a generous offer. You don't want to offend the Chief Magistrate to His Majesty?'

'I . . .' stammered Milagros again, having lost all trace of the haughtiness she had shown throughout the night.

Reyes took a step forward. 'Please excuse her, your excellencies. She is just overwhelmed . . . and confused. Your worships will understand that she is not used to such a great honour. She will sing in Madrid, of course,' she declared.

Milagros couldn't take her eyes off the Chief Magistrate's face, whose rigid features gradually relaxed as he listened to La Trianera's words.

'Excellent decision,' he said.

'My secretary and Don Antonio's will take care of arranging everything,' the count then added. 'Tomorrow . . .' He stopped, smiled and looked at one of the large windows through which the first rays of light were already coming in. 'Well, today,' he corrected himself. 'You are expected before nightfall.'

The aristocrats allowed her no more time than that. They bade the gypsies farewell, and with one man resting his hand on the other's shoulder, chatting, they headed towards the room's large double doors. The count's belly laugh woke Milagros from her shock; they were the only ones left in the parlour, except for the butler who was overseeing them and a couple of servants who, as soon as the echoes of laughter died down in the halls of the great palace, moved away from the walls where they had been standing solemnly still. One sighed; the other stretched to loosen his muscles. The sunlight and the candles that were still lit in the grand chandelier revealed a room begging to be returned to the splendour it had received them with: the furniture was jumbled; there were glasses here and there, cups stained with chocolate, trays, little plates with leftover food and even fans and articles of clothing left by the women.

'Madrid?' Milagros managed to ask then.

'Madrid!' La Trianera's voice reverberated against the room's high ceiling. 'Or do you plan to offend the Chief Magistrate and cause another rift between us and the illustrious of the kingdom?'

Milagros frowned at La Trianera. Yes, I will go to Madrid, she convinced herself. *Anywhere that's far from you and yours*, she thought.

They prepared to leave for Madrid in a large wagon that travelled between Seville and the capital once a week, covered with a canvas awning and pulled by six mules. The wagon was designed to transport fifteen passengers and their respective luggage, and they gathered around it that March morning of 1752.

This time, the gypsies were going to leave Triana with all their permits and passports in order, signed and sealed by as many authorities as were necessary, and with the safeguard of none other than the Chief Magistrate of Madrid himself, as stated in the letter his secretary had issued the day following the party – though not before he'd expressed his surprise at the old gypsy woman the Garcías tried to include in the retinue. 'Otherwise who will take care of the girl while she sings for his excellency?' had argued Rafael the patriarch. The secretary had shaken his head, but he didn't really care how many gypsies went to Madrid, so he agreed. However, he was quick to correct the reference made to his master.

'Make no mistake,' he warned. 'The woman will not sing for the Lord Chief Magistrate; she will do so in the Coliseo del Príncipe for all those who attend the comedies there.'

'But some day his excellency will attend, right?' Rafael García winked an eye at the functionary, trying to make him complicit in the story that Reyes, his wife, had exaggerated when telling of the scene in the count's palace.

The secretary sighed. 'And even the King,' he said sarcastically. 'His Majesty, too.'

Rafael García's face fell and he held back his reply. 'How much money will the Lord Chief Magistrate pay her?' he asked instead.

The secretary smiled maliciously, annoyed at having to deal with gypsies. 'I don't know, but I'm sure she won't take the leading lady's place. I suppose she will receive a wage of some seven or eight reals per day she performs.'

'Seven reals?' protested El Conde. The pocket watch Milagros had been given the night before was worth a hundred times that!

The other man's smile widened. 'That's the way it goes. New girls don't receive a regular salary, paid whether they work or not,' he explained at the gypsy's confused expression. 'She will be paid only for the day's work . . . Yes, seven or eight reals.'

Rafael García couldn't stifle a disappointed look. His son and the other two gypsies that accompanied him also showed their discontent.

'In that case . . .' The gypsy hesitated, but ended up making the threat. 'For that wage Milagros won't go to Madrid.'

'Listen,' announced the other seriously. 'She wouldn't be the first player who ends up in jail for refusing to accept the orders of the Chief Magistrate and the council that governs the theatres of the capital. Madrid isn't measured in reals, gypsy. Madrid is . . .' The man fluttered his hands in the air. 'There are many players in travelling companies and smaller theatres all over the kingdom who lose money when they are called to Madrid. You choose: Madrid or jail.'

Rafael García chose, and a month later his grandson Pedro watched smoking as Milagros loaded the few family belongings into the wagon and Bartola, her nanny, held their daughter in her arms.

Between bags, Milagros looked at the little girl. She was just like her mother, some said, while others were sure she took after her father and some looked for resemblances with the Garcías. No one mentioned the Vega family. She wiped the sweat from her brow with a sleeve. She didn't dare to baptize the girl with the name Ana. Many gypsies brought news of the imprisoned in Málaga, but none for her. She never asked them to talk to Ana Vega. She couldn't bear another response like the one she had received when she sent the Camacho! Perhaps some day . . . Meanwhile, she knew nothing about her mother, and that tormented her. However, she had baptized her daughter with the name María, in secret homage to the old healer who had been replaced by Bartola, who was going to accompany the family in their journey to the court.

Twelve more people got into the wagon after them: several couriers loaded down with packages; a Frenchified dandy who looked with disgust at everything around him; a timid girl who was going to the capital to work as a servant; a man who said he was a fabric vendor, two friars and a married couple. None of the gypsies had ever travelled in a wagon, and except for the couriers, who came and went between cities, it was clear than none of the other passengers had either, such was the aversion to travel in that period. The wagon was full and they all tried to get comfortable in a space without benches, among the piles of diverse merchandise and belongings they carried with them, on a floor that wasn't made of planks like the carts Milagros was familiar with, but instead of a network of strong cords on which the people and their baggage were randomly jumbled. They had to travel lying down, as the young woman saw one of the couriers do. Amid the pushing, the two gypsy women extended the straw mattresses they were carrying along one side of the wagon and sat down on them with their backs precariously resting against the straw mats that served as railings.

In such a way, accompanied by a cart transporting olive oil and another muleteer at the head of a train of six animals loaded down with merchandise, they faced the long journey. Milagros took a deep breath when the carter cracked the whip over the mules and they began their march, pulling the heavy wagon behind them. Then she let herself be rocked to sleep by the jingling of the animals' harness and the metal clatter of the pots and pans that hung outside the wagon. Every tinkle of those bells took her a bit further from Triana, from El Conde, from La Trianera, from the Garcías and from the misfortunes that had destroyed her life. Every once in a while, the crack of the whip sent the animals lurching forward for a few moments, until they resumed their apathetic gait. Madrid, she again thought. She had come to hate the capital when she found out about her grandfather's capture, but when a month later another courier arrived with the news that he had escaped, she, amid the swearing and cursing of the members of her new family, had been reconciled with that city. Would it be the same in a Madrid theatre, beside professional actors and musicians, as in the inns and parties of Seville? That uncertainty was the only thing that worried her. She remembered what torture it had been for her to sing Christmas carols in the Santa Ana parish, with the choirmaster reprimanding her constantly and the musicians looking down on her, and she feared that the same thing would happen. She was just a gypsy, and the *payos* . . . the *payos* were always the same with gypsies. Yet despite everything, Milagros was willing to suffer that ridicule, a hundred times over if need be, to get Pedro away from his family in Triana, from his indolent life and his nights spent . . . She'd rather not know where. She closed her eyes tightly and squeezed her little one against her chest. In Madrid, Pedro would only have her. He would change. What did she care about the money that the Garcías seemed so concerned with? Without it there would be no wine, no taverns, no bars, no . . . women.

Pedro had strongly opposed moving to Madrid, but El Conde had not budged, even for his favourite grandson. The freeing of gypsies had been suspended not long after José Carmona was freed; many trusted that some day the King would reconsider their situation. And they were fighting to achieve that. 'It's the Chief Magistrate of Madrid!' El Conde had shouted at his grandson. Then: 'Listen, Pedro,' he'd continued in a different tone, 'we are all getting closer to the *payos*. Soon, a few months at the most, we will present the rules of what will become the Gypsy Brotherhood to the Archbishop of Seville; we have chosen as its seat the monastery of the Holy Spirit, here in Triana. We are working on it. Gypsies with a religious brotherhood!' he added as if it were madness. 'Who could have ever imagined it? And we aren't just the Garcías, but all the families in the city, united. Do you mean to spoil that . . . for all of us, with a person as close to the King as the Chief Magistrate of Madrid? Go there. It won't be for ever.'

The gypsies had made such progress in their relations with the Church, which was capable of jailing or freeing people, that even the friars who went to Triana to hear general confessions had noted, over and above the other citizens, the piety and religious spirit of those who had come to confess.

'Refuse!' urged Milagros one day in the face of her husband's constant complaining. 'Let's go; let's run away from Triana. I married you against the will of my family – you can rebel too. Who is your grandfather to decide what we should or shouldn't do?'

But just as she had assumed, Pedro didn't dare to disobey his grandfather and from that day on there were no more arguments, although Milagros was careful not to show her happiness.

It took them eleven long days to reach Madrid. Days over the course of which other vehicles and travellers with the same destination joined them while others turned off at crossroads. The roads were bad and dangerous, so people sought each other out. Besides, the carters and muleteers enjoyed certain privileges that annoyed the locals: they could allow their animals to graze, or gather firewood in communal lands, and it was always preferable to defend such rights as a group. Numb, constantly trying to quiet the pathetic crying of a one-and-a-half-year-old girl unable to stand the tedium and monotony, Milagros was encouraged when she sensed they were getting close to the big city. Even the mules quickened their weary pace as the urban noise became increasingly noticeable. The sun had just appeared on the horizon, and the wagon they were in was squeezed between the hundreds of carts and thousands of pack animals that entered the city each day to supply the capital. A multitude of labourers, farmers, merchants and porters, either driving carts small and large, or walking, heavily laden, or leading mules and oxen, had to enter Madrid personally to sell their products and goods. To prevent the stockpiling and raising of prices, the King had outlawed dealers, traders and court suppliers acquiring edibles to resell on the outskirts of Madrid or on the roads that led to it; they could only do so after twelve noon, in the plazas and markets, after the inhabitants had had a chance to acquire them in the stalls at their original prices.

Through a slit in the tarpaulin that covered the side of the wagon, Milagros looked out at the jumble of people and animals. She shrank back at the shouting and chaos. What was awaiting them in a city that, day after day, required that entire army of suppliers?

They entered Madrid through the Toledo Gate, and on the street of the same name, in one of the many inns there, the Herradura Inn, they ended a journey that had seemed endless. They had been told to go to the Coliseo del Príncipe theatre when they arrived in order to receive instructions. Milagros and old Bartola fought with the other travellers to unload the mattresses and other belongings while Pedro got information from the carter and the couriers.

The sun of a cool but radiant day illuminated the colourful crowd that was entering the city and which they were now a part of. Pedro walked ahead, without any luggage, with the two women following behind dragging the bags and carrying little María. Not many people paid any attention to the group of gypsies as they went down Toledo Street towards the Plaza de la Cebada in one of the most populous and humble neighbourhoods in Madrid. The inhabitants wandered among the inns, bars, mattress shops, wicker shops, forges and barber shops that flanked Toledo Street.

Milagros and Bartola took turns carrying María. They were passing the girl from one to the other when Pedro, who had turned his head to see what the hold-up was, pounced on them just in time to keep the little one from grabbing one of the shirts that hung from the doorway of a miserable hovel that displayed used clothing.

'Do you want her to get sick?' he scolded them both. 'Nasty piece of work!' he announced after staring into the haggard face of the shop's owner.

His concern arose from the fact that on Toledo Street there were several second-hand clothing shops run by dealers whose gaunt faces showed the fate of many who, out of necessity, bought the clothes taken off the deceased in hospitals. While the gypsies burned the clothes of their dead after burial, the *payos* bought and sold them, not caring that in their stitches and seams lingered the seeds of all sorts of illnesses, and the skirts, britches and shirts, returned again and again to the shops to await a new poor soul to transmit them to, formed a vicious cycle of death.

Milagros hitched her girl up until she had her settled on her hip; she understood what had caused Pedro's reaction and she nodded before continuing walking. They reached the Plaza de la Cebada, a large irregular space where, besides executing the prisoners condemned to death by hanging, they sold grain, salt pork and vegetables. Many of the farmers who had walked up Toledo Street with them turned into the plaza. Around the market stalls loitered hundreds of people. Other peasants continued towards the Plaza Mayor.

Pedro, however, guided them to the right, towards a narrow

street that bordered the church and the cemetery of San Millán; they continued along it to the plaza of Antón Martín. There, while women and children cooled themselves in the fountain that spouted water from dolphins' mouths, he asked again for the Coliseo del Príncipe theatre. With no luck. A couple of men avoided the gypsy and hurried past. Pedro's jaw tensed and he stroked the handle of his knife.

'What are you looking for?' he heard when he was about to question a third person.

Milagros observed a constable dressed in black who, truncheon in hand, approached her husband. The men spoke. Some passers-by stopped to watch the scene. Pedro showed him his documents. The constable read them and asked for the performer referred to in the papers.

'My wife: Milagros of Triana,' he responded curtly as he pointed to her.

Beside the fountain, Milagros saw herself being scrutinized up and down by the constable and the onlookers. She hesitated. She felt ridiculous with the straw mattress rolled up under one arm, but she lifted her chin and stood tall before them.

'Pride comes before a fall!' shouted the constable in response. 'We'll see if you can stay so puffed up on stage, when the groundlings boo you. In Madrid we've got plenty of beautiful women but we're short on good comic players.'

The people laughed and Pedro made to turn on them. The constable stopped him by raising his truncheon to the height of his chest.

'Don't be so sensitive, gypsy,' he warned, drawling his words. 'In a few days, when the theatre season begins, all of Madrid and the surrounding areas will criticize . . . or praise your wife. It's up to her. There is no in-between. Come with me,' he offered as Pedro calmed down. 'The Príncipe Theatre is very close by. It's on my rounds.'

From the plaza itself they climbed a bit, around the Loreto school and into a narrow street to the right. Milagros struggled to maintain the same haughty bearing with which her husband paraded in front of the chorus of Madrileños who had witnessed the scene, but – weighed down with María on one side and the mattress on the other, followed by Bartola snorting and cursing into the back of her neck with the other two mattresses and the rest of the luggage – the few steps' lead that the constable and Pedro had on them seemed an insurmountable gap. 'We'll come to see you, gypsy!' Milagros heard, and she turned towards a short fat man wearing a large black hat that made him look like a mushroom. 'Don't make us waste our money,' she heard another shout. *Where is the luxury and pageantry of the Count of Fuentevieja's palace now?* she lamented, irked by the laughter and comments she heard as she passed.

One block more and they stopped at the side street that led to where the Príncipe Theatre was; a bit further on, from the corner of Prado Street, the constable pointed to his right, towards a building with straight lines and a sober stone face whose pitched roof extended far above its neighbours.

'There you have it,' he indicated proudly. 'The Coliseo del Príncipe.'

Milagros tried to get an idea of the theatre's dimensions, but the narrowness of the street she was facing made it impossible. She turned her head to the left, towards a continuous windowless wall that extended along Prado Street.

'The garden of the Santa Ana monastery,' explained the constable when he realized where the gypsy girl's gaze fell. Then he pointed to the upper part of the same street. 'There, in the atrium that leads to the monastery, there is a vaulted niche with a statue of the Virgin's Holy Mother whom many of your race come to worship. You should commend yourself to her before you go in,' he said, laughing.

Milagros left María on the dirt floor. Santa Ana! In her parish in Triana she had sung carols for the *payos* after being humiliated by the choirmaster and the musicians. How far off those days now seemed! Yet the same saint appeared beside the theatre where she would have to sing before *payos* again. It couldn't be a mere coincidence; it must mean something . . .

'Let's go!' The constable's order distracted her from her thoughts. The gypsies were about to head to the theatre when the constable stopped them with a wave of his truncheon and explained.

'That's the audience's entrance. The players go in through the back door, on Lobo Street.'

They went around the block until they found the door. The constable spoke with a doorman who watched the entrance and allowed them in without delay.

'Are you planning on going in with a straw mattress under your arm?' scoffed the man after inviting Milagros to follow him. 'The others can't come in!' he warned Pedro and Bartola right away.

Pedro managed to get through, as her husband. 'Who is going to stop me from accompanying her?' he said arrogantly. The mattress stayed outside, with Bartola, María and the other baggage. As soon as the door closed behind them, they found themselves in a large chamber on to which opened a series of rooms.

'The dressing rooms,' commented the constable.

Milagros didn't look at them; nor did she look at the various armchairs arranged beside one of the walls that had caught her husband's eye. The gypsy girl's attention was fixed on the back of the set: a huge, simple white canvas that, among pieces of stage machinery, almost entirely filled the space in front of the area reserved for the audience. Through it she could make out the shadows of people: some moved and gestured with their arms, others remained still. She couldn't make out what they were saying. Were they reciting? She heard a shouted order and there was silence, followed by another command. The figure of a woman gesticulated wildly. A shadow approached the woman. They argued. The woman's voice, obstinate, impudent, rose above the other until finally silencing it. The man was left alone. Milagros could see that his arms were slack at his sides. The woman disappeared from her vision, but not her shrieks, which gained strength as they approached along one side of the curtain.

'Who does that boor think he is!' The shout preceded the in-opportune appearance of a middle-aged woman, blonde, well dressed, as exuberant as she was agitated. 'Telling me, me, how I should sing my role! Me, the great Celeste!'

On her way to the dressing room, the woman passed by Milagros without even looking at her.

'This show won't last two days!' continued Celeste, indignant, but her discomfiture vanished as if by magic when she came across Pedro García a few paces further on.

The constable, by his side, removed his hat in deference.

'And who are you?' the woman questioned the gypsy, planting herself in front of him with her hands on her hips.

Milagros couldn't see the smile her husband received that sudden interest with: behind her, from the same place the woman had appeared, more than twenty people rushed in. 'Celeste,' clamoured a man, 'don't be upset.' 'Celeste . . .' They didn't notice her presence either; they passed her by, from right to left, until they were surrounding Celeste, Pedro and even the constable. Meanwhile, Pedro's gypsy gaze, with his eyes slightly squinted, had managed to make the woman stutter.

'No . . .' she tried to silence the requests that were coming in; she was captivated by the gypsy's lovely face.

'Celeste, please, think it over,' was heard. 'The leading man . . .'

At the mere mention of the leading man, the woman reacted.

'I won't hear of it!' she howled, pushing the others away from her. 'Where is my sedan chair? Send in my bearers!' She looked around until she located two scruffy men who quickly answered her call. Then she made as if to head to one of the sedan chairs, but first she drew close to Pedro. 'Will I see you again?' she asked in a sweet whisper, her lips brushing the gypsy's ear.

'As sure as my name is Pedro,' he promised in a similar tone.

Celeste smiled with a hint of naughtiness, turned and climbed the box of her sedan chair, leaving an aroma of her perfume behind her. The bearers grabbed the two poles, lifted the chair with them and, amid murmurs, headed to the door that opened on to Lobo Street.

'Too much woman for you,' the constable warned him when the door closed again and the murmurs turned into arguments. 'Half of Madrid is chasing after her and the other half wishes they had the balls.'

'In that case,' Pedro bragged with his gaze still on the door, 'half of Madrid will end up envying me and the other half applauding me.' Then he turned towards the constable, who was pulling down his hat, and drilled him with his gaze. 'What half are you in?'

The man didn't know what to say. Pedro sensed he might try to pull rank and he quickly said, 'There are always a lot of other beautiful women flocking around that type. You get me? If you stick with me . . .' The gypsy let a few seconds pass. '. . . you could also be the object of envy.'

'Who will be the object of envy?'

They both turned. Milagros had managed to make her way through the people and was now beside them.

'I will,' answered Pedro, 'for having the most beautiful wife in the kingdom.'

The gypsy draped an arm over his wife's shoulders and pulled her towards him. His attention, however, remained fixed on the constable: he needed someone to introduce him to the capital, and who better than a representative of the King? Finally, the man nodded.

'Let's find the director of the company,' he said immediately, as if that movement of his head hadn't been directed exclusively at Pedro. He grabbed an actor by the arm without thinking twice and asked, 'Where is Don José?'

'Why do you want to know?' the actor retorted, throwing off the hand gripping his arm.

The constable hesitated in the face of the actor's boldness.

'There is a new comic player,' he explained, pointing to Milagros.

Those around her leapt to get a look at her. The news spread rapidly through the rest.

'Hey . . . !' the actor tried to get his colleagues' attention.

'Where is the director?' insisted the constable.

'Crying,' joked the man. 'He must be crying on the stage. Nicolás and Celeste can't agree on anything when it comes to rehearsals.'

'If the leading man would treat her with more respect, the director wouldn't be in this fix.'

'The great Celeste?' A mocking expression appeared on the actor's face. 'Lofty, splendid, magnificent! If everything was left up to that woman's whims, or even those of the supporting actress, none of you would enjoy the shows.'

The constable opted not to argue, swatting the air with one hand and heading towards the stage. They reached it through one side of the set along with other members of the company. With Pedro's arm still around her, squeezing as if he wanted to protect her from the stares and whispers around her, Milagros stopped as soon as she stepped on the floorboards. Pedro urged her to follow the constable. She refused and shook his arm off her shoulder. Then, alone, she walked almost to the edge of the stage, where it rose above the pit. A shiver ran through her, which seemed to spread as some of the actors fell silent and watched the gypsy girl standing in front of the empty theatre, barefoot, her simple clothes dirty and wrinkled from her long journey, her matted hair stuck to her back. They knew full well how she was feeling: passion, yearning, anxiety, panic . . . And Milagros, her throat stiff, ran the gamut of those emotions as she looked around: at the front rows beneath her feet, the stalls behind, the upper balconies for the women and vendors; at the upper level, the hiding place for priests and intellectuals, at the dozens of unlit lamps, at the magnificent columns, at the boxes on the sides and the rounded boxes facing her that rose above her on three levels, of richly carved gilded wood . . . It was all so intimidating!

'Two thousand people!'

Milagros turned towards a gaunt bald man with a beard, who was the one who had spoken.

'Don José Parra, the director of the company,' the constable introduced him.

Don José greeted her with a slight nod of his head.

'Two thousand,' he then repeated to Milagros. 'That is the number of people who will be watching you when you get up on stage. Do you dare? Are you willing to be the object of that much attention?'

Milagros pursed her lips and thought for a few seconds before answering but Pedro spoke first: 'If she said she didn't dare, would you let us go back to Triana?'

The director smiled patiently before extending his arms; in one hand he held Milagros's papers rolled up in a tube.

'And go against the Council? If you are here you already know that isn't possible. Many comic players from out of town don't want to come to Madrid because they lose money. Isn't that right?' He directed his question at Milagros, who nodded. 'The Chief Magistrate told me about your arrival and he seemed enthusiastic. What is it that so impressed his lordship, Milagros?'

'I sang and danced for him.'

'Do it for us.'

'Now?' she objected without thinking.

'Aren't we a good enough audience to you?'

With the hand that held her papers Don José pointed to the people on the stage. There were about thirty: members of the company, both male and female, their understudies, the wardrobe master, the 'villain', the extras and the 'fools', the actor who played the old man roles, the prompter, the ticket collectors and the music conductor. Then there were the orchestra musicians, who weren't considered part of the company, the stagehand and the theatre staff who had rushed to see what was happening onstage when they were told the new player had arrived.

'My wife is tired,' interjected Pedro García.

Milagros ignored the excuse: her eyes remained fixed on Don José, who also disregarded her husband and held her gaze, smiling, provocative.

She accepted the challenge. She extended her right arm and with her hand open, fingers rigid, without accompaniment, she burst into a fandango in the style of those sung in the fields in the kingdom of Granada when it was time to harvest the green olives. The sound of her voice in the empty theatre surprised her and it took her a few more seconds to set her hands and hips to the joyful rhythm of those stanzas. The director's smile widened; many others got gooseflesh. One of the musicians made a gesture to run for his guitar, but Don José stopped him with a wave of Milagros's rolled-up documents and, brandishing them in the air, he indicated to the gypsy girl that she should turn and sing to the empty seats in the stalls.

30

MILAGROS ROSE UP on the tips of her bare toes, with her arms bent over her head, to end the fandango. However, the applause she was expecting didn't arrive. She was panting, sweating, she had given her all, more than ever before, but the cheers and ovations she thought she deserved were mere claps mixed with impertinent murmurs of disapproval that were increasing dangerously in pitch. She saw the hundreds of men who stood clustered in the pit, beneath the stage, not understanding where their apathy came from. She looked up towards the large closed-off balcony at the back where the women sat, chatting distractedly. She raised her eyes further, up to the boxes, filled with people: nobody seemed to be paying her any attention.

'Go back to Triana!'

Milagros's gaze searched for the groundling who had shouted from the orchestra pit.

'You're not worth what it cost to get you here!'

'Learn to dance!'

She turned her head to the other side, unable to believe what she was hearing.

'This is the great singer advertised on the sign in the Puerta del Sol?'

She felt her legs grow weak.

'With singers like you, the *chorizos* at the Teatro de la Cruz will be happy!' a woman shouted her head off, pointing at her over the railing of the balcony.

Milagros thought she was going to collapse and she looked for Pedro; he had told her that he would watch the show, but she couldn't find him. Her vision blurred. The shouting intensified and tears ran down her face. A hand grabbed her by the elbow just when she was about to let herself drop to the floor.

'Gentlemen!' shouted Celeste, shaking Milagros to revive her. 'We've already told you . . . ! Gentlemen . . . !'

The commotion didn't stop. Celeste's eyes questioned the royal magistrate who, along with two constables and a notary, remained seated on the stage itself, in one corner, to keep order in the theatre. The magistrate sighed because he knew what the leading lady was trying to do. He nodded. He hadn't even finished moving his head before Don José started giving instructions to the musicians to play the same piece that had just sunk Milagros.

Celeste allowed the strains of the violins to sound a couple of times before she began singing. The audience settled; the men in the orchestra calmed down.

'Now that's what I call a great singer!' echoed before she even started.

'Gorgeous!'

Celeste sang the first verse. Then, when it was time for her to begin the second one, she confronted the groundlings, as the music repeated, waiting for their decision. 'Is this the mercy we asked for during the presentation of a new player?'

Milagros, with Celeste still holding her elbow, remembered the entry to the *tonadilla*, a musical intermission that never went over half an hour and was performed between the first and second acts of the main show, although she had been told that the audience went to the theatre more for the *tonadillas*, the short farces and the *sainetes* that followed between the second and third acts, than for the main show. They told her that many even left after the *sainete* and gave the third act of the comedy a miss. During the presentation, Celeste herself, after introducing Milagros and extolling some of her virtues, which drew applause and whistles, had addressed the public begging for leniency with the new girl. 'She's only eighteen years old!' she shouted, eliciting exclamations. Several of the players had sung and danced together, leaving the closing act to Milagros alone, who had launched into it with the confidence of her years of experience singing in Seville. Yet her body did not accompany her magnificent vocal interpretation at any point. She had been warned.

'Stop!' Celeste had shouted as soon as she saw her dancing in the rehearsals. 'You'll be the ruin of us and you'll end up in jail if you do that in front of people.'

When she asked why, confused, they explained that the authorities did not allow dances as lascivious as hers.

'Such sensuality,' Don José had tried to teach her, despite the hesitation that showed in his face at the gypsy girl's ease with her body, 'it has to be shown in a more . . . more . . .' He searched for the right word as he shook a hand in the air. '. . . more artful . . . more concealed, covert . . . private. That's it, private! Your dances have to be sensual, because you are, because it comes naturally to you, never because you want to excite the audience. As if you were trying to hide your God-given charms and nurture restraint to avoid vulgarity. Do you understand? Restrained passion. Do you know what I mean?'

Milagros had answered yes, although she had no idea how to do that. She also said yes when they explained to her that those groundlings, and the women on the upper balcony, the noblemen and the rich in the boxes, and the priests and intellectuals in the gallery were not only expecting a good performance: they also wanted what she now witnessed from the leading lady. But she hadn't really under-stood anything; her dance movements had been rigid and coarse, she herself had seen that, and as for what those Madrileños were expecting of her . . .

'You're complaining about the girl's awkwardness, you of all people?' she now saw how Celeste brazenly replied to a blacksmith, known for his intolerance with players, who had complained about the gypsy girl's performance again. 'They say the first grille you forged couldn't even protect your daughter's virginity.'

The crowd burst into hearty laughter.

'Are you questioning—?' the man tried to respond.

'Ask the baker's assistant!' interrupted someone from the pit.

'He'll be able to tell you what happened to the grille and your girl's virtue.'

New laughter accompanied Celeste's graceful movement across the stage. At a sign from Don José, the music increased in volume when the blacksmith tried to make his way, pushing and elbowing through the motley groundlings in search of the one who had insulted his daughter. One of the constables was carefully watching to make sure it didn't go too far. Milagros remained alone in the middle of the stage, her gaze darting between the blacksmith and Celeste, who was now to one side. She didn't dare turn her back to the audience, nor to walk off the stage. She remained stock-still like a statue in a packed theatre on the first day of the season.

Celeste, in the corner, took up the song again. People began to sing along; she fell silent again and pointed to an obese, bowlegged, slovenly man with sweaty, bright-red cheeks. 'How can we actors ask generosity of those who use all theirs up on themselves?'

Before the crowd broke out into laughter, she began singing again and ran towards where Milagros was standing.

'Let your hair down,' she encouraged her between verses. 'You can do it.'

For a moment Milagros remembered Old María and Sagrario, who had given her her start in Bienvenido's inn in Seville. She had risen to the challenge then and she had become a success. She was a gypsy! She took a deep breath and sang with Celeste, until the leading lady gave her a little push towards the audience, encouraging her.

Thousands of eyes were on her.

'What are you looking at?' Milagros challenged the pit. She was tempted to swagger her body voluptuously, but instead she crossed her arms over her breasts with sham modesty. 'Don't your wives satisfy you?' The royal magistrate gave a start. 'Or maybe it's you who don't satisfy them?'

The insinuation earned her the applause and whoops of the women on the upper balcony. Milagros feigned shock at the string of obscenities that came from their mouths.

'So,' she shouted to be heard over the groundlings, 'what's happened to your manhood now?'

Many responded to the provocation by turning towards the balcony to argue with the women. The royal magistrate stood up and ordered Don José to end the act. One of the constables positioned himself on the edge of the stage and the other, with his back to the magistrate, whispered to the notary:

'Don't write down those last words.' The notary looked up in surprise. 'I know her. She's young. She's not a bad girl, she's just new. Let's give her a chance. You know that the Chief Magistrate . . .'

The functionary understood and stopped writing.

Rich men, aristocrats and clergy enjoyed the fight and the exchange of insults between the groundlings and the women. Gradually, for want of music, they calmed down and the audience focused their attention on the two women who remained still on the stage.

'My husband wouldn't know what to do with you, gypsy!' echoed through the theatre.

'Mine would shrink back in fear!'

There was more laughter and applause, which intensified when most of the groundlings, enjoying the scandalous festive atmosphere, joined in.

'You're beautiful!' someone from the stalls flattered Milagros.

On Easter Sunday, 1752, the first day of the theatre season, at three in the afternoon, Pedro García was watching his wife's inaugural performance among the groundlings, silent, without taking sides, holding back his rage at the booing. Then he went to look for her. A couple of soldiers on guard denied him access through the entrance on Lobo Street.

'Nobody comes in here, not even husbands,' one of them spat at him.

'And you can't just stand there waiting either; people are forbidden to congregate at theatre exits,' the other added.

Pedro waited around the corner, along with a group of the curious. He saw Celeste's sedan chair come out and he smiled as the leading lady's many admirers whirled around her and blocked her way. She would be his in an hour's time. They had already agreed to meet, like so many other assignations they'd had since his arrival in Madrid. The crowd continued to pursue the other players and at the end, when the streets began to clear out, Milagros made her appearance.

The gypsy girl seemed surprised by the fact that there was still daylight. She hesitated. She ran a weary gaze along Lobo Street until she recognized her husband, whom she walked towards, resignation in her gait and her face blank.

'Cheer up!' was Pedro's greeting. 'It's the first time.'

Her only response was a scowl.

'You'll do better tomorrow.'

'The magistrate warned me about my insolence.'

'Ignore him,' he encouraged.

'So did Don José.'

'To hell with that old man!'

'Hug me,' she implored, timidly opening her arms.

Pedro nodded slightly, came closer and embraced her tightly.

'Milagros!' shouted someone passing by. 'I *would* know what to do with you!'

A chorus of laughter accompanied the lewd remark while Milagros steadied Pedro's arm to keep him from pouncing on the man.

'Leave them be,' she begged him, stroking his cheek to get him to focus on her and not the offending group of men. 'Let's not look for problems. Let's go home, please.'

She pushed him gently along the entire block to Huertas Street; from there to their house was just a few steps, which Milagros used to seek out her husband's touch. She needed his affection. Her nerves, the theatre packed with hostile faces, the rushing, the shouting, the magistrate, the big city . . . She only had a few hours before she had to meet Marina and other players to study the new show, a couple of hours she wanted to spend with her family and even . . . why not? She had time. Enough to forget everything and feel her man strong inside her, his force, his thrust.

That yearning that ran up and down her back was interrupted by Bartola and their little girl, whom they ran into as soon as they turned the corner on to Amor de Dios Street. The old gypsy was looking after María as she played. Pedro grabbed the little girl and lifted her above his head, where he swung her around for a while as her mother looked on tenderly. Her man seemed content; perhaps coming to Madrid had been the right thing to do. Later, both laughing, Pedro handed the girl to her mother.

'I have to go,' he announced.

'But . . . I . . . thought . . . Come up with us, please.'

'Listen,' he cut her off. 'I have business to attend to.'

'What busi . . . ?'

Her husband's features tensed for a split second and Milagros was silent.

'Take care of the girl,' he said in farewell.

What business? wondered Milagros with her eyes fixed on his back as he headed into the distance. How could Pedro be doing business if they had no money?

Pedro García sighed in pleasure as fingertips slid down his back. Naked, satisfied after copulating, he remained lying face down in Celeste's bed.

'I wouldn't have done it for any other player,' whispered the leading lady just then, smoothing her blond hair. 'Although I didn't really do it for her, but for you. I don't want them to fire her.'

'So,' the gypsy interrupted her, 'you helped Milagros so you could continue to enjoy me. Therefore, actually, you did it for yourself.'

Sitting beside him, she gave him a loud slap on the buttocks.

'Big-head!' she scolded him before going back to running her fingers along his spine. 'I have all the men I could possibly want.'

'And have any of them given you the same pleasure I do?'

Celeste didn't answer.

'In the end your little gypsy girl did a good job of defending herself . . .' she commented instead.

'She's smart. She'll learn. She knows how to provoke, arouse desire.'

'I've seen that, but she'll have to be careful about it, or the magistrate or one of the censors will denounce her.'

'Isn't it all about having fun?' asked Pedro before letting out a long moan when she began to stroke the nape of his neck.

Celeste, also naked, sat astride the gypsy's back to continue massaging his shoulders and neck.

'That is the fun the theatre aspires to, just like at a party and even in church when noble ladies or maids flirt with their lovers while they pretend to be listening to mass; that's the story of humanity. Priests don't really approve of the comedies . . . even though many of them come to see them. The King and his councillors allow them to keep the people entertained, since if they are entertained and happy and at peace, they will have a lot to lose by rebelling against authority. You understand?' she asked as her hands squeezed his shoulders. The gypsy murmured in agreement. 'It's just one more way of keeping his subjects under control. But we can't go too far: we have to find the balance between what the authorities ask and what the clergy and censors are willing to allow. All the performances, even the one-acts, have to obtain permission from the city's ecclesiastical judge. Then they go to the High Court where they are censored again. And even then, the theatre magistrate controls the performance on the stage. It is only the authorities' interest in keeping the people entertained and all the money that the theatres make for the hospitals that allows us certain licence that we would otherwise never be able to take in this Spain of inquisitors, priests, friars, nuns and lay brothers and sisters. That balance is the most important thing for a player to know: if you don't reach it, you get booed and insulted; if you go too far, they clip your wings. Do you understand, my sweet little bird?'

Celeste leaned over the gypsy's back until she could nibble on the back of his neck. Then she lay down on top of him.

'I know your constable is keeping a lookout on the street, but I think my husband will be home soon. Make me fly up to the heavens one more time,' she whispered into his ear, 'and I will teach your little gypsy girl.'

The last thing I want is for her to learn, Pedro would have liked to reply as he felt her struggling to get her arms beneath his body. *Maybe then they would let us go back to Triana.*

'What are you mumbling about?' asked Celeste.

Pedro realized that he'd been thinking aloud. He turned over with difficulty, flipped Celeste over and settled on his side on one elbow.

'I said,' he answered, shifting his eyes from her large breasts, 'that the only heaven is between your legs.'

She smiled, purred like a cat, grabbed him by the neck and pulled him towards her.

Less than half an hour had passed and Pedro García was leaving Celeste's house along Huertas Street. Blas, the constable, who had already been waiting at the door when he arrived after leaving Milagros, approached him.

'You took too long,' he reproached him. 'I have to continue my rounds.'

'Your leading lady is an insatiable slut.'

The gypsy rushed to dig in his purse to contain the rage he saw in the officer's face, as always happened when he was rude about Celeste. He enjoyed provoking him. *How is it possible that this fool,* he thought the first time it happened, *is waiting on the street as a lookout while I fornicate with the object of his desire and then gets mad if I speak disrespectfully about her?* He pulled a couple of small coins out of his purse and handed them to Blas. Celeste gave him money: she was the only player in the company who had any to spare, because the others lived in misery, as he and Milagros did. *The constable has to be paid for his work . . . and his silence,* Pedro had demanded, but he kept most of it. Even though Blas hadn't yet got any women out of the deal, he settled for the few coins; he would have done it anyway just to be nearer to Celeste. *She must be why he gets angry,* concluded Pedro after the first few days. Blas adored her, accepted her fickleness as if she were a goddess, but he didn't allow anyone else to scorn her for her whims.

'If you talk that way about Celeste again—' the constable started to threaten him before the other interrupted.

'What? I'd say the same thing to her. Insatiable slut,' Pedro said slowly. 'My little whore. I whisper a thousand things like that into her ear when she's beneath me . . .'

He didn't have a chance to finish the sentence. Blas turned red and marched up the street without saying goodbye. The tapping of his truncheon hitting the walls faded into the distance, giving way to Madrid's church bells' call to prayer. Pedro grumbled. After the pealing of the bells people would emerge from their homes praying the rosary: all the pious citizens praying simultaneously before going to bed, as proper behaviour dictated. He was hungry. Celeste shared her bed with him but she said that she only shared her stewpot with her husband, since if she was cheating on him the least she could do was feed him well. 'Good consolation,' laughed Pedro as he went along Huertas Street in search of a tavern where he could have a few glasses of wine and some dinner, maybe even with her husband. He knew him: he worked in the company as the third male lead and he had run into him on other occasions in the month or so since they had come to Madrid; the man didn't seem too interested in the stewpot with which his wife attempted to restore his sullied honour.

Before reaching the side street called León, Pedro shifted his gaze to the left, where it led to Amor de Dios Street, where he lived with Milagros, their daughter and old Bartola in two miserable, damp and dark rooms on the third floor of an old house of malice whose rent ate up most of the wage his wife earned. Huertas, León, Amor de Dios, San Juan, El Niño, Francos and Cantarranas: all were narrow streets packed with very old buildings where, since the previous century, actors, poets and writers had lived.

'Cervantes lived in one room, in worse conditions!' replied the doorman of the theatre, who had accompanied them to their new home from the Príncipe, when Pedro complained. 'Lope de Vega, Quevedo, Góngora, they all graced these streets and buildings by living here. Are you going to compare yourselves – a band of gypsies – with the greatest of Spanish literature – what am I saying, of world literature?'

And the doorman left them there, marching off as they shouted and gestured wildly. From that day, Milagros had begun the comic players' routine: rehearsals in the morning and the afternoons devoted to learning the roles of the main production, plus the one-acts, dances and *tonadilla* songs. Once the season began, as Don José had already told them, they would continue to rehearse in the mornings, directed by Celeste as leading lady and by Nicolás Espejo, the one who had fought with Celeste that first day they arrived, as the leading man. The evenings were devoted to the performances, which had to last at least three hours, and the nights, to studying.

Milagros barely appeared in the main comedy, or the one-act farce that took place during one of the intermissions. She had been called there to sing and dance, but to take some of the work off other actors they would give her some minor role, even if it wasn't a speaking part: serving some jugs of wine, appearing as a washer-woman or as a street vendor . . . In any case, and as Celeste had predicted before storming out of the Coliseo del Príncipe that day, the show that had opened the season didn't last more than two days, so the very night it premiered, Milagros had to learn the role and the *tonadillas* of the show that would replace it.

'Once the theatre season starts,' Celeste had explained to Pedro, 'the actors have to work incredibly hard. The shows last as long as the audience is willing to keep the seats warm. Some only last one day, others two or three, most five or six, and if they last ten they're considered a big hit. Meanwhile, we have to learn new shows – or relearn them – at lightning speed, as well as the intermission pieces.'

'And how do you learn them?' asked the gypsy.

'That's even more complicated. As if having to learn them isn't enough, often we have only one copy of the author's manuscript to work with, which we all have to share and which will have been corrected by various censors. The same thing happens with the one-acts and *tonadillas*. We get together . . . there are some that don't even know how to read.'

Pedro García entered a tavern that was still open on San Juan Street. Milagros was one of those who didn't know how to read, so she had to work many more hours than Celeste, who didn't seem to worry too much about learning her roles. *What are the prompters for?* she would say. Until the start of the season, his wife's huge workload had given him a freedom that now . . .

'Gypsy!'

Pedro shook off the thoughts that had been filling his mind as he entered the tavern. He looked around him. Guzmán, Celeste's husband, and another couple of company members were sitting at a table, looking at him.

'Buy us a round!'

Pedro's smile was accompanied by an assenting hand motion towards the tavern keeper. He looked for a seat with the others and, when the man served them the wine, he lifted his jug, looked Guzmán in the eyes and made an ironic toast: 'To your wife, the greatest of them all!'

And who is paying for this wine, the gypsy added to himself as the glasses clinked. However, as he sipped that watered-down wine, he was forced to recognize that things had changed. Although not exactly for the better: in Triana he was the one who satisfied women's whims with the money Milagros made. In Madrid, however, he had to give pleasure to a woman twice his age just to get a few miserable reals. All . . . all to ingratiate himself with the *payos*!

'Barman!' he shouted as he crashed the jug violently against the table, splashing the others. 'Either serve us some quality wine or I'll slice you open right here!'

'La Descalza – The Barefoot Girl'. That was the nickname the groundlings at the Coliseo del Príncipe ended up giving Milagros. The gypsy refused to wear the dresses that Celeste and the other women in the company wore.

'How do you expect me to dance in that?' she claimed, pointing to the corsets and crinolines. 'You have trouble breathing,' she said to one actress, 'and you can barely move with that hoop skirt,' to another.

She did, however, agree to switch her simple garb for the attire of the *manolas* of Madrid: a yellow bodice that was close-fitting at the waist – with no boning – tight sleeves, a white skirt with green flounces that almost reached her ankles, an apron, green handkerchief knotted at the neck and a net pulling her hair back. No one could convince her to wear shoes. 'I was born barefoot and I'll die barefoot,' she declared over and over again.

'What difference does it make?' Don José said to the magistrate, trying to put an end to the discussion. 'Isn't there already a strip at the edge of the stage so the public can't see the actresses' ankles? So why would it matter if she's wearing shoes or not?'

Milagros soon lost her awe of that imposing theatre, which had managed to paralyse her muscles the day of the premiere, and she lost it because, except for the censors and the magistrates, no one else seemed to have any. The audience shouted and stamped. She found out about the rivalry between two Madrid theatres: the Príncipe and the Cruz, which weren't far from one another. There was a third theatre, the Caños del Peral, where they performed popular lyrical compositions. The people that liked the Príncipe Theatre were called *polacos* and those that preferred the Cruz were the *chorizos*. They didn't only fight each other, but they would also regularly attend the rival theatre to wreck the show and mercilessly boo the comic actors and singers.

And she not only understood that, no matter how well she sang, no matter how much passion she put into her songs and her dances, there would always be some *chorizo* fan who would dress her down, but she also discovered that there were players in the company who didn't put much effort into their work. A simple white curtain at the back of the stage and another on each side was all the set there was for the daily comedies, although other performances such as the elaborate comedies or the liturgical dramas, whose ticket prices were higher, enjoyed a somewhat more sophisticated set design. Between the curtains, there was merely a table with some chairs around it and a well or a tree as decoration to set the scene.

When she wasn't on stage in the main show, Milagros watched it from one of the benches of the front rows. Just like any other audience member, she was disappointed with the reciting by the members of her company: their gestures and movements bombastic and affected; their voices monotonous and even unpleasant. Behind the scenery she saw the prompter's shadow and the glow of the lamp that helped him read, as he moved incessantly from one side to the other to whisper the text the actors had forgotten or simply didn't know. It wasn't unusual to hear the prompter's words over the voice of the actor repeating them. The spectators tolerated the tedium of a low-quality repertoire, or one of the infinite revivals of the illustrious

Calderón, with actors who didn't even make an effort to identify with their characters: Greek philosophers wearing waistcoats, knee-britches and green stockings; mythological goddesses with panniers and feathered hats . . .

They were bored until they reached the intermissions, which featured *sainetes* and *tonadillas*. That was when both the audience and the actors enjoyed themselves. The *sainetes* were short, funny, popular parodies of social and family relationships. In them, the comic actors played themselves, their friends, relatives or acquaintances; most of the spectators saw themselves reflected and carried the players through the entire one-act with their shouts, laughter, applause and whistling.

As for the *tonadillas* . . . half of Madrid was now flaunting, as a sign of admiration for Milagros, green ribbons tied or sewn on to their clothes, the same colour as the handkerchief she always wore around her neck! Don José's advice had been hammering in her ears for days: 'Restrained passion, restrained passion.' And Milagros had been running it over and over in her head until one evening, standing on the stage, before starting to sing, when her gaze met that of a dirty, poorly dressed man, the kind that spent the six quarter-reals that he couldn't afford on a stalls ticket, probably before returning to his town near the capital – maybe Fuencarral, Carabanchel, Vallecas, Getafe, Hortaleza or some other . . . where he would brag about having gone to the theatre to become the object of envy and attention from his neighbours. The farmer, because he had to be a farmer, perhaps of muscatel wine grapes in Fuencarral, was watching her, captivated. Milagros took a few steps forward while holding the man's gaze, as he followed her gypsy stride with eyes like platters and mouth agape. Then she stood in front of him and gave him a faint smile. The man, entranced, was unable to react. The music of the two violins that came from behind one of the side curtains, where the meagre orchestra hid, composed of those violins, a cello and two oboes, repeated itself waiting for Milagros to begin. But she delayed it a few more seconds, enough to run her gaze along the groundlings in the pit and find some other faces similar to the vintner from Fuencarral's. Someone encouraged her to sing, others shouted compliments of 'beautiful!' and 'lovely!' Many asked her to begin. Finally she did, aware of their admiration and desire without needing to overstate her sensuality. Her dark skin, so different from the paleness that ladies insisted on even when it cost them their health; dressed as a *manola*, with clothes that symbolized the stubborn, silent fight against customs imported from France; proud like the Madrileños, just as haughty as those people who soon began to exalt her as a representative of the people.

'Restrained passion.' She finally understood it. She sang and danced feeling beautiful, not revealing herself, rising above the entire theatre like a goddess who had nothing to prove. She understood that a sigh, a wink or a droop of her eyelids towards the first few rows of the pit, a flutter of her hand in the air, a simple twist of her waist or the glow of the drops of sweat running from her neck to her breasts could ignite desire even more than cheek and effrontery.

'Neither the men nor the women want that,' explained Marina, a slight blonde who was the third lady, when Milagros confided in her one night about her worries. 'They need inaccessible idols; they need an excuse for not being able to win you over. If you go down to the pit and mingle with them, you will be of no use to them; you'll be just like any of the women they know in real life. If you are coarse, they'll compare you with the prostitutes who offer themselves on the streets and you will lose their interest.'

'And the women in the upper balcony?' enquired Milagros.

'Them? It's simple: they envy all that attracts their men more than they do.'

'Envy?' Milagros was surprised.

'Yes, envy. An itch that will make them do everything in their power to be more like you.'

Milagros not only learned to control her sensuality; she also knew how to give the public the repartee they expected from a good comic player. She left the orchestra's musicians disconcerted, although they gradually, blinded behind the side curtain but warned by the indications of Don José himself, got used to the gypsy girl's pace and the confusion she caused. Milagros would take her cue from the lyrics of the *tonadas* she sang and danced to.

'Where is that sergeant?' she asked on one occasion, interrupting a stanza that lamented a soldier's fruitless wooing of a countess. 'Is there a sergeant of the glorious armies of the King here in the house?'

Don José indicated to the orchestra that they stop playing and a couple of hands came up from the groundlings.

'Don't worry,' she then said to one of the military men, 'why aspire to a lady of noble birth when all those beautiful women up in the balcony are yearning for you to show them how you use your . . . sword?'

The magistrate shook his head as Don José, with an authoritative gesture, ordered the musicians to launch into the next bar to get Milagros to start singing amid all the lewd offers that were coming from the balcony.

She sang for the common folk. She talked to them. She laughed, she shouted, she cried and she acted out tearing her hair over the hard luck of the less fortunate. To the rhythm of her countless popular songs, she boldly pointed to the noblemen and the rich in their boxes while hundreds of pairs of eyes followed her accusatory finger towards her chosen victim, and she interrogated them about their habits and their excessive luxuries. Amid laughter, she joked about the wooing of ladies and about the friars and idle clerics who sought sustenance in the company of women of means. The whistles and boos from the pit and the balcony accompanied her scorn towards the mannered fops who, imperturbable, as if nothing could affect them, responded to her mocking with disdainful gestures.

In those moments, as the audience applauded, Milagros closed her eyes; when she did the entire theatre vanished and in her mind all she saw were those she wished to see among the audience. 'Cachita, María . . . look at me now,' she would whisper amid the cheers and praise. She was gripped by a strange anguish, though, when she thought of her mother and her grandfather.

Success brought more money. The Theatre Board decided to double her wage and include her among the company members who received a salary. Don José was surprised by the gypsy's reaction when he told her of their decision.

'Aren't you pleased?'

Milagros thanked him in a stutter that failed to convince the director.

Her success took Pedro further away from her. It wasn't much money, but enough for her husband to take to the streets of Madrid. 'Where's Pedro?' she would ask at lunch- or dinnertime, when she came back from the theatre to the rooms they had rented. 'We should wait for him.' Sometimes Bartola's expression soured and she looked at her as if she were a stranger. 'He's off doing his thing,' she would often answer.

'He's a man,' was Bartola's excuse for him. 'You're the one who is never at home. What do you want, your husband to sit around knitting like an old woman? Well, stop singing and take care of him and your daughter!'

Then Milagros could see the García blood in that woman who defended Pedro's excesses even when they suffered real hardship because he squandered the money she earned. Bartola was like Reyes, La Trianera and El Conde, like the entire family, who never hid their animosity towards her.

'We were better off in Triana,' she heard the old woman grumble. 'So many men fluttering around you with their green ribbons as a sign of . . . of . . .' Bartola gestured, unable to find the right word. 'How do you think your husband must feel?'

Milagros tried to find out, struggling against sleep and waiting up for Pedro, who almost always returned home as the sun was coming up. Most nights she couldn't manage to stay up, but the few times she did succeed in overcoming her weariness, and the drowsiness brought on by a silence broken only by the rhythmic breathing of her daughter and Bartola's snores, she received a man who staggering in reeking of alcohol, tobacco and sometimes other odours that could only fool someone who, like her, was willing to ignore them.

How did Pedro feel about the men who wore green ribbons on their clothes? She soon found out.

'None of your admirers give you gifts?' he asked her one night, as they both lay on the straw mattress, naked, after he had taken her to the heights of ecstasy once more. The pleasure, the satisfaction, that twinge of hope of recovering him for herself that she felt when he took her vanished even before he had finished his question. Money. That was the only thing he wanted! All of Madrid was taken with her, she knew it, men declared their love for her at the theatre and in the streets when they crowded around her sedan chair. They sent love letters to her dressing room, which, since she couldn't do it herself, Marina read to her: propositions and all sorts of promises from noble and rich men. She had soon decided to tear them up right away and return the presents. Of course they gave her gifts, but she knew if she accepted them, Pedro would turn them into more nights of loneliness. Comic actresses had the well-earned reputation of being frivolous and promiscuous; most of them were. Some changed Milagros's nickname from 'The Barefoot Girl' to 'The Aloof Girl'. All of Madrid desired her and the only man that she gave herself to willingly just wanted her money.

'They try to,' answered Milagros.

'And?' he asked in the face of her silence.

'You can be sure I would never put your honour and your manhood in question by accepting gifts from other men,' she replied after a few seconds of hesitation.

'And what about the parties and private performances that the company gives? They are well paid; why don't you do them?'

He could have imagined the parties, but how had Pedro found out about the private performances that the companies gave in the parlours and small theatres of large mansions?

'Here . . .' she responded, 'here your family isn't around to defend me. In Seville my honour is safe; your cousins and your grandmother make sure of that. Madrid isn't like the inns and palaces in Andalusia. I know because they tell me about them. Who can oppose the desires of a grandee? Do you want your wife's name to be on everyone's lips, like Marina or Celeste?'

Bartola's snores tore through the room for a good long while as she held her breath waiting for his reply. None came. Shortly after, Pedro murmured something unintelligible, turned his back and went to sleep.

Something changed that night for Milagros. Her body, usually exhausted after reaching climax, now remained tense, her muscles clenched, all of her restless. She couldn't fall asleep. The tears soon began to flow. She had cried, many times, but never like on that night when she understood that her husband didn't love her. She, who had thought that she would save her marriage in Madrid, realized that the big city was even worse than Triana. There, Pedro chatted with other gypsies on the alley and moved in known orbits, while here . . . Milagros knew that there were gypsies from his family. Pedro had found his García relatives; he had told her about it with his features twisted in rage. One of them had been beaten up by members of a brotherhood for insulting the Virgin on Almirante Street and had died. The rest of the family, men and women, were locked up in the Inquisition dungeons for crimes against the faith.

'It was all because of . . .' He hesitated for a moment. Milagros misinterpreted his silence; she thought that he didn't want to accuse her grandfather when what Pedro didn't want was for her to know that there were other Vegas in the capital. 'It was all El Galeote's fault. I swear to you that one day we will find him and I will kill him where he stands.'

She said nothing. It had been two years since Melchor had escaped from the Garcías. *Don't let them catch you*, she yearned in silence. Pedro's shouting gave her the impression that Melchor was no longer in Madrid; there were many gypsies who had scoured the entire city looking for him. Yes, Melchor's life was in danger. She consoled herself thinking that her grandfather liked it that way. Yet what about her? Everything had turned out badly: she had no one to turn to. Her father was dead, her mother was in prison and had disowned her, and her grandfather was on the run. Cachita and Old María had disappeared. Even the little girl who carried the healer's name seemed to be fonder of Bartola than of her! How could it be otherwise when she was never with her? And as for Pedro . . . He didn't love her; he only thought about the money he could get from her to enjoy with other women: she admitted it to herself for the first time.

The following day, at the Príncipe, Milagros lifted one arm to the heavens. With the other she lifted her skirt a few inches above her ankles and began to spin gracefully, wiggling her hips as she emptied her lungs in a finale that mingled with the audience's loud acclaim. That was all she had left: singing and dancing; taking refuge in her art as she had in Triana, when she had conceded a truce in the dispute with her mother and danced with her. Those who saw her applauded harder and harder, believing that the tears that ran down her cheeks were tears of joy.

31

CARIDAD HAD BEEN a prisoner at La Galera for almost two years when the riot happened. The insubordination of a couple of hardened prostitutes had driven the warden to impose a punishment that was as humiliating as it was novel: shaving their hair and eyebrows off. The decision infuriated all the prisoners; they could stand mistreatment, but shaving their heads . . . never! Many, taking advantage of the unrest, decided to insist on an old demand: that they be told the length of their sentence, since they had to watch the years pass without knowing when it would end. Passions were running high and the women of La Galera rose up in rebellion, breaking everything that was in their reach, arming themselves with planks, scissors and pointed sewing implements, and they took control of the prison.

When they closed the doors of La Galera and the inmates found themselves in charge of the building, a panting and enthused Caridad found herself with a stake in her hands. In her memory the running and shouting she had taken part in was still going on. It had been . . . it had been amazing! A mob of women, who until then had lived without free will or ever thinking for themselves, just like the groups of Negro slaves, had suddenly, instead of submitting to the master's orders, fought all together, like madwomen. Caridad looked around her and saw hesitation in her companions' faces. No one knew what to do next. Someone pointed out that they should prepare a brief addressed to the King; some supported the idea and others didn't; some suggested running away.

As they argued, a military detachment appeared on the street, preparing to attack the jail. Like all the others, Caridad ran to the upper galleries as soon as the first blow echoed against the door to Atocha Street. Many inmates climbed up to the roof. Shortly, the door was ripped off its hinges and close to a hundred soldiers with fixed bayonets scattered across the central courtyard and the inside of La Galera. However, to the surprise of the prisoners and the anger of the authorities and officers, the soldiers acted kindly. In one of the upper galleries, as the officers shouted to incite their men, Caridad found herself cornered by two of them. She naively raised her stake against their bayonets. One of the soldiers just shook his head, as if pardoning her. The other made a very slight motion with the tip of his bayonet, as if he wanted to let her know that she could escape. Caridad brandished her stake and slipped between them, while they just pretended they were trying to grab her. Something similar happened between the other soldiers and the rest of the prisoners, who ran from one side to the other in the face of the troops' passivity, if not outright collaboration.

The situation dragged on. Desperation appeared in the faces of some officers who shouted themselves hoarse demanding obedience, but how could they force those soldiers conscripted in miserable towns in rural Castile to contain the women? Many of them had been condemned to serve eight years in the army for mistakes like the ones those unfortunate women had made, and the prisoners kept reminding them of that during the siege. The authorities decided to have the detachment fall back and the women cheered their withdrawal, feeling vindicated: their triumphant shouts echoed throughout the night. The gate and surrounding areas of the La Galera were well guarded by the same troops that had refused to act against them but did clear out the crowd of curious onlookers that milled around Atocha Street.

At dawn the next day, however, the royal magistrates themselves showed up at La Galera leading an urban militia made up of some fifty God-fearing citizens, all well built and armed with whips, sticks and iron bars. They went in to subdue them ruthlessly and the women ran off in terror. Caridad, still brandishing the stake, saw two of the militiamen beating Herminia with an iron bar. Her blood boiled at the viciousness with which they were taking out their rage on the poor woman. Herminia, curled up on the ground, covering her face, begged for mercy. Caridad screamed something. What was it? She never was able to recall. But she pounced on the two men and hit one with the stake. Amid the barrage of blows that rained down on her, she could see how Herminia, from the ground, grabbed one of the men's legs and sank her teeth into his thigh. Her friend's reaction spurred her on and she continued blindly swinging her stake. Only the intervention of one of the magistrates kept her from being beaten to death.

One by one, the some 150 women prisoners were gathered in the courtyard of the jail, some limping, others with throbbing kidneys, chests or backs, their noses broken and their lips bleeding. Most of them hung their heads, defeated. Silent.

A couple of hours was all it took for the warden to take back control of the women's prison. With the rebellion snuffed out, he promised the prisoners that he would review all those sentences that had no fixed release date; he also warned of the harsh penalties that the instigators of the revolt would face.

Caridad, the Negress with the stake who had taken on two upright citizens, was the first to be pointed out. Fifty lashes was the punishment she would receive, in the prison courtyard, in full view of the others, along with three other women reported as having incited the mutiny by a treacherous woman imprisoned for peddling, who was rewarded with her freedom.

The lashes were merciless, cracking on the women's backs after a whistle that cut through the air. The authorities gave strict instructions for their harsh discipline; how else could they put an end to a revolt in La Galera when that was where mutinous women in other jails were sent as a punishment?

Caridad's last memory was the screams of the other women when the warden finally ended the horrific punishment and they dragged her out of the prison. 'Stay strong, Cachita!' 'We'll be waiting for you!' 'You can do it, *morena*!' 'I'll save you a cigar!'

'Be joyful and give thanks, sinner. Our Lord Jesus Christ and the Holy Virgin of Atocha do not wish you dead.'

She heard those words without realizing they referred to her. Caridad, having been unconscious for several days, had just opened her eyes. Lying face down on a cot, with her chin resting on a pillow, her vision cleared gradually until she was able to make out the presence of a priest by her bed, sitting on a chair with a prayer book in his hands.

'Let us pray,' he heard the chaplain for the dying poor order her before launching into a litany.

The only thing that came from Caridad's lips was a long, dull moan: the mere breath of the priest on her flayed back caused her as much pain as the whiplashes. Without daring to move her head, she turned her eyes: she was in a large vaulted room with lines of beds; the air was foul and hard to breathe; the wails of sick women mixed with the priest's chanting in Latin. She was in the hospital of La Pasión, right next door to La Galera, the one the inmates sewed the white gowns for.

'For the moment . . . your soul has no need of me,' the chaplain told her when he finished his prayers. 'Pray that I need not come to your deathbed again. One of your companions has already passed on to a better life. May God have mercy on her soul.'

As soon as the chaplain planted himself in the middle of the room, his eyes searching out some other woman in her death throes, another priest appeared, this one insisting on hearing her confession. Caridad couldn't even speak.

'Water,' she managed to articulate in response to the priest's insistence.

'Woman,' replied the confessor, 'the health of your soul is more important than that of your body. That is our mission and the objective of this hospital: taking care of souls. You shouldn't waste a moment before reaching peace with God. You can drink later.'

Confessions, communions, daily masses for the souls in those rooms; readings of the holy scriptures; sermons and more sermons to procure the salvation of the sick and their repentance, all in forceful tones, rising above the women's coughing, screams of pain and lamenting . . . and death. Thus spent Caridad that month in hospital. After the chaplain for the dying poor had confirmed she would live and the confessor was satisfied with her hoarse, stammering confession, one of the surgeons struggled to sew up her wounds, awkwardly mending the bloody mass her back had become. Caridad howled with pain until she fainted. Every once in a while, the doctor and his assistants, also under the watchful control of a priest, applied a salve to her back that made it burn as if they were whipping her with a red-hot iron. More often, however, the barber-surgeon would show up, one of the several advanced apprentices that went from bed to bed in both hospitals – El General and La Pasión – performing forced bloodlettings on the sick. He would perforate a vein with a cannula while she, impotent, watched the blood leave her body and drip into a basin. She witnessed how the second of the prisoners punished thus died, two beds away from hers. Weakened, pale and gaunt, she died amid prayer and holy oils after two bloodlettings: one on her left arm and another on her right. 'To even out the blood,' Caridad heard the surgeon say in a boastful tone. The third prisoner decided to flee, taking advantage of the commotion caused by a group of wealthy noblewomen who came to La Pasión each Sunday, dressed in coarse worsted linen for the occasion, to help the ill with their hygiene and bring them sweets and chocolate. Out of the corner of her eye, Caridad saw her get up and stumble away, while she, prostrate in bed, nodded time and again, promising to improve her conduct, before that grande dame, her attire as humble as her perfume was costly, who berated her for her faults as if she were a child, only to then reward her contrition with sweets and sips on the cups of hot chocolate they brought with them. At least the chocolate was delicious.

She never knew what happened to the runaway – Sebastiana she seemed to remember was her name – not even in La Galera when the doctors decided to send her back there. She enquired about her, but nobody could tell her anything. 'Good luck, Sebastiana!' she repeated to herself, as she had that Sunday night when the sister who guarded over them noticed her absence and sounded the alarm. She envied her. As she got better she even considered running away herself, but she didn't know where to go, what to do . . . Tears slid down her face when she was reunited with Frasquita and the other inmates, who received her with tenderness, feeling sorry that she had suffered a punishment that all of them equally deserved. She searched for Herminia with her gaze and found her to one side, hidden among the others. Caridad gave her a smile. Many of the inmates turned their heads towards the small blonde and opened a path through the group. After a few moments of silence, some encouraged her; others, who were behind Herminia, pushed her gently; they all applauded once the two women were standing face to face. The blonde went to embrace her, but Caridad stopped her – she couldn't bear having her back touched; instead they kissed amid tears and heightened emotion, both theirs and that of many of the other women.

What was I thinking? What would I do outside of here? Caridad asked herself in that moment. La Galera was still her home and the prisoners her family. Even the sentry and the ever-dour warden treated her with a certain benevolence, recalling the trail of blood she had left behind when she was taken to hospital. Caridad hadn't instigated the mutiny or participated more than the others, they both knew that. That compassion translated into her exemption from the harder tasks and a certain tolerance when the prisoners paid with their own money for some oil and rosemary branches to prepare a salve they used to soothe Caridad's deformed and still badly damaged back.

It was Herminia who offered to massage her friend after the guards extinguished the few smoky tallow candles that struggled to illuminate the women's gallery.

The scars that crossed her back didn't hurt her, what hurt her were her friend's hands slipping gently over her back: the sweetness with which she did it brought to her mind feelings that she thought she had forgotten. *Gypsy!* she thought, night after night, *What has become of you?*

'You needn't go on,' Caridad told her one night. 'The wounds have scarred over; the oil and the herbs cost money and they won't make them any better.'

'But . . .' objected Herminia.

'Please, I beg of you.'

*

One day Herminia was freed. Someone claiming to be her cousin came to get her as soon as her sentence was up. Caridad knew who that cousin was, the same one who had given her the two strings of garlic she'd been arrested and sentenced for. Some of the brotherhoods that helped the unfortunate showed an interest in placing Caridad somewhere as a maid, but she remained stubbornly silent, head bowed, when they asked her about her domestic abilities, wondering what sense it made to leave there only to fall into the hands of some other white man who would mistreat her. 'She's nothing more than a stupid Negro,' those who had offered to help her ended up concluding.

Herminia had also abandoned her.

'Dance for us, Cachita,' begged Frasquita one night; she was worried about her friend, who had been depressed for a couple of months now.

Caridad refused, but Frasquita insisted, and many others joined in. Seated on her straw mattress, she continued to shake her head. Frasquita shook her by the shoulder; she wriggled out of her grasp. Another woman tousled her hair. 'Sing,' she requested. A third pinched her side. 'Dance!' Caridad tried to get away from the clumsy slaps of the women surrounding her, but two prisoners pounced on her and started to tickle her.

'Do it, please,' insisted Frasquita, watching the three women wriggling around on the straw mattress.

The two women kept it up until they got Caridad to stop fighting and join in the laughter, panting, their tattered clothes dishevelled.

'Please,' Frasquita then repeated.

From that day on, Caridad decided to search for her gods through the frenetic, voluptuous dances that frightened even the most hardened prisoners. Whom else could she commend herself to? Sometimes she thought that her gods were indeed mounting her, and then she fell to the floor, unhinged, kicking and screaming. The sentry warned her once, twice, three times. Finally the warden was forced to put her in the stocks because of the uproar she was creating. Yet she continued to do it.

'And the little black girl did it,' sang Caridad then in a monotone, kneeling, her neck and wrists held in the planks of the stocks installed in the prison courtyard the last time she was punished by the warden, remembering the night when she gave into the pleading of Frasquita and the others. Just like the slaves on the tobacco plantation, she sang out her pain when they punished her in the stocks. 'The little black girl danced for her friends.' Motionless in the courtyard on those endless nights, her laments broke the silence and reached the upper galleries, disturbing the dreams of her fellow inmates.

'Shut up, *morena*,' shouted the sentry from the entrance, 'or I'll end up whipping you!'

'And the sentry came,' she continued in a whisper, 'the bad sentry! And he grabbed the little black girl by the arm . . .'

Dawn came and surprised her; she was defeated, her head hanging between the planks in an uncomfortable slumber. Her back hurt. Her skinned knees hurt, and her neck, and her wrists . . . Every second of that ill-fated life hurt her, bringing happiness so close she could reach out and touch it only to then refuse to make it hers! Drowsy, she thought she could hear the first movements in La Galera: the prisoners walking to mass, breakfast. When the others went up to the gallery to work, Frasquita brought her water and a crust of bread that she pulled into pieces to put it patiently and lovingly into her mouth. 'You shouldn't defy the sentry,' she advised her.

Caridad had again raised her voice in the night; she did it as she remembered Melchor, Milagros, Herminia. Caridad didn't answer; she chewed with no appetite.

'Don't dance again,' Frasquita continued giving her advice. 'Do you want some water?'

Caridad nodded.

Frasquita searched for the best way to bring the ladle to her mouth, although she spilled most of it on the floor.

'Don't do it, no matter who asks you to. Do you understand? I'm sorry I did . . .'

'What is it you're sorry for, Frasquita?'

The woman turned. Caridad tried to lift her head. The sentry and the warden were behind Frasquita.

'Nothing,' she answered.

'That is the problem you all have: you never repent for anything that you've done,' replied the warden rudely. 'Move aside,' he added as he gave the sentry a signal.

The man approached one side of the stocks and fiddled with the old lock that held the planks firmly in place. Frasquita watched, surprised; Caridad still had two days of punishment left. A sudden sweat made her body cold while the sentry lifted the upper plank on its hinges and freed her. Had they decided to whip her for singing during the night? Caridad wouldn't put up a fight.

'No—' she started to say.

'Silence!' ordered the warden.

Caridad got up slowly, stiff, leaning on the planks that had held her captive.

'But—' insisted Frasquita.

'Get to work.'

That time it was the sentry who interrupted her, beating her legs with his truncheon, which he'd retrieved just as soon as he'd finished opening the stocks.

'Not the whip, your worship,' implored Frasquita, dropping to her knees before the warden. 'The dancing is my fault. I am the guilty one.'

The warden, stern, kept his gaze on the women for a good long while, then shifted it towards the sentry.

'In that case,' he ordered, 'let her be the one to fulfil the two days of stocks left to the Negress.'

'It's not true,' Caridad managed to say. 'It wasn't her . . .'

The warden swatted the air with one hand and, while Caridad continued stuttering, she watched as the sentry indicated with his truncheon for her friend to get on her knees and place her neck and wrists in the holes of the lower board. The hinges creaked again and the upper board fell on to Frasquita.

'And you,' the warden then announced, addressing Caridad, 'get your things and leave. You are free.'

Frasquita scratched her neck as she instinctively turned her head towards her friend. Caridad gave a start.

'Why?' she asked innocently, in a thin wisp of voice.

The warden and the sentry laughed heartily.

'Because that is what the High Court ordered, Negress,' answered the first in a mocking tone. 'The judges have taken pity on us and are liberating us from your Negro dancing and singing.'

They didn't allow her to say goodbye to Frasquita. The sentry used his truncheon again to stop her.

'Good luck, Cachita,' she nevertheless heard being shouted from the stocks. 'We will meet again.'

'We will meet again,' answered Caridad as she crossed the court-yard on her way to the stairs. She turned her head but the sentry, behind her, blocked her view. Caridad doubted that her friend had heard her. 'We will meet again, Frasquita!' she repeated.

The truncheon hitting her side kept her from looking back. She went up the stairs with her stomach clenched and tears in her eyes because she knew it was unlikely that their wish to meet again would be fulfilled. After more than two years in that prison, what did she know about Frasquita? How could they find each other again?

'Who . . . ?' She cleared her throat. 'Who has vouched for me?' she asked the sentry before going through the door that led to the gallery.

'How would I know?' he answered. 'Some guy almost as dark as you. I don't care who he is. He brought the official letter from the High Court; that's the only thing I need to know.'

Almost as dark as she was? A single name came to her mind: Melchor. The gypsy was the only person she knew, thought Caridad as she obeyed the truncheon and entered the room. Stares from the prisoners, who stopped their sewing, surprised to see her out of the stocks, distracted her thoughts. She didn't know how to respond; she pursed her lips, as if she felt guilty, and ran her eyes over the gallery. Many others who were only now realizing what was happening also put down their work. Some stood up despite the orders of the guards.

'Don't dawdle,' urged the sentry. 'I have a lot to do. Grab your things.'

'You're leaving?'

It was Jacinta who asked the question. Caridad nodded with a sad smile. The girl had chosen not to give in to Don Bernabé's desires and seek a pardon that, her beauty now faded, she would probably not be offered again.

'Free, free?'

Caridad nodded again. She had them all before her, crowded together at a distance they seemed not to dare cross.

'Your things,' insisted the sentry.

Caridad ignored him. She had her eyes fixed on those women who had been her companions for more than two years: some old and toothless, others young, naively trying to protecting their freshness, all dirty and dressed in rags.

'Negress . . .' the man warned her.

'Am I really free?' she asked.

'Didn't I tell you that already?'

Caridad left behind the sentry, his truncheon and his demands, and crossed those few paces that symbolized the abyss that was opening up between freedom and those who – most of them unjustly – would continue to be subject to the truncheon that was raised above her threateningly in that moment. Caridad sensed it in the frightened faces of her friends.

'Cachita is free,' she heard a voice hidden among the women. 'Are they going to punish us all? Like in a revolt?'

Caridad knew that the truncheon had been lowered when the prisoner in front of her opened her arms. With her throat tight and tears springing to her eyes, she went to them. They surrounded her, patting her back, which was now healed. They hugged her and squeezed her. They congratulated her. They kissed her. They wished her luck. Caridad didn't want to enrage the sentry, who was stifling his anger, so she grabbed a threadbare blanket and the even more deteriorated remains of her slave clothes, which she still saved although she'd managed to replace them with others, and she went down the gallery stairs amid the deafening applause and cheers of those who remained behind.

It wasn't Melchor. For a moment she had imagined . . . but she didn't know the man who, papers in hand, visibly uncomfortable, waited beside the sentry's cubicle beyond the prison's entrance doors. He was shorter than her, thin, sinewy, with a bit of black hair visible beneath the cloth cap he hadn't removed. His unkempt beard was also black, on a harsh face with tanned weather-beaten skin. He dressed like a farmer: leather sandals tied at his ankles, brown flannel britches without stockings and a simple shirt that had perhaps once been white. The man looked her up and down openly.

'Here she is,' announced the sentry.

The other man nodded. 'Well, let's go then,' he ordered resolutely.

Caridad hesitated. Why should she trust this stranger? She was about to ask, but the rays of sun that lit up the gloomy prison room as the sentry stood aside to let them pass confused her vision and even her will. She unconsciously followed the farmer and went through the door, leaving behind more than two years of her life. She stopped as soon as she set foot on Atocha Street and closed her eyes, dazzled by the July sun that seemed different from the one that slipped in through the high windows of the galleries or illuminated the prison courtyard: this was cleaner, more alive, more tangible. She spontaneously breathed deeply, once, twice, three times. Then she opened her eyes and discovered little Herminia smiling at her from across the street, as if she were afraid to get close to La Galera. She ran to her without thinking twice. Many on the street complained but Caridad didn't hear them. She embraced her friend; her breathing accelerated and a thousand questions stuck in her throat as their tears blended together on their cheeks.

'You . . . ! Here? Herminia . . . Why . . . ?'

She couldn't continue. She felt faint. The long night in the stocks, the farewell to Frasquita and the other inmates, the hugs, the cheering, the sobs, the freedom . . . Herminia grabbed Caridad just as her knees gave out.

'Come on, Cachita. Let's go,' she said as she held her by the waist and led her to a small cart filled with melons. 'Grab on to this,' she added, bringing her friend's hand to one of the wooden planks on the side of the cart.

'Are we done?' asked the farmer brusquely.

'Yes, yes,' answered Herminia. Then she turned towards Caridad, who was clinging to the wooden plank. 'Now I have to help Marcial push the cart. Don't let go. We will go to the Plaza Mayor to sell the melons and . . .'

'We're very late, Herminia,' urged the man.

'Don't let go,' she repeated, running towards one of the cart's poles to push it with Marcial along the steep slope of Atocha Street.

Gripping the plank, Caridad let herself be dragged along. The hustle and bustle of people and carts coming and going was like a buzzing in her ears. She made out some places she had passed before: hospitals and churches, the fountain with the fish topped by an angel where she had been arrested, the immense prison building. More than two years in Madrid and that was the only place she knew in the city: Atocha Street. From the fountain with the little angel to La Galera, from La Galera to the High Court and back to the women's prison.

She had never been in Madrid's Plaza Mayor, but she had heard a lot about it from the other prisoners. She awoke from her confusion in a place that seemed vast, with boxes and stands for the market set up in the middle, surrounded on all four sides by the tallest buildings she had ever seen: six storeys high and narrow, covered in red brick, with wrought ironwork on the black and gold balconies on their façades. She was seduced by their harmony and uniformity, broken only by two sumptuous buildings that faced each other, although she knew that the interiors of all those houses were not like their majestic façades. She had heard that they were small, narrow, gloomy dwellings, for rent or inhabited by the merchants who ran the businesses in the plaza's arcades: one devoted to clothes, one to hemp cloth and one to silks, threads and sewing kits that covered two entire building fronts. It was there that they entered the plaza.

'Better?' asked Herminia when Marcial left them alone and went through the stalls to sell the melons.

'Yes,' answered Caridad.

People were constantly passing by them. The July sun began to burn and they took refuge in the shadows of the arcades.

'Why . . . ?'

'Because I care about you, Cachita,' she answered before the Negress could finish. 'How could I leave you in there?'

I care about you. Caridad felt a shiver; everyone who had said they cared about her, or loved her, had disappeared from her life.

'It wasn't easy,' said Herminia, interrupting her thoughts, 'to find a serious and solvent citizen who was willing to take responsibility for you before the High Court. Want a smoke?' She smiled and rummaged in her bag until she pulled out a cigar.

She asked for a light from a man passing by. They were silent as he lit the tinder and brought it to the tip of the cigar. Herminia sucked hard and the tobacco caught fire.

'Here.' She offered it to her friend.

Caridad took the dark, thin, badly twisted and scentless cigar. She sucked hard on it: bitter, harsh tobacco that was slow to burn. She coughed.

'I had better in La Galera!' she protested. 'Even there they don't smoke such bad tobacco.'

Herminia smiled. So did Caridad. They didn't dare to embrace in public, but in a single second they said a thousand things to each other in silence.

'Well, you owe your freedom to this disgusting tobacco,' said Herminia, breaking the spell.

Caridad looked at the cigar. A small clandestine tobacco plantation, that was what it was, explained Herminia. The priest of Torrejón de Ardoz kept a few plants on some land belonging to the parish. Until then, with the help of Marcial, who had leased the vineyards that hid the tobacco field from the parish, the priest had turned a profit with them through the sacristan, but the man was now too old to continue. 'I have a friend . . .' Herminia had said, taking advantage of the coincidence when she found out about the situation. It took her a while to convince Marcial and Don Valerio, the parish priest, but gradually their reluctance diminished when no other options appeared. Whom could they hire for such an activity, which was so harshly punished by the law? They accepted, and Don Valerio used some old contacts in the High Court so they would see Marcial and grant him custody of the prisoner. There was no problem: Caridad had completed her two-year sentence and the farmer could prove he was solvent and had a record of good behaviour. One day they informed him that the documents were ready.

Marcial came back to the arcades with the cart still piled high with melons.

'We got here too late!' he complained in a severe tone, blaming Herminia.

The delay caused by the paperwork at the High Court and La Galera had meant he was unable to sell his wares.

'None of the stalls want melons at this time of day.' Then he looked at Caridad the same way he had in the prison and shook his head. 'You didn't tell me she was so black,' he accused Herminia.

'At night it's not so noticeable,' interjected Caridad.

Herminia burst out laughing. The farmer raised his eyebrows.

'I don't plan on spending my nights with you.'

'Your loss,' added Herminia as she winked at her friend.

No. Marcial wasn't her husband, or her lover, not even a relative, Herminia answered, satisfying Caridad's curiosity as they walked behind the farmer with his small cart laden down with melons. He was just a neighbour. The house of Herminia's aunt and uncle, where she lived and where Caridad would now be living as well, was right next door to Marcial's, and despite the fact that the tobacco ought to be kept secret, half of the town knew about it. She had promised her aunt and uncle a small income in exchange for taking Caridad in.

'But I don't have any money,' she complained.

'That doesn't matter. You'll definitely get it with the tobacco. They will give you a part of the yield. The parish priest will decide what you get based on the results,' explained Herminia. 'Although your share will always be based on the finished product . . . Because you know how to work the leaf and make the cigars, right? That's what you told me.'

'That's the only thing I know how to do,' she answered when they reached an irregular plaza where there were gathered as many if not more people than in the Plaza Mayor. 'Although now I've also learned to sew.'

'La Puerta del Sol,' explained Herminia, noticing that Caridad had slowed her pace.

'Wait here,' shouted Marcial to the two women.

Herminia moved silently out of the path of the cart; she knew what the farmer was going to do as he turned down one of the narrow streets that led out of the plaza. In Madrid there were ten stalls authorized by the High Court to sell melons, where they were sold under the control of the authorities, who oversaw their quality, weight and price, but there were also many pedlars who, without a set location or any authorization, risked arrest and ending up in La Galera for buying and reselling fruit and vegetables illegally. The women who sold melons were scattered around the Puerta del Sol, and Marcial, cursing under his breath, went in search of them.

This is the famous Puerta del Sol? wondered Caridad. She had heard about that place too in La Galera: a gossip shop where people talked until they were convinced of the truth of rumours they themselves invented; a gathering place for idlers and layabouts, out-of-work bricklayers and haughty, impertinent musicians – some who had a chance and others who insisted on emulating them – waiting for some Madrileño to hire them to enliven one of the gatherings they often celebrated in their homes in the evenings.

Both women remained standing beside the monastery commonly known as San Felipe el Real, at one end of the plaza. Due to the irregular ground on Mayor Street, the church's long atrium, which had always been a place of meeting and entertainment for the Madrileños, rose above Herminia and Caridad's heads. Yet neither of them paid any attention to the laughter and comments that emerged from there.

'Would you like to go in?' invited Herminia.

Caridad remained absorbed in the row of caves that opened up beneath the steps of San Felipe. There were also small caves beneath the atrium of the church of Carmen and in some other places in that city built on hills, but none were as well known as the ones in the Puerta del Sol. In some they sold used clothes, but most sold toys that the merchants displayed to the public piled up beside the doors or hanging from their lintels in an attractive and colourful display that caught the eye of all passers-by.

'Can we?'

Herminia smiled at the naivety she saw in Caridad's round face. 'Of course we can . . . as long as you don't break anything. Marcial will still be a while.'

They entered one of the caves, which was narrow and long, dark and gloomy, with no natural light other than what entered through the door. The toys were scattered everywhere including over the floor: carriages, buggies, dolls, whistles, music boxes, swords and rifles, drums . . . They both jumped like little girls when a snake leapt out of a box to bite the finger of the woman who was touching it. The fat old woman who ran the business let out a laugh as she stuffed the snake back inside the box. The woman got over her surprise and asked how much it cost. As they negotiated the price, Caridad and Herminia amused themselves among the four or five people crowded inside, some fighting with the children who accompanied them and were demanding everything in the shop.

'Look at this, Cachita.' Herminia pointed to a blonde doll. 'Cachita?' she insisted when she got no response.

She turned towards Caridad and found her spellbound in front of a wind-up toy that rested on a shelf: on a small platform painted green and ochre, various figurines of black men, women and children, some loaded down with sacks, others with long sticks from which hung tobacco leaves, and a white overseer with a whip in his hand who finished off the arrangement, were placed around a representation of a ceiba tree and various tobacco plants.

'Do you like it?' asked Herminia.

Caridad didn't answer.

'Wait, you'll see.'

Herminia repeatedly turned a small key that stuck out of the base of the toy, let it go when it was wound as far as it would go and some little tinny music began to sound as the group of Negroes spun around the ceiba tree and the tobacco plants, and the white overseer lifted and lowered the arm that held the whip.

Caridad said nothing; one of her arms was outstretched, as if she wasn't sure whether to touch the toy or not. Herminia didn't realize that her friend was practically in a trance state.

'I'm going to ask the price,' she said instead, overjoyed, excited, heading over to the old woman who was watching them from the counter now that the woman with the snake in a box had left the cave. 'Not even if we saved all the money we made for several years!' she lamented on her return. 'Come and look at the doll!'

Marcial had to check several of the caves before he found them. His angry face was enough to make Herminia pull Caridad away. She knew what had happened: the pedlars had bought the melons for less than half what he could have made. They followed the empty cart through the plaza of the Puerta del Sol, slowly, despite the curses Marcial spat at the crowd to get them to make way.

Caridad saw the water carriers, all of them Asturian, gathered around the fountain they called the Mariblanca, with their pitchers ready to transport the water where it was needed. Jacinta was from Asturias and had told her about them. Was one of those men the relative who had brought her to Madrid, whom she hadn't wanted to disappoint with her pregnancy? She watched them; tough and rugged folk, Jacinta had assured her, most of them dedicated to harsh jobs such as water carrier, coal hauler or porter. On Fridays, from a pulpit set up in the plaza, between the church of Buen Suceso and the Mariblanca fountain, priests and friars preached sermons at them. From the looks of it they needed them: the rows between the water carriers and the neighbours who tried to help themselves in the fountains were constant, as were the quarrels they had between themselves when one of them tried to take more than was allowed on his turn: one large pitcher, two medium-sized ones or four small. Jacinta had also told her, wistfully, that the Asturians gathered in the Corregidor's Meadow to dance the *danza prima* native to their land. They all danced together but they always ended up fighting with rocks or sticks, divided into sides based on what town they were from.

As in the Plaza Mayor, around the Mariblanca fountain there were stalls and boxes for the sale of meat and fruits, but unlike the uniform, tall buildings there, the Puerta del Sol had few important constructions: the monastery of San Felipe el Real and, where it led to Mayor Street, a large house that took up an entire block with a corner tower demonstrating the nobility of its owner, the lord of the district of Humera; the church and the hospital of Buen Suceso, facing the tower on the other side; on one wall was the foundling hospital and, a little further on, the other side, the monastery of La Victoria, whose atrium was also a gathering place for Frenchified dandies. The rest of the buildings were nothing more than low houses, most of a single storey, narrow, old and crowded together, whose façades displayed both the clothes hung out to dry and the lack of privacy of the inhabitants. Rubbish collected in the doorways, and the excrement that hadn't been thoughtlessly tossed from the windows remained in front of the doors, in the chamber pots, waiting for the latrine cart to pass . . . if it ever did.

Among the crowd and bustle that seemed odd to her after two years of imprisonment, Caridad struggled to keep up with Marcial's pace as he pulled the cart. They passed the Puerta del Sol and entered Alcalá Street, with its press of carriages and carts going up and down, passing each other, stopping so their illustrious occupants could chat for a few moments, greet each other or just show off their wealth. Caridad tried to imagine what awaited her. Torrejón de what? She couldn't remember the name of the town Herminia had mentioned; she'd forgotten it as soon as Herminia told her about the tobacco, just a few plants, a priest and an elderly sacristan. 'Bad tobacco,' she added to herself. The rushing, the vehicles, the orders and insults hurled by the coachmen and the footmen who walked beside them forced Caridad to forget her worries and even kept her from looking at the ostentatious buildings erected by all sorts of wealthy people and religious orders on Madrid's noblest avenue, which ended at its eastern gate, the Alcalá Gate. Caridad left the city through its single arch, flanked by two small towers, just a few months after Milagros had arrived there.

Torrejón de Ardoz was four leagues along the King's Highway. They covered them in an equal number of hours, scorched by a summer sun that showed no mercy on them as they crossed through vast wheat fields. 'They grow tobacco here?' wondered Caridad, remembering the fertile Cuban plantation. She was reminded of her old straw hat: she hadn't needed it in La Galera, but on that road, beneath the burning sun, she missed it. It must have been left behind in the room of the secret guesthouse, along with her red clothes, documents and money. 'Strange freedom,' she said to herself. In two years she hadn't missed her red clothes, not even when she had to pay money for one of the tatty old shirts supplied by the *demandera*, and yet after a few breaths of freedom the memories were coming back to her.

Behind an irritated and silent Marcial, who dragged them along without compassion after having blamed Herminia, shouting, for the loss he'd had to sell the melons at, the two women had enough time to explain what they had been up to since they'd seen each other last.

'How is your back?' asked Herminia just as they were crossing a bridge. 'The Jarama River,' she announced, indicating the almost dry riverbed with her chin.

Caridad was about to reply about the state of her back, but the other woman didn't give her a chance.

'We have to get you some shoes,' she said, pointing to her bare feet.

'I don't know how to walk in shoes,' she replied.

They left behind the Viveros Bridge. There was still a league before Torrejón de Ardoz and Caridad already knew all about the family she was going to live with: Herminia's aunt and uncle, Germán and Margarita. He was a farmer, like almost everyone in the town, and his wife helped him when she could.

'My uncle is a good man,' murmured Herminia, 'like my father, although he was a bit obstinate. Uncle took me in as a girl, when my mother couldn't take care of her children and distributed us to various relatives.'

Caridad was familiar with the story; she also knew that Herminia had never heard from her mother again, just as had happened to her. She remembered the night that both of them had cried.

'Aunt Margarita is old,' she explained, 'and always sick with something or other, but she will treat you well.'

There was also Antón and Rosario. Caridad sensed a certain nervousness in her friend when she praised her cousin Antón, who worked the lands they had leased with his father, although he also often helped making tiles or transporting straw to Madrid.

'If your relatives are farmers,' Caridad interrupted, 'why don't they take care of the tobacco?'

'They don't dare,' she answered.

They walked a few steps in silence.

'Because you know that this tobacco business is dangerous, right?' asked Herminia.

'Yes.' Caridad knew it. She had talked to a prisoner who had been sentenced for trafficking in tobacco.

'You have to be careful with Rosario,' warned Herminia a bit later. 'She's vain, bitter and bossy.'

Her cousin's wife didn't help in the fields. She had four children whose names Caridad didn't even try to remember, and for years she had been making good money selling the breast milk that should have been theirs to the children of wealthy Madrileños. According to what Herminia told her, for almost six months now the son of a public prosecutor in the War Council had been living with them, the newborn having been brought to Torrejón by his parents so that Rosario could nurse him.

'And you?' asked Caridad.

'What about me?'

'What do you do there, in your aunt and uncle's house?'

Herminia sighed. Caridad stopped and Marcial got a few paces ahead; Herminia hadn't told her why she remained in her aunt and uncle's house.

'I help out.'

Caridad squinted at her friend's silhouette outlined against the fields while that sun that was so different from the one that shone in La Galera caressed her figure. 'You've never married?'

Herminia urged her to continue walking. 'We're almost there—' she tried to change the subject.

'Why?' insisted Caridad, interrupting her.

'A baby,' Herminia finally confessed. 'Several years ago, before prison. Nobody in Torrejón will marry me. And in Madrid . . . in Madrid the men are very reluctant to get married.'

'You never told me about any of this.'

Herminia avoided her eyes and they continued in silence. Caridad knew that men didn't want to get married. Many of the prisoners in La Galera complained about the same thing, that in the Madrid of civility and outrageous luxury, the men were afraid to get married. The number of weddings decreased each year and with it a birth rate that was replaced by people who came from every corner of Spain. The sole reason for this was the impossibility of meeting the costs of the luxuries, mostly dresses, that the women accrued as soon as they married in order to fiercely compete with others, both in noble and modest homes, each according to their means. Many men had been ruined; others worked ceaselessly to please their wives.

Torrejón de Ardoz was a town of little more than a thousand inhabitants located at the foot of the King's Highway that led to Saragossa. They passed the hospital of Santa María as they entered and dodged a couple of beggars who were harassing them. Another block and they went down Enmedio Street until they reached the town's main square. On Hospital Street, between the church of San Juan and the hospital of San Sebastián, they stopped in front of some low adobe houses, with back gardens that bordered the fields. The sun was still shining.

Marcial emitted a grunt in farewell, handed Caridad the papers confirming her freedom, pushed the cart against the façade of one of the houses and went into it. Caridad followed Herminia to the house next door.

'Hail Mary, full of grace,' she called out in greeting as she crossed the threshold.

32

ON 13 SEPTEMBER 1752, three years after the big gypsy round-up, 551 gypsy women plus more than a hundred children arrived at the Royal House of Mercy in Saragossa. All of them had boarded at the port of Málaga for Tortosa, in Tarragona, at the mouth of the Ebro River, from where they went upriver in barges to Saragossa, always in the custody of a regiment of soldiers.

Ana Vega squeezed little Salvador's hand when they saw the houses of the city and the towers that peeked out above them. The boy, almost nine years old, responded to his aunt's squeeze with one of his own, as if he were the one trying to give her strength. Salvador was a Vega and Ana had adopted him a little more than a year ago, after his mother's death in the typhus epidemic that devastated Málaga. It had ravaged the population of the coastal city and the gypsy women locked up on Arrebolado Street were no exception. The deaths ran into the thousands, more than six thousand they said, so many that the bishop forbade the ringing of the bells at the end of the viaticum and at burials. The priests distributed mutton rations in the houses of the sick, but none to the gypsy women and their children. Once the epidemic had passed, the famine of 1751 came, owing to the poor harvest. None of the numerous rogations and penance processions that the friars and priests convoked throughout Andalusia managed to put an end to that terrible drought.

Ana let go of the little boy's hand, tenderly stroked his shaved head and pulled him towards her. Saragossa opened out before them; the over five hundred gypsy women contemplated the city in silence as it drew closer. Most of those women, haggard, wasted, sick, many of them naked, without even a rag to cover their modesty, had no idea what fate awaited them. What other torments did His Majesty Ferdinand VI have in store for them?

The Marquis of Ensenada had the answer. The nobleman had not wavered in his obsession to exterminate the gypsy race. Many of those arrested in La Carraca had been taken from Cádiz to the El Ferrol arsenal, on the opposite coast, in northern Spain. As for the gypsy women, the marquis had to fight with the council that governed the House of Mercy in order to move them there. The Royal House of Mercy had been established to assist the poor and the vagrants who lived in the capital of the kingdom of Aragón. It deprived them of their freedom, forced them to work to be useful to society and in some cases even applied corporal punishment, but still the council didn't want to see it converted into a jail for delinquents. Saragossa had always considered itself an extremely charitable city, a virtue which only attracted more indigents to its streets. The 'father of the orphans' took care of the defenceless children and, every once in a while, organized the rounds of the 'poor cart': a barred wagon that went through the city to arrest the beggars and vagrants who loitered or asked for alms, and locked them up in the House of Mercy. How were they going to fit in these five hundred lost causes, plus another two hundred Aragonese gypsies who were still in the jail of the Aljafería castle and whom the marquis also wanted to send to that institution, when it was already packed with almost six hundred beggars?

The tussle between the council and the marquis was settled in the nobleman's favour: the State would take responsibility for the gypsy women's maintenance. Likewise, it would construct a new building to house them, make sure that they were always separate from the rest of the inmates and the field marshal would send twenty guard soldiers to watch over them.

The long line of dirty naked women, escorted by soldiers, caused so much excitement that a crowd joined the procession headed to the Portillo Gate, in front of the castle, where they entered the city. Not far from that gate was the Campo del Toro, on to which the grounds of the House of Mercy opened. Long brick and wooden buildings, one and two storeys tall, with pitched roofs and barred windows placed in no apparent order, made up the compound. Scattered among them were courtyards and open spaces, small service buildings and, on one end, a humble church with a single nave, also of wood and brick.

The warden of the House of Mercy shook his head at the sight of the women and children who came through the gate escorted by the soldiers. The priest, beside him, crossed himself repeatedly at the naked bodies, the gaunt faces, the bones jutting from hunger, the withered breasts revealed without modesty; squalid arms, legs and buttocks.

As soon as they had entered, they were pushed towards the building constructed expressly for them. Ana and Salvador, holding each other tightly by the hand, entered amid the mass of women and children. A simple glance was enough for the gypsies to see that they weren't all going to fit in there. The place was dark and narrow. The dirt floor was damp from stagnant water, and the unhealthy stench that came from it in the September heat without ventilation was unbearable.

The women began to complain.

'They can't put us in here!'

'Even animal stables are better than this!'

'We'll get sick!'

Many of the gypsies looked towards Ana Vega. Salvador squeezed her hand to encourage her.

'We won't stay here,' she declared. The boy rewarded her with a brilliant smile. 'Let's leave!'

She turned around and led the exit. The gypsy women who were still coming in backed up as they came up against Ana Vega. A few minutes later they were all on the esplanade that opened up in front of the building, complaining, shouting, cursing their lot, challenging some soldiers who questioned their captain. The officer turned towards the warden, who again shook his head: he knew it; he had foreseen that problem. It hadn't even been two months since the government council had warned the Marquis of Ensenada of the new construction's unhealthy conditions: there was no drainage and the waters stagnated in the gypsy building. There couldn't have been a worse beginning.

'Get them inside!' he then ordered over the din.

The roar hadn't stopped echoing when Ana Vega started hitting and biting a sergeant beside her. Little Salvador attacked another soldier, who threw him off with a slap before dealing with many of the gypsy women who followed Ana's lead. Others, unable to fight, cheered their companions on. After a few moments of confusion, the soldiers retreated, regrouped and fired some shots into the air that managed to halt the women's rage.

The solution offered by the riot satisfied the warden: he would demonstrate his authority and resolve the housing issue. Ana Vega and another five women who were identified as troublemakers would be whipped and then locked in the stocks for two days; the others could sleep outside the building, under the stars, in the courtyards and in the garden, at least as long as the heat that was turning the stagnant water bad lasted. After all, it was already September; the situation couldn't last that much longer.

In sight of the women and their children, Ana presented her bare back to the sentry; her jutting shoulder blades, spine and collarbones couldn't hide the scars from the many punishments she had received in Málaga. The whip whistled through the air and she gritted her teeth. Between whip strokes she turned her gaze towards Salvador, who was in the front row as always. The little boy, his fists and mouth clenched, closed his eyes every time the leather lashed her back. Ana tried to give him a smile, to reassure him, but all she managed was a forced grimace.

The tears she saw running down the little boy's face hurt more than any whiplash. Salvador had taken her as the substitute for his dead mother and Ana had taken refuge in the little one as the recipient of feelings that everyone seemed to want to steal from her. Twice she had disowned her own daughter. She had found out about what had happened in the San Miguel alley: La Trianera made sure to let her know. Milagros's wedding to Rafael García's grandson, that young troublemaker she'd once smacked, sank her further into despair. Her girl handed over to a García! On the other hand, her indifference to the news of her husband's murder, not feeling anything after so many years of sharing their lives, surprised and worried her, but she concluded that José hadn't deserved a different fate: he had agreed to that marriage. And as for the death sentence against her father . . .

'Do you have anything to say?'

The memory of that conversation with the soldier in Málaga interrupted her thoughts.

'Are they expecting a response?' she asked in turn.

The man shrugged.

'The gypsy told me that he would return once I had spoken with you.'

'Tell him that my daughter is no longer a Vega.'

'Is that all?'

Ana half closed her eyes.

'Yes. That is all.'

Some time later Milagros had sent Camacho to her. 'Tell her that I no longer consider her my daughter,' she'd declared. Was it true? Ana asked herself many nights. Was that what she truly felt? Sometimes, when her anger at the thought of Milagros in the arms of a García surfaced, the family hatred, the gypsy pride made her answer yes, that she was no longer her daughter. On most other occasions, what blossomed inside her was only infinite, indulgent, blind mother's love. Why had she said such a horrible thing? she would then torment herself. Rage alternated or mixed together with grief in her long dark nights of captivity; yet, either way, Ana ended up having to hide her tears and sobs from her fellow prisoners.

33

THE BUILDINGS WHERE Madrid's aristocracy lived weren't like the Sevillian noble houses, which had been erected at the height of the trade with the Indies and whose backbone and soul were their central courtyards filled with light and flowers and surrounded by columns. Except for a few exceptions, the many noblemen that settled in the capital – those whose titles had their roots in Spain's history were the most exalted by the new Bourbon dynasty – lived in stately homes with austere exteriors that differed little from the many others that made up eighteenth-century Madrid.

Philip V, grandson of the Sun King and the first Bourbon monarch – cultured and refined, timid and melancholic, pious, brought up in the submissiveness befitting the second son of the French royal house – spoke Latin fluently but took years to learn Spanish. He never liked the Royal Alcázar, which until his arrival had been the residence of his predecessors to the throne: the Habsburgs. How could that sober Castilian fortress squeezed atop a Madrid hill compare with the palaces that young Philippe had lived in during his childhood and youth? Versailles, Fontainebleau, Marly, Meudon, all surrounded by immense and well-tended forests, gardens, fountains and labyrinths. The Grand Canal built in Versailles, where young Philippe sailed and fished in a royal flotilla served by three hundred rowers, had more water by volume than the miserable Manzanares River that snaked at the foot of the palace. Surrounded by French servants and courtesans, the King alternated stays at the Castilian fortress with the Palace of Buen Retiro, until on Christmas Eve 1734 a fire that started in the drapery of his court painter's room devoured the entire Alcázar and led to the royal family moving definitively to the Buen Retiro. Despite the fact that Philip V himself had ordered a new palace to be built on the site of the fortress, some of the affluent followed the monarch's footsteps towards the area around the Buen Retiro and the avenues that developed in the adjacent fields. Still, most of the noblemen continued to live in what had been the epicentre of the city: the surroundings of the new royal palace whose colossal stonework was already visible by 1753.

It wasn't the first time that Milagros had been to one of those stately homes in the last few months. For a long time she had refused the invitations she received, telling herself that the money would only support her husband's dalliances, until there was one she couldn't refuse: the Marquis of Rafal, Chief Magistrate of Madrid and Judge Protector of the theatres, ordered her to sing and dance in a party that he was organizing for some friends.

'You can't turn down this one, gypsy,' Don José, the director of the company, warned her, after communicating the marquis's wishes.

'Why not?' she asked haughtily.

'You would end up in jail.'

'I haven't done anything wrong. Refusing to—'

The director interrupted her with a swipe of his hand through the air. 'There is always something that we are doing wrong, girl, always, and even more so when it depends on the decision of a nobleman whom you have scorned. First there would be a few days in jail for something petty . . . a rude remark to the audience or a gesture they consider inappropriate. And when you got out of jail, they would invite you again, and if you continued to decline, it would be a month.'

Milagros's features shifted from the initial scorn to intense fear.

'And they will insist again as soon as they free you again; noblemen never forget. For them it will be a game. Your obligation is singing and dancing in the Príncipe. If you don't do it or you intentionally do it badly, they will jail you; if you do it well, they'll find something they don't like—'

'And they will send me to jail,' said Milagros before he had a chance to.

'Yes. Don't make your life any harder than it is already. You will end up singing and dancing for them, Milagros. You have a young daughter, isn't that right?'

'What about her?' she spat out angrily. 'Don't you start—'

'The jails are full of women with their little ones,' he interrupted her. 'It's uncivilized to separate a child from her mother.'

Milagros accepted; she had no choice. The mere possibility of her daughter going to jail horrified her. Pedro's eyes sparkled when he heard the news.

'I'll go with you,' he declared.

She tried to object. 'Don José . . .'

'I will talk to him; besides, weren't you the one who said that you needed protection? I will find guitarists and gypsy women; the musicians at the Príncipe don't understand what those people want, they don't have the spark.'

Don José consulted with the marquis, who not only agreed to Pedro's suggestion but accepted it enthusiastically. Don Antonio, the Chief Magistrate, remembered how Milagros had inflamed the audience gathered in the Sevillian palace of the Count and Countess of Fuentevieja, and that was exactly what he wanted from her: the voluptuous gypsy dances that the censors banned in the Príncipe, the lascivious *zarabandas* so reviled by the pious and the puritanical, and those other rhythms that Caridad had taught her to understand and above all to feel, Guinean dances, Negro dances that were daring and provocative in their celebration of fertility: *chaconas*, *cumbés* and *zarambeques*. No member of the theatre company formed part of that group, not even Marina, despite Milagros's insistence, nor the great Celeste, with whom Pedro had broken the last ties. Except for Marina, who accepted her excuses, the decision earned Milagros the antipathy of the rest of the company, but Pedro didn't listen to her complaints. 'You are the one the audience at the Príncipe cheers,' he argued.

And it was true: people came to the theatre to see her, and when the *tonadillas* ended and Celeste and the others appeared to perform the third and final act of the comedy, most had left and the comic players found the place half empty and distracted.

After that first performance at the request of the Chief

Magistrate, there were many occasions when nobles, the wealthy and high-ranking officials required the presence of the famous Barefoot Girl at their many parties. Don José sent them directly to Pedro, who accepted all the invitations, and Milagros, after her performance at the theatre, went to those stately homes at night to indulge the sensuality of the civilized dignitaries of the kingdom and their wives.

That was why, on that spring night of 1753, Milagros ignored the anodyne appearance of the house's exterior. She knew that inside it would be crammed with luxury: huge living rooms, dining room, library, music and games room, sitting rooms, high-ceilinged parlours with spectacular crystal chandeliers that illuminated furniture embellished with mother-of-pearl, marble, bronze, painted glass or inlaid exotic woods, around the walls, almost always with a table in the centre accompanied by a few chairs at most; cornucopia mirrors that reflected the light from the oil lamps on their arms; carpets, statues, paintings and tapestries with motifs that had nothing to do with the Bible or mythology like those she had seen in Seville's noble homes. The same could be said of the fireplaces. In Madrid the large Spanish-style mantels were no longer fashionable. They preferred the French type, of marble and with delicate lines. The taste for French things reigned, to undreamed-of extremes.

In addition to the rooms, furniture, and the endless stream of servants, there was also a profusion of objects and decorations in gold, silver, ivory or hardwoods; porcelain china sets and rock-crystal cups that vibrated shrilly above the din when clinked together, raised in toasts around a competition of silks, velvets, moirés and lamés; feathers, flounces, tassels, bows, ribbons and blond lace; perfumes; extravagant hairdos on the women, powdered wigs on their companions. Luxury, ostentation, vanity, hypocrisy . . .

Milagros appeared indifferent to all that show. She didn't even wear the dresses she flaunted in the Príncipe, but her simple, comfortable gypsy clothes, combined with colourful ribbons and beads. Since she had been forced to visit the homes of the nobility, she had received gifts, some of them valuable, although they had done no good to those who tried to flatter and seduce her. All the gifts and money she earned for the performances went into Pedro's hands, who unlike her had significantly upgraded his wardrobe. That night he wore a richly embroidered bolero jacket, in the style of the *manolos*, silk stockings and shirt and shoes with silver buckles that he forced Bartola to polish time and again. Milagros, seeing him so splendidly turned out, elegant and dazzling, felt a stab of something. She wasn't sure if it was pain or rage. Pedro, in true gypsy form, addressed the Marquis of Torre Girón as an equal: they chatted, laughed and even slapped each other on the back, as if they were old friends. She could tell that many of the ladies there whispered with their gazes brazenly fixed on her husband. Even the Frenchified dandies that courted the ladies seemed to envy him!

Milagros passed before them with her nose in the air, as if challenging them. She knew the courtship game. Marina had explained to her that most of the ladies who filled the boxes at the Coliseo del Príncipe weren't accompanied by their husbands, but rather by the *chevaliers servants* who were courting them.

'And their husbands allow it?' she had asked, surprised.

'Of course,' answered Marina. 'Every evening they escort them to the theatre and pay for a good seat,' she commented in the dressing rooms, 'although sometimes the lady prefers to mingle with the women on the balcony, hidden beneath a good cloak: when she is in mourning, for example, and it isn't appropriate for her to be seen enjoying herself in the theatre or listening to the gossip of the vendors. In that case the suitor still has to buy her ticket and wait for her at the exit. Take a closer look!' she urged Milagros. 'I'm sure that even though they are covered up you can recognize them.'

'What else does the suitor have to do?' asked Milagros, her interest piqued.

'Well, he has to please the object of his affections,' explained Marina. 'He can talk only to her, not to any other woman, even when his lady is not present. Early in the morning, he has to go to her bedchamber to wake her up, bring her breakfast, help her to dress and converse with her while the hairdresser does her hair; then they go to mass. In the evenings, he escorts her here, to see the comedies.' Marina listed the suitor's obligations, counting on her fingers. 'Then, they take a long stroll through the San Jerónimo meadow in a fine open carriage, and at night it's time for gatherings, card games and contradances before dropping her off at home. Basically, the suitor must have permission from his lady for anything he wants to do.'

'That's all?' asked the gypsy in a mocking tone.

But, to her surprise, Marina continued. 'No!' she responded, exaggeratedly stretching out the vowel. 'I was just catching my breath.' She laughed with feigned affectation. 'That is what he should do. Then there's what he should pay for: the hairdresser, the flowers he has to send her every day and, above all, her clothes and accessories. There are some ladies who, before splurging, agree on a maximum amount for all those expenses with the suitor, but those are the cheap courtships. The true suitor has to open up an account at the best shops so that his lady can dress as is befitting, and he must also be up to date on the latest court style and everything arriving from Paris so he can offer it to her before everyone else is wearing it . . .'

'They must go bankrupt,' commented Milagros.

'Madrid is full of suitors who have lost their fortunes courting a lady.'

'Poor wretches.'

'Poor wretches? They enjoy the smile and company of their ladies, their conversation and their confidences . . . even their scorn! What more can a man aspire to?'

Remembering those words, Milagros revealed a smile that was misinterpreted by one of the young dandies invited to the marquis's party. *How much money do you have left?* she was tempted to ask him just as a couple of bold ladies separated from the group and approached the marquis and Pedro flirtatiously. Milagros hesitated over stepping into their path. He was her man! Wasn't he? There were more and more nights when he didn't even come home, but those foolish women who surrounded her in a cloud of perfume as they passed by her didn't need to know that. She did nothing. She turned her head and lost her gaze in the reflections of a large crystal chandelier as the two women launched their attack on Pedro.

With a party for almost two hundred guests, the Marquis of Torre Girón was celebrating the fact that the King had granted him, as a grandee, the privilege of keeping his head covered in the monarch's presence. Milagros sang and danced with the same passion as she did in the theatre. In those moments she was the queen. She could feel it; she knew it! Dukes, marquises, counts and barons surrendered to her voice, and in their eyes, then stripped of titles, money and even authority, she perceived nothing more than desire, the yearning to possess that sensual, lustful eighteen-year-old body as she danced and swirled about. And what about the ladies? Yes, the same ones who had gone after Pedro. They lowered their eyes, looking at their own hands or feet, some at their corseted breasts, probably lamenting how they fell flaccid as soon as they were released from their constraints. Even the youngest among them envied Milagros, aware that they were unable to use their charms the way she did. How could they emulate her, match her, in grotesque, ceremonial contradances? they thought. Not even in the privacy of their bedchambers would they dare to spin around and shake their hips like that.

The party was likely to last well into the night, probably until dawn. Still, Milagros was able to rest when the marquis, exultant after the coverage ceremony before His Majesty Ferdinand VI, entertained his guests with a puppet show.

So, while the marionettes performed – in front of more than one church provost – light, even comic versions of biblical stories, Pedro García was seated comfortably in the audience, beside a group of women who had come to captivate him, and Milagros and her accompanists were getting some refreshment in the kitchens after their first performance. The laughter from the audience at what more than one moralist would have deemed blasphemies, and the shouts of admiration from the ladies surprised by the cloud of smoke raised by an explosion of gunpowder when the devil appeared, echoed in the distance.

'What a disgrace!'

Some of the servants who were coming and going in the kitchens, holding trays with lit candles in the centre so the guests could see what they were being offered, stumbled at the marquis's sudden appearance. The rest shrank back at the screeching with which he had burst in.

'I cannot allow a princess such as yourself to be served in the kitchens,' he added, extending his arm to Milagros. 'Come with me, I beg of you.'

The gypsy hesitated before resting her hand on the arm outstretched before her, but the nobleman insisted and Milagros felt the eyes of the servants, guitarists and dancers fixed on her. *Will she be capable of refusing the courtesy the lord of the house honours her with?* they seemed to be wondering. *Why not?* she said to herself. She tilted her head to one side mischievously, smiled and accepted the invitation.

Joaquín María Fernández de Cuesta, Marquis of Torre Girón, was close to forty years old. Cultured and charming, quick with words, he hid a barely perceptible limp due to a fall from a horse. Milagros found herself enveloped in the perfume that the nobleman gave off as they went through the halls.

'I don't like marionettes,' he explained to her. 'The puppeteers are nothing more than a bunch of dissolutes who mock and call into question the people's most intimate convictions. They should be outlawed.'

'Then why did you have them come?' she asked.

'For the marchioness and her friends,' answered the nobleman. 'They are amused by them and I must humour them. Besides, you don't mean to compare them with the ignorant plebs!' They stopped in front of a door and Don Joaquín María announced: 'My private sitting room.'

They entered the room, which might or might not have been large. Milagros could get no idea of its true dimensions because of the countless books, pieces of furniture and objects accumulated there: on one of the walls was a prie-dieu with its kneeler and various carved images; a washbasin on the facing wall; beside it, a grandfather clock with many figurines; tapestries painted with forests and fields; mirrors and sculptures of mythological goddesses; crystal figurines; tables; chairs and armchairs . . . Milagros was captivated by a large golden cage with several metal nightingales inside it. The marquis came over and flicked a switch. Instantly, the little birds began to warble.

'You will like everything here,' he said, taking her by the elbow.

They went past a table with drawings scattered on it and the nobleman lit a light inside a box.

'Look through here,' he indicated, pointing to a hole located in a tube that emerged from its front.

Milagros covered her left eye and placed her right up to the tube.

'Versailles,' announced the marquis.

She exclaimed at the detailed sight of the immense palace. The nobleman allowed her to enjoy it for a few moments and then introduced another slide into the slot in front of the tube.

'Fontainebleau,' he then said.

They looked real! The marquis continued inserting slides as he explained what they contained. 'How beautiful! . . . Marvellous!' she exclaimed at the palaces, the immense, beautifully maintained gardens and the forests that he showed her through that box. Suddenly, with her eye still stuck to the tube, she felt the nobleman brush up against her. She held her breath and her body grew so rigid that the marquis moved away.

'Forgive me,' he murmured.

When they finished with the magic lantern, he invited her to drink sweet wine in some small crystal glasses he pulled out of a cabinet.

'To you,' he toasted, starting to raise his cup, 'the Barefoot Girl, the best player in Madrid . . . and the most beautiful.'

After the first sip, the marquis showed her, with a care and pride he couldn't hide, the many rare and curious objects that filled his sitting room. At first Milagros barely paid attention to the explanations that flowed from the nobleman's mouth. After turning in her hands, with extreme care and delicacy, the figurine of a goddess, Don Joaquín María opened a book with huge pages. 'Look,' he invited her.

She tried to keep her distance and she watched without getting too close; she felt uncomfortable being alone with a nobleman in his sitting room. He seemed not to see the problem and continued turning the pages, pointing out some magnificent drawings to her, while Milagros finished off the excellent sweet wine.

Why should I feel guilty? she asked herself. She had seen Pedro sitting in the audience, brazenly flirting with one of the tarts. She had done nothing wrong and the marquis seemed to respect her: he hadn't tried to grope her or made improper remarks, as usually happened at the inns. He treated her courteously, and except for that slight brush he hadn't shown any sign of coming near her. Milagros took a step towards the table the large book rested on and looked at the drawings. She accepted more wine, drank, and enjoyed examining all the different things in that room. She asked about the objects and furniture naively, where they were from, what they were worth, what they were used for, and she was pleased to see the efforts Don Joaquín María made to translate his cultured explanations into language she could understand, making them both laugh.

'Do you like it?'

In the palm of her hand Milagros held a gold cameo that showed the figure of a woman carved in white stone.

'Yes,' she answered distractedly, without taking her eyes off the medallion; it reminded her of the one that her grandfather gave to Old María in Triana.

'It's yours.'

The marquis closed her hand around the cameo. Milagros remained silent for a few moments, surprised by the touch of that soft hand, so different from the rough, calloused hands of the gypsies.

'No . . .' she tried to refuse.

'You would do me a great honour if you would keep it,' he insisted, squeezing her fist with his hand. 'Don't I deserve that?'

Milagros nodded. Of course he deserved that. They had spent some lovely time together. No one had ever treated her with such gallantry and attention, and in a room filled with precious valuables, in a great mansion . . .

'It's about time,' commented the nobleman suddenly after checking a large wall clock, releasing her hand and interrupting her thoughts.

Milagros raised her eyebrows.

'We should be getting back,' he smiled, offering her his arm, as he had done in the kitchens. 'The puppeteers must be finishing up their show, and I have no intention of causing malicious rumours.'

However, the rumours spread as soon as the spectacular bouquets of flowers started showing up every day at the Príncipe, addressed to Milagros, and they multiplied when she sang and danced with her gaze set on the nobleman's box.

'I haven't seen him since the party!' she defended herself when Pedro demanded explanations after slapping out of her hand one of the bouquets she kept showing up with day after day.

It was true. Don Joaquín María kept his distance, as if he were waiting ... Perhaps for her to make the first move? Marina encouraged her to do it, first excited and then visibly annoyed at her refusal. 'Are you crazy? How can I have relations with another man, no matter how rich and noble he may be?' let fly Milagros. And yet, at night, alone, while Pedro was in the taverns of Madrid with his women, she caressed the cameo that she kept among her clothes and she asked herself what was stopping her. The dawn, the hubbub that came up from the street, María laughing and running around the house made the fantasies of the dark disappear. She was a gypsy, she was married and she had a daughter. Perhaps some day Pedro would change.

'At the party,' her husband then insisted, 'you were with the marquis in his sitting room. They told me.'

'And where were you?' she replied with a weary voice. 'Do you want me to remind you?'

Pedro lifted his hand with the intention of slapping her. Milagros stood tall and tolerated the ploy, motionless, her brow furrowed.

'Hit me, and I will go to him.'

Their gazes clashed, both furious.

'If I ever find you with another man,' threatened the gypsy with his hand still in the air, 'I'll slit your throat.'

34

SHE COULD LEAVE, follow the golden trail that the spring night's full moon sent over the vegetable patch and the wheat fields that spread behind the house. The town was plunged in absolute silence, and that magical glow invited her to abandon the miserable little room beside the garden that they had let her stay in, and Caridad walked towards the moon with her gaze lost in the plains that extended before her. A shadow in the fields, sometimes still, awed by the immensity, other times walking aimlessly, as if hoping to find a path that led her . . . where?

Her reception months earlier into the new house had been mixed. Herminia's aunt and uncle had stifled their surprise. Too black, their eyes shouted. Antón observed her with a hint of lust that Herminia was quick to intercept by placing herself between them; Caridad didn't entirely understand that sudden reaction. The children's misgivings soon turned into curiosity, and Rosario welcomed her with a disgusted expression.

'Is she healthy?' she spat at Herminia. 'Are you sure she isn't going to give Cristóbal some Negro disease?'

The wet nurse's fear banished her to the garden, to a shed filled with farming implements, attached to the house, which reminded her of the one she had stayed in during the round-up, beside the house of the good Christians Fray Joaquín took her to for safekeeping. Instead of nets and fishing poles, this one had yokes and mattocks.

Cristóbal, the son of the prosecutor . . . how was she going to infect him with anything? The little boy looked more like a butterfly cocoon than like Rosario's boy, who was the same age; his mother topped up his share of her milk with bread soaked in wine and left him to be passed freely from hand to hand, when he wasn't on the ground. Each morning, after bathing Cristóbal in cold water and spreading flour between his legs, Rosario wrapped him in white linen from his feet to his shoulders, with his little arms stuck to each side to avoid deforming him with the tight fabric. That was how, like a little white cocoon from which only his head emerged, the boy spent his days, lying in the rustic wooden crib that Rosario only lifted him out of so he could latch on to one of her nipples. Once his hunger was sated, Cristóbal dozed, but most of his day was spent howling, unable to move, irritated by the urine and excrement trapped against his skin, which were cleaned up only grudgingly because swaddling him again was such a chore. Caridad felt sorry for Cristóbal. She compared him to the other kids who ran about the house, to the gypsy kids in Triana and even to the little mulattoes born in the shacks in Cuba; their mothers nursed them for two or three months and then they were left in the care of older slave women who were no longer useful in the fields. Always naked and free.

'All the wet nurses, even the ladies, swathe babies,' Herminia explained to her one day. 'It's always been done that way.'

'But . . . it's not natural!'

Herminia shrugged her shoulders. 'I know,' she agreed. 'Nobody would think to wrap a lamb or a piglet to make it grow healthier and better. There are wet nurses who have even broken one of their arms, or legs, or ribs . . . Many children end up deformed or hunchbacked.'

'So why do they do it?' asked Caridad, horrified.

'Because that way they don't have to watch them. And because they avoid accidents. If the wet nurse knows how to wrap, she will return the child alive to its parents. The deformities might show up, but always later on, over the years, and nobody will be able to say it was her fault. If they don't swaddle, they risk having to tell the parents that their child fell or broke a bone, or swallowed something and choked, or split open his head, or . . .'

Caridad silenced her with a disgusted expression.

Little Cristóbal occupied her thoughts on some of those nights in the fields: she was nothing more than a slave who was now free because the 'plague of the seas' had ended her master's life, although it could well be said that the insatiable plague had come with the intention of causing her the suffering that frail Don José was unable to inflict upon her himself. And yet, she could look up at the seductive moon over the Castilian fields. And Cristóbal, the rich son of a high-ranking official, was a slave to his swaddling linen. Sometimes she felt tempted to steal the boy and let him run through the fields . . . would he even know how to move? She remembered little Marcelo: even as a slave with his sight and mind disabled, he had lived in greater freedom than that poor boy.

'Women of means don't want to breastfeed their children, that's why they hand them over to strangers,' explained Herminia. 'They don't want to lose their figure, that narrow waist they fight with their corsets to achieve, or for their breasts to harden to bursting with milk only to droop flaccid over time. They don't want to be tied down and unable to attend social events, the comedies, the dances or the intellectual gatherings. But above all,' she added that Rosario had confessed this to her one day, 'they are afraid of not knowing how to soothe their child's crying and the possibility that their little ones could die in their hands . . .

'They prefer, if it has to happen, to just be shown the corpse!' Caridad remembered Herminia's outburst, her green eyes sparkling with rage, perhaps lamenting some personal experience. Caridad hadn't asked her about the fate of the child she'd told her about on their way there and even less who the father was, since for some time now she had been fairly certain it was her cousin Antón. It was a tacit agreement among all the members of that family: Rosario didn't want to get pregnant again, since that would mean the prosecutor taking his son out of her care and losing money; meanwhile, Antón brazenly approached Herminia, who was uncomfortable in her friend's presence and cheerful and obliging otherwise. Some nights Caridad hastened her steps towards the fields when she heard their frolicking. Then, in the moonlight, with the lovers' whispering drumming in her ears, she missed Melchor and cried remembering the nights beneath the stars when the gypsy had made her feel like a woman for the first time in her life.

In the months that had passed since her arrival, she'd met Don Valerio, the parish priest of Torrejón. She also met Fermín, the old sacristan who could no longer take care of the tobacco crops. Don Valerio had scrutinized her, as everyone did, while she tried to dispel the sacristan's misgivings. Fermín bombarded her with questions as if it pained him to leave his plants in the hands of a strange Negress.

'Sir,' Caridad eventually interrupted him with a certain harshness, tired of all the questions. 'I know how to grow and work with tobacco. I've done it all my life . . .'

'Watch your pride!' scolded Don Valerio.

Herminia was about to intervene, but Caridad beat her to it.

'It's not pride,' she replied to the priest, sweetening her tone. 'It's called slavery. White men like your lordship stole me from Africa as a girl and forced me to learn to grow and work tobacco. Everything I once was got lost because of that plant: my family, my children . . . I had two; one is still there, I sense it,' she added squinting her eyes for a few seconds. 'The other was sold very young to a sugar mill owned by the Church . . .'

'Your attitude is not that of a slave,' the clergyman scolded her again.

'No, Father. It is that of a prisoner who gave two years of her life to the King for letting those who call themselves good Christians treat her like a slave.'

'You've got a very free tongue,' persisted Don Valerio, raising his voice.

Herminia grabbed Caridad by the forearm, insisting that she stop, but it was the priest who overruled her that day.

'Let her go on,' he requested. 'I want to hear her.'

However, Caridad couldn't get past the sudden feeling brought on by that touch on her arm and her friend's pleading look. Perhaps it was true, perhaps she did have a very free tongue . . . Much had changed after two years in La Galera, she knew it, but at that moment she decided to keep quiet.

'I'm sorry to have offended you,' she apologized.

'Something you'll have to confess.'

She lowered her gaze.

That same afternoon Herminia accompanied her to the tobacco field. The vineyards Marcial cultivated were by where the Toroto Brook emptied into the Henares River and the flat landscape was broken by some little hills, olive trees and vines that replaced the extensive wheat fields in Alcalá de Henares, Torrejón's neighbouring town, which it had been separated from in the sixteenth century. A gully behind Marcial's vineyards served as a refuge for the tobacco farm, keeping it hidden.

Caridad looked at it from above: messy, wild, poorly maintained. It was July when she arrived in Torrejón and Marcial, following instructions from the sacristan, was harvesting; the man didn't even notice her presence. Caridad saw how he cut down the plants at the stem, with a machete, almost violently, like the slaves cut sugar cane. Then, with the leaves still on the stalk, he piled them up on top of each other on the ground, in the sun.

'What do you think?' Herminia asked her.

'Back on the plantation we chose leaf by leaf, each day choosing the ones that were ready, perfectly ripe, until the plant was just a clean standing stalk.'

Marcial turned when he heard their voices and signalled for them to come down.

'Caridad says that in Cuba they harvested leaf by leaf,' announced Herminia as soon as she reached the man.

To both of the women's surprise, the man nodded. 'I've heard that, but everyone who knows anything about tobacco assures me that in Spain it's always been done this way. The truth is, since all the farms are secret, nobody can prove it, although Don Valerio maintains that they follow this procedure in the monasteries and convents. He must know something about how the clergy do it.'

'What difference does it make—?' Herminia started to ask.

'The upper leaves get more sun than the lower ones,' Caridad answered before she could finish.

'That happens with all plants,' put in Marcial, adding with a smile, 'they grow upwards. The problem is that collecting leaf by leaf takes a lot of work . . . and knowledge.'

As if she wanted to demonstrate it, Caridad had gone off and was feeling and smelling the leaves of the plants that were still standing. She pulled off little bits and chewed them. Marcial and Herminia let her do it, spellbound by the transformation in her as she moved among the plants, enraptured and in her own world, touching one, cleaning another, speaking to them . . .

They decided not to change the harvesting system for the few plants that were left. 'It's not worth it,' confirmed Caridad. Marcial trusted her and let her choose some to obtain the seeds for the next year and, with the cart overflowing, they waited in the vineyards until it was night to transport the tobacco to the town. They shared bread, wine, cheese, garlic and onions and chatted and smoked, enjoying watching the immense sky above them fill with stars.

The tobacco drying room was none other than the attic of the church's sacristy, which a sleepy Fermín let them into. In the light of the oil lamp carried by the sacristan, who remained outside the door to the attic, Caridad could make out a large pile of plants on to which they hastily added the ones they had brought. How could they expect to get good tobacco with such carelessness? She stood up inside the attic. She grabbed one of the plants and wanted to bring it close to the light to . . .

'What are you doing, *morena*?' enquired the sacristan, moving aside the oil lamp.

'I . . .'

'You can't work here at night,' he interrupted, 'it's dangerous with candles or lamps. Don Valerio only allows it to be done with natural light.'

Caridad was tempted to reply that she didn't think that one would be able to work any better in there with natural light, but she kept quiet and the next morning, early, she showed up at the sacristy. She argued with Fermín until Don Valerio came up to the attic to sort things out.

'Didn't you say that you couldn't take care of it any more?' he reproached the sacristan. 'Then it will be as she decides.'

And Fermín let Caridad decide what to do and do it, but he kept his eye on her, sitting on a box and criticizing her every movement under his breath.

'Do you know what, Fermín?' said Caridad as she cut the leaves off a plant. 'When I got to Triana I met an old woman who you remind me a lot of: she thought everything was wrong.' The sacristan grumbled. 'But she was a good person.' Caridad let a few minutes pass in silence. 'Are you a good person?' she asked him after a little while, without looking at him.

That spring night, in the field, smelling of tobacco, Caridad was surprised to find herself thinking of Old María. Sometimes, in La Galera, she had come to her mind, fleetingly; now she believed she could feel her by her side and she could even hear her swearing break the silence.

'Why did you say that the old woman was a good person?' the sacristan asked her the next morning, as soon as he saw her at daybreak.

'Because I think you are as well,' she answered.

Fermín thought for a few seconds and held back a smile, before handing her the sticks that she had been wanting the day before. Unlike on the Cuban plantation, the attic was set up to hang the entire plant from some hooks stuck into the ceiling's wooden beams. 'In Cuba we string the leaves on to *cujes*,' she had told him, 'which are long sticks, to dry them.' Caridad was hoping to choose the best leaves and cure them the way she knew how to, but she had nowhere to hang them.

'Good *cujes*,' she lied, weighing the coarse, long sticks that Fermín handed her. 'Now we have to find a way to hang them.'

'I already know how.' The sacristan tried to add a wink to his statement, but his attempt was no more than the ungainly grimace of an awkward old man. Caridad looked at him tenderly and rewarded him with a smile.

With the help of a revived Fermín, who had been infected by her enthusiasm, Caridad chose the leaves one by one and hung them up, strung together in pairs on those knotty sticks. She hung them in silence, comparing them to the *cujes* used on the plantation, which were carefully chosen in the mangrove swamps and patiently worked so that they didn't imbue even the scent of wood on to the leaves. But what was the point of trying to keep that crude tobacco from smelling of wood when the incense that Don Valerio used to try to cover up their activities slipped in through every crack of the roof that led to the attic? She organized the leaves by their aroma, texture and dampness. She controlled the temperature and the atmosphere of the place by opening and closing the small windows, permitting or impeding air from running through depending on the moment. She incessantly ventilated and moved the leaves and the whole plants that hung from the roof to dry them better. She kept careful watch for insects and parasites. She devoted herself eagerly to it all until the midrib of the leaves was completely dry. Then she chose them from the *cujes* to pile up and tie together into small piles so they could ferment; Fermín knew very little about that procedure. Caridad calculated the temperature and dampness of the atmosphere and the water that the plants had had access to in the field. The size of the piles grew, and she moved the tobacco that had been in the middle to the top and put the new leaves in the centre, constantly tying up and untying the piles, smelling them, touching them, chewing the leaves, changing their location, moving them closer or further from the air currents, splattering the leaves with *betún*: a preparation she had made by fermenting the plant stalks in water.

During that season, her life was limited to walking at dawn the few steps from the house of Herminia's aunt and uncle to the church of San Juan. She went back for lunch, which she ate alone in the smelly, packed garden shed; Rosario didn't want her around the house, and Herminia was falling more in love with her cousin Antón each day, so she paid little attention to her. Caridad would have liked to talk to her about that, but her reproaches vanished when she remembered that Herminia had got her out of La Galera. She owed her gratitude. So she was forced to respect her friend's feelings and stopped seeking her out. As soon as she had finished the piece of bread and the bowl of chickpeas, haricot beans or broad beans, almost always without any meat, she went back to the church and when she left it again it was late at night and she blended in with the shadows.

Don Valerio spread the rumour that a personage of the court – 'How can I reveal his name?' the priest retorted when pressured – had begged him to take care of that poor Negro wretch who had been unjustly sent to the women's prison. So he had sought out the help of Marcial and got her a place to sleep, and Caridad's official documents fit with his story. He forced her to clean the church to justify her presence there, while the always willing parishioners gossiped, wondering which courtier it was and what his relationship was to the Negress. There were speculations about Don Valerio as well: some believed the priest; many others doubted him; and those who knew about the tobacco simply understood. The fact was that gradually that black woman, peaceful and solitary, who walked around barefoot and calm, became a part of the landscape; soon even the children stopped following her around and pestering her, and Caridad went out alone to stroll along the paths and fields, swaying in the spring breeze as she thought of Melchor, and Milagros, and Marcelo.

35

THE CONFINEMENT OF the gypsy women and their little ones at the Royal House of Mercy in Saragossa turned the charitable institution into a reform school, as much as the council regulating it refused to admit that. Punishments were widespread: whippings, stocks, fetters and being locked up with only bread and water. They suspended the practice of letting trusted women go out; they didn't allow the sick to go to hospital and they installed a basic infirmary; they separated the women from the children and from the girls who could work and they didn't allow them even the slightest contact with the other prisoners; they even suspended the masses and sermons because there was no priest who dared to stand in front of hundreds of half-naked women. The soldiers watched over them to keep the gypsies from running away, but, despite that, they managed what their husbands and sons were unable to in the arsenals and they made holes in the adobe wall that tried to protect the place. Then they ran through Saragossa until they were arrested or managed to outwit the soldiers and constables and hit the roads.

On one occasion about fifty of them managed to escape. The warden, enraged, ordered all the gypsy women to be sent to the gallery basements, which had no windows to the outside. There was no money for bars; there was no money, despite what Ensenada had promised, to feed that ragtag army; there was no money to provide them with beds – they shared in threes – or food, or blankets, or even plates and bowls for eating.

And the situation blew up. The gypsies complained about the

execrable slop they gave them and the conditions of the basements they were crammed into: damp and unventilated, gloomy and unhealthy. No one paid attention to their demands and they took it out on everything around them: they destroyed the cots and threw them along with the straw mattresses into the two blind wells at the House of Mercy. The poor health that followed the obstruction of the well began with a scabies epidemic that tormented the women. The itching kept them from sleeping and began between their fingers and toes, moved to elbows, buttocks and especially their nipples, and turned into scabs of dried blood due to the scratching, beneath which hid thousands of mites and their eggs. The scabs had to be ripped off in order to treat them with a salve made of sulphur that the doctor used to try to stop the disease; they also tried bloodletting, but the gypsies refused. Months later, the scabies reappeared. Some old women died.

Ana Vega was not one of those who fled that jail. Each day, morning and night, she tried to catch a glimpse of Salvador when, with other gypsy children and street kids, they took him to work on the properties owned by the House of Mercy. They left Saragossa to grow grain and take care of the olive groves and gather the olives to make oil. Despite the fact that all contact was banned, Ana and other gypsy women got as close as they could to the line of children heading off to the fields. They were punished for it. Some stopped, but she continued to do it. They punished the children; and they warned the women that they would do it again, saying: 'Yesterday they had bread and water because of you.' Although the others stopped, Ana refused to be convinced: something compelled her to dodge the sentry and approach them time and again. Salvador rewarded her by widening his mouth into a splendid, proud smile.

One morning the sentry that accompanied the children didn't flail his arms at Ana as he usually did to get her away from them. She was surprised, and even more so when she heard laughter in the line. She searched for Salvador. One of the boys pointed to him hidden among the other laughing lads and moved aside so she could see: Salvador wore a wooden collar that wrapped around his entire neck and forced him to walk upright, with his chin grotesquely raised. The boy avoided meeting her eyes. Ana could see the boy's gritted teeth between trembling lips that clenched at the others' mocking.

'You can take it off him,' she managed to say to the sentry with a trembling voice. The tears she hadn't shed over her whippings and the thousand other punishments ran down her cheeks.

Frías, the grim-faced and pot-bellied sentry, addressed her. 'Will you stop coming over?'

Ana nodded.

'Do you promise?'

She nodded again.

'I want to hear you say it.'

'Yes,' she yielded. 'I promise.'

Humiliation became the worst of the punishments that the cultured authorities of the period imposed on the minors. The gypsy girls that had been sent to the House of Mercy's sewing workshops refused to work when they didn't receive the food they were allotted. The warden's response was to take away the clothes and shoes they had been given and send them out with the others. Dozens of young gypsy girls suddenly found themselves naked in courtyards and galleries, ashamed, trying to hide their bodies, their pubic areas and their breasts, budding in some and developed in others, from the gazes of their mothers and the other prisoners. After a few days the government council cancelled the measure, but the damage was done.

Ana Vega, like many others, suffered during those days not only for the girls' disgrace but her own. Those young bodies, the modesty with which they defended their honour, led her to think about herself.

'What have they done to us?' she lamented over her flaccid, dry breasts, the hanging skin of her belly, neck and forearms, marked by lash welts and the effects of the scabies.

'I'm still young,' she told herself. It had been less than four years since her gait caught men's eyes and her dancing aroused their passions. In vain, she tried to relive the sparks of vanity she'd felt at those impertinent looks when she passed by; or at the whooping, clapping and shouting of the audience after a voluptuous shake of her hips; at the quick breathing of some man when they danced together and she brushed her breasts against him. She looked at her peeling hands. She had no mirror.

'What is my face like?' she suddenly asked, uneasy, in the basement where they were packed, without addressing anyone in particular.

They were slow to answer.

'Look at mine and you'll know.'

The reply came from a gypsy from Ronda. Ana remembered her from Málaga: a beautiful woman with blue-black hair and bright, inquisitive, slanted eyes the same colour. She didn't want to see herself reflected in that woman's face, in her wrinkles, in her dark teeth and jutting cheekbones, in the purple circles that now ringed her dulled eyes.

'Swine!' she cursed.

Many of the gypsies who found themselves near her looked at each other, recognizing themselves in the other women, sharing in silence the pain over the beauty and youth that had been taken from them.

'Now look at me, Ana Vega!'

It was a wasted old woman, almost bald and toothless. Her name was Luisa and she belonged to the Vega family, like about twenty of the gypsies who had been arrested in the La Cartuja settlement. Ana looked at her. *Is that my fate?* she wondered. Was that what old Luisa was trying to tell her? She forced herself to smile at the old woman.

'Take a good look at me,' insisted the woman. 'What do you see?'

Ana opened her hands in a gesture of incomprehension, not knowing what to respond.

'Pride?' asked the old woman as a reply.

'What good does it do us?' Ana asked with a disdainful shrug.

'It makes you the most beautiful woman in Spain. Yes,' affirmed Luisa at the indifference with which Ana received the compliment. 'The King and Ensenada can separate us from our men so we stop having children. That is what they say they are trying to do, right? Finish off our race. They can beat us and starve us to death; they can even steal our beauty; but they can never take away our pride.'

The gypsies had stopped feeling sorry for themselves and held their heads up high as they listened to the old woman.

'Don't back down, Ana Vega. You have defended us. You have fought for the others and they lashed your back for it. That is your beauty! Don't look for any other, girl. Some day they will forget about us, the gypsies, as has always happened. I won't see it.'

The old woman was quiet for a moment and no one dared to disrupt her silence.

'When that day comes, they shouldn't have managed to break us, do you all understand that?' she added in a hoarse voice, running her sad gaze over the basement. 'Do it for me, for those left behind.'

That same night, Ana ran to see the children who were coming back from working the fields.

'You promised me—' the sentry started to complain.

'Frías, never trust a gypsy's word,' she interrupted him, as her eyes searched for Salvador among the others.

36

'WE'RE LEAVING.'
It was night; the bells had already sounded the call to prayer. Milagros gave a start and turned towards her husband, who had suddenly appeared in the window opening. When she heard his tone of voice, Bartola, who was whiling away the time sitting lazy and indolent in a chair, hastened to take refuge in the room where the little girl slept.

'Where are you planning on going at this time of night?' enquired Milagros.

'We have an appointment.'

'With who?'

'A party?'

'I didn't know . . . what party?'

'Stop asking questions and come with me!'

On the street a carriage pulled by two richly harnessed mules was waiting for them. Its door boasted an engraved coat of arms picked out in gold. The coachman was waiting in the driver's seat with two liveried footmen standing on the ground with lanterns in their hands.

'And the others?' asked Milagros, surprised.

'They are waiting for us there. Get in.' He pushed her from behind.

'Where . . . ?'

'Get in!'

Milagros sat on a hard seat upholstered in red silk. The mules began to trot as soon as Pedro closed the door.

'Who's throwing this party?' she insisted as Pedro settled into the seat in front of her.

He remained silent. Milagros searched in the gaze her husband fixed on her and a strong shiver blended in with the carriage's jolting; it was an inexpressive gaze, which didn't show hatred, bitterness, excitement or even ambition. A few days had passed since their argument about the Marquis of Torre Girón. Pedro had stopped sleeping at home and she fantasized even more frequently about the attentions of that nobleman who had treated her with such courtesy when the puppeteers were performing. Marina encouraged her, day after day.

'Aren't you going to answer me?'

Pedro didn't.

Milagros saw that they were crossing the Plaza Mayor; from then on the carriage turned again and again through the dark, silent network of narrow, tortuous streets that surrounded the royal palace under construction. The carriage stopped in front of a large house whose side door was lit up by one of the servants when she stepped out. What she could clearly see, as soon as she set her bare foot on the ground and looked up, was that there wasn't going to be any sort of party celebrated there: the place was deserted and in silence, the house gloomy with no lights in the windows.

She was struck by panic. 'What are you going to do to me?'

The question was drowned in a sob when Pedro pushed her inside and shoved her behind a servant with a candelabrum through hallways, passing rooms and going up stairs; only the men's footsteps and Milagros's muffled crying broke the silence that enveloped the mansion. Soon they stopped in front of a door; the candlelight reflected in shards on the hardwood panels.

The servant knocked delicately on the door and, without waiting for a response, opened it. Milagros could make out a luxurious bedroom. She waited for the servant to enter, but he moved aside to let her in. She tried to do the same so that Pedro would precede her, but he pushed her again.

At that moment the impassive look her husband had been giving her over the entire journey took on hair-raising meaning; Milagros understood the error she had made in following him: Pedro wasn't going to allow her to go to the arms of the marquis. He thought that one day or another she would become his lover and stop singing for other noblemen; then he would lose control of her . . . and her money. Foreseeing that, her husband had anticipated the events. He had sold her!

'No . . .' she managed to implore, trying to back away.

Pedro shoved her violently and closed the door.

'Don't be afraid.'

Milagros shifted her gaze to the immense canopied bed on the opposite side of the room where, on an armchair, beside a fireplace of delicate lines in pink marble, sat a large man, with a pearly face and straw-like hair, dressed in a simple white shirt, britches and stockings. She knew him from some parties. How could she forget those cheeks that seemed to shine? He was the Baron of San Glorio. The man placed a pinch of snuff on the back of one hand, sniffed, sneezed, wiped his nose with a handkerchief and invited her with a simple gesture to sit on the armchair in front of him.

Milagros didn't move. She was trembling. She turned her head towards the door.

'You can't do anything,' the nobleman warned her with a calmness that frightened her even more. 'You have a husband who is too greedy . . . and a spendthrift. A terrible combination.'

While the baron spoke, Milagros ran towards a picture window and threw open the heavy drapery.

'We're three storeys up,' he warned. 'Would you prefer to orphan your daughter? Come here with me,' he added.

Milagros, cornered, looked around the huge room.

'Come,' he insisted, 'let's chat for a while.'

She turned to inspect the door.

The baron sighed, got up in annoyance, headed over there and opened it wide: a couple of servants were posted behind it.

'Shall we sit down?' he suggested. 'I would like . . .'

'Pedro!' Milagros managed to shout between sobs. 'For your daughter!'

'Your husband is kissing his gold,' spat out the baron as he closed the door. 'That is the only thing he cares about and you know it. Wasn't he the one who brought you here?'

The little hope that Milagros had been able to maintain about Pedro vanished at the crudeness of the baron's words. Money! She knew it. Still, hearing it from the mouth of an aristocrat was like being stabbed with a knife.

'Barefoot Girl,' the baron interrupted her reflections, 'my servants would pounce on you like animals in heat, and your husband is nothing more than a vulgar ruffian who sells you like a whore. In this house, the only man who is going to treat you gallantly is me.' He let a moment pass. 'Sit down. Let's drink and chat before . . .'

The gob of spit Milagros launched landed on one of the baron's legs. The man looked at his stocking; when he lifted his face, his pearly cheeks were red with rage. Only when she had him in front of her, infuriated, snorting, did the gypsy girl realize his true size: he was more than a head taller than her and must have weighed twice what she did.

The baron slapped her.

'Disgusting pig, son of bitch, heartless bastard!' screamed Milagros as she tried to hit him with her fists and legs.

The baron let out a laugh and slapped her again with incredible strength. Milagros staggered and for a second thought she was going to lose consciousness. When she began to recover her balance, the man ripped off her shirt.

'You prefer to act like a whore?' he shouted. 'So be it! I paid a fortune for tonight!'

He beat her to the floor. Milagros's screams and her struggles against his removing her clothes were no use. She bit him. She could taste his blood; he, blinded, seemed not to notice her teeth. Stripped of her clothes, which were ripped to shreds, the baron dragged her to the bed, lifted her up and hurled her on to it. Then he started to take off his clothes with feigned calmness, placing himself between the bed and the picture windows, in case the young woman was capable of throwing herself out through them. For a second, that possibility crossed her mind, but in the end she sank her face into the fluffy bedspread and burst into sobs.

'Get out of here!'

The shout came from the bed, from which the aristocrat had watched her efforts to cover herself with her destroyed clothes, which were scattered across the room. 'Would you rather my servants dress you?' he had mocked when he had kicked her out of the bed. She showed similar indecisiveness now in front of the bedroom door. She was crying. Pedro would be outside, and she didn't know how to face him after what had happened. She was overcome with conflicting feelings: guilt, hatred, disgust . . .

The nobleman's shouts silenced her doubts. 'Didn't you hear me? Get out!'

The naked man made as if to get up. Milagros opened the door. Her husband leapt on her, pushing aside the two servants and giving her a smack that spun her head.

'Why?' she managed to ask.

The cameo! Pedro held up the jewel the Marquis of Torre Girón had given her.

'No . . .' she tried to explain.

'You are nothing more than a harlot,' he interrupted. 'And that's how you will live from now on.'

That night Pedro hit her again. And he insulted her; he called her a whore a thousand different ways, as if trying to convince himself that that was what she was. Milagros accepted the punishment: her husband's violence distracted her mind from the memories; the pain transported her far from the touch of the baron's hands on her body, his kisses and sighs, his panting as he penetrated her like an animal blinded by lust.

'Go on! Kill me!'

Unhinged, she didn't hear her daughter crying in the next room, nor the shouts of the neighbours beating on the walls and threatening to call the patrol. Pedro did notice the neighbours' threats: he'd lifted his hand to smack her again, but let it drop. He had to preserve Milagros's face; that was what the audience admired.

'Strumpet,' he muttered before walking towards the door that led to the staircase, 'I have no intention of finishing you off. You won't be so lucky,' he added, his back to her. 'I swear you will be dead in life!'

The next day Milagros sang and danced at the Príncipe, though the emotions that filled her were very different from the ones she usually felt when she stepped on to the stage. She searched for the Marquis of Torre Girón in his box; he wasn't there, but some flowers did arrive, which she smelled, heartbroken.

Unfortunately for her, the Baron of San Glorio was soon boasting about his conquest, while keeping the price quiet. Milagros found that out a few days later, when she discovered that the marquis was in the theatre. He would be able to help her! She had thought about it during her sleepless nights. She had to escape with her daughter, leave Pedro, get away from the Garcías! Otherwise, what would they do to her next?

'His excellency says,' Don José informed her, when he returned from delivering the message that she needed to see him, 'that only the King is above him.'

Milagros shook her head, not understanding that reply.

'Girl, you made a mistake,' the company's director explained. 'The grandees of Spain never take second-best, and you, by agreeing to lie with the baron, have become that.'

Agreeing! Milagros didn't hide her tears from any of the comic players who milled around the dressing room area and looked at her, some out of the corner of their eyes and others, Celeste among them, blatantly. Agreeing?

'It's a lie,' she sobbed. 'I have to tell the marquis . . .'

'Forget about it,' interrupted Don José. 'Whatever happened, the marquis won't see you. He doesn't owe you anything – or does he?'

Celeste, who was bustling about by the dressing rooms, waited for a response that Milagros didn't want to give her.

Just like in Seville, when years back she had gone to the palace of the Count of Fuentevieja to beg for her parents' freedom. Noblemen, they were all the same . . .

The marquis's refusal put an end to her hopes. She remembered her grandfather, her mother, Old María . . . They would have known what to do. Although her husband seemed to know as well, showing up that same afternoon in the house on Amor de Dios Street, when Milagros returned.

'What happened to your marquis?' he taunted in greeting. 'Did he fight with the other nobleman over you?'

Her husband's cynical smile infuriated her. 'I will denounce you.'

He, as if expecting that threat, as if he had expressly sought it out, smiled with a gleam of triumph in his eyes; Milagros knew his reply before he even spat it at her. She had thought of it herself.

'And what will you say? That an aristocrat paid to have you? Do you think any judge will believe such an accusation? The baron can have any woman he wants.'

'Not me, not ever!'

'A gypsy?' Pedro let out a hearty laugh. 'A comic player? You gypsies are vile and dishonest, libertines and adulterers. The King says so, and it is written in his laws. And if that weren't enough, you are also an actress. Everyone knows the shamelessness of the players, their love affairs are common gossip, like yours with the marquis . . .'

'It's not true!'

'What does it matter? Do you know what they say about you and that marquis in the taverns of Madrid? Do you want me to tell you? There is even a song about the two of you.' He paused and continued in a cold voice. 'Go ahead. Denounce me. They will condemn you for adultery without thinking twice. The baron will make sure it's for life . . . and I will back him up.'

So she continued going to the parties and singing and dancing at the Príncipe, dissatisfied, unhappy with herself, although to her surprise the audience rewarded her with applause and cheers, which she received with apathy. Then she went home, where Bartola watched over her, not even leaving her alone in her own bedroom. 'Orders from your husband,' replied the old woman rudely when she remonstrated with her. 'Talk to him about it.' And she followed her with María if she went out on the street. The little money she was allowed vanished, and the García woman, just like Reyes in Triana, interrupted her conversations in the market, on the street or in the sweetshop on León Street, where she liked to buy treats, and put an end to them.

'You don't look well, Milagros,' commented the sweetshop owner once as she served her a couple of butter biscuits from the bakery. 'Is something going on?'

Her stammering response was interrupted by Bartola.

'Mind your own business, nosy!' she exclaimed.

A month and a half had passed since the night the baron raped her, when Pedro grabbed her by the neck and practically dragged her out of the bedroom. Downstairs two *chisperos* were waiting, along with some of the guitarists that usually accompanied them to parties and a couple of women she didn't know. The women received her with indifference. Pedro had mentioned another party before pushing her down the stairs. Who were those women?

She soon found out. She was singing and dancing for a small group of five aristocrats; they were in another large stately home with its display of furniture, carpets and all types of ornaments. At one point they interrupted the performance with passionate applause from their armchairs. *The dance isn't over*, thought Milagros in surprise, *why are they applauding?* She turned towards the new women dancing behind her: one of them had bared her breasts. A cold sweat soaked her entire body. She began to stammer; then she stopped singing and dancing, but the others continued to the rhythm of the guitar and the handclapping. The other woman also opened her shirt and revealed her large wobbly breasts. Milagros moved away from them and searched for a corner.

'What could it matter to you at this point, whore?' said Pedro, stepping in her path and pushing her back towards the centre.

A couple of noblemen hooted and laughed.

'Now you, Barefoot Girl!' shouted another.

Milagros was still in front of them, the frenetic strumming of the guitar and the clapping thundering in her ears. She tried to think, but the racket overwhelmed her.

'Take off your clothes, gypsy!'

'Dance!'

'Sing!'

The other two women did so brazenly, both now completely

nude. They danced around Milagros, touching her, encouraging her to join their shamelessness. Repulsed, she tried to get away from their caresses and pushed a hand off her inner thigh. Other hands groped her breasts and buttocks, pulled on her skirt and shirt as they spun and spun to the noblemen's delight. Behind her, someone grabbed her by the elbows and forced her to be still. Milagros managed to see that it was one of the *chisperos*. Pedro, beside him, tore his wife's shirt with a single knife slash and pulled on the cloth, which slowly came off her body as he mocked her. Milagros struggled, trying in vain to bite the arms that imprisoned her, but her resistance only excited the noblemen's lust, who came closer to help Pedro when he set to on her skirt and the rest of her clothes until she was left completely naked. She tried to cover herself with her hands and arms, her face filled with tears. They didn't allow her to: they pushed and hit her as the two women continued spinning in a dizzying dance, lifting their arms above their heads to show their breasts, swinging their hips to exhibit their pubes. Milagros's dark skin stood out against the other women's paleness and excited the noblemen even more, who awkwardly joined the dancing. Then they grabbed the women, groped them and kissed them, Milagros being their favourite target.

Right there, on the carpets, the noblemen fornicated with the two women and then, once, twice, three times . . . they raped Milagros, her pleading and howls of pain lost amid the sound of the guitars and Pedro and his *chisperos'* cheering and clapping.

THE BROKEN VOICE

37

How many times had Pedro sold her over the course of almost an entire year? Five or perhaps seven more times? He was aware that the situation would erupt at any point; that the rich Madrileños would lose interest in the Barefoot Girl as soon as the rumours got around their circles and enjoying her was no longer considered a triumph to boast about, so he sold her to the highest bidder.

María. Milagros sought refuge in her daughter, who was all she had. She hugged the girl, holding back her sobs, whispering songs in her ear in a broken voice, stroking her hair until the little girl fell asleep, and rocking her for hours and hours.

She learned to receive her laughter with feigned joy and play animatedly with her, even though she could still – and had done ever since that day – feel the disgusting brush of a brute's dirty hand on her inner thigh, on her nipples . . . and on her lips. In the end, most of the noblemen took her violently, blinded, screaming, biting and scratching her. It was as if they were beating her. But when they tried to seduce her, sure that their caresses and their words of love could bend her will as if they were gods, she felt even worse. Arrogant swine! Those were the memories, and not the violent ones, that Milagros couldn't shake; only the little brown hand of María running clumsily over her face managed to diminish the bitter feelings. Milagros nibbled her little fingers while the girl, laughing, pressed the other hand over her eye. And she sought out time and again the touch of her daughter's soft skin, the only balm for the sadness and humiliation that overwhelmed her.

I swear you will be dead in life. The autumn was ending when Pedro's threat exploded in her head after returning from the Príncipe and calling to her daughter several times and not seeing her come running.

'Where's the girl?' she asked Bartola suspiciously.

'With her father,' answered the García woman.

'When will he bring her back?'

There was no answer.

At nightfall, Pedro showed up, alone.

'María shouldn't live with a whore,' he answered harshly. 'It sets a bad example for such a young girl.'

'What . . . ? What do you mean? I'm no whore; you know that. Where is María? Where have you taken her?'

'She is with a God-fearing family. She will be better off there.'

Pedro looked at his wife: she was close to desperation and seemed to be trying to break her fingers, twisting them over each other, digging her nails into her hands.

'I beg you, don't do this to me,' implored Milagros.

'Whore.'

She fell to her knees. 'Don't take my daughter from me,' she sobbed. 'Don't do it . . .'

Pedro watched her for a few seconds. 'It's what you deserve,' he said, interrupting her pleas before turning his back on her.

Milagros grabbed his leg and shouted, weeping. 'I will do whatever you want,' she promised, 'but don't take my daughter away from me.'

'Don't you already do whatever I want?'

Pedro fought to be rid of his wife but she clung to him. He grabbed her by the hair and pulled backward until, gradually, her neck twisted, Milagros let go of his leg. Then she ran after him; Pedro smacked her on the landing until she went back into the house.

The next morning, a couple of nasty *chisperos* from the Barquillo neighbourhood were waiting on Amor de Dios Street to escort the sedan chair that arrived to pick up Milagros and take her to the theatre. Then they loitered on Lobo and Príncipe Streets until the rehearsal was over. In the evening, during the performance, there were two others as grim as the first pair; Pedro had enough money to hire an army of *chisperos*.

Milagros tried to find María. She didn't know where she was, but if she could find Pedro and follow him . . . From what she understood, he spent a lot of time in Barquillo. One night she waited until she heard the rhythmic breathing of the old García woman in the next room and she went down the stairs feeling along the walls with her hands. Bartola opened one eye when the door creaked, but she just rolled over on her straw mattress. Milagros didn't get past the landing; in the dark she tripped and fell over a *chispero* who was dozing there.

'Your husband has ordered us to kill you if necessary,' the grim-faced young man threatened when they both managed to get up. 'Don't make things difficult for me.'

He pushed her into the apartment. Desperate, Milagros even offered her body to the *chispero* on watch in exchange for helping her to find her girl. The man cynically weighed one of her breasts.

'You don't understand,' he argued as he squeezed it between his fingers. 'There's not a woman in the world who could tempt me enough to take that risk. Your husband is very good with his knife; he's shown that on several occasions already.'

On another day she got down on her knees at Bartola's feet and begged her, her face streaked with tears. The only response she got was insults and recriminations.

'None of this would have happened if you hadn't given yourself to the marquis, whore.'

Prostituted against her will, deprived of her daughter, controlled everywhere she went, Milagros was transformed into an empty, defeated, silent, distant woman, her eyes sunken into deep sockets that not even Bartola could cover up when it was time for her to go to the theatre.

'Keep her beautiful and desirable, Aunt,' demanded Pedro when he found out that Milagros was refusing to eat. 'Force-feed her if necessary; dress her well; make her learn the songs. She has to go on dazzling the audience.'

But the old García woman was getting desperate. Every time Pedro sold his wife to one of those noblemen, she came back in worse shape. With bites, scratches, bruises ... and blood: blood on her nipples, in her vagina and even in her anus. Bartola didn't spend money on potions and remedies; she just washed and tried to hide the unhinged woman's wounds. She hated the idea of taking care of a Vega, but she didn't dare stand up to Pedro, and day after day Milagros returned to the Príncipe, where she ended up thinking she could find some refuge and comfort. She made an effort to provoke warm applause from her public, and the compliments that came up spontaneously from the stalls or from the men gathered on Lobo Street when she passed in her sedan chair.

However, when she looked up from the stage at the box seats and she saw the nobles' glittering jewels and adornments, she would get distracted, thinking how one of them had taken her by force and that perhaps at that very moment he was bragging about it. And her voice would give way until she remembered the audience in the pit and the balcony. Probably many didn't notice, but she did, and so did Celeste, and Marina, and the other players waiting their turn to go on stage and their chance to get revenge on that vain and arrogant gypsy girl who had excluded them from the parties held by the powerful noblemen.

One evening, as the affected voices of the other players recited verses written by Calderón for *Love After Death*, Milagros found a bottle with some wine still in it beside the dressing rooms. She looked around behind the set on which Celeste was playing the part of Doña Isabel. The presence of the prompter, who followed the leading lady along the side of the dressing rooms to remind her of her lines, didn't worry her: the man seemed pretty busy. However, it was the prompter's comings and goings behind the curtain, with lantern and libretto in hand, that kept her from seeing a musician who played the viola da gamba beside the curtain that hid the orchestra.

'She drank desperately ... right out of the bottle,' he later told anyone who would listen. 'She almost fell over backwards trying to get the last little drop.'

What did Milagros care who it was that, from that moment on, left a bottle of wine in the dressing room every day? Maybe it was

Don José, she thought, because she herself believed she sang better and moved more freely on the stage, unconcerned about the boxes and the men inside them. 'Forget,' she repeated to herself with every sip, until the image of her little one's face faded with the alcohol.

Bartola soon realized the state in which Milagros was returning from the Príncipe every night; so did the *chisperos*: two good bottles of undiluted wine meant they had to hold her up when she got out of the sedan chair.

'And what do you want us to do?' they defended themselves to Pedro. 'They give her wine in the theatre.'

The old García woman was fed up with that life, especially since the little girl was no longer there. Only Milagros's obligations in the Príncipe were keeping her in Madrid. She missed Triana. Pedro now only set foot in the house on Amor de Dios Street when he came looking for the money Milagros earned in the theatre.

'No one will pay for her any more!' the gypsy confessed one day as he put aside some coins for them to live on. 'She earns more singing and dancing than if I sold her body on the streets . . . and it's more comfortable for me,' he added with a cynical sneer.

'Pedro,' argued Bartola, 'we've been in Madrid for almost two years and this last one you've made a lot of money off the Vega girl. Why don't we go back to Triana?'

The gypsy brought a hand to his chin. 'And what do we do with her?' he asked.

'She's not going to last long,' she answered.

'Well, I'm going to take advantage of her for as long as she lasts,' he declared.

Bartola didn't have to think twice: she would make sure she didn't last much longer. One day, with the food money, she bought a flask of wine and left it in the kitchen. Another day she brought distilled liquor. And sweet wine. And she always had spiced liqueurs made of distilled alcohol or wine, sugar, cloves, ginger, cinnamon . . .

All in Milagros's reach, and Milagros drank it all.

'Fools!'

Milagros felt as if her brain was exploding from the brusque movement to turn her head towards the curtain that covered the orchestra section. *Why aren't they playing properly?* she wondered, waiting for her vision to clear so she could focus on that part of the stage. *Are they trying to mess me around?* she thought.

'Fools!' she shouted at the musicians again, clumsily flailing her hands and arms before turning back towards her public.

The music sounded again in the Coliseo del Príncipe at the gypsy's sign, but she missed her entrance and her thick, slurred voice came in late. 'That's not the piece! Or is it? You are trying to ruin me!' She turned to the curtain again as boos came up from the audience. Cowards! Why were they hiding?

'Start again,' she ordered.

She thought she heard the music and she tried to sing. Her voice caught in her dry, burning throat. The words were trapped between her tongue and her teeth, stuck in her viscous saliva, unable to get away and slip out. The shouts of the groundlings drilled her head. Where were they? She could see one, two at most; the third was already blending into the lights, the golden reflections of the boxes and the jewels of those who had raped her. They were laughing. Didn't they understand it was the orchestra's fault? She stammered out the first verse of the song in a hoarse and ragged voice, trying to hear the music. She listened carefully. Yes. It was playing. Dance; she had to dance. She lifted her arms awkwardly. They didn't respond. She was dizzy. She couldn't control her legs either. She fell on her knees before the audience. Something hit her, but she didn't care. The entire theatre howled at her. And the applause? She hung her head. She let her arms fall to her sides. *Where is my little girl? Why did they steal her away from me?* she sobbed.

'Bastards, all of you!' she muttered when another object, soft and sticky, hit her body. Red, like blood. Was she bleeding? She felt nothing. Perhaps she was dying; maybe dying was this simple. She wanted it. Dying to forget . . . She felt them grab her by the elbows and drag her off the stage.

'Milagros García,' she heard once she was in the dressing room, as the theatre magistrate seized her roughly by the chin and lifted her head, 'you are under arrest.'

38

CONSTABLE BLAS PÉREZ rested his truncheon on the filthy dirt floor of Hortaleza Street one sunny spring morning when he was hurrying towards the Santa Bárbara gate, at Madrid's northeast edge. He didn't see José, the constable from Barquillo, until he almost bumped into him emerging from the side street of San Marcos.

'What brings you so far from your district, Blas?'

He stifled an irritated sneer; he didn't want to get into a conversation, he needed to find Pedro García, quickly. The gypsy had ordered him to keep his ears open for news about Milagros.

'An order,' he answered, lifting a hand, as if he were annoyed to find himself there.

He was about to say goodbye and continue on his way when he was forced to stop. 'Damn my luck!' he muttered.

In front of him, the sound of dolzainas and a drumroll from the Church of Saint Mary Magdalene announced the arrival of a priest wearing a black hat and carrying a simple bag containing the viaticum for someone dying. Many of the people on the street silently joined the procession behind the priest; those who didn't removed their hats, knelt in the dirt and crossed themselves as he passed. A carriage pulled by two mules stopped where Blas was kneeling. Three well-dressed gentlemen got out and offered the carriage to the priest, who got in. The gentlemen joined the procession and followed the Holy Sacrament on foot as soon as an altar boy indicated to the coachman where the dying person was and he drove the mules on.

Blas remained on his knees as the procession passed him by.

'Rodilla's wife,' murmured the other constable, who had come to kneel beside him. 'The accountant of the congregation of Our Lady of Hope – do you know him? He's very upset.'

Blas shook his head; his thoughts were elsewhere.

'Sure you do,' insisted José, 'one of the brothers of the mortal sin patrol.'

'Ah!' was all Blas said, nodding.

He must know him; more than one night he had run into those brothers of the congregation who went through the streets of Madrid asking for alms and calling the licentious citizens to order, trying to interrupt their indecent carnal relations with their chanting and their prayers, warning them that they were committing a grave sin and that if death called for them in that moment . . .

Surely he knew Rodilla, like many of those who walked behind the priest and would squeeze into the sick woman's room as he attended to her. *The death rites*, he thought. Even the King gave up his carriage to the viaticum and walked behind it! What Blas wasn't sure about was whether His Majesty had ever gone into the dying person's bedroom after paying homage to the Holy Sacrament. He, Blas, because of his position, had done it on several occasions: the priests extracted protestations of faith and acts of contrition from the sick person to help him die well even at the cost of his precarious health: penitential psalms; ejaculatory prayers; litanies; praying to the saints . . . A deployment of prayers for each of the seconds of agony that the mourners accompanied with their compassion, until some indication – perhaps the frightened eyes of someone seeing death draw near, maybe an incomprehensible babbling, foaming at the mouth or uncontrollable convulsions – signalled the presence of the devil. Then the priest sprinkled the bed and the entire room with holy water and, to the horror of those who witnessed it, lifted the Holy Sacrament over his head and challenged Satan.

'Do you need my help with your order?' the constable from Barquillo interrupted his thoughts.

They both got up and wiped the dirt off their stockings. Blas didn't need help. He didn't even want the other constable to know where he was headed.

'I appreciate it, José, but it's not necessary. How are things going?' he asked only so he wouldn't seem rude.

The other man sighed and shrugged. 'You can imagine—' he began to say.

'The procession is getting away from you,' interrupted Blas. 'I don't mean to keep you.'

José shifted his gaze to the backs heading down Hortaleza Street. He sighed. 'She was a pious woman, the accountant's wife.'

'I'm sure she was.'

'Everyone's time has to come.'

Blas didn't want to get into that discussion and he kept quiet.

'Well,' added José after clicking his tongue, 'I'll see you soon.'

'Whenever you'd like,' agreed the other as José prepared to follow the viaticum.

Blas waited a moment and then set off again, passing in front of the Saint Mary Magdalene Home for Reformed Prostitutes: the viaticum had left from its church and the mortal sin patrol would also emerge from there. He slowed down and even tapped his truncheon against the ground, slightly worried. The death that comes to everyone – sin, the devil that the priests were trying to expel – made him doubt what he was going to do. He could change his mind. He smiled at the idea of having regrets right in front of the place where fifty loose-living women, who'd been touched by the hand of God, had voluntarily decided to be confined under the auspices of Mary Magdalene, living a cloistered life of prayer and self-discipline and never again leaving the home unless it was to embrace religion or marry one of those honest men that the Brothers of Hope procured for them.

The repentant women had to pay one hundred *reales de vellón* and four pounds of wax to enter the Mary Magdalene Home and be locked up for life! One had to pay to repent. He didn't even have that much money. So he couldn't repent, he concluded, finding a certain satisfaction in the argument: the poor couldn't do it. Besides, he didn't want to renounce the money he was hoping to make that day.

He continued on, turned to the right at Panaderos Street and headed towards Regueros Street.

'Hail Mary,' he called as he opened the door to a small single-storey house, whitewashed on the outside, neat and clean on the inside, with a vegetable patch out at the back, crammed among nine similar dwellings.

'Full of Grace . . .' was heard from inside. 'Ah! It's you.' A pretty young gypsy woman came out of an inner room. A girl's head peeked out from behind her.

'Pedro?' was all the constable asked.

The young woman had gone back into the room but not the girl, who remained still, with her large eyes fixed on Blas.

'At the tavern,' shouted the gypsy woman from the room she was rummaging around in, 'where else?'

The constable winked at the little girl, whose expression didn't change at all.

'Thank you,' he answered with a disappointed look.

The girl no longer smiled the way she used to, when she lived with her mother, on Amor de Dios Street. Blas tried again with the same results. He frowned, shook his head and left.

Regueros Street was a single block that was just a few paces from the tavern on the corner of San José and Reyes Alta, beside a patch of open ground bordering Madrid's wall; there rose the monastery of Santa Bárbara with its discalced Mercedarians and the Carmelite convent of Santa Teresa. Beside them, Queen Barbara of Portugal, wife of Ferdinand VI, often ill and a book lover, had ordered a new convent built, devoted to teaching noble girls under the auspices of Saint Francis de Sales, in 1748. It was said that the Queen had planned the part of the building that overlooked the gardens as a private residence to escape her husband's stepmother, Elisabeth Farnese, and as a place to retire to if the King died before her, since they had no issue and the crown would pass to Charles, Elisabeth's son, then King of Naples. In 1750 construction began; it was to be the largest and most sumptuous convent ever built in Madrid: alongside the new church devoted to Saint Barbara was erected a colossal palace with French and Italian influences using the finest materials. The compound would be surrounded by gardens and vegetable plots that would extend alongside the wall, from the Recoletos

Meadow and Gate, almost all the way to the Santa Bárbara Gate.

That spring of 1754, Blas observed the construction, which was already quite far advanced. The Queen was sparing no expense. It was rumoured to have cost more than eighty million reals in total, although there were also those who lamented (Blas among them) that it was spent on the Queen's glory and tranquillity instead of on a great cathedral. There were nearly 140 churches that celebrated mass daily, thirty-eight monasteries and almost as many convents, plus hospitals and schools packed into the walls that surrounded Madrid . . . Yet despite all that religious magnificence, the largest and most important city in the kingdom had no cathedral.

Blas cleared his way into the tavern with blows of his truncheon until he found Pedro, sitting at a table and drinking wine with various *chisperos* who were working as blacksmiths on that vast construction.

The gypsy, always vigilant, noticed the constable's presence as people moved to avoid his truncheon. Something important must be happening for Blas to show up there, so far from his district. They both stepped away from the crowd as soon as they were able to.

'She's been released,' whispered the constable.

Pedro maintained his gaze on his companion's face; his lips were pursed, his teeth were grinding.

'Is she still under contract at the Príncipe?' he asked after a few moments.

'No.'

'That's just going to cause me problems,' he commented to himself. 'She needs to be finished off.'

Blas had been sure that would be the gypsy's reaction. Almost two years by his side were more than enough for him to know his character. Violent rows, revenge to the point of murder. He had even sold his own wife!

'Are you sure . . . ?' He hesitated.

'If they let her go it's to avoid a scandal that could taint some grandees. Do you think that anyone will care what happens to a drunken whore?'

*

Everything had happened the way Pedro had imagined: they dragged Milagros off the stage at the Príncipe after the theatre magistrate ordered her arrest. The constables brought her straight to the royal jail, where she slept it off. The next morning, excited, nervous, restless from the lack of alcohol but sober, Milagros entered the court of law.

'Your highness should ask the Baron of San Glorio,' she challenged the magistrate who was presiding over her trial for scandalous behaviour and a long string of other crimes, after the process had begun by asking her name.

'Why should I do that?' The magistrate immediately regretted that spontaneous question, but he'd been confused by the gypsy woman's cheekiness.

'Because he raped me,' she answered. 'He must know my name. He paid a lot of money for it. Ask him.'

'Don't be impertinent! We have nothing to ask the baron.'

'Then ask the Count of Medin—'

'Silence!'

'Or the Count of Nava—'

'Sentry! Make her shut up!'

'They all forced themselves on me!' Milagros managed to shriek before the sentry and his truncheon reached her.

The man covered her mouth. Milagros bit his hand, hard.

'Do you want me to tell you how many more of your aristocrats have raped me?' she spat when the sentry pulled his hand away in pain.

The gypsy woman's last question floated over the courtroom. All three magistrates looked at her. The prosecutor, the notary and the lawyer for the poor waited for their response.

'No,' replied the president. 'We don't want you to tell us. Session adjourned!' he then decided. 'Take her to the dungeons.'

Milagros spent several days in the royal jail, enough for the court magistrates to consult with the councillors to the King and eminent noblemen. Although not all were in agreement, most rejected the idea that such illustrious surnames were mixed up in such a disagreeable matter. Finally, someone maintained that the matter tainted the King himself, because one of his councillors was a relative of a nobleman who'd been implicated, so they ordered the matter buried and Milagros was set free.

Despite the magistrates demanding discretion and the notary destroying the records of the trial proceedings and all references to her arrest, the matter got out and reached many ears, including those of Constable Blas.

'This very night,' ordered Pedro as they walked back to the house on Regueros Street. 'We will do it this very night.'

We will do it? That statement surprised the constable. He was about to object, but kept silent. He remembered the gypsy's promise the day he had arrived in Madrid: women. He had enjoyed some in the nocturnal adventures he'd shared with Pedro; however, he was less interested in those idle pursuits than in the money he got out of the arrangement. Despite that . . . would he take part in a murder? Was the gypsy right about no one caring?

With those thoughts running through his head, he went into the house that Pedro shared with his new companion.

'Honoria!' he shouted in greeting. 'We're here for lunch!'

They ate stew and, for dessert, chestnut compote and quince jelly that the gypsy woman had made. Blas watched how Honoria tried to control little María's sweet tooth. She failed; her nervousness grew as the girl disobeyed. As hard as she tried, thought the constable, watching María push away the young gypsy woman's hands with her own, she couldn't replace her mother. Although officially she was her mother! Pedro had got false papers which listed Honoria as the girl's mother. He had showed them to the constable: 'Pedro García and Honoria Castro. Married with one daughter.'

'Are you insane?' Blas had asked him when he saw them.

The gypsy waved off his question.

'And what if someone finds out? People know Honoria; they know she isn't married to you. Anyone could . . .'

'Denounce me?'

'Yes.'

'They wouldn't dare.'

'Even so . . .'

'Blas. We are gypsies. A *payo* will never understand. Life is a moment: this one.'

That was the end of the conversation, although Blas tried to work out why the gypsy behaved as he did. He was unable to, just as Pedro had said, but he did manage to understand why the gypsy people always had a sparkle in their eyes: they bet it all on every hand.

After lunch, Pedro satisfied the constable's expectations of his generosity and promised him more after the 'job' was done.

'Remember,' he said in parting, 'tonight, after the chiming of the bells.'

They found Milagros prostrate and dejected in a corner of her room, with her gaze fixed on a single point on the ceiling and an empty bottle of liquor by her side.

'Aunt,' announced Pedro to Bartola, 'we're going back to Triana; gather your things and wait for me downstairs.'

Bartola García motioned towards Milagros with her chin. 'What about her?'

Pedro let out a guffaw. 'Don't worry, no one will miss her.'

His laughter broke the long silence that had stretched out between the two women all day, since Milagros had compulsively polished off the liquor.

Milagros reacted and looked at them with bloodshot eyes. She stammered something. No one understood what she was saying.

'Shut up, you drunken whore!' spat Pedro.

She waved a hand clumsily through the air and tried to get up. Pedro ignored her; he waited impatiently for Bartola to gather her things and leave.

'Come on, come on, come on,' he urged.

The constable, at a distance, standing almost in the doorway, watched how Milagros tried to use the walls to help her stand up, but, weak, fell again. He shook his head as he watched her try once more. She leaned precariously on the wall, struggling to stay on her feet, as Blas tried to remember if he had ever witnessed a young woman's murder. He searched through his memories of the city, where a motley horde of nobles, rich men, beggars and criminals – arrogant people quick to fight – mingled. As a constable he was familiar with all sorts of crimes and wickedness, but he had never witnessed the murder in cold blood of a beautiful young woman. His stomach shrank when he moved aside to let Bartola out, with a straw mattress beneath her arm and bundles of clothes and goods in her hands. The old woman didn't say a word; she didn't even look back. The few seconds it took her to drag her feet out of the room multiplied in the constable's senses. Then he turned and blanched as Pedro reacted immediately, going over to Milagros and lifting her up mercilessly by the hair.

'Look at her!' he said, holding her upright. 'The biggest whore in Madrid!'

Blas couldn't take his eyes off the woman: beaten, helpless, lovely in spite of her filth and raggedness. If Pedro let go of her hair she would be unable to stand. *Is it really necessary to finish her off?* he wondered.

'I promised you women,' he was surprised to hear the gypsy say then, reminding him of their first conversation. 'Here's one: the great Barefoot Girl!'

The constable managed to shake his head. Pedro didn't see him, he was too busy ripping off Milagros's shirt.

'Fuck her!' he shouted when he got it off, pulling Milagros's head back to show off her firm breasts, which were surprisingly magnificent.

Blas was disgusted. 'No,' he objected. 'Stop this. Kill her if you want to, but don't keep up this . . . this . . .'

He couldn't find the word and he just pointed to her breasts. Pedro looked daggers at him.

'I'm not going to take part in such vileness,' Blas added in response to the gypsy's challenge. 'Finish it, or you're on your own.'

'I pay you well,' Pedro retorted.

Not enough, Blas thought to himself. And if the gypsy really was going back to Triana, there would be no more money. He looked at Milagros, trying to see some pleading in her eyes. He couldn't even find that. She seemed resigned to her fate.

'Up yours, gypsy!'

Blas turned and went down the stairs, expecting to hear Milagros's death throes and feeling sorry for her. But he didn't hear anything.

With his free hand, Pedro García pulled his knife from his belt and opened it. 'Whore,' muttered the gypsy as soon as the constable's footsteps disappeared in the distance.

He slid the blade from Milagros's neck to her bare breasts.

'I have to kill you,' he continued, 'just like I killed the healer. The old lady fought more than you will, surely. Braggarts . . . The Vegas are nothing more than conceited braggarts. I'm going to kill you. What would happen if you showed up in Triana? Honoria would be furious with me, you know?'

Milagros seemed to react to the touch of the knife tip on her nipples. The gypsy smiled cynically.

'You like that?' He played with the tip of the knife, feeling his own excitement grow as her nipple hardened.

He cut her skirt and continued slipping his knife along her belly and pubis until she sighed and a fetid cloud of liquor smell reached his face.

'You're putrid. You smell worse than an animal. I hope you meet up with all the Vegas in hell.' He raised his knife to her neck, now ready to slit her jugular.

'Halt!' suddenly echoed through the room.

39

'SHE'S DRUNK!'
'She can't stand up.'
'What a disgrace!'

The comments of the ladies who accompanied him in one of the side boxes at the Coliseo del Príncipe joined the booing and shouting from the groundlings and the women's balcony. The orchestra had attempted the *tonadilla* several times without Milagros managing to sing along to the music. The first two times she gestured furiously at the side curtain behind which were the musicians, blaming them in clumsy gestures; the other times, as the words stuck on her thick tongue and her arms and legs refused to follow her orders, Milagros's rage transformed into dismay.

Fray Joaquín, his stomach churning and his throat clenched, tried to hide his trembling hands from the ladies and their escorts as he looked at Milagros. There was no longer any music on the stage that the day before had seemed barely large enough to contain her dancing, smiles and brazen remarks, but which now seemed vast with her kneeling in the middle, defeated and downcast. Someone threw a rotten vegetable at her right arm. The groundlings came prepared. Rumours had gone around Madrid in the last few days about the state of the Barefoot Girl: her recent performances had showed signs of her deterioration. Some said she was sick; many others recognized the effects of alcohol on her cracked voice and disjointed movements.

Milagros didn't even react to the rotten vegetable, or when a tomato burst on to her shirt and set off laughter throughout the theatre. Above the stalls, leaning on the box's railing, Fray Joaquín shifted his gaze to find who had thrown the tomato.

'Stupid!' he muttered.

'Did you say something, Reverend?'

The friar ignored the question from the lady sitting beside him. From the stalls they were now throwing all sorts of rotten fruits and vegetables, and the people were tearing off the green ribbons that had adorned their hats and dresses in a sign of admiration for the Barefoot Girl. The magistrate assigned to the theatre sent two constables to take Milagros offstage. She seemed resigned to the punishment. 'Why doesn't she leave?' the priest asked himself.

'Go, girl!' exploded Fray Joaquín.

'Girl?' asked the lady, surprised.

'Ma'am,' he answered without thinking, his attention focused onstage, 'we are all children. Wasn't it Jesus Christ who declared that he who was not like a little child would not enter the kingdom of heaven?'

The woman was about to question the priest's words but instead she opened up a lovely mother-of-pearl fan and waved it in front of her face. Meanwhile, the two constables dragged Milagros offstage by her elbows amid a rain of fruit and vegetables. As soon as the gypsy disappeared behind the curtain and the shouts from the stalls and the balcony transformed into a murmur of indignant conversations, Celeste appeared on the stage while three men continued cleaning up. Victory gleamed in her eyes.

'The Marquis of Rafal,' commented one of the noblemen who was standing at the back of the box, referring to the Chief Magistrate of Madrid, 'should never have replaced the great Celeste.'

'And certainly not with a gypsy who sells her body for two reals!' exclaimed the other.

Fray Joaquín gave a start when Celeste began to sing and the two noblemen joined in with the audience's warm applause.

'Didn't you know, Reverend?' The lady with the fan spoke with her face hidden behind it, leaning back slightly in her chair, 'If your reverence would honour us more often with your presence at our gatherings . . .'

I would have heard, he finished to himself, in silence, the sentence she left hanging in the air.

'Personally,' said the woman, 'I can't imagine what Our Lord Jesus Christ would say about that girl.' She stretched out the last two words in disdain. Then, bringing her chair closer to the clergyman's and using the fan as cover for her brazenness, she began to list the Barefoot Girl's affairs, multiplied in the whispers of such gatherings.

Amid vivacious Celeste's singing and the applause and shouts of the fickle audience, again devoted to the leading lady, Fray Joaquín interrupted the woman, who turned towards him and unconsciously began to fan her face. She knew that he was sensitive – all his acquaintances praised him for that quality – although she had never suspected that the news of a simple gypsy girl's dalliances could turn him almost as pale as a corpse.

Fray Joaquín was thinking of Milagros: beautiful, cheerful, charming, clever, joyful . . . clean . . . virginal! The memories came flooding back to stab his stomach and paralyse the flow of his blood. She filled his nocturnal fantasies and made him feel that guilt he had so often tried to atone for with prayer and punishments: her rejection, after he suggested she run off with him, had driven him to the roads, doubting that there was a sacrifice capable of purifying him in God's eyes. Since then, that dark face had followed him wherever he went, overwhelmingly beautiful: encouraging him, smiling at him in moments of adversity. But now, what had happened to that strength of spirit? She was a drunk. He had seen that. And a prostitute, from what he had heard . . .

Before the evening when Milagros collapsed onstage at the Coliseo del Príncipe, her image came to Fray Joaquín's mind every night as he walked with all his senses alert along the dangerous streets of Madrid towards his house. When that happened, the memories of Milagros took hold of him. Fray Joaquín lived in an apartment on a tiny block with only three buildings, all narrow and so long that they stretched from the façade overlooking the silversmiths on Mayor Street to the

San Miguel Plaza at the back. Francisca, the old servant who took care of him, got up sleepily to help him despite knowing how he would respond: 'May God reward you, Francisca, but you can go back to bed.' Still, the woman insisted every single night, eternally grateful for having a roof over her head, food and even the meagre salary that the friar gave her for the efforts she put into her limited tasks. Francisca had never been a servant before. Widowed, with three ingrate children who had abandoned her in her old age, she had devoted her life to washing clothes in the Manzanares River. 'I washed so much,' she had bragged to Fray Joaquín, 'that I needed a porter to help me deliver the washing to their owners.' But as happened to all those women who, day after day, year after year, went into the river with their washboards to clean other people's dirt – whether it was wintry cold and the water frozen, or in the heat of the summer – her body had paid a high price. She had swollen, stiff hands, atrophied muscles, and permanently aching bones. And Fray Joaquín would run to pick up the saucepan that had slid from her awkward hands to avoid the torment it gave her to kneel down. The priest had rescued her from the streets when the coin he gave her as alms slipped through the washerwoman's unbending fingers, clinked on a stone and rolled far away. They had looked at each other: the old woman, unable to chase the coin; Fray Joaquín glimpsing death in her dull eyes.

After ordering her back to bed, the friar compared the slow movements that would take Francisca to her straw mattress, at the feet of the marvellous statue of the Immaculate Conception, with the vitality and happiness of the movements that Milagros had offered her public. He was watching from one of the boxes, like the noble and rich women did almost every day with their suitors and escorts. Marvellous! Prodigious! Enchanting! Such was the praise that echoed in his ears when he first set foot in the Coliseo del Príncipe, soon after he'd arrived in Madrid from Toledo. The Barefoot Girl. And that first day he jumped in his seat.

'Is something wrong, Father?' they asked him.

Something? It was Milagros! Fray Joaquín was almost on his feet. He stammered out something unintelligible.

'Are you feeling poorly?'

Why am I standing up, he asked himself. He apologized to his pupil, took his seat again and listened to Milagros sing, rapt, as he discreetly fought to stop the tears that filled his eyes.

Since his arrival in Madrid, the Coliseo del Príncipe and Milagros's performances had become a site of pilgrimage for Fray Joaquín. If some evening, Dorotea – the young woman from Toledo whom, at her father's insistence, the priest had accompanied to the capital after she married the widower Marquis of Caja – decided not to attend, Fray Joaquín excused himself and paid, out of his own pocket, for a ticket in the pit or the upper gallery with the other religious men. The first time he felt lost at the eight doors that led to the different self-contained areas – the pit, the upper gallery, the boxes, the door just for women that led to their balcony – but soon he had won the regard of the ticket sellers and the honeyed-wine vendors beneath the women's balcony. The friar sat through the whole show and many times, while watching a bad play with even worse acting, he struggled not to join in the surge of people mocking the comedy's final act and leaving the theatre after the Barefoot Girl's performance. He didn't want to be known as yet one more of those who just went for the *sainetes* or intermissions. When it ended, he applauded the author and the players even though he only had the gypsy girl's voice in mind, her measured dances that – without striving to – aroused the desire and fantasies of the public with their voluptuousness. He trembled at the memory of her insolent remarks towards the audience, to the groundlings among whom he hid. And he shrank back when Milagros ran her gaze over them, afraid she would recognize him.

'What do you say about the unjust Chief Magistrate?' she asked, interrupting her song in which a poor peasant was jailed by the King's magistrate.

The booing and whistles, with arms raised, allowed the priest to stand up straight again in the confusion.

'Louder, louder! I can't hear you!' shouted Milagros, encouraging them with her hands before launching herself into the next song, competing with the crowd's shouts.

And she won. Her voice lifted above the fray and Fray Joaquín felt himself grow faint as his throat clenched. One evening, perhaps after too much wine at the meal with the Marquis and his wife, the friar got a bit closer to the stage and didn't move when Milagros looked out over the theatre's seats. His knees shook and he didn't have time to turn his head when she ran her gaze over the groundlings who cheered her on, right where he was standing. Maybe he wanted her to discover him. But she didn't see him and Fray Joaquín surprised himself by relaxing as he released the air he'd been holding in his lungs. He didn't know why he'd done it, but that day he felt her near, as if he could even smell her.

After that visit to the theatre, before dinner and the gathering he would attend with Dorotea, Fray Joaquín locked himself in the clock room of the marquis's home, overwhelmed by conflicting emotions. He scolded himself for the fact that the room the marquis used to display his power and his good taste, confirmed by all who admired his collection, and where the priest usually sought refuge, soothed him more than prayer or reading holy books. He stopped in front of a grandfather clock as tall as he was, in ebony adorned with engraved gilded bronze. The Englishman John Ellicott had made it; he had signed its face, which depicted a lunar calendar and a celestial globe.

Milagros was happy, he had to admit as the second hand ticked. She was a success! *Why should I intrude on her life?* he asked himself later, before an elaborate table clock with bucolic figures by Droz, a Swiss watchmaker according to what the marquis had told him. How did they make such marvels? More than a dozen were displayed in the room. Musical clocks. Would Milagros like them? Some even had a dozen little bells . . . How would her voice sound beside them? Pendulum clocks, huge with a mechanism of gears and perpetual movement; there was one that even did arithmetic calculations. Automatons that played the flute: he loved to listen to the shepherd's flute or the barking dog . . .

Milagros had refused him once already. What did she say then? *I'm sorry . . . It just could never be.* Yes, those had been her words before she fled towards the Andévalo. *Why do you insist, you idiot?* he said to himself. If in that moment of desperation, at the time of the big round-up, frightened at having to flee Triana, with her parents arrested and her grandfather missing, Milagros had been unable to find a scrap of affection for him inside her, what could he expect now, when she was a star and adored by all of Madrid?

Even so, he never stopped going to the theatre, not even when, months after his arrival, he had to leave the house of the marquis and the woman who had been his pupil and move to the narrow, long house on Mayor Street that he shared with Francisca. During that time, Dorotea had gradually become caught up in the capital city's seductive habits, so different from those in Toledo, and she stopped needing the friar, who up until that point had been her teacher, confidant and friend. Don Ignacio, the marquis, father of three children from his previous marriage, was a man as rich as he was carefree.

'It pains me to say this, Don Ignacio,' explained Fray Joaquín – both men were seated in the clock room one morning, having coffee and sweets – 'but I consider it my duty to warn you that your wife is on a worrisome path.'

'Something scandalous?' queried the marquis, so shocked that he almost spilled coffee on to his waistcoat.

'No, no. Well . . . I don't know. I guess not, but in the gatherings . . . she is always whispering and laughing with someone or another. I know that they are courting her; she is young, beautiful, refined. Doña Dorotea isn't like the other women . . .'

'Why not?'

It was the friar's turn to be taken aback. 'You allow her to be courted?'

The marquis sighed. 'Who doesn't, Father? Men in our position can't oppose it, no matter how uncomfortable it makes us. It would be . . . it would be uncivilized, impolite.'

'But . . .'

The marquis elegantly lifted one of his hands, asking for silence. 'I know it's not church doctrine, Father, but in these times marriage is no longer the sacred institution it was for our ancestors. Marriage, at least for the lucky such as ourselves, is based on courtesy, respect, politeness, sensitivity . . . They are nothing more than mere marriages of inclination.'

'It's not as though there were that many marriages of love before,' the friar tried to disprove him.

'That's true,' the marquis was quick to admit. 'But we no longer have terrified women locked up at home by their husbands. Today even destitute women, however humble they may be, want to show themselves off to men; perhaps they don't have the sensitivity and culture of ladies, but that doesn't stop them from displaying themselves on the streets, in theatres and at parties. True, they don't have as many emotional needs either, their lives are too precarious for such luxuries, but no mother exists who doesn't want to teach her daughter, alongside the Christian virtues, to sing and dance, as well as the silent art of body language that they know full well dazzles men with its "will-she-won't-she".'

Fray Joaquín cleared his throat, about to answer, but the marquis continued talking.

'Think of Doña Dorotea. You taught her Latin in her father's house; she knows how to read and she does. She is cultured, refined, sensitive; she knows how to please a man.' Don Ignacio picked up a piece of sponge cake and bit into it. 'What do you think most pleases my wife about the courting game?' he then asked. The friar shook his head. 'I'll tell you: it is the first time in her life that she has the chance to choose. Her marriage was imposed upon her, like everything else since the moment she was born, but now she will choose her courtier and after a while she will leave him for another, and flirt with a third to arouse the first, or the second . . .'

'And if . . . ?' Fray Joaquín stuttered. 'If it leads to adultery?' He immediately regretted the question. 'Doña Dorotea is trustworthy and honest,' he hastened to add, swatting the air as if he had said something ridiculous. 'However, the flesh is weak, and women's flesh . . . even more so.'

Yet the nobleman did not show the rage one might expect of someone who has just had his wife's virtue questioned. Don Ignacio sipped coffee and for a few moments his gaze lingered on those clocks he so admired. He finished inspecting them with a grimace.

'They say it's sexless love, Father, and most courtships are. Don't think that we haven't discussed it extensively between us, but who knows what goes on inside a woman's bedroom? Publicly it is merely gallantry, simple flirting. And that is what is important: what others see.'

So, freed of the hindrance of that friar she'd brought from Toledo as a tutor, the marchioness learned to use her fan to communicate in the secret language that everyone employed to send messages to the dandies: touching it, opening it, fanning herself quickly or languidly, letting it drop to the floor, closing it violently . . . Each action meant something. She was also soon using beauty marks on her face to show how she felt inside: if she painted one on her left temple it meant she already had a suitor, if it was on her right it showed she was tired of him and accepting others; next to her eyes, lips or nose were all different ways to show her mood.

The rift between Fray Joaquín and that young woman from Toledo to whom he had taught Latin and the classics had grown as Dorotea learned the game of courtship. In the mornings, not even her husband could go into his wife's bedroom. 'The marchioness is with her hairdresser,' replied the maid like a warden, in front of the locked bedroom door. Fray Joaquín saw the current suitor enter, a young man, clean shaven and powdered, smelling of lavender, jasmine or violet, sometimes wearing a wig, other times with his hair moulded with tallow and lard by a hairdresser, but always decked out with a thousand details: cravat, watch, eyeglasses, cane, rapier at his waist, lace, embroidery and even bows on colourful silk suits with golden buttons. The marquis, the friar also noticed, did his best not to run into the suitor who feigned dignity as he snorted snuff while waiting for the butler to be called to escort him to the bedchamber. *What do they do inside there?* wondered Fray Joaquín. Dorotea would still be in bed, in her bedclothes. What would they talk about for the hours it took the marchioness to emerge from her chambers? Why had he worked so hard to teach his pupil the most modern doctrines regarding the feminine condition? All those affected dandies that pursued ladies were as vainglorious as they were uncultured, something he had seen in the gatherings; he'd been shocked at the stupidity he heard.

'Madam,' one of them boasted, 'Horace was too dogmatic.'

'Without Homer, what would Virgil have been?' said another.

Names and quotes memorized just to impress: Periander, Anacharsis, Theophrastus, Epicurus, Aristippus, were dropped here and there in the ladies' luxurious salons. And Dorotea smiled, mouth agape! They all haughtily disdained the slightest criticisms and mocked those that were presented as authoritative opinions, until, by using such tricks, some managed to gain a reputation as a sage in the eyes of a feminine audience, utterly taken in by their braggadocio.

Ignorance. Hypocrisy. Frivolity. Vanity. Fray Joaquín exploded when he listened to a dandy, who was battling to win Dorotea's favour, begging her to give him a bottle containing the water she had washed herself with in order to use it as medicine for a sick maid. The blood left the friar's face and gathered in his stomach, all of it, a flood, leaving him livid, watching how the young woman with whom he'd declined Latin and enjoyed reading Father Feijoo was thrilled to comply with the ridiculous request, supported by some of the ladies who applauded the initiative and others who insisted, for the good of that poor ill maid, that she agree to the cure.

Fray Joaquín was familiar with the controversial modern theories around treatments based on water. Their proponents were called 'water doctors'. Not even Feijoo had been able to call them into question, but that was a long way from giving a sick girl a lady's dirty bath water, no matter how young, beautiful and aristocratic she was.

'I can no longer continue living in this house.'

Don Ignacio curved his lips in something similar to a smile. *Sad, melancholy?* wondered Fray Joaquín.

'I understand,' he said, comprehending perfectly the reason that brought the clergyman to that decision. 'It has truly been a pleasure to have you here and converse with you.'

'You have been really generous, Don Ignacio. As for your chapel—'

'Continue with it,' interrupted the marquis. 'I would have to find another priest and that would be a bother,' he added, screwing up his face. 'And otherwise you wouldn't be able to enjoy my clocks, and you know that satisfies my vanity.'

The marquis smiled; the friar thought he was sincere. 'I consider you a good person, Father. I'm convinced that the marchioness will not object.'

Dorotea didn't. In fact, she bade him farewell coldly and hurriedly – her friends were waiting, she excused herself, leaving him unable to say his piece – so Fray Joaquín continued looking after the marquis's private chapel, generously compensated for the few masses he said for the souls of the nobleman's ancestors, which were only attended by a few servants.

Where was Milagros? In just one evening, Fray Joaquín saw all his principles come crashing down. Despite his desires, he had managed to remain on the margins: idolizing Milagros. However, after witnessing her fall, he was overcome with doubts over what he should do. She was married, but how could her husband allow . . . ? Had she really sold her body? The expression on the Marquis of Caja's face, when the friar finally made up his mind to ask him, confirmed it.

'It can't be!' escaped his lips.

'Yes, Father. But not with me,' added the nobleman quickly, seeing the friar's expression. 'Why are you interested?' he enquired when Fray Joaquín asked him if he knew where the Barefoot Girl lived.

The friar pursed his lips and didn't answer.

'Very well,' yielded Don Ignacio at his silence.

The Marquis sent his secretary to find out about her situation and in a few days he called for the friar. He told him about the High Court's sentence. 'It is undoubtedly the easiest thing for them to do,' he added in passing. 'They just released her today.' Then he gave him an address on Amor de Dios Street.

The friar stationed himself there. He only wanted to see her and help her if necessary. He banished from his mind his worry about what he would do when that happened . . . if it happened. He didn't want to get his hopes up, as he had that day he ran after her in Triana. The problem he came up against was that there were three buildings marked with the number four in Amor de Dios Street.

'There's no way of knowing,' answered a parishioner he asked. 'Look, Father, the thing is when they numbered the buildings they did it going around the blocks, so a lot of numbers are repeated. It happens all over Madrid. If they had done it linearly, by street, like in other cities, we wouldn't have that problem.'

'Do you know . . . do you know which one the Barefoot Girl lives in?'

'You aren't saying that a religious man like you . . . ?' the man reproached.

'Don't jump to conclusions,' Fray Joaquín defended himself. 'I beg of you.'

'That was where the sedan chairs stopped to take her to the theatre,' grumbled the man, pointing to a building.

Fray Joaquín didn't dare go up to the house, or ask a couple of the neighbours who entered or left the building. *Really, what am I after?* he asked himself. He was still pacing up and down the street when night fell. It was a mild night yet he closed the neck of his habit and took refuge in the facing doorway. Perhaps he could see her the next day . . . He was thinking that when he saw two men head towards the building. One was a constable, with his truncheon tapping on the ground; the other, Pedro García. He had no trouble recognizing him. More than once he had been pointed out by a pious parishioner in Triana because of those love affairs that his grandfather, El Conde, then had to rush to fix. *Milagros's husband,* he lamented. He could do little with him there. How had he allowed his wife to prostitute herself? Was that what he would say to him if he stepped out into his path? Both men entered the building and the friar priest remained waiting, not really knowing why. Some time later, an old woman emerged, loaded down with a straw mattress and two bundles. She was also a gypsy, he could see her face in the light of the moon and her dark skin gave her away. It seemed they were getting ready to leave, moving out of the house. Fray Joaquín was nervous. His hands were sweating. What was going on up there? Soon he saw the constable leave the building.

'Get away from that beast or he'll kill you too!' he heard him warn the old gypsy woman.

He'll kill you too?

Suddenly, Fray Joaquín found himself in the middle of the street.

'He will kill her?' he stammered before the constable.

'What are you doing here, Father? At this time of night . . .'

But the friar had already started running up the stairs. *He will kill her* echoed frenetically in his ears.

'Halt!' he ordered, gasping for breath. He had just stuck his head through the only open door and found Pedro about to slit a woman's throat.

The gypsy turned his head and was surprised to recognize Fray Joaquín.

'You're very far from Triana, Father,' he spat, releasing Milagros and facing him, knife in hand.

The sight of Milagros's naked body distracted Fray Joaquín for a moment.

The gypsy drew closer to him.

'You like my wife?' he asked cynically. 'Enjoy her because she'll be the last thing you see before you die.'

Fray Joaquín reacted but he didn't know what to do against that man: strong, armed, oozing hatred from every pore. In a split second his testicles shrank and a cold sweat soaked his back.

'Help!' he then managed to scream as he backed up towards the landing.

'Shut up!'

'Help me!'

The gypsy launched a first stab. Fray Joaquín stumbled as he dodged it. Pedro attacked again, but Fray Joaquín managed to grip his wrist. He wouldn't be able to hold it for very long, he realized.

'Help!' He used the other hand to aid the first. 'Help me! The patrol! Call the patrol!'

Pedro García was kicking him and beating him with his free hand, but Fray Joaquín was only focused on the one that held the knife near, already brushing his face. He continued screaming, ignoring the beating he was getting.

'What's going on?' was heard from the stairs.

'Call the patrol!' exclaimed a woman.

Fray Joaquín's screams in the night were joined by the

neighbours in the building and even the buildings opposite, men and women sticking their heads out over their balconies.

Footsteps and more shouting were heard on the stairs.

'There!'

'Here!' Sensing that help was on the way gave Fray Joaquín the strength to continue screaming.

Someone reached the landing.

Pedro García knew that he had lost. He let go of the knife just as the friar released the grip he couldn't hold any longer, at which point the gypsy pushed past him and ran down the stairs, knocking down the people on their way up.

40

ALL THAT SHE needed to heat the small single-storey house on the outskirts of Torrejón de Ardoz was a couple of logs. It was just a dining room beside a hearth and a bedroom. In the silence of the night, the smell of burning wood mixed with the scent of the tobacco Caridad exhaled in long spirals. Alone, seated at the table, she put the cigar down on a little clay plate to wind the tobacco plantation toy again. The repetitive, tinny music she knew so well filled the room as soon as Caridad let go of the little key she had turned as far as it could go. She picked up the cigar, pulled hard on it and released a slow mouthful of smoke over the little figures that spun around the ceiba, the sacred tree, and the tobacco plants. On the other side of the world, beyond the ocean, many Negroes would be cutting and loading tobacco at that very moment. The Jesuits at the Casa Grande in Torrejón had assured her that the hours were reversed, that when it was night here, it was day there, but no matter how many times they tried to explain the reason to her, she still didn't understand it. Her thoughts flew to the slaves she had shared her suffering with: to María . . . María was the third of that row of tin figures that spun and spun; she thought she could see a resemblance, although she barely remembered her friend's features by this point. She ended up identifying little Marcelo with the boy who turned ceaselessly, loaded down with a leather bag. When Marcelo passed by the overseer who lifted and lowered his arm with the whip, Caridad closed her eyes. *What has become of my boy?* she sobbed.

'All the Negroes love him; he's always laughing,' she had

commented to Father Luis, one of the Jesuits of the Casa Grande, one day when she brought over a shipment of fine tobacco.

'Caridad, if he's anything like you at all, I have no doubt,' he declared.

Father Luis promised her that he would bring her news of Marcelo. 'As long as you keep bringing me tobacco,' he added with a wink.

The Company of Jesus, like other religious orders, owned those sugar mills worked by Negroes. She felt irritated listening to the Jesuit proudly list some of their names: San Ignacio de Río Blanco, San Juan Bautista de Poveda, Nuestra Señora de Aránzazu and Barrutia . . . Why would someone who believed that slavery was good take an interest in the fate of a little black boy?

'Is something wrong, Cachita?' asked Father Luis, noticing the sudden change of expression on Caridad's face.

'I was thinking of my boy,' she lied.

But she did remember him, along with many others like Melchor and Milagros, while she watched the wind-up toy in that little house that, through Father Valerio, she rented from the Jesuits. The silence and loneliness of the long Castilian nights made her sad. So, despite its high price, she'd decided to buy the toy she had seen in the little cave in the Puerta del Sol that made her feel closer to her loved ones, to the Negroes and those who were no longer with her. After all, what did she want money for?

Caridad had been living in Torrejón de Ardoz for less than a year when Herminia ran off with her cousin Antón. She did it one night, without even saying goodbye to her. Instinctively, Caridad shut off the hurt. Another person disappearing from her life! She poured herself into her work with the tobacco, and when she went home she was always tense, always on watch for what might happen, because of Rosario's shouting and anger over her husband's betrayal. For a few days, Herminia's aunt and uncle didn't know what to do with Caridad, who at that point still lived in the shed attached to the house. It was the public prosecutor of the War Council, Cristóbal's father, who decided for them. After he found out from the town authorities what had happened to Rosario, the man showed up unannounced, with a doctor, a secretary and a couple of servants. Without paying much attention to little Cristóbal, wrapped like a cocoon in his white linens, he demanded that everyone who lived there present themselves; right then and there, shooting disdainful glances at Caridad all the while, the doctor subjected the wet nurse to an exhaustive examination. He inspected her body, her hips, her legs and her large breasts, which he weighed approvingly in his hands. Then he focused on her nipples.

'What do you use on them?' he enquired.

'Virgin wax, sweet almond oil and whale blubber,' Rosario answered solemnly, as she handed him a bottle of salve, which the doctor smelled and touched. 'Then I wash them with soap,' explained the wet nurse.

The most important, however, was the milk. The doctor, as if it were a complex operation, extracted a glass bottle with a long neck from his satchel and heated its base on the fire. He grabbed the bottle with a rag, introduced a nipple into the mouth of the neck and pressed it up against the breast so no air would enter. As the bottle cooled, Rosario's milk poured into it.

With the prosecutor by his side, the doctor held it up to the light, stirred it, sniffed it and tasted it.

'It doesn't smell,' he commented while the other man nodded, 'it is creamy and sweet; bluish white and not too thick.

'Come closer. Over here,' he then ordered Rosario's oldest son, who didn't come forward until he was pushed by his grandfather. The doctor pulled the boy's head back, opened one of his eyes and spilled a few drops of milk into it. 'It isn't an irritant, either,' he declared after a few minutes.

Based on the doctor's recommendation, the prosecutor allowed Rosario to continue nursing Cristóbal.

'His excellency will not consent to his son living with a Negress,' his secretary added rudely when the others were already on their way to the door.

Don Valerio quickly came to her aid and offered her the little house: he wasn't going to allow Caridad to have any problems. Her dedication and seemingly tireless hard work had achieved excellent results. The parish priest trusted her, letting her do things her way, and Caridad modified the entire system that Marcial and Fermín had been using up until her arrival. She chose the seeds and planted the seedlings. Throughout the month they took to grow she prepared and ploughed the earth thoroughly in order to transplant the seedlings she thought were the best. Day after day she watched over the tobacco's growth; she used a short hoe to weed the plot; she topped the plants and removed suckers so the leaves would grow more and better, and they even saw her hauling buckets of water when she felt the crop needed it. She harvested leaf by leaf, as they did in Cuba; she handled them, smelled them and sang constantly. She urged old Fermín to get her good *cujes* and, with the sacristan, she sealed the slits in the attic beams so the smell of the incense wouldn't seep in from the church. She patiently took care of the drying, curing and fermentation, and when it was still young, unlike the tobacco they worked with in Cuba, she made cigars right there in the attic. While they didn't completely satisfy her, their quality and look was far better than the ones Herminia had given her after freeing her from La Galera.

Don Valerio praised her work and proved himself generous. Suddenly Caridad found herself with money and living in a house where no one bossed her around. *You are free, Negress,* she often said aloud to herself. *What's the point?* was her immediate retort. Where were her people? And Melchor? What had become of the man who had shown her that she could be woman and not just a slave? She often cried at night.

The inhabitants of Torrejón de Ardoz – there were more than a thousand of them – had two hospitals with a couple of beds each as a refuge for pilgrims, the sick and the strays; likewise they had a church, a butcher's shop and a fishmonger's that also sold oil, as well as a haberdashery, tavern and three inns. There were no more businesses; they didn't even have a bakery. Those, like Caridad, who didn't knead their own at home, bought it from the vendors who brought bread from the nearby towns each day. In that closed environment, Caridad was forced to expand her horizons a bit. The protection of Don Valerio and the kindness of the Jesuits guaranteed her freedom of movement, but most of the town's women were suspicious of her, and those who weren't found her to be a woman of few words who didn't seek out anyone's company and who, for all that she had changed, still instinctively kept her gaze on the ground when a strange white man addressed her. As for the men . . . she was aware of the lasciviousness with which many of those rough farmers watched her walk. A new world opened up for her and it was old Fermín who accompanied her in her progress: he taught her how to shop and use those coins whose value she was unfamiliar with.

'Herminia told me that it cost a lot of money,' said Caridad when she found out that the sacristan was going to Madrid and, to the man's consternation, gave him all she had and asked him to buy her the wind-up toy.

Fermín also taught her how to cook stew, and Caridad, happily singing to herself, would indiscriminately toss in all the ingredients she had and that, along with the bread and some fruit, became her regular diet. Still, what pleased her the most were the candied almonds made by the cloistered nuns of San Diego in Alcalá de Henares, which could only be bought through the convent turntable. Don Valerio, and even Don Luis or any of the other Jesuits, would give her those delicious sweets after they'd gone to the neighbouring town for whatever reason, and on those occasions, when her work was done, she would sit at night in the doorway of her house with the vast wheat fields, the moon and the silence as her only company, and savour them. Those were moments of calm in which her loneliness ceased to torment her and Melchor, Milagros, Old María, Herminia and her little Marcelo vanished as she tasted the syrup on her tongue and constantly debated whether she should save some of the candied almonds for the next day. She never did.

On one of the nights when Caridad was distracted by her treat – just like a little girl – a man's voice made her jump.

'What are you eating, Negress?'

Caridad hid the packet of candied almonds behind her back. Despite the silence that reigned, she hadn't heard them coming: two men, dirty, dressed in rags. *Beggars*, she said to herself.

'What did you just hide?' one of them asked.

Fermín had warned her. So had Don Valerio and Don Luis. 'A woman like you, alone . . . Bolt your door.' The beggars approached. Caridad stood up. She was taller than them. And she must be stronger, she thought as she looked at those haggard bodies devastated by hunger and misery; but there were two of them, and if they were armed, there was little she could do.

'What do you want?' The forceful tone of her voice surprised her.

It surprised the men as well. They stopped. They didn't pull out any weapon – maybe they had none – although Caridad saw that they carried rough walking sticks. It pained her to drop the packet of candied almonds but she did; then she grabbed the chair and held it between her and the men, slightly raised, threatening. The beggars looked at each other.

'We only wanted something to eat.'

Their shift in attitude emboldened Caridad. Hunger was a sensation she knew well.

'Throw those sticks aside. Far,' she demanded when the others were about to obey her. 'Now you can come closer,' she added, still holding fast to the chair.

'We don't mean to do you any harm, Negress, we just . . .'

Caridad looked at them and felt strong. She was well fed and had been working hard in the fields, ploughing and planting many, many furrows. She let go of the chair and knelt to pick up the almonds.

'I know you won't harm me,' she then asserted, turning her back to them. 'Not because you don't wish to, that I can't know, but because you can't,' she added, to erase the smile she found when she turned to face them again.

Servando and Lucio were the names of those beggars Caridad fed with the leftovers of her stew.

The following night she bolted the door; they banged on it and begged, and finally she let them in. The day after they didn't even wait for her to finish her work in the attic of the sacristy: they were loitering around her house when she arrived.

'Out!' she shouted at them from a distance.

'Caridad . . .'

'For God's sake . . .'

'Get gone!'

'One last time . . .'

By that time she had reached them. She was about to threaten to call for the constable, which was what Fermín had suggested she do when he found out who they were, but she noticed a small ember in Servando's hand.

'What's that?' she asked, pointing to it.

'This?' the man asked in turn, showing her a cigarette.

Caridad asked him for it. Servando handed her a small tube of ground tobacco rolled in thick, rough paper, which Caridad examined with curiosity. She was familiar with *tusas*, thin cigars like that, but rolled with cornhusks. Nobody wanted to smoke them.

'It's cheap,' Lucio put in. 'That's what people buy when they can't afford cigars like the ones you smoke.'

'Where do they sell them?' she asked.

'Nowhere. It's illegal. Everyone makes their own.'

Caridad took a drag on the cigarette. It was hot. She coughed. Disgusting. In any case . . . she thought, she had plenty of tobacco scraps that, when she had time, she ground up and rolled into cigarettes that not even Don Valerio would accept any more. That night, Servando and Lucio came back to eat stew. That night and many more. They brought her paper, anything they could find, and Caridad cut it up into small rectangles and filled it with the cut tobacco. She gave them the first cigarettes on credit. They paid her when they came back for more. Soon, Caridad had to start choosing the worst tobacco leaves, which she had used to make cigars before, to grind up and wrap in little paper rectangles. She continued to make the cigars for Don Valerio and the Jesuits, choosing the highest quality leaves; she also kept her own smoke aside, of course, but the rest went into the cigarettes.

The day came when Fermín had to go all the way to Madrid to exchange two sacks filled to bursting with *reales de vellón* and *maravedís* into a few marvellous gold doubloons. The sacristan didn't approve of Caridad's activities and he warned her.

However: 'I don't know why but I've grown fond of you,' he admitted after scolding her and handing her the gold doubloons.

'Because you are like that old woman I told you about when we first met: grumpy, but a good person.'

'This good person won't be able to do anything for you if you get arrested—'

'Fermín,' she interrupted, stretching out the last vowel. 'They could also arrest me for making cigars for Don Valerio, but you didn't warn me about that.'

The old sacristan lowered his eyelids.

'I don't like those two you're working with,' he said after a little while. 'I don't trust them.'

It was Caridad who was silent then for a few seconds. Soon she smiled and, though she didn't know why, Melchor's face came into her mind. What would the gypsy have answered?

That spring night, as she watched the wind-up toy spin, Caridad remembered the reply she had given the sacristan.

'They didn't fail me today. Tomorrow . . . we'll see.'

41

'CALL THE PATROL.'

'What happened?'

Many of the neighbours in the building milled around the friar. A couple of them carried oil lamps. 'Are you hurt?' repeated a woman who kept touching him. Fray Joaquín was panting, flushed, trembling. He couldn't see Milagros inside the apartment. Yes, she was there: she had slid down the wall and remained crouched down, naked. He managed to see through the faint light, the people crowding the landing. 'Did that ruffian hurt you?' insisted the woman. 'Look,' he then heard. He was filled with anguish when he saw how most of the people turned and focused their attention on the young woman. They shouldn't see her naked! He shook off the impertinent woman who was feeling his arms and he managed to shove his way through the crowd.

'What are you looking at?' he shouted before closing the door behind him.

He could hear the sudden silence and looked at Milagros. He wanted to go over to her, but instead he remained by the door for a moment. The gypsy girl didn't react, as if no one had come in.

'Milagros,' he whispered.

She continued to look off into the distance. Fray Joaquín went over and knelt down. He fought to keep his eyes from dropping to her breasts or . . .

'Milagros,' he hastened to whisper again, 'it's Joaquín, Fray Joaquín.'

She lifted an empty, blank face.

'Holy Mother, what have they done to you?'

He wanted to hug her. He didn't dare. Someone knocked on the door. Fray Joaquín looked around the room. With one hand he picked up the gypsy's torn shirt from the floor. Her skirt . . . They knocked harder.

'Open up in the name of the law!'

He couldn't let them see her naked, although he didn't dare to dress her, or touch her . . .

'Open up!'

The priest stood up and took off his habit, which he placed over the gypsy girl's shoulders.

'Stand up, I beg of you,' he whispered to her.

He crouched and took her elbow. The door burst open at a constable's violent shoulder slam just as Milagros was docilely obeying and getting to her feet. With trembling hands, ignoring the people who were entering the room, the friar buttoned the hook and eye on his habit over Milagros's breasts and turned to find a pair of constables and the neighbours from the landing, who were watching the scene, perplexed and disconcerted, although the closed cassock fell plumb to the floor and kept them from seeing the woman's body. Suddenly Fray Joaquín realized that they weren't looking at her, but at him. Stripped of his habit, all he wore was an old shirt and some simple threadbare underwear.

'What is this scandal?' enquired one of the constables after looking him up and down.

The priest was embarrassed by the way they were staring at him.

'The only scandal I can see' – he turned on them as if he could get the upper hand that way – 'is that you have broken the door.'

'Reverend,' replied the constable, 'you are in your underwear with . . . with the Barefoot Girl,' he dragged out his words before continuing, 'a married woman who is wearing your cassock and who seems . . .' He then pointed to Milagros's legs, there where the habit opened slightly and revealed the shape of her thighs. 'She is naked. Doesn't that seem like enough of a scandal to you?'

The murmurs of the neighbours accompanied his declaration.

Fray Joaquín demanded calm with a motion of his hands, as if that could put a stop to the accusations of those observing him.

'I can explain everything . . .'

'That is exactly what I asked you to do in the first place.'

'Very well,' he yielded. 'But is it necessary that all of Madrid listen in?'

'To your homes!' ordered the constable after a few moments of reflection. 'It's late and tomorrow is a work day. Out!' he ended up shouting to finally get them going.

In the end he didn't know how to explain it. Should he denounce Pedro García? He hadn't injured her; no one would take it into account. The gypsy would come back . . . On the other hand, if they believed the denunciation, what would then happen to Milagros? Sometimes witnesses were jailed until the trial, and Milagros . . . she had already had enough problems with the law. What was he, a friar, doing there in the Barefoot Girl's house? the constable asked him again with his eyes still on Milagros, who stood there in the cassock, indifferent to what was going on. Fray Joaquín kept thinking: he wanted to be with Milagros, help her, defend her . . .

'Who attacked you on the landing?' the constable wanted to know. 'They neighbours said . . .'

'His Excellency the Marquis of Caja!' improvised the priest.

'The marquis attacked you?'

'No, no, no. I mean that the marquis will give you all the references you need about me; I hold the benefice at his private chapel . . . I am . . . I was his wife's tutor, the marchioness, and I—'

'And her?' The constable pointed to Milagros.

'Do you know her story?' Fray Joaquín pursed his lips as he turned towards the gypsy. He didn't see the constables, but he knew they had both nodded. 'She needs help. I will take care of her.'

'We have to inform the High Court about this incident, do you understand?'

'First speak with his excellency. I beg you.'

She was awoken by the bustle of Mayor Street; it was strange, different from Amor de Dios Street. The light that came in through the window hurt her eyes. Where was she? On a rickety old bed. A narrow, long room with . . . She tried to focus her vision: a statue of the Virgin presided over the room. She shifted on the bed. She moaned when she felt she was naked beneath the blanket. Had they forced themselves on her again? No, it couldn't be. Her head wanted to burst, but gradually she began to remember Pedro running the knife-point over her body, her neck, and her husband's murderous gaze. And then, what had happened then?

'Are you awake at last?'

The imperious voice of the old woman didn't match her slow, pained movements. She approached with difficulty and dropped some clothes on to the bed; her own, Milagros saw.

'It's almost noon, get dressed,' she ordered.

'Give me a bit of wine,' Milagros asked.

'You can't drink.'

'Why?' ·

'Get dressed,' the old woman repeated brusquely.

Milagros felt unable to argue. The old woman walked wearily to the window and opened it wide. A stream of fresh air entered along with the noise of the merchants coming and going and the carriage traffic. Then she walked towards the door.

'Where am I?'

'In Fray Joaquín's house,' the woman answered before leaving. 'It seems he knows you.'

Fray Joaquín! That was the missing link she needed to connect her memories: the fight, the screams, the friar kneeling beside her, the constables, the people. He had shown up and saved her life. It had been five years since they had last seen each other. 'I told you he was a good person, María,' she mumbled. Flashes of happy times in Triana forced a smile to her face, but she soon remembered that when the friar burst into the house she had been naked. She saw him again kneeling before her when she was naked and drunk. The burning in her stomach rose up to her mouth. How much more did he know about her life?

It calmed her to learn from Francisca that Fray Joaquín had gone out earlier. 'To the house of the marquis, his protector,' the old woman added. Milagros wanted to see him, but at the same time she was afraid of doing so.

'Why don't you take advantage now?' the old woman interrupted her thoughts after bringing over a bowl of milk and a piece of hard bread; the gypsy was already dressed.

'Take advantage . . . to do what?'

'To leave, go back with your people. I'll tell the friar that . . .'

Milagros stopped listening to her; she felt incapable of explaining that she had no one and no place to go to. Pedro had tried to kill her in her own home, so she couldn't go back there. Fray Joaquín had saved her and, even though she couldn't find an explanation for his presence there, she was sure that he would help her.

'I have to find my daughter.'

With those stammering words, she received the friar priest. She was standing waiting for him, with her back to the window that overlooked the street of the silversmiths. She heard the door to the house open and Fray Joaquín whispering with Francisca. She looked at her clothes and carefully smoothed the skirt with one hand. She heard him walk through the hallway. She smoothed her rough, spiky hair too.

He smiled from the door to the room. Neither of them moved.

'What's your daughter's name?' he asked.

Milagros closed her eyes tightly. Her throat was seized up. She was going to cry. She couldn't. She didn't want to.

'María,' she managed to articulate.

'Pretty name.' Fray Joaquín's words were accompanied by a sincere, kind expression on his face. 'We will find her.'

The gypsy girl collapsed at the simple promise. How long had it been since anyone had shown her affection? Lust, greed; they all wanted her body, her songs, her dances, her money. How long had it been since they had offered her comfort? She sought support in the window frame. Fray Joaquín took a step towards her, but he stopped. Behind him appeared Francisca, who passed him without even a glance and approached Milagros.

'What are you planning on doing with her, Father?' she asked in annoyance as she escorted the gypsy to the bed.

Fray Joaquín stifled an impulse to help the old woman and watched how, with difficulty, she managed to lie Milagros down.

'Are you OK?' he asked.

'She'd be better out of this house,' replied Francisca.

Milagros dozed for what was left of the day. Although her body needed it, she was tormented by dreams that didn't let her sleep. Pedro, knife in hand. Her girl, María. Her body in the hands of noblemen, abused. The groundlings at the Príncipe booing her . . . However, when she opened her eyes and realized where she was, she calmed down and her senses grew drowsy until she fell asleep again. Francisca watched over her.

'You can rest for a while if you'd like,' offered the friar to the old woman after a few hours.

'And leave you alone with this woman?'

From her room, Milagros heard the voices of Fray Joaquín and Francisca, arguing.

'Why?' he repeated for the third time.

She hadn't seen him once the entire morning. 'He's out,' was all Francisca answered before going to mass and leaving her alone. Milagros had heard them both return, but when she was about to go into the hallway, the voices had stopped her. She knew that she was the reason for the argument and she didn't want to witness it.

'Because she's a gypsy!' the old washerwoman finally exploded at the priest's insistence. 'Because she is a married woman and because she's a whore!'

Milagros dug her nails into her hands and clenched her eyes shut.

She had said it. If Fray Joaquín hadn't heard about it before, he knew it now.

'She is a sinner who needs our help,' she heard him answer.

Fray Joaquín knows about it! thought Milagros. He hadn't denied it, his words showed no surprise: a 'sinner' was all he had said.

'I've treated you well,' Fray Joaquín proffered. 'This is how you thank me for it, abandoning me when I need you most.'

'You don't need me, Father.'

'But she . . . Milagros . . . And you, where will you go?'

'The priest at San Miguel promised me . . .' confessed the old woman after a few seconds of silence. 'It is a sin to live under the same roof shared by a prostitute and a man of religion,' she offered as an excuse.

The parish of San Miguel was where Francisca went to mass every day. The old woman begged him with a weary gesture to let her leave and Fray Joaquín stepped aside to let her pass.

Don Ignacio, the Marquis of Caja, had not been exaggerating at all. *Every door in Madrid will slam in your face*, he had warned him when the friar insisted on continuing to live with Milagros. Luckily, the nobleman had taken care of the denunciation.

'I can intercede before the ministers of His Majesty and the High Court,' he had told him, 'but I can't silence the rumours that the neighbours and the constables have spread . . .'

'There is nothing sinful in my behaviour,' he said in his defence.

'I am not the one judging you. I think highly of you, but people's imaginations are as vast as their ability to slander. Maliciousness will bar your access to all those people that up until now rewarded you with their friendship or simply with their company. No one will want to have any link to the Barefoot Girl.'

How right he had been! But it wasn't only the nobles. Not even Francisca, the washerwoman he had saved from certain death on the streets of Madrid, accepted the situation. *You are ruining her life, Father*, Don Ignacio warned him.

The house fell silent when Fray Joaquín closed the door. He looked towards the room where Milagros was. Was he sure that there was nothing sinful in his behaviour? He had just given up the marquis's chaplaincy for that woman. He'd lost a chapel benefice over a gypsy woman . . . Suddenly, Francisca's betrayal had turned the marquis's warnings into a painful reality and he was overcome with doubts.

Milagros heard the friar head towards the room that overlooked the San Miguel Plaza, on the extreme opposite side of the narrow dwelling. She thought she could sense the feelings overwhelming the friar priest in the slowness of his steps. Fray Joaquín knew about her life; she had spent the whole morning speculating about the sudden, unexpected appearance of the friar and she couldn't explain it . . . She thought she heard a sigh. She left the room; her bare feet muffled the sound as she went down the hall. She found him seated, downcast, his hands intertwined across his chest. He sensed her presence and turned his head.

'It's not true,' professed Milagros. 'I am no whore.'

The priest smiled sadly and invited her to sit down.

'I have never given myself willingly to any man that wasn't my husband . . .' she began to explain.

They didn't even eat; their hunger disappeared as Milagros's confessions spilled out. They drank water as they spoke. He observed her first sip with some suspicion; she was surprised to taste a drink that didn't scratch her throat or dry out her mouth. 'Cachita,' Fray Joaquín whispered nostalgically when she told him about her father's death. 'Don't you cry,' scolded the gypsy, her voice choking as she told him about her first rape. The darkness surrounded them, seated facing each other. He tried to find, in that face marked by hardship, a trace of the sauciness of that girl who stuck out her tongue or winked at him in Triana; she explained herself, her gaunt fingers flying in front of her, allowing her to cry unafraid as she regurgitated her grief. When there was silence, Milagros didn't lower her gaze; Fray Joaquín, perturbed by her presence and her beauty, ended up looking away.

'And you?' she broke the silence, surprising him. 'What brought you here?'

Fray Joaquín told her, but he kept quiet how he'd tried to free himself of her memory by flagellating himself during the missions, in the darkness of the churches in remote Andalusian towns, or how little by little he ended up taking refuge in her smile, or how eagerly, when he reached Madrid, he went to the Coliseo del Príncipe to listen to her and see her perform. Why was he hiding his feelings? he admonished himself. He had dreamed of that moment for so long . . . And what if she rejected him again?

'That's my life up to now,' he declared, burying his doubts. 'And yesterday I gave up my benefice at the marquis's chapel,' he added as an epilogue.

Milagros straightened her neck when she heard the news. She let a second pass, then two . . .

'You gave it up . . . for me?' she asked after a little while.

He half closed his eyes and allowed himself the trace of a smile. 'For me,' he declared categorically.

They both agreed that Blas, the constable, was the person who'd come with Pedro when he tried to kill Milagros. Fray Joaquín told her about the old gypsy woman he'd seen leaving the building with a straw mattress and some bundles.

'Bartola,' said Milagros.

'She was moving out of the apartment,' maintained the priest. He also told her about the constable's words that had alerted him as to what was going on upstairs.

'Blas. It must have been him,' said Milagros, although she didn't even remember him being there. 'He is always with Pedro. If anyone knows where my husb— where that rogue is,' she corrected herself, 'it's Blas. He has to know where my daughter is.'

The next morning, early, after buying freshly baked white bread, some vegetables and mutton in the Plaza Mayor, and paying an Asturian from the Puerta del Sol to escort him back home with a large pitcher of water, Fray Joaquín was finally ready to set out in search of the constable. Milagros was in the doorway. 'Go on!' she ordered to put an end to his list of warnings: *Don't go out; don't open the door to anyone; don't answer . . .*

'Get going once and for all!' shouted the gypsy, expecting to hear his footsteps fading into the distance.

Fray Joaquín rushed downstairs like a naughty boy caught red-handed. The bustle of Mayor Street and the urgency of finding the constable, of helping Milagros, of making sure that the spark he saw in her eyes when he solemnly promised to find María didn't go out, made him banish all doubt. Not so for Milagros, who paced through the house from the room that overlooked San Miguel Plaza, where Fray Joaquín had slept, to the one over the silversmiths, where she had lain down.

During the night she hadn't been able to fall asleep. And he, was he sleeping? she'd asked herself over and over again as she lay in bed. It must have been the first time in her life that she'd spent the night without the company of one of her kind, and that made her nervous. After all, the friar was a man. She trembled at the mere thought that Fray Joaquín . . . Cowering in her bed she let the hours pass, aware of any movement in the hallway, as the faces of the noblemen who had forced themselves on her paraded before her eyes. Nothing happened.

Of course not! she told herself in the morning, after Fray Joaquín left; the sunlight erasing suspicions and nightmares. *Fray Joaquín is a good man. Isn't that right?* she asked the Immaculate Virgin who presided over the room; she ran a finger over her blue and gold robe. The Virgin would help her.

María was the only thing that mattered to her now. But what would she do after getting her girl back? Fray Joaquín had made her a proposition years back, but she couldn't be sure of his intentions now. Milagros hesitated. She felt a deep fondness for him, but . . .

'Why are you looking at me?' she addressed the statue again. 'What do you want me to do? He's the only thing I have; the only person willing to help me; the only one who . . .' She turned her head towards the straw mattress. A cloak, a headscarf, the sheet . . . She pulled on it and covered the image. 'When I get María back I will decide what to do about my relationship with Fray Joaquín,' she declared to the wrapped statue in front of her.

You see that, girl? Then the words of Santiago Fernández when they were walking through the Andévalo echoed in her ears, as if he were beside her, as if those vast stretches of arid land opened up before her as the old patriarch pointed to the horizon. *That is our route. For how long? What does it matter? The only important thing is the present moment.*

'The only thing important is the present moment,' she told the Virgin.

Fray Joaquín had trouble finding the constable. 'He patrols Lavapiés,' Milagros had assured him, but that day they were opening Madrid's new bullring, built beyond the Alcalá Gate, and people had taken to the streets expecting a great bullfight. The priest walked along the streets of Magdalena, La Hoz, Ave María and many others until, once again in the Lavapiés plaza, he saw a couple of constables dressed in their black suits with ruffs and with their truncheons. Blas recognized him and, before the friar could reach them, he excused himself and went over to Fray Joaquín.

'Congratulations, Father,' he exclaimed once he was standing before him. 'You did what I didn't dare to.'

Fray Joaquín stuttered. 'You admit that?'

'I have been thinking a lot about it, yes.'

Were his words born of his fear of being denounced or were they sincere? The constable imagined what was going through the friar's head.

'We all make mistakes,' he tried to convince him.

'You call a woman's murder a mistake?'

'Murder?' Blas feigned ignorance. 'I left the gypsies in an argument between husband and wife . . .'

'But on the street you warned the old gypsy woman to be careful, that he would kill her too,' the friar interrupted him.

'A figure of speech, a figure of speech. Was he really trying to kill her?'

Fray Joaquín shook his head. 'What do you know of Pedro García?' he asked, and immediately waved his hand to silence the constable's excuses. 'We have to find him!' he added firmly. 'A mother has a right to see her daughter.'

Blas snorted, pursed his lips and looked at the point on the ground where he rested his truncheon; he remembered the little girl's sadness.

'They left Madrid,' he decided to confess. 'Just yesterday they got on a wagon headed to Seville.'

'Are you sure? Was the girl with him?'

'Yes. The girl was with him.' Blas looked the friar in the eyes before continuing. 'That gypsy is a bad person, Father. There was nothing more he could get out of Madrid, and after you intervened, he was sure to have problems. He is going to take refuge in Triana, with his people, but he will kill the Barefoot Girl if she dares to go anywhere near, I assure you. He will never allow her to reveal to the others what happened these past few years and ruin his life.' He paused and then added seriously, 'Father, make no mistake about it: before getting on that wagon back home, Pedro García will have paid one of his relatives to kill the Barefoot Girl. I know him; I know what he's like and how he behaves. I'm sure of it, Father, sure. And they will follow through. She is a Vega and no longer of any use to anyone. They will kill her . . . and you along with her.'

Triana and death. With his stomach clenched and his heart beating wildly, Fray Joaquín rushed back home. It was public knowledge that he had taken Milagros in: Francisca, the priest at San Miguel, the constables, they all knew; the marquis had warned him about that. What would whoever wanted to know her whereabouts do? They would start by going to the neighbours and from there anybody could find out where she was living. And what if someone was bursting into the house in that very moment? Desperate, he raced back. He didn't even close the door behind him and ran up to Milagros's room, shouting her name. She received him standing, worry reflected in her face when he burst into the room.

'What—?' the gypsy started to ask.

'Quickly! We have to . . .' Fray Joaquín stopped talking when he saw the Immaculate Virgin covered with a sheet. 'What's that about?' he asked, pointing to it.

'We were talking and couldn't come to an agreement.'

The friar priest opened his hands in confusion. Then he shook his head. 'We have to get out of here!' he urged.

42

AS HAD BEEN happening throughout that day, Melchor once again forgot about his own worries and held his breath, as did most of the thousands of people watching the bullfight. As did Martín, who stood tensely beside him, when he watched how the horse his older brother Zoilo was riding was tossed into the air by a bull. After stabbing its horns into the animal's belly, the beast lifted it over its sturdy neck as if it were a marionette. The horse was left on the ground, kicking out its death throes in a huge puddle of blood, just like the other two the nineteenth bull of the day had killed. The picador, who had flown out of his saddle, soon became the new target for the furious, aggressive, raging animal. Zoilo tried to get up, fell, and crawled quickly until he reached the long lance he had lost. The cheers broke out again in the arena when, standing, the gypsy faced the bull just as it charged at him. He managed to jab the lance into one of its sides. Not enough to stop the animal, but enough to get away from it. Still, the animal turned, and was about to sink his horns into Zoilo, who was now defenceless, when two matadors came out to distract the bull. They managed to catch its attention with their red capes, getting it to focus on their movement and forget about the gypsy.

Martín finally released his breath. Melchor did too and, among the large audience that spring day in 1754, they applauded and cheered for Zoilo, who waved victoriously to the people before getting on another horse that his father, El Cascabelero, rushed into the ring. Melchor slapped Martín on the back.

'He's a Vega,' he told him.

The young man nodded and smiled, but somewhat tiredly. It was starting to get dark and they had been at the bullfights all day. Nineteen bulls that, except for one, had been goaded six, seven and up to ten times with the lance. Eleven horses had died that day along with some dogs who were thrown to the one bull that was too docile and ended up dying in canine jaws.

The simple folk of Madrid were enjoying the festivities: the bull-fights were inaugurating the new masonry bullring that replaced the old wooden one. All the *manolos* and *chisperos* in Madrid had shown up that day, either in the stands, outside the arena, or in the field that extended from the Alcalá Gate: men and women, all happy and elegantly dressed. The French Bourbons didn't like the bloody spectacle, so removed from the elegance and preciousness of the court at Versailles. Philip V had banned them for almost twenty-five years, but his successor, Ferdinand VI, once again allowed his subjects such entertainment, perhaps to distract them, as was the case with the comedies; perhaps for the income earned that went to charities, or perhaps for both reasons. However, in a period where reason and civility reigned, most of the noblemen, high-ranking citizens and intellectuals opposed the bullfights and called for their prohibition. In 1754, when Martín and Melchor went to the ring, it was no longer haughty noblemen who faced the bull for honour and prestige, with servants waiting in the wings to attend to them at all times. The people had made the bullfights theirs; the gentlemen were replaced by picadors who only tried to stop the animal's charge time and again, instead of killing it, as the noblemen had, and the servants became matadors on foot who harpooned and grappled with the animal, finally ending its life with sword thrusts.

Once he had recovered from his fear for Zoilo's life, Melchor was plunged back into his own worries. He had spent more than three years smuggling in Barrancos, where he'd met up with Martín again. The Vega boy had made himself useful to Méndez in just a few months, as El Galeote had advised him to when the lad had had to flee Madrid. With Martín he worked all along the Portuguese border, in Gibraltar and wherever there was even the slightest possibility of making some money. Tobacco was the best merchandise, but his need for income led him to deal in all sorts of products, from precious stones, fabric, tools and wine, which were brought into Spain from hand to hand, to pigs and horses that they stole and brought to Portugal on their return trip. Melchor had never worked so hard in his life and he had never, despite the coins clinking in his bag, led such an austere life as the one he decided to tolerate in order to obtain his daughter's freedom. Martín supported Melchor's obsession as if he were his grandson, and he made the older gypsy's hatreds and hopes his own, although he continued to have doubts about Ana being able to fix the situation with Milagros and the Garcías. He only once dared to insinuate those doubts to Melchor.

'Because she's her mother!' muttered the other, ending the discussion.

He had shown the same stubbornness when, a few months after his arrival in Barrancos, they had run into a group of gypsies in the Aracena mountains who spoke about those in Triana. Melchor hid his identity and introduced himself as a native of Trujillo, but as the conversation wore on, Martín sensed the hesitation in El Galeote's face: he wanted to know, but he didn't dare to ask.

'Milagros Carmona?' one of them answered the boy. 'Sure. Of course I know her. Everyone in Seville does. She sings and dances like a goddess, although now she just had a baby girl and no longer . . .'

A baby girl! Vega blood, Melchor Vega's own, united with García blood. That was the last thing that Melchor wanted to hear. They never asked again.

On the harsh roads and mountains, Martín became a strong, handsome man, a real gypsy; a Vega who drank from El Galeote's spirit and listened with respect, fascinated, when he told and showed him things. Only one secret seemed to come between them, between the trust and fraternity they shared as they roamed, always hidden, those inhospitable lands: the one that often disturbed Melchor's dreams. 'Sing, *morena*,' the young man heard him whisper in the night as he tossed and turned, while they both lay on simple blankets stretched out on the ground under the stars. The Negress that he had gone to look for in the secret guesthouse, Martín said to himself, the one who had been sentenced to death in Triana, the one he had asked him not to talk about. He didn't. Perhaps one day Melchor would tell him.

Each year they had secretly returned to Madrid with the money they'd earned. Melchor ran to hand it over to the notary while Martín waited for him on Madrid's outskirts: he didn't want to run the risk of bumping into any of his relatives or other gypsies that might recognize him. He had argued with his father and other members of his family when he talked to them about freeing Melchor. Despite the warnings that El Galeote had given him when they parted, the boy couldn't help bragging about his feat, with the vanity and pride of a child, before an audience whose faces shifted gradually from surprise to indignation. 'Everyone will know it was you!' spat out his sister. 'I told you that the other families had decided not to get involved!' added his father. 'You've brought us certain ruin,' chimed in Zoilo. They shouted. They insulted him and finally disowned him. 'Get out of this house!' ordered El Cascabelero. 'Maybe that way we can save ourselves.'

'They take years to grant pardons!' Martín tried to reassure a despairing Melchor, after they had met up beyond the Manzanares River following his second meeting with the notary. 'I've heard of people who have been pleading for years: pardons, wages, jobs, clemency . . . An entire army moves around Madrid pleading, but the King is slow. There are many gypsies pleading for their family members. Don't worry, Uncle, we will get it.'

Melchor knew of the royal administration's apathy. He had been in jail for more than a year and a half before they decided what galley to take him to and the documents for his transfer arrived. He also knew of the requests for mercy that carried on until, years later, they were resolved one way or the other. No. That wasn't what was worrying him; he was concerned that the notary might be cheating him. Doubt and suspicion gnawed at him every day that he denied himself a visit to a tavern or a decent bed to sleep in: was the notary just keeping that money he worked so hard to save?

But he could never have imagined that things were going to end the way they did. He had dreamed of hearing the words: 'Your daughter is free.' Although perhaps some day the notary would show him a piece of paper he couldn't read where it would say that the King denied the pardon. Sometimes he imagined himself stabbing the man, gouging out his eyes, once his treachery was revealed. But the news of the notary's death disconcerted him. Dead. Simply dead. He had never considered that possibility. 'Fevers, from what I understand,' said the woman who now lived in what had been his office. 'What would I know about his papers or the clerk who worked with him? When I rented the house it was already empty.' Melchor babbled. 'Fixer?' the woman asked in surprise. 'What fixer?' There was nobody there. Her husband was a pastry cook. Melchor insisted to the point of appearing naive, 'And now what do I do?'

The woman looked at him incredulously, then shrugged and closed the door.

The gypsy asked other neighbours in the building. No one had any news for him.

'He was definitely shady,' one old woman tried to explain. 'Mysterious. Untrustworthy. Once I myself . . .'

Melchor left before she had even finished her sentence. The first thing he did was head to a tavern and order wine. Just as when he abandoned his search for Caridad, he grieved with a cup in his hands. Madrid didn't bring him luck. More than three years ago he had fled in search of money, and now?

'Would you like to go to the bullfights?' he had asked Martín, to his surprise, when he heard that they were inaugurating the new ring the next day. 'Your brother might be there.'

The young man thought about it. How long had it been since he'd seen any member of his family? In the arena he would be hidden among the crowd; they wouldn't recognize him, so he accepted the invitation. They retraced their steps with the setting sun at their backs. Melchor tried to put his arm around Martín's shoulders, but he was already taller than him. He looked at the young man: strong, tough . . . Perhaps he was the only one he could still rely on.

They didn't even look for a place to spend the night. They stretched out their dinner of slices of bread, toast soaked in water, fried with lard and sprinkled with sugar and cinnamon; chicken stewed in a sauce made of its own crushed liver; almond biscuits and doughnuts for dessert, vast quantities of wine and, once they'd had their fill, they spent the last few hours of the night asleep under the stars.

The bullfight ended and the people continued the festivities on the field that surrounded the arena. Thousands of them, dressed in typical Spanish style, sang and danced their traditional dances, shrieked and laughed, bet and gambled; they drank and fought, some with canes and others with sticks. In the pell mell and noise, Melchor kept spending his money. 'There's nothing to be done,' he had told Martín during the bullfight. Then he explained it to him. No, he didn't know the fixer, he answered the boy. He had never known who he was . . . if he ever existed.

'And what if they recognize us?' asked Martín as Melchor bragged about his money and ordered more wine. 'There could be Garcías around here.'

Melchor turned slowly and responded with a calm that seemed to silence the din that surrounded them. 'Boy, I have spent enough time with you to be sure that, if it comes to pass, I won't have to come to your aid. Let all the Garcías in Madrid and in Triana come at us together. You and I will deal with them.'

Martín felt a shiver. Melchor nodded once he'd finished speaking. Then he turned and shouted for his wine.

'And tobacco!' he demanded. 'Do you have any good tobacco?'

The man, behind the box he used as a counter, shook his head as he rummaged around. 'All I have is this.' He showed him a few paper cigarettes in the palm of his hand.

Melchor let out a laugh. 'I asked you for tobacco – what's that?'

The other gave an indifferent shrug. 'Cigarettes,' he answered.

'Now they sell them already rolled?'

'Yes. Most people don't have the money to buy a piece of Brazil cord and scrape it every time they want to roll a cigarette. This way, they buy only what they want to smoke.'

'But then they can't check the quality of the tobacco they're smoking,' Melchor pointed out.

'Yes, that's true,' agreed the man. 'But they are good quality. They say they're made by a Cuban Negress who knows about tobacco.'

A shiver ran through the gypsy.

'The Negress's cigarettes, they call them.'

The music stopped in Melchor's ears and the people seemed to vanish. He could sense . . . He picked up one of the cigarettes very delicately and smelled it.

'*Morena*,' he whispered.

43

IN THE YEAR 1754 the briefs and requests to the authorities for pardons on behalf of detained gypsies multiplied. The pleas had never stopped coming. In the towns they continued to process the secret files, despite the fact that the Marquis of Ensenada had ordered years back that they were no longer relevant, and the town councils claimed the gypsies as residents in their districts, most of them smiths by trade, a job the old Christians didn't do because they considered it beneath them.

More than four years had passed since the big round-up, and that was the jail sentence that vagabonds were given. Since they hadn't been told how long their jail term was, the gypsies tried to compare themselves to the vagabonds. They hadn't committed any crime, they maintained in their petitions, and they had been doing forced labour for years.

The governor of the arsenal of Cartagena even began to support freeing the gypsies, and he proposed that, if the authorities didn't attend to their requests, they should at least designate a length for their jail term.

The gypsies' pleas were unsuccessful. In fact, the authorities ordered the governors of the arsenals to stop dealing with their petitions, as if they were merely a nuisance. Some specific requests did succeed, tenaciously filed by women unrelenting in their efforts to free their relatives, but those arbitrary decisions only managed to infuriate the vast majority who continued to be held in captivity.

Meanwhile, the conditions both the men and women were living in got worse. The arsenals in Cádiz, as well as those in Cartagena and El Ferrol where some of the prisoners had been sent after an arduous sea voyage that ended the lives of many, still lacked the facilities to house them. And those men who had been separated from their families – injured, treated worse than slaves, desperate in the face of lifelong sentences – continued to rebel, mutiny and even run away. Few of these escapes ended well, but that didn't keep the gypsies from trying, even shackled.

The women, locked up in the House of Mercy in Saragossa and in the provisional jail in Valencia, suffered, if that were possible, greater hardships. They weren't productive; no one had managed to make them work, and the money from the King to support them wasn't forthcoming. Hunger and misery. Diseases. Attempts to flee, some successful. Constant disobedience and rebelliousness. While the men were fettered, the women were kept almost naked, covered at most with simple rags even at the risk of being unable to find priests willing to preach to that flock of lost souls. The authorities maintained that when they gave them clothes, they ran away.

Families were scattered and married couples separated by hundreds of leagues. The girls remained with their mothers, if they still had them, and fate had kept them on the same course; the boys suffered more injustices. In the big round-up, those older than seven had gone with their fathers, uncles and older brothers to the arsenals, but those that were initially in the women's group grew up in captivity. Once in the provisional jail in Málaga, before being transferred to the House of Mercy in Saragossa, the gypsy women had tried to hide the boys that were over the age where they were expected to start working. Since they had seized their papers, the authorities governing the provisional jails couldn't know their exact ages, which their mothers lied about, taking advantage of their scant growth due to poor nutrition. Still, before their departure, twenty-five of the older boys were separated against their will from their mothers and taken to the arsenals. The same thing happened in Valencia, where almost five hundred women were crammed together. There forty boys were violently taken away from their mothers and relatives. Some managed to find their fathers and brothers, others discovered that they had been taken to a different arsenal, or that their family members had been transferred to another – as happened to those in Cádiz, who were taken to El Ferrol – or that they had simply already died.

The boys held in the Royal House of Mercy in Saragossa were no exception. That year, 1754, almost thirty – Salvador among them – were sent to the arsenals; the fields where they had slept out in the open were used to plant wheat, according to the instructions given by the Countess of Aranda when she was made aware of the decision.

Close to five hundred gypsy women witnessed the departure of the boys amid the tough security measures adopted by the warden, who asked for reinforcements and lined up the soldiers between them. Their weapons – with their bayonets fixed – were at the ready to open fire on the young men. The soldiers' presence intimidated the ragged women who, holding hands, crying, sought support from each other while the others silently watched the slow march of the line of boys who struggled to maintain their composure. All the women felt like mothers and sisters. Almost five years of hardship, hunger and misery; their efforts, their resistance, their struggle seemed to vanish with the march of those boys whose only crime had been to be born gypsy. Ana Vega, in the front row, with her flooded eyes fixed on Salvador, felt just like many others: those young men had symbolized the future and survival of their race, their people; the only hope they had left in that senseless prison.

A deep, long, shattered wail rose from among the motley group of women. Some trembled, cowering. 'Deblica barea!' Ana Vega heard someone shout at the end of the first stanza. The boys firmed their steps and lifted their heads as their magnificent goddess was praised; some of them raised their hands to their eyes, quickly, furtively, as they went through the gate of the House of Mercy. The *debla* accompanied their steps and continued to shred the gypsy women's souls, no longer hounded by the soldiers, but standing motionless until long after the shadows of their sons faded into the distance.

Melchor realized that the threats he'd used on the wine seller outside the bullring to get him to reveal where he sourced the Negress's cigarettes weren't going to work this time. The man had refused, but then the tip of Melchor's knife on his kidneys had made him change his mind. The cigarettes were distributed by Madrid's ragmen, who went through the streets of the capital collecting the rags, papers and all sorts of cast-offs and scraps that they traded in. Since olden times, the ragmen had also taken care of the many animals that died in the city and transported their bodies to a dungheap on the outskirts, beyond the Toledo Bridge, where they would skin them for leather.

Melchor observed the place in the night: blended into the smoke from the bonfires where they burned the bones and other animal remains, close to a hundred ragmen were dealing with the horses killed that day in the bullring: some were skinning them, others struggled to keep away the packs of dogs that wanted to make off with the scraps. He had asked one of them, a man covered in blood who held a large flaying knife in his hands.

'Cigarettes? What cigarettes?' he answered curtly, without even stopping. 'Nobody knows about that here. Don't go looking for trouble, gypsy.'

They were hard men and women, toughened by privation, who wouldn't hesitate to fight with them. Melchor wondered if he should offer them money for the information. They would just rob him; then they'd carve them up right there and toss them into the fire . . . Maybe they wouldn't even bother. He saw how the ragman he'd asked was talking to others and pointing at them. A group came over to them.

'Go, Martín,' he whispered as he hit the lad in the side.

'Uncle, I've been hearing you sigh in the night over that woman for years . . .'

'You two!' one of the ragmen then shouted.

'I wouldn't miss this for anything in the world,' the young man finished saying.

'They are as afraid we'll denounce them as they are of losing the business,' Melchor managed to warn him before the five dirty, scruffy ragmen covered in blood planted themselves a step away from them, all armed with knives and tools.

'What's your interest in the cigarettes?' enquired a wrinkly bald one, slighter than the others.

'I'm not interested in the cigarettes, I'm interested in the Negress who makes them.'

'And what's the Negress to you?' put in another of the ragmen.

Melchor sketched a smile. 'I love her,' he confessed openly.

One of the ragmen gave a start; another cocked his head and squinted his eyes to scrutinize him in the darkness. Even Martín turned towards him. Melchor's sincere declaration of his love seemed to lessen the tension. Laughter was heard, more joyful than cynical.

'An old gypsy and a Negress?'

Melchor tightened his lips and nodded before answering. 'Do you know her?'

They shook their heads no.

'If you heard her sing, you would understand.'

The conversation caught the attention of the other ragmen; men and women joined the group.

'The gypsy says that he loves the Negress who makes the cigarettes,' one of them explained to the others.

'And she . . .' It was a woman who quickly formulated the question. 'Does she love you back?'

'I believe she does. Yes,' he affirmed categorically after thinking it over for a second.

'Let's finish them off!' proposed the small bald one. 'We can't trust . . .'

A couple of men came towards the gypsies resolutely, leading with their large knives, while the others surrounded them.

'Gonzalo, all of you!' A woman, with a naked little girl clinging to her leg, interrupted the attack. 'Don't ruin the only nice thing that has ever happened in all this . . .' She waved her hand over the foul dungheap, the smoke rising from the bonfires in the night, everything scattered with dead bodies and remains. '. . . all this filth.'

'The gypsy will take over the business,' complained one of the men.

Melchor decided to stay silent in the face of those two men's knives; he knew that his and Martín's fate depended on the sensitivity of a group of women who probably hadn't even heard the word love in a long, long time. *Morena*, he thought then, tense, *another fix I'm in because of you. I must love you!* He sensed Martín's nervousness; they could fight off the two they had in front of them, but the others would pounce on them mercilessly. He could already smell death when a third woman intervened.

'And what would he do, sell the cigarettes across the entire city? We're the only ones who can do that.'

'Some day we'll be found out and we'll be sorry,' the woman with the little girl added despondently as she stroked the girl's dirty cheek. 'There's already too much talk about the Negress's cigarettes. The next time it might be the patrol instead of the gypsy; you see how easy it is to find out what we are up to. We would lose our husbands and sons. I would almost prefer the gypsy take over the business.'

'I don't want to take over anything,' Melchor then interjected. 'I only want to find her.'

In the gleam of the bonfires on the men's faces, Melchor saw them looking at each other.

'She's right,' he heard one of them say behind him. 'The other day, a tavern keeper on Toledo Street warned me that the constables of the patrol are asking questions about the cigarettes. It won't be long before they find someone who will rat on us. Why kill these two when tomorrow we might not have anything any more anyway?'

The sun was coming up when they reached Torrejón de Ardoz. Servando, one of the beggars who acted as an intermediary, had come by that very night to collect what must have been a lot due to the bullfight, and he stubbornly protected the secret that was so profitable for him.

'Gypsy,' said one of the women, tired of the discussions that were delaying their work with the dead horses, 'you get him to take you to your beloved yourself.'

Servando took a few steps back as soon as the ragmen resumed their duties and he was left alone with Melchor and Martín.

'What's the name of the Negress?'

That was the only thing they talked about with the beggar on their way to Torrejón. Melchor needed to hear it, to confirm his hunch.

'You want to find her and you don't know her name?'

'Answer me.'

'Caridad.'

When Servando pointed out the small adobe house that bordered the wheat fields, Melchor regretted not getting more information out of the beggar. A lot of time had passed. Would she still be alone? She could have ... she could have found another man. The chaotic mixture of wonderful hopes that had enlivened his steps when he heard Caridad's name now faltered when he saw that little house that seemed to shine in the light of the first rays of springtime sun. Would she still love him? Maybe she was bitter over being left in that hostel ... The three men paused at a slight distance from the little house. Servando urged them to continue, but Martín stopped him with an authoritative sweep of his hand. What had her life been like all these years? Melchor asked himself, unable to control his anxiety. What paths had led her here? What ... ?

The door to the little house opened and Caridad appeared, her attention focused on the fields, greeting the day.

'Sing, *morena*.' His voice came out in a croak, hoarse, weak, inaudible!

A second passed, two ... Caridad turned her head slowly towards where they stood ...

'Sing,' repeated Melchor.

'Stay here,' Martín threatened Servando in a whisper when he made as if to follow the gypsy, who was walking tall towards Caridad. Her round black face was already marked with shiny tears.

Melchor was crying as well. He fought not to run to her, not to shout, not to howl up towards the heavens or down to hell; yet he did nothing to hold back his tears. He stopped close enough to touch her by simply extending his arm yet he didn't dare.

Standing before one another, they looked into each other's eyes. He showed the palm of one dark hand with his fingers outstretched. She sketched a smile that was soon overcome by her trembling sobs. He frowned. Caridad looked up at the sky, for just a moment, then tried to smile again, but her tears got the better of her and Melchor saw a face clenched in a maelstrom of emotions that were bursting inside her. Still, he thought he could recognize them: happiness, hope, love . . . and he came closer.

'Gypsy,' she then blubbered.

They melted in an embrace and silenced the thousands of words in their throats with a thousand kisses.

44

AFTER LEAVING THE apartment over the silversmiths, Fray Joaquín pulled Milagros to a house on Pez Street, a road crammed with buildings filled with proud, haughty Madrileños, just as in Lavapiés, Barquillo and the capital's other districts. The priest, fearing rumours, didn't even dare go to a secret guesthouse, so he negotiated the rent of a couple of dingy rooms from the widow of a soldier who slept by the hearth and didn't ask questions. Along the way, he told Milagros about his conversation with Blas.

'Well, then let's go to Triana,' she said quickly, grabbing him by the sleeve to stop him as they went up Ancha de San Bernardo Street.

The crowd went happily in the opposite direction, towards Alcalá Street and the bullring.

'Pedro would kill you,' the priest objected as he examined the buildings and side streets.

'My daughter is there!'

Fray Joaquín stopped. 'And what would we do?' he asked. 'Go into the San Miguel alley and kidnap her? Do you think we have even the slightest chance? Pedro will get there before us, and as soon as he does he will spread all sorts of malicious lies about you; the entire gypsy settlement will consider you a . . .' The friar stopped there, his words hanging in the air. 'You wouldn't even get as far as . . . we wouldn't even get across the pontoon bridge. Come on,' he added tenderly a few seconds later.

Fray Joaquín kept walking, but Milagros didn't follow him; the flood of people seemed to swallow him up. When he realized, the friar retraced his steps.

'What does it matter if I get killed?' she murmured between sobs, tears already running down her cheeks. 'I was already dead before . . .'

'Don't say that.' Fray Joaquín was about to take her by the shoulders but he stopped himself. 'There has to be another solution, and I will find it. I promise you.'

Another solution? Milagros frowned as she clung to that promise. She nodded and walked beside him. It was true, she admitted to herself when they turned down Pez Street: Pedro would defame her, and Bartola would obediently confirm all the slander the bastard could think up. A shiver ran down her spine as she imagined Reyes, La Trianera, vilifying her. The Garcías would enjoy publicly repudiating her; the Carmonas would do it too, their honour offended. Milagros had broken the law: there were no gypsy prostitutes, and all the gypsies would turn against her. How could she show up in the San Miguel alley in those circumstances?

However, the days passed and Fray Joaquín didn't fulfil his promise. 'Give me time,' he asked her one morning when she insisted. 'The marquis will help us,' he assured her the next day knowing that he wouldn't be able to go to his house. 'I wrote a letter to the prior of San Jacinto, he will know what to do,' he lied the third time she reminded him what he had promised.

Fray Joaquín was afraid of losing her, of her getting hurt or killed; but to avoid facing up to her questions he left her alone in a filthy room with a rickety bed and a broken chair as its only furnishings. 'You shouldn't go out, people know who you are and Pedro will have the Garcías looking for you.' Echoing his excuses, with the laughter of her little girl ringing constantly in her ears, Milagros gave in to her tears. She was sure that the Garcías would mistreat her. The images of her daughter in the hands of those heartless people were too much for her. Sober, she couldn't bear them . . . She asked for wine, but the widow refused to give her any. She argued in vain with her. 'You can leave if you like,' the woman replied. 'Where?' Milagros asked. Where could she go?

He always came back with something: a sweet; white bread; a

colourful ribbon. And he would chat with her, cheering her up and treating her with affection, but that wasn't what she needed. Where was his gypsy pluck? Fray Joaquín was unable to hold her gaze the way the men of her race could. Milagros sensed that he followed her with his eyes the entire time they were together, but when she faced him, he pretended he hadn't been. He seemed content with her mere presence, with smelling her, brushing past her. Her nights were filled with bad dreams: Pedro and the parade of nobles attacking her. Yet she began to reject the idea that Fray Joaquín could act like them.

In a couple of weeks they were out of money to pay the exorbitant rent charged by the widow to guarantee her silence.

'I never thought we would need it,' said the friar, contrite, as if he had failed her.

'And now?' she asked.

'I will find—'

'You're lying!'

Fray Joaquín wanted to defend himself, but Milagros didn't allow him to.

'You lie, you lie and you lie,' she shouted with her fists clenched. 'There's nothing, isn't that right? No marquis, no letters to the prior, nothing.' The silence confirmed her doubts. 'I'm going to Triana,' she decided then.

'That would be crazy.'

Milagros's decision, the need to leave those squalid rooms before the widow threw them out or, even worse, denounced them as adulterers, the lack of money and, above all, the mere possibility that she would leave him, made Fray Joaquín react.

'This is the last time I'm putting my trust in you. Don't let me down, Father,' she relented.

And he didn't. The truth was that he did nothing else for the next few days except think about how to resolve the situation. It was a preposterous idea, but he had no alternative: he had been dreaming about Milagros for years and he had just given up everything he had for her. What could be more preposterous than that? He went to a second-hand clothing shop and exchanged his best habit (of the two he owned) for coarse black women's clothes, including gloves and a mantilla.

'You want me to put that on?' Milagros tried to refuse.

'You can't walk along the roads as a gypsy without papers. I'm just trying to keep us from getting arrested on our trip . . . to Barrancos.' The clothes slid from Milagros's hands and fell to the floor. 'Yes,' he said before she could speak. 'It's not that far out of our way. It's just another road, a few days more. Remember what the old healer woman said? She said something like if there was any place your grandfather could be found, it was Barrancos. The day we spoke, you told me that you didn't make it there after the round-up, and things haven't changed much since then. Perhaps . . .'

'I spat at his feet,' Milagros then said, reminding him of the rage she had shown towards her grandfather. 'I told him—'

'What does it matter what you did or said to him? He always loved you and your daughter has Vega blood. If we can find him, Melchor will know what to do, of that I'm sure. And if he isn't there any more, maybe we can find some other family member who wasn't arrested. Most of them deal in tobacco and we can probably find news of someone.'

Milagros was no longer listening. Thinking of her grandfather filled her with both hope and fear. She hadn't heeded his warnings, or her mother's. They had both known what would happen if she gave herself to a García. The last thing she had heard about her grandfather was that he had been captured in Madrid and had managed to escape. Maybe . . . yes, maybe he was still alive. And if anyone could face up to Pedro, it was Melchor Vega. But . . .

She knelt down to pick the black clothes up off the floor. Fray Joaquín stopped speaking when he saw her. Milagros didn't want to think about the possibility that her grandfather had disowned her and would refuse to help her out of spite.

'Hail Mary, full of grace.'

'Conceived without sin,' said Milagros, downcast, to the young maid who opened the door to the house. She knew what she had to do next, the same thing she had done a league back, in Alcorcón: intertwine the fingers of her gloved hands, showing Fray Joaquín's rosary that she carried between them, and murmur what she could remember of those prayers Caridad had taught her for her baptism, which the friar repeated insistently along the way.

'Alms to send this poor, miserable widow to the Dominican convent in Lepe,' begged Fray Joaquín, lifting his voice over her chanting.

Through the black mantilla that covered her head and hid her dark face, the gypsy looked at the maid out of the corner of her eye. She would respond like all the others: refusing at first only to end up opening her eyes incredibly wide when Fray Joaquín revealed the beautiful face of the Immaculate Virgin he was carrying. Then she would stutter, tell them to wait, close the door and run in search of her mistress.

That was what had happened in Alcorcón and in Madrid as well, before they went through the Segovia Gate. Fray Joaquín decided to alleviate their poverty by joining the army of pilgrims and alms-seekers who carry saints through the streets of Spain. The former dressed in capes adorned with shells, sackcloth, staffs taller than they were, gourds and hats for supposed pilgrimages to Jerusalem or countless other foreign locations. The latter were friars, priests or abbots asking for a mite for all sorts of pious works. The people gave alms to the pilgrims in exchange for kissing their relics or scapulars that they claimed came from the Holy Land. With those who carried saints, they prayed before the images, stroked them, kissed them and drew them close to children, the elderly and especially the sick before dropping a few coins into their almsbox or bag.

And of all the sacred images, there was none like the Immaculate Virgin that Fray Joaquín unveiled to the shock of the maids in the wealthy homes. As Milagros had foreseen, the same thing that had happened in Alcorcón happened again in Móstoles, little more than three leagues from Madrid. Soon after, the lady of the house opened the door, spellbound before the beauty and opulence of the statue of the Virgin, and invited them in. Milagros did so cowering, as Fray Joaquín had instructed her, murmuring prayers and hiding her bare feet beneath the long black skirt that dragged along the floor.

Once inside, the gypsy sought out the furthest corner from the makeshift altar where Fray Joaquín placed the Virgin, while he introduced her as his sister who had just been widowed and had promised to enter the convent. They didn't even look at her; all eyes were on the Immaculate Virgin. 'Can she be touched?' they asked cautiously. 'And kissed?' they added excitedly. Fray Joaquín led prayers before allowing them to do so.

And while they made enough money to continue their journey, eat and sleep in the inns or in those same houses if there were none – Milagros always separated from the rest, taking refuge in her supposed vow of silence – their progress was slow, irritatingly slow. For safety they always looked for someone to travel with, and sometimes they had to wait, as when the ladies of the house insisted on demanding the presence of their husbands, children and, on occasion, even the village's parish priest, with whom Fray Joaquín would converse until he had convinced him of their good intentions. The shows of devotion and the prayers dragged on endlessly. When they needed money they spent entire days showing the Virgin, like in Almaraz, before crossing the River Tagus, where they were well paid for allowing the statue to protect a sick man in his room.

'And what if he doesn't get better?' Milagros asked Fray Joaquín when he brought her food to eat in the room they had given her so she could remain in her self-imposed silence.

'Let Our Lady be the one to decide. She will know.'

Then he smiled and Milagros, surprised, thought she could make out a hint of mischievousness in Fray Joaquín's face. The friar had changed . . . or was it she? Perhaps both, she told herself.

Milagros found the nights particularly hard; she was abruptly awoken by nightmares, sweaty, confused, short of breath: men forcing themselves on her; the entire Coliseo del Príncipe laughing at her; Old María . . . Why was she dreaming of the old healer so many years since last seeing her? While her nights were torturous, during the day the mere possibility of seeing her grandfather again gave her the courage to tolerate those coarse black clothes that chafed her skin. The tedium of the prayers and the hours spent alone in homes and inns, so their hosts wouldn't discover their lies, became time to fantasize about Melchor, her mother and Cachita. She often had to make an effort not to launch into singing those prayers that

Caridad had taught her to the rhythm of fandangos. How long had it been since she had sung? 'As long as it's been since you last drank,' Fray Joaquín had answered her, ending the conversation when she brought it up. The sun and her yearnings managed to keep the bitter, torturous dreams at bay, as if enclosed in a bubble, and the hope of being reunited with her family opened out before her. That was the only thing that really mattered: her daughter, her grandfather. The Vegas. In the past she hadn't understood that, although she consoled herself by using her youth as an excuse. Sometimes she also remembered her father. What had the Camacho told her when he came back from talking with her mother in the makeshift jail in Málaga? *He knew what the deal was: his freedom for your engagement to the García boy. He should have refused and sacrificed himself. Your grandfather did what he had to do.*

When she recalled those words, Milagros struggled to banish the memories and think about her grandfather again. Only with his help could she get her little girl back and, with her, her joy in life. Each town they passed brought her a little closer to that goal.

Sometimes, after hearing him lie to the naive, pious people who wanted to get close to the Virgin, Milagros also thought about Fray Joaquín, and when she did she was filled with conflicting emotions. The first days in Madrid, when they started using the Virgin to make money to pay off their onerous debt to the widow, she was exasperated with his stammering. She silently asked him for firmness and conviction, but she got even more nervous when she could see, through the lace of the mantilla, how he was constantly looking at her out of the corner of his eye to make sure she was playing her part. *Worry about yourself, friar. How could anyone recognize me in these clothes that cover me from head to toe?* As Fray Joaquín grew more confident in his role, his attitude towards Milagros changed, as if he took strength from his self-assurance. He didn't seem as fraught over her presence and he sometimes even held her gaze. Then she would feel, even if only for a few moments, like a girl, as she had been back in Triana.

'Aren't you attracted to me when I'm dressed in black?' she asked him brazenly one day.

'What . . . ?' Fray Joaquín went red up to his ears. 'What do you mean?'

'Just wondering if you don't like me in these . . . these rags you force me to wear.'

'It must be the Immaculate Virgin, who strives to avoid temptation,' he joked, pointing to the sculpture.

She was about to reply but didn't, and he thought he understood why: inside her was still that mistreated woman, humiliated by men.

'I didn't mean—' Milagros started to apologize before he interrupted her.

'You are right: I don't like you in those widow's clothes. But I do like,' he added quickly, seeing her sad expression, 'that you are joking and worrying about your appearance again.'

Milagros's face changed again. A shadow of sadness marred her gaze. 'Fray Joaquín, we women were brought into this world to give birth in pain, to work and suffer men's perversion. Hush,' she said, seeing that he was about to reply. 'They . . . you men rebel, struggle and fight against evil. Sometimes you win and become the triumphant hero; many other times you lose and then you turn brutally on those weaker than you to cover up your failure, and vengeance becomes your only goal. We have to shut up and obey; it has always been that way. I finally learned that and it cost me my youth. I don't even see how I can fight for my daughter without the help of a man. Yes, thank you,' she added before he could intervene, 'but it's true. All we can do is fight to forget our pain and suffering, to overcome them, but never to take revenge for them. We cling to whatever hope we have left, and in the meantime, once in a while, only once in a while, try to feel like women again.'

'I don't know what . . .'

'Don't say anything.'

Fray Joaquín shrugged as he shook his head, his hands extended out in front of him.

'Someone who tells a woman that he doesn't like her' – Milagros raised her voice – 'no matter how black her clothes, how old or ugly she may be, has no right to say anything.'

And she turned her back on him, trying to swing her hip enough for him to see it through her shapeless clothes.

The proximity, the common goal, the constant anxiety over the danger that someone would discover that the respectable and pious widow beneath that disguise was nothing more than a young gypsy – the Barefoot Girl from the Coliseo del Príncipe in Madrid, in fact – and that the friar was lying when he asked for alms for her to enter a convent, brought them a bit closer each day. Milagros did nothing to avoid brushing up against him; she felt the need for that respectful, innocent human contact. They laughed; they opened up to each other – she as never before, observing the man who hid beneath his habit: young and handsome, although he didn't seem strong. Except for that round bald spot on the top of his head, he could be considered attractive. Although maybe his hair would grow back . . . He was definitely no gypsy, he lacked decisiveness and haughtiness, but he showed plenty of devotion, sweetness and affection.

'I don't think we'll get any alms here,' Fray Joaquín lamented in a low voice one evening, when they reached a miserable group of shacks that they had been led to by a couple of farmers returning from work, the only companions they found on the road.

'Perhaps not with the Virgin, but surely we'll find someone who would pay to have their fortune told,' she bet.

'Nonsense,' replied the friar, dismissing the idea with a wave of his hands.

Milagros grabbed one of them in mid-air, instinctively, just as she had done so many times in Triana with men or women who were reluctant to spend a few coins.

'Would his eminent reverence,' she joked, 'wish to know what the lines on his palm have in store for him? I see . . .'

Fray Joaquín tried to pull his hand back, but she didn't let him and eventually he gave in. Milagros found herself with the friar's hand in hers, her gloved index finger already running along one of the lines on his palm. As she slid her finger, she felt a disturbing tingling in her belly.

'Wow . . .' She cleared her throat and shifted restlessly.

She tried to blame her nervousness on the uncomfortable clothes she was wearing. She took off her glove and swiped the mantilla away from her face. She took his hand in hers again and felt its warmth. She observed the white, almost delicate, skin of a man who had never worked in a forge.

'I see . . .'

For the first time in her life, Milagros lacked the effrontery to stare into the eyes of the man whose fortune she was reading.

They were getting close to the Múrtiga River, with Encinasola at their backs and Barrancos rising over their heads. Milagros ripped off the mantilla and threw it down; then she did the same with the gloves and lifted her face to the radiant late May sky as if trying to capture all the light she'd been denied over the almost month and a half on the road.

Fray Joaquín contemplated her, spellbound. Now she forced the hooks and eyes of her black bodice open so that the sun's rays could caress the top of her bust. The long pilgrimage, which in other circumstances would have been gruelling, had had the opposite effect on Milagros: her weariness made her forget; the constant worry of being discovered eliminated any other concerns; and imagining the reencounter to come softened her previously contracted and permanently tense features. She knew she was being watched. She let out a spontaneous shout that broke the silence, shook her head and turned towards the friar. *What will happen if we don't find Melchor?* Fray Joaquín then asked himself, fearful at the wide smile Milagros was rewarding him with. She struggled to undo her bun and release her hair, which refused to fall free. The mere thought of not finding Melchor made Fray Joaquín put down the statue of the Virgin so he could pick up the mantilla and gloves.

'What are you doing now?' complained Milagros.

'We might need them,' he responded with the mantilla in his hand; the gloves were still lost among the brush.

He had trouble finding the second one. When he stood up with it, Milagros had disappeared. Where . . . ? He ran his gaze over the area in vain; he couldn't find her. He went around a little hill that allowed him to see down into the Múrtiga riverbed. He exhaled. There she was, sleeves rolled up and on her knees, putting her head into the water again and again, scrubbing her hair frantically. He saw her get up, soaked, with her plentiful chestnut-brown hair falling down her back, sparkling in the sun in contrast to her dark skin. Fray Joaquín shivered as he contemplated her beauty.

The people of Barrancos received them with curiosity and suspicion: a friar carrying a parcel and a lovely, haughty gypsy woman who was looking curiously at everything around her. Fray Joaquín hesitated. Not Milagros: she confronted the first man she came across.

'We are looking for the person who sells tobacco to smuggle into Spain,' she said; the man was elderly and overwhelmed by her. He stammered out some words in the local language, unable to take his eyes off the face interrogating him as if he were guilty of some crime.

Fray Joaquín sensed Milagros's tremendous anxiety and decided to intervene. 'May peace be with you,' he greeted the older man calmly. 'Do you understand us?'

'I do,' he heard someone else behind the man say.

'It's very dangerous,' repeated Fray Joaquín a dozen times as he approached the group of buildings that had been pointed out to them as making up Méndez's establishment. The place was a nest of smugglers. Milagros walked decisively, with her head held high.

'At least cover your face up again,' he begged her, quickening his step to offer her the mantilla.

She didn't even answer. Countless possibilities, all of them terrifying, were going through the friar's head. Melchor might not be there; he could even be this Méndez's enemy. He feared for himself, but above all for Milagros. Few people failed to notice her presence; they stopped, they looked at her, there were even some who complimented her in that strange language they spoke in Barrancos.

What have I got Milagros into? he lamented just as they went through the gates of Méndez's establishment. Several runners were lazing around the large dirt courtyard that opened out in front of the smuggler's headquarters; one of them whistled when he saw Milagros. A couple of shady-looking women, peeking out of one of the windows of the bedroom that extended over the stables, screwed up their faces at the friar's arrival and a band of half-naked little kids who ran among the sleepy mules tied to posts stopped to go over to them.

'Who are you?' asked one of the children.

'Have you got any sweets?' enquired another.

They had already reached the main house. None of the men who were watching them made any motion towards them. Milagros was about to swat away the pestering kids when Fray Joaquín intervened again.

'No,' he said before she could deal out the brusque gesture, 'we don't have sweets, but I do have this,' he added, showing them a two-real coin.

The children milled around the friar with their eyes bright at the sight of the copper coin.

'I will give it to you if you let Mr Méndez know that he has visitors.'

'And who is asking for him?'

The children were silent; some of the runners stood up and the prostitutes in the window stuck their heads out even further.

'The granddaughter of Melchor Vega, El Galeote,' Milagros answered then.

Méndez, the smuggler, appeared in the door of the main house. He looked the gypsy woman up and down, cocked his head, scrutinized her again, let a few seconds pass and then smiled. With a snort, Fray Joaquín let out all the air he had been holding in his lungs.

'Milagros, right?' the smuggler asked then. 'Your grandfather has told me a lot about you. Welcome.'

One of the children demanded Fray Joaquín's attention, pulling on the sleeve of his habit.

'For that coin I'll take you to El Galeote,' he offered.

Milagros jumped and leapt on the little boy.

'He's here?' she shrieked. 'Where? You know where...?' Suddenly she was wary. What if the kid was tricking them just to get the coin? She turned to the smuggler and questioned him with eyes that could penetrate the entire building.

'He arrived a couple of weeks ago,' confirmed Méndez.

With the smuggler still in front of her, Milagros stammered something that could have been a thank you or a farewell, grabbed the end of her long black skirt, revealing her ankles and, with it hiked up on one side, prepared to follow the little kids, who were already waiting for them amid laughter and shouts beside the entrance gates to the smuggler's establishment.

'Let's go!' one of them urged.

'Let's go, Fray Joaquín,' Milagros hurried him, already a few steps ahead.

Unlike Milagros, the priest said goodbye in clear voice. 'I can't go carrying the Virgin,' he then complained.

But Milagros didn't hear him. A girl had grabbed her by the hand and was pulling her towards the road.

Fray Joaquín followed them unhurriedly, exaggerating the weight of the statue he had carried with no problem over half of Spain. Melchor was in Barrancos, thanks be to God. He had never really believed they would find him. *I would kill for her. You are a payo . . . and a friar as well. You could renounce your vows, but not your race.* The warning the gypsy had given him one day on the banks of the Guadalquivir, at the possibility of a relationship with his granddaughter, had gripped his stomach as soon as Méndez had confirmed his presence in Barrancos. El Galeote would do anything for her! Hadn't he already killed Milagros's father for allowing her to marry a García?

'What are you doing?'

Two of the kids were fighting to help him with the weight of the statue of the Virgin.

'Give it to them!' ordered Milagros, ahead of him. 'Or we'll never get there!'

He didn't hand it over to them; he wasn't sure he wanted to meet Melchor Vega face to face.

'Get out of here!' he shouted to the pair of runny-nosed kids who, despite everything, continued to try to help him to carry the parcel. They were more of a nuisance than anything else.

Milagros waited for him, holding up the hem of her skirt,

impatient. The girl accompanying her stayed by her side, hands on her hips, imitating the gypsy woman's stance.

'What's going on with you?' Milagros asked him, puzzled.

I'm going to lose you, that's what's going on. Don't you realize? he wanted to say.

'What are a few minutes after we've come so far?' he answered instead, more gruffly than he would have liked.

She misinterpreted his tone and her expression soured. She looked at the kids, who continued running happily ahead, silhouetted against the sun. She was overcome by doubts.

'Do you think . . . ?' She let her arms drop to her sides. Her skirt fell. 'You told me that my grandfather would forgive me.'

'And he will,' Fray Joaquín assured her, to keep himself from suggesting they run away together again, that they take to the roads with the statue of the Virgin.

But the friar's despondency came through in his voice. Milagros sensed it and adapted her pace to match his.

'She is a García too,' she murmured.

'What?'

'My little girl. My girl, María. She is a García too. My grandfather's hatred of them is greater than . . . everything! Even the affection he once had for me,' she added in a thin voice.

Fray Joaquín sighed, aware of the contradictions that lashed his soul. When he saw her happy, excited, he despaired, terrified at the idea of losing her, but when he saw her suffering, then . . . then he wanted to help her, encourage her to go to her grandfather.

'A lot of time has passed,' he said without conviction.

'What if he doesn't forgive me for marrying Pedro García? Grandfather . . .'

'He will forgive you.'

'My mother disowned me for it. My mother!'

They reached the foot of a hill, outside the town. The oldest of the children was waiting for them there; the others were already running uphill.

A single solitary house atop the hill overlooked the lands; several of the kids pointed in that direction.

'He's up there?' asked Fray Joaquín, taking advantage of the pause to place the statue on the ground.

'Yes.'

'What's Melchor doing up there, alone?' he wondered, surprised.

'He's not alone,' said the boy. 'He lives with the Negress.'

Milagros wanted to say something but the words didn't come out. She trembled and sought out the friar for support.

'Caridad,' he whispered.

'Yes,' confirmed the boy. 'Caridad. They are always there, see them?'

Fray Joaquín sharpened his gaze until he could make out two figures sitting in front of the house, on the edge of a cliff.

Milagros, her eyes damp and her senses clouded, couldn't see a thing.

'Since they arrived,' the boy continued explaining, 'they've gone out a few nights to smuggle. Every time they came back with sweets! Caridad loves sweets . . . and she shared them with us. And Gregoria, the girl . . .' The boy scanned the path. '. . . that one, you see her? The first one, the little one who runs the fastest, well, they brought Gregoria some sandals because she couldn't walk, she had huge gashes on the soles of her feet. Look how she's running now!' Fray Joaquín watched little Gregoria leap. 'But the rest of the time they spend sitting up there, hugging each other, smoking and looking out on the fields. We sneak up a lot, but they always catch us. Gregoria can't keep still!'

'Hugging?'

The question came from Milagros, who tried to dry her eyes to focus them on the top of the hill.

'Yes. All the time! They pull each other close and then El Galeote says to Caridad, "Sing, *morena*!"'

Sing, *morena*! Milagros was starting to be able to make out the peak. Cachita! That friend whom she'd hit and insulted, whom she'd said she never wanted to see again for as long as she lived.

'Gregoria is already at the top!' exclaimed the boy. 'Let's go!'

Both Fray Joaquín and Milagros straightened up. The two seated figures stood when the little girl reached them. Gregoria was pointing at the foot of the hill. Milagros felt Melchor's gaze on her as if, despite the distance, he was right beside her.

'Let's go!' insisted the boy.

Fray Joaquín knelt to pick up the statue of the Virgin.

'I can't,' Milagros groaned.

Caridad grabbed Melchor's hand and squeezed it. The touch of his coarse, rough palm, hardened by ten years rowing on the galley ship, calmed her. They were the same palms that had run over her body countless times since Melchor had showed up in Torrejón; the same ones that she had bathed in tears as she kissed them; the ones that he had brought to her cheeks waiting for a reply when just a few days later Don Valerio forbade her to live in mortal sin with a gypsy. 'This set-up with the ragmen isn't going to work,' Melchor warned her. 'They will catch us; they'll end up arresting us. Let's go far from here. To Barrancos.' Caridad's smile sealed the pact between the former slave and the gypsy with a gleam in his eye and a face grooved with lines. Barrancos, where they'd first fallen in love, where she'd felt like a woman for the first time, where the law couldn't reach them. They paid plenty, travelling quickly in a covered wagon to Extremadura, eager to leave it all behind.

Melchor, stock-still, expectant, with his gaze and his other senses trained on the foot of the hill, responded by squeezing her hand in return. On that occasion, the gypsy's touch didn't calm her: Caridad knew she was part of his whirlwind of worries, because she felt them too. Milagros! After so many years . . . Without letting go of his hand, she shifted her gaze from that figure dressed in black to the universe that opened up at her feet: fields, rivers, valleys, untilled lands and forests; each and every one of them had absorbed her songs as they sat, looking out on the horizon, in that new life that fortune had afforded them. She would oblige Melchor and lift her voice, a voice that she often left hanging in the air to follow its reverberation along the paths they had travelled together, loaded down with tobacco and a love that quickened their steps, their movements, their smiles. They had gone out again by night with their backpacks filled with tobacco. They didn't need the money; they had more than enough. They only wanted to travel those paths again, cross the river again, run and hide at the crunch of a twig, sleep out in the open . . . make love under the stars. They lived for each other, with nothing better to do than look at each other while they smoked. Nights of caresses, smiles, conversations and long silences. They consoled each other over bad memories; they promised each other, with a simple touch, that nothing and no one would ever separate them again.

'Why doesn't she come up?' she heard the gypsy ask.

Caridad felt a shiver: the breeze from the fields hitting her face warned her that Milagros's arrival would affect her happiness. She didn't want her to come up, she wished she would turn around and retrace her steps . . . She looked again at the foot of the hill just as the gypsy woman began her ascent. Melchor squeezed her hand harder and held it while they approached.

'Fray Joaquín?' he said in a surprised tone. 'Is that Fray Joaquín?'

Caridad didn't answer, although she too recognized the friar priest. Even the children grew silent and moved to the side, serious, solemn, at Milagros's arrival. The stifled sobs of the gypsy woman masked any other sound. Caridad noticed a tremble in Melchor's hand, in his entire body. Milagros stopped a few paces away, with Fray Joaquín behind her, and she looked up towards her grandfather; then she shifted her gaze to Caridad and then back to Melchor. The silence dragged on. Caridad stopped feeling El Galeote trembling. She was the one who trembled now at Milagros's tears, at the storm of memories that came rushing to her mind. She heard again those first words from the gypsy girl as she lay in the small courtyard on the San Miguel alley after Melchor found her feverish beneath an orange tree; remembered the pontoon bridge and the church of the Negritos; the gypsy settlement on the grounds of the Carthusian monastery; the cigars and her red outfit; Old María; the round-up; the flight through the Andévalo . . . She spurned her fears and let go of Melchor's hand. She stepped forward, a small, indecisive step. Milagros's eyes begged her to take another, and Caridad ran into her arms.

'Go to him,' she said after the first embrace.

Milagros shifted her gaze towards Melchor, stern and proud up on his hill.

'He loves you,' added Caridad, sensing the young woman's hesitation, 'but, for as much as he hides or denies it, I know that he fears you haven't forgiven him for . . . for your father. Forget what happened,' she insisted, pushing her gently from behind.

Milagros left Caridad and Fray Joaquín and walked uphill. Her own tears prevented her from noticing Melchor's damp eyes. How many times had she tried to convince herself that what had happened to her father had been done in a fit of rage? She wanted to forgive him, but she couldn't be sure if he had forgotten what he considered a worse betrayal of her Vega blood: her marriage to Pedro, another link in the chain of hatred that set the two families against each other. How was Melchor going to forget the Garcías? Just a few years ago the Garcías had tried to kill him . . .

'Damn the Virgin of Bonaire!'

The gypsy stopped at her grandfather's curse. She looked at Melchor in horror and then behind her and to both sides. What was he trying . . . ?

'What are you doing dressed in sinister black?'

She looked at her mourning clothes as if it were the first time she had seen them. When she looked up she saw Melchor was smiling.

45

'I GOT THE WRONG MAN.'
Melchor's words made Caridad cower, even more than she had been doing as she listened to Milagros's long, cruel story. The four of them were around the table: Melchor and Caridad in their regular chairs with willow-cane seats, while Milagros sat on the stool they kept for Martín's visits each time his contraband brought him to the area; the friar was standing, uncomfortable, looking here and there for a place to lean, until Melchor pierced him with a look and he was still for a while.

Caridad looked for a tiny bit of the tenderness in Melchor's gaze, but she found his eyes pinched and his pupils ice-cold. The gypsy spoke few words over the course of his granddaughter's story: a curt 'thank you' to the friar when he found out that he had saved Milagros's life, and brief questions about the daughter she'd had with the García boy. His most important question, 'Do you have any news of your mother?' was met with a sob from Milagros. Caridad sensed how her man was repressing his emotions. *Start swearing!* she wanted to encourage him, still shaken up by Milagros's words, seeing the tension that gripped Melchor's body, his fists clenched on the table. *Damn all the gods in the universe!* she was about to shout when she managed to stop listening to the horrible story of rapes that Milagros was telling them and she turned towards Melchor with her throat seized. The veins on his neck were swollen and throbbing. *They're going to burst, gypsy,* she thought, growing even more distressed. *They're going to burst.*

She knew that she shouldn't follow him when, after the conversation ended, he got up and headed towards the door to the house.

'I got the wrong man,' he said before leaving.

As those words echoed, Caridad watched the gypsy head out into the reddish dusk that floated above the peaks; he was challenging the entire world, even the air he was breathing had become his enemy. A thousand stabs then reminded her of the scars on her back, which Melchor had caressed and kissed. The whip cracked again in her ears. Slavery, the tobacco plantation, La Galera prison . . . She thought . . . she thought she had left all that behind for ever. How naive she had been! She was enjoying happiness with the gypsy, in Barrancos, far from it all, 'close to heaven,' as she had whispered with excitement and gratitude when Melchor showed her the house he had rented on top of the hill. How stupid! What a fool! She fought against the tears that flooded her eyes. She didn't want to cry, she didn't want to give in . . . She felt Milagros's hand on hers.

'Cachita,' she sobbed, lost in her own pain.

Caridad was slow to respond to her touch. She tightened her lips, although not even that managed to control her trembling. She felt weak, dizzy. She had listened to Milagros's story with her spirit torn between the granddaughter's pain, the grandfather's rage, and the premonition of her own unhappiness, leaping frantically from one to the other following their words, gestures and silences. Milagros pressed on her hand, searching for a comfort that Caridad wasn't sure she wanted to offer her. She met her gaze, her doubts fading when she saw her friend's flushed face, her bloodshot eyes, the tears running down her cheeks. She surrendered to sobs.

From one corner, distressed, Fray Joaquín watched as the two women got up awkwardly, and hugged each other, and cried, and tried to look at each other and, tongue-tied, stammer out unintelligible words, before embracing again.

Night fell and Melchor still hadn't returned, and Caridad prepared dinner: a nice loaf of white bread, cold cuts, garlic, onions, oil and quince jelly that Martín had brought them. They didn't talk much. Fray Joaquín tried to break the silence by asking about

Caridad's life. 'I've survived,' she offered as the only explanation.

'What could Melchor be doing?' the friar asked again, after a long silence.

Caridad looked at the piece of onion she held between her fingers, as if surprised by its presence. 'Demanding the devil give him back his gypsy spirit.'

The mix of bitterness and sadness in her response kept the friar from making any other attempts. She wasn't the newly freed slave who dropped her gaze before white men, nor the woman who offered a piece of tobacco leaf in the church of San Jacinto while she sang softly and rocked back and forth on her knees before the Virgin of Candelaria. She was a woman hardened by experiences she didn't want to recount to them, different from the one he had met in Triana. It wasn't difficult for Fray Joaquín to understand Caridad's concerns: their arrival had shattered the hard-won happiness she'd achieved. He turned towards Milagros, wondering if she also noticed it: she was chewing on the dried salted meat apathetically, as if she were being forced to eat. She hadn't made any comment about Melchor and Caridad living together. The house only had one bedroom, and in it there was just one straw mattress. Here and there, the few belongings they had were mixed together: a bright red short jacket with gold piping and buttons that Melchor had forgotten, beside a wool shawl that surely belonged to Caridad. One object stood out among the routine practicality of the others: a wind-up toy on a stone cupboard. On numerous occasions over the course of the evening, whenever Melchor shifted his gaze on to Fray Joaquín as Milagros referred to him in her story, the friar had looked at the toy. *Does it still work?* he wondered, trying to distance himself from the suspicions he sensed in Melchor's gaze. Fray Joaquín knew that he wasn't welcome there. Melchor would never accept him; he was a friar and a *payo* besides, as he had warned him in Triana. Wasn't he himself living with a Negress? But Melchor would never allow his granddaughter, a Vega, of the Triana Vegas from the settlement at La Cartuja, to be with him. What Fray Joaquín didn't know was what the gypsy woman thought.

'I need to rest,' murmured Milagros.

Fray Joaquín saw her point to the straw mattress in the next room, asking Caridad for permission. She nodded her head.

Caridad left the house as soon as she heard Milagros's slow breathing. Fray Joaquín was wrong when he thought she had gone out in search of Melchor. She headed to Méndez's establishment, asked for him, and urged him to find Martín that very night.

'Yes, tonight,' she insisted. 'Have all the runners you can round up go out in search of him tonight. The entire town of Barrancos if need be! You have our money invested in the tobacco,' Caridad reminded him. 'Pay what they ask, just find him.'

Then she went back to the house and sat in front of the friar, attentive to the slightest sound that might come from outside. Nothing happened, and with the first light of dawn, she stretched and began to prepare a bundle with her belongings and some food.

'What are you doing?' asked Fray Joaquín.

'Haven't you realized yet, Father?' she asked, her back to him, hiding her tears. 'We're going back to Triana.'

A simple exchange of glances was enough for Melchor and Caridad to tell each other anything they needed to. *I have to do it*, morena, said the gypsy's. *I'm coming with you*, replied hers. Neither of them discussed the other's decision.

'On the road,' ordered Melchor later, addressing Milagros and the friar, both seated at the table waiting for him to return.

Melchor put on his short red jacket calmly; he didn't need anything more. Caridad tossed the bundle on her back and prepared to follow him. Milagros had nothing, and the friar felt ridiculous when he picked up the statue of the Virgin.

'And . . . ?' asked Fray Joaquín, pointing to that object that stood out atop the cupboard: the wind-up toy.

Caridad frowned. *They are going to kill Melchor!* she could have answered. *And me too, probably. This is our house and here is where it should be*, she would have added. *This is its place.* She turned and headed towards the door.

Caridad and Melchor began the march, with Milagros behind them and Fray Joaquín lagging somewhat, as if he weren't part of the group, all in silence, the leaders choosing the same paths they had taken so many times with tobacco on their backs, passing where they had hidden when they suspected a patrol, crossing the river at the same point where they had been together for the first time.

Milagros, unlike Caridad, who had already accepted her man's fate, was plunged in doubts as she walked: neither she nor her grandfather uttered any recriminations over what had happened in Triana. They hadn't talked about her father's death, or about her marriage to Pedro García. They'd just hugged each other as if the mere gesture itself would banish all the heartache into the distant past. How was her grandfather planning to get María back? Milagros asked herself again and again. *I got the wrong man,* he had said. It seemed that the only thing he was interested in was taking revenge on Pedro, on the Garcías . . . How could he do that alone?

She slowed her pace until Fray Joaquín, who kept wondering if he had done the right thing by going to Barrancos, reached her.

'What is he planning?' asked Milagros as she pointed to her grandfather's back with her chin.

'I don't know.'

'But . . . he's not going to go into the alley, like that, alone, without backup. What is he going to do?'

'I don't know, Milagros, but I'm afraid that is his plan.'

'They'll kill him. And my girl? What will become of her?'

'Melchor!' The friar's shout interrupted Milagros.

He turned his head without stopping.

'What's your plan?'

GALLEY LAMENT

46

THE ONLY PLAN Melchor had in mind was entering Triana along the road from Camas and crossing it until he reached the entrance to the San Miguel alley. And that was what he did after a week of travelling, despite the doubts and objections raised by both Milagros and the friar priest, who, in spite of it all, continued walking through the outskirts of Seville.

The early summer sun was high in the sky and drew glints from the gold accents on the gypsy's jacket. Melchor stopped before the entrance to the alley, in front of the others and with Caridad by his side, and stroked the knife handle that emerged from his sash while some men and women looked at him in surprise and others ran to their forges and their homes to warn of his arrival.

Soon the hammering stopped. The smiths came out of their forges, the women peeked out of windows and the children, infected by the tension they sensed in the grown-ups, stopped playing.

Caridad recognized some of the men and women and, gradually, as the rumours died down, silence was heard. Everything had started in that alley, and everything would end there, she lamented. Suddenly she felt strong, invincible, and she wondered if that was what Melchor was feeling, what had led him to act the way he did, scorning the dangers. She had had her own doubts along the way, hearing the constant complaints from Milagros and the friar priest, their warnings tinged with a dread that she too shared. She didn't speak, she didn't admit her fears, she supported Melchor with her silence, and now, resigned to the fate that awaited her man, and probably her too, before men and women whose initial surprise had turned to rage, she thought she finally understood the gypsy's character. She drew herself up straight and felt her muscles tense. Surprised by her own assurance, she shared Melchor's defiance. She lived in the present, that very moment, completely removed from what could happen in the next.

'Gypsy.' Melchor didn't move, but she knew he was listening to her. 'I love you.'

'And I love you, *morena*. I will miss your singing when I'm in hell.'

Caridad was about to respond when what the crowd gathered in the alley was waiting for happened: Rafael García, El Conde, and his wife Reyes, La Trianera, made their way slowly towards them, both of them older, stooped. They were followed by various members of the García family and other gypsies that joined the ranks. Caridad and Melchor waited motionless; Milagros, behind them, took a few steps back, searching for Pedro with her restless gaze. She didn't see him. Fray Joaquín tried to hold the Immaculate Virgin firmly in his grip as she slipped from his sweaty hands. The appearance of the patriarch emboldened the others. 'Murderer!' someone shouted. 'Son of a bitch!' another insulted Melchor. 'Swine!' A group of women came over to Milagros and spat at her feet as they shouted 'Harlot!' An old woman tried to grab her by the hair and she drew closer to Fray Joaquín, who managed to scare off the aggressor. The insults, threats and obscene gestures continued as El Conde moved towards Melchor.

'I come to kill your grandson,' he spat above the din before they reached him.

Hearing Melchor's cold, steely, cutting words, Caridad clenched her fists. Yet the threat didn't intimidate the patriarch who, knowing he was protected, continued walking with an impassive face and his eyes fixed on Melchor.

'You've been sentenced to death . . .' replied Rafael García before the crowd's shouts thundered again through the alley.

'Let's kill him!'

Caridad turned towards Melchor as some of the gypsies were

already heading towards them, hurling curses and insults. How could he take on the entire alley?

'Melchor,' she whispered. But he didn't move; he remained still, tense, defiant.

His fearlessness sent a shiver down Caridad's spine.

'Gypsy!' she then exclaimed in a very clear, powerful voice. 'I'll sing for you in hell!'

She hadn't finished the sentence before she pushed aside a man who was coming for them and leapt on to Rafael García, knocking him down. The attack surprised the gypsies who, watching Melchor, were slow to react. Tangled on the ground, Caridad searched frantically for the knife she had seen in the patriarch's sash. She would kill him for her man!

Melchor was also surprised by Caridad's unexpected assault. It took him a few seconds to pull out his knife and hold it up at several of the gypsies who surrounded him. He tried to think, keep cool, as he knew he should in the face of the weapons he was up against, but the shouting from behind his opponents – where Caridad was – clouded his senses and led him to launch countless random stabs in order to make his way towards her.

'Do you want us to kill your Negress right now?'

Melchor didn't even hear the threat. Then a gap opened up between the gypsies surrounding him and he found himself stabbing the air in front of Caridad, who was struggling to get out of the arms of the two men who had her immobilized. He stopped the last stab, suddenly, in mid-air.

'Keep going!' she urged him.

Someone slapped her. Melchor thought he could hear that arm whistling through the air and felt the blow himself, with more violence than the whiplashes on the galley. He shrank back in pain.

'Keep going, gypsy!' shrieked Caridad.

No one hit her that time. Melchor, shaken up by the trickle of blood that flowed from the corner of Caridad's mouth and ran down her chin, red on black, regretted having allowed her to come with him. Two more men were needed to contain Caridad, who shook and screamed when she saw others attacking Melchor. Defenceless and defeated, they disarmed him and, like an animal being led to sacrifice, bent over, they presented him to Rafael García, who had already recovered from the attack, amid the cheers and acclaim of the gypsy settlement.

'I'm sorry, *morena*, forgive me.'

Melchor's apologies were lost in her sobbing and the orders with which El Conde received his enemy.

'The whore!' he shouted, pointing to Milagros. 'Bring me the whore, too!'

The women near Milagros pounced on her and immobilized her without the slightest resistance; her attention was focused on her grandfather, her hopes dashed at the sound of four simple shouts and about the same number of threats.

Fray Joaquín, still carrying the sculpture of the Virgin, couldn't do a thing and just watched as Milagros let herself be carried off amid shoves, shouts and gobs of spit. Suddenly, the men and women focused their attention on the friar priest, who had been left alone at the entrance to the alley.

'Leave, Father,' Rafael García threatened him, 'this is a matter between gypsies.'

Fray Joaquín was surprised by the hatred and rage reflected in many of their faces. Yet his fear turned into anxiety when he saw Milagros beside Melchor, with her head down. What had become of the promises he had made to her?

'No,' replied the friar. 'This is a matter for the King's justice, like everything that happens in his lands, whether or not gypsies are involved.'

Several of them ran towards him.

'I am a man of God!' Fray Joaquín managed to shout.

'Halt!'

Rafael García's order stopped the men. The patriarch squinted his eyes and sought the opinion of the heads of the other families: the Camachos, the Flores, the Reyes ... Some shrugged indifferently; most shook their heads. It was unlikely that anyone in the alley would break gypsy law and speak about Melchor, Milagros or even Caridad, El Conde thought then, and if they did, the authorities wouldn't say a word. They'd just conclude it was another gypsy scuffle. But detaining a clergyman was different. Perhaps one of the women or the children might let it slip, and then there would be terrible consequences for them all. They had worked hard with the Church; the young folk went there to learn their prayers, and almost the entire alley attended mass with feigned devotion. The brotherhood was up and running. Less than a year ago the archbishop had approved the rules of the Gypsy Brotherhood and there were already quite a few problems. They hadn't been able to establish it at the monastery of the Holy Spirit in Triana and they were still trying at Our Lady of Pópulo. They wouldn't achieve their goal if the Augustinians found out about this. They needed to maintain good relations with those who could jail them. No. They couldn't risk offending the Church by taking action against one of their own clergymen.

Rafael García gestured to the men and they moved away from the friar priest. But he wasn't planning on doing the same for those Vegas . . .

'Release them,' Fray Joaquín interrupted his thoughts.

El Conde shook his head stubbornly and then Reyes came over and whispered in his ear.

'She,' the patriarch pointed to Milagros after his wife stepped aside, 'stays here with her husband, which is where she belongs. Or am I wrong, Father?'

Fray Joaquín went pale and was unable to answer.

'No. I see that I'm not wrong. As for the other two . . .'

Reyes was right: who could know about or prove the murder of José Carmona besides the gypsies? No one had reported it to the authorities; they'd buried him in an open field and the crime had been dealt with in the privacy of the council of elders. How could *payo* law intervene?

'As for them,' he repeated smugly, 'they will remain with us until the officers of the King whom your reverence spoke of come looking for them. You understand,' he added, pleased with himself, as some of the gypsies in the crowd smiled, 'we are making sure they are safe. Someone could hurt them.'

'Rafael García,' threatened Fray Joaquín, 'I will come back for them. If anything happens to them . . .' He stammered; he knew that he would achieve nothing alone, that he needed help. 'If anything happens to them, the full weight of the law and divine justice will fall on your head. On all of your heads!'

47

'THEY'VE GONE,' announced Rafael García.

'What . . . ?' shouted Fray Joaquín angrily, waving his arms wildly.

But he kept quiet after an order from the prior of San Jacinto.

'When did they leave?' asked the friar priest.

'Shortly after Fray Joaquín left,' responded Rafael García as if it were the most natural thing in the world. He stood at the entrance to the smithy, beneath his apartment, where his large family continued working, completely unconcerned at the visit of the five friars, including the prior of the San Jacinto monastery, who accompanied Fray Joaquín.

The gypsies who wandered through the alley didn't seem interested in the scene either. Only Reyes, above them, hidden behind a window on the first floor, perked up her ears to listen in on the conversation.

'They said they were going to look for you,' added Rafael, looking directly at Fray Joaquín. 'Didn't they find you?'

'No! You're lying!' accused the friar, who fell silent again at the request of his superior.

'And why did you let them go?'

'Why wouldn't I? They are free; they've committed no crime. I don't know . . . they can come back whenever they want.'

'Fray Joaquín maintains that you were holding them with the intention of killing them. And—'

'Reverend Father . . .' El Conde interrupted him, showing the palms of his hands.

'And I believe him,' said the prior before he could go on.

'Kill them? How barbaric! It goes against the law, against the divine precepts! We wouldn't harm anyone, your eminence. I don't know what to tell you. They just left. Ask around.' Rafael García then indicated to several of the gypsies on the alley to come over. 'Isn't it true that El Galeote, his granddaughter and the Negress left?' he asked them.

'Yes,' two of them answered in unison.

'I heard them say they were going to San Jacinto,' added an old, toothless gypsy woman.

The prior shook his head, as did two of the friars who accompanied them. Fray Joaquín's face was still enraged, his fists clenched.

'Your reverences can search the alley,' El Conde then suggested. 'Every house if you wish! You will see that they are not here. We have nothing to hide.'

'Would you like to start with my house?' offered the old gypsy woman with feigned earnestness.

Fray Joaquín was about to accept her offer when the prior's voice stopped him.

'Rafael García, the truth always comes out, keep that in mind. I will be watching, and you will pay dearly if anything happens to them.'

'I already told . . .'

The prior lifted one hand, turned his back and left him with the words still on his lips.

That night, guitars were heard in the San Miguel alley. The weather was splendid; the temperature, mild; and the gypsies, mainly the Garcías and the Carmonas, were in the mood for celebrating. Men and women sang and danced fandangos, *seguidillas* and *zarabandas*.

'Just kill them,' La Trianera urged her husband. 'We'll bury them far from here, beyond the lowlands, where no one can find them,' she added at Rafael's silence. 'No one will ever know.'

'I agree with Reyes,' declared Ramón Flores.

'Pascual Carmona has to kill them,' stated Rafael, who still remembered the rage and violence with which Pascual, the head of the

Carmonas since old Inocencio's death, had burst into his house after Melchor's escape in Madrid. He shook him and threatened him, and if it weren't for the intervention of his own relatives, he would have hit him. 'I'd like to do it myself, I would pay to execute El Galeote, but the revenge belongs to the Carmonas; it is theirs by right of blood. It was a Carmona El Galeote killed, Pascual's brother in fact. We should wait for his return. I don't think he'll be long. Besides . . .' El Conde pointed with his chin past the dancing gypsies, where Fray Joaquín remained leaning against the wall of one of the buildings. '. . . what's he still doing here?'

Fray Joaquín had refused to return to San Jacinto with the prior and the other friars. He stayed in the alley, asking everyone he met and always getting the same answer.

'Father,' complained a gypsy woman when he grabbed a boy by the shoulders and shook him after he answered him with hesitation in his eyes, 'leave the little one alone. I already told you what you want to know.'

He went into some of the apartments clustered around the court-yards. The gypsies allowed it. He walked through them with children and old ladies observing him closely. He inspected the squalid rooms and, desperate, even shouted out Milagros's name: his words echoed strangely in the courtyard. Someone started tapping a hammer to mock the impertinent friar's heartbroken screams. The incessant, monotone banging of the hammers accompanied some verses that urged the friar to leave. 'I won't go,' he decided nonetheless. He would remain there, in the alley, alert, for as long as it took: someone would make a mistake; someone would tell him where to find them. He began to pray, contrite, repentant at turning to divine help that he didn't believe he deserved after having run off with Milagros and having used the Virgin to cheat people.

'The friar?' spat La Trianera. 'We'll see if he stays there once Pedro comes back.'

Hearing the name of La Trianera's grandson, Ramón Flores made a face that didn't go unnoticed to Rafael, who in turn shook his head, his lips pursed. He had sent a couple of boys to try to find him and let him know about Milagros's arrival. He told them to search for him in the many inns and bars of Seville where he whiled away the hours and spent the plentiful money he had brought back from Madrid, wine and women flowing. *Where had he got so much money?* El Conde wondered. The boys had come back in the mid-afternoon with no news. Rafael insisted, sending two young men who could continue searching by night, but they still didn't know where he was.

'Melchor Vega is a lucky man,' pointed out La Trianera, interrupting her husband's thoughts. 'He survived the galleys. For years he's been smuggling tobacco and the patrol hasn't caught him, and he even escaped from the Garcías in Madrid. It seemed impossible, but he did it. I wouldn't wait another minute before finishing him off.'

Rafael García turned his gaze to Fray Joaquín again. He was wary of his presence, the prior of San Jacinto's threat still present in his memory.

'I told you that Pascual is the one who should kill him. We will wait for him.'

The dawn found Fray Joaquín sleepy, sitting on the ground and resting against the wall, in the same place he had been standing until well into the early hours, when the gypsies went back to their homes. Some even wished him a sarcastic good night; others mocked him with a greeting in the morning. The friar didn't answer in either case. He felt as if he hadn't slept a wink, but he had; enough to not realize that Pedro García had returned. The darkness was almost absolute. Pedro had looked at him in shock, sprawled out there. He didn't see his face, so he couldn't be sure it was him. He thought about kicking him, but decided against it and headed towards the apartments.

'Is that friar who I think he is?' he asked his grandfather after waking him up rudely.

'It's Fray Joaquín, from San Jacinto,' he answered.

'What's he doing here?' Pedro wanted to know.

La Trianera, who was sleeping beside her husband, closed her eyes tightly after seeing her grandson's nervousness. Although Bartola consistently backed his story, and the García and Carmona families insulted Milagros and repudiated her, La Trianera had doubted Pedro as soon as she saw him show up with that pretty gypsy girl from Madrid, little María . . . and his purse filled with money. 'He must have stolen it from the whore when he found her out,' answered her husband when she revealed her doubts. But La Trianera knew that wasn't the case. After escorting her to all those performances and parties, she knew the Vega girl . . . and she never would have prostituted herself voluntarily; she had been raised with gypsy values. Days after their arrival, she questioned Bartola, just the two of them; her evasive answers were enough to convince her.

'Where is Milagros?' asked Pedro before his grandfather had finished explaining.

Rafael García violently shook off the hand his grandson had around his arm and got up from the straw mattress with surprising agility. Pedro almost fell to the floor.

'Don't you dare touch me,' El Conde warned him.

Pedro García, his balance regained, took a step backward. 'Where is she, Grandfather?' he repeated without hiding his anxiety.

Rafael García turned his head towards La Trianera.

'The pit in the forge,' guessed Pedro, 'that's where you're keeping them, right?'

A simple hole in the ground, covered with planks where the Garcías hid goods and chattels, especially stolen goods, in case a constable came into the forge. It wasn't the first time they had used it to hide someone, they'd even tried it during the big round-up, but they had crammed so many in that the King's soldiers had laughed when they arrested them.

Milagros lifted her head as she heard the planks moving. The faint light of an oil lamp revealed the three of them sitting on the ground, hands and feet tied, packed together in the meagre pit. Above, she could make out the shapes of three men arguing. The oil lamp made one of their jackets glitter and Milagros screamed. Caridad could see the terror in her friend's eyes before she pulled her knees to her chest and tried to hide her head between them. Then she looked up towards where Melchor was: the argument was getting worse and the men were starting to tussle. It took them a while to recognize Pedro, who got free of the others and jumped into the pit with a gleaming knife in his hands.

'Don't kill her!' they heard Rafael García say.

'Whore!'

Pedro's shouting was lost amid Caridad's and Melchor's voices.

One of the gypsies leapt in and managed to grab Pedro's wrist just as he was about to stab his wife. A moment later there were two more holding him back.

'Bring him up here!' ordered El Conde.

A brutal kick in the face clouded Milagros's vision. Her head hit the wall violently.

'Leave me be! She's a whore! Let me finish her off!' shouted Pedro García. Unable to free his arm, he kicked her furiously.

Amid the blows and screams, Milagros thought she heard her grandfather's battle cry.

'Bastard dog!' she reacted and lifted her feet, still tied together, to kick back at her husband. She hit him on one thigh, not hard, but the blow calmed the pain of the others she received: on her face, chest, neck . . . She tried to land another one, but the two young men who were guarding the pit were already lifting Pedro up, as he kept kicking the air.

Milagros and Pedro exchanged a glance. He spat; she didn't even move. Her eyes oozed hatred.

'Have you gone mad?' Rafael García accused his grandson even before his body was entirely out of the pit. 'Silence!' he demanded, putting an end to the resistance with which Pedro returned to the surface. 'Don't let him anywhere near here again, do you understand?' he ordered the two guards. And turning to his grandson he added, 'Leave Triana. I don't want to see you here again until you get a message from me.'

While El Conde headed towards the door of the forge to look out at the alley, Milagros and Caridad communicated in a glance. Melchor remained downcast, mortified at not having been able to defend his granddaughter. *We are going to die*, the two women said to each other silently. Their faces hardened, since they didn't want those bastards to hear them cry.

Rafael García checked that the alley was deserted and in silence. He pricked up his ears and heard how that stillness was broken by a murmur the patriarch was slow to recognize: Caridad and Milagros's muffled singing down below in the pit. One began to softly sing her Negro songs and the other followed along, trying to overcome her fear with a fandango. A monotone rhythm joined by an upbeat one. The planks over their heads didn't allow them to see the gleams of the oil lamp.

'Shut up!' the gypsies guarding the pit ordered.

They did not.

Melchor listened to the songs of the two people he loved most and he shook his head, his throat choked. Why did it have to be here, now, when he finally heard them sing together? They continued in the darkness, Caridad gradually adding joy to her songs and Milagros drinking in the sadness of the slave melodies. Then they matched their rhythms. A shiver ran down Melchor's spine. Without music, without words, without shouting and clapping, the now fused, single song sung by the two women resounded off the planks that covered the pit, filling it with pain, friendship, betrayals, love, experiences, lost hopes . . .

Up above, when Pedro had left the smithy far behind, the two young guards questioned the patriarch with their gaze. Rafael didn't answer, transfixed by the women's voices.

'Silence!' he shouted nervously, as if he had been caught out. 'Be quiet or I will finish you off myself,' he added, kicking the planks.

They ignored him. El Conde eventually shrugged, ordered the young men to bolt the doors of the smithy and went home. Caridad and Milagros kept singing until dawn broke, though they couldn't see even a glimpse of its light.

Sitting on the ground, Fray Joaquín felt how the passing hours transformed the space that surrounded him: the din of hammering and the clouds of smoke that came from the lower levels of the forges; the shouts and playing of children and the gypsies coming and going, or simply chatting and loafing about.

He couldn't stop what he was sure was going to happen. He couldn't even count on his religious community. A plague of locusts was destroying the Sevillian crops, and the friars were needed to recite rogations against that divine punishment that so frequently laid waste to the harvests, leaving hunger and epidemics in its wake. The prior, spellbound by the statue of the Immaculate Virgin, had asked to carry it in the procession. It would always be better than excommunicating the locusts, as some priests did. Fray Joaquín wondered about appealing to the authorities, but he desisted at the thought of the questions they would ask him. He didn't know how to lie, and the officials weren't interested in gypsy quarrels. Giving himself up to them would do no good.

Reyes and Rafael watched him from the window of their home.

'I don't like having him there,' commented the patriarch.

'And Pedro?' she asked.

'He left. I ordered him not to return until I say so.'

'When is Pascual Carmona coming back?'

'I've already sent for him. According to his wife, he's in Granada. I trust they will find him soon.'

'We have to resolve this quickly. When are you going to hand the Vega girl over to Pedro?'

'When I've finished with the others. El Galeote is what concerns me. I don't want anything to get in the way of Pascual slitting his throat. After that, Pedro can do what he likes with the granddaughter.'

'Fine.'

Those were her last words before falling silent, looking out pensively on the alley, just as her husband did, and just as Fray Joaquín did. Suddenly, like everyone there, they focused their attention on a woman who had stopped at the entrance to the alleyway. 'Who . . . ?' some wondered. 'It can't be!' doubted others.

'Ana Vega,' murmured La Trianera in a halting voice.

Many were slow to recognize her; some didn't manage to at all. Reyes, however, could even sense the spirit of her enemy asserting itself on the skinny, wizened body that held it, in the haggard face and the gaze that emerged from deep eye sockets. She was barefoot and raggedy, her dirty hair white, and she wore old, stolen clothes.

Ana ran her eyes over the alley. It all seemed the same as when she had been forced to leave, years earlier. Perhaps there were fewer people . . . She stopped a second too long when she came across the friar, leaning on the wall, and for a brief instant she wondered what he was doing there. She recognized many others as she searched for Milagros: Carmonas, Vargases, Garcías . . . *Where are you, my daughter?* She sensed misgivings from the gypsies; some even lowered their heads. Why?

Ana had been walking for almost two months since leaving Saragossa; she had fled the House of Mercy with the fifteen Vega women who were left, including girls, after Salvador and the other boys were sent to the arsenals. No one followed them, as if they were pleased they were running away, content to be rid of them; they didn't even report their escape. They divided into two groups: one headed towards Granada; the other to Seville. Their thought was that that way some would make it. Ana headed the Sevillian party, which carried old Luisa Vega. 'You will die in your homeland,' she promised her. 'I'm not going to let you die in this disgusting jail.' They walked those two months before stopping in Carmona, just six leagues from Triana, where they were taken in by the Ximénez clan. Old Luisa was worn out and the others could barely continue carrying her. 'We're almost there, Aunt,' she tried to encourage her, but it was the old woman who objected. 'Let's rest here, where we're protected and safe,' replied another Vega. 'We've been gone for years, what could a few more days matter?' But they did matter to Ana: she needed to find Milagros, she wanted to tell her that she loved her. Five years of hunger, illness and punishments were enough. Gypsy women from historically embittered families had ended up helping each other and smiling at each other while they shared their misery. Milagros was her daughter, and if the quarrels between families had vanished over the years of adversity, how was she going to hold a grudge against someone of her own blood? What did it matter whom she had married? She loved her!

She continued the path alone and when she arrived at the alley she was met with sullen looks; whispers; gypsy women who turned their backs on her and ran to their houses, stuck their heads out of the windows or doors and pointed her out to their relatives.

'Ana . . . ? Ana Vega?' Fray Joaquín approached that woman who was looking at the street, perturbed.

'You still recognize me, Father?' she asked sarcastically. But something in the priest's face made her change her tone. 'Where is Milagros? Did something happen to her?'

He hesitated. How could he recount so much misfortune in a few sentences? Even the hammering in the forges stopped as Fray Joaquín told her what had happened.

Ana shouted to the heavens.

'Rafael García!' she howled soon after, running towards the patriarch's house. 'Son of a bitch! Bastard! Mangy dog . . . !'

No one stopped her. The people moved aside. Not even the Garcías, who remained in the door of their smithy, tried to keep her from entering the courtyard. She shouted to Rafael García at the foot of the stairs that led to the upper levels.

'Shut up!' shouted La Trianera from above, leaning on the railing of the long gallery. 'You are nothing more than the daughter of a murderer and the mother of a whore! Get out of here!'

'I'll kill you!'

Ana flew up the stairs. She didn't get to the old woman. The gypsy women in the gallery pounced on her.

'Get out!' ordered Reyes. 'Throw her down the stairs!'

They did. Ana stumbled down a few steps before she managed to grab hold of the railing and slid down a few more. She recovered.

'Your grandson sold my daughter!' she shouted, trying to go back up.

The García women in the gallery spat on her.

'That's every whore's excuse!' replied Reyes. 'Milagros is nothing more than a common harlot, the shame of gypsy women!'

'You lie!'

'I was there.' It was Bartola who spoke. 'Your daughter sold herself to men for a few *cuartos*.'

'Lies!' repeated Ana with all her strength. The others laughed. 'You lie,' she sobbed.

After a couple of attempts, she understood that no one would deal with her if the friar was there. Ana needed him: he was the only one who could speak in Milagros's favour to contradict the story Pedro had spread and La Triana had exaggerated, but finally she was forced to yield to gypsy customs.

'Go, Father,' she urged. 'You will only make things worse,' she insisted when Fray Joaquín refused. 'Can't you see? This is a gypsy matter.'

'I can go to the Chief Magistrate in Seville,' offered Fray Joaquín. 'I know people . . .'

Ana looked him up and down as he spoke. His appearance was as deplorable as his words were fiery.

'I don't know what interest you have in my daughter . . . although I can guess.'

Fray Joaquín confirmed her suspicions with a sudden flush.

'Listen to me: if a constable shows up here, the entire gypsy settlement would join forces with Rafael García in defence of gypsy law. They wouldn't listen to reason or arguments then . . .'

'What reason?' he exploded. 'There is no sentence on Milagros like there is on Melchor . . . and Caridad. Let's suppose she had become a harlot, that it were true, why keep her? What will they do to her?'

'They will hand her over to her husband. And after that nobody will worry about what might happen to her; nobody will ask about her.'

'Pedro . . .' muttered the priest. 'He may have already killed her.'

Ana Vega remained in silence for a few seconds.

'We must trust that he hasn't,' she finally whispered. 'If they are hidden here, on the alley, neither El Conde nor the other patriarchs would let them do that. A corpse always brings problems. They will demand that it's done outside of Triana, in secret, with no witnesses. Leave, Father. If we have any chance . . .'

'Leave? From what you say, if Milagros is in the alley, Pedro will have to take her out of here. I will wait at the entrance until Judgement Day if necessary. You do what you need to do.'

Ana didn't argue. She couldn't have, because Fray Joaquín turned his back on her, headed towards the entrance and leaned against the wall of the first building; his expression made it clear that he had made up his mind to stick it out there as long as he had to. Ana shook her head and wondered whether she should go over and tell him that there were many other ways to leave the alley: the windows and some of the back gates . . . Yet, she observed him and saw the blindness of someone in love. How long had it been since she'd seen passion in a man's eyes, the fear of his beloved being hurt, rage even? First a García and now a friar. She didn't know whether Milagros returned his feelings. In any case, that was the least of her worries. She had to do something. She didn't have the Vega men here to back her up. The women in the settlement at La Cartuja had always been hated by the people in the alley, who wanted to keep the peace with the *payos*, do business with them; it would do her little good to go to them with this problem.

She tightened her lips and began a pilgrimage that was much more difficult than the long, hard road from Saragossa. Forges, homes and courtyards where children played and women wove baskets. Some didn't even bother to turn their heads and listen to her pleas: 'Let my daughter defend herself from her husband's accusations.' She knew that she couldn't plead for her father. Gypsy law would be fulfilled: they would kill him, but the terrible anguish she felt over it was eased by the opportunity to fight unrelentingly for her daughter despite the weakness she felt. She got some reactions.

'If what you say is true,' replied a woman from the Flores family, 'why did your daughter allow it? Answer me, Ana Vega, wouldn't you have fought to the death to defend your virtue?'

Her knees were about to fail her.

'I would have ripped my husband's eyes out,' muttered an old woman who seemed to be dozing beside the first. 'Why didn't your daughter do that?'

'We shouldn't interfere in other people's marriages,' she heard at another house. 'We already gave your daughter another chance after the death of Alejandro Vargas, remember?'

'I won't lift a finger.' 'She deserves what she gets.' 'You Vegas have always been troublemakers. Look at your father.' 'Where's your haughtiness now?' The recriminations followed her wherever she went. Her hands were trembling and she felt a crushing pressure in her chest.

'Besides,' admitted a woman from the Flores family, 'you won't find anybody willing to challenge the Garcías. Everyone's afraid of going back to the arsenals, and El Conde has gained a lot of power with the *payos* and the priests.'

'Kill me instead!' Ana ended up screaming in the middle of the alley, defeated, desperate, when the sun was starting to set. 'Don't you want Vega blood? Take mine!'

No one answered. Only Fray Joaquín, at the other end of the alley, came to her, but before he reached her, another gypsy did. Ana didn't recognize him until he was quite close: it was Pedro García, who had returned, disobeying his grandfather's orders, when he found out that Ana Vega had showed up in the alley. In his arms he held a small girl who struggled and tried to hide her face in his neck, ever more anxiously as her father brought her closer to the madwoman screaming with her hands held high in the middle of the alley. The friar had told her about her granddaughter, and Ana recognized her in that girl. Pedro García stopped a few paces from her, stroked the little girl's hair, pulled her to him and then smiled. It had been worth arguing with his grandfather just to see the pain in the face of the woman who had dared to smack him in public some years ago; that was what he told El Conde, and Rafael García had finally understood and allowed it, with the promise that he would disappear again until El Galeote had been executed.

Ana fell to her knees on the ground, defeated, and broke down in tears.

48

AFTER A NIGHT of grieving, Ana came to believe that she had no tears left in her. Fray Joaquín was awkward in his consolation because he too was struggling to hold back his emotion. The temperate summer sun didn't improve her mood. The gypsies in the alley passed them by without even a glance, as if what had happened the day before had put an end to any dispute. Ana Vega saw the backs of those leaving the alley as she waited for the arrival of Pascual Carmona. When the head of the Carmona family arrived the sentence would be carried out, they had told her in one of the forges. Pascual was her last hope: he wouldn't yield on her father's death sentence, that she knew. José had hated Melchor, Pascual did too, many of the Carmonas had made her husband's feelings their own, but even so Pascual was Milagros's uncle. She was the only daughter of his murdered brother, and Ana trusted that there was still some affection left in the gypsy for the little girl he used to play with.

'Pray in silence, Father,' she urged Fray Joaquín, tired of his constant murmur, which only increased her anguish as it mingled with the blacksmiths' irksome hammering.

She was planning to approach Pascual before he entered the alley, begging him on bended knee; humiliating herself, throwing herself at his feet, promising him anything he asked for in exchange for her daughter's life. She didn't know if she would recognize him after five years. He looked somewhat like José, but taller, considerably stockier . . . surly, dour . . . but he was the head of the family and as such should defend Milagros. She looked at the people passing, between La

Cava, the Minims and San Jacinto, and she envied the laughter and the seemingly carefree way they went about their lives on that magnificent sunny day that was witness to her misfortune. She saw a couple of gypsy girls following after a *payo* asking for a coin and her expression soured. The man brushed them off rudely and the youngest fell to the ground. A woman ran to help her while the others chided the *payo*, who hurried on. Ana Vega felt the tears she thought had run out return to her eyes: her friends from captivity. Old Luisa was the first to see her; the others were still insulting the man. Luisa hobbled over to her, pain showing in her face at every step. The others soon joined her, though none of them dared to pass the old woman: seven women in rags walked towards her, filling her blurred vision, as if nothing else existed.

'Why are you crying, girl?' asked Luisa in greeting.

'What . . . what are you doing here?' she sobbed.

'We came to help you.'

Ana tried to smile. She was unable to. She wanted to ask how they had found out, but the words didn't come. She took a deep breath and tried to calm herself down.

'They hate us,' she replied. 'They hate the Vegas, my father, Milagros, me . . . all of us! What can we do, just us?'

'Just us?' Luisa turned and pointed behind her. 'The Ximénez came too, from Carmona; some others from El Viso and a couple from the Cruz family in Alcalá de Guadaira. You remember Rosa Cruz?'

Rosa peeked out from behind the last of the Vegas and blew her a kiss. This time, Ana's mouth widened into a smile. It was the same gesture that Rosa had made when Ana stayed behind, in the night, watching her back as the other fled through a hole in the wall of the House of Mercy. That had been two years ago.

'There's one from Salteras,' continued Luisa, 'and another from Camas. Soon they'll be arriving from Tomares, Dos Hermanas, Écija . . .'

'But—' Ana Vega managed to say before the old woman interrupted her.

'And they're coming from Osuna, from Antequera, from Ronda, from El Puerto de Santa María, from Marchena . . . from the entire kingdom of Seville! Just us, you say?' Luisa stopped speaking to catch her breath. No one in the group surrounding the two gypsy women added to the conversation; some had their teeth clenched, others already had tears in their eyes. 'Many of them shared jail with us . . . with you, Ana Vega,' continued the old woman. 'They all know what you did. I told you one day: your beauty is in the gypsy pride you have never lost. We are grateful to you; we all owe you something, and those who don't are in debt to you through their mothers, their sisters, their daughters or their friends.'

While Melchor, Caridad, Milagros and Fray Joaquín had taken a week to travel from Barrancos to Triana, Martín Vega took just three days to gallop from the Portuguese border to the city of Córdoba. The people Méndez sent to find him ran into him already on his way back to Barrancos, two days after Melchor and the others left. He listened to the smuggler's explanations, aware that El Galeote was headed to certain death. No one would defend him; there were no Vegas in Triana, nor in Seville. Most of the Vegas from the settlement of La Cartuja had been arrested in the big round-up and they were still prisoners in the arsenals, unable to prove they had lived according to the laws of the kingdom and particularly the Church; the few who had escaped the King's soldiers were scattered along the roads. There were some, however, in Córdoba, one of the cities with the most gypsies. Distant relatives, but with Vega blood. Martín knew about them from the sale of a good shipment of tobacco. He knew how to ride a horse from when he used to help out his brother Zoilo, and he rode the one that Méndez gave him almost into the ground. He was searching for help from the Vegas in Córdoba, a help they refused him.

'By the time we get to Triana,' said the patriarch as an excuse, 'Melchor will already be dead.'

He knew he shouldn't insist. In Córdoba, just as in Seville, Murcia, El Puerto de Santa María and many other places where gypsies resided, the men knew the arsenals; the women the incarcerations; they all knew the separation of married couples, children and loved ones. Some had managed to return to their homes, and they were forbidden to leave the city. How were they going to go to Triana to fight with the families there? There would be bloodshed, injuries and perhaps deaths. The authorities would find out. *Don't ask us for such sacrifice*, pleaded the old gypsy's eyes.

'I'm sorry, boy,' the patriarch lamented. 'By the way,' he added, 'three days ago one of our women came across a group of famished gypsy women trying to get discreetly across the bridge over the Guadajoz River.'

'So?'

'They told her they had escaped from the House of Mercy in Saragossa and they were headed to Triana.'

When he heard Saragossa, Martín sat up straight in the chair he had collapsed into after the patriarch's refusal. Could it be?

'They were Vegas. All of them,' the old man said, confirming his premonition.

'Was . . . was Ana Vega among them?'

The patriarch nodded.

'I remember very well,' affirmed a woman whom they had called over right away. 'Ana Vega. I couldn't tell you the other names, but Ana Vega's for sure. She was the one in charge: Ana this and Ana that.'

'Where could they be now?' asked Martín.

'They were exhausted and they were even carrying an old woman – I don't know if she was sick, but I'd swear she was. They were arguing over whether to rest here for a while, but Ana Vega said they shouldn't stop in the large cities, that they'd stop in Carmona, with the Ximénez family. Maybe they've arrived. We fed them and they continued on their way.'

Martín didn't hesitate; he took off at a gallop towards Carmona. If they had stopped there, it wouldn't be hard to find them. The Ximénezes were well known among gypsies throughout all of Andalusia because their family was one of the few, perhaps the last, still ruled by the matriarchy. Ana Ximénez, the matriarch, like her mother, demanded that all the daughters in the family continued to use their maternal last name: the sons were given their husbands' name, but the girls proudly bore their maternal ancestors'.

He found them and was unable to recognize in any of those

scrawny women the daughter whose virtues Melchor extolled. 'Ana continued on to Triana,' they explained. The two old women, Ana Ximénez and Luisa Vega, were the first to sense problems when they saw the expression on the young man's face upon hearing the news. 'Melchor Vega . . . that crazy old man!' blurted out the Ximénez matriarch after hearing Martín's hasty explanations. 'A real gypsy!' murmured Luisa proudly. Martín was unable to clear up the many questions they all posed. 'Caridad says . . .' 'Caridad warned . . .' 'Who is this Caridad?' the Ximénez leader burst in again. 'She says they will kill them all: Melchor, Milagros and her,' was his only response.

'The only one who came to Triana to die was me.' With those words, Luisa broke her silence following her praise of the old gypsy. 'You forced me to come,' she chided the others. 'You told me that we would find our people; you promised me that I could die in my home-land. You dragged me across half of Spain, over leagues and leagues to the torment of my legs. Why are you silent now?'

'What do you want us to do?' answered one of the Vegas. 'You see that those in Córdoba are unwilling—'

'Men!' Luisa interrupted her, her eyes shining as they hadn't in years. 'Did we need them to survive in Málaga or in Saragossa?'

'But gypsy law . . .' one of them began to object.

'What law?' shouted Luisa. 'Gypsy law is the law of the roads, of nature and the earth, the law of freedom, and not the law of some gypsy men who allowed those of their race to be locked up for life while they lived like cowards among the *payos*. Cowards!' repeated the old woman. 'They don't deserve to call themselves gypsies. We have suffered humiliations while they obeyed the *payos*. They've forgotten the real law, the law of our race. We have put up with blows and insults, and suffered hunger and illnesses that have ruined our bodies. They separated us from our families and we never stopped fighting. We have defeated the King and his minister. Aren't we free? Well, we should now fight against those who call themselves gypsies and aren't really!'

'Ana helped one of my daughters,' the Ximénez matriarch then murmured.

'That is the only law,' declared Luisa as she saw how the faces of

her relatives were starting to light up. 'She also helped La Coja. Remember La Coja? The one from Écija, near here. She escaped Saragossa a year before us. And the two from Puerto de Santa María? The ones with the first pardon . . .'

Old Luisa continued listing all those who had been freed before them. However, it was Ana Ximénez who made the decision.

'Martín,' she said, addressing the young man and silencing Luisa. 'Ride to Écija. Right now. Look for La Coja and tell her that Ana Vega needs her, that we all need her, that she should head to Triana without delay, to the San Miguel alley. Urge her to send word to the other gypsy women she knows in the nearby towns, and have each of them spread the message.'

Marchena; Antequera; Ronda; El Puerto de Santa María . . . Martín received similar instructions for each of those places.

It was the third time that the people of the San Miguel alley were surprised by an unexpected arrival: first it was El Galeote with his group; then Ana Vega; and now almost fifty gypsy women headed by Luisa Vega, with her spirits and her strength renewed, and Ana Ximénez, the matriarch of Carmona, who tried to walk upright while leaning on a lovely two-pointed gold staff that sparkled in the sun.

'What are we going to do?' Ana Vega asked in a whisper as she continued walking beside the two old women.

'Never let men,' replied Ana Ximénez in the same hushed tone, 'take the initiative; it makes them bolder.'

'Wouldn't it be wise to wait until there are more of us? Yesterday . . .'

'Yesterday no longer exists,' replied Luisa. 'If we wait, it will be Rafael García who will have the chance to decide. We could be too late.'

As they talked, the women following them looked at the people of the alley. They knew many of them. Some were even relatives, the product of marriages between families. There were a few smiles, some greetings, incredulous men's faces in the distance, because the women didn't hesitate to approach them and ask what they were doing there, what they were planning. Fray Joaquín followed a few paces behind them, praying for that motley group to pull off the seemingly impossible.

They reached the door of the Garcías' house and shouted for El Conde to come and receive them.

'Rafael García,' Ana Ximénez confronted him when El Conde finally appeared in the alley, flanked by the heads of some families, 'we have come to free El Galeote and his granddaughter.'

Ana trembled. Freeing her father wasn't something she had even dreamed of. She didn't think it was possible that the death sentence could be annulled, but as she turned her head and saw the gravity in the faces of Luisa Vega and Ana Ximénez, she began to nurture some hopes.

'Who are you to come here, to Triana, to free anyone?'

El Conde's powerful voice interrupted the murmurs with which most of the gypsies in the alley had received Ana Ximénez's words.

Luisa spoke first. She forced her voice, which emerged hoarse, cracked: 'We are those who suffered for being gypsies while you and yours were living here, in Triana, under the yoke of the *payos*. Rafael García: I didn't see you in Saragossa fighting for your people, the ones you claim to represent as head of the council. That gold you wear' – she pointed with disdain at the large, shiny ring on one of the patriarch's fingers – 'shouldn't you have used it to buy the freedom of some gypsy?'

Luisa was silent for a few moments and stared at the heads of families who accompanied El Conde; one of them was unable to hold her gaze. Then she turned her back to them, and pointed a finger at the men of the alley.

'I didn't see any of you either!' she reproached them in a shout. 'There are still many of us imprisoned!'

Some of the people lowered their eyes as Luisa, Ana Ximénez and the other gypsy women looked at them with scorn.

'What could we have done?' was heard from among them.

Luisa waited for the murmurs of assent to end, arched her eyebrows and turned her head towards the corner where the question had originated. For a few moments the alley was overtaken by silence. Then the old woman gestured to the gypsies that were behind her to clear the alley, took Ana Vega by the arm and planted her in the middle.

'This!' she screamed, tearing off Ana's raggedy shirt.

Ana was left naked from the waist up. Her breasts hung flaccid over ribs that proclaimed the hunger she had suffered.

'Stand up straight!' muttered the old woman.

The skin on Ana Vega's belly didn't even become taut when she obeyed, standing up tall and proudly challenging the entire alley.

'This!' repeated Luisa, grabbing Ana and forcing her to turn around and show the dry welts that crossed her entire back. 'Fight!' shouted Luisa. 'That is what you should have done: fight, you cowards!'

The old woman's coughing was clearly audible in the reverent silence with which the alley took in her accusations. Ana thought she could see blood in her spit. Luisa struggled to breathe but couldn't. The other woman took her in her arms before she collapsed and the others quickly surrounded her.

'Fight,' Luisa managed to articulate. 'You've done it, Ana Vega. I will die in my homeland. Now do your duty to your family. Triana is ours; it belongs to the gypsies. Don't let them kill Melchor.'

She coughed again and her mouth was filled with blood.

'She's dying,' confirmed one of the Vegas.

Ana looked around for help.

'Fray Joaquín!' she shouted. 'Take care of her,' she added after he came over and knelt down, embarrassed, struggling to keep his eyes off Ana's bare breasts.

'But . . . I . . .'

'It's not your time yet,' Ana encouraged the old woman, ignoring the friar's excuses. 'Take care of her. Cure her,' she demanded, placing Luisa in his hands. 'Do something. Take her to a hospital. Aren't you a friar?'

'I am a friar, but Our Lord didn't bless me with the ability to revive the dead.'

Luisa's body, more slight and vulnerable than ever, hung inert in the friar's arms. Ana was about to say her goodbyes when four words stopped her.

'Don't let her down.'

That voice . . . She searched among the gypsy women. La Coja! She wasn't among the women who had come with the Vegas. La Coja nodded to confirm what was going through Ana's mind. *I came to your aid*, her eyes said, *and I didn't come alone.*

'Don't let us down, Ana Vega,' she then said, as she gestured with her head towards the entrance to the alley.

Ana, along with many others, looked where she indicated: two more gypsy women appeared at that instant. A whirlwind of feelings confused Ana Vega. Her breasts were still bared, showing her scars and her ravaged body beneath a radiant sun determined to highlight her among the crowd; she wanted to cry over Luisa's death, go over to her before her body grew cold, and hug her one last time. They had suffered so much together! And, meanwhile, her father and her daughter's fates were still in the hands of their bitter enemies, while gypsy women from all around left their families to come to help her.

'Rafael García, give us El Galeote and his granddaughter!'

The Ximénez matriarch's emphatic order brought Ana back to reality and she rushed to her side. The other women, as if one, huddled around them. Fray Joaquín was left behind, holding Luisa Vega's lifeless body.

Rafael García stammered. 'I have no intention . . .' he managed to get out.

A string of insults rose from the gypsy women. 'Dog!' 'Let them go!' *'Payo!'* 'Bastard!' 'Where are they?'

Someone from the alley revealed their hiding place in a whisper. 'In a pit in the Garcías' smithy!' repeated a voice, this time shouting.

The group of gypsy women moved towards the forge, which was in front of them, pushing Ana Vega and Ana Ximénez. The matriarch lifted her staff when she was about to bump into the men. The shoving stopped to allow her to speak.

'Rafael, you have the chance to—'

'The vengeance belongs to Pascual Carmona,' El Conde interrupted her. 'I shouldn't . . .'

'Vengeance belongs to us!' was heard from behind. 'It belongs to the women who have suffered.'

'To the gypsy women!'

'Move aside, you son of a bitch.' Ana Vega spat out those words just one step away from the old patriarch, who looked for help among the other family heads, but they moved away from him. Rafael García lifted his eyes up to the window, in search of his wife's support, and he sighed in disappointment when no one answered. Not even La Trianera dared to face up to these gypsy women.

'Are you going to let them oppose a sentence set down by the council and allow a killer to escape?' he shouted nervously to the other gypsies of the San Miguel alley, most of them clustered to the sides and behind the women.

'Are you going to kill them too, all of them?' replied someone.

'You don't care about avenging José Carmona's death!' shouted a woman. 'You just want to kill El Galeote!'

El Conde was about to answer, but before he had a chance, he found the end of Ana Ximénez's staff against his chest.

'Move aside,' muttered the matriarch.

Rafael García stood strong. 'Don't let them get in,' he then ordered his people.

The Garcías, the only ones who barred their way into the forge, tightly gripped the hammers and other tools they had in their hands, and raised them up.

The threat created an expectant silence. Ana Vega was about to pounce on El Conde when an old woman from the Camacho family came forward, approaching them from one side.

'Ana Vega has paid enough for what her father did and what her daughter might have done. We all witnessed it! Luisa even died for the same freedom the Vegas demand. Rafael: move your people aside.'

The old woman sought out and received a sign of approval from the head of her family before continuing.

'If you don't do it, we Camachos will defend them against your men.'

A shiver ran through Ana Vega's spine. The Camacho family, from the very San Miguel alley, were defending her and defending a pardon for her father! She wanted to thank the old woman, but before she could go over to her, two other women, these ones from the Flores family, joined the first one. And another, and another. All from different families, as their men looked on with resigned and relenting expressions. Ana smiled. Someone tossed a large fringed yellow kerchief over her shoulders just before she headed into the forge. No one dared to stop them.

49

ANA HUGGED HER daughter as soon as they managed to get her out of the pit, to the applause and cheers of the crowd that were squeezed into the forge. Dazzled by the scarce light that streamed in, Milagros heard her, felt her, smelled her and held her tightly. She asked for her forgiveness a thousand times; they kissed, stroked each other's faces and wiped away each other's tears, laughing and crying at the same time. Then Melchor insisted they untie and pull a bewildered Caridad out of the pit. As soon as she could see again, she went into a corner, followed by the curious eyes of those who didn't know who she was. Finally, the gypsy who had gone down into the pit helped Melchor out.

'Father!' shouted Ana.

Melchor, stiff, let himself be embraced but was barely able to return his daughter's displays of affection and he hastened to free himself from her arms, as if he didn't want any other emotion to cloud his spirit. His actions made Ana's blood run cold.

'Father?' she asked, separating herself from him.

The gypsy women's applause and comments stopped.

'And my knife?' demanded Melchor.

'Father . . .'

'Grandfather . . .' Milagros approached him.

'Rafael!' shouted Melchor, pushing aside both women.

El Galeote tried to walk, but his legs failed him. When his daughter and his granddaughter tried to help him, he let go of their hands. He wanted to stand up on his own. He finally managed it and took a step forward. His blood was flowing again and he took another.

'Where is your grandson?' howled Melchor. 'I came here to kill that mangy dog!'

Ana Ximénez, who stood in front of him, moved aside; the other women followed suit and opened up a passageway to the alley. Ana and Milagros hesitated, but not Caridad, who ran after her man.

'Cachita,' Milagros begged her, brushing one of her arms with her hand.

'He has to do it,' declared Caridad without stopping.

Mother and daughter rushed to follow her.

'Where is your grandson? I told you I came to kill him,' said Melchor to Rafael García, who hadn't moved from in front of the door to his house.

Caridad clenched her fists and teeth in support of the gypsy's words; Ana Vega, on the other hand, only noticed the arrogance with which El Conde received his threat. Without the gleam of a knife blade in his hand, her father looked small and defenceless. The years had taken their toll on him as well, she lamented. The women exchanged glances. *What determination in the* morena's *face,* thought Ana, so different from the last time she saw her, fallen on the ground, innocent, covered as always with her straw hat, as Ana begged her to take care of Milagros! Her daughter had changed too. She turned towards her; where . . . ?

'I thought you would run away amid all these women,' she heard Rafael García reply just then, in a powerful, sarcastic voice.

Between El Conde's response and her not being able to find Milagros, Ana felt terribly dizzy. Where . . . ? She feared the worst.

'Father!' she shouted when she saw that Milagros was already crossing the threshold that led to the courtyard of the Garcías' apartments, a few steps past the door to the forge.

Ana set off after her daughter before Melchor understood what was going on. Some women followed her. Milagros had reached the gallery of the upper level when Ana entered the patio.

'Milagros!' she called out, trying to stop her.

Milagros jumped over the remaining steps. 'Where's my little girl?' She pushed two old García women and made her way along the gallery. 'María!'

Bartola's head peeked out of the door of one of the apartments.

'Bitch!' Milagros screamed at her.

From the stairs, Ana saw her, dressed in black, running and entering that apartment. 'Quickly!' she urged the women who followed her.

When they crowded into the apartment, the women found the girl, who was crying and struggling, in the arms of a beautiful young gypsy. Milagros, in front of them, panting and with her arms extended towards her daughter, had frozen when she saw the cold looks Bartola and Reyes, La Trianera, gave her, as if she were afraid that taking another step could put little María in danger.

'She is my daughter,' whispered Milagros.

'Give her her child!' Ana ordered the young woman.

'She won't do that without the father's consent,' objected La Trianera.

'Reyes,' growled Ana Vega, 'tell her to hand over the girl to her mother.'

'To a whore? I will not—'

La Trianera couldn't continue. Milagros pounced on her, roaring like an animal. She pushed her with both hands and they fell to the floor, where she began to hit her. Ana Vega didn't waste any time: she went up to the young woman and grabbed María from her without any resistance. The little girl's crying and Milagros's shouts filled the room and reached the alley. Ana held María close to her and watched the beating that was Milagros's revenge for years of torture. She did nothing to stop her. When the people piled up in the door and Ana sensed the presence of some men, she went over to Milagros and knelt down.

'Take your daughter,' she told her.

They left the room just as Rafael García was reaching the gallery. They passed each other. Milagros tried in vain to calm the little girl down. Her hands were shaking and she was out of breath, but her gaze was so bright, so victorious, that El Conde grew alarmed. He dodged them, worried, and quickened his step towards his house.

'Show her to your grandfather. Put the girl in his arms. Run, my daughter. Maybe that way we can avoid tragedy. When we did that with you, years ago, it worked.'

While Ana was trying to keep Melchor from challenging Pedro García to a duel, La Trianera, sitting bruised on the floor of the room, was condemning the old gypsy.

'Go and find Pedro,' she told her husband. From the window, she had heard Melchor's threat. 'Have him fight El Galeote. He should have an easy time of it with that old man. Tell him to kill him, to tear out his eyes in front of his family, to rip out his guts and bring them to me!'

Below, on the alley, Melchor didn't want to touch the little girl.

'Pedro will kill you, Father. You are . . . you're much older than he is.'

Milagros brought the girl over to him again. Caridad was watching from a certain distance, still and in silence. The gypsy didn't even stretch out his hand.

'Pedro is evil, Grandfather,' she pointed out with her arms extended, showing him the girl, who was still sobbing.

Melchor made a face before answering. 'That son of a bitch still has to meet the devil.'

'He will kill you.'

'Then I'll be waiting for him in hell.'

'Father, we are all alive,' interjected Ana. 'We've found each other again. Let's make the most of it. Let's leave here. Let's live . . .'

'Tell him not to do it, Cachita,' begged Milagros.

Ana's eyes joined Milagros's plea. Even Ana Ximénez and some other women who were listening attentively to the conversation turned towards Caridad, who remained in silence until Melchor fixed his gaze on her.

'You taught me to live, gypsy. If you don't challenge Pedro, will you feel the same when you listen to me sing?'

His silence was answer enough.

'Finish off the bastard, then. Don't be afraid,' she said with a slight sad smile. 'Like I told you, I'll go down to hell with you and I'll keep singing for you.'

Ana bowed her head, defeated, and Milagros hugged her daughter against her chest.

'Galeote!'

El Conde's shout, as he stood at the entrance to the courtyard, silenced all conversations and made everyone stop in their tracks.

'Here!' He tossed a knife at Melchor's feet. 'When he gets here, you'll have your chance to fight my grandson.'

Melchor bent down to pick up his knife.

'Clean it well,' added El Conde seeing how he rubbed it against his red jacket, 'because if Pedro doesn't finish you off, I'll do it myself.'

'No!' objected Ana Ximénez. 'Rafael García, Melchor Vega: this fight to the death will end it all. If Pedro wins, no one should bother the Vega women . . .'

'And the girl?'

'What do you want Vega blood in your home for?'

El Conde thought for a few moments and finally nodded.

'The girl will stay with her mother. No one will seek further revenge on them! Not even your grandson, understood?'

The patriarch nodded again.

'Do you swear? You swear?' insisted the matriarch at the simple nod with which he wanted to seal his commitment.

'I swear.'

'If it is Melchor who wins . . .' Even she hesitated at her own words, and she couldn't help a pitying glance at El Galeote, as did many of the women present. 'If Melchor defeats Pedro, the sentence will be considered fulfilled.'

'The vengeance belongs to the Carmonas,' El Conde then declared. 'And Pascual isn't here to swear on it.'

Ana Ximénez nodded thoughtfully. 'We can't all wait here for him to return. Gather the council of elders,' she said then. 'Including all those from the Carmona family.'

That very afternoon, the matriarch represented the interests of the Vegas in an emergency council meeting. The family heads attended, along with the Carmonas, many of the gypsies from the alley and some of the gypsy women who had come from other towns. Others wandered through Triana and the ones who remained stayed with Ana and Milagros, crying over Luisa's corpse, which up until then Fray Joaquín had been taking care of, and they settled it in one of the courtyards.

It was a long courtyard that opened up between two rows of small, single-storey houses. There soon rose from it a constant wail from the gypsy women. Some of their displays of grief were restrained but most were overwhelming. Exhausted by the long torment she had suffered since Pedro had stolen her daughter from her in Madrid, Milagros sat on a stone well attached to one of houses, and there she sought refuge in the girl she had just got back, cradling her and staring into her face with love. As she felt María falling asleep in her arms, relaxed, tranquil, trusting, she forgot all her suffering. She didn't want to think about anything else until, from between the long skirts of the women gathered, she recognized Fray Joaquín's sandals and habit standing before her. She lifted her face.

'Thank you,' she whispered.

He was going to say something, but she was already absorbed in her girl's sweet features again.

Despite her sadness over Luisa's death, Ana Vega didn't let herself get swept up in the dismal atmosphere looming over the courtyard. Fray Joaquín had told her about the relationship between her father and the *morena*, but she'd had trouble really believing him until she had seen the bond that clearly united them. She found Caridad, alone, just a few steps away from Melchor.

'I don't want Pedro to kill him,' Ana said to her after going to her side.

'Neither do I,' answered Caridad.

They both looked at Melchor, standing in a corner, still, expectant.

'But he will,' avowed Ana.

Caridad was silent.

'You do realize that, right?'

'What would you choose, his life or his manhood?' Caridad asked.

'If he loses his life,' replied Ana, 'his manhood will be of no use to me . . . or to you.'

Ana waited for Caridad to react to her acknowledgment of their relationship, but she didn't. She continued contemplating Melchor as if spellbound.

'You know that isn't true,' Caridad then responded. 'I felt him tremble when Milagros told him how she had been prostituted by her husband. I feared he would burst. Since then he hasn't been himself. He lives to avenge her—'

'Vengeance!' Ana interrupted her. 'I have spent five years locked up, suffering, only to escape and return to my homeland, with my people. I know what happened to Milagros was terrible, but just one day ago I had given both of them up for dead . . . all three,' she corrected herself. 'Now we have the chance to start again—'

'What?' Now it was Caridad who interrupted her. 'Five years locked up? What's that? I've been a slave my whole life, and even when I gained freedom, I continued to be one, right here in Triana and in Madrid, too. You know something, Ana Vega? I'd rather have a second of life beside this Melchor . . . Look at him! That is what I learned from him, from you all! And I like it. I prefer this moment, this second of gypsy pride, than spending the rest of my days with a man full of resentment.'

Ana couldn't find the words to answer. She noted her father's impassive figure blurring as tears came to her eyes, and she left. She searched for Milagros, and she saw her absorbed in her little girl and with the friar close by, but the other Vega women approached Ana as soon as they saw her blend into the group. They accompanied her over to Luisa, where the gypsy women who continued to stream into the alley from various towns in Seville gathered. She knew some of them, from Málaga, from Saragossa; others introduced themselves as relatives or friends. She tried to smile at them, aware that they had come to support her. Many had even argued with their men to do so. They had risked being arrested by travelling to Triana without passports, and they had done it for her. Gypsy women! She looked at Luisa's squalid, shrunken corpse. Yet how great she had been! *They can never take away our pride*, Luisa had said to them in the House of Mercy to spur them on. *That is your beauty*, she had flattered her later. And that very night, breaking her promise, Ana had run to watch Salvador coming back from the fields. Her stomach shrank at the memory. Then they had sent him to the arsenals, perhaps because of her stubbornness, but Salvador, like the other boys, had left with his head held high.

'Are you feeling ill?' asked one of the Vega women.

'No . . . No. I have something to do.'

She left them all behind and ran towards Melchor.

Kill him, Father. Finish him off. Do it for Milagros, for all of us.

Ana's words of encouragement to Melchor not long before were still echoing in Caridad's ears. At that moment they all left the courtyard and went out on to the alley. She didn't need to tell him anything. She'd had the feeling that Ana had come to take her place when she'd returned to the corner where Melchor was, to ask for her father's forgiveness. Ana had cried as she reproached herself and encouraged him with all her heart before embracing him. However, during that hug, Melchor had turned towards Caridad and smiled at her, and with that smile she knew that she was still his *morena*.

Caridad let Ana be the one to accompany Melchor. She walked behind, with Martín, who had shown up at the alley on a different horse – 'The other one didn't last,' confessed the young man – with an old gypsy woman, from the Heredia clan in Villafranca, on its hindquarters. That had been shortly before Ana Ximénez arrived in the courtyard to report that the council had made a decision: the fight would end it all. There would be no more revenge taken and Milagros would be free with her daughter. The Garcías had accepted, and the Carmonas – even though Pascual wasn't there – had as well. She didn't tell them that it had been easy to achieve that pledge because no one believed that Melchor would be victorious. 'Just another way to carry out the sentence anyway,' the matriarch had heard one of the Carmonas saying before the others nodded in satisfaction.

They were saying that the Garcías were searching for Pedro in Seville. Caridad prayed to the Virgin of Candlemas, and right there, from the tobacco Martín had given her, she tossed some leaf pieces to the ground begging her Orishas to have Pedro fall into the Guadalquivir drunk, or get arrested by the constables, or stabbed by a cuckolded husband. But none of that happened, and she knew he had arrived when the murmurs in the alley grew.

Melchor didn't wait, nor did Ana. Milagros refused to go.

'He is going to die because of me,' she tried to offer as an excuse to her mother.

'Yes, my daughter, yes. He will die for his family, like a good gypsy, like the Vega he is,' Ana objected, forcing her to stand up and go with them.

'Don't worry, Father, Luisa isn't going to run away,' quipped a gypsy woman when she saw the doubt in Fray Joaquín's face as he realized that everyone was leaving the wake in the courtyard where the corpse lay.

Some laughing was heard, though it couldn't break the tension that reached its highest point at the series of clicks Melchor's knife made as it opened; those clicks seemed to rise above every other sound, including the laughter. Caridad took a deep breath. The gypsy didn't even wait for people to make way for him. Caridad saw him grip his knife and cross the alley towards the Garcías' apartments. Men and women moved aside as he walked.

'Where are you, you son of a bitch?'

Caridad realized that Melchor didn't even know Pedro. He probably hadn't seen his face the night he jumped into the pit, she thought, since she hadn't either. And, when they lived in Triana, why would Melchor notice a young García boy? She was tempted to point Pedro out to him herself.

It wasn't necessary: Pedro García separated from his family and walked towards Melchor. The gypsies opened into a circle. Many were still talking, but they fell quiet when the two men began to jab their knives into the air, their arms outstretched: one with rolled-up sleeves, young, tall, strong, agile; the other . . . the other one old, skinny and wasted, with a haggard face and still wearing his red jacket trimmed in gold. Many wondered why he didn't take it off. It seemed to be interfering with his movement.

Caridad knew it wasn't the jacket. The wound from his fight with El Gordo burned, and his movements registered the pain. She had cared for him tenderly, in Torrejón, in Barrancos. He'd resented her attentions, but in the end they'd laughed together. She looked over at Ana and Milagros, both in the front row: one cowering, on the point of collapse at the terrible odds; the other crying, hugging her little daughter's face tightly against her neck to keep her from seeing the scene unfolding before them.

Pedro and Melchor continued to circle around, insulting each other with their eyes. Caridad felt proud of that man, her man, willing to die for those he loved. A shiver of that pride ran down her back. Just as she had felt upon her arrival at the San Miguel alley, when they'd captured them, she felt in herself the power that Melchor radiated, the power that had attracted her from the first time she laid eyes on him.

'Fight, gypsy!' she then shouted. 'The devil is waiting for us!'

As if they had been holding themselves back, the crowd watching the duel broke out in cheers and insults.

Pedro attacked, spurred on by the throng. Melchor managed to dodge it. Their eyes challenged each other again.

'Conceited braggart,' spat out Pedro García.

Conceited braggart . . . Pedro's words set off a spark in Milagros's mind and she saw an image of Old María. Pedro had confessed to it in Madrid, but she had been drunk and unable to remember it. *Conceited braggart*, those were the words he had said to her that night. Pedro had killed the old healer! She felt weak; luckily someone managed to take the little girl from her arms before she fell to the ground.

'Careful, Melchor!' warned Caridad when Pedro García launched towards him, taking advantage of his shifting his gaze towards his granddaughter.

He dodged his thrust again.

'The Vega line ends with you,' muttered Pedro, 'all your descendants are women.'

Melchor didn't answer.

'And they're all whores,' those who were closest to Pedro heard him say.

Melchor swallowed his rage, Caridad could tell, then she saw him provoke his enemy with his free hand. *Come on*, it said. Pedro accepted the invitation. The crowd broke out in whispers when García's knife cut El Galeote's forearm open. In just a moment the blood dyed Melchor's sleeve dark and he responded to the wound with a couple of ineffective charges. Pedro smiled. He attacked again. Another stab, this one to the wrist that Melchor used to protect himself. The crowd fell silent, as if they could foresee the outcome. Melchor attacked clumsily. Pedro's knife reached his neck, near the nape.

Caridad looked at Ana, who was on her knees, lifting her head with difficulty, her hands intertwined between her legs. Behind her was Milagros. She brought her gaze back to the fight just in time to feel, as if in her own flesh, the stab that Melchor got in his side. As the blade went into him it was as if it were wounding her. Beyond the knives, she saw Reyes, and her husband, and the Garcías and the Carmonas smiling. Melchor was dragging one leg, panting . . . and bleeding profusely. Caridad recognized that her man was going to die. Pedro was playing with his rival, delaying his death, humiliating him by dodging his weak thrusts easily, and laughing heartily. *Devil*, thought Caridad, *how does one go down to hell?* She turned towards Martín, who was motionless by her side, and tried to grab the handle of the knife that emerged from the young man's sash.

'No.' He stopped her.

They struggled.

'He's going to kill him!' moaned Caridad.

Martín didn't yield. Caridad finally gave up and she was about to jump in to help Melchor with her bare hands when Martín grabbed her. They struggled again, and he hugged her as tightly as he could.

'He'll kill him,' she sobbed.

'No,' he assured her into her ear. Caridad wanted to look at his face, but he didn't let up on his grip and continued speaking. 'He doesn't fight like that. I know. He taught me how to fight, Caridad; I know him. He's letting him get a few stabs in!'

A second passed. She stopped trembling.

Martín let Caridad go, and she looked back at the fight when Pedro, exultant, sure of himself, looked at his grandparents as if he wanted to dedicate the end of this enemy to them, now that he was about to strike the definitive blow. La Trianera was slow to grasp what was going on, and tried to react when she saw her grandson attack El

Galeote languidly, filled with vanity. The warning died in her throat when Melchor dodged the stab aimed right at his heart and, with a vigour born of rage, hatred and even pain itself, sank his knife to the hilt in Pedro García's neck, who stopped short with a grimace of surprise, before Melchor viciously dug deeper, until he finally pulled it out with a spurt of blood.

In the most absolute silence, the old gypsy spat on the body lying on the ground, still gushing blood. He wanted to look over at the Garcías, but he was unable to. He tried to stand up straight. He couldn't do that either. He only managed to fix his eyes on Caridad before collapsing. She ran to his side.

50

TWO DAYS HAD passed since the fight. Melchor woke up in the middle of the night and adjusted his eyes to the faint light of the candles in the empty apartment on the alley where they had set themselves up; he looked at Ana and Milagros, who stood at the foot of the straw mattress.

Then he asked them to take him to Barrancos.

'I don't want to die near the Garcías,' he managed to mutter.

'You aren't going to die, Grandfather.'

Carmen, a gypsy healer whom Ana had called from Osuna, turned towards her and shrugged.

'Whatever will be, will be,' she confirmed. 'Here, in Barrancos . . . on the road to Barrancos,' she said, anticipating Milagros's question.

Melchor seemed to be listening to her.

'You shouldn't stay in Triana,' he managed to say. 'Never trust the Garcías.'

Several of the gypsy women in the room nodded their heads to the sound of Melchor's laboured breathing.

'And the *morena*?' he asked.

'Dancing,' answered Milagros.

The answer didn't seem to surprise Melchor, who moaned as he smiled.

Caridad watched over Melchor during the day. She followed the healer's instructions and, with Ana and Milagros, changed bandages and dressings, and replaced the damp cloths on his forehead to combat the fevers. She sang softly as if Melchor could hear her. One of the gypsy women tried to stop her, making a displeased face when she heard the Negro songs, but Ana shot her a severe look and Caridad kept on singing. When night fell she slipped away and ran to the orange grove where she had first met the gypsy. There, timidly at first, and later with wild abandon, a convulsive shadow among the shadows, hitting sticks together in her hands, she sang and danced to Eleggua, he who decides men's fates. She hadn't earned his favour, but the supreme god hadn't yet decided to take her man either. Melchor had made her a woman; he had taught her how to love, how to be free. Could it be that was the lesson she was missing? Knowing the real pain of losing the man she loved? She had been just a girl when they took her away from her mother and siblings; the pain was then blended with her childish lack of understanding, and it was tempered by the distractions of new experiences. Years later Don José had sold her first son and he ended up separating her from the second, Marcelo; Caridad was a slave and slaves didn't suffer, they didn't even think, they just worked. On that occasion, the pain came up against the impenetrable scab with which slaves covered their feelings in order to keep on living: that's how things were; their children didn't belong to them. But now . . . Melchor had destroyed that scab, and she knew, and felt; she was free and she loved . . . And she didn't want to suffer!

'Don't let her go to the fields alone,' said Melchor.

'Don't worry, Father, Martín is watching out for her.'

The gypsy was satisfied, nodded and closed his eyes.

'It doesn't seem prudent to take Melchor to Barrancos.'

The comment, directed at both mother and daughter, came from Fray Joaquín. Once the fight was over, the priest had followed them discreetly, as if he were part of the family, blending in with the other Vegas who had nowhere to go and some of the gypsy women who were delaying their departure awaiting what they saw as an imminent denouement. Many gathered around the house. With Melchor's anguished situation as he hovered between life and death, the burials of Luisa and Pedro, the crying and moaning in the funeral, the tension over what could happen with the Garcías despite their promises . . . nobody was paying much attention to Fray Joaquín.

'Prudence has never been one of my father's virtues, wouldn't you agree, Fray Joaquín?'

'But now . . . in his state, you are the one who should decide.'

'While he still has a single breath of life, he will decide, Father.'

'It isn't a good idea,' insisted the friar. He words were addressed to Ana, but his gaze was fixed on her daughter. 'You should find a good surgeon who—'

'Surgeons cost a lot of money,' interrupted Ana.

'I could . . .'

'Where would you get the money from?' interjected Milagros.

'From the statue of the Immaculate Virgin. Selling it. It was valuable before, but now it's even more so. It seems the locusts jumped into the river at the sight of her.'

'Thank you, Fray Joaquín, but no,' Ana refused his offer.

Milagros studied her mother carefully. No, Ana repeated with her head. *If you let the friar make another sacrifice for you, you won't be able to refuse him*, she wanted to explain to her.

'But . . .' Fray Joaquín started to say.

'With all due respect, I think my father would feel humiliated if he knew that a Virgin had had to help him out with money,' Ana said as an excuse, while thinking it was probably true.

'Are you sure, Mother?' asked Milagros after the downcast friar left them alone.

Ana hugged her, and they both looked at Melchor, lying with cloths and bandages all over; the worst injury, the worrying one according to the healer, was the stab in his side, near where El Gordo had wounded him. Ana squeezed Milagros's shoulder before answering.

'Are you sure, my daughter?'

'What do you mean?'

Her mother's look was explanation enough.

'Fray Joaquín has treated me very well,' said Milagros. 'He saved my life and then . . .'

'That's not enough. You know that.'

She did know it. Milagros shivered.

'In Madrid,' she whispered, 'when he saved me, I thought . . . I don't know. Then later, on the way to Barrancos . . . you can't imagine how well he took care of me, his attentiveness, his efforts to get money, food, places to sleep. All I had was him and I thought . . . I felt . . . But then I found Grandfather, and Cachita, and you, and I got my girl back.' Milagros sighed. 'It's . . . it's as if the love I thought I felt for him has been diluted by the others. Now I look at Fray Joaquín with different eyes.'

'You have to tell him.'

Milagros shook her head as she made a dismayed face. 'I can't. I don't want to hurt him. He gave up everything for me.'

Ana Vega made a meaningful gesture towards one of the Vega women, who instantly took their place at the foot of the straw mattress, and she gently pushed her daughter towards the door of the house. The heat of the night was oppressive and humid. They walked through the courtyard in silence and then they sat down on two rickety chairs.

'The friar will understand,' said Ana.

'And what if he doesn't?'

'Milagros, you have already made one mistake in your life. Don't make another.'

Milagros played with a ribbon she wore around her wrist. She was dressed in a simple red skirt and a white shirt, which she had swapped for the black clothes she'd brought from Madrid. They had also given her several colourful ribbons.

'A very big mistake,' she admitted after a little while. 'I didn't heed your warnings then. I should have—'

'It was probably my fault,' her mother interrupted her. 'I didn't know how to convince you.' Ana put her hand over Milagros's. Her daughter grabbed it.

'You know?' Her voice was trembling. 'Things change when you're a mother. I hope that some day my daughter is as proud of me as I am of you today. All of Andalusia came to your aid! No. It wasn't your fault. When you have a daughter, things look differently from how they did when you were fifteen. Now I understand: your family comes first, the ones who won't let you down; nothing and no one else exists. I trust I'll be able to teach that to María. I'm sorry, Mother.'

The ones who won't let you down echoed in Ana Vega's ears as she shifted her damp eyes towards the house where her father lay. *El Galeote is strong; all sinew*, the healer had said to cheer her up as Melchor struggled to curse all the women who were badgering him. *Don't give up, gypsy*, she had heard Caridad say when his teeth chattered from the fever. She remembered the almost superhuman effort that Melchor had made when he found out that Pedro had killed Old María, as if he wanted to get up off the straw mattress to run and kill him again. They had hesitated over whether to tell him about it after Milagros had told them the story. *And what if he dies without knowing that he also avenged Old María?* said Caridad, ending the debate. It was Milagros who told him. *Your family, the ones who won't let you down* . . . Ana hugged her daughter.

'Fight, my father, fight!' she whispered.

The sun was high in the sky the following day when Martín entered the house looking for the women.

'I've got everything prepared,' he announced.

Caridad made no motion to leave, as she was busy feeding Melchor a cold broth. Ana sensed Fray Joaquín perking up his ears.

'You go and have a look,' she then said to Milagros.

The friar soon followed her to the alley, where they found a ramshackle cart with two wooden wheels, without sides or a driver's seat, and a miserable old donkey yoked to its shaft.

Milagros examined the straw on which Melchor would travel.

'Back to Barrancos,' said Fray Joaquín.

Martín looked the friar up and down before leaving him alone with Milagros, who continued moving the straw around as if she were looking for something.

'Yes,' she confirmed, still rummaging through the straw. 'That's what Grandfather wants.'

The silence extended between them.

Finally, Milagros turned.

'What does my hand foretell?' Fray Joaquín surprised her by holding it out for her to read.

She didn't touch it.

'Fortune telling . . . You know that's all just bunk.' Her voice scratched at her throat; she didn't want to cry.

'It depends on what the gypsy who reads it wants to see,' insisted Fray Joaquín, extending his hand further, encouraging her to take it in her own.

Milagros wanted to lower her head, hide her gaze. She didn't because of the memory of her childhood in Triana, his help in Madrid and on the way to Barrancos, his having saved her life and all the tenderness and affection he had showed her afterward. Yet she said nothing.

Fray Joaquín pulled back his hand at the commotion raised by Melchor's exit; he was walking very slowly, held up by Martín on one side and Caridad on the other. Ana walked behind him with the girl and the others. All that, however, wasn't enough for Milagros to take her eyes off the friar's face: tears were running down his cheeks.

'Don't cry, please,' she begged him.

They stood there motionless, in the way of Melchor getting into the cart.

'You are a good man, Father,' put in the old gypsy with a reedy voice when he reached them. 'Don't ask for more,' he advised him then. 'Continue with your God and your saints. The gypsies . . . as you can see, we come and we go.'

Fray Joaquín questioned Milagros with his gaze. 'Don't leave me again,' he pleaded in the face of her silence.

'I'm sorry,' she managed to say.

The friar didn't have time to respond before Melchor intervened again, as they tried to lift him on to the straw in the cart. 'Oh, Father!' Melchor called him over as if he wanted to tell him a secret.

The friar priest looked at him. He didn't want to leave Milagros's side, but the old gypsy's eyes – as glassy as they were penetrating – convinced him to go over.

'Don't let them cheat you with the snuff,' whispered the old gypsy with feigned gravity. 'If it looks red, no doubt about it, it's cut with ochre.'

When the friar rushed to search out Milagros's eyes again, he was unable to find them.

He will get better in Barrancos. They wanted to believe it. They had repeated it to each other over the long, laborious journey through the mountains, trying to lift their mood as they walked behind the cart where Melchor lay in the straw. Martín led the donkey that he had swapped in Triana, together with the cart, for his horse.

When they reached the foot of the hill, Caridad looked up at the house that touched the heavens: her house. They went up and stopped at the peak. Martín helped Melchor to get down from the cart. Ana and Caridad tried to help also but he refused, trying to hide his pain.

The day was clear; the summer sun outlined fields, rivers and mountains, emphasizing their vivid colours. Silence pervaded the scene. Melchor hobbled towards the edge of the cliff that opened out on to the vastness. Milagros handed the girl to Martín and prepared to follow her grandfather, but Caridad stopped her by extending an open palm, with her gaze on her man, who now leaned against the large rock that had been witness to the dreams and hopes they had shared.

'Sing, gypsy,' she then murmured, her voice catching in her throat.

A few seconds passed.

It began with a whisper that gained strength until it became a long, deep wail that echoed against the very heavens themselves. A shiver ran down Caridad's back; her whole body shook and her fine hairs stood on end. Milagros hugged her mother, to keep from falling. None of the three women sang, all bewitched by the cracked voice that melded with the breeze to fly off in search of freedom.

'Sing, Grandfather,' whispered Milagros. 'Sing until your mouth tastes of blood.'

Author's Note

'A lirí ye crayí, nicobó a lirí es calés.'
[The King's law destroyed the law of the gypsies.]

'El Crallis ha nicobado la lirí de los calés.'
[Charles has destroyed the gypsies' law.]

IN 1763, FOURTEEN years after the big round-up, by which time the Marquis of Ensenada had fallen into disgrace, King Charles III pardoned the gypsies for being born gypsies. There were still about 150 of them held in the various arsenals, and it would take years for them to be freed. In the Royal House of Mercy in Saragossa there were only a few remaining gypsy women without any family. Those who hadn't run away, more than 250, got their freedom by taking advantage of King Ferdinand VI's long demise, after which that institution settled the gypsy problem and could devote itself to recovering its original mission.

Twenty years later, in 1783, Charles III himself passed a proclamation aimed at assimilating the gypsies. It reiterated the prohibition of the use of the term 'gypsy' – 'those who call themselves gypsies are not, either by origin or by nature' – as had been ordered in previous resolutions, albeit with little success. But besides that reiteration, the King established that the gypsies did not come from 'tainted roots', which granted them the same rights as the rest of the population.

Despite continuing to outlaw their clothing and their language, he allowed them to choose their profession freely – with some exceptions, such as innkeeper in a desolate location – the ban on moving about the kingdom was lifted and they were allowed to live in any town, except in the capital and royal seats, where, in spite of everything, they continued to do so, as Minister Campomanes had been careful to underscore when lamenting the failure of attempts to banish them from Madrid.

The enlightened spirit behind the 1783 proclamation was supported by reports from several courtrooms, some of which pointed out the constant discrimination, harassment and unfair treatment that the gypsies had been subject to by the public, in particular officers of the law and clergymen, owing to their lifestyle and the fact that they lived outside of society.

Suffice to remember the paragraph with which Cervantes began his novel *The Little Gypsy Girl*:

It seems the gypsies were born into the world merely to be thieves; they are born of thieving parents, they are raised with thieves, they study to be thieves and, finally, they end up polished and perfect thieves, in whom the desire to steal and stealing are inseparable, and only eliminated by death.

According to the courtroom reports, the gypsies preferred to live alone and isolated than alongside those who mistreated them.

Even taking that into account, it is still true that gypsy society is an ethnocentric one. There is no written tradition in that community, but there are many authors who agree on a series of values that characterize the gypsies: racial pride and certain guiding principles: 'Li e curar, andiar sun timuñó angelo ta rumejí' (freedom to work, according to their own wishes and benefit); 'Nothing belongs to anyone, everything belongs to everyone,' attitudes which are difficult to reconcile with habitual social norms.

From that, the two quotes which begin this note are understandable. It seems that the legal comparison between *payos* and gypsies established by King Charles III's proclamation disappointed the latter.

'Charles has destroyed the gypsies' law.' Is this *victimismo* – a tendency to see themselves as being victimized? Rebellion, perhaps? That is for the scholars to decide.

The gypsy capacity for adaptation, if not assimilation, into diverse environs, is a constant demonstrated by scholars of this people. In the eighteenth century in Seville, counting Triana, there were almost fifty penitent brotherhoods, most of them with a long tradition, including the Negritos', although this was probably a common name and doesn't appear in books until the 1780s, after the ending of this novel. The Gypsy Brotherhood, so beloved today, wasn't founded until after the big round-up, and didn't appear in the Holy Week processions until 1757. Around that same time the missionaries emphasized the great devotion and penitence of the gypsies of Triana in the general confessions that were held.

It is surprising that in the Spain of the Inquisition, missions and religious fervour, the gypsies, who were constantly accused of being ungodly, impious and irreverent, weren't persecuted by the Inquisition. Neither the Holy Office nor the Catholic Church seemed to pay them any attention. Unlike other communities similarly persecuted throughout history, the gypsies were able to withstand and get around difficulties, almost as if it were a game, mocking the authorities and their constant efforts to repress them.

On the other hand, the gypsy community has contributed like none other to the art of flamenco, now declared part of the Intangible Cultural Heritage of Humanity by UNESCO. I am not the person and this is not the place to go into depth about whether the gypsy people brought their own music – the *zíngara* – with them to Europe or not, or if it originated on the Hungarian plains; in any case the gypsies became virtuosi of its performance, as would happen in Spain with a music that during the eighteenth century, when this novel takes place, scholars now call 'pre-flamenco'. Out of that grew a type of song that, since the late nineteenth century, with its *palos* and structure defined, would be known as flamenco.

The scholars also seem to agree that those songs were probably the result of the fusion, by the gypsies, of their own music with the Spanish tradition, the Moorish tradition and the Negro tradition, whether of slaves or freed slaves: what is called the music of 'ida y vuelta' [roundtrip] because it travelled from Spain to Latin America and back again.

Three persecuted peoples, some enslaved, others exploited and banished, all scorned: Moors, Blacks and gypsies. What emotions could be born of the fusion of their music, singing and dancing? Only those that reach their climax when one's mouth tastes of blood.

Triana, in competition with other parts of Andalusia, is considered the birthplace of flamenco. The San Miguel alley, where the gypsy family forges were clustered, disappeared in the early nineteenth century.

Perhaps the flamenco song as it is commonly recognized was born in the early twentieth century, but that shouldn't detract from the depth and bitterness, the *jondura* of the eighteenth-century gypsy songs. El Bachiller Revoltoso, witness to life in Triana in the mid-eighteenth century, writes:

> A granddaughter of Balthasar Montes, the oldest gypsy in Triana, goes to the main homes of Seville to perform her dances, accompanied by two men with guitar and small drum and another who sings when she dances. These songs are begun with a long breath they call the galley lament, because a gypsy forced to row would thus moan and it would spread to the other benches and from there to other galley ships.

It must be left to the reader's imagination and sensibility the vision of that gypsy for whom freedom is the greatest treasure, singing to complain about living fettered to the oars of a galley that few would get out of alive; a long breath, as the contemporary author describes it, that was later reproduced in the parlours of the noble and illustrious.

It is also El Bachiller Revoltoso who tells us of a gypsy who worked in a tobacco factory, who was smuggling some powder out – inside his body – when the pig intestine it was wrapped in burst. The smuggling of tobacco, a product that was monopolized by the royal tax office, was at the time – and continues to be – among the most lucrative activities, and the Portuguese town of Barrancos was one of its main hubs. Scholarly works are unanimous in including clergymen in this practice.

The eighteenth century also was one of great change for the city of Madrid. The advent of the new Bourbon dynasty brought new tastes and customs to the court. The Enlightenment provoked the creation of Royal Academies, economic societies, state-owned factories and workshops and a series of urban reforms that reached their height during the reign of Charles III, nicknamed 'the best mayor' because of the reforms he spearheaded in the capital.

One of those was carried out by Philip V on what had originally been the open-air Corral de Comedias de la Pacheca, turning it into the Coliseo del Príncipe Theatre, which later became the Teatro Español when it was reconstructed after two raging fires; it is located in the bustling Plaza Santa Ana, situated in turn on the site of the former convent of the Discalced Carmelites.

While comedies were banned in Seville, they were performed daily in Madrid in the Príncipe and Cruz theatres. Many scholars agree that the people attended them not only for the dramatic works but also for the *sainetes* and *tonadillas*, which had replaced the classic Baroque intermission pieces and become autonomous one-acts between the larger pieces.

The staged *tonadilla* reached its height in the eighteenth century, separating from the *sainete* over the course of the 1700s only to be completely forgotten by the end of the 1850s.

The *tonadillas* were short works, mostly only sung and danced. Their themes dealt with local customs and were satirical, exalting the common folk and criticizing the upper classes and their Frenchified ways. One of its most notable characteristics was the interaction the *tonadilla* players had with the public, which meant that their wit, self-assurance, sarcasm and, of course, sensuality were talents as important as their voices and grace as dancers.

The humble people of Madrid extolled many of those *tonadilla* players who sang for them. *Manolos* and *chisperos* are typical representatives of those appealing Madrileños, so proud of their city.

My thanks, as always, to my wife, Carmen, and my editor, Ana

Liarás, to all those who helped and collaborated in the making of this novel and, above all, to you, the reader who gives it meaning.

Barcelona, June 2012

Ildefonso Falcones' first novel, *Cathedral of the Sea*, became a publishing legend with over a million copies sold in Spain alone. It has since been published in over forty countries, becoming a European bestseller. In *The Hand of Fatima*, Falcones marked the four hundredth anniversary of the expulsion of the Moors from seventeenth-century Spain. His latest novel, *The Barefoot Queen*, has already sold over a million copies in Spain. It tells of the tumultuous birth of Flamenco in Spain. Falcones is a practising lawyer in Barcelona, where he lives with his wife and four sons.

Mara Faye Lethem has translated novels by David Trueba, Albert Sánchez Piñol, Javier Calvo, Patricio Pron, Marc Pastor and Pablo De Santis, among others. Her translations have appeared in *The Best American Non-Required Reading 2010*, *Granta*, *The Paris Review* and *McSweeney's*. She is currently working on a novel by Jaume Cabré.